Swords of Steel

Omnibus Edition

Introduction by D.M. Ritzlin

Artwork by Martin Hanford (front cover), Lauren Gornik (back cover), Ralph Torres (page 9), Eva Flora (page 125), Bob Byrne (page 183), Scott Waldrop (page 259), and Pan-Spec (page 341)

ISBN 978-1-7334086-1-5

Cover design by Michael Greylord

Want to get an e-book for free? *The Infernal Bargain and Other Stories* is available exclusively for DMR Books mailing list subscribers. Go to https://dmrbooks.com/ and get your copy now!

ALSO AVAILABLE

The Chronicles of Caylen-Tor by Byron A. Roberts – The Wolf-King of the north, Caylen-Tor, does battle with imperial armies and sorcerous serpent-men in three exciting novellas! Spectacular sword-and-sorcery by the lyricist of Bal-Sagoth.

Lands of the Earthquake by Henry Kuttner/Under a Dim Blue Sun by Howie K. Bentley – The first split release from DMR Books in the tradition of the Ace Double series! *Lands of the Earthquake* is a classic science-fantasy adventure from the pulp era that has never been published in book form before. On the flip side you'll find a brand new sword-and-planet tale. A US soldier hijacks a Nazi spaceship and lands on a planet threatened by snake-men! This title is available exclusively from DMRBooks.com.

Death Dealers & Diabolists – Eight action-packed tales of swords and sorcery! Includes stories by Keith Taylor (author of the *Bard* series) and Buzz Dixon (writer for *Thundarr the Barbarian, G.I. Joe* and *Transformers*).

Warlords, Warlocks & Witches – Eight more fantastic tales of action and adventure! Features stories by David C. Smith *(Red Sonja, Oron)* and Geoff Blackwell *(Swords of Steel)*.

CONTENTS

COSMIC HORROR

NAUTICAL ADVENTURES

Introduction

It's hard to believe it's been over five years since I first came up with the concept for *Swords of Steel.* Manowar is responsible for it, of course. One day, while listening to their song "Dark Avenger," I became fascinated by the lyrics. I was reminded of the sort of sword-and-sorcery stories that appeared in '70s anthologies like Andrew Offutt's *Swords Against Darkness*, but have long since fallen out of favor with mainstream publishers. I began to wonder if any heavy metal musicians had tried their hands at penning this type of fiction. They write lyrics with this subject matter, so why not short stories or novellas? Then I recalled reading interviews with a few musicians (Byron Roberts and E.C. Hellwell, specifically) who said they had written some stories, but they were never published. Someone should publish them, I thought.

Why not you? an inner voice asked me. Well, why not? Apparently no one else was going to do it. Sometimes when you want something done right, you've got to do it yourself. Once I had the idea, I had to go through with it. It was too good not to. I contacted various band members (and a few contacted me!), and before I knew it, I had enough stories to fill a book.

Swords of Steel (which was also the first DMR Books release) debuted on February 21, 2015. Two more volumes followed. All three were published in what I call "classic size paperback" format, 6.5" x 4.25", because I wanted the books to fit on my shelf alongside all my vintage Robert E. Howard and Michael Moorcock paperbacks. Besides, the contents were a throwback to the good old days of pulp fiction, so I thought the format should reflect that as well. Unfortunately, doing things the old fashioned way (i.e. having a shop print up 500-1000 copies and then wondering how you're going to move them) isn't terribly efficient in this day and age. For one thing, with such limited distribution, it's extremely prohibitive for readers outside the US to acquire copies.

Hence the need for the *Swords of Steel Omnibus Edition.* This massive tome contains all twenty-three stories that appeared in the three SOS volumes, and includes three brand new ones as well. I'm pleased to present these fantasy stories (both heroic and horrific) to the wide audience they deserve.

I'd like to thank the following for their help and support: All the authors and artists who participated in this project, Eva Flora, Deuce Richardson, Michael Greylord, Jon Zaremba, Bob and Shane (Legions of Metal Festival), Doug Ellis (Windy City Pulp and Paper Convention), John O'Neill (Black Gate), Morgan Holmes (Castalia House), P. Alexander (Cirsova Magazine), Marco (Ride Into Glory), Robert M. Price, and David C. Smith. Special thanks to Manowar and Orson Welles for composing and performing "Dark Avenger."

Swords of Steel Omnibus Edition is dedicated to the memory of Mark Shelton, mastermind of the legendary epic metal band Manilla Road. Mark tragically passed away in July 2018 after suffering a heart attack while Manilla Road performed a headlining set at the Headbangers Open Air Festival in Germany. Even though Mark was idolized by thousands of fans and musicians around the globe, he was one of the friendliest and most down-to-earth individuals in the scene. He was a big supporter of *Swords of Steel* and DMR Books from the very beginning. In the last email he sent me, he joked "If you get rich off this, don't forget about me!" It remains to be seen whether I'll get rich or not, but one thing is certain: I won't forget him. No one who met him ever will.

Up the hammers!

—D.M. Ritzlin

In Memoriam

Mark Shelton

December 3, 1957-July 27, 2018

Eldritch Deities

All Will Be Righted on Samhain

By Howie K. Bentley and David C. Smith

Prologue:

Revenge Against Rome

By 60 CE, the Roman Empire stretches from the deep, black forests of Germany in the north to the rocky deserts of Galilee in the east, from broad fields of wheat and spelt in the south, in North Africa, to the flowery meadows of Britain in the west. In Britain, an uneasy peace exists between the Romans and the Kelts. The Romans have built towns and encampments of stone and wood in the east of Britain, along the English Channel—Camulodunum, a settlement for retired soldiers, and, farther south, Londinium, a commercial center that sits in the marshland of the Thames River. Near Camulodunum lives the tribe of Kelts whom the Romans call the Iceni. Prasutagus, the king of the Iceni Kelts, accepted Roman rule, but upon his death, Nero, the young emperor in Rome, eager to expand the empire he has inherited from the emperor Claudius, his uncle, breaks his agreement with the Iceni and orders all their lands and property to be seized by his governor, Gaius Suetonius Paulinus, who resides in Londonium.

The Iceni Kelts rebel. With their king dead, their complaints are voiced by Queen Boadicea, Prasutagus' proud, fiery-tempered wife. Roman response is swift and unconditional. Suetonius's procurator, Catus Decanius, and his officials strip Boadicea of her throne and governing rights. They rape her daughters, Bunduica and Voadica, in front of her; then Helga, Decanius' amazonian German torturer, publicly whips the former queen, naked, before her people and before the Roman officials and soldiers who have intruded on the village of the Iceni.

Voadica, ill, dies within the year. Boadicea patiently waits until the proper moment to strike back at Rome. At last, Andraste, the great Keltic goddess of victory, promises the queen many bloody sacrifices in her victory over the Roman invaders. Boadicea sends her surviving daughter, Bunduica, to hide in safety with the druids under their leader, Balor, in a secret sanctuary deep in the forest. Then the Iceni, led by the proud queen, join other local tribes of Britons to move against the Roman occupants.

Camulodunum falls first beneath the swords and knives of the angry

Briton tribes of Iceni and Trinovantes. The terrified inhabitants of Camulodunum gather in the temple erected in honor of Claudius to make a stand until help arrives from the IXth Legion. They do not know that Boadicea's army has already ambushed the IXth on the road to Camulodunum and slaughtered the centurions nearly to a man. The Romans in the Claudian temple are also butchered, although Boadicea is disappointed to discover that Catus Decanius and his perverted, whip-wielding German amazon are not among the corpses. The proud Roman and his company have already fled for safety to Gaul. The fearful Governor Suetonius has left, as well; no longer in Londinium, he stays on the move, trying to build a force sufficiently large to confront the inflamed Kelts.

Emboldened by their victory at Londinium, the combined tribes under Boadicea now comb the countryside for Roman and pro-Roman settlements and savage them in bloodbaths, one after another. The Britons are particularly brutal in their revenge at the settlement of Verulamum, home of the traitorous Catavelaunii. Of all the Briton tribes, none was more accommodating to the Romans or more hated by their neighbors than the Catavelaunii. Boadicea's army heaps the carnage high, and the kites and scavengers feast.

Governor Suetonius at last raises an army sufficiently large to withstand the onslaught of the Kelts and makes his stand against Boadicea and the allied Britons southeast of the settlement of Atherstone. The battlefield is not to Boadicea's advantage: she must attack from a wide, open field, whereas the Romans have an entire forest at their backs for protection. But the queen of the Kelts has an army of 200,000; Governor Suetonius's combined Legions II, XIV, and XX comprise only 13,000 men.

Yet Boadicea is confronted by a bad omen. Before each prior attack on her enemy, from Londinium to this field, the queen had released a hare from under her cloak. The hare is a familiar sent from the goddess Andraste. Boadicea had once told Bunduica that Andraste had come to her in a dream and whispered into her ear the secret of divining the outcome of a battle: when the rabbit returns, the Kelts will be victorious. This morning, however, when Boadicea releases the hare, it does not return.

Has Andraste abandoned her?

Those closest to Boadicea hear the queen say, under her breath, "... and if she won't help me, I will destroy them without her." She then mounts the step of her chariot and shakes her spear in the direction of the Romans. Her wild, waist-length red hair beats in the wind like a mighty flame. Her muscular frame taut, she calls out to her tribes: "See them on the hill with the trees to their backs! Cowards who whip and rape defenseless women! Grown men who sleep with little boys! Let them run to the trees and hide! Have I not shown you the Goddess is on our side? She has sated her thirst on our crimson-stained altars! We have reveled in her name! Let the men of Briton go home even. The women can finish this battle on their own!" In response to her exhortation, the Kelts raise their voices as one and thrust their weapons in the air.

Confronting this display, Suetonius turns his horse and shouts to his men, "Keep close order. When you have thrown your javelins, push forward with the bosses of your shields and swords. Let the dead pile up. Forget about plunder. Win the victory, and it's all yours."

With awful shouts from both sides that rock the sky, the Kelts advance. The Romans hurl javelins, and many Britons drop. The Romans charge in a wedge formation, like a mighty battering ram, crowding in the tribes and going to work on them with short swords and spears designed for fighting in close quarters. The Britons, wielding their otherwise effective long swords, are caught. Before their families, whom the tribes had invited to watch this spectacle, the Britons go down in defeat. Hemmed in by their own wagons at their backs, the tribes are unable to retreat. The Roman cavalry has them flanked on both sides. By the end of the day, the dead lie in tall piles.

Boadicea, having survived the slaughter and aware that her daughter is safe, takes poison that the old druid Balor had given her should she and the tribes confront defeat at last. Forsaken by Andraste just when she most needed the Goddess's strength, the flame-haired queen now is dead and her revolt at an end.

This last battle, however, has driven Suetonius out of his mind. He has become almost more animal than man, drunk with power, enraged at the Kelts, as bloodthirsty as a wolf. His desire is to continue killing and torturing Britons endlessly. Learning of this, Nero sends Julius Classicanius to Britain to replace the rapist Catus Decanius as procurator, and Classicanius sends Governor Suetonious back to Rome so that he will cause no more trouble in Britain.

There has been enough already.

Chapter I

The Sacrifice

A slow wind moaned through the endless forest of tall, great trees. Bending strongly, heavy branches beat together and knocked out an unaccompanied nighttime dirge. The argent moon frowned on the Briton forest, watching like an eye as Bunduica weaved her way among the dark, gnarled boles. In her right hand she carried a torch; under her left arm was a wiggling bundle; slung over her back was a sack that contained fresh water and some few provisions.

Trees began to change, and before the young woman's eyes, as she hurried, the very light of the moon came alive around her. The old druid's mistletoe concoction, which the girl had drunk before entering this heavy forest, was taking effect. Immediately, everything around her burst alive—and Bunduica was walking in two worlds at once.

Here was the forest, ripe with fearful things and the expectancy of the evil to come, and here was the world alongside it, the sinister prelude of the forest and her immediate surroundings—the original world. Here lakes of blood ran in red waterfalls, and men and women took the forms of written characters—ancient runes—and shape-shifted into horse- and boar-headed chimeras. As Bunduica hurried on, one of these boar-headed men, standing now not far away, looked at her and, lifting his right arm, showed her the decapitated head of a man. He threw back his head, exposing freshly blooded fangs, laughed—and vanished, turned into fog.

The inhabitants of this damned world moved like ghosts free to pass through or pass over time. They shifted and dissolved as scenes of aeons came and went instantly, like the dreams of stars, all around the dazed Bunduica. A flaxen-haired woman, bare-chested, with a well-muscled abdomen but only half-human, slithered through the trees, her head and breasts and arms swaying atop her lower body, which was that of a large serpent. Curling and uncurling, the snake woman moved past a long row of impaled torture victims, some of whom yet lived, writhing and sweating, in the starlit mists. Her head swiveled completely around as she examined these bloody trophies; the back of her head, revealed only briefly as it revolved, was the face of a beast that Bunduica could not identify.

The young woman tried to keep her attention focused on her mission. This other world, she understood, was the result of the druidic potion, and she must not allow it to stand in her way or distract her from her purpose. She had suffered much already, but she was strong. Indeed, she looked like a younger version of her mother, the great Boadicea, with her flaming red hair, taut but feminine physique, alabaster skin, and piercing green eyes—eyes full of haunted memories. But Bunduica had her mother's iron will, too, so she walked on through the grim forest with complete determination, as if in a trance.

A crunch of autumn leaves beneath a booted foot not far away reminded her that she was not alone. The two boys, one tow-headed and the other red-haired with freckles and a perpetually sour look on his face, watched her through the trees from a distance. They had been following her for some time. Bunduica was aware of them, but they did not know that. Since ingesting Balor's mistletoe concoction, Bunduica felt as if all of her senses had become heightened to a nearly agonizing level. The boys were undoubtedly following her to spy on her and report back to the Roman officials. Most likely they were of pro-Roman families. It didn't matter. She knew that tonight there would be a reckoning.

She walked past a tree with a leering skull-like face that had been carved by no human hand. The jaw moved as the face tried to whisper to her. As she went by the skullface, Bunduica began to wonder just how far into the forest she would have to travel before she found the place. Suddenly a sharp voice inside her head said, "Look! There it is. To your left!"

Balor's voice, or her mother's? Or her own from deep within her? Bunduica saw a copse of four thick, gnarled old oaks, their tops leaning into each other as if they had grown together in a knot to make a roof. Balor had told Bunduica that when she saw this sign, she would have found the very place where the ritual must be performed.

Now she entered the grove and laid her torch and the writhing bundle on the altar of black stone that sat far beneath the knotted roof. On the sides of this carven block of onyx, strange characters had been chiseled, much like those she had seen in Balor's book. Had this slab of stone really been brought from another world, as old Balor had said? Bunduica shrugged the pack from her back, removed a flask of spring water, and set about quenching her thirst.

She then closed her eyes and made sure that she could recall the rune sounds and words Balor had taught her from his old tome. He called it the *Book of Dead Runes*. This grimoire, written on leaves of strange parchment and bound in skin with clasps of iron and bone, had been ancient even when fabled Valusia, the great kingdom, was young, its first trees green, its skies bright. Balor had given Bunduica the book when he decided at last that the child had nothing to live for but the vengeance she craved. She had spent months begging the blind old man for the occult knowledge she needed to take her revenge.

Balor had said to her, as he made his fateful decision, "You will be working in magick and summoning forces the druids have shunned since before the great cataclysms of old." The powerful magicks within the book were like trickster spirits, he told her; they would likely destroy the user as well as those against whom they were used. He recited the history of the *Dead Runes.* The fierce grimoire had first been in the possession of the race of Serpent Men, the unhuman creatures that had tried to topple the line of the ancient Great Kings who had reigned before the oceans engulfed Atlantis. It was this race of Serpent Men, some said, that had bound the book in the age-grayed human flesh that now covered it. Much later, it had been held by a sect of sorcerers in a land far to the east, Stygia. The sorcerers of Stygia had used the book to rule that dusky kingdom; with it, they brought down death and terror on all who opposed them. Even these workers of darkness, however, feared to utter spells contained on certain of the book's leaves. "Stygia long ago collapsed into dust," Balor told Bunduica, "and the book came to be held by two ancient enemy tribes called the Aesir and the Vanir. Through them, it reached my hands. I can tell you that there is a race to the north of the Briton Isles that will one day wash this land in blood, but not in your lifetime. They use written characters similar to those in this book to divine the future, but their runes are a very mild corruption of the dead runes. Some wise person knew what he was doing when he disarmed such knowledge. This will be the last that men will know of the book."

Balor had concluded with a dark warning. "This tome may not even have been born on this earth. Some say that it was brought down from the stars or from another world. What we know, Bunduica, is this: our world sits on top of, or passes through, the world as it truly is, not as it appears to be. For there surely are such other worlds beside ours. Bunduica—when you summon the rune forces, it isn't known whether the dark entities evoked will appear to the human eye, or are invisible demonic entities, or are forces of nature. I myself have not spoken these passages aloud. What I do know, myself, is from the undisputed testimony passed down through druidic tradition since before Atlantis sank. The rune forces are most potent—and utterly dangerous."

And the key to the living forces of the runes, he emphasized, lay in the proper pronunciation and vibration of the sound that each rune represented. "You must practice each patiently. And know that the ritual formula prescribed herein must be followed to the last letter and sound. There is no room for error. Do you understand?"

She had promised him that she did. And now she wished that his ancient strength were here with her. Old Balor, her mentor and foster father since her mother's death, had been wise in the ways of all things. He had been tortured and his eyes burned out when Suetonius, during the rebellion, had destroyed the druid sanctuary on Mona.

Taking in a deep breath, Bunduica unraveled the blanket. As the cold autumn air hit the baby, he began to cry. Bunduica clenched her teeth and reached for the athame at her belt. The dagger had a black handle that looked as though it could have been fashioned from the same material that the altar was hewn from. She paused as her hand touched that handle, and her green eyes burned with an unholy light. If those who had known her mother could have seen her at this moment, they would have sworn that Bunduica was Boadicea returned.

She began chanting the incantation in a whisper. The sonorous rhythm of the rune sounds lifted above the trees to pierce the silvery moon and grip the sky of the late October night. The sounds grew louder, and louder still. Even in the chill of the cold autumn night, sweat poured down Bunduica's face and drenched her back and her breasts as she intoned the malefic words over and over, calling louder each time. At last her chant built to a crescendo, and she screamed in a language that had never been intended for human organs to resonate: *"Tree-Micalazoda Yom-Gurd! Deesmees! Jeshet! Bonedose! Feduvema! Enttemoss!"* Then, *"Open wide the Gates! Manifest Rune Thorn!"*

Down her fist slammed, driving the dagger into the crying baby's heart. The thrust made a thumping sound like that of a bursting melon. Blood spurted in jets, landing on the surface of the black stone altar. Bunduica wiped a dripping stream of blood from her eyes and grinned. She dipped the fingers of her right hand into the blood and drew the Thorn rune on her forehead, then smiled.

Before her on the darkened slab running with crimson lay her own dead child—the bastard son of Catus Decanius.

Chapter II

The Horned God

Bunduica lifted her hands and, in answer to her, the sky split with a crack of thunder that shook the floor of the forest. It was then that she heard the boys break and run.

The people of this land had seen many cruelties and torments visited on human beings, and even for children, such things were common. But the two boys, Tow and Red, had never witnessed such savagery in the context of a ceremony—a ceremony that immediately answered prayers with an earth-shaking retort.

They felt evil coming. They felt it in their bones. They ran screaming in fear of their lives from the blood-spattered witch as rain started to fall in heavy drops.

Bunduica laughed hysterically at them, shouting, "Run, little piggies, *run!*" She snatched the torch from the altar, wheeled with the ritual dagger in her other hand, and gave chase.

The breathless boys now regretted following the young woman, but they had been lost; that was all, and trying to find their way out of the woods. Seeing a woman going into the deep trees alone on this night, of all nights, was an uncommon thing and could mean only mischief. A fellow Briton who was certainly up to no good—the Roman officials would surely pay a nice little reward to them if the boys had just a little more information on this woman.

Just as Bunduica was gaining on the two, she heard a crashing through the trees to her left. Immediately she stopped and, panting, hid herself behind a thick birch. Peering carefully from behind the tree, she saw a hunting party going by. Because her vision was partly obscured by the trees, she only caught a glimpse of the leader of the hunt.

He was a giant. He had long red hair and wore some sort of helmet with horns that dipped and pointed upward. His upper torso was bare and seemed to be inhumanly white although, after he had passed by, Bunduica reflected that the giant's skin might actually have been a funereal greyish-blue. Was he dead? Dying?

Behind him loped a band of hunters with the heads—not of human beings—but of boars and horses and of beasts that Bunduica did not recognize. Most were men, but there were a few women. The strange animals that came behind these hunters, sniffing the ground as they went, looked like giant dogs, but their brilliant red eyes cut through the darkness. These demonic animals, all lean and athirst, made loud panting noises. More of them came then; the hounds seemed to materialize from cracks in the shadows or from the misty air that formed sharp angles and opened suddenly, bringing them forth.

Bunduica herself saw through one of the angled openings only briefly. Close to the opening, just inside it, a goat-legged satyr approached. He was standing inside a scarlet circle that rolled like the rim of a wheel. This rolling circle stopped short just of the opening, and the goat-man pointed a finger at the strange hunting party. He said, "There it is." The abhorrent hound beside him shot out of the angled crack in the atmosphere and joined the hunting party.

The last figure to ride by was a woman with a lizard-like head. She gripped her horse's reins with the clawed pincers of a large crustacean. As she passed by the birch tree, she turned her head with a sly grin, as though knowing that Bunduica was hidden there. Bunduica saw the lizard woman's horse open its mouth in a saber-toothed snarl as the woman's forked tongue flicked in and out of her mouth. They rode on.

Powerful visions, nether-worldly scenes, images from nightmares and dreams. Bunduica judged that these powerful visions were the effects of the shamanistic potion of the druids that Balor had given her. But she now realized that what she had just seen go past was no vision or dream but rather a manifestation in this world, this level of existence, of what she had seen earlier in visions. The visions were as real as she was.

For there surely are such other worlds beside ours.

Bunduica recalled the tales told about this one night of the year. Throughout the warm months of spring and summer, the Goddess would walk the earth. It was then that life was given, and all things thrived. Tonight, however, was the night that the Goddess went away. Now the Horned God of the Hunt would rule, for it was the winter of the world, and death incarnate walked the earth tonight, reaping the harvest—the Wild Hunt. Here was the reason why Balor had chosen the night of Samhain for her to call on the force of the Thorn rune in the name of revenge. The angry dead gods, the vengeful spirits and creatures of the other world—this was their night to pass into our world if they could, forcing their way through and taking whatever they might to carry with them when they returned to the dead land of everlasting storms and shadows.

When the Horned God and his party had passed by and were out of sight, Bunduica left her hiding place. She realized that her two young spies were well away from here, probably on their way back to their village with a worthwhile bit of information—which may or may not be believed by the Roman officials. It began to rain hard now, and she decided it were best to be on her way, back to the secret catacombs of the druids, deep underground, where the Romans would never find her again.

After an hour had passed, however, in the deep of the chill night, Bunduica realized that she still had not been able to retrace her steps to the path she had first taken into the forest. Losing her focus by chasing the two spying youngsters had been a foolish act. The rain was now beating down in torrents. She needed to find shelter quickly, but she was unable even to find her way back to the black stone altar, which at least offered the cover of its oaken roof.

Panic was beginning to overtake her. Was she dying? Or had she died somehow already, and was she now between the worlds, or in the world of the Hunt? None, she had been told, who witness the Hunt, its dead gods and its memories and angry spirits, survives to speak of it. Suddenly, the same voice from deep within that had helped her find the altar said, "Look to your left! Shelter!"

Bunduica saw it. There, in the depths of the forest, was a house, all alone. It was a tiny, rustic stone cottage with latticed windows, no two of the same size, and a thatched roof. Vines had climbed all over it, and a stone path before it led straight to a thick oaken door. The door, Bunduica saw through the heavy downpour, was arched and had some sort of hide nailed to it. As she drew nearer, she saw by the light of the crackling sky that the hide resembled the form of a small human being.

If the hide were a warning meant to dissuade visitors, Bunduica was not convinced. She reached the door and lifted a hand to knock on it, but then it opened on its own. Bunduica looked into the single room of the cottage and saw an old woman, a crone as ancient as the trees themselves, stooped before a bright, snapping fire and stirring at a great black cauldron with a large spoon fashioned from a gourd. The woman was dressed in a black cowled robe made from some type of coarse material. Bent as she was, stirring her brew, the old woman turned her head to meet Bunduica's gaze.

"Come in," she said. "I have been expecting company." She then let out a loud laugh, a high cackle, and returned to her work, mumbling about company and chanting under her breath.

Bunduica was fearful but, as in a dream, she eased forward. Behind her, the great oak door fell closed.

Perhaps the wind of the storm had pulled it shut.

Chapter III

Thorn

Bunduica sensed something familiar about the old woman—but what? As she came closer, she recognized that the old woman was working particular spells, turning the ladle around and around, dragging the bottom of the cauldron as though stirring a hearty soup. When Bunduica was sufficiently close to see what was in the great pot, she saw strange skulls floating near the top, bobbing up and down. One head still had strings of flesh on it, although its eyes were hollowed out. One skull was human in shape but displayed the fangs of a vampire. Bunduica could also see the occasional arm swirling in the cauldron's liquid and, as big as the pot was, once thought she even saw a torso lift to the steaming surface and sink again.

The crone again turned her head to Bunduica and said to the young woman, as though she were annoyed at the interruption of her chanting, "The chair on the other side of the table—sit and wait. Soon there will be a rendezvous at the little cottage in the woods." Then she laughed, cackling, as though she had amused herself.

The table and chairs were set against a wall just beyond the witch. Bunduica carefully looked around the cottage as she moved to her seat. The wall opposite the one where the witch worked had an enormous, cobwebbed bookshelf filled with a host of dusty tomes. Bunduica surmised most of them to be grimoires that dealt with the very darkest of the black arts. As Bunduica settled uneasily in the creaking old chair, she tried to look away from the bubbling morass of slimy, green liquid in the witch's cauldron, although she wondered, *Have I created this with Balor's spell? Did I open a gate to welcome this crone into the world?*

To her right was a fireplace. The crackling logs in the grate kept the room moderately warm and also served to illuminate the dim cottage. At each end of the stone mantle of the fireplace was a candle. Each candle was made from the withered left hand of a hanged man and encased in wax. The hand on the farther end of the mantle had a silver ring on each finger. Bunduica saw that the four rings appeared to be identical except each had a different blackened rune engraved on the front of it.

The remainder of the cottage room was dimly lit by candles of various sizes, shapes, and colors. Where it was dark, the darkness in the room was profound and drank the light like a succubus taking her lover's fluids.

Now Bunduica noticed a little girl in one dim corner. She was dirty, wearing a dress made from a sack, and had only whites for eyes. Her mouth had been sewn shut, and her neck craned back so that she could look at the ceiling. But she didn't move at all. She was dead. As Bunduica's eyes adjusted to the gloom, she saw where the girl's head had been severed from the neck and sewn back on. Bunduica wasn't even sure that it was the child's own head because it did seem rather large in proportion to the small body.

Bunduica saw two old broken chairs and others that, although not damaged, were situated in impractical positions for furniture. What things came into the cottage to be seated at such odd angles, leaning against walls or lying on the floor? The wall directly opposite the table where Bunduica sat, on either side of the cottage door, contained more shelves, these lined with the many instruments of witchery. There were a mortar and pestle for crushing herbs, and all sorts of cups and beakers for mixing potions, as well as jars filled with human and animal fetuses embalmed in green liquid that resembled that in the cauldron. Bunduica thought she saw one of the fetuses move, as though it still retained some measure of life. There were dolls on the shelves, both male and female. Most of them looked like actual miniature human beings, and she saw that the heads of all of them had been sewn on. One person had a dog's head in place of a human head; a small figure of a dog kneeled beside him with a human head in place of its own.

The hag turned from her infernal broth and brought a dish of some sort of meat to Bunduica. "Eat!" she commanded the young woman. "This will give you strength!" She set down a large foaming jack of some pleasant-smelling libation and said, "Drink! This will steady you for what is to come."

Bunduica pushed away the dish. She didn't know what was in it, but she could guess. She hauled up the drink, however, and quaffed deeply.

As she set the cup down, the door to the cottage slammed open. Bunduica started at the figure stepping through the arched doorway. It was the giant she had seen earlier, or dreamed that she had seen. He must have been seven pedes in height; he had to crouch deeply to make his way inside, he was so tall. His skin was alabaster, startlingly white in contrast with his long, red hair. In shape he looked human, except for his face, which was fixed in a rictus of evil. The curved horns that Bunduica remembered protruded from his head—they dipped toward the ground, and thrust back up in defiance of the heavens. His eyes burned a horrible red. Bunduica couldn't stand to look into them. Two dark bundles hung from his wide belt.

The stranger opened his mouth, showing the elongated fangs of the vampire, and said in a deep, resonating voice, "I don't suppose these two will be troubling you anymore." He reached to his belt and lifted the decapitated heads of the two boys, Tow and Red.

Bunduica almost felt pity for the two young spies.

The demonic stranger tossed their heads onto the floor at her feet. They were nothing more than garbage to him.

Bunduica became dizzy; the room tilted away from her, then toward her, the deep shadows and the candlelight blurring to her vision. Seized in the grip of vertigo, Bunduica tried to look away from the creature's red eyes. They burned. They were awful. She turned to look at the old witch, and saw that the old witch was now gone. But where *could* she have gone?

The horned man came across the floor and sat at the table directly across from Bunduica; the chair was small for him, and she wondered that it hadn't broken beneath his weight. Perhaps it had changed shape in the same way that the witch had disappeared. He asked Bunduica in a booming voice, "Don't like the sight of what you have wrought, woman?"

She summoned the courage to look upon him. Slowly she felt her head begin turning toward him, but against her will. To Bunduica's astonishment, a handsome man with long red hair and a well-groomed beard and mustache now sat across from her. He seemed to have shrunk in size, and horns no longer protruded from his head.

But his eyes were still horrible to look upon. The moment Bunduica looked into them, the red orbs shifted into several pairs of burning slits, and abruptly, a sort of hazy field floated in the air before the creature's eyes. To Bunduica, it looked like a miniature ocean in which demonic eyes awoke and pierced a cosmic veil to penetrate this plane.

She looked away, still facing him, but not staring at those red eyes.

He smiled at her then—and gone were the fangs of the vampire. Remarkably, he was now clad in a black silken tunic and breeches fit for a nobleman. He again spoke in a voice that resonated with a more human timbre. "Is this better? We have much to discuss and little time to do so."

Bunduica felt her heart racing and thumping. Her mouth was dry. Trying to speak, in a quavering voice she managed to ask, "W-who are you? What do you want of me?"

"I think it is my place to ask you those questions, woman. It was *you* who summoned *me.*"

Bunduica's eyes went wide. "You are the demon sent by the rune? How—?"

"I *am* the rune. I am Thorn. I am king of Hel-Valha—and anywhere else I care to tread. The spirit of the child you dispatched to me now screams in agony, awaiting my return. When dawn comes in this world, woman, I must be away to my kingdom. You have offered me a most precious gift with this child you have damned. Now it is I, by my own law, who must give you a gift of vengeance in return. Name your price!"

Bunduica gained strength, then, looking at Thorn, as though he had lent it to her in some fashion, guiding her. She said to him, "This is my price—the torture and death of him who raped and impregnated me, Catus Decanius."

Thorn again took on his original demonic form. From somewhere below Bunduica's line of vision, blocked by the edge of the table, he drew forth a human heart that, she understood, had once belonged to the spying red-haired boy in the woods. In his claw-like grip, he showed it to her and squeezed it. As it dripped blood, the heart formed into a glowing round orb.

Bunduica looked in amazement as a scene inside the glowing ball unfolded before her. Catus Decanius was in his chambers lying in bed. He was not alone. With him were a mother and her son. The mother wore a collar about her throat; attached to it was a leash that hung down one side of her—a leash, as though she were no better than a dog. The boy couldn't have been more than ten years old.

Standing at the edge of the bed, holding her whip, was Helga, the tall muscular German, bare breasted, her bronzed skin glowing. Taken at thirteen from her tribe in a border war with the Romans, unfit for life in a harem and enrolled in the Ludus Magnus, the largest gladiator school in all of Rome, Helga had bought her freedom after much success in the coliseum, then hired herself out as an assassin to any politician willing to meet her price. Hired by Catus, a man with tastes as debased as her own, the amazon was barking orders now at the mother and child as the procurator laughed and squealed with delight, anticipating what he planned to do with the boy, his usual practices.

Helga took hold of the mother's leash and yanked her away, leaving the boy in the company of Catus.

Bunduica looked away in disgust. This was what she had endured when she was raped.

Thorn withdrew the glowing heart and replaced it in a small pouch at his belt. "The worlds have met. I know where he is. Before your sun rises again, Catus Decanius will begin screaming in eternal agony."

"I want to see it."

"You will see it all."

"Then I will come with you?"

"No, Bunduica. You move too slowly. My time is only until daybreak. I must be seated on the throne of Hel-Valha before it is again daylight in this world. But I will return to show you my work before your accurst sun rises. But you—once I have left, wait here inside the cottage. Do not leave for any reason. This is the law."

Thorn departed through the arch of the cottage. The rain had dwindled now to little more than a drizzle.

Bunduica, however, daringly followed behind him, standing just beyond the threshold of the cottage.

Outside, waiting on Thorn, was an enormous horse with the giant, veined wings of a bat and eight legs. Oddly, when Bunduica looked at the eight-legged steed, she saw four men moving beside it, carrying a corpse in a casket. She was reminded of her father's funeral ceremony. He had died leaving half of his kingdom to the emperor, hoping by that generous gesture that the Roman officials would show respect to his family and tribe.

Thorn mounted his great winged steed. It reared on its hind legs and kicked its hooves while flapping the mighty leathern wings. The horse screamed its terrible jubilation to the sky and bared awesome fangs. To be away into the fray of carnage and bloodshed—these excited the beast nearly as much as they did his demonic rider.

Thorn held the fanged, flying beast's reins in one hand and thrust his mighty war hammer, Jolnir, above his head in the other. He screamed the primal war cry that had felled armies and destroyed nations. "Away, Sleipnir," he shouted, and horse and rider soared into the air, mounting the sky of night as though it were a solid road beneath them.

They would fly far to the south, three hundred *millaria*, to the Gallic town of Lugodunon. As Bunduica watched, lightning flashed high above her, and a door with many corridors opened in the sky as Thorn waved his hammer and roared a loud incantation. A door that traversed time and space. He steered the winged beast through the door, and the tear in the sky closed behind them.

Bunduica saw them vanish in the middle of the sky, and she wondered in despair if the demon truly would return. Or perhaps she was indeed dead, now. Or was it that all that she had seen and heard this night had merely been the musings of she herself… finally gone mad?

Chapter IV

Revenge

Catus Decanius' sleep was fitful. Although he had satisfactorily spent himself in a long evening's debauchery with his slaves and now lay in his comfortable bed, covered with a warm downy blanket to stave off the Gallic autumn chill, something was wrong. His dreams had begun pleasantly enough, with the procurator recalling how he had forced himself on the two daughters of an Iceni noblewoman, taking turns with each before he was spent. His pleasure had been heightened by the fact that their mother was bound, stripped, and alternately whipped and molested by Helga while forced to watch his performance with her daughters. His exhibitionism sent a surge of pleasure coursing through him, and in this pleasant dream, just as Catus was starting to build to another climax, the scene changed.

He was still in his sleeping chambers, but he was in the present, awake. Two burning red eyes looked down on him in the darkness. The head of the horned watcher pushed forward from the darkness. The horrible head hovered in the room and now erupted silently in a flaming inverted star and stared down on the Roman disapprovingly.

Catus mumbled, still certain that he was asleep, "No, no, not me. I was just taking what was mine to take." His bed and blanket were now drenched in his feverish sweat. Finally, he cried out and awoke.

Weeping, he slowly let out a sigh of relief. A bad dream. Perhaps he had overexerted himself tonight. Too much wine.

But as he went to call for a slave to enter and change his sweat-soaked bedclothes, the procurator heard a faint sound. It was the odd noise of someone in the distance beating on a wall. With each strike, the noise sounded louder and came nearer. Now it was like a giant battering ram, crushing stone and splintering marble.

Catus pushed himself from his bed to investigate, but then paused. The room had abruptly gone quiet—which was shattered by the crashing of a giant war hammer through the wall opposite his bed. Catus fell backward, onto his fine blankets. Another blow—and an alabaster giant with long red hair and jutting horns appeared where the wall had been.

The stranger's terrible face, fixed in a rictus of hate, was the same face Catus had seen inside the hovering, burning pentagram a moment ago in his dreams.

The snow-colored giant bellowed, "It is time, Catus Decanius. I've come to carry you home."

Catus began weeping again and, in fear, wet his comfortable bed. He called for his guards, but no sound came from his throat. Was he still inside a dream?

His sleeping chambers were situated in the middle of the upstairs in the villa. The guards' chambers were off to each end. The two guards on the south end of the hallway slept in the same room, and they were asleep now: Helga had given them the grieving mother slave to play with after she herself was done with her. They heard their procurator's commands, but his voice at first was no more than part of their own dreams.

The giant leaned close. Gripping Catus by the face in his powerful right claw, Thorn dug in until the head dripped blood, then dragged the Roman through the doorway that opened onto the massive hall of the villa.

The hallway was illuminated by torches ensconced at intervals along the walls. Thorn, still holding Catus by the head, slammed him down onto the stone floor of the hallway, pushing him and knocking the breath out of him. Each time the shivering Catus tried to get up, Thorn threw him down again, and each time, bones broke.

Thorn had his back to the first guard who managed to reach the doorway. The delighted giant was watching Catus trying once more to get to his feet despite some freshly broken ribs, a shattered collar bone, and mangled right arm. Thorn leaned with his left hand wrapped around the handle of Jolnir, his war hammer, with his right arm crossed over his left. The head of the hammer rested on the floor.

As the first guard charged in from behind to run Thorn through with his *spatha*, Thorn swung his war hammer up and, without even turning to look, smashed in the soldier's face with a backhanded blow. Bones crunched and teeth and blood flew all over the hallway. The soldier, spinning around, slumped to the stones face first, into a widening pool of his own blood.

A second guard arrived. He hadn't had time to get into his armor, but he had managed to come armed with a shield. He was further armed now with knowledge of his foe, having just seen for himself the death-work of this giant, truly the most formidable opponent he had yet faced in his service to the procurator.

Thorn slammed a booted foot onto Catus's lower left leg, and more bones crunched. Catus brought up his insides, emptying his guts and doing his best to wipe the remaining vomit from his mouth with his jittery left hand.

Holding the procurator to the floor, Thorn watched the circling guard. Sweat washed down the Roman's face as he tested Thorn's reflexes with a jab toward the abdomen. He moved in several times, feinting, then quickly drew back. The rune was amused, watching this Roman trying to calculate how best to deal with the demonic figure before him.

Then came the wild war cry of the German amazon as she rushed over the top of the stairs at the other end of the hallway.

Moving so quickly that the motion was a blur, Thorn hefted his war hammer and threw it. The great weapon slammed full force into the Roman guard's shield. The force of the blow carried the fighter through the open wall and into Catus' sleeping chamber, the impact breaking his neck and back and crushing his internal organs beneath smashed bones.

The naked, charging Helga fell into a crouch. Thorn crossed his arms and stood as still as a statue, watching her. Quick as a panther, Helga threw three *pugios*, one after another. Thorn quickly caught the leaf-shaped daggers in his left hand. Nostrils flaring, the amazon, dressed only in her weapon belts and scabbards, drew two swords, one with each hand, and spun them in a blinding whirl that cut the air and made whistling sounds as they moved.

The rune was clearly not as moved by her exhibition with weaponry as he was by her nudity. Whatever else he was, the rune was male, with instincts for women, and aside from her close-cropped blonde hair, this fighter was an attractive woman. It was apparent that she didn't care for body hair, however; the only hair she tolerated was the little on her head. She was more than six *pedes* tall and was muscular, yet still retained just enough body fat to be appealing in a feminine fashion. Her breasts were large with big nipples, and her skin was well tanned; surely she spent much time naked in the sun. The rune approved.

Thorn's simultaneous indifference to her display of martial skills and clear appreciation of her body infuriated Helga. She snarled, a wild beast. No man had ever stood before her in battle, ogled her bare body, and lived. This demonic figure, whether he were a specter or a man—he would die. His head was that of a demon, but his body was that of a man and would surely bleed like those of all the other men who had had the misfortune of confronting Helga at arms.

By now all ten of the procurator's remaining guards had donned their armor and arrived from the north end of the hall.

Helga hissed at them, "Stay back! He is mine!"

All stopped where they were. Aside from the procurator, Helga largely ran the household; and if the truth were told, every man in the villa feared her as he had never feared any man.

The German shifted her weight onto her right foot, slowly rolling the short swords in front of her. Both swords had been made especially for her. They were each two *pedes* long, the length of a normal *gladius*, but these blades had jagged edges spaced six thumb-lengths, six *unciae*, apart, going all the way down them on both sides. Wielding such blades in battle gave Helga an immense sense of pleasure, as they caused her victim so much more pain than the clean death of a stab wound from the standard *gladius*.

Thorn calmly unfolded his right arm from his left; his mighty war hammer shot back from the crushed guard's corpse in Catus' bed chamber into his fist, seemingly of its own volition.

Helga winced, a look of wonder on her face. Sweat rolled down her body, and her sienna skin glistened as if she had been rubbed down with oil. "Who are you?" she growled. "*What* are you?"

She was used to being answered immediately by anyone within the sound of her voice, but the giant rune did not react at all. Thorn's silence set her off; as superbly and swiftly as she had ever moved in her fighting life, Helga swung the right-handed sword around for a decapitating blow as the left came up to gut him. No one in the hallway saw Thorn's sword rise, but there it was, in his left hand, deflecting the blow aimed at his neck just as the handle of the massive war hammer knocked aside the German's left-handed sword.

Immediately Thorn lashed out. The head of Jolnir struck Helga in her chest, above her moving breasts, knocking the air from her. Before she could recuperate from that blow, Thorn punched her in the face with his left hand. The German dropped her swords and folded at the waist, staggering backward.

Her nose was broken; the bottom half of her face was red with the running blood. The guards in the hallway stood unmoving then as Thorn retrieved Helga with one hand around her face, lifted her, and tossed her. When she landed farther down the hallway, she rolled headlong down the stairs, out of sight, making a final loud thud as she hit the bottom, then letting out a long moan.

The procurator, seeing this and nearly out of his mind from pain, shouted, "Guards! Fools! Take him!"

Swords slid from their scabbards in the torch light as the score of guards came charging in, shields in front of them. Thorn threw the war hammer into the cluster of men. Howls lifted as men were crushed beneath Jolnir, chests and backs and legs broken apart and heads crushed beyond recognition, as the force of the flying hammer pushed them backwards into walls or caused their own blades to cut them backwards along the throat and face. Thorn held out his left hand; Jolnir returned to his fist; then the rune drew his sword and waded into the seven Romans left standing.

The first man came charging in with his head down and thrust his sword low in an attempt to disembowel the demonic warrior. Thorn brought Jolnir down on the man's head; the helmet cracked like a nut, and the legionnaire's brains came out and slid down his neck as he dropped. Another Roman stepped forward to thrust his sword, point first, into the giant's heart. Thorn parried the blow with his heavier blade and slit the man's throat with the backhand return.

Two others, wielding daggers, tried to tackle Thorn and drag him down; Thorn laughed as the two thrust the daggers into his sides. These were men well trained in their craft, but their cuts were an annoyance to the rune, nothing lethal. As the two continued to strike, another guard jumped onto Thorn's back and tried cutting his throat with his *spatha*. Thorn reached back behind him and plucked the man from his back, digging two fingers into the screaming man's eye sockets to get a grip. He lifted the guard over his head and dropped him onto the floor in front of him. The man groaned, eyeless and bleeding to death from the empty sockets. Thorn then grabbed the two digging steel into his sides, gripping them by their heads and slamming them together. Skull and neck bones cracked, and the two dropped strengthless to the floor.

Three remained—one of whom had survived the force of Jolnir's initial blow. Now he was trying to rise. Thorn grinned, stepped over the two corpses on the floor before him, and swung his sword at the guard's heavily muscled neck. In a moment, his head slid from his shoulders and rolled onto the stones, his face locked in an expression of great surprise.

The two Romans left standing now ran for their lives.

Catus, only somewhat lucid, crawled weakly on the floor. Thorn was showing blood down his sides and legs, but already the wounds had closed up and turned to scars, and the scars themselves were vanishing as if he had never been stabbed. The rune grabbed Catus Decanius by the hair and started dragging him down the stairs. "Your time has come, Procurator."

Regaining consciousness, with a broken nose, smashed left hand, and the multiple cuts and bruises she had suffered from her fall down the stairs, Helga fought to get to her feet. She heard the din of battle and screams coming from upstairs. The demonic stranger was slaughtering everyone in the household. Her ankle was sprained, but she had survived much worse. She hurried away from the stairs, down the corridor, half dragging and half running on her lame foot. *I can be free of this place in a moment*, she told herself. *Rouse the local praetorians. Not even the demon can stand before an army of disciplined Roman steel.*

Ignoring her pain, Helga reached the arched doorway. *The portico. The stables. Then I am free.* She threw the bolt and was through. Outside. Free—

She let out a piercing scream.

There was a flurry of hooves. The two remaining household guards lay one to each side of the doorway, mauled and mutilated. Helga saw the giant, eight-legged horse as it flapped its membranous wings and bared its terrible fangs. She saw its burning red eyes.

Then it was on her.

Chapter V

"You Are the Witch."

Bunduica had pulled a chair up to the small fireplace to bask in its warmth. She had been drowsing for only a few minutes when the door to the cottage slammed open again.

She was sure she must be dreaming. Could Thorn have returned so soon? Because it could have been no more than half an hour when the rune had taken to the sky on his flying beast, headed for Gaul.

She came wide awake as Thorn snorted, pushing his way through the opening, and dropped Catus Decanius at her feet. The Roman was bound hand and foot and grimacing in pain from his broken bones and lacerations.

Bunduica stood, looking at her enemy—*"Open wide the Gates! Manifest Rune Thorn!"*—and slowly drew the athame from her belt.

Thorn threw up his hand. "Hold, woman!"

Bunduica stopped close, looking up at him.

"A hunter hunts for food to fill his stomach," said Thorn, "but he does not discard the hide. He needs it to cover himself against the elements in winter. Every death serves many purposes for the hunter. A god is no exception. Know this: It is a god's pleasure to feed on the spirits of human beings. Their lives—every pain, sorrow, and misery—each of these is a delicacy for the god's consumption. A sorcerer possessing the knowledge of a god can do many things."

Thorn walked outside and reached into the saddlebag on Sleipnir. He returned and threw a large book onto the cottage table. It was identical to the *Book of Dead Runes*, the grimoire from which Balor had taught her the runic incantation.

Bunduica was puzzled. "I don't understand. Balor's book?"

"My book," Thorn told her. "It was I who brought it to your world. I wrote it. There are two other copies of it in your world now, but the only one in the possession of a human is the one your druid retains."

Thorn reached down and grabbed Catus Decanius, throwing him hard against the wall so that he was in an upright, seated position. Catus grunted but could do no more. Thorn had gagged him with a strip torn from the procurator's own sleeping robe so that he wouldn't have to endure the annoyance of Catus pleading for his life during the return to the witch's house.

Squatting, Thorn touched his hand to Catus' head and, with an almost pious look on his face, as if in mockery of some sacred religious ritual, he recited an incantation. Catus shook as if he were having a seizure. His face turned purple, and he foamed at the mouth.

Bunduica moved forward one step, then stopped.

As if in response to her apprehension, Thorn told her, "He is not dying. Quite the contrary. Now he cannot die until his body is all gone. Each part of him that you sever will die, but as long as any part of him is left intact, he will feel pain. And so this will go until he is no more."

Thorn grinned as he saw understanding in Bunduica's eyes.

"There is more." The god walked to the fireplace mantle and took one of the silver rings with the rune on it from the wax-covered, withered dead man's hand. He turned and slipped it onto Bunduica's forefinger. Thorn then reached down and with his clawed finger tore Catus' right eye from the socket. Blood spurted onto the cottage floor as Catus jerked and shook in agony.

"Hold his eye in the hand on which you wear the ring," said the rune.

Bunduica took Catus Decanius' eye in her hand. As she did, there was a swirling of darkness before her, and a window opened in the midst of the room.

"This ring will help you translate the language in the book. Each severed part of a human's anatomy opens a door by which knowledge may be procured and wonders may be experienced. Do you wonder what is happening and what will become of Catus' henchwoman? Squeeze the eye gently in your hand and look into the window."

A rich, purple-hued pattern pulsated, then exploded inside the strange window. It was replaced by a clear image of Helga lying in a bed. Her eyes were rheumy as she beheld sights not of this world, as if she were dying. Her tanned face had turned a pale, ashen grey. Helga's forehead was beaded with sweat. Two servants of Catus' household now tended to the amazon and wiped the sweat from her fevered brow. Her stomach was swollen as if she would explode. Her feet and legs were tied to the bed, and her mouth was opened in what could only be a scream. Suddenly her stomach exploded and a demonic head burst through.

Blood and offal struck the walls and covered the nearest servant. The servant woman who had been tending the amazon was screaming as she held her hands out and frantically tried to shake the demon's blood from them. Helga, opened from the breastbone down, lay unmoving as everything that been inside her now lay steaming on either side of her. And still, the demon that had come from her struggled to move from the bed, awkwardly moving itself over her bound legs.

Bunduica had seen Helga die giving birth to a creature with the misshapen head of a monster, the face of a human, and the body of a horse. She saw it as it ran from the mansion of Catus Decanius, screaming its hatred at being born, as its eight horse's legs carried it away into the night.

Thorn then slipped another ring on her middle finger. He drew one of the leaf-shaped daggers that Catus' amazon had thrown at him and grabbed Catus by the wrist. Catus kicked and tried to get away. Tears rolled down his face. Thorn then severed Catus' index finger near the base and squeezed the blood out of it. Catus, kicking and squirming, had vomited from the pain but had been forced to swallow most of it back down because of the gag in his mouth.

Thorn removed a jar of reddish liquid from behind some tubes on the shelf of witches' tools and set it down on the table by the book. He then plopped Catus' severed finger into the jar and told Bunduica, "Soak the index finger in the jar for three days, then dry it by the fire until it withers. Wear it about your neck when you wear this ring on your finger, and no human or animal eye will detect your presence. The rest you may learn of your own accord, as I have provided you with the book and the instruments."

Bunduica held out her hand and gazed wide-eyed in awe at the rings. A smile crept over her face. "Might you destroy the whole Roman army and the emperor, too?"

Thorn shook his great head. "I am a god of the old world. As I have told you, the new gods feed on the pain, suffering, and sacrifice of human beings. I am an exception. I am the oldest god not to have fallen into oblivion. There is no greater morsel for me than feeding on the very essence of another god. The stronger the god, the greater the hunt, and the greater the feast."

He continued, "It is a new era. Many young gods are being born. There is an upstart god worshipped by a tribe far from here, in the east. This tribe is called the Hebiru. Almost one hundred years ago, the Hebiru god sent forth a son. The god is a war god, but his son preaches peace as a facade to attract and enslave the masses. Over fifty years ago, the Romans put this man to death because of the trouble he caused them. In the years to come, the Romans unknowingly will pave the way for the upstart war god of the Hebiru. Their cult will spread to the far corners of this world. As the faith in this god grows, so shall his strength grow. I will return one day, and I will slay him when the fruit is ripe for the harvest. Then there will be a feast fit for only such a king as myself."

Bunduica remembered Suetonius. "There was a Roman general who was responsible for my mother's death. He took the old druid's sight. They burned his eyes out."

Thorn grunted, whirled, and shoved a clawed hand through Catus' chest. It made a squishy, tearing sound as he quickly withdrew Catus' heart from behind his ribs. Blood sprayed all over the room. Catus, lying on the floor, coughed profusely and gasped as if he were dying. Thorn reassured the girl, "He won't die. He can't until he is all used up." Thorn then squeezed the remaining blood from Catus' heart and held it up to look at it closely. The heart formed into a glowing globe; in it, Thorn saw flashes of battle and wholesale death, and he saw Suetonius' insane glare. The general's face became that of a demonic woman with piercing evil eyes; then it flashed back to Suetonius' grinning leer.

Thorn smiled, a look of pleasant surprise on his face, and he said, "Ashteroth!"

Bunduica cocked her head slightly to one side and gave Thorn an inquisitive look.

The rune told her, "Your people refer to her as Andraste."

Bunduica's face lit up. "My mother called on Andraste to grant her victory in her war against the Romans. She gave thousands of lives to Andraste on her bloody altars. But when my mother needed her most, this goddess turned her back on her."

Thorn continued gazing into the glowing orb. "Andraste didn't just turn her back on your mother. She clothed herself in the very flesh of the man who destroyed your mother. She now possesses Suetonius."

Bunduica was stunned.

Before she spoke again, Thorn said to her, "Oh, yes! To drink the essence of one of the Ancients again. I am sure that you want to shell the nut that is hiding in that woman. Remember what I said about the hunter and how he wastes nothing valuable? Study the book."

"I am the hunter?"

"You are the hunter, woman. Now… when Catus Decanius is no more than a stump, summon me again. I will take his Ka. That is when the great suffering shall begin."

"His Ka?"

"The Ka is the spirit that leaves the body once it truly dies. Once I have his Ka, I will sever it into seven layers, the Ka still existing, but in turn branching off into the Ren, Sekhem, Akh, Bau, Sheut, and Sekhu. Each will suffer its individual torments but, at the same time, each will bear the pain of the others, as well as feel all of the suffering at once again, as a whole. Study well the *Book of Dead Runes*. With the ring and the finger charm, you may come and go between this cottage at the edge of the world and the world of men."

Bunduica asked him then, the rune, Thorn, this strange man or god-man whom she had, with Balor's magic, called down to exact her revenge on Rome, "Tell me… am I dead?"

"Dead?" he said to her.

She had spoken the runes, sounding the syllables perfectly. Under fear of the storm and the wild hunters, she had hurried to this witch's cottage—whoever or whatever the witch had been. She had feared then that she had died and was only her spirit, whatever remained of herself. What had Balor said to her? *"You will be working in magick and summoning forces the druids have shunned since before the great cataclysms of old."*

Thorn, sensing her concern or reading her mind, said to her in a voice now more placent or soothing, "No, Bunduica, you are not dead. Through your courage, you have earned your place. Here you may stay. You are the witch you first met here. Although this place borders on space and time, your accurst sun still rises here, and so I must be away. Know that I will return in four months, as you reckon time, on the eve of Brigid, in the heart of winter."

And he was gone.

All of it—storm, boys, book, babe, hunters, witch, bloody vengeance—a dream, a dark dream, no more than that?

Feeling the strength that Thorn had left her with, Bunduica slowly turned and glared at the mutilated but yet living figure lying on the floor. She smiled, and the smile rose to her eyes and imbued them with a maddened glint.

She went to Catus and removed his gag.

He vomited everything within onto the cottage floor. Then he screamed, and he screamed, and he screamed. And that was just the beginning of eternity as he was to know it.

Chapter VI

Feeding on the Essence of Another God…

In a far corner of the throne room in the great palace of Hel-Valha, the Ka of Suetonius Paulinus was stretched out on the floor and was skinless. His flesh had been neatly peeled away from his body and was now spread out and fastened to the floor by hooks made of fire. He could still feel the pain of suffering that torture. He—his Ka—was held in place by vine-like tendrils with suction cups that sent a burning serum coursing throughout him. His sightless eyes stared, as though keeping them open might somehow grant him some sign of light. He opened his mouth and screamed repeatedly, but no one present could hear him.

In fact, no one anywhere could hear him aside from himself. The sound that escaped his throat was silent to those outside his own head but amplified infinitely inside him. The deafening roar of his screaming served only to heighten his pain and confusion, but the actual physical pain to his Ka was such that he could not cease, and he could not die.

His Sheut was nailed to the wall with daggers. His Sheut was himself, precisely similar to his body as it had been on earth, but it was a complete shadow of that body from head to toe. The hilt of each dagger was an elongated reptilian head that bit him over and over, and his body shook in convulsions, wracked with venomous pain. His head leaned forward, and from his mouth drooled spittle. The falling drool was the shadow of spittle as it hit the floor and vanished as though it had never existed. Suetonius' Ka felt the venom coursing through his veins, felt himself dying the death that he could never partake of. His Sheut, in turn, felt the acid boiling through the veins of the shadow; heard the deafening screams amplified infinite times over. Each of the seven aspects of his being was isolated in separate viewing chambers by invisible barriers, and each felt the pain of the other, and all felt the torment collectively.

The Ka of Catus Decanius was in another far right corner of the throne room. Catus slowly slid down the spear he was impaled upon as it rose out of the floor in an endless upward motion. It was the Spear of Endless Ascent. Blood ran out of his mouth, and he moaned. His arms had been removed, and his legs were now in their place. His arms were where his legs had been, and he wore his internal organs on the outside of his body—intestines, heart, liver. His Ren, which was his true name, stared into the Mirror of Truth at his own jackal head and wept in shame. He couldn't stop weeping at the revelation of what he truly was and always would be. He wanted to try to find a place to hide, perhaps to curl up, to become a child again, but he was frozen in front of the magick mirror, and always would be.

To all of this Thorn gave no heed as he lolled on his throne. The throne was carved of solid onyx, and the top corner posts were adorned by the ancient horned and fanged vampire skulls of his ancestors set into the onyx. On each skull sat the two ravens, Hugin and Munin. They took many forms and flew throughout all the worlds and dimensions, gathering whatever information Thorn required.

At the rune's feet, gorgeous women of all shades writhed in an orgy of unending pleasure. There were goddesses and succubi of all types intertwined. Some looked like mortal women, some were snow white and had red eyes like Thorn, and some had wings and were covered in thin fur, as are bats. There were sirens with the bodies of mermaids and mouths of fangs, and there were those who were mortal in form but colored like various jewels. Transparent beasts, lions, apes, and man-sized lizards casually loped in and out of the throne room. They looked as if they were made of crystal.

Thorn slumped on his throne in the ecstasy of the greatest intoxication a god can experience. The smoking pipe that now lay on the arm of the onyx throne gave out the remaining mists of what was left over from the previous session of his feeding. Rubbery vine-like tubes ran from the pipe and were fastened with suction cups along the body of Andraste.

Andraste was securely fastened by multi-colored, jewel-like bands to a stake that rose from the floor. She writhed and burned in a fire that sent out waves of flames in all colors, some visible to the human eye, many outside the range of what humans recognize. The burning goddess was contained in an invisible, cylindrical barrier, penetrated by the suction-like, flexible tubes attached to Thorn's pipe. Her screams, like those of Catus Decanius and Suetonius Paulinus, could be heard only inside her being, infinitely amplified as they were.

Thorn was taking her very essence into him, and this act had left him in a slumber, within the Great Dreams that only an Ancient can hope to dream. The rune was intoxicated by all seven layers of the goddess' spirit, and he would revel in the visions and dreams that were the wondrous events actually taking place on another plane. When this euphoria was complete, he would awaken ten times stronger than he had been before taking up his pipe.

Even now, the light was diminishing in Andraste's piercing, evil eyes as the fire consumed her. As she burned, she shifted and changed into the various incarnations she had assumed down through the ages, from the demonic appearance of the platinum-haired, terrible goddess of victory down to the dark-headed, full-bosomed peasant girl she had assumed to waylay hapless men and drag them down to their doom. Only a few more burnings remained before Thorn would consume her essence, before Andraste fell into oblivion and become as if she had never been.

Thorn smiled the smile of an Ancient in the throes of the Ecstasy of the Great Feast.

Epilogue

Bunduica's prowess in the black arts had grown so rapidly and to such an astonishing degree that it had surprised even Thorn. Upon the witchmaker's last visit to his prodigy at the cottage at the edge of the world, Thorn had concluded his stay with, "I don't think you will be needing me for anything else."

She had thanked the rune and wished him well on his next hunt.

Occasionally Bunduica would look in on old Balor. The old man swelled with equal parts pride and awe each time he heard the voice of the woman that he considered the daughter he had never had.

Aside from visiting the old druid, the witch's trips into the world of men became less and less frequent as her strength in her art had grown. She much preferred the company of succubi, incubi, lamiae and the associations with assorted other-worldly creatures at the celebration of the sabbat.

With the overwhelming number of feats that she had rapidly been capable of performing, it had only recently dawned on Bunduica what results the practice of necromancy might yield.

* * *

Just a shadow of a woman was cast on the faintly candlelit wall of the cottage on Walpurgisnacht. The shade spoke in a waning voice like one who is dreaming aloud. "You have done well by your tribe. You have avenged the Iceni, and you have avenged your kin. I will always love you."

Tears rolled down Bunduica's face as she sobbed. "I will always love you, Mother."

Faint, and fading back into the world of shades, Boadicea trailed off. "I… know…"

…Leaving Bunduica alone in the empty room.

In the distance, she heard the ecstatic cries of the demons, devils, nymphs, and satyrs reveling in the sabbat, her new home.

Vengeance of the Insane God

By Jason Tarpey

INTRODUCTION

This was an age of silver light, an age of steel forged out of darkness. Before it, the things of chaos crawled and swam and devoured. After it, darkness and chaos would reign again. It was a time as brief and thin as a moonlit blade swung in the night.

The dark below Vyntane was absolute. It was the space between the stars, or a night without them. What was thrown into the darkness will prosper in it—it will hate and feed and grow. The white horde has waited an aeon, long enough for the truth to become legend, long enough for vengeance to invoke the Gods.

Chapter I

Landing

"Time to rise!" the captain barked from the foredeck to the men in the berth below. Sunlight was leaking through the cracks in the deck above and the planks creaked under the weight of the heavy commander, known only as Wolfhair to the Arginese men aboard his charter ship, *Seasplitter.* "Man the oars, we're approaching the cliffs of Vyntane!"

Rænon lifted his pounding head, rubbed the crust from his eyes. He emptied the rest of his nearly depleted wineskin and splashed water on his face from a nearby wash bowl. "Now, you drunken dogs!" Wolfhair was only a charter captain now, but he carried with him a reputation as a ruthless warrior and former commander of a fleet of raider ships from the north in Haiklan. Rænon would oblige him but only to avoid the annoyance of the captain's chiding so early in the day.

As he ascended the stairs and stood on the forecastle, he could see the dark cliffs of Isahin through the morning mist, like a huge black blade fallen from the hand of a god, landing sideways into the ocean.

Rising steeply, the cliffs held a perfect shape and singular altitude for miles, save for the port of Vyntane, which clove the only break in the sea wall and held only one accessible harbor.

As he took up his oar and started to row with the others, Rænon reflected on the last two weeks since he left his home in Maehlin, sold his horse in Runefare, and bought his way on Wolfhair's ship to Isahin.

It was summer now. His father, a Guard of Lourn, had been slain that winter by Navordian jackals who ambushed him and his riders while they were crossing the River Bruna returning back into Aelbrond. Firing arrows at their back, his company was dragged out downriver, their horses taken and belongings stripped, and their bodies laid bare on the banks of the Bruna on Aelbrond's side.

Rænon wanted vengeance for his family. He had pyre-forged Pitkeeper with the spirit and strength of his father's ashes; now the blade held his whole line of ancestors. He would take it to Navordi, to find the band of thieves responsible for his father's death.

Alas, by himself, and with no way of finding his father's slayer in the murderous capital of Kynara, he resolved to sail to Isahin. The Guards of Lourn would do their own investigating; for now he would delay his vengeance to see the city his ancient ancestors built, to learn the art of the metal-folding swordsmiths of Vyntane, and chiefly, to be alone with his grief.

Seasplitter made port and the five other men, Haiklaners like Wolfhair, disembarked the vessel. They were sailing south to the small isle of Larion on a modest craft docked at the opposite end of the pier.

Rænon looked back at Wolfhair who was still standing on the gangplank, rubbing his long grey beard and looking disdainfully on the populace of the harbor. Rænon called, "If I wish to return to Aelbrond, can I find you at this harbor for a trip back?"

"I won't make port here again and I cast off at dawn. I have heard rumors of The Starless Night and a boiling evil beneath this city. The wise move would be to return to the mainland with me now—for a fee, of course," the grizzled captain replied with a grin.

"Double your money for a short cruise across the Arginese? I'll take my chances with the 'boiling evil!'" Rænon offered sarcastically.

Wolfhair only grumbled a curse and disappeared into his quarters.

The Starless Night. The name troubled Rænon. It seemed familiar to him from the stories of his childhood but he could not recall from what legend it came. Wolfhair had made a few ominous insinuations about Vyntane during the long trip from Runefare, but Rænon had dealt with evil before, and he remained ardent.

It was good to be on solid ground after sailing for ten days. He felt the cool sea breeze on his face. He took in the briny air and gazed up at the towering black cliffs rising sharply above him. The spires on the walls of The Iron Castle peaked over the edge, like the claws of a hawk perched on a ledge about to leap.

Rænon walked along the wharf leading to the main road which wound up the steep crack in the cliff and up to Vyntane. Two merchant ships from Arginor were docked and unloading goods to trade for the iron mined on Isahin. The ore pulled from the western coast of the isle was more easily accessed than the iron mines in Aelbrond in the mountains near Shunned Albrunn, a range that the hardened Aelbronders would rather cross an ocean to avoid.

He saw a Mareship from Haiklan, with its carven prow resembling a long-maned horse, docked and unloading lumber. The other vessel was a large galley from Tarsul, bringing in fabrics and a brightly colored harvest. Rænon overheard from his fellow passengers on *Seasplitter* that the desert-dwelling mystics of Kynara sailed their sleek vessels to Vyntane, bringing wine and women. On occasion, it was said, a tattered ship from the barren and disdained southern continent of Nitaar would enter Vyntane's harbor, having not much to offer but relics and antiquities that only a few scholars and collectors on Isahin would be interested in.

Ropes and pulleys led down from the city high above the harbor and baskets were filled with goods from the ships. The loaded baskets were led up and fed back down with the iron ore that many of the merchants were trading for. Large carriages filled with people were being pulled up to the city as well. In the chance a Vyntanite didn't fancy climbing the steep and long road up the chasm and back into the city, they could pay a fee (which not many could afford) to ride up.

He paced along the quayside and peered down the alleys looking for a suitable place to quench his thirst but there was nothing in sight. Turning down the last alley at the very end of the harbor he spotted The Cormorant, a dingy tavern with one window and a tattered wooden sign that hung unevenly from a rusted chain.

As he approached, Rænon saw a figure walking towards him from beyond the tavern. At first, he saw only a faint red shape emerging from the darkness of the alley. He slowed his pace as the figure gave him a feeling of unease. The young barbarian gripped the hilt of his sword and noticed that the dark robed, crimson turbaned figure walked with both arms outstretched, holding out what appeared to be a small body or dead animal, wrapped in tan cloth and bound in silver thread.

They passed one another silently. Without the dark robed man looking at him directly, Rænon could swear that the ghoulish man had a ruby tint to his pupils and an unhealthy smile on his dark lips. Before reaching the mouth of the alley and the beginning of the wooden pier that lead back to the ships, the man holding the wrapped mystery bent down and began descending a stairway that Rænon was embarrassed to admit he didn't notice before. *Those steps must lead down below the ocean,* he thought to himself, for the sea was crashing into the rocky cliffs not thirty feet from where he stood in the alley at the very end of the harbor.

He walked farther down the alley which was carved out of the black cliff, past The Cormorant, to find out from whence this shadowed figure had appeared. There was nothing past the tavern, no other doors, no rooms. The alley terminated into a steep slate rock wall that rose and became the cyclopean black cliff below Vyntane.

His gut turned, told him that he needed to keep his wits about him in this new place, and then he remembered the legends passed down by his people, tales of the first men from Maelhin to sail to this isle and what they encountered here.

The barkeep eyed Rænon closely as he walked through the doors of The Cormorant. He stood out as a barbarian from Aelbrond. The heavy longsword at his side with a bear's head pommel gave him away as a Maehlin warrior. He was over six and a half feet tall and the corded muscle of his scarred and bulky frame belied his young age and quiet manner. His umber hair fell below his broad shoulders and his leather breeks and bear fur coat were unique amongst the more colorfully dressed patrons of The Cormorant.

Though it was barely midday the tavern was already full with traders from Haiklan, a few whores lounging with merchants on the benches towards the back, and a small group of dark-featured Kynarans drinking their wine in a solitary corner.

Rænon gave the Kynarans a baleful look as he called the barmaid for a brew. She smiled at him, which didn't go unnoticed by her father, the barkeep and owner. She brought him an overfull cask of ale. It sloshed as she walked, the foam falling on her hand, which she casually wiped on his bear fur. He grumbled, astonished at her gall but allowing it to use the moment she looked down to admire her breast falling out of her shirt. "Do you have rooms for rent here at The Cormorant?" he said as he averted his gaze.

She bent down to speak quietly to him. "The only rooms are above the harbor in Vyntane and any visitor must report to the city guard before being led through the gates and into the city." She turned to walk back to the bar.

"This is not a free place?" he called back to her.

She cocked her head back. "No longer. Not free, not safe."

He turned and sat at a table by the window facing the alley where he passed the robed figure. He sat there and brooded. His cold northern disposition kept him from starting conversation with strangers and his quiet nature prevented him from making companions. Instead, he stared at the black walls of the tavern that were carved by hand out of the sable cliffs and then back through the filthy pane, into the dark alley, wondering if it was a mistake to travel so far only to be met with such unwelcome portents.

He downed a barrel of ale, it seemed to the barkeep, but Rænon sat stoically, undaunted by the strong Isahinian brew. He sat for hours drinking until most of the other patrons had spilled out of the tavern, all except for a few of the merchants and whores in the back, and a lone woman sitting separate from them at a booth, talking to the barmaid. Multiple times the woman in the booth noticed Rænon looking at her, and after a few awkward glances she stood up and sauntered towards him with a plate of half-eaten fish in one hand and a cask of ale in the other.

She was light of hair but dark of eye, tall and shapely, with fair skin and deep scarlet lips. She wore a long olive-colored thin shirt, methodically unbuttoned. She bore little else save for her leather sandals and her belt, worn high on her waist a few inches below her large breasts. On her side she holstered a dagger with a golden handle, embellished with rubies and strange blue gems, its craftsmanship unlike anything he had seen in Aelbrond.

"I cannot afford you," Rænon uttered. "Besides, it is time I head up the road to Vyntane and find a place to sleep."

Her smile turned. "If I were a whore, do you think I would bother with an obviously destitute barbarian like yourself?"

He grabbed the cask and plate from her. "Fair enough. That food is welcome, as is your company, girl." Rænon slurred, the strong Isahinian ale finally impeding his better judgement.

"My name is Aren, mainlander, and you're welcome." She eyed him carefully. "Are you from Aelbrond? Why have you come so far to Isahin?"

"I've come to work, and learn the ancient skill of my forebearers. My name is Rænon. Am I so transparent that I've come from Aelbrond?"

She smiled again, her initial impulses to walk away leaving her. "You could've found work somewhere in Aelbrond, I'm sure. And if you wish to learn a trade you could have went to a more hospitable land to do it. They won't be kind to a stranger up at the gates. Travelers are usually turned away to find passage back to the mainland on their own. Not many ships coming and going anymore."

Rænon scowled. "That bastard Wolfhair said nothing of the guard turning men away."

"Wolfhair? Is that who brought you here!" She laughed. "That old dog has brought his last ship of fools it seems. There is a chance you can convince the guard to grant you entrance to Vyntane if you tell them you wish to toil in the mines, otherwise I doubt they will let you in."

"I'm not worried about getting into the city, and if the guardsmen want to keep their guts, they will be kind to a weary traveler." He took a drink from his cask and hailed the barmaid to bring him another. "I have little reason to return to Aelbrond, and even less to return to Maehlin. My father was slaughtered by Navordian scum before he could return home and finish my training. I wish to finish that training here, in the city my people built a thousand years ago." He waited for her reply, feeling foolish for being so open. He resolved to leave the tavern before he gave anything more away.

She clasped her hands together and nervously wove her fingers. "I am from Kynara. I escaped Navordi as a child after my family was also killed. I walked for days into the Kynarian Desert until I was discovered, nearing my death, by a traveling caravan of entertainers. They were singers, actors, seers… I was trained as an actress and court dancer. I sailed here two years ago from Tarsul to serve in the court of King Tavrik, Vyntane's loutish ruler. I've heard Navordi has since become a corner of rotting hell. No doubt there are thousands of men there who would kill any riders from Aelbrond they passed."

Rænon stared at her bitterly. Though she too was a victim of the Navordians, he held the unreasonable notion that all in Kynara had turned to treachery or dark sorcery. It was a thought he knew he must let go of, even if the land had been overrun with an evil that he didn't even respect, an evil born of weakness and deceit.

Aren continued, "I'm also afraid to tell you that this place has become just as dangerous. The Starless Night are now leaving the castle and roaming the streets. Fewer beggars are seen littering the alleys and even some of my friends have gone missing in the last few weeks. Their disappearances have been ruled as suicides, but I knew the girls in my troupe, and though Vyntane is gloomy, they would not hop into the cold ocean like some forlorn lover. No, I fear an even worse fate has befallen them. I came down to the harbor this morning to make sure my friend over there is safe." Aren pointed to the barmaid that had been bringing Rænon his drinks, and she smiled back at her.

"That's the second time someone has warned me against The Starless Night," Rænon uttered. "Why would I fear a small cult of dwarfish men? I think I passed one in the alley outside before coming in this place. Do they wear dark robes and red turbans?"

"Gods, they are coming down to the harbor in the light of day?" Aren said in a shaking voice. "Where was it going?"

Rænon gave a curious look. "It? Well, *it* was going down a stairway, carved down into the cliffs by the pier. *He* was holding what appeared to be a body, wrapped so completely in cloth I couldn't discern what kind of body it was."

Aren drank down her entire cup, set it down, her hands trembling. "They might be taking children down now, and all the entrances to the caves below Vyntane have been left unguarded by our foolish leader King Tavrik. I swear he is in league with those demons and I have seen them for what they are, creatures from the Pit. The ones you see in The Iron Castle can pass for men, their hellish features and small curled horns hidden beneath their headwrap. They are the caretakers of the world below Vyntane."

This Aren was being very honest considering they had just met, Rænon thought. She seemed scared enough to be telling the truth, but he couldn't trust her so quickly. She was Kynaran, after all. "And how would you know this?" he asked suspiciously.

She took a long breath and continued nervously, "There are tunnels descending down below the castle that lead to the carved-out halls that the first men who came here built, your ancestors, it seems. Below those halls and crypts of men lie the caverns which lead down and spread out in every direction all over Isahin. That's where the true Starless Night resides…"

"I recall the legend," Rænon interrupted. Aren glared at him and continued.

"One night, less than a month ago, after I entertained the King and his nobles, and they lay about drunk on the floor, I slipped away, down to the kitchens to gather some bread and dried meat to bring back to my camp. Foolishly, I kept going down, past the food stores and weapon keeps, beyond the Crypt of Kings, into a great hall with a colossal iron statue of your god, Farick. In a far corner of that hall I noticed a hole, blasted through the stone floor by some unholy force. I looked into that pit and saw nothing—the unlit blackness of nothing. No steps could be seen, the sheer sides of the hole were only discernible for a few feet until disappearing, but what I could see looked like the walls of a cave. That must be the end of man's domain and the beginning of the sulfurous bowels of Isahin."

Rænon looked unsatisfied. "So you saw nothing in the pit? I have seen caves before, girl, and they are usually dark."

She stared at him crossly. "You will remember my name or I will leave you here, with no further warning of what you've foolishly landed on." Aren's voice shook. "It wasn't what I saw in the hole, but what I saw behind me when I turned to leave. A pale thing, hiding behind the giant god statue. Its skin was white as the moon and completely hairless. It stood upright, bobbed its head and looked at me with lidless crimson eyes. It bared its yellow fangs like a rabid hound and then came rushing at me. From behind the statue its head looked like a man's, but as it neared I realized it was but a gruesome mockery of man, apish, with small ram's horns on the side of its skull. I could hear its hooves clacking louder on the floor, like the legs of a giant crab on the stone flags. Somehow I fought the urge to faint and grabbed the dagger from my belt. It was almost upon me when it leapt high above my head and went straight down into the pit. I didn't hear a sound, no thud or splash of water, just the awful shrieking it made as it jumped and fell into the abyss."

"And you think this creature you saw and the man I passed in the alley outside are one and the same?" Rænon remained skeptical. "I've heard the tales of the warriors from Maehlin who built Vyntane and what they fought back into the earth. Remember my people are the guardians of The Summoner's Pit, my line are the keepers of The Waste of En-Faln. I have heard tales like this for twenty years. I am not afraid."

"Hearing tales and seeing them in the flesh is very different, swordsman. I think The Starless Night that we see in the city are more man than demon in appearance, but make no mistake, they are not men. I have met a lord from The Red Jewel, his name is Sanhar, who told me that the acolytes of The Starless Night have been breeding with King Tavrik's degenerated line for hundreds of years. That is why a small fraction of these demons resemble men. That is also why Tavrik allows them to worship in their caverned temples under the city, offering sacrifices to their insane god, and to be hidden in plain sight as caretakers of Vyntane's historic underworld."

Rænon entertained her, "Why would you stay here one moment longer if you believed this to be true?"

Aren looked straight into his eyes. "I am leaving in two days. Lord Sanhar is coming from The Red Jewel and I will return with him to serve in his court. I suggest you leave with me as well. There won't be as many ships coming to port anymore. King Tavrik has increased the tax on ore so much that no one will buy or trade, and rumors of his lunacy and depravity are spreading among the merchants."

He sat still and silent, then finished his brew. "I will not leave because some pale goats are stealing beggars and hopping around in their caves. I thank you for sharing your story but I'm not sailing anywhere just yet."

"Very well, swordsman, but remember the tales from your own people. If one summoner can call up from the pit The Wyrms of Fire and Frost, imagine what an army of sorcerous creatures can invoke." She paused, feeling embarrassed to be offering this wild tale as a truth. "I don't know why I've shared this with you, but something tells me you should be forewarned if you expect to survive in Vyntane."

Aren rose and walked back to her friend the barmaid, looking back once. She gave him a graven glance as if he were already dead and she looked upon his pyre-forge.

Rænon left a stack of coins on the table and stepped outside the tavern. It was now dark, later than he wanted to start his trek. *Too much time listening to the ravings of a scared dancer*, he told himself silently.

He walked down the alley toward the pier, this time staring down into the passage that he saw the acolyte carry his burden into. He knelt down next to the edge of the stone stairs and listened. It was only the sound of the waves crashing against the cliffs, of the noisy seabirds nesting high above him. He rose to his feet and started to walk toward the main road.

Was there a faint sound of beating drums? He walked back to the underground passage and listened again. At first just a hum, it swelled louder into the sound of rolling, sinister chanting.

Chapter II
Vyntane

Rænon walked down the unlighted pier and into the night, up the steep road toward Vyntane. He stopped halfway up to get a pull from his wineskin. Each side of the path rose into the steep, slick rock wall, always at least fifty feet high, trapping those on the road to travel up or down, never around. He could see *Seasplitter* still docked in the harbor far below. The other two ships he saw earlier were already gone.

His mind went back to the tavern. What was it that he had heard coming from the passage down in the alley? He could still hear the hum faintly in his mind, the horrible chanting reverberating in the back of his skull.

He fought the urge to sleep, resolving to get into Vyntane's gates before finding quarters and getting rest. Only a mile or two left. He stood up and began the march toward the city.

The dawn was shining its golden light upon the monolithic stone gate of Vyntane when Rænon finally crested the hill. This was surely the work of his ancestors, and he looked proudly upon it.

The gate itself was chiseled out of the top of the cliff, using Vyntane's natural defenses to reinforce man's short domain over Isahin. It rose to a high arch where the dark green turf covered its precipice. Nothing could be seen beyond the gate. It was the only way into Vyntane without sailing around the isle, and the only opening through the cliff face was a few chariots wide. In this small opening stood three guards. Their helms lay on the ground as if they were too uncomfortable to suffer and their swords remained sheathed as Rænon approached.

"Hold right there!" one of the guards shouted at Rænon as he stood not twenty feet from the opening of the gate. "What's your business in Vyntane?" the guard questioned.

Rænon knew within a breath that these three couldn't prevent him from passing through the gate any more than they could prevent the tide. "I've come from Aelbrond, to work on Isahin and learn the skills of Vyntane's warrior smiths."

"Then you have come very far for nothing, Aelbronder. King Tavrik has sealed this gate. No strangers allowed entrance," the guard yelled back.

Rænon scowled. "I am no stranger. I am from Maehlin. My people built this gate and the city beyond it."

The guardsmen laughed. "Aye, that may be true, but now King Tavrik sits the throne and he doesn't honor past deeds or allegiances. He pays us well to keep mainlanders out of Vyntane. Now head back down the road and return to your mountains."

It had been months since Rænon had drawn his blade, even before his father was murdered, and now all the anger of that injustice swelled up in him, ready to be unleashed on whomever was the first in his path.

He continued to walk towards the gate. The first guard, the one who spoke, unsheathed his sword and pointed it at Rænon. "Do not test my steel, foreigner! I would send you rolling back down that hill headless!"

Before he could finish speaking Rænon had drawn Pitkeeper, crouched, pivoted quickly, and swung his broadsword through the guard's waist, almost chopping him in half. The gatekeeper fell and screamed for his gods, staring at his twitching legs and emptied torso. The other two guards moved in slowly, disheartened to see their fellow dispatched so quickly.

Rænon could feel the ire rising in him. He ran straight at the two remaining men, throwing his axe into the chest of one and cleaving the other through his skull down to his breastbone.

He yanked his sword from the middle of the guardsman and retrieved his axe from the other, flinging the gore from both.

He looked down upon the three ruined corpses. Perhaps he was quick to act. Vyntane's guard would now be on high alert and this was no place to linger. He left the bodies where they lay and walked through the carved opening of the rock wall gate and saw the city of his ancestors for the first time.

Vyntane spread out before him like a tattered blanket of black cloth, revealing through the holes patches of rich green turf and giant oaks. What wasn't forged from iron was carved out of cyclopean blocks of black stone. In fact, like the harbor below, much of the city's structures were built right on top of, or rather, out of the rock, making it hard to discern where the natural terrain ended and where the dark iron architecture of men began.

Pitch-shaded buildings, as tall as smoke pines, tapered sharply toward the heavens. On the far northern side of Vyntane a temple shaped like a gigantic sword thrust into the earth rose from the ground with an immense anvil altar in front of it. A forged statue of Farick kneeled in reverence before the gigantic steelwork. It was unlike anything he had seen in Aelbrond, or anywhere in Arginor for that matter.

The Iron Castle, of which Aren spoke the night before, was near the edge of the cliff on Vyntane's eastern side. He could see the onyx rock at its base that crept up into the dark metal bulwark of the castle. It had three main towers. The central tower reached the highest and terminated into a faceted, gemlike structure. The other two towers were wider, with terraces built incrementally and at their precipice each flared into identical half spheres. It was protected on its seaward side by the sheer drop of the unscalable cliffs and its other three sides were guarded by a crescent-shaped perimeter of high walls and sentry towers.

The edges of the city seemed to be mostly small houses, modest in design, but built with sleek and stable craftsmanship. Beyond these low-laying common areas there were no more buildings dotting the landscape, just rolling emerald hills with patches of dark viridian oaks and giant shards of the black rock of Isahin, jutting impudently out from the ground.

Rænon walked down from the gate, toward the western edge of the city. He had blood on his hands and face, he stood out as an Aelbronder, and Vyntane's guard would be looking for strangers as soon as the bodies were discovered. It was time to find a change of clothes and a room to wash in.

He walked along a small cart path which ran along the southwest edge of the citadel. Hoping to avoid any passersby, he kept the lush green land of Isahin on his left and the dark citadel on his right until he came to a small bridge over a sparkling rivulet. This must be the River Deene, which travelled down from the hills, through the middle of Vyntane and ran off the cliff behind The Iron Castle. Rænon walked under the bridge, washed the dried blood from his body, and drank the cold, metallic-tasting river. Even the water on Isahin was rich in iron.

Beyond the bridge he could see a market. He heard the yelling of merchants, the barking of dogs, the welcomed sound of chaotic commerce. Faintly, he could discern the sound of a smithy, the unmistakable high-pitched ting of hammers striking anvils.

He walked towards the market that wove along the path on both sides. These were truly his people. Most were Rænon's size, with straw colored hair and fair skin. The men holstered longswords and the women wore smaller broadswords. There were covered stalls selling food, jewelry, fabrics, honeywine, and ale, most things familiar to him from his home.

The people eyed him strangely. Aelbronder or not, they were not used to seeing new faces. A burly voice called out to him from behind, "Hey, a true Maehlin warrior has come to the isle, and with the blood-stains to prove it!" The man behind Rænon was standing at a table of furs in a stall comprised mostly of hammered armor and things made from horn. He looked to be a northerner from Haiklan judging by the amulet around his neck; the Hand of Ylar, which is sacred to those from the frozen waste. "Don't worry, Aelbronder, if you got through the gate then I imagine you must've sent a few of Tavrik's dogs to Hell. That is something the folk around here would reward."

"Aye, a few drops of blood at the gate. I had no choice. I've come to stay on Isahin as it is my right." Rænon palmed the hilt of his sword but remained calm.

The merchant smiled. "It is your right, barbarian. Most people you see here share your Maehlish blood. Their steel is forged with their ancestor's ash, just as yours is. My name is Hrukir. Please, step inside." Rænon entered the tent cautiously. Hrukir went on, "Tavrik has not let anyone into Vyntane for months, and word has come from the mines that he has ordered them closed. Apparently he has declared that we will no longer take from the 'womb' of Isahin. One by one he has ordered his nobles to be executed, guilty of some treason. The only advisors that remain in his court are of The Starless Night."

Rænon gave a concerned look. "Perhaps Aren was right."

Hrukir raised an eyebrow. "Aren? Do you know her?"

Rænon cracked a smile. "I met her last night. She warned me of The Starless Night as well."

Hrukir looked down gravely. "And she was kind to do so, stranger. She didn't come up on the lift last night and I fear for her safety. Too many folk gone missing lately."

"I'm sure she stayed at The Cormorant. Her friend was in the tavern with her," Rænon tried to assure him.

"I pray to Ylar that you are right. Now put these on." Hrukir handed him a pile of white furs with bronze detail and dark, almost black, breeks made from elk leather. The white fur coat had a hood, which Hrukir suggested he wear up while walking around the city.

"I suppose you could pass for a Haiklaner!" Hrukir chuckled as

Rænon handed him his old clothes.

Rænon held out a few silver coins. "Here is what little I can spare."

Hrukir put up his hands in refusal. "No slayer of Tavrik's guards will pay me anything! Now, what will you do now that you are here?"

Rænon looked outside the tent to the busy street. "I came to study under the warrior smiths of Vyntane. There is not much left for me in Aelbrond. One day I'll return but not until I have finished my training."

Hrukir smiled under his bushy beard. "There is a smithy down the way a bit. Old Aarna knows the ancient secrets of Vyntane's sorcerer smiths. I believe he's in need of an apprentice, but you will have to prove yourself a pyre-forger before he will share them with you."

Rænon looked down proudly at the sword at his side. "My steel is thousands of years old. It has been reforged with the spirit of a hundred warriors of my line. Any sorcerer smith of Vyntane will see that."

"Then you had better get going," Hrukir said jovially, "and tell Aarna that I sent you."

"Thank you northman," Rænon offered sincerely.

"May Ylar's hand guide you," replied Hrukir, and Rænon walked out of the tent.

He passed many merchant stalls on his way down to the smithy. Old Hrukir was right, he wasn't attracting much attention.

Soon upon his left he came to the only solid building on the street, a brothel, by the looks of it. He heard the hammers striking in the background. The smithy was close, just down the road, but as he looked inside the open doors of the brothel he could see vaguely the shapes of women lying about the room, naked and writhing like a den of snakes. His youthful lust clouding his better judgement, Rænon stepped inside.

The windowless room was lit by a blue-green fire set in a flambeau in the middle of the large chamber, and around it spread out every kind of debauchery and decadence. Whores, unclad and gleaming in the weird light, lay around the fire, moaning and caressing. On a large divan against the far wall there were two girls chained together around the neck, already staring at Rænon. As they saw he noticed them they began gesturing and beckoning him to approach. One of the girls poured wine down the other's breasts and licked it off thirstily.

Against the opposite wall gamblers, likely from Tarsul, cast their bone die into the large skull of a sea-beast and argued loudly.

From a dark room at the back of the brothel a voice called to him,

"Welcome, swordsman." The shape of a pale, naked female form started to appear from the darkness. "I don't recognize you. It's not often we see a fresh face in here." She was tall, with coal-black hair and ice blue eyes that pierced Rænon from across the room. She wore a gold chain mail garment across her waist and nothing else. Her skin glistened with sweat and her massive breasts heaved as she approached him, casually stepping over the orgy in the center of the room. As if in a spell, Rænon found it hard to turn from her stare.

"A Haiklaner with a Maehlish sword, now that is a sight. Tell me, warrior, how have I not seen you before?" she said in a quiet, smoky voice.

Rænon pulled his white fur hood back, looked down and admired her buxom form. "I have been here for a year, working in the mines until Tavrik closed 'em a few days ago."

She squinted her eyes suspiciously. "I hope you are a better lover than you are a liar, Aelbronder." She cracked a wicked smile at him and pulled at his arm. Rænon pulled away and started to turn back towards the door. His bluff wouldn't work here and already too many of Vyntane's citizens were aware of his presence.

She tugged him back and put her hands down the front of his leather breeks. "Stay for a while. I have some wine in the back. Share a cup with me."

He relented; it had been months since he had felt a woman. She led him back into the shaded room from whence she came.

It was lit by a few candles. He could make out several tapestries on the black rock walls. Some illustrated scenes of men and women copulating with demons; a few depicted the most popular forms of Brakur, The Insane God. On the far wall, bigger than the other tapestries, was a battle scene. It appeared to be the legend of the Maehlin warriors driving back into the pit a host of gruesome white creatures.

Rænon recoiled, but the whore pulled him down upon her large divan and sat upon his broad chest. She poured him a cup of wine and put it to his lips. "Drink, Aelbronder, and I will show you pleasures that your mountains have kept hidden from you all your life."

He sipped the strong wine. It warmed him within and tasted like mead but with a slight copper taste, like blood or the spring water from the River Deene. Almost immediately his head started to swim. *What a fool, taking wine from a stranger in a strange place*, he thought.

Rænon grabbed her by the throat. He tried to crush her neck as she laughed at him but his arms went numb. He fell back onto the divan. His vision blurred and he felt vertigo as if he stood on the ledge above a bottomless chasm. Into the doorway stepped a figure. His vision was leaving, but he could make out a dark robe, a crimson turban and a pair of unwholesome ruby eyes. Then, nothing.

Chapter III

Under the Iron Castle

Rænon awoke to the sound of screaming. His arms and legs were bound by chains and he was laid upon a great stone table. High above him was a vaulted ceiling supported by gigantic iron columns which resolved in bas reliefs forged into the heads of beasts, and gods, and the enemies of gods. He was in a great hall, which must be in The Iron Castle.

He looked to his right side and saw a group of chained women being led by a small number of The Starless Night down into an opened vault below the hall. He noticed one girl, either dead or nearly so, being carried by two of The 'Night down the giant stone stairway. He could swear the girl was Aren, but his vision was still blurry.

On his left he saw a giant throne, and upon it could only be King Tavrik. Dwarfed by his royal seat, which was carved out of a cave formation that jutted out of the ground and into the throne room, he sat and grinned maliciously at the proceedings.

He was like most kings that Rænon had seen before: fat and vainglorious. His curled grey hair fell onto his white embroidered shirt, which was stained and greasy with wine and spilled food. He was tended to by three women with skin whiter than fresh cream. They wore red scarves around their heads and no hair escaped below their wraps. Their mouths were full of yellow, rotting teeth. Their eyes, like those of the men of The Starless Night, were an awful vermilion color.

There were no members of Vyntane's guard, no court advisers, just The Starless Night positioned around the room and protecting all exits. Most carried spears with obsidian heads. None carried swords, a strange thing.

"So our trespasser is awake!" Tavrik yelled as he noticed Rænon struggling against his chains. "First I should like to thank you for killing the last of my guard. That was something I would have had to take care of myself."

"That was my pleasure, Tavrik, as it will be my pleasure to tear out your heart when I'm free of these chains," Rænon growled.

Tavrik laughed heartily. "Well, you will have to use your hands, Aelbronder, because I think I will keep this sword." He held Rænon's brand aloft, admired the carved inscriptions traveling up the fuller groove. "Keeper of the Pit, it says, and this is pyre-forged, I would assume? Your line is in this blade, and if the bards sing true then it may well have been on Isahin before. Furthermore, I think this steel and your blood troubles The Starless Night greatly. Your landing on the isle has seemed to speed things up quite a bit. In fact we are preparing to offer up the whole of Vyntane to Brakur tonight."

Rænon looked into the king's eyes. "Brakur the Formless is an insane god, Tavrik. Only a fool would put faith in Him. I have heard the legends. I have heard what happens to those who summon Him."

"Aye, pitkeeper! You dwell near Shunned Albrunn and beyond it, En-Faln. You know the things that dwell beneath Aelbrond are kin to the things that dwell below Isahin, and Kynara, and Nitaar! That is why sacrificing you will bring me favor with The Formless One." The king reclined back in his throne.

"In whatever form Brakur comes, He will feast on your soul, Tavrik, and I will be the one to deliver it." Rænon eyed his sword leaning against the throne. He resisted against his bonds and felt a few of the rivets were coming loose of the rock they were driven into. He pretended not to notice.

Tavrik shook his head and replied, "The Starless Night were born of this isle when Brakur fell here from His cosmic throne. His blood soaked the earth and bore The 'Night and now they will gorge on Vyntane's flesh, for your steel offends them, this castle offends them, and killing you with your own sword will bring form and glory back to Him!"

Tavrik finally rose from his throne, walked toward Rænon, and continued, "My blood offends them as well, for my line has ruled this isle since the Maehlish first sent them back into their caves a millennium ago. I have done penance for my crimes. I, like my father and grandfather before me, have been laying with The Mothers of Night for a hundred years. Suut, I suppose under the command of Brakur, demanded a deal be struck, and that bargain spawned those you see around you. My sons and daughters look enough like us right now, but soon you will see everything as it truly is!"

The sound of chanting arose from the aperture in the floor, and mixed among the low guttural chants of the ghoulish cult were the high-pitched screams of the women being tormented in the chamber below them.

King Tavrik was now standing right next to the stone table to which Rænon was chained. "The Starless Night will rise and feast on these offerings, then they will cover Isahin, sparing none save for myself and my queen, Narila, whom I believe you've met."

From behind Rænon a soft hand caressed his head. A woman stepped to the side of the table—the woman who drugged him.

"The Queen of Vyntane is a common whore? Your depraved house has fallen low, Tavrik." Reanon spoke venomously. Narila grabbed Pitkeeper and held it to Rænon's throat. "I was squeezing every last bit of pleasure out of Vyntane's doomed citizens when you arrived, foolish dog. Kaur, one of The 'Night's carriers, spotted you and your Maehlish sword down at the harbor last night. I knew to wait for you in the brothel because you Aelbronders are a predictable race." She lowered Rænon's sword from him and laughed.

"And you do not share our Maehlish blood then? Tavrik, where did you find such a crusty harlot?" Rænon jabbed, obviously growing weary of the parley.

"I am from Navordi," Narila said haughtily. "And this will be my most cherished pleasure of Vyntane's demise!" She raised Pitkeeper again but her last statement had already sent Rænon into a fury.

He ripped his left-side bracket loose of the stone table and grabbed Narila by the arm which held his sword. Narila screamed, dropped Pitkeeper and scratched at Rænon's wrist.

He sat up quickly, grabbed Narila by the hair and dashed her skull against the stone table twice. He dropped her limp form, stood up and pulled at the right-side bracket until it came loose as well. He jumped down from the sacrificial dais, recovered Pitkeeper, and struck the chains from his wrists.

Tavrik yelled for The Starless Night to protect him. The frightened king ran towards the open aperture in the throne room's floor. Rænon was already on his heels when a spear shot in front of his face. One of the king's degenerated spawn was sprinting towards him from the entrance to the hall behind him, and two more came from each side. He would have to let Tavrik run. There was nowhere for him to go but below the hall in any case.

The acolyte to reach him first was the guard approaching from behind. Howling and barking like a beast, it hurled its last flinted spear at the Aelbronder. Rænon dodged it easily and waited for the foul thing to get close enough to attack. Once near, it ducked Rænon's first strike and slashed open his side with sharpened claws. He ignored the pain and brought down Pitkeeper again, this time hacking into the fiend between the neck and shoulder, splitting it in two.

The other four guards slowed their pace as they surrounded the warrior from Maelhin. They held their spears out but it only allowed Rænon to cut each of their weapons into a useless dowel. The first two he beheaded with one stroke. The next he grabbed up, held high above his head and brought down onto his knee, cracking the creature cleanly so that the two halves fell to the floor separately, connected only by its skin. The last of Tavrik's guardians jumped at the barbarian. Rænon snatched it by the neck and skewered it on Pitkeeper like a piece of mutton. He snatched the wrappings from its head. It shrieked at him and clawed at his face while he looked in horror upon the loathsome creature. Small curled horns protruded from its pale, black-veined head. It spit at him from a yellow fanged mouth and its cerise, dying eyes stared hatefully into his own. He flung the ghoul from his sword and ran toward the opening in the floor.

Directly below The King's Hall was the weapons keep. Rænon descended the stairs carefully, although there was no Starless Night guarding the way. He snatched up a shield and continued down the piceous stone staircase that led down into the Crypt of Kings. He could hear the chanting of The Starless Night getting louder, such a low bellow that he felt it vibrating the walls of the chamber and the floor beneath him. The crypt was narrow and continued back so far that Rænon could not see its end. The stone slabs of the sepulchers rattled on the tombs of kings.

It seemed as though there was thunder coming from the core of the island but this was not from The 'Night's chanting, it was more like an army approaching from the center of the earth on horseback.

There was a pale orange light glowing in the opening of the floor of the crypt which led down into the next level. Rænon peered over the edge and espied a giant iron statue of Farick. This must be the hall that Aren spoke of.

In the colossal chamber he saw a circle of the ebon-shrouded Starless

Night, forty or less, standing around the orifice that was blasted through the hall from the cavern underneath. Some held spears, others held torches. They were keeping their sacrifices at spearpoint, close to the edge of the pit. The women trembled and wailed as the chanting of The Starless Night grew louder.

Some of the acolytes stripped away their robes and turbans. They hopped around the great statue of Farick, blaspheming and gesturing at the idol. Some hurled their spears at it, others spat upon it. Rænon cursed the creatures and swore to gut every one of them.

He could see King Tavrik at the edge of the circle, chanting with the rest. He was almost certain he also saw Aren at the edge of the gaping maw, cursing and throwing stones at the robed demons.

He walked down the stairway slowly until finally reaching the base of Farick's Hall. At the same time he could see something gain the edge of the pit.

A pallid, hairless, ruby-eyed thing pulled itself up onto the floor of the hall. Aren was right, this one was not like the others. It had claws the length of daggers and a fang-filled mouth that opened wide enough to take the head from a man. Its horns twisted and coiled down like the mountain rams from Shunned Albrunn. The creature's anklebones bent backward, allowing it to jump abnormally high, and its arms almost met the ground. It let out a high-pitched scream and The Starless Night ceased their chanting.

The great thundering from below still rumbled, and the ground still shook, but all were silent in the great hall. The pale thing walked forward on cloven hooves that clacked on the stone flags, its red eyes glaring insidiously at the offerings of Vyntane's women.

In one quick motion it grabbed one of the girls, took her into its arms, and jumped screaming back into the pit as the other girls cried hysterically. Rænon started toward the ghastly proceeding but as he did, another form rose from the maw. It was a creature, like the last, but much larger. A few feet taller than Rænon, it had an intelligence in its face that the other creatures did not possess. King Tavrik bowed as the abomination came forth. This must be the archdemon Suut, with whom King Tavrik had made his infernal pact. It bent its head down to the king and spoke in a low voice that Rænon could not hear, or likely understand. The king shook his head in agreement and pointed at the one who looked like Aren. The archdemon turned toward her and approached.

Rænon had witnessed enough. He emerged from the shadows and

strode toward the pit. "So Tavrik, this is your demon lord? It looks like a scrawny goat, too old to fight, too dumb to reason with. You are a fool, my liege!"

Tavrik was startled. He jumped when he saw Rænon approach and ran behind the archdemon. Rænon drew his sword and raised his shield as Suut growled rabidly and began to run at him on all fours, its head slightly bent down like a ram's. Rænon let it run close, almost close enough to strike with its overlong arms, then he threw his shield into its face and slid under the demon as it passed over. Rænon lifted Pitkeeper and sliced the thing from breastbone to abdomen, spilling its black entrails on the floor of Farick's Hall. It bayed as a dying bear would. Slowly it stood on two hooves again, holding in its guts with one hand and clawing at Rænon feebly with the other. Rænon jumped to the side of the archdemon, then behind it. It kicked like a steed, driving its cloven hoof into Rænon's gut. He flew back, sliding across the stone floor to the edge of the blasted pit. His breath was gone for a moment and his bottom two ribs were most likely cracked, but he rose quickly and ran at Suut once more, this time parrying the demon's strike with his sword and in turn slicing off its long-clawed hand. Again he sank Pitkeeper into the wounded goat-lord's side and climbed upon its back. Rænon grabbed it by the horns, positioned his feet on the giant's shoulders, and pulled up as hard as he could. He twisted the head of Suut until the wan skin tore away, and with a sickening crack, snapped its head from its limp body.

Rænon threw the horned head at the circle of The Starless Night. Most of them jumped into the pit, shrieking in fear. Now only a few remained in the hall, and those that did faced the wrath of the captured women who began to take up fallen spears against them.

The sound of marching hooves from below was still getting louder in the hall, pieces of stone ceiling were starting to fall, and Rænon had lost sight of Tavrik. Had he jumped into the abyss? No, too bold a move for such a feeble man, he thought. Then he saw the king's robes behind the forged effigy of Farick.

"You may hide, king, but it does not mean that you are hidden. Come die with honor, don't bring further shame on your line. Your archdemon is dead, your bargain died with him I'm sure. I will give you a clean death here, for your crimes against Vyntane, or you can be eaten alive by the horde, which you deserve."

The king rose from behind the statue. "Please have mercy, warrior of

Maehlin. I deserve to die but if you let me live I will show you a way out of here before they rise from that cave," Tavrik pleaded.

"Rænon! Kill him!" He turned quickly. Behind him stood Aren, pulling a spear from the eye socket of one of Tavrik's sons. "He has destroyed Vyntane. The citizens are not prepared for this attack. The king has offered them up to these demons as a feast. Soon, all of Isahin will belong to the Blood of Brakur!"

Rænon was surprised to see her alive. The other women had fled up the stairs while the rest of The Starless Night lay about the floor of the hall, dead or dying. He smiled back at her. "Don't worry, Aren, the king knows he is dead."

Tavrik dropped to his knees. "There is a doorway behind that statue. I was trying to open it when you saw me there. We can make it down to the coast while The 'Night overwhelm Vyntane from the castle. Now please, spare my pitiful life!"

Rænon raised Pitkeeper and brought it down, severing the king's arm completely. The king cried out, pleading for Brakur to save him. Rænon finished quartering him, allowing the king to feel the deepness of regret, then mercifully and effortlessly took the head of Tavrik from his shoulders. The king's bloody pate rolled past Rænon towards Aren, who kicked it into the pit.

Rænon sheathed his sword and motioned for Aren to follow. "A shame we couldn't spend more time prolonging the bastard's death, but I think we had better move before we are overrun." He knelt behind the statue and tugged at the iron door. It creaked open and Aren grabbed a torch.

Just as they were both climbing down into the secreted passage, the true Starless Night began their assault.

At first, ten rose out of the pit, then in seconds a hundred. Rænon rushed Aren down into the passage and waited a few moments more before he shut the iron doors above him. There were now at least a thousand of the pale creatures in the hall. Some were already feasting on the parts of Tavrik that lay near the edge of the pit. They gnashed their teeth and sent their high-pitched screams echoing through the halls under The Iron Castle. Rænon shut the doors and closed the bolt securely.

The people of Vyntane were about to be slaughtered by a hungry, depraved, and scorned army. Rænon's heart felt heavy. He had come all this way to learn, to see the work of his ancestors, and now he would only see the end of that culture. There was nothing he could do to prevent it.

Spiraling into the nighted depths of the narrow tunnel, they rushed down the stairs for hundreds of feet until they could hear waves crashing right outside the lapidarian walls of the passage. "We must be close. If we go any lower we will be underwater," Aren shouted.

Finally they came to a large room carved out of the atramentous rock. The tunnel continued below the room, seemingly below the sea level. In the far corner of this large chamber there was another staircase. In the gleam of Rænon's brand they could see the stairway led up into the open air. They ran across the room and up the stairs. Once they were out of the antechamber Rænon realized where they were.

"The Cormorant!" Aren yelled and hugged Rænon hard. They were in the harbor's alley where he first spotted one of Tavrik's spawn going into the selfsame passage from which they just arose.

They started down the wharf hoping there would be at least one vessel to escape on. As they rounded the corner of the bluff there was a lone ship, bearing the flag of The Red Jewel. "Lord Sanhar's ship!" Aren exclaimed.

Just then, right in front of them something crashed through the planks of the harbor, then another. Rænon looked up and saw a score of The Starless Night falling through the air towards them. He could see flames at the edge of the cliff, and in the pale firelight high above it seemed that the demons were jumping to their deaths willingly.

They caterwauled as they fell. Some were clinging to men and women of Vyntane, taking them along into the cold ocean grave. Then Rænon observed that some fell, already dead with swords and axes driven through their colorless bodies. He was glad that not all of Vyntane were going without a fight.

They sprinted towards Sanhar's ship. Scores of bodies were now splashing into the sea. Rænon could see that the ship's crew was casting off the docklines that held the vessel in port. Behind the ship he spotted the merchant's lift coming down. It was full of people screaming in horror. Aren arrived at the gangplank first. She called to Sanhar who was standing on the forecastle staring up in disbelief at the demonic mass suicide. "It is The Starless Night!" he yelled back at her. "We must leave now! They are trying to summon Brakur!"

Rænon waited for the citizens from the lift to arrive at the ship. Seven had made it. He helped them onboard before casting off the plank.

The ocean seemed to boil around the ship. At least a thousand of the demons had jumped into the sea but no corpses floated atop the water. The bodies of the men they carried down with them also stayed below the torrid, bubbling surface.

Everyone on board picked up an oar, Sanhar not excluded. Even an old man and two small children from the lift started to row vigorously with the others. They sped a few hundred feet away from the cliff below Vyntane. No more demons fell around the ship but Rænon could still see a few of the pale shapes falling against the pure ebon backdrop of the cliff.

The water around the harbor was now a roaring cauldron. It was hard to see in the wan light of the moon, but Rænon could swear there was a shape rising from the waves.

Slowly at first, what seemed to be the arm of a giant lizard broke the surface and gripped the face of the cliff. The arm was almost the length of the harbor itself. Then, another arm shot out, its clawed hand gripped the cliff face and slowly began to pull its bulk out of the water. The Starless Night were successful; this was the insane god.

His head arose between the massive reptilian arms. From behind, Rænon could see it was hairless, but crested with spines that continued down His back. His viridescent skin was like that of a salamander, smooth and fleshy. As the god rose higher out of the sea the crew stood mesmerized, staring in horror at the lower half of Brakur. His soft flesh became rigid. Six more legs, three on each side, gripped the bluff. They were jointed and armored like a giant crab from the lightless depths.

Brakur was halfway up the cliff when He finally turned His head towards the ship. Rænon heard Aren and the children from the lift scream in terror, then become suddenly quiet.

It was a human shaped face, but it was a travesty of humanity. Instead of two eyes He had ten, black and emotionless, like a spider. His mouth, also spider-like, was an open, drooping maw with fangs horizontal, and molten rock came vomiting from it, setting ablaze the harbor below.

Brakur turned His face back toward the cliff. He looked up at Vyntane and let out a siren cry so high-pitched and tortured that Rænon knelt on the deck, pawing at his ears in agony.

The Insane One finally crested the bluff. The ship was far enough away that Rænon could see the towers of The Iron Castle. He watched Brakur, who was more than half as tall as the keep, hold the two shorter towers in His clawed hands. He ripped them out as if they were sticks in mud and cast them into the sea. Any hope Rænon had for the people of Vyntane was surely gone now. The foe of sanity had come to reclaim His abode.

The Aelbronder looked back upon the deck of Sanhar's ship. The rest of his crew had fainted, all except Sanhar. Likewise, all but one of the rescued Vyntanites lay unconscious upon the deck, a giant man that wore the leathers of a smith.

The three of them stood silent for a few moments. Finally Sanhar spoke. "I suppose that this is the beginning."

Rænon looked at him, confused. "The beginning? It looks to be the end."

Sanhar stepped forward. "The end of Vyntane perhaps, but the beginning of a new age. An age where The Gods dwell among men. Two days ago, a lord's messenger from Haiklan arrived on The Jewel. He said that Ylar's tomb had been opened and lay empty. That is a strange thing because her tomb may only be opened from the inside."

The smith stood next to Rænon and put his hand on his shoulder. "Aye, Aelbronder, from your sword I can see you are from Maehlin. I'm sure you have heard the bards sing of Farick's awakening. If he should break free of his chains in the heart of Shunned Albrunn, I will forge him a sword myself, one great enough to bring here and cut from Brakur His profaned head."

Rænon smiled at that, despite the proceedings. "And what is your name, friend?"

"I am Aarna," he replied, "now the last of Vyntane's sorcerer smiths."

The Mirror Beguiling

By James Ashbey

Telekir gazed with malice into the black face of the Mirror Beguiling. For long years the Mirror had been his chief ally, residing as it did in the uppermost chamber of Wistwood Tor. It was his window on the world, casting his sight far into the lands of those who had hounded and shunned him. Now, in the winter of his long life, Telekir clung like a limpet to the edge of civilisation, his thoughts ever bent on revenge.

Turning from his dark divinations, he shrieked in the direction of a small wooden door in the corner of the room. "Grubbin! Attend me, you miserable woodlouse!" A few moments passed, then his call was answered by the sound of bare feet frantically ascending stone stairs. The door opened, and Grubbin entered.

"Command me, high one!" mewled the newly arrived creature, his filthy garments clinging limply to his wasted frame. He was one of the forest-kin by birth, though there was scant sign of this proud breeding left in him. Twelve years as Telekir's lackey had seen to that.

"Grubbin, I have looked into the Mirror."

The wretched slave gritted his teeth, silently damning the tedium that was to follow. Then he uttered the obligatory response: "What has been scried, O Telekir Fargazer?"

"Many things, fool. The glass is of Alandian make, and heeds not the petty laws of nature." Grubbin rolled his eyes discreetly as Telekir continued. "Foremost in my scrying was a means to destroy the hateful city of Kuwatash, and all who dwell therein."

Grubbin's interest grew. His master's revelations were typically vague at best, and often gibberish. But this time there was a clear note of purpose in the old man's ravings; perhaps even the prospect of action.

"Grubbin, I have learnt of a foul creature living at the uttermost rim of the world. He broods amidst the Qalati Mountains and spends his days in bitterness, nurturing to life plagues of shocking virulence which he stockpiles towards some unknown end. Men call him Arath the Exile, but of his true name and pedigree one should ask the bitumen canvas of night, whence came he in an epoch too remote to fathom. And there would come no answer, only the cold glare of alien stars."

It was hopeless, thought Grubbin, his curiosity extinguished. He had long known that his master's mind was as frail and worm-eaten as the parchment of his books, but it seemed at last to have crumbled to dust. He edged towards the door, hoping to leave Telekir alone to his ramblings.

Suddenly his muscles froze, and a sensation of extreme cold coursed through his body, emanating from the torc of twisted iron that he wore around his neck. "Slave, I am not finished!" boomed the voice of Telekir. "You well know what power I hold over you by virtue of that fine neckpiece you wear, but do not think you have felt its fiercest bite. Untold agonies are the wages of true disobedience."

The icy chill subsided, and Grubbin slumped to the floor, shivering helplessly. Telekir walked to a wooden cabinet at the side of the chamber, and produced from it a small velvet pouch.

"I have gathered intelligence from far and wide," he resumed, turning back to face his thrall. "I have weighed my options with the Mirror's aid, and there is one man alone who would seek out Arath in his mountain lair, and see his pestilent gifts delivered to the streets of Kuwatash. A man to whom morality is ash, and chaos the only creed. A man whose name is whispered by the weak, and cursed by the strong… his services will not be cheap." With a thin smile Telekir turned out the contents of the velvet pouch onto his opened palm.

He held in his hand a ruby of immense size. Its deep red colouring seemed to pulse in the candlelight like a beating heart freshly torn from a sacrifice. Grubbin had seen nothing of its like before.

"Listen very closely, Grubbin. Here is what you must do…"

* * *

There are men in the wild reaches of the world whose only calling is combat. They care nothing for the colonnades and fountains of the great cities, nor the timid songs of harp and flute. Indeed, their cares of any kind are few: the clamour of battle and the besting of one's foe; the writhing contours of a young woman; the savouring of fine drink and hearty food. Such things alone can stir the soul of the warrior.

Rúga Hawkhand mused on this theme, fancying that by night's end he would achieve in full that catalogue of triumphs which most fire a man's heart. It had been a day rich in bloodshed and rapine, and he and his men had removed deep into their native wilderness to toast the audacity of their raid. Three of their comrades had been freed from the dungeons of Gharboud, and much pillaging was had at the expense of their jailers, the wicked monks of Nesh.

Rúga knelt alone on the food mat in the centre of his spacious yurt, a kingly platter of meat, fish, and fruit arrayed before him. He selected an attractive cut of venison, fresh from the hunt, and followed it with a gulp of the intense wine for which the Purthian coast is famed.

The sound of light breathing and shifting fabric caught his attention, and he looked over to the silken drapes that surrounded his sleeping pallet. The light of the tent's oil lamps shone through the thin hangings to reveal the soft female form of Stasha, his favourite plaything. Rúga sipped more of the Purthian wine, his eyes following the gentle undulations of Stasha's body as she stirred from sleep. This is how the mighty live, he thought to himself.

Outside the yurt the noises of the warband's merrymaking came to a sudden halt. Rúga tensed instantly, his feral instincts taking over. He heard the gruff voice of Octar, his lieutenant: "Who in Grod's name are you?"

In moments Rúga was on his feet and bounding to the tent's doorway, not waiting to be summoned. He emerged to find his warriors scattered around the camp, each of them looking towards the newcomer who trespassed on their revelry: a thin childlike figure, shambling wearily through the camp's perimeter. His garments were ragged, and a torc of twisted iron encircled his neck.

"Name yourself!" growled Octar again. The massive fighter pointed his spear at the intruder menacingly.

"I am named Grubbin, a lowly servant of Telekir the Sage. I have trekked here from Wistwood, countless leagues hence, seeking the one named Rúga Hawkhand."

"You have found him," responded Rúga himself, striding forward. "What business does your master have out here on the Great Steppe, and why should I entertain a runt sent in his stead?"

"My master is aged and frail, too weak of body to leave his high tower. He sends me in his place to bring you a great gift, and a greater proposal."

Rúga gave Grubbin a long scrutinising look. He thought himself skilled in the reading of others, but this odd little creature vexed him. It was a marvel that he had survived the journey this far into steppe country; more marvellous still that he had found their ever-roving camp.

There was more to him than met the eye. "I will listen," concluded Rúga bluntly. "But we will sit alone; my men have lost enough drinking time for one night."

Grubbin sat opposite Rúga in his yurt, relaying Telekir's designs as best he could while the famed marauder selected morsels from the food mat. Grubbin reached the end of his master's message and waited nervously while Rúga noisily defleshed a peach.

"Your enslaver plots a terrible end for Kuwatash," muttered Rúga at length, wiping peach juice from his thin black beard. "I am no friend of that louse-nest myself, but what are its crimes to deserve such punishment?" The question was inevitable, and its response had been much rehearsed by Grubbin on his long quest.

"For one, my master was gravely wronged by the lords of Kuwatash, many years ago. They stripped him of his vestments as a Priest of Penumbra, and cast him into the wild like an animal. But much more than this, they now plot a dreadful new empire that will stretch from the east sea to the west, bringing a long age of darkness and misery to all who fail to kneel." These latter falsehoods came out just as Telekir had dictated; a fact that filled Grubbin with a faint sense of pride.

Finally he produced the velvet pouch which had been his burden on his long journey, and emptied its precious contents onto the food mat.

"This is the Huhraan Ruby. It was mined in the Pordur Valley when the world was young, and once adorned the brow of Zirgos the Vile. It is now yours, as a small flavour of the greater riches that will pass to you on completion of this deed." Anxiety bubbled behind Grubbin's calm delivery; Rúga had given no indication of a decision, and Telekir's instructions were running dry.

At last the barbarian chief made his decision. "We will ride to the Qalati Mountains. We will seek out this beast you describe, and there judge for ourselves if this cause be worthy." He picked up the ruby and rotated it before his eyes, studying the way it glimmered in the lamplight. "You can tell your cowering master that I ride not for riches; many men have misjudged me so, to their doom. I ride because I would dwell in no land where strange creatures and their powers are unknown to me. My fighters, however, are simpler in their motives; your master's treasury will be empty before they are truly satisfied. As ever, it will fall to me to retain their loyalty."

Grubbin bowed humbly and, with some final instructions given, made his preparations to leave. As he moved to depart, Rúga spoke once more. "We are unalike, slave, except in one ultimate respect: we are both survivors. It would serve you well to remember that nothing truly separates emperor and serf if both share the will to endure. What else matters in the end? The survivor may be dragged through thorns, he may be engulfed in smoke and flame, and he will emerge unscathed, because his impulse to prevail burns stronger. All the riches of the earth are no substitute for that."

Grubbin shuffled out of the tent and into the thickening darkness of night, Rúga's parting words resonating in his mind like a deep and ominous gong.

* * *

The full story of Rúga Hawkhand's journey to the Qalati Mountains would be long in the telling. With flowing mead and an eager audience it might be sung in sequence across a span of many evenings, and its listeners would go late to their beds to rehearse its many episodes in their drunken dreams. They would hear of how the warband went first to the holy Mundzuk Tree to speak their accustomed vows and to call forth the protection of the great Wild; they would see in dream the robed assassin of Nesh who shadowed the company's camp for days, and finally met his end at the edge of Rúga's knife; they would relive the brave sacrifice of young Ellac, who stole a guarded vessel with which the warband crossed the Foothill Fjords, but died from the wounds he was dealt. But the closing verses of the tale must here be sung in full.

Rúga and his men reached the Qalati Mountains on a crisp morning of autumn. The snow upon the peaks had begun to thicken, and the warriors were glad for the heavy pelts and furs they had carried with them from the steppes. Far overhead the silhouette of Charaton, Rúga's faithful hawk, could be seen wheeling in the ice-blue sky, his swift eyes ever attuned to his master's whereabouts. He watched as the company trekked across sweeping heights and hushed valleys, and descended to his master's hand when finally they entered a ravine of dark stone, carved by glaciers in ages past. At last they had reached the destination Grubbin had described.

A deeper silence pervaded this new landscape, as though the nomads from the steppes were trespassing upon some solemn rite not of this world. The ravine had widened into a rocky plateau, devoid of vegetation and punctuated only by a broad pool of crystalline water. It was an oppressive place, more deathly than any tomb delved by men.

Suddenly Charaton shrieked and tore himself away from Rúga's gloved hand. The men quickly spotted what the hawk's keen eyes had sighted first: a host of shadowy forms rising from the pool, like fumes from a deep-sea vent. Impossibly, they seemed to take on human shape, and wore on their nebulous limbs the wargear of bygone empires. Before Rúga could cry out, the spectres rushed forward with preternatural speed, as though blown by ill winds.

Octar hurled his spear at the lead spectre, only to watch the weapon pass through its target and clatter impotently to the rocks behind. The nimble pickpocket Uldin fared little better, jinking to avoid the swing of a terrible vaporous arm and then loosing a stone from his sling that ricocheted harmlessly off his enemy's heavily plated shoulder. Contradiction hung thick about these dreadful guardians, being here a diaphanous wisp, there a solid mass of ancient armour, immaterial yet momentous in their advance.

Rúga found himself confronted by a towering mass of black smoke clad in a coat of antique mail. He ducked as the nightmarish thing made a lunge for his throat, then drove his spear-point clean through the rusted links guarding its flank. Dark fumes billowed from the sundered armour, but the attacker seemed unslowed by the wound and readied itself for another strike. Casting a quick glance to his comrades, Rúga saw that Denzic the bowman lay stricken on the ground, engulfed by a roiling cloud of evil. Meanwhile Charaton dived fearlessly in and out of the fray, but his beak and talons proved as ineffective as the warriors' steel.

Rúga's battle-honed mind surveyed the arena in moments, noting how the spectral aggressors had quickly circled to cut off any retreat back through the ravine. The only egress was straight ahead, but that way lay nothing but the eerie pool from which the smoke-fiends had risen. Looking to the pool, Rúga saw that a strange light now glowed from somewhere in its depths, and that the water itself, previously glass-still, now bubbled restlessly. Could it be some aqueous portal to Arath's domain?

Again the terrors attacked, and again the human weapons claimed no victories. Denzic lay lifeless on the rocks, and more of the fighters looked soon to follow him, each now coughing and choking as the foes tightened their final suffocating embrace.

"Into the water, steppe-men!" roared Rúga, conceding that defeat was imminent. "Swim to the light and remain masters of your fate; we will drink again together, whether it be in halls of men or gods!" With that he plunged into the pool, barely pausing to abandon his heaviest furs and armaments.

The surviving warriors looked on with bewilderment as their chief vanished into the icy deeps, but their hesitation was brief as the black fog of doom rolled ever closer. All soon followed Rúga's example, discarding their weightiest garments and committing to what seemed a madman's escape.

At the water's edge the ethereal victors stopped dead. A fell wind howled through the ravine and across the rocky plateau, and each of the vapours surrendered its body to the breeze, dissipating utterly into the cold mountain air. Vacant armour collapsed to the shoreline, and then all was still.

* * *

Rúga slowly opened his eyes. The sound of dripping water echoing on rock had roused him from a fey slumber. How long had he lain in the clutches of delirium, adrift in those strange realms of faery which should belong alone to the undines and the drowned? He had no memory of his descent into the mountain pool, nor of any agency that had plucked him from its chill waters.

As Rúga's vision returned he found that he lay in a narrow stone cell, barely large enough to contain him. A sickly yellow glow indicated that one end opened onto a larger chamber, and so he crawled out to face whatever fresh malevolence had brought him to this purgatory.

He found himself in a circular atrium, its walls honeycombed with cells much like his own. A single arched doorway led off into darkness, while beside each cell a small lamp flickered, casting feverish shadows across the walls.

Rúga pulled the nearest lamp from its fitting and used it to explore the room. He was reminded of the Catacombs of Sharazad, the labyrinthine tombs cut into the volcanic ash beneath that city to house its wealthiest dead. He had plundered those graves frequently as a boy, daring to venture where no other street urchin would. But in these alcoves there was no sign of glittering grave goods to loot; only the dormant forms of his comrades, each in his own gloomy sepulchre. What armour and weaponry they had taken with them into the water was nowhere to be seen, and all now wore grey linen shrouds as though primed for burial.

One by one the men shook off the sleep spell, waking to see for themselves where the pool had led. As ever, they looked to Rúga for answers.

"What devil's pit is this?" hissed Volga, a veteran of the group. "I'd sooner be slain in battle than rot alive in a crypt."

"Aye, this is no warrior's end," agreed Dargor the tall Thurnian, ever Volga's ally. Their complaints echoed sullenly around the chamber.

"Return to your coffin-holes if you deem your journeys ended!" responded Rúga venomously. "Me? I have not travelled this far to lie corpse-like and waste away. I would seek out he who dares to garb me in funeral robes and rob me of my blade. I would see an end to this wretched quest, and spill the blood of any beast that slows my homecoming. I would die on my feet, in a manner worthy of song! If any here feels different, then consider this farewell." With these words he strode through the great arched doorway, desecrating its darkness with his lamp.

The murky passage sloped deeper and deeper through the damp rock, squirming this way and that like the innards of a horrible worm. Shamed by Rúga's fighting talk, the whole troop followed behind him.

Finally the tunnel opened out into a vast glistening cave. Pearls of phosphorescent water dripped from countless stalactites, splashing into pools and streams which filled the cave with an unearthly half-light.

The warriors picked their way further into the great hall of stone, edging around crags and stalagmites, gullies and sheer chasms. They noticed precious gems twinkling in the rocks around them; small and sparse at first, but growing more frequent and sizeable with each step. Verdant emeralds shimmered alongside huge studs of sapphire and turquoise, and, further on, shocking seams of diamond mimicked the trickling waters.

Unable to resist the tangible bounty before him, Dargor the Thurnian reached out to dislodge a chunk of diamond from the rock.

The moment his fingers touched the jewel a great thunder-clap filled the cavern, and the soft half-light of the waters plunged to a deep crimson. Through this new darkness the men saw a mighty form rise shudderingly upward, as though a segment of the cave-floor itself had broken loose and come to life. With cruel inevitability the warriors' eyes adjusted to the gloom, until they saw that which loomed before them.

The thing was massive in size, towering almost to the cavern's roof; a hulking, saurian form, stooped in gait, clad in scales which had in them the light of unknown constellations. With each shift of its posture these lights seemed to ripple and realign, as though they rehearsed some cosmic narrative charted by no stargazer. But there was no light in its eyes; only two blank sockets in an ox-sized skull, as black as primordial chaos. With the creature's coming a great reek filled the air, as of sulphur and blood and incense, combined to herald an ineffable power.

"At last my guests awake, and find their way to the World's Tomb. Welcome Rúga Hawkhand, and your attendant mortals." Tremors shook the rocks as the beast spoke, its voice a chilling blend of serpent and man, nightmare and reality.

Many of the warriors cowered in awe, primal fear overcoming their usual bravado. But Rúga stood firm, weaponless and draped in the ragged linen of the grave, an avatar of defiant mortality. "Explain yourself, beast! If you are he named Arath, then our miserable hunt is over, and I demand answers. What breed of creature dwells in deathlike caves beneath the world, guarded by blasphemies in smoke? And where are our stolen weapons?"

While Rúga spoke the reptile's blank eye-holes gaped towards him, as though they drank in not light but sound, or some more vital essence.

"Indeed I am Arath," it continued sonorously, "though I prefer the names bestowed on me by my kin, long before your pallid sun was kindled. Once I was Abouelauthargon, and Tzaagthaal, and Crestyzin-Ka, and other names not for human ears. These dark caves have been my abode of late, but I once bestrode the firmament, and reigned in spheres too lofty for man's reckoning."

Arath's scaly hide shimmered mysteriously as he spoke of his past, but he was soon back to the present. "It pleases me that you have come; my faith in your temerity was well-placed. You have braved ice and smoke and death to seek out that which was merely rumoured to you by an inferior, risking everything to conquer the unknown. Such is the doom of the hero, is it not?"

Rúga was unsatisfied. "You speak as one who expected us... how is this so? What do you know of our cause and he who sent us?"

Rumbling laughter filled the cavern, and Arath's huge form shook with mirth as he relished in his guest's confusion. At length he answered: "Perhaps I can offer you... clarity."

Before the echoes of Arath's words had died, an impossible scene unfolded. At no apparent signal the water dripping from the cave roof surged in intensity, and instead of falling straight as gravity would dictate, the droplets flew obliquely through the air and came to a stop in front of Arath, joining with countless others until a floating disc of water was formed, defying all natural law.

"Behold, the true Mirror Beguiling," Arath announced proudly. "It has many imitators throughout the world; many pale reflections, many scattered shards that speak treacherously to the foolish. All of them are slaves to my will. Allow me to demonstrate..."

The watery disc shimmered like molten pewter, and then the men saw a strange vision appear. The face of a haggard old man came into view, smiling with evil satisfaction. At random intervals he broke down into convulsive cackling, although the scene remained eerily soundless.

"Here at last you see Telekir, the craven architect of your quest," Arath resumed. "See how he stares into his own Mirror Beguiling—a deceitful mockery of its namesake—and sees therein sights that greatly please him. But the lesser mirrors are mine to command, and reveal only what my whim dictates. Telekir thinks he witnesses the triumph of his designs and the fall of Kuwatash; in fact he is a powerless thread in a tapestry of my weaving, and has gleaned nothing of my true purpose."

The Mirror shimmered again, and the vision changed. Rúga instantly recognised Stasha. She appeared to be seated in an ornate ship's cabin, and wore fine courtly robes.

"See now the true face of courage and perseverance," continued Arath. "She sails for her homeland, laden with the riches given to her in exchange for the Huhraan Ruby. She saw her freedom in that gemstone, Rúga, and fled with it on your fastest steed when you were too drunk to notice." A mixture of anger and admiration welled up in Rúga, conceding an act bravely committed.

"But enough delay. Telekir's delusions are now at an end." At these words the old sorcerer's wicked face filled the Mirror once more, though now he wore an expression of shock, followed by despair. For the first time his Mirror revealed a truthful sight; the terrible eyeless visage of Arath the Exile leering back at him, with Rúga Hawkhand and his surviving men visible behind.

The old man's mind quickly pieced together this new revelation—no plagues had been delivered to the streets of Kuwatash, and the monster Arath had known all, manipulating him like a tattered puppet—but his realisation was too late.

Telekir let out a panicked scream as Arath pushed his gargantuan arm straight through the rippling surface of the Mirror and closed his talons around the wretched man's neck. Then Arath pulled back, and along with his arm there came a billowing black vapour, identical to the hellish guardians of the pool. Telekir's very soul had been dragged through the Mirror to become yet another smoke-servant of Arath; yet another blackened spirit undeserving of rest.

As the evil cloud faded into the shadows of its new prison, the Mirror Beguiling at last surrendered itself to gravity, losing its shape and crashing to the cave floor in a single watery mass.

For all his fearlessness, Rúga knew when he was beaten, and this serpent from the stars whose claws could claim a man's very soul was an adversary too far. With no weaponry in his men's hands, assaulting the beast would be insanity. Instead he stepped forward, seeking answers if nothing more.

"Arath, your mighty power is clear. We are simple mortals who do not wrong the undeserving; tell me, what doom have you deemed we deserve that has caused you to bring us here and strip us of all that defines the warrior?"

Arath towered over Rúga, his scales now gently twinkling like the first stars of evening. "You are free to go," he said simply, and gestured behind him to the mouth of an upward-sloping tunnel. "Like you, my quarrel is not with the innocent; their earthly lives are tiresome to spectate, and their souls make feeble and humourless minions." He lumbered aside to allow passage to the tunnel.

The steppe-men stood still, baffled by Arath's words. Overcome with anger, Rúga's lieutenant Octar suddenly spoke for the group. "Why then did you bring us here, beast? You could have claimed Telekir's soul whenever you pleased, and now you expect us to face the frozen mountains in nothing but rags. Our sacrifices have been for nought!"

"You will find all the necessary furs, boots, and food at the end of the tunnel," Arath said. "Your weapons and armour I shall keep, however. These were the reason for your visit; my soul-pets are playful things, and they like some variety in the trinkets they amuse themselves with. I allow them this small boon, but it requires me to replenish my stocks from time to time. I assure you your wargear will be put to good use, like that of all my other visitors through the centuries.

"Now go, for I am sure your faithful hawk is waiting—and as you do, claim from this cave whatever jewels you can carry by way of payment. But remember this, Rúga Hawkhand: a warrior is not defined by the blade he carries or the riches he hoards; it is only the deathless flame in his heart that burns his name into eternity."

* * *

In the dank cellar of Wistwood Tor, Grubbin was awoken by a terrible scream. He raced up to his master's chamber, and there he found the empty robes of Telekir lying crumpled at the foot of the Mirror Beguiling. The sinister frame of the Mirror still hung on the wall, but its dreadful black glass lay in smithereens on the floor, each shard smouldering as though struck by lightning.

As Grubbin stared at the scene in bewilderment he felt the iron torc around his neck slacken and then disintegrate, falling away as a fine dust.

It was several moments more before Grubbin smiled, then laughed, then danced and skipped ecstatically round the chamber. He was free at last from Telekir's cruel dominion; free to return to the forest, and never again fear the icy wrath of the torc.

With a final glance around Telekir's empty lair, he set a blaze in the evil place with what remained of his master's candles, and bounded off into the night, shouting a triumphant salute to Rúga Hawkhand, wherever he might be.

"The survivor has prevailed!"

The Heart of the Betrayer

By Howie K. Bentley

Chapter I

The Hero and the Wolf

The clangor of steel on steel resounded across the battlefield. A few of the remaining villagers crossed swords with a handful of the invaders as three of the local men gathered around a large wolf that was tearing a man's throat out on the ground. Man after man had fallen before the wolf. Before any of the beast's victims could strike a blow with their swords and spears, the monster had darted out of their midst and back in, hitting one man like a lightning bolt before jumping on another and savaging his face. One of the fallen man's eyes was torn out of its socket and lying on the ground as he held his hand to his bloody face and screamed in agony. The next man struck at the wolf with his sword, but the creature was already behind him, crushing the back of the villager's head with its powerful jaws. The man's brains oozed out onto the ground. The last villager to face the beast realized that this was no ordinary wolf, while he watched the monster stand on its back legs like a man, towering over him as it snarled its razor-sharp fangs into a rictus—casting its cruel arrogant gaze on the horrified villager. Before the man could raise his spear, the monster leaped, dragging his human foe down to his death on the cold earth.

Argantyr was surrounded by four warriors. His long black hair and lengthy beard were speckled with blood, and his steel sinews rippled as he stepped into a fighting stance, holding his large broadsword in both hands. His emerald eyes sparkled, and he grinned as the first man rushed in and brought his blade up and down at Argantyr's head. Argantyr blocked the blow with his sword and made a quick arc with his blade, coming back around to slit the man's throat. Another foe moved in quickly, thinking that he would have time to sink his dagger into Argantyr's ribs while he was regaining his balance from the blow he had just dealt. Argantyr's blade came through and cut down his adversary with the return. A third man came in with a short axe, but Argantyr was on him and quickly cut him down before the man knew what was happening. The blade made a thumping sound as it sliced through the man's abdomen, and his innards spilled on the ground.

There was a loud growling as a bear-of-a-man came into Argantyr's view. Argantyr gritted his teeth and braced himself as the giant came wading through the dead bodies of his enemies. The large man's braided beard and square-cut brown mane were caked with the blood of those who had the misfortune to step into the path of his battle-axe as it had wheeled and spun out the fates of Argantyr's falling comrades. The man stood at least a whole head taller than Argantyr. A deep booming command issued forth from the bellowing giant: "Tell your companions that Ursas sent you to join them in Hel!"

Argantyr barely ducked the blow of the giant's axe in time and heard the whistling of the steel as it went over the top of his head. Ursas was deceptively fast for a man nearly the size of a bear, but Argantyr moved at twice the speed of the giant and drove upward with his sword into the man's guts while he used his left hand to cut the big man's throat with his long dagger. This man was defending his village, but Argantyr had killed men for as long as he could remember. The remaining villagers fell before the swords and axes of the marauders. The battle was over.

Where the huge supernatural wolf had been, there now stood a man with a grizzled red beard and a shock of dirty tangled hair. His head was cocked to the left, and his icy-blue eyes were void of sanity while he leaned on his axe and stared into cosmic vistas undreamt of by anyone save the fey—those touched by the twisted and unclean things that rule the outer gulfs. His mouth, mocking human flesh, formed into a lopsided grin. Foam gushed from his mouth. He wore the hide of an oversized wolf like a cape on his back. The skin of the beast's head and its ears came up and fit over his head like a cap. The man's name was Klak, but those who followed him called him "the Wolf." He was the leader of the band of marauders who had just taken the city of Horan. Horan was like so many other settlements in the far western corner of Gorn, barely ruled by feuding nobles, since Gorn had been torn apart by civil war. Horan was like all of the rest—a ripe fruit for the plucking for a marauding band of seasoned fighters made up of murderers, criminals and sellswords like Argantyr.

Argantyr's companions who yet lived gathered round him and fell behind him. Since Argantyr had joined the Wolf's band of marauders, he had quickly earned their respect, not only by his skills in battle but by the amount of wine and ale he could imbibe, his skills at gambling with dice, and his ability to wench all night and fell his foes like chaff before the sickle the next day.

The men had their backs turned to Klak as they bragged about how many men they had killed to each other. Klak heard one man say loudly, "…and Argantyr slew that tree-of-a-man like Donar felling an Ice Giant."

Klak wrinkled his nose and spat. "This will all change when I reach Aroon-Joon," he mumbled.

* * *

The scene before the sorceress receded as she drew back from the glowing green scrying orb in which she had just viewed the battle where Klak and his mercenaries had taken Horan. A beast-like sound of heavy breathing issued from behind her. She said to the horned figure who sat languorously in the darkness, "Soon we shall have the *Talisman*, my love." She looked to be no more than a maiden, but her deeply resonating, husky voice and confident mien betrayed her years. "Soon you shall taste the essence of gods and the souls of men again, and you will revel in the bloodshed of war. Know this thing and persevere, Witch-Maker!"

Chapter II

Conspiracy

Klak handed the crying infant to Tharat as the wizard told Klak, "You will need to get this powder into his wine cup. It will turn the bravest champion into a cowering cur." Tharat held up the vial of white powder for Klak to see. "He won't be able to lay a hand on a weapon without emptying his stomach and groveling before you." The old wizard had thin white hair, and his filmy blue eyes shifted when he talked. He looked at Klak and snapped his teeth. His right eye was larger than the other and looked off to the far right. He was wearing a dirty brown robe and his tiny, sharp teeth were white as ivory. "This thing will not be easy. The problem will be getting the powder in his cup without him noticing." The dirty little wizard snapped his teeth again after speaking.

Klak glared at Tharat, his voice becoming deeper as he told the little man, "You will stop snapping your teeth at me like an old fox getting ready to go into a hen house if you value your life, wizard!" Klak knew that Tharat ate human flesh, but he didn't care. Klak himself had consumed the flesh of another human being on several occasions when he was changed into the werewolf but had no taste for it when he went about on two legs as a man. He would have long ago dispatched the corrupt little wizard to Hel had it not been for Tharat's usefulness as a dealer in magickal items and potions that truly worked. The dirty little man fell silent, fearing the Wolf's ire.

Klak broke the silence. "I don't care to hear your tales, wizard. I have already taken care of arrangements to get Argantyr to drink the powder." Klak made a cruel barking sound as he laughed. "His woman is a sloe-eyed slut we took in a raid to the Far East. She is called Arju-Lao. He hasn't wenched a night since we took her. He tried to set her free, but she wouldn't go. He thinks that he saved her from me and my men taking her and doing what we want with her, but when Argantyr is deep in slumber or away, she comes to my sleeping quarters and asks me to do as I like. She likes to be treated rough. Once Argantyr is out of the way, I will give her a good beating and put some cuts and bruises on her. She told me how much she likes it. If that fool only knew! He trusts her. She will have no problem getting him to drink the powder." Klak barked out another laugh. "Once I am shed of Argantyr, I might even brand Arju-Lao and keep her around for a while."

Tharat's eyes shifted nervously, and his tongue lashed out and licked around his mouth. "You know that if you take her while you are changed to the Wolf, she will be like the others? Her body torn and mangled—her…"

Klak's glare penetrated into the deep recesses of Tharat's brain—those pre-human levels that control the survival mechanism. There was a long pause as the Wolf's eyes burned through Tharat.

Uncomfortable, Tharat changed the direction of the conversation. "Be careful, Wolf. I have seen visions of a battle between a wolf and a great demon that grows out of a man—a demon of such a magnitude as I have never seen before. This man who spawns the demon is…"

Klak growled, "Here is the rest of your payment, wizard!" The Wolf threw the sack of gold coins to the ground at Tharat's feet and wrenched the stoppered vial containing the powder from the wizard's hand, nearly knocking the little man down.

* * *

As Klak rode back to the nobleman's home that he had taken as a temporary residence—a part of the spoils of his growing band of mercenaries' war on Horan—he stopped to look out over some ancient ruins. He felt a chill go up his spine as he recalled old legends of a cruel wizard's imprisonment and torture of an elephant-headed god from beyond the stars. The particular wasteland that Klak looked upon was supposedly the site where a great warrior had destroyed the wizard and, in turn, crumbled his weird spiraling tower to dust. This was said to have been a part of Aroon-Joon when it was called *Zamora*—in times long past. Klak spat and mumbled to himself, "Legends… it probably never happened." He rode on, but Klak was uneasy all the way back to Horan.

* * *

Argantyr and the rest of Klak's men sat around the table at their wine cups and foaming jacks of ale. They were in the dining room of the manor that the Wolf and his men had appropriated from the now deceased Count Dagnus, whose decapitated head rested on a spear in front of the house. Arju-Lao carried a cup filled with wine to Argantyr. As she passed Klak, the Wolf told her, "Make sure that Argantyr drinks it!"

A mirthless grin spread across her face as she said, "Assuredly, sire. He has already imbibed one cup containing the powder. This will be the second." Her almond eyes gleamed an inhumane light. The Wolf reflected her gaze with his own leer and smiled at her assiduousness.

Arganytr didn't seem to notice Arju-Lao or anyone else in the room as the exotic beauty set the fresh cup of wine on the table before him. He was deep in thought—*spiraling back down a path that he had forgotten in his youth—admiring a butterfly as it landed on a flower—the sweet smell of spring and a joyous occasion around a campfire with his family—a gift of fruit from a little girl who was his dear friend in times fell to dust—just like her frail body had returned to the dust when the sickness had taken her. A tear rolled down Argantyr's cheek—what was wrong with him? He had forgotten how to cry long ago—even before he had killed his first man.*

Arju-Lao told Argantyr, "Drink, my love! Celebrate victory once again! You have earned it. You all have earned it."

Arju-Lao's words brought Argantyr out of his trance, *but he still felt much remorse for what he had lost—and what he had become.*

Argantyr picked up the cup and stared into it. The Wolf was watching him. At first Klak thought that Argantyr knew the wine was tainted and this made him uneasy. Argantyr was like a lion in battle. Klak had watched the man surrounded by foes, cutting them down like blades of grass before they could even close in on him. Argantyr had saved the Wolf's life twice. Once when Klak's attacker was poised to run him through from behind with cold steel—Argantyr had stopped the man in his tracks with an axe thrown to the head. Another time, the Wolf had been wounded and fallen to his knees. A Gornian chieftain gripped Klak by the hair and had his knife on his throat—when Argantyr had rushed in at the last moment and toppled the chieftain's head from his body with a single stroke of his sword. Argantyr was a formidable foe, and Klak was uncertain about his ability to best Argantyr unless Klak was changed into the werewolf—even then Argantyr might not be so easily vanquished. This way was better; it would show to all that even Argantyr would cower before the mighty Wolf.

Klak breathed a sigh of relief when Argantyr tilted the wine cup to his mouth and started on his second glass of ensorcelled wine. The Wolf had had only a few drinks of wine, but was feigning drunkenness. Arju-Lao moved over close to Klak. Argantyr had nearly finished his second glass of wine when Klak wrenched his sword from its scabbard and bellowed out into the feasting hall for all to hear, "Any man who can best me at arms can have all of the plunder taken from the raid on Horan yesterday!"

The Wolf looked around the room at the men as they cast their glances down at their cups or upon other parts of the room. A few of them shot quick glances at Argantyr, but he seemed to be deep in his own thoughts and to not hear Klak's challenge.

Klak shouted out louder a second time "I said, 'Anyone who can best me at arms can take the spoils from yesterday!'" He reached over and roughly pulled Arju-Lao to him, adding, "I will even give you this whore to play with!" making sure that Argantyr saw him squeeze Arju-Lao's left breast hard with his right hand. Argantyr snapped out of his trance. His limbs would barely move. His hand went to his sword hilt, but he fell upon the floor. Argantyr tried to rise and felt his stomach churning. He vomited the wine up on the floor. The Wolf roared with laughter. He went over to where Argantyr was lying prostrate on the floor, trying in vain to lift himself up. Klak squatted beside Argantyr. He drew Argantyr's own sword from his scabbard and put it in his hand saying, "Take your sword and fight, champion, or your woman will be servicing your fellow dogs tonight… and me. It's not as if I haven't had her already."

Arju-Lao burst into bell-like, high-pitched laughter. "Argantyr knows how to take a man's life on the battlefield, but he has no idea about how to take a woman in bed." A few of Klak's men laughed at her jest, but most remained silent.

Arju-Lao told Argantyr, "Why don't you take your sword and face Klak? I always suspected you were really a coward. A woman wants to be taken by a real man, not made love to by a timid sheep." Arju-Lao pulled Argantyr's head up by his hair and spit in his face.

The Wolf nodded his head in Argantyr's direction as the fallen warrior was still struggling to rise from the floor. Most of Klak's men went over and started beating Argantyr. The few who straggled behind just watched. Most of these men were hardened at birth. Some of them were from tribes who cast newborn babies into embankments of snow to prove that they were worthy of life. Some of them were orphans who had grown up in the streets of cities such as Tulanarth and Taktreer, doing whatever they had to do to survive. If they hadn't been shaped into what they now were as children, life would have made them murderers and cut-throats somewhere along the way.

When the men were finally finished beating Argantyr, Wintaun drew his sword and looked to Klak for his approval. Wintaun had always resented Argantyr for his martial prowess and his luck with the women. The Wolf's face split into a horrible grin as he shook his head and said, "No. Dump him in the ruins on the outskirts of Aroon-Joon where they say it is haunted; in the place they called the city of *Zamora* in ages long past. He can bleed to death there, or let the devils that haunt the place have him. You dogs worked him over pretty well. Not even Argantyr could survive such a beating. Likely, he'll die before you get him there. Either way, we won't be seeing the cur again."

The men picked Argantyr up and made for the door of the manor. Arju-Lao walked over and leaned back against Klak. The Wolf put his arms around her as they grinned like hyenas at the broken and bloody body of the dying man leaving their sight.

Chapter III

Rescued by the Witch

Argantyr opened his eyes. Everything was blurry. He heard a woman speaking. "You are fortunate to be alive. If I hadn't found you when I did, you would most certainly be dead." Her voice was deep and resonating, but feminine, nonetheless.

Argantyr choked out, "Where am I? I need to…"

The woman's voice fell to a soft whisper like a mother comforting her child, "Shhh… What you need is rest… Then you can tell me."

The woman laid her cool hand on Argantyr's forehead; when she did so, his sight receded into darkness. As he fell off into slumber he mumbled, "I need to kill the Wolf… need to kill…"

The woman said, "All in good time. You need rest now."

* * *

Dreams assailed Argantyr like an invading army. *He crouched within himself like a child hiding in the cool forest while murderers and rapists rained terror down on peaceful villagers with fire and sword. As he receded into himself like a fetus in its mother's womb, he felt the spring breeze touch his face and savored the aroma of the honeysuckles and lilacs in bloom. The earth was a living, breathing entity again; and Argantyr was glad to be a part of this wonderful sentient being. He saw his parents waving to him as he made his way to the forest. He heard his mother call to him, "Be back by supper!" His father was gathering branches for the bonfire that they would have that night.*

The severed tree limb in the forest became his sword as he pretended to slay Ice Giants and imagined the tales that would be told of his valor in Cruach's feasting hall that evening. Of a sudden, there came the rumble of horses' hooves. Argantyr heard the curses of men without gods or souls as they crashed through the forest close by. Argantyr ducked behind some trees into the fort that he had recently constructed of branches with newly grown green leaves.

He heard the shouting of the village men as the steel entered their guts and cut their throats and the cries of the women as they were defiled. He thought that he heard little Bessa screaming. Argantyr shook with rage and fear and tried to withdraw further into himself as he lay there hidden in the trees. A man came riding back his way—one of the marauders. He looked directly into the tree limbs where Argantyr was hiding. The man knew he was there. Argantyr looked out through a space be-

tween the limbs. When he did, he saw the man glaring directly into his eyes. The man was Argantyr—Argantyr himself. Argantyr, killer of men.

Argantyr the man woke up screaming. His fever had broken. He managed to stumble out of the bed and reach for a sword that had been lying by his bedside. When he picked up the sword, a shock ran through his body that knocked him sprawling onto the floor. He tried to raise himself up but could not. The mysterious woman was kneeling by his side, helping him back into the bed.

She told him, "You are getting stronger; soon, you will be ready."

"Ready for what?" he inquired.

"Ready for what you have to do. Vengeance burns in your heart. I can see it surrounding you."

"The Wolf—I have to kill him."

"I know," she said as her piercing green eyes bored into him. He noticed what a beautiful woman had been caring for him. She was petite and had long wavy red hair. Her body was taut and muscular, and her low-cut dress revealed the top of her ample bosom. In spite of her athletic build, she was beautifully feminine in every respect.

As she looked into his very being, she spoke as if she were far away. "My heart once burned for vengeance too. And I got it. The men who had destroyed my life, destroyed my sister and my mother. The men all died. I had the satisfaction of seeing them suffer. I helped them suffer, and suffer they did—endlessly. My mother fought them for a while. She raised a great army. But their army was greater. She made them pay in blood, but finally they defeated her; and she took her own life."

The woman spoke as though she were entranced. "Then I called Him—the Rune—Thorn, the Witch Maker. The one before whom no man or army can stand."

Her face snarled into a rictus, and her green eyes blazed—a hellish emerald fire. Her sultry voice rumbled, and she growled like a demonic priestess singing praises to a patron devil. "Not even the mightiest of gods can vanquish him, for he feeds on their very essence!"

"What is your name, woman?"

"My name is Bunduica," she said, seeming to become aware of her surroundings again. "But all of that of which I told you happened in ages long past—or yet to come. I have travelled through time so much that I am not sure when it was."

"I am Argantyr. I was once a killer of men, but now I cannot bring myself to pick up a sword."

"I know this, but you will be able to kill again. You have lain in a fever dream for weeks now. We had best lay plans for you to exact your revenge and destroy those who tried to kill you."

"Why are you helping me?"

"We… I have been watching you for a while, Argantyr."

"Watching me?" Argantyr asked, experiencing a feeling of unease at the woman's answer.

Bunduica turned and picked up a round object that immediately blazed into a glowing green luminescence. She held the glowing orb before Argantyr and said, "Look! Even now you can see your former comrades and their werewolf chieftain."

Scenes quickly played out before Argantyr's eyes—scenes of wholesale rapine and murder. Klak and his men took another city—then another—then another. More women and children screamed. More men died. Klak's army rapidly grew and swelled with each city that fell along the way. The marauders sat at the table of a recently appropriated villa and Arju-Lao bounced on Klak's lap as he and his men laughed in drunken revelry.

Bunduica made a gesture and moved her hand over the top of the orb and the light was extinguished.

Argantyr still stared at the scrying orb in amazement. "Arju-Lao yet lives?" he wondered aloud, doubting what he had seen.

"Aye. That is one more reason why we need to quickly set things into motion. The *Talisman* that I need is still in the werewolf's possession." Bunduica poured some liquid into a cup. "Drink this while I explain to you all that is involved."

Chapter IV

Thorn's Armor

Argantyr and Bunduica walked along outside. It was night time, but the skies were a dim red instead of black; Argantyr could still see quite well. Trees whispered to one another and walked around on their roots—the roots lashing themselves into the ground when a tree stopped in a new position. Bunduica told him, "Do not fear the *Irminsuls*. They will not harm you." *This was a strange world that Argantyr had found himself in since he had awoken from the fever dream.* He wondered aloud if he were dead, but Bunduica assured him, "No, you are not—and soon you shall be more alive than you have ever before been."

Bunduica led Argantyr deep into the hilly forest, to the mouth of a cave. As they stood before the yawning cavern, Bunduica told him, "Inside you will find it—the suit of armor that will make you invincible. The mightiest army will not be able to defeat you."

"But how am I to fight when I can't even pick up a sword?" asked Argantyr.

"You shall be as a monstrous war machine to anyone who stands in your path—man, god, or demon. I shall go in with you and show you, but you must don the armor and experience Thorn's power—alone. Your being must merge with the essence of the Rune to regain what you have lost—and then some. You shall see through the eyes of Thorn. As he passes some of his strength to you, so you will pass some of your strength as a living being to him."

"'Thorn?' You have told me of Thorn before, but I still don't fully understand what or who it is that you speak of."

"I told you that long ago I delved deeply into the blackest of arts to gain the knowledge to destroy those who murdered my family and outraged me." Argantyr nodded. "The old druid Balor was my mentor," Bunduica continued. "He was like a grandfather to me. He presented me with the *Book of Dead Runes*, the most powerful book of magick on the earth or any other world that I know. After much study and connecting with the runes in the book, I summoned the Thorn rune. I did not know what to expect. But a mighty warrior king came. He was larger than a man and had hair the color of freshly spilled blood, while his skin was white as snow. He is what some would call a demon. Call him what you will, but he is the physical manifestation of the Thorn rune, as well as he is the Rune itself. Thorn told me that he would destroy the Romans, and he did. But we tarry too long; come inside and see for yourself!"

Bunduica entered the mouth of the cave, and Argantyr followed. As they entered the cave, Bunduica took a torch from a bracket in the wall. She held her hand over the top of the stick, and it burst into flames. Argantyr could see written characters on the walls. Argantyr nodded his head. They looked similar to those used by the priests of the Aesir and Vanir—warlike races that dwelled across the sea and to the far north of his Tuathic people.

The cave was dank and smelled of earth, even though Argantyr wasn't sure that they had entered the earth that he knew. They went through a large chamber that contained doors to several smaller chambers. Bunduica pointed to the doorway of the far left antechamber, and they passed through it. There were life-sized figures displayed there. As Argantyr looked at a serpent-man, Bunduica explained that these were trophies of Thorn's many hunts and battles. They walked on. Argantyr marveled at the regal skeleton of a large man sitting on a throne clutching a mighty broadsword. Bunduica told Argantyr, "He was a great Atlantean king, whom Thorn had admired. Thorn keeps his skeleton and Hel-forged sword here to honor the warrior king."

Argantyr gazed upon the jewel-encrusted crown of the great king. *Those jewels would buy a kingdom in this age.*

They walked on past a silver-winged minotaur and stopped in front of a suit of armor. Argantyr estimated that the armor was nearly seven feet in height. Argantyr wondered how he was to move in armor of such girth and stature as his eyes took in the details of the eldritch suit. The whole suit was of a shiny black color and looked as if it were made of polished stone. There were runes all over the armor—they appeared as though they were etched into the suit. The helmet would cover the skull and had eye holes and a cheek guard. The suit of armor seemed to stand there of its own volition—sentient. The helmet rested on top with nothing visible to support it other than a black void.

Bunduica spoke. "I must now leave you. Come back to the house—to the spot that I showed you near the black stone. There you and Thorn will find Æbbath. You… Thorn will know what to do." With these words, she turned and made her way out of the cave.

As Argantyr buckled on the last piece of armor and slipped the helmet over his head, he felt an incredible surge of power starting at the top of his head and moving down into his forehead, through his throat, through the heart region, into his groin, down to his feet, and then into the ground. He felt heat moving through his body; then at the base of his spine, he felt the power spiraling back up toward the base of his skull. When it reached his head, he heard strange music as he had never before experienced. The agony and the ecstasy of the experience brought him to his knees. Glimpses of another life flashed before him. *He was wading knee deep through serpent-men as he hacked and slayed his way to a destination that he didn't remember. A naked barbarian queen screamed behind him as the serpent-men clutched at her to take her away to their breeding camps. Long daggers shot out of Argantyr's gauntlets. He spun around and threw a dagger with each hand as one found its way into the heart of one serpent-man; the other blade went into the second reptilian's throat. Argantyr quickly turned to face a serpent-man rushing upon him with a battle-axe. He hacked into the monster's belly with his mighty broadsword and the greenish-yellow reptilian ichor sprayed into the air before him and spattered his armor.*

Argantyr could feel his body changing. He was growing in both girth and stature. He tried to rise to his feet, but screamed in agony and fell to his knees again as horns sprouted from his head—horns that curved down and jutted back up in defiance of the heavens. His hair turned red as blood and grew even longer to fall down over his swollen, rippling muscles. Argantyr rose to his feet, standing nearly seven feet tall. The suit of armor had all melded together forming one piece. As Argantyr looked down and flexed the mighty sinews of his arm, he saw that the armor had molded itself to fit his body like a second skin. Argantyr grinned a razor-sharp smile, baring the elongated fangs of the vampire in realization of what he had become—he had now merged and become one with the Rune—Thorn; God—Demon—Witch Maker—King and Warlord of a strange empire that existed in ages undreamt of by man. Time was merely relative. Thorn had been here before man, and he would exist long after man was no more.

More visions came to Argantyr: *Beings with long triangular heads formed of opaque crystal surrounded Argantyr—Thorn. The beings were cloaked in white robes and they ordered Argantyr to kneel before a god made of white light sitting upon a throne before him. Argantyr heard himself laugh; gruff booming laughter that sounded as if it issued from the throats of ten hellhounds. A host of tendrils shot out of Thorn's weirdling armor and penetrated the light-god's very core, draining it of its essence as the temple dimmed to darkness and started crumbling around him.* Argantyr realized that these memories belonged to Thorn and that both he and Thorn were now two entities sharing one physical body. Argantyr could feel Thorn's thirst for sustenance as the Rune sensed Argantyr's yearning for vengeance, and Thorn answered him, "We give strength to one another. I will grant you vengeance, and you will, in turn, bring me the *Talisman* that will give me life in this domain—for I have stayed far too long here and am beginning to fade. Once you have faced your greatest adversary, and we have the *Talisman*, our bargain will be complete." They turned and left the cave.

Chapter V

The Battle Commences

Æbbath burst forth from the ground. The colossal creature's skin looked as though it were cut from a polished red ruby. Its membranous wings spread as dirt and rocks exploded into the air and trees were uprooted. Thorn charged in and jumped on the creature's back, getting a hold of its horns, and then shifting his grip to the reins that Bunduica had fashioned from the hide of a young child. The beast flicked its forked oily black tongue out of its mouth like a serpent. Argantyr knew that Bunduica had made arrangements for their swift travel, as Klak's ever-growing army was rapidly marching hundreds of miles to the north of Aroon-Joon; but Argantyr hadn't known the specific means of travel that she had planned for Thorn and Argantyr. Thorn shouted commands as Æbbath took to the skies with the armored giant on the back of the Hel-born creature. Maybe Bunduica thought that Argantyr would fear Æbbath, but at that moment Argantyr heard his own cry of jubilation issue forth from Thorn as the Rune threw his head back and roared Argantyr's battle cry—the battle cry that Argantyr thought that he himself would never raise again. Thorn and Argantyr raced out on the winds of dusk on the back of Æbbath as the beast dipped its elongated neck and screeched its own awful shout to mimic that of its rider.

* * *

"Do you think that I am pretty?" Arju-Lao taunted the girl in the cage. The prisoner did not respond to Arju-Lao's question, though she understood what her tormentor had asked her. The caged girl had yellow hair that had been made much lighter by the sun since her days in captivity. The prisoner couldn't have been more than thirteen years old.

Arju-Lao's face split into a sinister grin, and her dark almond eyes pierced through the girl. "When we get you out of this cage, you will talk plenty once the Wolf squeezes those firm little breasts of yours hard and feels you up with his manhood. I think that will be more than you can take; and I am going to help him."

The girl's heart pounded, and she felt as hopeless as the rest of the prisoners who had survived Klak's last few raids. The Wolf had heard that the auction blocks in Quan-Kara would pay nicely for young female slaves, and these unfortunates who were in Klak's captivity were bound for a life of servitude to the cruel, wealthy merchants and nobles of the city. The young men who yet lived were made to march along behind the cages. The males were used for labor until the whole army had reached the city—there, the prisoners would be put to the sword once they had served their purpose.

Tarac had been taken in the raid with his younger sister, Taren. He was a few years older than the yellow-haired girl that Arju-Lao took much pleasure in tormenting. The heat and long days of marching had finally taken its toll on Tarac and he dropped to the ground. A soldier immediately kicked the fallen boy and yelled, "Get up!"

Taren gripped the bars of the cage so hard that her knuckles turned white as she cried out, "Tarac!"

Arju-Lao laughed, "You do know how to speak, slave girl."

One of Klak's men rode his horse to the back of the line and told the mercenary who was kicking Tarac, "Go ahead and cut his throat. Klak says his sister should see this, so that she will learn how to behave, if she knows what is good for her."

The soldier reached down and pulled Tarac up by his hair. Taren was in tears and screaming hysterically. As the mercenary brought the long knife up to the boy's throat, a demonic screech issued from the sky; and the monster swept down into the ranks of Klak's men. The men scattered, taken by surprise. The armored demon riding the winged creature swung his battle-axe and severed heads from the bodies of several men while Æbbath sped through the host of Klak's army. Æbbath and the rider were again borne aloft while the soldiers fell back. "Archers, forward!" Klak ordered. "The rest of you, fall back! Bring the beast down and hack it to pieces with your swords and axes! I want that rider taken alive! He is to be made a *hymnar*; he is to be shorn of his arms, legs; his tongue cut out. I will carry the torso in a box to show men what happens to those who dare to defy Klak, the Wolf!"

No sooner had Klak made his boasts than the beast plunged downward again. The bowmen let loose with their volleys, but the creature quickly flew upward and out of the reach of the arrows and then rapidly plummeted again, landing to the rear of Klak's army. Thorn leaped from the beast's back and crouched down, one knee touching the earth. He pressed the palms of his armored hands on the ground, and flames exploded from where his hands touched the earth and raced out into the ranks of Klak's army. The men screamed in torment and rolled on the ground in an effort to extinguish the fires that singed their flesh and burned them to death. Wagons burned, and the men were in disarray. Thorn was already among the soldiers—hacking and slaying with his battle-axe. His axe whirred and whistled, singing its song of slaughter; and Æbbath took to the skies with a man in his clutches as the soldier's sword and helmet fell to the earth.

A mercenary met Thorn with an axe. Thorn leaned back as he heard the wind whistle off of his adversary's weapon. The Rune immediately retaliated by bringing his own battle-axe over his head and splitting the man's skull. His enemy's helmet was shattered in twain, and blood spurted up as the man's brains seeped out onto the ground. The runes embedded in Thorn's armor glowed with a hellish red luminosity as he felled foe after foe with his battle-axe.

Thorn was like a lion surrounded by packs of hyenas. His axe moved so fast that it was a shining silver blur of death. One mercenary managed to get in and ram his sword into Thorn's back, but the sword vanished when it was pulled through the eldritch armor and disappeared into another dimension. Thorn bashed the man's head in with the butt of his axe handle and roared with laughter. A few soldiers were able to briefly move in and strike a blow here and there while their comrades died. Those who managed to use their swords in an effort to penetrate Thorn's armor realized too late that no weapon could bite into the strange suit.

Argantyr remarked to Thorn, "It is easier making war than I had remembered."

Thorn snorted, "The real struggle is ahead. To completely break the curse that was placed on you, you must fight Klak alone."

"Fight the Wolf alone?" Argantyr exclaimed in wonder.

"No… Not the Wolf. Klak!" Thorn growled. "The spell preventing you from fighting is temporarily broken, and you are gaining some of your strength back. The potion closed off corridors in your brain that allow your skills in combat to surface. As long as you are in this suit and joined with me, those doorways are open. Do you remember what I told you about how we lend strength to each other?"

The voice that was Argantyr inside of Thorn's body answered, "You told me that we are joined together by this suit of armor, and that we give each other strength."

More blood splattered on the polished jet-black jewel-like surface of the fantastic armor, and the runes etched deep into the armor glowed as red as the freshly-spilled blood. Thorn grunted while he finished splitting one of Klak's men down the torso, "Indeed, I told you that we lend strength to one another; but that is not all—the bargain must be finished by you obtaining the *Talisman* that will rejuvenate me, and you alone facing the man responsible for your binding, to finish breaking the spell of the potion."

"But I am in a weakened condition outside of the armor, and Klak is more than a man. He is a werewolf!"

Thorn growled, "He won't be for much longer!" as he quickly swung his battle-axe twice, decapitating the two men facing him. They were still holding their swords as their heads landed on the ground with a resounding thump.

Thorn had smote and heaped the bodies high as he waded through the dead mercenaries that had made up the Wolf's shattered army. The remainder had fled; so had Klak's prisoners who had once been bound for the auction block in Quan-Kara and a life of bitter servitude at the hands of cruel and perverse masters. All that was left were the dead and the dying, aside from a lone figure that stood leaning on the hilt of his great scabbarded broadsword across the smoking battlefield from Thorn. The man had tangled hair and a red beard, and he wore a large wolf skin that covered his back like a cape with the beast's head draping over his own head. Klak and Thorn were separated by only a few stacks of dead bodies. The stench of charred flesh, freshly-butchered human meat, and death itself were overpowering.

"*Who* are you? *What* are you?" Klak asked as he looked at Thorn with both a sense of hatred and wonder.

Joined together as they were inside of the suit of armor, Thorn could feel Argantyr's tension mounting as Argantyr hissed through clenched teeth, "Be careful—the werewolf!"

Thorn responded to Argantyr's unease by turning the head of his battle-axe to the ground and leaning on the handle. Thorn's face split into a hateful grin, and he growled in a voice that sounded like ten angry men speaking in unison, "I am Thorn, and I deliver your death to you, Wolf!"

Klak's face wrinkled and moved uncontrollably, a look of uncertainty spreading across his countenance.

Thorn continued, "You do remember the man who saved your life on more than one occasion? The man who you thanked for his service by stealing his woman and trying to kill him."

Klak looked away from Thorn's gaze. *Even with all of the evil that Klak had perpetuated, nothing could begin to approach the horror and agonizing insanity that he knew that he would experience if he looked into those burning red eyes. They held both that which is too good and that which is too evil for man and those two elements combined and created its own entity that entwined and swam in an eternal lake that was the beginning and the end.*

Klak shouted, "It wasn't me that wanted Argantyr gone! It was that slant-eyed whore that took up with us when we took Jade-Chuan-Kune!" Klak was biting down hard on his lower lip and mumbling something between his words to Thorn. "She wanted us—all of us to use her, and use her rough; but Argantyr was in the way!" Klak was frothing at the mouth as he mumbled something again in a language that was not intended for the human tongue.

"Incantations! This is how he does it—changes. I have seen it many times!" Argantyr put in hastily.

Thorn showed no concern for action as Klak burst into laughter and went on, "There she is now! Argantyr can have her back! You can take her to him, demon!" Arju-Lao sprang from behind an overturned wagon and started to run.

"Should we not stop her?" Argantyr asked of Thorn.

Thorn calmly answered, "There will be time for that later, Argantyr. You are getting ready to fight a battle, and the prize is you get to reclaim your manhood."

The change came on fast when the snout burst forth from Klak's face and his body quickly covered in hair as he bared razor fangs and ascended in height. He had much experience at quickly changing to the giant wolf on the battlefield and the transformation, once it had started, had only taken seconds. The werewolf snarled and sprang at Thorn. Thorn quickly stepped to one side and tossed the Wolf to the ground. The werewolf rolled over and came up, baying its awful war cry, which Argantyr had heard many times just as a battle was brought to a close.

The werewolf leaped onto Thorn and tried to get its claws into the Rune's throat. Thorn picked the Wolf up by one powerful claw of his own—the Rune's mighty sinews flexing inside of the armored sleeve that clung to him like a second skin. Thorn slammed the supernatural beast onto its back and growled, "I could end this now, Wolf; but I made a deal and there is another who must see to your death."

The Wolf leaped to his feet and stood up on his hind legs. Argantyr thought he saw a cruel and arrogant expression that looked like a smile. Argantyr braced himself for the attack inside of Thorn's body, but before the werewolf could leap, tendrils shot forth from varying points in Thorn's armor and penetrated the heart, throat, forehead, stomach, and groin areas of the creature. Thorn breathed deeply as he absorbed the very essence of the beast. The werewolf was being drained of its vital energies as Argantyr watched the coruscating colors: reds, blues, yellows, and greens, which were the very physical manifestations of the Wolf's essence that were riding Thorn's breath as he inhaled the energy into himself.

Thorn remarked approvingly, "A substantial morsel—for a minor god. Klak used the enscorcelled werewolf's skin to invoke one of the Fenrir and become a werewolf—a manifestation of the Wolf God who devours worlds when they have come to their end. Except now he is the one being devoured. All that is left on your enemy's back is the mangy hide of a dead animal now."

Klak was kneeling on the ground breathing deeply. Thorn took one last deep breath as Klak, who was once called the Wolf, collapsed on the ground. Thorn removed the scabbarded sword from his side and let it fall to the ground as he said, "Reclaim what you have lost, Argantyr, and don't forget your part of the bargain." Thorn then stepped forward and left Argantyr standing alone. The armored Rune and Argantyr were again two separate beings, and Thorn was nowhere to be seen. Darkness assailed Argantyr as he collapsed on the ground a few feet away from where Klak lay.

Chapter VI

One Man Must Die!

A booted foot to the ribs nearly brought Klak off the ground as Argantyr growled, "Get up and meet your death, Wolf that is a wolf no more." Argantyr had regained consciousness several moments erenow and was waiting on Klak to stand and draw his sword.

Klak coughed and a wicked grin spread across his face. He found his feet and barked, "Give me space, dog!"

Argantyr stepped back, drew his sword, and with a sweep of the blade, indicated that Klak now had space to prepare himself for combat.

* * *

Dusk was rapidly approaching under the graying sky while steel clashed on steel and curses and oaths were exchanged between the two men. Argantyr cautiously circled Klak. Though he was no longer able to change into the great supernatural wolf anymore, Klak was still a deadly swordsman and as formidable a foe as any Argantyr had faced on a battlefield. As the two men circled and parried, Argantyr caught a glimpse of Arju-Lao watching the combat between the two swordsmen. She quickly ducked her head behind a charred wagon that had been used to hold prisoners. The distraction of Arju-Lao nearly cost Argantyr his life as his sword came up at the last moment and stopped Klak's sword from cutting his throat; the impact of Klak's blade cut Argantyr's face instead. Argantyr paid no heed to the wound that Klak had just dealt him; he had been scarred by countless such savage fights as this one. The two men winced as they strained iron sinews and, steel on steel, pushed away from each other. Klak came in again and aimed a disemboweling thrust at Argantyr's lower torso. Argantyr managed to turn to the side as Klak's sword raked his ribs. Argantyr could feel the blood trickling and mixing with his sweat.

Argantyr's strength ebbed while visions of his past life flooded into his brain: *His parents and friends gathered around a bonfire—singing—someone made a jest—laughter—running through the grassy fields with his best friend, Bessa; she was a beautiful little girl—they were only months apart in age.*

Klak moved in and swung his sword at Argantyr's head; Argantyr brought his sword up and deflected the blow as he arced back around and stabbed into Klak's thigh with the tip of his blade on the return. Klak's leg buckled.

More visions from Argantyr's past: *A village left in smoking ruins. Argantyr was now an orphan; he looked upon his mother's and father's funeral pyres. His father had fought valiantly, but there were too many of them. His mother had been defiled and viciously slaughtered like the rest of the women of his village. He saw little Bessa lying on a bed coughing as the fever took her after what the men had done to her.* Argantyr gritted his teeth and, as spittle flew from his mouth, he shouted, "No more! I buried you all! I buried you and myself with you!"

Argantyr sprang like a tiger and rained blow after blow of steel so fast that the stunned Klak barely managed to counter his enemy's assault in time. Argantyr's head momentarily filled with visions of his family and tribesmen growing dim as they waved to him from the bank by the creek where his home had been in what was another life. He shook his head and dealt blow after blow, each one faster than the previous attack. Klak was gasping for breath and bleeding heavily, but Argantyr had never felt as alive as he now did—the blood pumping through the iron sinews that gripped his steel. Klak tried one last desperate attempt; marshalling all of the strength left in his battered body, he struck a quick blow at Argantyr's head but was still far too slow for the panther-like reflexes of his adversary as Argantyr stepped back and brought his own broadsword down on Klak's weapon, breaking Klak's blade in twain. Argantyr wasted no time in bringing his sword back through and slitting Klak's torso open. Blood frothed from Klak's mouth as he dropped to his knees and looked up at Argantyr. Argantyr kicked the hilt and shard of broken steel jutting out of it towards Klak and growled at the man, "Pick it up! Pick it up and fight, *Wolf!*"

Klak held onto his stomach in an effort to prevent his innards from tumbling out onto the ground as Argantyr bitterly stated, "It wasn't so long ago that I was on the ground due to you and your concubine's treachery. I at least gave you a chance to fight. It appears as though the Norns have woven out the final thread of your *wyrd*, Klak." As soon as Argantyr spoke the last word his sword flashed in a deadly silver arc that sent Klak's head flying from his shoulders and rolling on the ground.

Klak's dead face looked up from the ground in horror. Arju-Lao ran and dropped at Argantyr's feet, clutching at the man's legs, groveling and crying, pleading with him. "The terrible things they made me do. They hurt me so badly! They told me they would kill you if I didn't go along with Klak's plan. That is the only reason that I did it! Argantyr! You have to believe me. I could love only you. Tell me you believe me! Tell me, Argantyr!"

Argantyr breathed deeply and clenched his jaw; he squinted—eyes full of pain. He looked down at the girl groveling before him and helped her get to her feet. Arju-Lao wrapped her arms around Argantyr, and he slowly raised his arms to return the embrace. She clung to him tightly and for several moments. Finally Argantyr whispered to Arju-Lao, "We must be gone now."

"But where will we go?" Arju-Lao asked, realizing for the first time that the course that her life had been on had changed significantly.

Argantyr responded, "I need to go see some… friends. I have to complete a bargain that I made."

Arju-Lao looked all around the smoking battlefield. The wagons had all burned and all of the horses that were left living had long ago fled. She said, "It will take several days on foot to reach civilization. How far away is our destination?"

Argantyr was watching the sky. Arju-Lao cast her gaze aloft and saw what Argantyr had been staring at: a horned and winged creature bathed in the light of the moon. The thing's appearance reminded her of the stories in her homeland of the legendary dragons of Jade-Chuan-Kune.

"Traveling on foot won't be necessary," Argantyr said quietly. He waved his sword in the air, threw back his head and shouted, "Ho! Æbbath!" The flying beast acknowledged Argantyr's call by dipping its head and plummeting earthward.

Chapter VII

The Sinister Talisman

Arju-Lao was seated across from Argantyr in the candlelit dining room, watching him savagely tear into the roasted boar as he grabbed a loaf of freshly baked bread with his other hand. He had not eaten anything in two days, and he was famished. Arju-Lao delicately pecked at a plateful of roasted potatoes and vegetables cooked in herbs. The dish reminded her of the food of her homeland, but in place of the rice, there had been potatoes.

Their hostess had been absent only briefly when she returned to the dining table with a glass of red wine and set it before Arju-Lao. Still chewing a mouthful of the roasted boar, Argantyr burst out enthusiastically, "This is Bunduica's special wine that I told you about, Arju-Lao! The best in these parts! Fit for a princess!"

Arju-Lao forced a smile at Bunduica seated on the end of the table. Arju-Lao didn't like the way Bunduica's cat-like eyes shone like fiery green emeralds, cutting through her as though she could see every secret of her soul and was privy to every wicked thing Arju-Lao had ever done. Arju-Lao noticed that there were four plates set at the dinner table, but only she, Argantyr, and Bunduica were present. Arju-Lao's almond eyes squinted, looking as though they were nearly closed. "Bunduica, where is this other person who is to dine with us?" she asked.

Bunduica responded in a voice as smooth as silk, "Oh, he is out hunting. He is a hunter."

"What does he hunt?"

"Gods," Bunduica answered with a wry smile.

Arju-Lao pretended to giggle like a young girl at Bunduica's jest. "He-he! Gods!" There was an uncomfortable moment of silence as Arju-Lao's feigned laughter stopped as quickly as it had started.

Bunduica's gaze shifted to Argantyr's eyes and back to her own wine cup when suddenly Argantyr boomed, "You haven't tried the excellent wine yet, *my love.*" The words almost choked Argantyr to say and prompted him to empty his own vessel and put it back down. Bunduica lifted her cup and thrust it forth, silently toasting Arju-Lao. Arju-Lao wrinkled her tiny nose at the sanguinary liquid and quaffed deeply, half-emptying the cup in one drink. The wine immediately went to Arju-Lao's head. It had a sweet taste going down, like a burning amalgamation of chocolate, caramel, and liquid flowers. Made uncomfortable by the silence, she finished draining the cup as an excuse to ask Bunduica for some more, just to get the woman to leave the room. No sooner had Arju-Lao brought her wine cup back down and set it on the table than her head followed the vessel to the table with a thump as the young woman became unconscious and her brain swam in a sea of primordial darkness.

* * *

A blast of light becoming a single source of illumination in the darkness that was before the beginning—and would be there when all had ended... The light was a sun shining in the night that radiated rays of runic shapes from its core.

The light receded and became smaller as the woman drew back with her candle from where Arju-Lao lay on the cold black stone altar. Arju-Lao could hear voices. *But where was she? The last thing she remembered was dining with Argantyr and his friend, Bunduica... and the wine. The wine! She had been drugged.*

As if they could both sense her realization of what had happened, Bunduica laughed and Argantyr said, "I guess this makes us almost even now, Arju-Lao. You put powder in my wine, and now we have put powder in your wine. Though, I don't think that you are going to be faring as well as I have in the aftermath."

Arju-Lao tried to move, but her limbs were bound by red vines—supernatural tendrils that were much stronger than she was. She tried to let out a scream, but her mouth held a gag to prevent any sound from issuing forth.

Bunduica gruffly chuckled, saying, "I would have liked to have heard you, Arju-Lao—it is exciting—but your *lover* told me how he loathes to hear a woman scream. He said it brings back bad memories of when he was a child."

Arju-Lao tried again to move her limbs, but her resilience availed her not, for she was much too firmly bound.

Bunduica had placed a pillow under Arju-Lao's head so that the woman could witness what they were doing in the room. For the first time, she noticed the demon in the darkness. His skin was alabaster, and his long hair was red as blood. His large muscular frame lolled on the ebon throne he sat, and he breathed laboriously. Something was wrong with him. He was the one on the battlefield. The one who destroyed Klak's army and brought Argantyr to kill her true lover, the Wolf.

Tears welled up in the girl's dark almond eyes and she began to tremble with fear as her brain tried to correlate all that had happened and simultaneously started to speculate on what was happening at that moment.

As if in answer to the questions that raced through Arju-Lao's head, Bunduica broke the silence. "Yes, Arju-Lao, Thorn is the demon who destroyed Klak's army. With help from Argantyr, of course. Thorn has stayed too long in this world that we inhabit tonight. He is weak. The synchronicity of Thorn and Argantyr in Thorn's suit of armor lent strength to both men temporarily. The curse that you helped Klak put on Argantyr is now completely broken, but I made a deal with Argantyr, and there is one last thing he needs to do to fulfill our bargain."

Arju-Lao strained at her bonds on the altar as tears rolled down her face onto the cold black stone beneath her.

Bunduica continued, speaking as if she were in a dream, "Once… ages ago, I was the daughter of a proud queen. Her name was Bodicea. My father had died and left Bodicea as the ruler of a wild race of warriors known as the *Iceni*. There was a mighty empire to the east called Rome. Even before my father Prasutagus had died, there had existed, at best, an uneasy peace between the *Iceni* and the Romans. One day, the Romans came… They came and took away my mother's governing rights. They tied her up and whipped her. Made us, me and my sister

Vodicea, watch while they did it."

Bunduica had raised her voice to a crescendo, and her piercing emerald eyes gleamed with madness. Arju-Lao's heart was pounding as though it could burst from her chest at any moment.

Bunduica looked at the floor and fell silent for a moment. Lowering her voice, she regained her composure and turned her head to the side and continued, "They raped me and my sister. Both of us. Over and over again. My sister, Vodicea, died shortly thereafter; but I survived on the hatred in my heart alone... I went to the deepest, darkest recesses of my mind, and I opened up corridors that, it is said, that no human being should open. One night, I made the ultimate sacrifice that a mother can make. I sacrificed my own son in a ritual, and Thorn came. Thorn came, and he destroyed all of those who'd had a hand in our downfall; and he made them suffer; and O they did suffer for aeons! But he didn't stop there; he knew that I loved him like I could never love a man, and he took pity on a poor broken girl whose only reason to live was the vengeance in her heart—and now that that was sated… what was left? I will tell you! He taught me the secrets of black arts that no wizard on this earth knows. He showed me wonders that no other human eyes have looked upon. But now he is weak and dying, because he has spent so much time with me here, in the House on the Edge of Time, and has been long absent from his kingdom of Hel-Valha. He needs the sustenance to open doors that only he can open and return himself home; and the last object that I need for the spell is in you; and it has to come out!"

Bunduica drew a long dagger and, holding it flat in both hands, offered it to Argantyr. The dagger was etched deeply with runes like those on Thorn's armor. Bunduica cast her penetrating gaze upon Argantyr and said, "It is time to fulfill your part of the bargain."

Bunduica raised her arms and chanted, "*U-u-ur! U-u-ur! Come forth from the Land of Castles where the towers spiral into forever and timeless-time where time and space have no meaning. Come forth, cause of all causes. Origin of all creation. Origin of immortality! Origin of all law and of chaos. And origin of all vibration in which the great secrets of truth abide! Come forth, thou ghosts of the Runestorm, and heal the one who is stricken with torment and fading into the darkness that was here before time and surely will be here when time is no more. For he is of your essence, though he manifests in matter. U-u-ur! U-u-ur!*"

Argantyr stood over Arju-Lao, both hands clutching the hilt of the long rune dagger as Bunduica's incantations heightened to a fevered pitch. Arju-Lao saw weird angles opening and tumbling in the air all around her and she screamed into the cloth that muffled her cries. Bunduica shouted, "*Tree-Micalazoda Yom-Gurd! Ho-dag nona nu nak no! Deesmees! Jeshet! Bonedose! Feduvema! Enttemoss! Open wide the Gates! Manifest Ur!*" Bunduica screamed as loud as she could, "Now, Argantyr! Bring forth the *Talisman*! Do it now!" Argantyr drove the dagger down with all of his might into Arju-Lao's breast. Blood jetted up, and the angled openings in the air about the room shot forth a glowing green light that coalesced and was absorbed by the rune dagger. Argantyr gritted his teeth and shifted the blade of the dagger around, deep in the dying woman's chest. He then reached into her bloody breast and pulled out her heart—still beating due to Bunduica's sorcery. Argantyr turned and handed Arju-Lao's heart to Bunduica, saying, "Our deal is finished, witch woman. You now have your *Talisman.*"

Argantyr watched as Bunduica walked over to the demon sitting on his throne—dying. As Bunduica held up the *Talisman*, she said to Thorn, "Here, my love, the still-beating Heart of the Betrayer torn from her breast by the one whom she betrayed; the *Talisman* needed to restore you to life so that you can open the corridors leading back to Hel-Valha."

Bunduica put her arm around Thorn and held the heart up to him, slowly feeding him the delicacy, a treacherous and evil heart sustained by sorcery, the sinister *Talisman* that gave him life.

Chapter VIII

Road of the Lone Wolf

The four soldiers sat at their foaming jacks and wine cups around a table at the Wolfshead Inn. It was a crowded tavern in Horan, being one of two that hadn't been burned to the ground in recent years. One of the men at the table slapped Taren on her behind and gripped it as he chuckled through rotten teeth. "How much for a night's pleasure, serving girl?" he inquired. The man sitting next to him laughed at the girl's silence.

The innkeeper saw Tarac's face turn red and knew the boy seethed with rage at the expression of fear and humiliation on his younger sister's countenance. As the young man reached for the knife at his hip, the portly, balding barkeep shot Tarac a disapproving glance. "Not if you want to keep your job—or your life," he said. "I gave you two a place to stay and the means to make an honest wage when you came here begging for food and shelter, and telling your story about being taken in a raid on your village, but I sense trouble, and I would wager that the two of you are hiding from the authorities somewhere. If you are going to live in this city, then you are going to have to obey the laws of this city. I see no harm in charging a small fee for them to sleep with her. We could split the pay, say, sixty-forty. That would be sixty percent for me and forty percent for you and your sister—split between the two of you, of course."

An old one-eye sitting at the table of the soldiers chortled with a phlegmy drawl. "Now, hold on, barkeep. Who said anything about money? You know what you just told them youngsters about obeying the law. Well, we *are* the law; and *we* say what is right here."

Another man sitting nearby spoke. "If we knew you was going to be selling those kinds of sweets, we would have done had our turn with her, barkeep. I'll offer you good money for that."

Suddenly, a man who had been sitting in the corner for some time listening to the conversation got up and walked over to Tarac and his sister. "I have a better deal for both of you than any of these pigs can offer you." He placed two sacks of jewels on the bar and nodded to the two siblings. "Go ahead, take them and leave this pig-sty. You can buy ten dung heaps like this one with one of what is in that sack."

The whole room fell silent as Taren looked at the man and picked up the bag; her brother followed her example. The man who had given the jewels to the youths was an imposing figure, dressed in black accoutrements fit for a nobleman and wearing knee-high leather boots, silk breeches, a shirt of fine dyed wool, and a cape of black silk lined with red. He gestured toward the door of the tavern and solemnly commanded Taren and his sister, "Now, get out, and don't come back here."

As the two siblings exited the tavern, the old one-eye sitting at the door was the first to break the silence. "Who are you that comes in here and interferes with the law, dog? Your neck could be in a noose as soon as I say it."

Without turning to look at the man the stranger replied, "There has been no law here since Count Dagnus' head was set on a spear in front of his house in Horan, and Klak and his men sat feasting at Dagnus' table; and even at that, there wasn't much law before then. The whims of a few cutthroats do not concern me any more than I value their lives."

The one-eye nodded to the other three men at the table. The room exploded as the soldiers' table was overturned and flashing swords came out of their scabbards while the barkeep ducked behind the counter. The first man to rush forward caught a dagger in his chest. As the stranger drew his sword, he threw his cape over the next soldier rushing him while his steel met another mercenary's sword and came back around and slit the man's throat. He threw another dagger into rotten-teeth's thigh, and the wounded man dropped to the floor as the soldier with the cape over his face worked free; but it was too late for the man, as the stranger drove his cold steel into the man's guts and the mercenary dropped to the floor—blood gushing from his mouth, and his intestines spilling out onto the floor.

Rotten-teeth tried to rise, but the stranger's broadsword hacked at the man's neck, and his head rolled on the floor, face leering upward in a black-tooth grimace. The fight had been over as soon as it had started.

The stranger looked behind the bar at the cringing barkeep and laid two small jewels on the bar. "Use this to pay for the damage and get some real whores around this place so the sell-swords will stop trying to rut with children."

The stranger then walked out the door of the Wolfshead Inn to where his horse was tethered in front of the tavern. As he prepared to mount the great white steed, a young girl's voice cried to him, "Wait, sire! Where are you bound? We have no home, nor way to travel." It was Taren.

The stranger answered, "I am bound for Tuatha, where I hail from; but first, I have business on the outskirts of Aroon-Joon. You can follow me until we get to Arthing; then we must go our separate ways. Take the horses that belonged to the soldiers; they have no need of them now. Mount quickly and let us be gone before more soldiers come."

Tarac and his sister mounted the mercenaries' steeds. "What is your name, man?"

"My name is Argantyr! Now make haste before you become a guest in someone's dungeon!" The three raced off for the outskirts of Aroon-Joon.

* * *

Tharat sat alone at his supper table savoring the flesh of the slow-roasted urchin who had had the misfortune of becoming lost deep in the woods and ensnared in one of the old wizard's traps. Tharat snapped his teeth as he dipped his spoon into a bowl of boiled potatoes and spooned some more out. No sooner had he brought the oversized wooden spoon up to his mouth than there came a knock at the door. Tharat was immediately wary. *No one knew where he lived. It must be someone who had gotten lost and was seeking shelter for the night. A wide grin split the wizard's face and he became excited about the potential opportunity and the possibilities. A slow roasted babe or a small child was tender; but a fully grown adult human would supply him with meat for some time. What if there were more than one person?* His heart raced and he snapped his teeth together. The rapping at the door came again.

"One moment!" shouted the wizard as he got up and ran over to the door. "Now, who is it?"

The voice of a young girl answered, "I am just a poor girl with an infant who seeks shelter this night." The excitement was more than Tharat could contain. He hurriedly flung the front door wide and saw a girl standing in the doorway with a bundle. Tharat grinned and gestured for the girl to enter his home as he stammered, "Right this way! Right this way, you poor child. Poor child with a child. How fortunate for me. Fortunate for me, that is, because I am all alone and welcome your company..." His words trailed off as he turned to shut the door to his house, but instead his throat was seized in an iron grip. Argantyr commanded Taren, "Now take your blanket and get back to the horses and wait with your brother. I will join you ere long."

Tharat's eyes were wide with fear as Argantyr held him against the wall and strangled him—recognition upon the dying wizard's face. Argantyr growled at Tharat, "I know you know who I am, Tharat. The witch showed me what Klak and Arju-Lao did to me in her scrying orb. She also showed me your part in it, and for that you are going to pay with your life! Just as they did."

* * *

Argantyr released Tharat; the wizard had expired some moments agone. Argantyr rummaged through the dead sorcerer's house looking for something of value. Argantyr did not need any gold or jewels; he had taken all that Klak's mercenaries had amassed when he and Thorn had destroyed the Wolf along with his entire army. Argantyr took what spoils that he could carry with him, and the rest he had hidden in a secret place to gather upon his return. *No, he knew that Tharat dealt in unique magickal objects that the old wizard would trade for the human flesh that he craved.*

Argantyr found one room in the house that was locked. He kicked the door in with a loud thud and looked upon the chamber. The room was lined with shelves of books on all sorts of *gramarye* and dark magicks—books dedicated entirely to subjects as varying as necromancy and shapeshifting to pacts with demons and vampirism. Argantyr's eyes scanned the room by the light of a large candle he had taken from Tharat's dining table; he looked upon daggers and swords of various makes and sizes—most of them covered in runes similar to those that were on Thorn's armor and the dagger that he had used to kill Arju-Lao. He saw scrying orbs, pendulums, and rings and pendants with mystical signs and sigils. With a snort, Argantyr turned to leave the room but stopped as his eyes lighted on a familiar sight. Hanging in the corner was a large wolf's hide like the one that Klak had worn and used to shapeshift into the werewolf that had made him nearly invincible in battle. Argantyr stepped forward and took the magickal cloak down from its hanger. He threw it over his shoulder and walked back to the bookshelf. Argantyr removed the book dedicated to shapeshifting titled *On the Black Art of the Fenrir and Becoming the Lycanthrope.* With the book in one hand and the wolf's skin thrown over his shoulder, Argantyr stepped over the dead wizard's body and left the house.

Taren and Tarac had heeded well Argantyr's instructions and waited with the horses. They stared at the weird wolfskin draped over the man's shoulder as they all mounted their horses, but thought it better not to ask any questions of the man who had agreed to be their protector until they had reached the more orderly and civilized lands of Arthing.

Argantyr was a man of scant words. After imbibing a few cups of wine around the campfire on the first night of their journey, Tarac had asked the warrior, "So what will you do once you reach your native land of Tuatha, Argantyr? Live a life of wine, women and song?" Taren sat listening intently to every word; she was concerned about parting company with this strange man who had saved her virtue and, she was certain, the life of her brother back at the Wolfshead Inn.

Argantyr answered the boy in his deeply resonating voice, "Aye, Tarac, I will live a life of wine, women, and song; but first, I must satisfy my wanderlust. I will go to Gurmania and raise a band of mercenaries; then, carve a kingdom for myself to the north in Scaldavia, perhaps all of the way from Aesirland to Vanirland." Taren and Tarac sat quietly as they realized that they could not follow Argantyr; his life was to be one of conquest, usurped thrones, and blood-soaked crowns. "Best get your blankets and get some sleep," Argantyr told the youths. "There is a long day's ride ahead of us on the morrow."

As Argantyr drifted off to sleep he heard the baying of a lone wolf in the distance; he wondered to himself, "What will it be like…?"

Return to Stynar Vort

By Joe "Deathmaster" Minichino

"There is no hell for those who rejoice at their damnation,
And no heaven for those without need of salvation"
—The Uncrowned

Part I: The Fall of Stynar Vort

I

It was sunset when the relentless snow joined forces with Helved in the storming of the walls of Stynar Vort.

From the snow-blasted battlements an archer shouted: "The enemy is in! The north wall is breached!" as the Helvedians broke the defensive line.

"Sound the—" The archer's cry was silenced by the blade that pierced his back and emerged a foot out of his chest. His killer retracted the sword and with a jubilant cry hurled the body headlong into the castle courtyard.

Huethys, commander of the army of Stynar Vort, instinctively grabbed King Gaetys' arm just in time as the falling soldier crashed, head-first and helmetless, not three feet away from him, spraying blood and brains.

"Huethys, sound the retreat!" the king roared at his commander and friend. "Get the soldiers in the citadel, then find me in the throne room!"

Huethys hurried up the stone steps to the unused altar to the long forgotten blood god Styne. Amidst flying arrows, he climbed the altar, which lay atop a rock in the middle of the courtyard, and from there he repeatedly blew the retreat with his horn and shouted battle-tongue commands.

At the signal, the soldiers on the wall-walks ran into the bastion towers, bolting the doors behind them, then flowed into the courtyard like streams of incandescent iron. The exalted invaders crowded the *chemin-de-ronde* and began ramming the doors that led into the bastions, when Huethys' sustained horn note rang their death sentence. Seven soldiers of Stynar Vort in a concealed room in the entrance tower of the citadel pulled seven levers, and the seven wall-walks swung freely, hinged on their respective towers, dropping hundreds of intruders to their death. A deafening unison of horror and panic ended with the clangor of hundreds of armour-clad bodies being crushed nearly at once. The spectacle was so revolting that several of Stynar Vort's soldiers wretched and turned their eyes away from the death pile in disgust. Huethys loudly exhorted the soldiers to resume their retreat into Styns-Ueg, the inner citadel of Stynar Vort, on a background of cries and moans of the dying crushed Helvedians.

The ruse of dropping the wall-walks had gained the defenders enough time for a safe retreat.

But commands in the Helvedian tongue rang out from the battlements: soldiers knotted ropes and secured them to the battlements and began descending the titanic walls of the fortress, wearing their shields on their backs to protect them from missile attacks.

Twenty times a thousand men of Helved entered the virgin walls of the mythical Stynar Vort.

II

"No one has ever breached Stynar Vort. I would give my soul to go out there and tear the jugulars from their necks!" growled a feral King Gaetys. Taking a breath to regain his poise, he continued, "The citadel's resilience has never been tested, and we have to protect the people. We need to lead them out through the tunnels of Swartheime. And beyond that… I do not know."

"The enemy is climbing the walls of Styns-Ueg as we speak. Whatever we decide to do, we must do it immediately," said Huethys. "As for the Swartheime tunnels… I am not even sure they are more than a legend. And if they are there, we do not know if they are viable or to where they lead. What will our people do once they reach an exit? I say let us make a last stand, and die honourably."

"The passages exist, Commander Huethys. I have been there," interrupted old Bedar, the King's Counsellor. "And so does Styne's Chamber, which many believe to be a story. I have been there as well. And I propose we use both," he said, with a solemn air.

"I know nothing of this, Bedar. How come you possess knowledge I do not have?" Gaetys questioned his white bearded counsellor. His hand stealthily and subconsciously reached for the handle of the long dagger at his side.

"It is a little known fact—my Lord—that the King's Counsellor is also the High Priest of Styne," explained Bedar. "According to the Mountain Scrolls, the fortress is a manifestation of the Blood God himself. Let us follow the custom of our ancestors, and let the king ask for protection at this desperate hour."

"So what do you propose we do?" asked Gaetys.

"Lead the people out by the tunnels," answered Bedar. "They will only have to wait until Styne has saved us all from the Helvedians. Meanwhile, Your Majesty, Commander Huethys and I will descend into Styne's Chamber, to perform the Eternal Life ritual, and conjure Styne's supernatural help."

"What will be the price of Styne's help?" asked the king. "Would it not be better to ride to battle, one last time, and die for our home?"

"I would rather die by the friendly taste of steel which I understand, than be saved by that which I do not," interjected Huethys.

"There is no honour if there is no legacy!" exclaimed Bedar, uncharacteristically shouting, his beard shaking in great wrath. "Your name is not going to be in any song! What is the value of sacrifice if it does not yield salvation? Put down your sword and your pride and put the lives of the people of Stynar Vort ahead!"

"Perhaps you are right, Bedar. Whatever the price, we will pay it," answered King Gaetys. "Huethys, call the royal guard to accompany us to the—"

"No!" interrupted Bedar. "That would be sacrilege! When performing the Eternal Life ritual, only the High Priest and two individuals, representing the sacred virtues of Death and Rebirth, are permitted in the chamber."

III

The stairs to the chamber were only reachable from Bedar's room, which was the top floor of a tower adjacent to the main building in the citadel. Before entering the passage, Bedar warned the others: "I have only been to the Chamber once, many years ago. It's an exhaustingly long descent. There are no windows, and it is easy to become overwhelmed with panic when you are hundreds of feet from the outside world and just as many from reaching our destination."

The king glanced out the window at the very moment when Helved's soldiers opened the Blood Gates of Stynar Vort against the backdrop of a sunset snow storm. The massive blood-tinted metal doors creaked with the strain of disuse since they had not been opened in memory of man. The triumphant roar of the invaders flooded into the courtyard.

"They are in…" the king mumbled.

"Then we have to be fast," answered the commander, "or all will be lost."

The door to the passage was a grotesque relief of a man struggling with a gigantic serpent, something Gaetys recognised as "The Taming of Seyden," a scene of one of Styne's legends from his childhood. Bedar operated a mechanism which he purposely shielded from view with his body, and the relief opened like a door, beyond which was a narrow passage leading to spiral stairs.

Bedar took three torches, lit one, and gave Gaetys and Huethys the other two. "One torch at a time, torchbearer at the back. The stairs are so narrow and steep that anyone walking behind a torchbearer would be too close to the flame and unable to see ahead."

The three proceeded into the passage and down the steps for what seemed like an interminable time. Bedar kept his lucid and composed demeanour, while Gaetys and Huethys seemed much more uncomfortable, at first because of the oppressing closeness of the walls. Then the king and his commander started hearing distant echoing voices of tormented souls, the growls and grunts of unseen creatures of the darkness, and a barely audible laughter of demoniacal madness.

Huethys became convinced that each brick in the wall was a face, frozen in terror and covered in blood. At last, far beyond the point where an untrained mind would have given in to the temptation of going insane, a dim glow faintly lit the steps ahead of the three men. The stairs terminated their dizzying spiral to straighten into wider steps that descended into the greenish light.

Bedar led the way into the Chamber, and paused for a brief moment under the stony arch of the entrance to the sacred place.

Two glowing yellow-green flames were suspended in midair in the room, and the air was heavy with dampness and the smell of mould.

Despite being out of the oppressive spiral of the stairs, the atmosphere was of unadulterated evil as it became clear the room was a subterranean temple: an imposing and finely decorated altar stood at its centre, raised from the floor by a few steps, and oriented so that the performant of whatever dark and perverse ritual was taking place in this temple would be facing the farthest wall. On this wall was an enormous, vitreous hemisphere that looked as if made of transparent marble. The altar's surface was strangely shaped, in that it was slightly slanted, and on its lower end the otherwise flat surface formed a funnel with a hole carved into the altar itself. Precisely above the funnel, a slanting pipe, piercing the chamber's ceiling, stood some six feet above it, as if whatever liquid the pipe conducted was meant to fall straight into the altar's funnel.

The decorations on the altar's side represented scenes of stories untold, with demonic looking figures, serpents, chains and daggers, mountains and people marching. Scattered everywhere within the decorated strip of stone were eyes made of the same material as the great hemisphere on the wall. Bedar looked back to Gaetys and Huethys, and gestured them to wait at the entrance of the chamber at the bottom of the stairs. He climbed the dais to the altar. Placing his left hand over the funnel, he reached with his right hand to his belt, extracted a carefully hidden long-bladed althame, and ran its blade on the palm of his left hand. He clenched his hand into a fist to squeeze blood down the funnel, then pronounced the prayer: "Take my blood, O Styne, made pure by Seyden's Tooth, the sacred althame."

A low hum, almost imperceptible to ears, suddenly rang through the air, but while it was hard to hear, its vibration could be felt in the eardrums and teeth in the most uncomfortable way. The glassy hemisphere on the wall instantly lit up like the eye of a colossal cat, staring directly at Bedar. The old man tried to hide his incredulity and addressed the eye on the wall, looking at the floor and his voice breaking with fear. "Almighty Styne, protector of the Mountain, it is your servant Bedar, High Priest of Stynar Vort, who asks for your help in this desperate hour of need."

"Humans," answered a deep cavernous voice that had not spoken in a thousand years. "Ungrateful, forgetful, unfaithful creatures. That is what humans are!

"I gave you an unvanquishable home, and eternal protection, in return for blood. But you have forgotten me, for a thousand years… and you forgot the blood you promised… and now you want protection. You have sinned for generations. You owe me *all* that *blood*… a thousand years of it."

"I will restore your cult as the rightful protector of Stynar Vort," answered Bedar, "and I can give you the blood you want, all of it, today. But we are moments away from extermination, and if we are defeated, then you will be forever forgotten and no blood will ever run from the altars of Styne again…"

"I see intruders in their thousands in my fortress… So much blood… Proceed, priest, with the ritual of Eternal Life," Styne ordered eagerly. "Take Gaetys' life on the altar to represent Death, and Huethys to represent Rebirth. I will take their blood and their souls and turn them into Kruhd'asra, the Undead Blood Fury, who shall bring you victory."

Bedar turned to King Gaetys. "Your Majesty, this is the price. I will ensure that everyone in Stynar Vort knows that the king and his commander sacrificed their lives and souls for their salvation."

Gaetys and Huethys looked at each other in horror, then the king spoke with hesitation in his voice: "Bedar, this is… much to ask. Our souls?" He looked at the old priest, hoping he offered some kind of alternative.

"My King, you wished to kill the enemy on your own, and you said you would offer your soul for that opportunity…"

"Are you ready to die, Huethys? Ready to die with me, for our people?" asked Gaetys, trying to find consolation in sharing the same fate with his commander.

"I am," answered Huethys, as devout and impassible as ever.

The King of Stynar Vort stepped up to the altar and lay upon it, his head on the lower end. He turned to Huethys and with a strangely serene tone of voice said, "You were a good friend and I am glad to die for our people." Huethys nodded.

Bedar murmured words not known to common men, then paused. With his eyes closed, he violently stabbed Gaetys in his heart. With his left hand he hammered Seyden's Tooth deeper into Gaetys' chest until the tip of the blade stuck out of the king's back. Then, with an almost sadistic expression, the priest turned the blade in Gaetys' chest. Blood started dripping from the king's body into the funnel.

Styne's voice boomed suddenly: "Rise again, as the Slayer King, and kill every enemy of Stynar Vort within her walls and on this mountain. I will drink the blood of the slain, and the people of Stynar Vort will hail their saviour who gave up his life and came back from the dead to deliver them." As blood flowed into the altar, the two yellow-green flames gained a more crimson hue, and slightly grew in size. Styne's cavernous voice broke the silence of the chamber to recite words of a language unspoken by Man.

Gaetys lay immobile for a brief moment, then a strong smell of burned flesh began permeating the room. His garments turned increasingly black as if burnt by invisible flames, then crumbled to ashes on the floor to reveal the corpse's blistering skin suffering the same inexplicable fate. What once was Gaetys stood slowly up from the altar, shedding the last of his skin. He faced the eye of Styne, who welcomed his demoniacal creation with a cry: "Another Son of Styne is born. Join the eternal fight, my child!" The bare muscles of Gaetys' body became covered by a black and silver armour. In one hand appeared a silver hilted black blade, in the other a black shield with the silver emblem of a serpent. He jumped off the dais and ran to the dark wall near Styne's eye, to disappear in the darkness.

Bedar turned to Huethys, knowing what was expected of the king's commander. Huethys slowly walked up the altar, and lay on it. As Bedar approached him with the althame, he blocked the old man's arm and punched him under his chin, causing the priest to fall senseless on the floor. Styne's eye glowed crimson and yellow. With maniacal eagerness he shouted, "What are you doing? You owe me your blood!"

"I do not owe you anything," answered Huethys. "If it is blood you want, I will give it to you—Bedar's blood!"

"So be it then," answered Styne. "You are now the High Priest, Huethys. Now give me Bedar's blood! Your god commands it!"

"Not before you show me the way out of here."

At that moment, blood started dripping from the pipe that came through the ceiling onto the altar. Gaetys was massacring the enemy, and Stynar Vort was drinking the blood of the slain, to feed its God and Creator, Styne.

"Ahhh… blood, here it comes. My child is reaping lives!" Styne cried.

"How do I escape?" Huethys insisted, finding himself shouting at the god.

A faintly lit tunnel appeared in a dark corner near the stairs that lead down into the chamber, and Huethys paused to plan his moves.

"I held up my end of the bargain," said Styne. "You are the High Priest. Complete the ritual of Eternal Life. Give me the blood that represents Rebirth! Stynar Vort will fall if you do not!"

Huethys grunted. Reluctantly he leaned toward Bedar, then stabbed the old man in the heart, retracted the blade and immediately ran toward the tunnel. Blood was copiously dripping down the ceiling pipe, and Styne's voice became inebriated, drunk on his everlasting lust for it. While the blood-obsessed god sang his pleasure, Huethys disappeared down the tunnel, running as fast as he could, with the dripping althame still in his hand.

Part II: 25 Years Later

IV

A shuffle of leaves broke Thruen's concentration and he turned his head to identify the source of the noise. "Ah, it's you, King Huethys..." Thruen said, barely hiding his irritation, and resuming his carving of the mythological scene of "The Swallowing of the Moon" on a staff.

"Yes, I came here because I knew you would be alone. We must talk," said the king.

"It sounds important," answered Thruen.

"Yes. You are to be king, my son," Huethys said, getting straight to the point.

Baffled, Thruen looked at him and commented: "I am the commander of Helved's army, and your protector. You are the king. I do not understand."

"Thruen... I have spent the last twenty-five years festering inside, eaten by guilt and remorse. I am the worst sinner the Gods have ever known. Now I am old, and I need to atone before my physical and mental faculties abandon me and impede my ability to seek repentance... This is a quest from which I will not return."

Thruen's precise age was unknown. He was perhaps in his early thirties, but the scars on his face made him look older and—in combination with a tall muscular build, long plaited dark red hair and beard—decidedly menacing. His eyes were a bright grey, like those of a blind man, and there was a cold liveness in them, like a wolf observing prey from a distance. He stood up and said, "Then I am coming with you. And you will come back. And you will continue to be king."

"You are like a son to me Thruen," Huethys said. "I cannot ask you to do this... and I know you too well. You are fretting to return to your carving right now, and after dinner you will want to continue your studies. What did you say you are learning now… herbalism? Tomorrow you will want to practice archery, then sword fighting, then preparing ink. In this precise order. Yes, I noticed the hawthorn berries ready to be boiled. You have your whole life ahead of you, with that mind of yours. A mind so fine that it made you an unbeatable sword master and the perfect commander of the guards. Let go of old Huethys. My beard is white… When I drink wine I fall asleep before I can get drunk… I have been living on borrowed time for twenty-five years. It's time I face my past."

"Have you abdicated yet?" asked Thruen.

"Yes, it's in the hands of the council now. You are to be crowned king soon, and you are already the regent by law."

"Perfect. Then I command you to bring me with you on your journey," said Thruen with his usual monotone voice. Then he sat down and resumed chiseling the profile of a wolf eating the moon.

V

"Helved was my sworn enemy, and now I am its king," said Huethys breaking the silence of the ride. "Now that my life is coming to an end, I want you to know that I am a native of Stynar Vort."

"Is this the same place of the Lost Army of King Hruath? That's just a legend… I thought?" Thruen interjected.

"It is a magical place, and it is real," answered the old king. "Everyone knows that King Hrauth the Greedy claimed he had found the mythical Stynar Vort, with its jewel encrusted walls, and set off to conquer it. No one ever returned from the expedition. What people do not know is that they all died within the walls of Stynar Vort. So yes, as far as the people of Helved know… Stynar Vort is indeed just a legend."

Huethys recounted the events of his last night in Stynar Vort. He told of King Gaetys, supposedly trapped in the fortress as Kruhd'asra, the demon guardian, forever nourishing a blood-obsessed god.

"I swore revenge on those who invaded and destroyed my home, and I exacted it by grabbing Helved's crown, by treachery, murder and sheer bravery," the old king continued. "But as soon as that crown rested on my head… revenge felt empty and futile. Most importantly, all that was left was guilt. I betrayed my friend and king at the time, and abandoned him to an eternity of torture. I am going back to Stynar Vort to rectify this. I will kill him with this althame." He gestured to the weirdly decorated dagger on his belt. "Then I will take his place as the demon guardian. But let us find a suitable place to spend this last night now. We have just enough time to hunt some game before it gets dark. We should reach the fortress tomorrow."

As night fell on the travelers, they enjoyed a meal of pheasant roasted over an open fire, and a flask of the finest ale in all Helved, which Huethys reserved for what he thought to be his last night. The tired old king lay on the ground, as comfortable as any veteran soldier, pillowing his head with his arms. In his drunken sleep he mumbled "...forgive me, my King..."

That night, Thruen immersed himself in his meditative state, and remembered the day when Huethys first found and rescued him from his solitary confinement in the darkness of the basement of a Godanian monastery. It probably—Thruen could not be sure—was the place where he had learned to replace sleep with meditation. Thruen was perhaps seven or eight then, and twenty-five years had since passed. A part of him feared this was indeed his last night with his saviour and adoptive father, and, in his sadness, he was grateful for the years spent together.

The following day was decidedly harsher on the two travelers. As they reached for higher altitudes, mist turned to drizzle, then drizzle turned to sleet, and sleet into light snow.

Huethys halted his horse and took a long look at the surrounding peaks, barely visible in the mist. "The entrance to Stynar Vort is behind that boulder," he declared. "I used this tunnel to escape all those years ago, and I would not dare enter through the gates knowing Gaetys is guarding the courtyard."

Before entering the tunnel concealed behind the great rock, Huethys grabbed Thruen's arm and said: "You have been a great commander, a great son, and an even greater friend."

"I will be bringing you home, Huethys," coldly replied Thruen, still unaccepting of Huethys' conviction of his imminent death.

"Stubborn to the end. How unsurprising," commented Huethys.

Huethys touched the rock forming the arched entrance of the tunnel and murmured unintelligible words, and a small floating yellow-green flaming orb appeared on his hand.

"You never told me you were a sorcerer," Thruen said with a slight tone of disgusted surprise.

"That's because I am not," answered the old king. "But I am a priest, and this is one of very few tricks I possess. It only works here anyway, so do not think I withheld these abilities in the past..."

"I'd be upset to know you willingly put me through the ordeal in the tunnels of Sevar," said Thruen, referring to an adventure the two shared years before.

"How can I forget? No, I would not willingly subject us to that oppressive inferno," said Huethys. "You are awfully talkative today, Thruen. Come, follow me."

VI

The old king and his commander walked down a narrow tunnel which gently sloped down into the earth for what felt like an eternity. Then at last, a brighter light in the distance signified the end of that highly uncomfortable journey.

"Stand back, Thruen, let me explore first," whispered Huethys.

He glanced around the corner of the wall at the temple that he had left twenty-five years before.

Huethys was catapulted back to his last day in Stynar Vort, when he descended the spiral stairs with his king and friend Gaetys, and old Bedar showing the way. He decided to take another very cautious step forward so to reconnoiter the room further. But before he could do so, he heard a whisper, a repetitive sound, coming from the centre of the room, and clicking noises. The whisper gradually became clearer as it got closer, and to Huethys' horrified amazement the word being repeated was his own name.

"Huethyyyyssss... Huethyssss..." the voice repeated continuously as it began to move farther away. Huethys glanced again at the temple, and discovered the supernatural source of the noise: a skeleton wandering aimlessly around the temple, still dressed in Bedar's rotten robe. The undead priest repeated his name endlessly, at times stopping to look around, checking the empty scabbard hanging at his belt, while conjuring yellow-green flames in his bony hands and empty eye sockets.

Huethys took a couple of steps back towards Thruen and described the scene. "It's as if he is suspended in a limbo unable to fully die, his skeleton and his will lingering."

Huethys paused for a moment then regained focus. "To the right of the altar there's a wall. On that wall you will notice a gigantic glass hemisphere, and beyond that is the entrance of a tunnel that leads into the fortress. We should try to reach it without being noticed by that monstrosity."

"Something tells me he sees in spite of his empty eye sockets," Thruen said while extracting his sword, "so I will prepare for the worst."

"Bedar can have my life if he wants it so badly," added Huethys, "so long as I have freed Gaetys' soul first. I die today. Once I achieve my goal then it is of little importance who will have taken my life."

Thruen flattened against the wall and took a few steps to the right, then signaled Huethys to follow him. The two kept shifting in the darkness of the shadows that pervaded the periphery of the chamber, slowly and stealthily making their way toward the glass hemisphere.

"Huethyyyyysssss…" hissed again the robed undead, turning toward the two men in a slow and menacing way, positioning his hands in front of his rib cage with palms facing each other. Between the undead priest's hands an orb of light appeared, which quickly became oblong and assumed the shape of a viper's head, and a glowing green serpent oozed out of the orb as if made of liquid light.

"That's the Serpent of Light," whispered Huethys. "It's lethal and invincible, but it only lives in the temple, it cannot go outside this room. We need to reach the exit!"

"Can you run?" asked Thruen nervously.

"Yes," answered the old king.

The two ran the length of the naked rock wall and snuck under the protuberance formed by the glass hemisphere on the wall. Thruen made a quick turn into the tunnel, while the luminous serpent slithered its way toward the two intruders. Then, while the viper wraith hissed a hellish noise that would terrorise a god, Bedar growled *"Huethyyyyyssss!"* and in an instant Huethys' leg was caught in the supernatural grip of the serpent's fangs.

Huethys fell to the floor with a choked cry, as if the air was being sucked out of his lungs, while Thruen observed the terrifying spectacle of the old king's blood running through the glowing and transparent body of the serpent. Bedar moved closer to the two men and as blood from Huethys reached his hands he started to grow what looked to be muscle fibers and organs, and eyeballs were forming in his sockets, and a heart appeared in his empty rib cage. Thruen leaped toward Bedar and aimed at his heart, but the undead priest was quick to parry the blow, and in doing so, his hands disconnected and the Serpent of Light disappeared. Bedar grabbed Thruen's throat and squeezed against the warrior's corded neck muscles. In an effort to free himself from the deathly choke, Thruen grabbed Bedar's skull with his left hand, pressing on the forming eyeballs, while thrusting his sword blindly into the undead's body. Bedar groaned and with his other hand grabbed Thruen's shoulder and crushed the plate of armour covering the warrior's upper arm. A piercing and unnaturally cold pain ran through his entire body as Bedar's hand pulsated of a strange and icy blue light. Thruen pulled his hand out of Bedar's skull, ripping the abhorrent eyeballs out of the sockets. As Bedar released his grip on Thruen's shoulder to prepare for a final crushing blow, Huethys cried "Thruen, here!" and threw the althame. The red haired commander caught the flying dagger by the blade. He flipped it in the air, spraying blood from the new cut on his palm. He grabbed it by the handle and struck straight into Bedar's heart. The undead priest's heart exploded and the skeleton shattered, leaving the once gold-adorned blue robe to flop onto a pile of blood, malformed guts and bones.

VII

Huethys fell back, semi-conscious, and Thruen immediately tended to him.

"That was horrible. I am drained," whispered Huethys. "That wraith was sucking my soul as well as my blood," he added, looking deathly pale and trembling, "but it takes more than a little bloodletting to kill this king."

"Can you walk?" asked Thruen.

"Yes, barely, but we are nearly there, and that's all the energy I need to muster," answered Huethys.

Thruen helped Huethys to his feet and the two resumed their quest by walking into the dark tunnel that opened in the wall near the glass hemisphere.

After a long and strenuous uphill walk, the tunnel turned into a short flight of stairs which lead into a room on the first floor of the citadel. From here, Thruen and Huethys glanced out the window and were stricken with horror at the sight of what had become of Stynar Vort: the courtyard of the fortress had turned into a lake of blood, with the remains of countless soldiers stacked to the side of the lake. At its center, an altar stood on top of a massive rock emerging from the lake. The altar was horrific to behold, for it was washed in blood, with dried rivulets running down its sides. Huethys remembered standing on it to blow the retreat twenty-five years earlier.

"That was the sacrificial altar to Styne," said Huethys. "Once a month and before every battle the people of Stynar Vort used to sacrifice a willing victim to propitiate good fortune."

"That is horrendous."

"Yes it is… was… but prayers were answered. Styne was our god, our benevolent protector."

"So where is Gaetys?" Thruen asked, changing topics to a more relevant one.

"I do not know… but he is guarding the fortress, of that I am sure."

The two quickly made their way to the courtyard, and gained a deeper, more traumatising appreciation of the lake of blood and its bone-dressed shores. The skulls had expressions of horror and desperation, and the cries of torment and pain could still be heard echoing.

Huethys noticed that the rock of the altar was accessible from a bridge made of more bones and human remains arranged to form an isthmus, like what you would see only in the inner seas of Hel.

Thruen followed Huethys to the bony bridge, then took a step on it. As he did so, a deep, raspy grunt reverberated in Stynar Vort.

A figure slowly stood up from behind the altar at the top of the rock, and revealed itself in all its magnificent abhorrence: King Gaetys, now the Slayer King Kruhd'asra, the Undead Blood Fury, clad in an armour that was fused to his own muscles, deprived of all skin. He took a small and precise jump onto the altar, then stood in an animalistic crouch ready to leap on his prey.

From this position he uttered one word: "Hueeeeethyyyyyyyys…"

Huethys answered with a voice broken by the swirling emotions inside of him: "I am here, my friend. I am here to atone, to pay for my sins, to give you freedom…"

"I am in no need of freedom, this is paradise to me," answered the demon that was once Gaetys. "Styne, the God Demon, left this world, and his parting gift was turning me into Kruhd'asra. Now I rejoice in immortality, in the ecstasy of murder, in the pleasure to kill… I shall gladly take your life and that of your friend."

"You are a blasphemer! This can't..." said Huethys, but as he cried his indignation out to the world, Kruhd'asra leaped into the air and landed a few feet away from Thruen, who unsheathed his sword and assumed his fight-ready crouched pose.

Kruhd'asra unceremoniously assaulted Thruen with a barrage of lightning-fast thrusts and swings, slashing and ripping at every move with blade-sharp bone barbs that protruded through his muscles and the bracers on his forearms. Thruen barely kept on his feet parrying the whirlwind of strikes, all the while trying to shield Huethys from the demon guardian.

"Gaetys, you were my friend, I have come to free you!" shouted a desperate Huethys, but the demon was completely taken over by his lust for killing.

Thruen gradually overcame the shock of the assault and regained his concentration, reacting more and more swiftly to the demon's attacks. By invoking his ancestral strength, he grew feral and brought powerful blows to the demon's body. But Krudh'asra's strikes were furiously fast, and deep cuts from the demon's bone blades and weapon opened on Thruen's body, as if the air itself had claws wrought of steel.

With infernal precision, Kruhd'asra's sword pierced Thruen in the same shoulder that only a few moments earlier Bedar had struck with his icy magic grasp. The blade's tip stuck out of Thruen's back.

Thruen grabbed the corner of his cloak and wrapped his palm with it before grabbing the demon's bladed forearm, then pulled him closer, causing Kruhd'asra's sword to transfix his flesh even further. With the calculated rage that characterised him, Thruen pounded the undead's face with his bare fist, surprising the demon who also seemed strangely inebriated by the blood that sprayed from Thruen's shoulder onto his face. Thruen's sanity left his eyes and they turned into glazed vitreous spheres of pure hatred. He shouted and cursed in a language unknown and unguessed even to himself as he hit everything in his vicinity at an inhuman speed. Huethys knew that when this beast that lived inside Thruen was unleashed, there was no chance of survival for mortal and immortal beings alike. The ferocious struggle continued as the two combatants, locked in a mortal grapple, rolled down the side of the mound of bones that formed the bridge to the altar and plunged into the lake of blood.

After a few moments, Kruhd'asra emerged from the blood in a frenzy, shaking and screaming as if on fire.

The top of Thruen's head emerged from the lake. Back in full possession of his faculties, he noticed that Kruhd'asra was too distracted to focus on him. He moved closer, sword in hand but kept under the surface, ready to strike.

Entirely covered in thick blood that was kept liquid for twenty-five years by the most unthinkable demonic sorcery, Thruen advanced close enough to attack, his lips retracted in a feral snarl. But as he bent his legs ready to deal a death blow, the tip of the althame suddenly pierced Kruhd'asra's chest, having been pushed all the way from his back through his heart by Huethys, who at his old age still retained his ability to move as stealthily as a cat. Kruhd'asra stopped his shaking, with a frozen expression of terror on his face.

"I am saving you, my friend..." said Huethys as he thrust Seyden's Tooth deeper into the demon's back and further out his chest.

"I do not... want... your salvation..." grunted the dying demon. He turned his sword toward himself and thrust it hilt-deep into his own heart, skewering both Huethys' and his own body. He grinned with the maniacal satisfaction of a last killing.

The two fell into the blood. Thruen walked incredulous toward Huethys, dragging him out of the lake, but fully aware that Huethys' life had already abandoned his body.

Thruen loomed precariously over Huethys' corpse and spoke with a very uncharacteristic and soft tone, for he was overwhelmed by sorrow of the death of his long-time friend, father-like figure and king, and dazed by the wounds and blood loss. "Huethys... what nonsense it was... to spend a life in the rotting stench of guilt, feeling like a sinner in the eyes of a god that does not exist... To decide for others what mercy and salvation are, and to impose it on those who had no desire for them... and to give purpose to a damned child's life, only to take that purpose away. Nine times nine words, and perhaps I shall see you soon at the Ramparts of Eternity..."

Thruen dropped to one knee and loosened the grip on the sword's handle, letting it slowly fall to the ground. He surrendered to the exhaustion and fell on his back, staring at the sunset-tinted snow falling on Stynar Vort.

Masters of Magic

Journey in Somnamblia

By Jean-Pierre Abboud

Beyond the alchemical order of the city Weydan, a bleak wood stretched across a long, dismal valley. The lifelike mouth of the forest enveloped the land with a winding, monstrous tongue; a yawning road in disrepair. Towering in the distance monolithically, the city endured another day like any; uninterrupted commerce from its fixed populace swelled and contracted. The road leading out, usually vacant, unfurled an abnormality as four sojourners came into view from the city's horizon. Scuttling along the earth in secret, the group took care to not leave a trail. Seeking encampment, their eyes fell upon an under hill pass one hundred meters ahead. Under a pallid blaze, childhood fears of the wood gripped Merik. "These trees… I've never felt so uneasy," he quietly complained. An orphan gypsy of age twenty, urban stories of taboo and the forbidden filled his mind; Merik's prior band of thieves spoke of trees and flora which sup their energy from unknown sources, eschewing sunlight. Coming closer to the arching foothill, the four travelers moved towards safety.

"Before we begin the second phase of this journey, I want to thank the three of you for all your bravery thus far!" Mataera Nom's voice carried from the top of the hill, echoing with a fatigued defiance under the shadow of monstrous limbs and branches. They knew escape from the city, however painstaking, was of the simplistic and familiar; the unknown lay beyond the borderline. Mataera, studying their surroundings, eyed the terrible wood with a knowing consignment. Her tall frame, wild lavender hair and pitch black skin stood at the forest entrance like an apparition; a silhouette in traveler's garb. Merik's meek, pale-white and wide-eyed visage under an oversized brown cloak projected the illusion of a familiar. Feeling comforted, he threw up a visible smirk under his large hood. "Remember how swiftly I burgled the 6th gate key? I could have returned it in gift wrap if Abon weren't so slow!"

Abon and his partner Risten ambled close behind the two before setting up camp under the hill. Red and sun-beaten, they spent their formative years in Weydan learning the trade of street performance. With Risten's small, wiry build a common type opposite Abon's oversize brawn, they also performed spells on the black market (mostly mild sick-healing, divination, and of course binding). Fingered as fringe sorcerers by the

5th Magister, they had arranged a meeting with Mataera through various confidants, preempting their flight. "If we all moved like you, our blood pressure would keep us from magick!" cackled Risten, her body leaping about, imitating Merik's frantic, wide-eyed movements. "All your undisciplined pacing about," Abon interjected gravely, "will get us killed in this place."

Forbidden as it was to leave, Merik understood beyond his years the futility of a thief's life in Weydan. A bellicose fool's paradise of retrograde spell-scrolls and potions, dilapidated talismans and stones, lay before any quick-handed chaser; food and drink, while sparse for orphan children, still flows in green-grey and crystal abundance. "I started stealing to feed myself, that is, until I learned to be smart about it," Merik recalled his words before his thief's initiation rite. Mataera led his former band, prior to his entrance. He remembered when it was all he wanted, but then tugged at his brown cloak in a feeling of shame; he knew Mataera understood realms beyond the corridors of the city, beyond the engineered confines of the lotus field.

"We cannot travel through the forest without a spell of concealment," she disclosed. "The entire forest is under surveillance, all entrance and exit anticipated."

Abon dreaded the thought. He and Risten never attempted a spell of concealment. Although both were adept hobbyists at advanced spells and master practitioners of general magick, the physical and mental requirements for such a spell were excruciating. "More secrets withheld, I suppose," whispered Risten to Abon. "I wonder if she had the kid get them." *Them*—referring to the various herbal and liquid elements required to disapparate, foremost a volatile concoction of trefoil, rue, and molten lapis lazuli (requiring its own spell).

"Our destination is to the northwest," Mataera continued. "It will be three days of travel on foot with no sleep, keeping the spell intact. This will require all our power; Abon, you will need to cover us all with the concealment cloak for the entire journey. Risten, I need you to hold concentration with me to power the spell. Merik, you will be our lookout and help to orient our direction; our roles in the spell cannot be interrupted."

"Of course!" replied Merik, preparing a cauldron with a small kindling.

"Where does one find lapis lazuli of purity entailing magickal properties," wondered Risten. "I can see why she's kept so quiet up to now..."

"Do you need me to melt the stone?" asked Abon, bluffing.

"There's a special alchemistic consecration we can perform to melt the stone, you may know of it. We broke out two nights ago for the moon. Tonight, our blue stones will run like water beneath black candles. While Risten and I cast this spell, you can get some stones as well. But make them red, and let's enjoy our last meal before we toil in the unknown."

* * *

Under the full moon's eyes, the party did their best to conceal the encampment. Escape through the city walls had slowed no one's pace, as eluding the magistrates' forces unseen and unheard could only propel them further onward. Mataera, uttering incantations, fixed her onyx eyes on the stone, now levitating above the cauldron brew. Her right arm, shaking with unnatural force unfurled a long slender finger scornfully pointed at the floating rock. Exploding in a flash of royal blue, which would threaten their position had not Mataera known this particular moon would yield no passers-through, ribbons of molten lapis lazuli slowly trickled down. Supping blue lava beneath, the cauldron began to heap and gasp as Mataera collapsed in agony. Merik prepared a makeshift bed, having anticipated such recoil. A spell of this sort can wreak considerable damage on the caster's liver; with the moon's power and a complex series of summonses pertaining to the organ's ability to break down matter, the organ itself comes away several years on. Though one-hundred-percent accuracy must be held with such advanced magick under risk of death, considerable physical damage remains. Mataera had planned for this, as her weakened state after such a consecration necessitated a party for the following spell.

Fearful visions ran through Risten's troubled brow, those that only scarce whispered tales from Weydan's ravages could conjure; savage highwaymen wielding powerful weapons and even stronger sorcery. Placing her tiny hand on Mataera's marble bound lackyre shoulders, she observed her eyes—within the oft-jet black pupils raged a pale blaze of emerald. In her face, Risten sensed a knowing born of her current weakness, reflected in a glance back to Abon.

"Are we coming to? I have salves and herbs for you," Merik eagerly cooed, relieved Mataera's color had returned.

"We can use the compound to attempt the spell now," she replied with a lucid sense of purpose.

"I only meant to ask if you felt better!"

"No time."

"All right, then!" bellowed Abon, hungry for the challenge, worried the others sensed his ambivalence. Risten nodded as the four gathered 'round the cauldron. Deeply fatigued, Mataera began to chant, beckoning a call and response. Merik's involvement with the circle served a perfunctory purpose. Mataera's power amounted enough for three bodies; his knowledge of this lesser burden drove him to silent curses. Another tug of shame, knowing the severity of his companions' burden compared to his own.

A terrifying light crackled above the cauldron as Abon and Risten chanted with Mataera's throaty invocation. The time of the Magister's return, as she knew it, had not come to pass, with the distance from the darkened wood shielding spectral bursts of royal blue. Mataera's back arched upward in painful immediacy, consciously feeding blaque energies through Abon and Risten's now-vessel-bodies. Merik, enthralled with the imposing might of Mataera's magick power, felt relieved by waves of hardened contentment.

* * *

Abon's strength seeming a match, the party adeptly strode forward over the last two days, cloaked in a viscous star-shine band, unseeable by outsiders or the forest's infected flora. Risten squinted hard under tremendous migraine pain previously unfathomed in her small time sorcery. Mataera knew this pain well, and derived a sort of polymorphously perverse pleasure familiarly offsetting the quick unpleasant pain below. Her darkly slender side, still reeling from the previous alchemistic spell, stayed strong as her concentration kept the band intact. Risten slowly began to realize her lack of control in her own motions, feeling as though her body traded sight for all other faculties. "The thief moves as though there is no magick binding him… Abon ambles behind like a golem now… I cannot break concentration… I want to… but I cannot…" Paranoia began to overtake her thoughts, as Mataera's manipulation kept their bodies moving, working, powering the spell.

"i am walking death"

"i am living excrement"

"no more than a blank vessel"

"i own nothing"

"i am nothing."

Risten's struggle to control her now-eggshell mind bled into the starshine, difficultly traipsing through the second half of the woods' northwest passage. Merik, sensing movement ahead, slowed the pace of the group as its eyes, ears and front. Shaking in terror from the burdensome mental storm the spell wrought on his companions, he spotted a caravan ahead.

"Magisters…?" he whispered to himself.

Chained in single file, twelve horrified, pathetic bodies seeming only alive in movement shuffled down the path. Covered head to toe in scars and lesions, driving them forward were the distant figures of two magisters. Hardened albino nobles draped in crimson red, they seemed to Merik ironically featureless compared to the suffering chain of broken mages. "Mages…"

Supping the deep concentration of magick aura from the slaved, the two magisters conversed loudly and boisterously on the subject of water. Irrigation kept Weydan running as an insular dominion, where its citizens could drink deep of a perpetuating well and enjoy its abundance. Laughing at the feeble waifs in subjugation, the magister highwaymen beat their caravan of emaciated male and female bodies forward. The party, ambling as quietly as they could within concealment, still strode on with the visibly daunted Merik. Terror undertook the young thief, gazing at a catatonic Risten, realizing her body would not survive the spell. Unerring doom seemed inevitable, no longer lying in wait.

"Taken as slaves…" Already burdened with turmoil wrought from the concealment spell, Merik's mind ran wild projecting violent flashes of primary reds and blacks. Irrational rage married his continuous worry, channeling visions of dread begetting a furious anger.

"*Die*, pig slavers!"

Merik rushed as the spell broke, the band shooting off in all directions into the sky. Risten's lifeless body collapsed on the ground. Like a berserker, Merik's young slender hands attacked with an acute fierceness befitting a hardened street fighter. As he battered the brutish form of the first magister, it was already too late. The second magister, reaching out his chalk-white hand began to hold sway over an enslaved female on the chain. Weaving synchronous energies through her skeletal frame, he concentrated a flash of material breakdown. Her stomach visibly pulsating, a voiceless, sickened cry echoed through a series of contortions. Merik looked up and suddenly felt a million needles of pain spark through his body as his skull began to cave in. Mataera, fallen and confused from the break, watched in disbelief, locking eyes with Merik's. Triggering such a deep sensation of pain, all that could be heard was horrific laughter as his head crumbled into putty. Weak and battered, gazing round in utter defeat, Mataera observed the slaved and the mage-slavers. She stared as they slaughtered now-mindless Abon like cattle, her lamenting eyes resigning themselves to death.

* * *

When Mataera awoke, she quickly realized her destination had been reached. Outside the forest to the northwest, she gazed upon the mage slaver encampment which the party had sought to liberate, eying familiar faces from Weydan's dire underground. Casing her surroundings, her back suddenly doubled forward with a heinous snap.

"So blackened princess, we've been watching you since the 6th gate. Say no words, you cannot, we know where you've come from and where you have been. Eschewing provided comfort for a taste of the outland, were we? Your amateurish concealment spell might impress those pathetic street vermin you somehow convinced to help your misguided flight. Don't you understand the sustenance of order? Its importance in our lives? Weydan powers not only itself, but this whole land with our magick, and as you must have been taught, those of the lower sub-simian mind cannot handle such responsibilities. Give them their spells of love, materials, or binding, provide a framework for their intentions, and our world moves in harmony. We are building a new dam, and Weydan will have more food and water; someone with power such as yours can head this operation, lighting the minds of these slaved in synchronous task. You may have done so with the dominance of a mage vessel, but no longer. We know who you are, but there are... penalties for leaving the city. We all saw such potential in you, not to mention your beauty, which with good luck may keep within your first year under my hand. A fine boon for the young magisters!"

Mataera did not look up. This voice with no face needed no introduction. Her eyes, only now a withered gray in her terrific weakness still burned in defiance. "It doesn't matter if I die here," she sorrowfully whispered to herself, "we transcended Weydan, and we now know… someone else will know…" Submitting to brutal colloidal manipulation of her body's minerals, the pain could only conjure Merik's horrified eyes, beating upon her with the weight of all time.

Eldon

By Chris Shoriak

A young child raised not of nobility or wealth but raised from the land, the earth, the wilds. Displaced from his own people before possessing memories, he grew as a pariah amongst his peers and a house servant to those of adulthood. You see, he was quite different, different at least from most. His kin was the woods, and his people born of it; traded away at a young age to the growing ranks of the plains-folk, he had known nothing of free life, finding wholeness only in nature and the time bade spent foraging for wild edibles. Though still a slave by all accounts, his masters were fair and generous. Their children, though cruel as children are, still regarded him as a sibling, a member of the family. He respected and even grew to love them, at least to his best impression of the word. A slave by every account, but destined for far more than toiling for the rest of his days.

The outer-lying forest was ancient, lush and vast. Moss and fungi covered woods of decay, abundant with life and death, all in a marriage of verdant splendor. To flee the village, Eldon could quite contentedly and effortlessly live there; but to what end? Always inflated with a greater sense of purpose; to live as a slave and be accepted, or free alone lacked any great meaning.

The world was large, and he longed always to explore and learn of it. There was no sense of contentment in the confinement of the village. Cursed with the mystery of an unknown past, there was always a secret longing to gain knowledge of his people, and one day perhaps reunite with them. Though, to be under ownership bears no light repercussion, and he well knew that the dream of freedom was just that, a dream; a virtually impossible boon to attain, a reality enjoyed only within his wandering mind.

His adoptive village perched iconically upon coastal headlands, thrusting skyward above a seething, unforgiving ocean. The looming woods crept just barely to the edge of town, standing as a sinister, foreboding world; a world forever attempting to swallow the plains-folks' way of life. Though to Eldon the wood felt welcoming and calming, the other villagers had heard only legend of lurking evils and unnatural things. His very nature was what kept him useful, and his contentment therein bestowed the village a previously untapped resource. He possessed untold knowledge and as he grew older, so did his almost innate ability to commune with the woods themselves; to notice things previously unseen, to glean uses from plants and fungi previously unknown. It was as if, as he grew to adulthood, deep seeded knowledge crept from his subconscious.

As he matured to adulthood the village grew wary of him: skeptical, fearful, questioning his furtive motives. In truth, beside his desire to explore the world and his past, he possessed very little ill will towards the townsfolk, and desired greatly for some general acceptance. Time had crawled onward since his youth, and the apparent need for a skilled ranger seemed superfluous at this point. All the minute buildings and developments had grown; agriculture and trade had trampled much of the need for hunting or gathering, and Eldon was thrust out of the general public's need. His adoptive family, as it were, still cared for him though, and he would regularly still forage and hunt for them. His brothers and sisters had grown appreciative of him as they grew older, and his owners very affectionately considered him their son. He loved them, and they him, enough so to recognize that with the growing development he would soon have no place amongst them. What contentment can a man out of time, out of place, locked in a dying skill-set possess in a world so quickly evolving?

A frigid mist swept gently through the town and over the bluffs, returning to the sea from whence it came. The coastal fog lay dense in the air, and the brisk wind chilled all who meandered about. It was morning and Eldon was about to begin his daily jaunt to the woods. The clouded shroud provided a calming cover of sorts, concealing Eldon from possible hunting prospects, and deadening noise would allow him to travel more stealthily. Gathering his bow and various accoutrements to embark, his mother approached, and placed a light hand upon his shoulder.

Her gaze moved toward the floor to avoid his. "Eldon," she calmly uttered, "you have lived here your whole life, and have grown skillful with your talents. Though you are not our blood we have grown to call you 'son.' When first we found you, we never could have known that we would grow to care for you so. While in the eyes of the other townsfolk you are considered our servant, we have perhaps only in the beginning ever considered you so. As you have probably noticed, your talents have until recently been quite helpful, but as of late, we rarely call upon you. Our village is changing, and we've no need of the woods anymore save for timber. Thusly you have gained your freedom. As time moves on, the others will merely grow more dubious of you. Though we love you, there is no place for you here anymore. Please, I urge you, do not return."

She clasped his hand, placing a small gold-pouch in his palm; it wasn't much, but could conceivably attain lodging for a few nights, perhaps some modest rations. With that, Eldon calmly nodded, and with pain in his heart gathered his few belongings. Not being one for many words, he approached his adoptive mother, hugged her, and set out.

His heart was in pain. He felt bitter and unwanted, and though he oft felt excommunicated, this was different. As if he had lost a sense of identity a second time. Detecting a certain sense of urgency from his mother, he opted not to bid farewell to his siblings and father; the pain would merely mount more heavily. While the angst of separation was ever apparent, he was overwhelmed with a sense of wonder; the one thing he had wished desperately for since childhood he had now attained. He was free to pursue his dreams; exploration of a new, almost infinite world, to learn of his people and past.

Stepping heavily forward, Eldon began to saunter confidently into the forest. Even though he was fraught with sorrow, his newfound liberation seemed to carry him effortlessly toward whatever he may find.

Trees loomed high above, twisting and writhing into all manner of shape and torturous image. Ferns blanketed the earth, and clung defiantly to vertical trunks and earthen walls. Scintillating drops of dew fell rhythmically from the shadow-shrouded canopy high above, clapping loudly upon leaf-litter below. Ever present radiant light defiantly penetrated the blackened roof above, reflecting off all wet surfaces and dew soaked mosses.

Carrying a methodical pace, Eldon continued onward, tempestuously winding his way about the trees and shrubs. Desperately wishing he'd had more knowledge of where to start he pressed eastward. There were vague rumors of a great city that lay east beyond the behemothic woods, but he knew naught of the validity, or actual location. All had been overheard in villagers' passing banter, and none were ever approachable enough to inquire further.

Light was hastily fading and shelter had to be addressed before the pitch darkness of the eve set in. Any and all navigation would be virtually impossible in nightfall's abyss. As per Eldon's better sense for the surroundings, he had been gathering food as he traversed the landscape, and was quite contented with the knowledge he would have a substantial meal before slumber. Beneath a lichen-cloaked boulder there lay a small outcrop where he laid soft boughs in preparation for rest. After a brief meal and a rummage through his supplies for a wool blanket, Eldon finally lay to dream.

His dreams were vivid that eve; the liberated, unchecked rest within the forest brought other-worldly visions to mind. Hazy images of forest folk, old knowledge, and arboreal spirits flooded in and out of his consciousness. In particular, a hoary, ancient, bearded old man stood out as a lasting significance amidst the ebb and flow of visions.

It was in this way he continued to travel onward: using wind, moss, and sun to navigate due east. Bedding down in hollows and improvised shelters, always foraging and hunting when an opportunity presented itself. The forest was larger than he could have ever imagined, and a fortnight had already elapsed. All the while the nightly visions grew stronger, forever dominated by the recurring image of the old man. What was his significance? Who was he? All thoughts seemed to return to him. Eldon knew that he couldn't have fabricated the old man from his own subconscious; the image was far too vivid.

After several more days and nights had elapsed, Eldon found himself crossing over a defined threshold between what appeared to be rolling grassy hills and the dense vegetation he had been clamoring through. He had finally reached the edge of the wood, and he was quite elated. Though the woods were calming to him, the visions were becoming excessively overwhelming, and served to make him quite uncomfortable. For the first time since his departure Eldon longed for some of the comforts of the village: a bed, the warmth of a hearth, and the murmur of a household of voices. He knew those would be comforts he would never again enjoy in the context of home.

In the distance, beyond the emerald-green rolling hills, a spire glistened blindingly in the midday sun. This could only assumably be a part of the great city he was seeking. With a rearward glance he pressed onward shuffling deftly through the knee-high grass. Wind cascaded across the rolling field, forming a veritable ocean of waves and currents, hypnotically churning, almost carrying Eldon forward toward the white spire.

Two giant, dark oaken doors lay open, welcoming, stretching upwards high above the path leading beyond. Elegant parapets crowned all the walls surrounding the great city. Eldon had never witnessed anything nearly so grandiose in all his years, save the woods, which were as beautiful to him as any man-construct. To gaze upon a city though, even from the outside, filled him with excitement and anticipation. Upon crossing through the archway threshold a single guard, clad in ornate reflective armor, pike in hand, approached and spoke quite clearly.

"Good day good sir, welcome to Shoryal, the unmovable mountain in the emerald sea. While within these walls I expect nothing less than your best behavior, you should know most of the people in this city do not take too kindly to the plains-folk. Not all of us discriminate, we've just had a lot of crop raiding as of late, and I didn't want you finding any trouble for it."

Eldon steadily nodded and started down the cobbled path that looked to cut straight through the towering city. He laughed inside briefly; the irony was not lost on him, given he wasn't even technically from the plains, but he understood he was clad in the garb of his adoptive town.

Stone and brick buildings sprouted from either side of the path, dwarfing all that lay beneath them. Indescribable scents, colors, and sounds abounded, most of which he could not have ever imagined. He was filled with overwhelming desire, and longed for nothing more than to taste, listen, and gaze upon all these newfound interests. The odd and sometimes even fuming glances toward him were becoming ever more noticeable, more apparent. Though he impulsively wanted to approach many of the vendors littering the streets, their general off-putting demeanor and his lack of wealth kept him at bay.

Wandering aimlessly for several hours, he figured seeking accommodations for the eve would probably be in his best interest. He felt like a child, unprepared for this world, quite socially uncomfortable, fearful, tentative, hesitant, and still burdened by the loss of his adoptive family. After all, he really didn't even know why he was there. What purpose would his visit to the city even serve?

The city folk gave him discomfort to a point he couldn't rightly grasp. Of the strange interests and aversions, he was realizing very quickly that large groups and social gatherings made him quite uneasy. The banter of merchants beckoning him to make a sale; the howls of infants and children; the unwanted advances of courtesans and insistent beggars; all blended together adding to his mounting anxiety.

His sordid contemplation was suddenly interrupted as he felt a sharp tug on the waist of his pants. His immediate impulse was that he had been robbed, but was quite stunned as he whirled around to see a young child standing confidently awaiting his attention.

"Sir," he said with poise. "Your presence has been greatly anticipated. My master hath bade me gather Eldon for a special meeting." The child wasn't dressed of nobility, but clearly wasn't of a poor household either. Rather neutral and nondescript.

Sensing his own naivety heavily now, Eldon was absolutely dumbfounded. He knew better than to accompany anyone he didn't know, let alone someone who knew him by name. How on earth could anyone know him? He was merely a slave: no identity, no distant relations. Though to have nothing bestows a certain sense of haphazard action. What was there to lose in following the boy, his life? For that he hadn't even found a purpose yet. Against all better judgement he decided to follow.

All questions regarding the nature of the meeting, or with whom it was to be attended, were met with a stern "all will be answered when we arrive."

The guided stroll through the city continued, serpentining past rising towers, ornate fountains, and incredible sculptures. Shoryal was very clearly not lacking in scientific and artistic advancement. The architecture alone was otherworldly. Breathtaking murals and sculptures adorned all the grand, larger buildings, which in form seemed to teeter with unprecedented balance and form.

The pair sauntered through an open, intimidating iron-bar fence, and descended a staircase entering a sprawling estate encircled by a thick, towering brick wall. Crawling, blanketing ivy lay thick upon all surfaces within the brick fortification, save the imposing mansion in the center and the well-maintained grass covering the grounds. The large multiple-storied building penetrating the center of the grounds felt ominous, foreboding, but Eldon freely continued trailing his guide across the grass toward it. Throughout the property trees had been planted at regular intervals, all quite aged, all covered in the ivy-shroud. To Eldon these actually brought a certain comfort to the estate-grounds; the very notion that nature hadn't entirely been eradicated from the city, and was even being cultivated and nurtured.

Just as they had crossed about halfway across the far-reaching lawn, Eldon's attention was startled by an ear-piercing crash of the gate that lay behind them. With a short glance he noticed it had been shut securely, looking almost overgrown with the same ivy that dominated the bricks, shrubs, and trees. The realization that they were now essentially enclosed in what appeared to be an impenetrable fortress was very apparent, but even so, Eldon well knew that by accompanying the boy to begin with he was to be at his unknown host's mercy.

The large mansion now before them appeared to be wrought from solid wood, with such spectacular wood-carving craftsmanship as to look as though it was comprised of still-living branches. They approached two solid iron doors resting on deep set hinges, and it was clear this place was to double, in some capacity, as a fortification. Without warning, both gates yawned wide and warm hearth air heaved from the bowels of the structure. Now side by side, they both stepped through the vaulted doorway.

The entryway opened into a large hall. Each wall held several lit candles casting dim lighting about the walls and ceiling. They did little to actually light the path, but more bestowed a certain calm ambience. Though the building was sprawling, the foyer seemed to just stretch forward, with an illuminated door at the end. No entryways lay to either side, just a bare hall, save the candles and their dull glow. Eldon assumed the floors and walls to be wood, but no answer could be ascertained without closer inspection, and some substantial light.

The boy stepped forward and Eldon continued behind, both moving toward the glowing entryway at the end of the hall. Eldon was perplexed by how such a well-constructed building could be so humble, plain, and almost cave-like. He had expected bright white ceilings hanging high above and staircases ascending to all manner of extravagant rooms.

Entering the brightly lit doorway, Eldon's expectations were met slightly more accurately. Long stretching beige wooden planks made up the floor. The room opened up to two large staircases at either side of the boy and him. An aged, drooping willow lay in the center of the room, apparently still growing, despite the ceiling blotting out all sunlight. Its tendrils arched high overhead, draping partially above both staircases and the entry. At the far wall ahead of them a fireplace glowed from behind the massive tree's twisted bole.

The boy bowed and held his hands out, beckoning Eldon. "Proceed forward," he said.

Eldon cautiously walked toward the large tree, sidestepping around it when he neared close enough. It appeared to be fused to the floorboards, but was most likely the product of the skilled wood-working he had seen on the exterior. As he shifted past the willow trunk he noticed that two green armchairs faced the warm fire ahead. Both chairs faced away from him, and he could not tell whether or not they were occupied.

"Come, sit." A warm voice boomed out from the seating area.

Eldon resumed his creeping gait toward the turned armchairs. Two legs, one folded, outstretched from what appeared to be the occupant of the chair to the left.

The unassuming voice bellowed again. "Please, come sit. I've been expecting you for quite some time."

Eldon crossed to the right, navigating around the outer edge of his intended chair, keeping it between him and the denizen already seated. Stepping around to face the sitting individual, Eldon felt a shudder stab through his whole being.

Silver tinged grey hair hung raggedly from a defined chin, while two steely eyes stared intensely. Before Eldon sat the old man; identical to the visions from the forest. The same eerie and unsettling sensation from the woods crept over Eldon, and he felt himself overwhelmed; the need for escape. He was transfixed, unmoved; entirely unable to find the wherewithal to flee.

The old man calmly spoke again. "Please sit, my friend. It will all get easier with time."

Shaken, Eldon weakly lowered himself into the chair. He found it hard to meet the man's eyes. It felt as if they pierced directly through him, directly to his subconscious.

"Who are you?" Eldon demanded loudly.

The man calmly shifted in his chair. A glowing smile crawled across his wrinkled, wise face. His blue eyes averted from meeting Eldon's, as if aware of the discomfort they were bringing.

The grey, wrinkled fellow cleared his throat and met Eldon's question. "My name is Sillot, and your presence is most welcome. What you're feeling is a sensation I thought I would never share in again. You see, we are one and the same; in a manner of speaking. I've no idea how you've eluded me, but we are of the same ilk; kin to the forest. I haven't seen another person of the wood for some time. Are there more of you?"

As Eldon stared toward the ancient man, he found the flood of emotions and overwhelming thoughts subside to a manageable level. He composed himself and stammered, "I am the only one I've ever known of. My adoptive family told me I was traded away at a young age. Why haven't you seen any forest folk? What happened to them?"

The old man shook his head subtly, and gazed back at Eldon.

"That's a conversation for a different time, boy. For now, let's get you acclimated. I've a spare bedroom for you to stay in. I encourage you to remain here for a duration of time, as to learn more of our people. For now, just relax, and listen.

"I know what you're feeling must be overwhelming. You see, us forest-folk have a unique connection to nature, as well as with one another. Through the woods we can communicate, sense things; we share an almost collective consciousness with nature itself and each other. What you're feeling right now, these disjointed thoughts and feelings, are coming from my consciousness."

Eldon felt uneasy, unsettled, perhaps even slightly violated, but quite intrigued.

In a still warm voice Sillot continued on. "I first sensed you when last you were in the woods. You must not have ever spent an extended stay there before, because I would have long ago sensed you. I know this must all be quite a shock to you, but as it stands I intend to pass along all my wisdom regarding our ability. It is no mere coincidence that you arrived here. You were drawn here, partially by the draw of your kin, but actively by my will as well."

Eldon's instinctual sense would have him remain skeptical of the old man's words, but he couldn't deny the very direct connection he felt. There was a certain sense of wholeness within he had never experienced before. He felt a growing sense of overwhelming trust for this stranger.

"As I have grown old I have learned our abilities far exceed that of merely observing through nature. There is far more to all of it." The old man paused for a moment and looked intently upon Eldon. "You're tired; you should get some rest. All will be made clear in the morn." He gestured toward the staircase behind Eldon. "All accommodations shall be met: food, ale, bathing, rest, clothing; all will be taken care of. If you require anything simply call out to Rel, he will aid you."

"I thank you, sir. Good eve." With that trailing sentiment, Eldon turned and began ascending the curving staircase. He felt bewildered and beleaguered, yet oddly reassured. How could all have come to pass in so short a time? What kind of a legacy did his people possess? With thoughts all swirling he crossed the threshold atop the stairs and lay to rest in the quarters provided.

His dreams that eve, while as vivid as those within the forest, possessed far more clarity and direction. He found himself not overwhelmed, but calm, collected; curious to see more of this strange shared consciousness.

Upon awaking from what proved to be one of the most restful nights he'd had, Eldon noticed his clothing had been removed from where he had lain it, and in its place lay a cleanly folded black cloak and shirt, deep forest-green pants, and some weathered brown boots. A breakfast of fruit and toast rested on a plate just beside the clothing. After eating, he lazily dressed himself and proceeded back down the picturesque curved staircase. The boy, whom he could only imagine was Rel, awaited at the bottom of the stairs.

"Good morn, sir. The master awaits in the forward wing. You may follow me."

Following the boy, as he had before, he was led to the mansion's front entrance. Within the dimly lit hallway, there were now several doors to either side. These seemingly new doorways appeared to be of the same exquisite carving as Eldon had seen before. It was as if the walls were now made of vertical hanging vines which stretched away from one another to create an opening. Eldon could swear that this anomaly had been quite newly formed, and could most assuredly not have been carved by hand.

Rel directed Eldon through one of the passages and within was the old man pouring over a stack of elaborately bound books on what appeared to be a wicker desk. Oversized wooden bookshelves reaching high above abutted every wall, all heavily laden with multicolored tomes of varying sizes.

"Thank you Rel, you may go," said the old man, attention unmoved from his studies. Rel exited the room.

"Please, sit." The old man motioned to a wooden chair beside him, attention still unbroken.

"Rel has been assisting me with tasks about the grounds for several years now. He's a good fellow. Truth be told: our friendship isn't nearly as formal as he'd like to think. I found him at a young age in a slavers' encampment by the edge of the wood, and freed him. Since that day he seems to have felt obligated to repay the favor, and I subsequently have become his family and employer." The old man chuckled for a moment and drew his eyes away from his reading, upward toward Eldon.

Eldon, feeling far more at ease this meeting, sat down in the wooden chair and prepared to listen intently to the old man's words.

"Like I said, my name is Sillot, and I've beckoned you here for a very specific reason. I can sense your distrust, and skepticism, but I assure you I've no ill intentions. Merely probe my thoughts, and you will see the truth." Sillot grinned wide.

Strangely Eldon somehow knew, with absolute certainty, that the old man was uttering the truth.

"You see," the old man began talking again, "it's abilities like that which are inherently present within our people. The forest-folk possess many almost supernatural abilities. It is these that I wish to share, to teach you. I want to answer any mysteries of your past, to inform you of all the qualities of your birthright, your legacy."

The aged man adjusted rusted spectacles on the bridge of his nose and continued.

"I have grown quite old, and fear that knowledge of the wood-folk will die with me. Though I fancy myself living until the end of time, we both know that mortality is ever-present, and whether it's my silver hair, wrinkles, or failing eyesight, I think it's pretty apparent that my youthful years are behind me." He smiled humbly. "I intended to at least pass the memory of our people to Rel; so at least someone would know of the wood-folk, but to have by happenstance found you, I think it far more fitting to share our legacy with kin."

Eldon wanted to let loose a barrage of inquiries, but somehow knew all would be answered by the wise old man before him: all in due time.

The old man continued. "I can't tell you how much it warms my heart to see one of your age clothed in the garb of our people. It has been so long. Now come. We've many questions to be answered and much training to complete. You know in your heart that no question will be left unanswered."

Sillot winced as he pulled himself upright from the chair, and began shambling toward the doorway. Eldon, still quite intrigued by the flood of knowledge and emotion, stood, and patiently followed Sillot's crawling pace.

Over several months Eldon and Sillot became quite close. Day by day Sillot would reveal, almost unrelentingly, knowledge about the past of their people. He would regularly meditate with Eldon, teach him how to control his mental focus; show him how to share the consciousness of anything from a single blade of grass, to a whole grove of trees. They would regularly take trips to the edge of the woods, where more training and honing of skills would take place with rapid progress. As time passed and Eldon's mental connections to his natural surroundings increased, they began to work on his ability to alter nature as well.

Eldon was astounded to learn that not only could his kind commune with nature, they could control it: will it to grow in a specific fashion, to move, to die, to reproduce.

All the while teaching Eldon of his new abilities, Sillot continued to educate Eldon of their people: the fact that they couldn't adapt to the growing technological advancements, their persecution, their beautiful culture and love for the earth, and their eventual demise at the hands of religious zealots and growing encroachment of cities and technology.

It was now known to Eldon, the grim reality that he would never know the joy of meeting other wood-kin. Sillot would be his only window to this lost world, and Sillot was quickly slowing from age. The time spent communing with the woods and one another, and the training sessions spent willing plants to bend and change, quickly became some of the fondest memories Eldon would ever have. He had grown skilled, proficient, aware, whole. Though he still hadn't found his direct purpose, he was content and longed only to hone his abilities to absolute mastery.

Forced to practice in the woods as to avoid unwanted public suspicion, Eldon was already willing ivy to quickly envelop and constrict surfaces, to raise a full meadow of grass to head-height in mere seconds, to make trees sway and bend with the same speed and precision as his hand. He now felt powerful, and invincible. Even the mystery of the mansion had been solved to him: it was growing, constantly changing, being altered to fit Sillot's needs, and expertly so.

Much time had passed, and Eldon sensed Sillot's passing was near. Bade by their connection, Eldon met Sillot in the large room with the hearth and willow tree.

Sillot sat at the base of the ancient willow with a hand resting on its exposed roots.

"Come sit beside me, Eldon." He gestured toward the tree.

"You have already sensed I am soon dead. To return to the nature I so powerfully loved. I have taught you all I can, save one memory. Place your hand upon this tree with me."

Eldon slowly lowered himself to the base of the giant tree, and outstretched a hand to it. Both men closed their eyes, and a flood of visions filled Eldon's consciousness.

A village of the forest-folk, completely crafted from living matter, peacefully rested in a small clearing within the woods. Eldon quickly realized he was viewing this sight from Sillot's perspective.

Carefree people, all laughing, smiling and talking, milled about the landscape: foraging, hunting, crafting from nature. All wore the black and green garb of which Eldon had grown quite fond. None appeared angry, none sad. All appeared gentle, beautiful. Eldon was filled with wonder, comfort, and a certain familiarity with the scene. It was beautiful: the very essence of his people's way of life; the way he himself wished to live.

Screams. Screams of pain and suffering Eldon could scarcely believe rang out. Wild, soulless people flung themselves heedlessly upon the unsuspecting forest-folk, savagely cleaving limb from body, head from shoulder. Deep crimson blanketed the moss-covered earth, and stained all that had been vibrant green before. The clothing was unmistakably that of the plains-folk, and they fought with an inhuman vigor and bloodlust Eldon could barely comprehend. Terror continued to ensue as those not yet under attack attempted to bend the will of nature to their defense. Outnumbered as they were, most of the forest-dwellers were cut down before they could mount any kind of defensive blow.

Amidst the fray several recognizable faces pierced through Eldon's heart. He saw his adoptive mother violently dragging a screaming child from one of the shelters. His adoptive father wailed with near-delight as he mercilessly bit his blade into a would-be defender and proceeded to throw a torch upon a shelter. Several other members of Eldon's plains-community could be seen burning, raiding, and killing the peaceful folk who moments ago lay blissful.

In the end pure numbers surrounding the small village put a quick end to all who resisted or submitted. None were left alive save the screaming child dragged brutally from his home. This Eldon recognized to be himself.

The vision abruptly ended and upon gazing down to Sillot he realized tears were covering both of their faces.

Staring coldly downward Sillot coughed, and whispered, "I fled, I was scared. I found the road and a man saw my terror. He took me back to his house. The house we currently sit within. I assisted him here for years until he passed and I inherited this estate."

Sillot laboriously craned his head upward, looked Eldon in the eyes, and spoke his last words. "That is our people's fate... The skills I have shown you far exceed those of our forbearers… I will die with my own kind, of my own age: in peace… Always remember…"

Sillot's body went limp and slumped forward, sliding down the trunk of the willow until lying on the floor. Eldon stared into the foggy lifeless eyes of his mentor and only kin, tears filling his own.

Several roots of varying sizes arose from the base of the tree and began enveloping Sillot. They twisted and wrapped him, covering all but his head. They pulled him earthward gently, unhurriedly; until his form lay no longer visible, and the floor lay as it did before.

Eldon leaned against the willow staring blankly toward the entrance that brought him to this crossroad. He loudly called for Rel, but there was no answer. Eldon would miss the wise old man...

It was then that Eldon had found his purpose, the reason for which to train, to learn, to love, to hate: revenge. He had always known he was destined for something more, and now the scope of that was fully realized.

Eldon hastily wandered through Shoryal, down the cobbled streets amidst barking vendors and beggars, through the chaos, the sickening, the depraved. He reached the gates of that cursed testament to triumph over nature, and proceeded toward the forest.

The journey was long, but passed quite hastily in the fog of rage.

The woods brought no comfort, no respite from pain, just power. Sensing the consciousness of the forest he learned of where his coastal village lay. The place he once called home, the place he loved with the people he loved.

Eldon stood calmly on the edge of the wood. Gazing into the once quaint village ahead, Eldon noticed how much it had grown since he had left, how bustling and successful it had become.

With two hands raised skyward Eldon experienced his legacy. He would cast away his pain; he would avenge his people. He knew now what Sillot had trained him for. The purpose of his newfound knowledge.

Vines, lightning fast, stretched out into the village. Shrubs and grasses violently protruded from beneath the earth's surface. All the ground was boiling and crumbling, as villagers in fear fled their homes. Ivy lashed out at hysterical, running villagers, dismembering some, crushing others. Trees arose from the earth, crumbling foundations, destroying homes and fences; all structures torn and bent as if delicate in nature. Screams rang out deafeningly; screams ten-fold that of the forest village. Terror was cast upon all faces. Those who fled were cast to the earth violently where they were then enveloped by vines and undergrowth. Blood splattered all the vegetation, slaking the thirst of the earth; all was red, deep red. Buildings toppled, and structures splintered as all manner of vegetation seemed to penetrate the heart of the village. The piercing screams seemed unending, but were becoming fewer and fewer in number.

Eldon gazed to the building that was once his home. It lay untouched by the chaotic natural environment wreaking havoc upon the rest of the village. The last memories he would possess of that home were the familiar voices of his adoptive family; their screams and cries as he lay waste everything before him...

Where the village once stood, now only nature and crumbling structures could be seen. The forest had expanded to cover what was once a place of development, growth, and a way of life. Eldon turned to the woods that lay behind and as he first stepped into them, he would do so again: alone…

Beyond the Mirrors of Faellnoch

By D.R. Lackner

I

The needle lifted from the fallout groove with a mechanical click, and the Earth Warrior opened his eyes.

All around him was an inky black void. He felt no weight of gravity, and was not falling, but was cradled in the nothing which surrounded him. The silence made the ringing in his ears grow to a deafening howl. As he began to wonder to where he had travelled, a small yellow light began to glow at what seemed to be a distant point. While he stared, the yellow light became brighter and wider. His eyes struggled to adjust, and he could see what appeared to be a circular opening in the dark void; it was wreathed in slow coiling mist which dissipated into the blackness surrounding it. Within this window, he could see a bleak landscape of craggy mountains and burnt, dying vegetation clinging to the rocks. A narrow path crested the slope of the mountainside and overlooked a barren plain. Upon the peak was a rock formation which appeared as a skeletal hand grasping at the uneasy skies.

From behind this cruel formation rose a solitary humanoid figure, unnaturally tall compared to one of earthly origin. It wore a flowing robe of deep yellow and a gray hooded mantle which obscured its features. Below on the plain could be seen the fires of a war camp, crowded by ragged canvas tents and standards flapping in alien winds. Gathered in the center of the camp were racks of jagged weapons, forged of a yellow metal. Stands like husks of great insects rested there bearing cruel armor.

From the tents lurched cruel monstrous humanoids, their hunched forms bearing deformities both horrific and pitiful. The hooded figure reached the apex of the overlook and with outstretched arms shouted a rallying cry, followed by fierce declarations in a language the Earth Warrior knew was not of his home world, nor the common tongue of Eyrn. While the words were obscure, it was clear that these were not creatures of peaceful desires. The sounds of these words echoed in the blackness enveloping the warrior; they seemed to push him away from this vision with their weight. As the war camp howled and clattered in their armaments, building their fires with furious hatred, the mist wreathing this vision began to close in and obscure the warrior's sight. Coiling inwards, it brought with it blackness until the vision was gone and the warrior was alone once more in the dark. He felt weightless in the dark, floating yet motionless. He looked in all directions for a sign, a point of reference, and yet found none. Time passed, and the silence once again grew to envelop him. The warrior closed his eyes for a moment, and when he opened them, he was suddenly once again in the tavern in Ardona, sitting by the fire.

II

The Tower Keep was no more, and yet, no rubble lay in the city of Ardona. The people there will tell that on that night, the tower began to crumble and rise upward into a swirling vortex in the sky. It left existence piece by piece, leaving only the stony mount on which it once stood. Only the Earth Warrior knew what had come to pass there in the chamber of evil magick. Only he knew of the world beyond.

The people of Ardona had crowded into the streets. The Tower Keep had stood as a beacon of darkness for a thousand years, and a sign of hope for thousands before that. Many fled at this omen, whatever the meaning. Many feared for what it could mean. The wise men of the city knew the legends, and knew of the prophecies foretold in a distant time.

The Earth Warrior rose to his feet. He slung his ancient shield across his back and sheathed his sword. He stepped out into the night, among the clamor and bustle of the people. He could hear song. He could hear cheer. He could hear laughter. In the midst of this celebration he noticed unsavory types gathering their wares and belongings into carts and onto horses, leaving the city with haste. Their time and grasp of the city had come to an end. He took some comfort in knowing that the people here would not bother him, knowing nothing of what had taken place up in the Tower Keep. They would not know, unless he saw fit to tell them, that he had dispatched the evil wizard Vael, and they would also not know of the prophecy which he set into motion. In his heart, he knew the doom which he had brought unto this world by unearthing the Eye of the Kings in the deep dungeons of Evermorn, yet he knew that fate was the only thing which would remain constant in his unstuck existence.

III

The warrior walked through the streets, seeing no sign of the Lady in Blue, the guardian who had spoken to him of the Eye of Kings which had brought him here. He walked with a lingering pace, listening to the songs of triumph recounting the night's events, and hearing the lively talk from all corners. He offered himself a few moments to escape in thought, experiencing joy vicariously through the revelry which surrounded him. He sauntered through the streets of Ardona, unrecognized as the hero of legend long foretold, and seen only as an adventurer on his way. As he rounded a corner onto a side street, a figure in a gray cloak stood in his path. He slowed to a halt, and the cloaked figure raised his head and spoke.

"Warrior, I know well the prophecies which once lined the great rising halls of the Tower Keep. In a distant time, the Council of Wizards made the Tower a place for all to feel welcome, and artists were invited to study the carven forms you no doubt saw in your ascent. Magick and sciences of this world flourished there once, but no more. These things took place eons ago, and yet, my Order has preserved parchments which contain the full prophecy. Come with me, we have much to discuss."

The warrior said nothing, and followed the old man, who turned quickly and led him to a narrow alleyway. Normally, the old man would look over his shoulder to ensure no one would see this secret entrance, yet at this late hour of triumph, all were distracted by ale and song. The warrior followed the old man down the dark alley until he stopped, not at a door, but at what appeared to be simply part of the brick wall. The old man reached out to a brick with what seemed like a crudely scrawled word of graffiti in some runic character unfamiliar to the man from Earth. He traced the lines of this word with a bony finger, and the lettering began to glow bright green. As it did so, the grout lines of the bricks around it also began to glow, outlining the form of a door. It swung inwards, leading to a stair descending into the earthen lair.

"Quickly!" the old man said as he motioned the warrior inside. The old man took a lit torch from the wall and began his descent into the earth. The warrior's weariness was catching up with him; the adrenaline of battle now fading and leaving an ache in his bones. He followed the old man down the long stair, which carved a path into a hidden hall beneath the great house above. Before him, the warrior saw a warmly lit room, furnished with deeply carven wood and rich tapestries on the walls. Within the underground hall, several adventurers were gathered. They spoke in hushed tones, and the warrior could not make out their speech as it was not in the common tongue he understood. A few sat at a large table, piled with not only a feast of strange roasted meats, but weapons, flagons of ale, and mysterious tomes, while there were others obscured in the shadowed recesses of the hall. Large wooden shelves bearing bound books and iron stands which held candles lined the walls. Piles of armor were carelessly strewn and alchemical tools sat piled upon an altar on one side of the room.

"My friend! I am Immerus, and these are the Guildsmen of Eyrn," the old man proclaimed, gesturing to the ragged adventurers. "Among us are protectors from each of the Four Kingdoms of the old wizards whose Council found a home in the Tower you sent spiraling off into oblivion. As foretold in prophecies long ago, you have arrived, both to our doom and to our hopeful rebirth. When you brought the Eye of the Kings back into the light of day, you sealed the fates of many; and yet, you have set into motion what generations have prepared for.

"Here is he," said the old man. "Here is he who has slain Vael!"

A rush of silence fell over the room. The Earth Warrior caught the eyes of each adventurer. Each bore a ferocity unique. About the subterranean lair were warlords from the far corners of Eyrn. In a gloomy corner outside the light thrown from the fireside, the warrior saw the maiden from beyond the sea clad in an azure cloak.

Immerus turned to the Earth Warrior, and spoke to the room. "This man has defeated the demon of Evermorn, and recovered the Eye of the Kings. He ascended the Tower Keep to recover the Talisman which once housed the Eye from the Forgotten Plane of Oxuul. This Warrior has come from faraway lands unknown, as foretold in the legends of Eyrn, both to destroy and create a world anew!

"Earth Warrior, these men have gathered here in Ardona, for the sages of their kingdoms have each kept the lore of old. For one thousand years had Vael corrupted the once great refuge of wisdom and hope, and now I present to you those who would die in service of the council of the nine wizards."

The wise man motioned to a man seated at the heavy wooden table in the center of the room. "From the northern kingdoms of Irethorne, Arnyr has joined us." The Earth Warrior saw a man in a golden chainmail hauberk brooding over a flagon of ale, fiery hair and beard in braids of war. He wore the talismans and runic glyphs of his people on his arms and face, no doubt as permanent inscriptions of ink. Arnyr stood with a clamor and raised a large, two-handed axe in salute.

"At his right is Wrathcloak, the scout from the western wilds. His allegiance lies with the kingdom of Westfold, yet this is a man of the wilderness." A man in a wide brimmed hat looked up from a vellum scrawling and flashed a glance at the warrior, one hand holding the work of mysticism which he studied, and the other at a dagger on his belt. His cloak and tunic were the color of dust, and were threadbare with age and abuse.

"At the far head of the table, I present Grothymn from the savage jungles south of the Mad River. The tribal council of Uthynk has sent him on behalf of their War Chief." The Earth Warrior looked to the eyes of this warlord and saw both the fury and wisdom that the wilds will teach. Grothymn rose from his seat bearing what resembled a steel mace, barely concealing a mechanism of death within. He wore a belted hide of soft dark leather and bracers of steel. His face and exposed arms were scarred deeply from battle. He wore no beard and had wild dark hair bound back.

"Finally, Aktai from the nomadic tribes of the east comes to our aid." A fierce looking man in a strange hat looked to be deep in thought, smoking a long pipe; at his back was a finely crafted bow and quiver of red fletched arrows. He wore a caftan of coarse black fabric and a wide five-buckled belt. Leaning against the table at his side was a large sword, most suitably used with two hands.

"The time to fulfill the prophecies has come, my friends!" said Immerus. "We go now to our fate, and death or glory!"

A great cheer erupted from the room as the adventurers leapt to their feet, raising flagons of ale in a great foamy uproar. The mood of the room abruptly changed from the hushed tones and uneasy greetings. The adventurers began to sing songs of old, songs of their making, songs of their fathers, bellowing and booming joyously. The day of reckoning had finally come for the evils of the realms.

"We have prepared a room for you. Rest," Immerus said to the Earth Warrior. The maiden rose and guided him without a word to a corridor beyond the great hall to a room as richly furnished as any noble's quarters.

"Once again, we meet," stated the warrior. "I have many questions troubling me. This world is strange, and yet these things, these people, bear resemblance to my own world. I feel as if I have always known this prophecy, and I feel my old world slipping from memory. I was a child there, and through mists of time I have wandered, between worlds where time has stretched and turned. These things follow an order of their own, one not bound by reason or time." The warrior entered ahead of the maiden to see the room contained a great wooden bed and a large shelf of ancient tomes. He laid down his shield and looked to the maiden who stood at the door. "I have met the others at the table and we have spoken, and yet, I know not your name." His words were met with silence.

She cast a short smile as he stared with wonder and closed the door. The light faded, as did the sounds of revelry from the great hall.

IV

Again the warrior was in darkness. He dreamed of great armies amassing. Hulking forms were pillaging and ravaging, forging cruel armor and crude weaponry. He saw the nightmarish yellow-clad figure standing tall on a war chariot driven by beasts unknown which snorted and howled under the yoke of oppressive force. The gray ragged mantle lay about the figure's broad shoulders, and the hood obscured its face. The armies raged through a desolate land. Burning clouds billowed uneasily in the skies above. Thunder cracked through canyons of chaos where gravity seemed wrong. Pyramids of mad design dotted the horizons, in ruinous formations of ragged stone.

A chasm spit lava down into a valley.

Smoke and fire: torment and sacrifice.

Lightning cracked the terrible skies, and blood ran over the land.

When the warrior awoke, he was alone in the darkness. He stirred and arose, feeling for his sword, which lay beside him in the great wooden bed. Raising the sword of steel, he fumbled in the dark and felt for the door. As he opened it light spilled in from the corridor.

V

As the warrior entered the light, he was greeted not by revelry but by plotting. The guild did not notice him at first, until the old man who had retrieved him from the world above caught glimpse of the weary Earth Warrior.

The warrior with no name gathered his wits as he poured water from a clay jug into a tumbler. He looked about the room, imagining the strange lands each of the adventurers had traveled from, the misty jungles and tall hills. He imagined the many thousands of years of culture which brought them here to this place. Some of their garb appeared familiar, as if ripped from the history of his own Earth, while others were clearly from lands altogether strange to him. He thought of his home plane of existence, and the great forgotten civilizations, lost to him here. They were paying little attention to him as they talked and pored over manuscripts.

"We know that within the Tower Keep there was a doorway to another world: the Realm of the old gods known here as Faellnoch within the dark dimension of Oxuul. The wizards of old had split the Talisman of Kings into two parts, the Eye and the Claw. The Warrior found the Eye in Evermorn in the belly of a demon, and the Claw about the neck of one of the old gods of Faellnoch." Immerus walked to a large table, littered with books and scrolls. The script was not familiar to the man of Earth, but the imagery depicted the things he had seen in striking detail. "Within these texts are the prophecies of our world, and are these things foretold. We have only the prophecy of destruction, beyond this, we know nothing, other than fate will deal a fitting end by his hand." Immerus looked down at the dusty tomes as his mind wandered. "In the night, we received word that Portals have opened, and there are strange reports of creatures not of this world lurking in the shadowy recesses of the forests."

"I have seen them," the Earth Warrior interrupted. "In dark visions. I have seen armies amassing under cruel banners. There is a figure in a cloak of yellow whose rule is harsh and filled with anger."

As he spoke these words, the guildsmen looked up with fear in their eyes, for they knew of these things, if only from study and the words of their forbears.

"While our respective kingdoms serve the ancient ways of the wise elders, there are those who would bring this King in Yellow to our world, to the certain destruction of all," said Immerus. "These cultists will have learned of the fall of the Tower Keep, and they will know the prophesized times have come. Our spies have infiltrated their ranks, and have learned of their plan to sacrifice themselves to their gods by opening a portal to Faellnoch and spilling their blood on its soil. Warrior, you must pose as a devotee and enter their cult in order to travel to that forsaken realm. You have traveled there before, for it is where the claw of the Talisman of Kings was hidden. In this realm, you must find the King in Yellow, and destroy his efforts to enter Eyrn. You must sever his line of demons who serve the old gods. All the while, the King in Yellow will undoubtedly send his warriors to Eyrn through their cursed portals. The guildsmen will return to their respective kingdoms and raise armies of their own, to protect against these attacks, wherever they may lay siege." Immerus looked to the room, scanning the faces of the warriors of this realm, and turned to the Earth Warrior. "The cultists of Faellnoch have been seen in the mountains to the north of Ardona. Their green fires will be the sign."

The Lady in Blue approached the Earth Warrior from the far corner of the hall. The candlelight flickered as she passed. "Since ancient times of this world, my order has held objects of power. We served the old wise wizards of the past, and guarded their secrets down through the ages." She held out what appeared to be a strange key of a bronze-like metal, etched finely with runic markings. At its end was a fiery crimson gem, which changed appearance as the light moved about it. The key was fastened upon a sturdy chain. "This key will aid you on your quest to Faellnoch, yet, I know not what creation of evil it opens."

"I thank thee, lady of the wise wizards, and would that I might see thee again upon my return," the warrior replied, as he tied the chain upon his studded belt.

The Earth Warrior gathered supplies for his journey then: dried meat and a skin of water. The guildsmen and the Lady in Blue bid him farewell as he passed the heavy door which led back up the stair to Ardona. His boots fell hard on the stone.

VI

At the top of the stair, the warrior saw an iron lever protruding from the wall. As he pulled the lever, the doorway began to glow, and the stones moved free by forces of ancient magick. Dim light poured into the stairwell and he entered Ardona once more. It was now midday, and the townsfolk were bustling in the streets. It was the first day free from the villainy of Vael, and as the warrior exited the alleyway into the main streets of the city, he saw that a small militia of men had taken it upon themselves to cast out the remaining vile folk who once thrived here. They brandished ceremonial swords of their fathers against stone-hurling and club-wielding brigands. The militia pushed them toward the gates, ignoring their wicked threats. These things were of little concern to the Earth Warrior. He strode through Ardona and headed for the main gate house himself.

At the iron mouth of the town, he turned back, and looked to the grey mountains off in the distance where the once mighty Tower had stood. He took to the fields beyond the town. As he walked, the crashing and shouting of the city streets faded into the soft winds that bent tall grass. Soft earth and sounds of birds gave him much needed peace, and his mind began to dream. He passed stony monuments to forgotten gods, buried by moss with inscriptions faded by centuries.

The hills beyond Ardona began to roll as he drew nearer to the mountains. The Earth Warrior turned back to see the yellow stone walls of the city, cracked by time but strong and thick. There was no Tower which rose above them any longer. New Towers will be built, and will fall in time, as all things will. The warrior had outrun time and reason, but not fate. He turned back to the mountains, and continued his journey until nightfall.

The warrior made camp beneath the evergreen trees of this world at the base of the stony gloom of the mountains. He struck a fire and sat for an evening's rest. He lay back and closed his eyes as the howling of distant beasts sang their song of the night.

In the darkness, the warrior saw a stone castle appearing in crimson hues against a violent orange sky. Cracked towers wound upon a complex structure, buttressed against harsh stony peaks. Great lizards forced their forked tongues between cruel teeth as they dominantly stalked the parapets. Torches and banners lined the walls and glowing fire could be seen through arrow slits in the many towers. A bridge of arched stone led up to an iron gate over a chasm many hundreds of feet deep. About the mountainous base flowed a river of fuming lava, and beyond lay the war camp of monstrous creatures he had seen once before.

The warrior awoke to find his fire naught but ashes. He gathered his supplies once more and wove a path into the mountains. The wind howled between the jagged peaks and down through the mountain passes, beckoning him to his doom. He began his ascent up the blocks of granite-like stone at the side of a pool of spring water, which flowed down from the heights of the mountain. Step by careful step, he climbed the stony walls, following the spring upward.

After many hours of climbing, the warrior reached a plateau which overlooked the forest and field, and he viewed Ardona as a tiny glowing dot far off in the distance. Upon this shelf of stone he took rest in an oasis of evergreen trees, which buried their roots at a clear pool fed by a waterfall. A refreshing mist filled the air, and the warrior bent to drink. He gazed upon his reflection, and did not recognize his face. His helm had gathered rust and dents since his adventure began. His features had hardened as well. He looked overhead and saw the bright birds of this world take flight from the canopy, crying strange songs into the sky. He looked down once more at the pool and saw another face, grey and cruel. As he puzzled, the face pushed forward to break the surface of the water, and a jagged sword pierced the waterline into the air of Eyrn. The Earth Warrior jumped back and drew his sword. Here was a creature of his visions.

"Warrior! We have seen you. We have seen what you have done in our world," the creature rattled with a hard low voice. "Your blood will spill upon these rocks now, as our dreaming god has died at your hand."

The creature lunged forth out of the pool, water spilling from its harshly forged armor of unearthly metal. He swung his blade upward at the warrior's torso, aiming to cleave him in two, but the warrior drew back and blocked his strike. The Earth Warrior kicked the creature in the chest. It fell back with a gasp. He then raised his sword and came down on the center of the creature's head, splitting it down the middle into its body. As the two sides fell unto its shoulders, oozing yellow blood gushed to the surface and stained the crystal clear water. Steam arose from the water and the remaining air from the creature's lungs bubbled to the surface. The body of the creature liquefied and vaporized, leaving behind only the crude armor and blade sinking to the bottom of the shallow pool. The warrior knelt to examine the armor and found a talismanic amulet, bearing a mysterious symbol. He took this and tied it onto his belt, and cleansing his sword of the alien blood, he continued on his trek.

VII

The warrior ascended the waterfall at the base of the pool, and came upon a hedge which bordered a grassy clearing, bound at the sides by stony heights. He heard murmuring and chanting in a language unknown to him. Remaining hidden behind a boulder, he peered between the leaves of the hedge. From here he could see an ancient stone altar alight with sickly green fire. It was ringed by standing stones; upon each was perched a human skull. At the far edge of the clearing was a canvas tent of golden yellow. Two guards in crimson hooded robes stood at its entrance. It was dusk now, and as the light faded, figures emerged from the forest to stand among the nine stones. Eight figures came forward, leaving one stone unattended. Each devotee was bound to their stone with black cords by the crimson guards. As the moon rose above the altar, the opening of the tent parted and a figure came forward with golden scepter in one hand. The eight figures began a haunting chant as this high priest entered the ring of standing stones and approached the altar.

"My children," he said, "you have come to this site of your forbears, to stand among the relics of the old wizards. We spit on this world as we welcome the doom of this planet. The Tower Keep has fallen at last, and you come here now to travel to Oxuul, and to spill your blood on the soil of Faellnoch. Let us greet oblivion at last!"

The chanting continued to a rising crescendo, and the warrior looked down at the talisman upon his belt. He tore it free and walked with it in hand toward the hedge. He parted the branches and entered the clearing as the cultists looked on in amazement and ceased their chant.

The high priest said, "You, who walk among us, you dare to enter our ritual space bearing this amulet from beyond? Guards! Kill this infidel!"

The guards drew black daggers of volcanic glass, similar to the one once held by Vael, and moved toward the warrior around the ring of standing stones. The warrior raised the talisman he had plucked from the fallen creature high above his head.

"Come forward and kill me if you wish, but my blood is better spilled on Faellnoch," the Earth Warrior proclaimed. "I come here as a pilgrim to my doom. Let me sacrifice myself that the world of Eyrn be forever dust in the void of space."

"It is as prophecy foretold, that a stranger would come to us to bear sacrifice among our final ritual," said the high priest. "Guards! Tie this man to the ninth stone, that he might take the place of the ancient wizard of Ardona."

The guards took hold of the warrior's arms and pulled him to the standing stone. They bound his wrists with black cord and wrapped it around the mossy stone. The high priest raised his hands and the chanting began once more, rising wildly into the night sky. The warrior fell into a daze as the chant grew and swelled in rhythmic complexity. He looked about him at the faces of the cult. They were humans of all races of Eyrn, their brains tainted by evil and misanthropic zeal.

The high priest stood at the altar, upon which lay a large tome of black writs; he spoke words from the page with fury and hate. The ancient tongues of dark wizards came alive; magick smoke poured from the high priest's mouth as he uttered the incantation. It lingered in the air above them in a haze. Within the cloud of smoke, jolts of electricity flickered and cracked, flashing gloomy blue light onto the stones. With a clap of thunder, a golden shimmer began to grow in the center of the cloud, widening into a circle. The chanting continued at a feverish pace, and the high priest began to intone the final lines of the evil spell. The portal above their heads grew wider and extended out to the edges of the standing stones. The Earth Warrior looked up into the void and saw the skies of Faellnoch and smelled its sulfurous air. As he stared up into the magick void, the portal began to move down toward their heads slowly. The other victims of sacrifice looked around in a panic, yet did not cease their dark chanting. The golden vortex came lower now, encompassing their heads and necks. The weight of another atmosphere bore down onto them. They looked around at the new world they found themselves partly in. Bizarre structures appeared on unfamiliar horizons, yet their feet remained on Eyrn. The warrior of Earth recognized these pyramids from his travels, and they reminded him of those on his home world, yet there remained a desperately wrong aspect to them which shook his very being. The portal reached the ground and fire leaped up from the stony soil of Faellnoch, spiraling around the ancient standing stones and vanishing off into the sky as the chanting ceased.

One by one, the guards loosed their bonds, and the victims approached the altar. They stretched their necks across the stone, baring flesh unto the cold moonlight. The high priest drew again his dagger of volcanic glass, and cut their throats with no hesitation or pageantry. The blood spilled forth, pouring down the stone and wetting the soil beneath. A great pool of blood grew around the stone altar, and the high priest grinned, baring white teeth in madness. With each sacrifice, the bloody pool around the stone grew, and soaked the robes of each victim as they approached. The guards who had tied the warrior freed him from his bonds and drew again their swords, only to fall on them: their blood was not fit for sacrifice, and yet, they were not permitted to live. The high priest laughed and pointed toward the Earth Warrior. Now was his time.

"Priest! Now will be the ninth sacrifice, but it will not be my blood upon the soil of this forsaken planet!" the warrior shouted as he drew his blade and lunged at the high priest. His first strike was blocked by the obsidian blade, which shattered on impact, and sent black glittering shards flying into the heavy air. The priest gasped and jumped away from the altar, sliding in the blood of his coven and falling to the ground.

"I have come as prophesized, not to end my life in honor of the dreaming gods, but to seal this world off and be forgotten in the seas of time. You have come here only to bring about the doom of the gods you wish to serve. Contemplate this in your final seconds of life!" With a shout, the warrior raised his sword above the high priest. The priest knelt and bowed his head low as the warrior freed it from his neck. Blood spilled again on the soils of Faellnoch.

VIII

Familiar restless inky hues swirled in the skies of this forsaken land, and the warrior's footfalls met the ground with strange heavy thuds. The physical laws of this realm were not as in Eyrn, or as in his home world. His travels had taken him here once, and he had hoped to never return. The rocky landscape spat forth harsh vegetation. What appeared as fleshy trees with pod-like fruits, large as a man, sprouted in a vast oily forest. Their deep blue hues contrasted with the red umber soil. He stood in a clearing, as a mirror of the ritual grounds on Eyrn, and looked about him to see the crooked mountains on a horizon which defied the logic of his familiarity. He knew not which direction the lair of the King in Yellow lay. He looked to the key which he had tied about his belt and felt it twitch with arcane magick. He lifted the heavy chain and held the key with arms outstretched. Closing his eyes, he turned in the clearing. He felt a pull, as if a ghostly hand had grasped for the key in the darkness of his mind, and walked on to meet it.

The Earth Warrior came to the edge of the clearing and turned back to see that the rocky soil of the ritual ground had drank the blood of sacrifice: it had pulled the life-force of the cultists in to feed the heart of the dreaming planet. The bodies lay strewn, withered, and contorted. Turning back to the rim of the forest, the warrior trudged carefully, edging carefully through the darkness of the leathery trees. They seemed to be aware of his presence, and appeared to move slightly as he passed. On the forest floor, he observed small pale white mushroom-like growths sprouted close together. When he trod on them, they let out tiny gasps of pain. Ever on his way he felt watching eyes upon him.

Hiking through these strange woods, the warrior all the while felt the pull on the key which he had carried from Eyrn, following it like a compass on Earth. After walking over lumbering hills and shallow valleys, he heard a muffled cry from beyond a rocky pass at the edge of the wood. He approached the pass and quickly entered between the sheer cliff sides. When he reached the far end, he saw another fleshy blue tree, much larger than those of the forest. It moved with a slow slither, its branches coiling like snakes. Near the ground, one of its leathery pod-like appendages closed with the legs of a man extending out of the far end. The warrior heard muffled screams from within, and unsheathed his sword as he ran forward. Several branches cracked like whips and struck him, flinging him to the ground as the pod began to rise up from the ground. The warrior got back to his feet and lunged forth, cutting the slithering arms of the creature. Oily black liquid spewed from the fresh wounds. He leaped as the pod lifted into the air, and slashed at the stem which held it onto the leathery blue trunk of the tree creature. As the pod slopped to the ground, many more appendages desperately reached for him and were cut in a series of flashing sword strikes. The warrior took to hacking away at the trunk, giving the tree creature little time to recover. As he cut away at the base of the carnivorous plant, black ooze gushed and foamed, and as his strikes reached the core, the snake-like limbs went slack and wilted in the dank air.

The warrior approached the fallen pod as the creature withered and let out an alien moan in the heavy night. He pried open the petals, and pulled at the pair of legs which moved only slightly now. Covered in the sap, or blood, of the entity was a man, haggard and wearing tattered clothes. He raised a hand to wipe the oily material from his face. He regained his senses and stood slowly.

"I never thought that I would see a human face again. I do not know how long I have been here, but it feels like an eternity," the man said. "All I can remember now is looking into a mirror in my home on Eyrn, and a grotesque grey face replaced my own as brutish arms grabbed and pulled me through. That evening, I had been preparing for my journey to the city of Ardona on behalf of the Kingdom of Westfold. I'd received dire word from our castle sage that a time of strife had arrived, as had a warrior from distant lands. I then found myself here in this forsaken place, tortured and deserted by my captor, left to wander the wastes, until I found myself in this living forest. I thank thee for saving my life, even though I was better to have died. I was once called Ruhgar… that was my name." The bedraggled man scratched his head, and looked down at the forest floor, lost in thought. The warrior wiped the black blood from his blade and sheathed it at his back.

"You may yet see the skies of your home world, and you may know more of this world than you think. I have trodden the lost roads between worlds, and I know your kingdom of Westfold and of a roguish Wrath-cloak who arrived in your stead, but these things are little importance to us here in this wasteland," said the warrior from distant lands.

"I seek the King in Yellow, and I have traveled here to unseat him from his throne," continued the Earth Warrior. As he spoke, he looked about him. The slain tree creature stood in an enclosure of rock, with craggy walls stretching upward high into the spinning skies of Faellnoch. The key pulled to the far end of the stony canyon. "We must scale these walls with all the haste you can muster." Ruhgar nodded silently, as he wondered whether he had the strength left. The two lost adventurers searched for some time at the base of the rock face for a suitable path upward, and began their ascent.

IX

Attended by a gray humanoid creature with two pairs of human arms and wings resembling those of a bat, the King in Yellow sat upon his throne in a crimson hall. The King waved his hands in the air, and an image appeared of armies amassing in the stony landscape of Faellnoch. They marched through fallen cities, dotted with crumbling columns and misshapen pyramids. Their heavy boots fell as the beating of deep drums. As the King in Yellow viewed this vision, a warlord of his troops entered the hall, and approached the bat-winged champion, uttering an ancient, ugly language in a hushed tone. The bat-winged creature drew a large battle axe and chopped at the neck of the war leader where he stood, and the head bounded down the stairs away from the throne as the lifeless body fell at his clawed feet. The King in Yellow swiped at the vision before him, and it melted into the air. He turned to the bat-winged creature, who relayed the message of the now dead warlord. The King in Yellow drew his hand into a fist and pounded the arm of his throne, which cracked upon this blow.

X

Ruhgar and the Earth Warrior neared the top of the rock wall, and could see a vast ruinous land before them. Upon the sandy plain was an ancient city. A series of stout pyramids was arranged around the remains of a colonnade about a stone foundation. The pyramids on the far side glowed with flickering red-orange light, the source of which was a river of lava. Beyond the lava, a jagged stony peak rose from the earth, and upon this mountain, the King in Yellow lay in wait.

"When I arrived in this land, I found myself within those castle walls," Ruhgar huffed as he pointed toward the castle beyond the ruins. "My captors tortured me until they realized I had no information to tell them. They led me out into the wild wastes in a chariot driven by strange bird-like creatures. I was lowered into the pit of the tree creature and left as sacrifice to it. I long for vengeance, and will guide the way back."

After crossing a desolate rocky plateau, the warrior with no name and Ruhgar descended into the ruinous valley of ancient stone structures. The warrior recognized this as the place where he had once battled the metal monster and retrieved the claw talisman. To the far side of the valley lay the cracked pyramid where he had placed the completed Talisman of Kings upon its high altar; it was there where the dreaming god fell into the widening volcanic pit, and where a portal drove him back to the Tower Keep. The pit was now a river, barring the way to the plains beyond.

They walked on, crossing the center of the crumbling colonnade. In the recesses and shadows, slinking silhouettes could be seen scratching along the fallen stones. The warrior reached for his sword, but did not draw it, as the creatures scurried off into the darkness.

Once they reached the cracked pyramid, they could feel the heat of the boiling stone within the fresh chasm. They searched for a way to cross, and after scaling the stone steps of the pyramid, found that near the apex was a space which could be leapt across. First, Ruhgar attempted, and as he did, a large chunk of stone splashed down into the inferno below. His trajectory faltered, and his hands narrowly grasped the opposite edge. The Earth Warrior quickly jumped across, although he felt again the oppressive effects of the gravity of this world while in the air. He reached down to grab the arm of his guide and pulled him to safety.

"That's twice," Ruhgar said shortly as the Earth Warrior nodded.

From the top of the pyramid they saw fields of dead and dying vegetation. Far off into the plains was one lonely peak where stood the castle of the King in Yellow. The warrior took the steel dirk from his belt and handed it to Ruhgar.

"Take this as defense in these, the enemies' lands."

They continued on their quest, edging with caution. Among the singed and burnt leafy plants were the bones of alien creatures, strange and terrible. The warrior mused that these were remains of the creatures who had stalked them out of sight. The grand towers of the castle beyond stood proud against the whirling orange sky. Lizard beasts from the Earth Warrior's vision stalked the parapets and a strange glow illuminated stone crenellations. Each step drew them closer to doom, and the foreboding weight of the Faellnochian atmosphere fell heavy on their shoulders.

At the base of the mountain, Ruhgar turned to the Earth Warrior. "It was near here where I was removed from the castle dungeon," he said.

They peered beyond a large chunk of stone and saw two grotesque guards armed with spears standing watch on an iron gate, torchlight flickering and glinting off their crude armor. The warrior drew his sword silently. From his back he slung his shield, which bore the ancient winged predator insignia of the forgotten lore of Eyrn. Ruhgar drew his dagger and they made their attack, charging at each of the guards with fury. The mutant guards readied their position with spears pointing to their assailants. The Earth Warrior deflected the oncoming spear thrust and forced it against the guard as his sword pierced its throat. Ruhgar grabbed the spear of his guard, then buried the dagger in the creature's heart. Both mutants fell, their thick yellow blood oozing and bubbling onto the stony ground. The Earth Warrior searched the fallen corpses and found a crudely formed key, which he fit into the slot on the iron gate. It turned with a crunch and the gate creaked open. Ruhgar took a torch from the rock face and led the way inside. They stalked slowly inside, and found that they were in a passage of crumbling brick with many heavy doors lining the walls.

"We are in the castle undercroft; this place is a labyrinth of sorts," said Ruhgar. "Beyond each door is a series of shifting paths. The very walls here are alive. When the guards dragged me through these halls, they became lost several times and argued in their harsh, primitive language. We may remain lost here."

The warrior with no name nodded. He approached a door and pulled the iron latch. As the hinges spoke, the door swung open. The warrior peered into the blackness. Something shuffled heavily in the darkness within. Again he took the key given to him by the Lady in Blue and held it in hand with his sword. As he did so, his sword swung away from the open door, and pointed to another door further down the hall. This door seemed to be turning to dust where it stood. The warrior approached it and grasped the latch. It pulled free and crashed to the stone floor. He kicked at the door and the rotten planks splintered. Ruhgar approached the passage and lit his torch. Within were a continuing series of claustrophobic stone hallways. The adventurers walked along, twisting and winding further into the labyrinth, always following the pull of the magick key.

XI

The four warriors sent from the far regions of Eyrn had left the guild hall. They were to return to their kingdoms and raise armies fit to fight the demons of a faraway planet. The Lady in Blue and Immerus now sat at the guildhall table, deep in thought. Their prophecies had only revealed how this tale would begin. Now fate's hands were shrouded in mystery.

It was after their would-be protectors had left that the guildhall door burst open, and a war band of mutants crashed into the room. The Lady and Immerus leapt from their seats to draw weapons against the beasts, but were too late. Immerus was cut down by a nameless demonic creature of the Oxuul dimension. His blood spattered across the table onto the tomes and vellum scrolls, and the Lady was bound and taken. The cruel captors shouted at her in their wicked tongue. She did not understand the words, but ceased her screaming. The creatures barricaded the entrance to the hall and threw her into the room at the end, barring the door.

As these things transpired, a great army of grey humanoid creatures amassed in the forests surrounding Ardona. Trees were felled, and crude siege engines were built. Through mirrors and still waters, more barbaric hordes crossed over to the planet Eyrn. In the very homes of the citizens of this world creatures were emerging, shouting and pillaging. The dark days had arrived, and the Lady thought of the Earth Warrior.

XII

After navigating the maze of corridors, Ruhgar and the warrior with no name arrived at the end of a long stone hall to find a door unlike any of the others they had seen. The door was of a shining crimson lacquer, seemingly untouched by the dust and grime which coated the stones of the maze they had navigated. Ruhgar first reached out to the golden ring at its center and paused. As his fingers touched the yellow metal, a low rumbling laugh echoed through the halls, its reverberations bounding down through the darkness. The deep sounds rumbled, then a rattling sound grew to replace it. Ruhgar turned to light the passages opposite the crimson door, and saw nothing at first. The sounds grew louder, and the clanking of metal arose to join the chatter.

Again they lit the halls with the torch and saw a company of skeletal undead warriors, each wielding a sword and shield of rusty iron, running down the hall towards them at a great pace. The Earth Warrior charged forth into the first three skeletons. The reanimated bodies broke on his shield like a wave of bone meal and dust. Ruhgar turned to face two oncoming skeletal abominations and thrust the torch into one's ribcage, igniting the dry bone instantly. The flaming mass crashed into his comrade and the fire spread. The flaming undead gasped ghostly cries as they crumbled to the floor in smoldering ash. The low rolling laugh began again as the crimson door clicked open.

XIII

A wide stair of perfectly carved crimson stone lay before them. It was buffed to a mirror shine, and glimmered in faint torchlight from above. Thin green mist arose from the piles of bones around them and crawled up the stairs, clinging to the ground, moving almost as if in reverse as the laughter continued.

"Enter my court, travelers, and behold your doom," a voice called after them, seemingly in many simultaneous tones.

Brandishing their weapons, the adventurers climbed the stair and entered into a hall of mirrors. As they stalked past, their reflections refracted into disfigured and bizarre forms. The reflections they could see were altered beyond recognition by evil magick. The warrior turned to gaze at his reflection, and the mirrored room around him and Ruhgar melted away.

He was at once alone in his bedroom, a child on Earth, the album sleeve for Rush's *Caress of Steel* lay beside him on his bed. The stereo crackled:

"The men are free to run now
From labyrinths below
The Wraith of Necromancer
Shadows through the sky
Another land to darken
With evil prism eye"

The final line distorted as the record slowed to a halt. Flame shot up all around the walls of his room. Posters curled and framed pictures crashed to the floor, and the room was consumed in fire. He raced to the door. He reached for the knob and it burnt his hand with a sharp hiss. He backed into the center of the room as all around him burned, and smoke filled the air. He lowered himself to the ground, covering his head as the black smoke rose.

When he raised his eyes, he had returned once again to the court of the King in Yellow: the Necromancer. Again there rolled the now mania cal laughter from beyond. Ruhgar, who had walked ahead, turned back to see the warrior rising from the ground.

"What happened?" said the rogue.

"A vision of another time: a cage of mirrors," the Earth Warrior answered. "There seems to be no end to the court. The mirrors go on out of sight."

As he spoke these words, the terrible form of the King in Yellow appeared in each of the mirrored panes, grey hood obscuring his face. The warrior, in anger, crashed through a mirror on the wall near him, plunging his sword into the chest of the reflection. The laughter rolled on, coming from nowhere and everywhere. The floor beneath his feet disappeared into a black void of nothing. He began to slowly sink into the darkness. He reached to the edge of the crimson floor, pulling himself back up and out. The warrior got to his feet, and rejoined Ruhgar, huffing with rage.

"There must be an answer to this riddle," said Ruhgar, puzzled. "This is dark magick, but there must be a source."

The warrior again held out the key given to him by the Lady in Blue.

He closed his eyes and felt it twitch. He followed the force which pulled on the key and walked blindly. After many paces, he heard the chime of metal on glass, and stood back, raising the ancient sword he wielded. His reflection shifted violently into that of the King in Yellow, his cloak billowing in unearthly winds with a bony hand outstretched. The warrior brought his blade down with a crash on the mirror in front of him. Shards of glass fell to the ground, glittering in the air as they fell. Beyond the mirror lay a small room, lined with glossy crimson stone. At the center the square room was a golden picture frame of elaborate design standing upright on a pedestal of white marble. The picture frame housed a smooth golden panel with a keyhole at its center. Ruhgar ran to catch up with the warrior and peered into the room.

The warrior placed the key into the keyhole, and it turned with a mechanical click. As the key turned, the golden surface of the panel floated back and out into darkness, taking with it the key. A low rolling wind began to howl from within. The golden picture frame grew larger and wider, and the blackness within grew deeper. The adventurers backed out of the room as the darkness spread, engulfing the room which held the box and moving onto the court. The marble pedestal broke with a snap as the void of golden darkness continued to grow, cracking and shattering the mirrored walls as it expanded. The winds from within picked up, pulling the shards through the air and cutting the adventurers in their flight. The court rumbled and shook and a harrowing voice rang out.

"Gaze at the void in despair! The dreams of gods lie within and are beyond time." The adventurers watched as the shards of mirrors and crimson polished stone flew into the golden gateway before them. They turned to see that one mirror behind them remained intact, and within it stood the King in Yellow, who walked toward them through the glass as if it were air. He towered over them, his yellow cloak flowing wildly in the dark wind.

"Secrets beyond time I hold," he said. "Great mysteries of all life and existence await. Faellnoch is a dying world. Join me in cosmic travel: I can return you to your home-world, Earth Warrior. You may yet breathe the air there again."

The warrior searched his soul, and thought of his burning bedroom on Earth. This illusion was part of the cage of mirrors he had destroyed. He walked toward the King in Yellow, who awaited his response. The Earth Warrior bent to pick up a single crimson stone which lay in the black void. He looked into the eyes of the King in Yellow, and they flashed at him in panic. The Earth Warrior hurled the stone at the remaining mirror, and instead of crashing through, splashed as if into a pool of water. It was then that the very form of the King in Yellow shattered into thousands of tiny shards, which were pulled through the air into the void opened by the ancient key. As the ripples in the mirror cleared, a familiar reflection appeared. Within the gateway, the warrior recognized the room he had rested in the guildhall of Ardona. He and Ruhgar made a dash and leapt through.

XIV

With a crash the adventurers landed on the floor in the room of the guildhall, its fixtures utterly destroyed by the forces of the King in Yellow. The two found that the main room where the Earth Warrior had met with the guild had also been destroyed. Upon the floor lay the bloody remains of Immerus. With sword in hand, his strength was outmatched in the end. The Earth Warrior knelt to close the eyes of the fallen sage, and solemnly the adventurers exited the guildhall to seek the streets of Ardona. Once they opened the secret door, they found naught but carnage. The city was set aflame, and the gray mutated troops of doom ransacked the buildings in careless greed and plunder. Distant screams of the villagers filled their weary minds. The adventurers then sought cover behind destroyed crates of supplies and bore witness to a strange scene. The King in Yellow drove his chariot through the city streets with triumphant swagger, shouting eerie commands in a wicked tongue. Strange reptilian creatures toiled and pulled the demonic entity along the cobbles, forked tongues probing the air.

"This cannot be," mused Ruhgar. "He was all but devoured by the void on Faellnoch."

"It may be that time between the worlds moves differently," the Earth Warrior suggested. "Let us remain hidden and find a way out of the city."

The adventurers continued on their way toward the city gates, ever wary of threat of discovery. Great violence and bloodshed was unfurled in the city, and the Earth Warrior held the secret hope that the four kingdoms of Eyrn had not failed in their quest. As they neared the gate, they caught the eye of a guard lagging behind his company of raiders. The Earth Warrior raised his sword in fury; Ruhgar sneaked up behind him and cut his throat, spilling the vile yellow blood upon the street. The body hit the ground, kicking up a cloud of dust. Ruhgar and the Earth Warrior ran through the unguarded gates for the cover of the tall hills at the edge of the fields. They reached the cool shade of the evergreens and made camp in silence.

XV

Beyond the walls of the city, far into the hills, a vast army amassed, comprised of the four kingdoms of Eyrn and lead by their warlords. They made their council in a ragged canvas tent which had seen many bloody campaigns. They discussed the sack of Ardona. They wondered the fate which befell Immerus and the Lady in Blue, who had remained. The force of Eyrn mustered, and began their march to Ardona in the evening. As they neared the gate, they discovered the humble camp of Ruhgar and the Earth Warrior.

Once cool night fell, a great storm of war crashed upon the gates of Ardona. The mutant army had slammed shut the iron gate and gathered in formation. The archers of the nomadic eastern tribes launched volleys of arrows over the walls, while the Northmen of Irethorne used a make-shift battering ram to crush the gates into a mangled heap. Raiders of Westfold lobbed grappling hooks over the high walls and breeched the stronghold. As the heavy iron gates crashed to the ground the Uthynk tribesmen fell in with the Northmen, sweeping the city and overtaking the gray humanoid creatures. The streets ran with blood and carnage. Cries of fury and pain filled the air as the city burned.

The Eyrnian forces swept through the city, hacking their way through hordes of vile hulking creatures. The armies of the four kingdoms pushed their way through to the mount on which the Tower Keep had stood, backing the gray mutants against the rocks. The creatures made a final stand, but were overtaken and slaughtered to the last. As the Eyrnian forces shouted and cheered in their glory, a lone figure emerged. From atop the mount the King in Yellow appeared with arms raised. Behind him was the winged demon with the Lady in Blue captive in his four armed grasp. She struggled not, but her azure robes billowed in the winds of sadness and defeat. The King in Yellow bellowed in the common tongue of Eyrn:

"You who stand before me have borne witness only to the slightest of the storms of Oxuulian nightmares. My word holds the power to crack this planet to its core, and the vengeance of dreaming gods! They will seek further vengeance upon thee in eternal suffering and pain! Hear now the song of your doom!"

The King in Yellow raised his hands and his ragged hood fell back to reveal a grotesque undead countenance of white bone and sinewy strands of rotten flesh. He began to chant a lyrical and wicked incantation. The air seemed to vibrate, and the Eyrnian forces clasped their ears in a violent fury, falling to their knees. Buildings shook and chunks of stone fell to the street.

The horrid words of the King in Yellow reverberated through the land; winds howled and buildings crumbled into heaps. The men of the four armies looked to each other, and hope failed as panic took hold. The song of doom reached deafening heights, and it seemed that all was in vain, when the spell suddenly weakened. The armies looked up again to see that the eyes of the Yellow King glowed white, and that the winds grew still. Light poured forth in thin beams into the blue midnight. Gleaming cracks started to form over his face, and spread out through his arms and down to the edges of his yellow tattered cloak, and a single crimson stone burst forth to land at the Earth Warrior's feet. The cracks grew wider, finally shattering the demonic entity into thousands of razor slivers, bounding and breaking onto the sandy street.

The demon holding the Lady in Blue released her and took to the air in retreat. His bat-like wings were silhouetted against the moon as the nomadic archers loosed their arrows into the creature's heart. The demonic entity dissolved into dust as it fell. The Lady in Blue caught the eye of the Earth Warrior and ran to him. He crushed her white form in his battle-scarred arms, and a roaring cheer emerged from the victorious forces of Eyrn in unified glory. The gateway was closed once more.

Uncertain years lay ahead, and new hulking towers of stone were built. The portals of time rested as dreaming gods: in uneasy slumber. Catastrophic evil must balance unwavering good, as utter chaos rivals tidy order. The Earth Warrior traveled onward to meet his destiny, with crimson stone and ancient steel in hand, as dreams of Earth haunted the darkness of his mind ever on.

The Darkness Among the Trees

By Max Birbaum

The sun was setting in the land of Darfar.

Shadows crept slowly across the vast cliffs of the coastline. They lingered and danced between the enormous trees and voluptuous plants, grew taller by the hour and threatened away the remnants of the fading day. A man stood among the trees watching the waves crash against the shore through a clearing in the thick undergrowth. Even the foam of the waves seemed to have lost all of its colour and structure. The man made a noise of disapproval. He wore the remnants of what might have been a uniform of some kind. His breeches seemed to have been of a clear white once but had faded into something that looked like tainted ivory. A curved knife was hidden within each of the almost knee-high boots he wore. The long rapier at his side seemed out of place in such primordial and untamed surroundings, civilization being hundreds of miles away. Yet the figure seemed lithe like a panther and emanated a natural confidence. Those tender hands with its long fingers suited those of a poet, but they could also weave death. The vulture-like nose gave the man something savage in his appearance, but there were wrinkles around his eyes too, which came from laughter. A blood-red bandana was wrapped across his forehead. He rarely went without it.

The person was Sir William Archibald, but men mostly knew him by a different name. "My, how I hate this place!" he remarked as the sun sank into the waters on the horizon.

William Archibald resumed his march through the jungle of Darfar without haste. As he had travelled far and wide in his life and known many rough places, he trusted his instincts and abilities to survive in such a hostile environment. Just when he was about to call it a day and find a place to rest, he smelled something in the air. His body went erect and finally he quickened his pace. There was smoke in the air coming from a fire, accompanied by screams and other sounds of pillage and murder. The Englishman started to run.

After a short time he reached a wide clearing filled with crude huts of timber and mud, the roofs being made from the leaves of some bizarre plant of the jungle. The village was burning and blood-smeared corpses littered the ground. The dead seemed to be natives, as the ebon skin of the mutilated and torn bodies indicated. "Blast it, there is evil afoot here!" said Archibald as he tore the rapier from its sheath. Carefully he advanced to the center of the burning village, all senses alert. Before him lay a huge pit surrounded by a circle of huts. The pit was obviously intended to be used for cooking, but now it was filled with bodies. From one of them emanated a quiet moan. Archibald hurried to the pit and found a boy of maybe twelve years. He could see with an expert gaze that the child was dying. The boy started to speak slowly in a slightly altered dialect of one of the river-tribes of West Africa. Archibald had learned it during his past negotiations with this peaceful folk to establish trade with the Empire.

"Are they gone?" whispered the boy. "The If'truul, the shadows of the grasslands! My eyes seem to fool me, I can't seem to see or hear them anymore, but they were everywhere! Are you too a devil then?"

"I won't do you any harm," said the Englishman. "Who did this to you and your people?"

"The devil priest Yarguu and his followers, the If'truul, did this! They worship the gorilla-god of Gullah and have killed my people and stolen away our beloved priestess Itlinaa. Mercy! Oh, the shadows among the trees…!"

The boy closed his eyes and died. Archibald held his hand for some time before he stood up and gazed into the dim jungle before him. "Heads will roll for this!"

"Now look at this, *camaradas!* What have we here, a white man lost in this wasteland, eh?"

William Archibald turned towards the speaker. A group of eleven men bearing torches had arrived from the near jungle. They were white like himself. Their faces, grimly lit by the fire, looked cruel and worn. Gems and golden rings glittered in pierced ears. All of them wore heavy cutlasses or scimitars.

Archibald knew exactly with whom he dealt here. "And what are Spanish buccaneers doing in this part of Darfar?" he asked.

The leader of the pack, the one who had first addressed him, gave a sneer. He was a strongly muscled brute whose long arms looked more like those of a primate. In one hairy paw he gripped an axe, in the other, a curved blade. "You shut up!" he said. "I ask questions here! You kill those tribesmen? We see fire, come through jungle." He looked around the burned village and its dead inhabitants. "No looting here, unfortunately. And you? We got attacked while being in jungle, many of me men were killed by some strange beasts, only these few remain! Maybe you sent those monsters, eh? Maybe we just kill you too, did not have much fun lately, no!"

The Englishman didn't move, yet a sly smile reached his lips. "You try that, pirate, and you meet your maker!"

The brute instantly raised his weapons, froth on his lips. "Wait, Galvez!" suddenly cried one of the buccaneers. "I think I know who this is! The rapier! The red bandana! We are dealing with William Archibald, who is also called '*Sans Pitié*!" An excited mumble went through the group of pirates. Obviously the name was known. Only their leader Galvez didn't seem to be aware that he was in danger.

"Sans Pitié?" he pronounced with some difficulties. "Ho ho, so a damned Frenchman this is?"

"I am surely not a Frenchman, rover! I am but a blade of the Empire and a torch in the hand of the house of Tudor! Yet I gained my battlename in the finest duelling courts of Malnéant and Orléans!"

Galvez started to laugh mockingly. "What are duels of a Frenchman to Sergio Galvez? But be sure I will kill you, you English mongrel, and send your carcass back to your wretched queen!"

Archibald started moving slowly towards Galvez, the hand that held his rapier folded behind his back. Suddenly, too fast for the eye to see, he broke into a small sprint. Like a snake hidden in the grass, his blade licked forth and pierced the heart of Sergio Galvez, who died in an instant and dropped to the earth. There had been no time for him to raise his weapons. His comrades drew their swords now, but hesitated.

"Ha, another heart pierced by vanity!" exclaimed Archibald loudly as he wiped his blade clean. "If you wish to insult me, fine! A duel might be adequate then, for no revilement should ever remain unpunished! But if you insult the Empire or the house of Tudor, I warn you! You shall sail the rivers of Hell then and deal with the Devil only! But well, no more of that!" He looked up. "What are Spanish rovers doing in Darfar? I don't like to repeat my questions too often, gentlemen!"

A giant negro stepped forth slowly, scimitar in hand. "I am Song. We are indeed buccaneers, paid by the Spanish crown. We were sent here to convince the local tribes to trade with the Spaniards and no one else. We might have burned a few villages while negotiating, but things like this happen, you know."

"Certainly!" Archibald wasn't smiling. "I can imagine your way of negotiating quite well. And what about the attacks in the jungle your former leader was talking about? He sounded like the sun of Darfar had taken its toll on his head!"

Song looked uneasy. "Galvez might have been a fool, yet he spoke truth here! We went through the jungle, thirty-two men, fully armed! Then the jungle came alive! Something was hiding in the trees! Something that tore, scratched and bit! We managed to fight those shadows off, yet many of us were killed in battle! We surviving few started to run, I don't know for how long. We then saw smoke drifting through the branches and came here!" Song looked at William Archibald curiously. "And what is *Sans Pitié* doing in the African jungle? I have heard tales about you, how you fought the harpies and its queen in the Pyrenees. The fire that devastated Izmir, said to have been caused by a genie and its curse. How you wanted to charge the walls of besieged Lissabon with a sabre only and five men had to hold you back! What brings you here?"

"Ask your Spanish lords, for a start! They sank my ship! I was harrying one of their galleons that fled when they sighted my banner. Unfortunately two more of their war-ships appeared on the horizon, but alas, I don't like to give up a merry chase like this so easily! I might have misjudged the coming battle a little then, I must admit. My ship was destroyed, masts and rigging were broken, and my crew sank to the bottom of this cursed ocean! I swam to the shore, the lone survivor. Blast those Spanish cowards! They are becoming quite impertinent since we sank their Armada!" He scratched his cheek absently. "And it was not a genie that burned Izmir, but an Ifrit. A spirit of fire, summoned by the local grand vizier. They always do things like this, blast grand viziers too!" Then Archibald was smiling again. "So, what now, gentlemen? As I see it, we are hereditary enemies and I have sworn to avenge those villagers and save their priestess, which was abducted by some madman! You can choose to fight me and fewer of you will return to their homes. You are also free to leave and try the jungle again on your own—yet I would not advise to do so."

"The Spanish crown doesn't mean anything to us!" rumbled Song. "We are but its ugly and ferocious dogs that do the dirty work, but we would more likely meet the gallows in Cádiz than receive the gold owed us! We are not frightened of the Spaniards. It's this jungle that haunts us!"

"Then join me!" said the Englishman. "I've got a feeling that there is a connection between the evil priest Yuurga and those things that attacked you. We rest here for the night. Keep a fire burning and post guards!"

The night remained silent and uneventful for several hours, until Song called Archibald to see him. "After I finished my watch, I sought out a hut to rest in," said Song. "Look at what I found inside."

Archibald entered the ruined hut and examined the small carving which lay on the floor. It portrayed a beast of some kind with furry hair and huge eyes, jaws agape and threatening. "Where did you find this?" he asked. "Looks like a spiritual idol or totem to me!"

Song shook his head. "It was placed here. Left by someone. Or something!" He made an obscure gesture with his right hand. "I was born on this coast. I know what this is! This is the gorilla-god of Gullah! I have only seen it once in my life, far away from here, in another land. I had thought this cult extinct in these latitudes!"

The Englishman raised his brows. "Let me assure you that the real gorilla-gods reside in Westminster. Yet I sense something here. 'Tis a thing of evil, I think. I have seen several totems and idols like this in the past, indeed, I have known ancient gods and witnessed foul magic! Yes, I can sense something. This idol is old. Very old!"

Song refused to touch the idol in any way, so Archibald picked it up and hurled it into the center of the burning campfire, where the coals were scorching hot. Black smoke engulfed the carving, then vanished. "Dawn is near," said Archibald.

The band of warriors left the burned village at the first light of day. William Archibald and Song, both skilled pathfinders, were able to follow the tracks of the mysterious attackers. Yet even an amateur would have been able to do so in most places, for the abductors had left a trail of destruction in the undergrowth. Branches had been cut and broken, plants were ripped from the earth with bad intent and left to die. There were marks of huge claws in the trunk of a palm tree. Archibald placed his hand on the trunk beside the scratchings. "Looks like a panther claimed its territory here, only it must have been a panther of twice the normal size," he mumbled, more to himself than to one of the bystanders. Then he remembered something and turned to Song. "Do you know what an If'truul is? One of the villagers mentioned them. I have never heard the name before."

Song watched the palm tree bend its shape in the light wind before he answered. "The If'truul are said to be the servants of the gorilla-god of Gullah," he said slowly. "They are the hunters of the grasslands. It is said amongst my people that long ago they were men who defied Father Leopard. This Father Leopard was worshipped by all tribes in the riverlands and they offered him water and meat. In return Father Leopard kept his brethren, the lions, from entering the jungle and scared away the lesser beasts. The gorilla-god, who felt jealousy and envy toward Father Leopard, wanted to be worshipped too; worshipped and feared. One day he approached a tribe of the lower deltas and talked them into betraying Father Leopard. The men refused to offer their sacrifices to Father Leopard any longer, and in return the gorilla-god sent them his little servants, baboons, bonobos and mandrills. The inhabitants of the village became lazy and vile. When Father Leopard visited them to eat their food and drink their water, the villagers laughed at him and told him to disappear. The monkeys screamed and yelled and laughed. Father Leopard then became very angry and let out a mighty roar, which made all monkeys immediately flee to the treetops. Since that day monkeys fear the leopard most of all other beasts. Then Father Leopard wove a mighty magic and said to the villagers: 'You have betrayed me and are therefore exiled to the grasslands, where you shall dwell forever with the lone winds and the darkness! Thy image shall resemble that of the false god you fell for and his madness shall be yours!' Since that day, no one ever saw those villagers again. Yet warriors spoke in fear of the grasslands shortly after this."

After two days of steady marching the band of rogues reached the edge of the jungle. Before them lay the grasslands that stretched across their entire field of vision. "If only we had a map!" said Song angrily. "We have to be careful that we do not lose their trail here!"

Archibald looked more confident. "If a map of this place existed, it would probably say *'Hic sunt leones'* only." He gave a short laugh. "And this time it would be true!"

Song and Archibald were able to track down the abductors' trail even through the high grass, where no other paths of any kind existed. At night there were indeed roars of lions around their provisory camp, but the great predators left them alone and did not attack. None of the buccaneers slept well that night. Even Archibald had to admit, to himself at least, that he felt a little concerned.

On the third day Archibald and the band of rogues could finally see a mountain that seemed to tower in the sea of grass surrounding them. Sharp rocks pointed to the sky like skeletal fingers, burning in bright red and copper.

"All the tracks lead there!" said the Englishman. "Let's hurry. I don't like the thought of a priestess locked up in such a place!"

Eventually they reached the foothills and started to climb under the merciless and fierce sun. A path led up the crimson mountain toward a ridge. From time to time during the ascent the rovers passed ruins of broken walls and towers that breathed antiquity. When they finally reached the summit, they found that the top of the mountain was a flat, circular plateau surrounded by crumbling walls. The buccaneers hid behind a group of rocks, for what they saw made them hold their breaths.

In the middle of the plateau was a crude altar, made from the same copper stone as the rest of the mountain, though Archibald wasn't sure if there was dried blood involved too. Bound on the altar lay a young girl, lithe and beautiful, that struggled against the ropes that held her. This could only be Itlinaa. In front of her stood a massive figure with pointed teeth and opal-like skin. He wore the skull of a wildebeest on his head and carried a huge axe made of flint. Yuurga was chanting, speaking an old and forgotten language, his voice rising and falling like the tides of the Nile in ancient Egypt. He spoke words of evil and dread. But even stranger than this man were the creatures that danced around the altar in seemingly maddened ecstasy. They indeed resembled gorillas, yet smaller and with a shaggy, grey fur. From their faces protruded tusks like those of the mighty elephant or the wild boar of the steppes. Talons glittered in the sun, yellow fangs dripped saliva and blood.

"Iftruul!" murmured Song. He grasped his scimitar tighter until his knuckles stood out white.

One of the pirates was hiding a little apart from the others, crouching behind a splintered piece of wall. The man was nervous. Riding the waves and scaring villagers was one thing. Hunting primordial beasts and rushing after black magicians was something far different.

The pirate detected movement to his left. He raised his short spear, its blade sporting cruel hooks. He saw nothing, but felt wind. Gravel dropped onto him from above. Suddenly the pirate understood. He looked up. On top of the wall it sat. It sprang. The pirate screamed.

William Archibald rushed to the luckless buccaneer as soon as he heard the scream. The Iftruul that had slain the man made a barking noise and menacingly rushed towards the Englishman. Archibald evaded his clumsy attacker with a slight shift of his hip. He gracefully whirled around his rapier and pierced the heart of the grey beast. The other

Iftruul and Yuurga were alarmed by the noise. The priest of evil shouted orders. Archibald charged toward the altar and Song and the buccaneers followed close behind. The black magician Yuurga laughed and raised his mighty axe, trying to behead the bound priestess before anyone could reach them. With a swift motion Archibald drew a dagger from one of his boots and threw it. It pierced the right hand of Yuurga, causing him to drop his axe. The dark one stared at the blade stuck in his hand. Laughing with his unhuman, deep-booming voice, he withdrew the dagger and let it fall to the ground carelessly. Then he raised his hands and started to chant. The ground shivered and from a hole in the rocks emerged a giant, yellow-scaled serpent.

"U'rasha!" yelled Song, who was fighting right next to Archibald. "*Sans Pitié,* it's U'rasha, the strangler of the river! Free the priestess! We will fight off the enemies!"

Archibald slowly backed away from the two Iftruuls he was duelling at once. "Serpents! It's always serpents that belong to the wielders of black magic! Yet keep in mind, magicians and their minions both share the same weaknesses. They both die if you cut off their heads!" Song laughed at this and swung his bloody scimitar.

Archibald evaded three attacking Iftruuls and cut down two others before he reached the altar. As fast as possible he cut the cords holding down Itlinaa. She stared at the white man in bewilderment, yet thanked him in the river-dialect.

"My staff!" she exclaimed, pointing at the ground where Archibald stood. "Hand me my staff, the totem of the coast!" The Englishman picked up the strange looking clam-adorned stick that was obviously made from driftwood found on the shores. Itlinaa started to chant and suddenly the beating of wings was heard. A croaking filled the crimson peak and from the skies dropped hundreds of seagulls and their brethren, the white albatross of the coves. They aggressively descended upon the Iftruuls and the mighty serpent U'rasha, who had entangled Song in its coils. A dozen of those birds of the sea attacked the monstrous snake with their beaks. U'rasha twisted and tried to devour its winged assailants. The distraction allowed Song to break free from the grip of his grisly foe. With a great cleave he brought down his scimitar and the head of U'rasha was severed.

"Seagull and albatross!" he mused. "My, how their sorrowful singing lured me to the seas long ago when I was a boy! And now they return when I am in need, close to death, fighting devils! May the gods bless their feathers with their breath!"

A black chasm yawned behind the altar. Beside it Archibald faced Yuurga, the priest of evil. The dark one had reclaimed his axe and stared at the Englishman with hatred and scorn.

"Your rule of terror has come to an end, devil!" said Archibald. "Normally I'd say the first strike goes out to the challenger, yet you are not what I would deem a true gentleman! So, *en garde, prêt, allez!"* Fast as lightning Archibald struck, yet Yuurga simply stopped the blade of Archibald with his hand. Though it cut him badly, he didn't seem to feel any pain. Yuurga grinned at the smaller man, who tried to wrangle free his blade. Using the skull of the wildebeest he wore as a weapon, he head butted the Englishman, knocking him to the dusty ground several paces away.

Slowly Archibald rose. Pointing at Yuurga, he said, "Chivalry is languishing in these lands, blast you! You don't hit people with wildebeest skulls! I miss my England sometimes, ah!" Then he rushed at the priest again, evading a powerful thrust of Yuurga's axe. He slid through the giant's braced legs and cut the sinew behind one knee. The black priest tumbled and Archibald was behind him in an instant, piercing his heart and ending his life. The English explorer wiped the sweat from his face and fastened the red bandana around his head. "Another heart pierced by vanity!" he said and looked at his companions. *"À raconter ses maux, souvent on les soulage!"*

Only two of the buccaneers besides Song yet lived. The others had been slain by the serpent U'rasha, the priest Yuurga, or his Iftruul-servants. Song stood still as a statue, blood-splattered, but alive. He was grinning. "A good fight, *Sans Pitié!* Tonight a crimson sun will set in the west!"

"Where will you go, friend?" asked Archibald.

Song laughed loudly. "Ha, I shall return to the coast with these two rats here. We shall build a raft and conquer a new ship for myself, this time as a captain! Merchants will shiver and the jungle will whisper my name fearfully! Ho ho, the plunder and the wine!"

"And what are your plans for the future, William Archibald, called *Sans Pitié?"* asked Itlinaa, speaking for the first time. "Today we were victorious and I am thankful for your heroic actions. Yet Yuurga was only a minion, a minion on the hunt for this talisman of mine!" She showed the men a necklace made from ivory, adorned with strange carvings. "Yuurga's masters have sent him after this. The black circle of the Drakensberg has risen again and wants me dead! They shall not have the amulet of the Elephant! They will look for me and I shall fight them, alone if needed!"

William Archibald rubbed his chin. "What you say sounds grim and dangerous, indeed! My old friend Henri Estienne, once of Paris, used to say *'Chacun pour soi et Dieu pour tous'*—every one for himself and God for us all!" He looked at the African sky above. "I don't necessarily agree with everything my friends say. Those in need I aid, whether God may be with me or not! Itlinaa and I shall travel southwards, for I have already heard of the Drakensberg and its horrors. Ah, will I ever see the white rocks of Dover again?" He kicked at the sand at his feet. "My, how I hate this place…"

Mythical Monsters

The Forgotten City of Tehm

By Ernest Cunningham Hellwell

It was a time when many deities ruled the minds of men across the lands. A time when kings and queens were the final justice for all. When the art of war was changing due to a few ingenious metallurgists who had discovered how to make weapons of steel. A time when legends were born from the doing of heroic deeds and the spilling of blood.

The land of Khosh! Mostly rugged and barren terrain except for a few oases in the desert region, the Khijar Valley in the north, and the fertile region around the plush city of Khotar in the southwest. To the north of Khotar is the salty Sea of Baal which runs along the western coast of Khosh. To the east across the desert are the steppes which in turn incline into the Himla mountain range that most consider impossible to breach. A finger of the Himla Mountains splits off of the range north of the Khijar Valley and extends west to the coast of the Sea of Baal, making for a seemingly impassable natural border between Khosh and the kingdom of Tarran to the north.

Almec Khan, the self-proclaimed ruler of Khosh, rules from his seat of power in the city of Khotar which is in the only region of the kingdom that is truly satisfactory for farming. It is the major trade hub for most of the Khoshite tribes. Khotar is also near the borders of the neighboring western kingdoms of Camoria and Arcania and it is trade with these kingdoms that has helped Almec Khan gain his wealth and warlord status.

Many different Khoshite tribes are scattered across the kingdom with most of them being nomadic. Some of the tribal chieftains do not recognize Almec as the true Khan of Khosh and oppose him and his dealings with the western kingdoms. They raid his caravans that travel between Khotar and the trading post of Rho Thule to the north in the Khijar Valley, sometimes referred to as the Khijar Pass. Even though Almec Khan is a very powerful ruler with a standing army, his troops have recently proved to be very unsuccessful at protecting the trade route to Rho Thule. Because of this situation Almec Khan conscripted the services of mercenaries from Arcania and Camoria to help protect the caravans from the Khoshite bandits. The majority of these mercenaries are veterans of the bloody war between Camoria and the land of Skythia which ended in treaty some fourteen moons past. Arcania became ally with Camoria during the war. The resulting onslaught of the Arcanian Legion across the Skythian border caused the ruler of Skythia, King Nimneth, to finally sue for peace and eventually sign the treaty that has since held.

The caravan trail from Khotar to Rho Thule is long and arduous with only the Tijem Oasis between, providing water and safe haven. The Oasis of Tijem is manned by a garrison of Almec Khan's troops of such strength that the bandit tribes do not chance attack. It is the trail that continues north to Rho Thule where the bandits prefer to strike, being at farthest point from the city of Khotar and beyond reasonable reach of the Khan's army. The trail leads northeast to the more fertile lofted mountains of the Khijar Valley with its wooded hills full of game and vineyards. On both sides of the Khijar Valley are steep rocky mountains with perfect vantage points for defense. Within these mountains are many minerals and gems that are mined by the hands of the Khijar tribe, along with slaves provided by Almec Khan. Wine, hides and precious ore are the commodities most exported by caravan to the city of Khotar from the trading post of Rho Thule. In trade the Khijar tribe receives weapons, grain and fine imports from the rich lands of Camoria and Arcania.

Even though Rho Thule is a great distance from the exotic towers of Khotar, the chieftain of the Khijar tribe, Haru Pesch, is ally with Almec Khan and recognizes him as the true ruler of Khosh. But Haru Pesch refuses to extend his reach beyond that of the Khijar Valley and Pass. A decision well made, for no other tribe has ever been successful in attempts to invade the easily defended pass. Therefore Haru Pesch maintains the safety of his people and their way of life by remaining within the fortified valley and not expanding beyond its boundaries.

* * *

A slight mist was to be felt in the air as dusk fell upon the trading post of Rho Thule. Six well-armed warriors dismounted their steeds at the entrance of the great wooden hall of Haru Pesch. Three of these men were of Almec Khan's army, wearing the traditional padded leather armor and teardrop-shaped helms of the Khotarian Guard, spears and shields in hand with *tulwar* sword at their side. Another was a tall, slender

Khoshite of typical dark complexion and black hair by the name of Tarrak. Being a man of many tongues, Tarrak was in the hire of Almec Khan as a scout and translator for the caravan's commanders from the west. His attire was much more typical of the Khoshite people with turban upon brow, loose fitting cloth shirt, pantaloons, sandaled feet and a scimitar dangling in its sheath from his waist belt.

The other two were not of the kingdom of Khosh. Both were brown-haired lighter-skinned men, obviously from the western lands. Braxus, a large hunk of a man, tall and muscular, was raised in the farmlands of Camoria. He was freshly out of the Camorian army in which he had fought bravely against the painted Skythian warriors in the war not so long past. Cape and hood partially covered his banded leather armor, animal skin loin covering, padded leggings and sandaled feet. His arms were a circular metal shield strapped upon his back and a medium length sword in scabbard at his side. Next to him was Argus, a man of medium frame and height but muscular in build and extremely fit. A retired Legionnaire of the Arcanian army and also a veteran of the Skythian war, he still wore the chest-fitted metal cuirass, *pteruges* skirt, bracers, greaves and leather boots that are the common armor and dress of an Arcanian soldier. At his side, a sheathed medium length *gladius* sword made of the finest Arcanian steel.

The Khijar tribesmen that guard the great hall of Haru Pesch eyed the men carefully as several stable boys relieved the men of their horses. Brushing the dust of the trail off his armor, Argus told Tarrak to dismiss the three Khoshite guards that accompanied them. Tarrak obeyed and excused the Khan's men in their native tongue. Argus and Braxus both traversed the steps to the doors of the great hall with Tarrak following.

"I would have words with your chieftain!" exclaimed Argus. Both guards looked at each other with uncomprehending eyes.

Tarrak moved between Argus and Braxus. "They know not the tongue of your western lands, my lord! Allow me." Tarrak spoke to the guards in their own language. Another guard was summoned to escort the three travelers into the hall to appear before the Chief of the Khijar tribes, Haru Pesch.

The great hall was lit by torches along the walls and a large fire pit burning brightly in the center of the structure. Just beyond the fire was a small elevated dais. Upon the dais was an ornately carved wooden chair in which rested the chief of the Khijar. He was a short but stout Khoshite of full graying beard. A scar across his left eye hinted that this man had seen his share of battle in years past. Cloaked in animal furs and guzzling wine from a tankard, he stood from his makeshift throne to welcome his guests.

Tarrak stepped forth and began to address the chieftain in his own language only to be interrupted by Haru Pesch in the Arcanian tongue. "Damn you, Tarrak! Spare me your slithering words. If I wish to hear the hiss of a reptile I will call upon you." Tarrak bowed to the chief and recoiled slightly as Haru began to laugh exuberantly. "It is all too rare that I have reason to speak in the tongue of the west. I am honored to receive you, my friends. I hear that you have saved my caravan from raiding bandits, a feat not easily achieved. You must be Argus?" Haru approached Argus, eyeballing the Arcanian at great length. "I have received messages from the great Khan regarding you and your friend Braxus the Bull. His trust must be well placed, seeing that you have repelled those bandit bastards from pillaging my wares."

Argus bowed and raised his gaze to the chief. "We have heard tales of the great Haru Pesch, and I am sure that in younger days thou wouldst have dispatched the outlaws with little effort thyself. They were but a small band easily fought off."

Haru busted out in laughter. "Flattering words will achieve much with me! I think we shall get on splendidly. Let us take food and drink. I'm sure you are ready for finer delights than the trail can provide."

The chieftain clapped his hands and sputtered some words in Khoshite as scantily-clad servant girls brought food and wine to a large table that looked to have been hewn from a single tree. "Please, my friends, sit. I think you will find Khijar hospitality unequaled in this life." All sat at the table except for Tarrak who stood by with his head bowed. "Stop pouting, you spineless worm!" Haru commanded. "Sit and par take, Tarrak! You see, Tarrak's father and I shared many battles in the days of old and upon his death I decided to keep an eye on the boy. Now he is a young man of great knowledge of many tongues, educated in Khotar where they teach skills of the mind instead of the blade. It is time for him to travel amongst the real men and learn the ways of the warrior class now. So you said it was a small band that was upon you?"

Braxus was stuffing his mouth with food and drink by now, leaving Argus to respond. "Yes, my lord. They were but a dozen and in my mind ill-equipped for the task. They were easily hastened off as soon as they gave witness to Braxus offing two of their comrades. We stand forty men at arms camped at the southern mouth of the pass, waiting to return the caravan that you send to Khotar. You will find that your men already took possession of the incoming caravan's wares once we arrived at the opening of the valley."

Haru rose from the table and walked behind Braxus. "I am sure that the sight of The Bull coming would hasten anyone to flee but I must compel you to caution. I fear this raid was but a test of numbers and strength. I think it best if you are most watchful upon your return to Khotar. What you take back is much more valuable than that which you brought to Rho Thule."

Braxus washed down a mouthful of meat with wine, sputtering, "The only way they will have your goods is over our rotting corpses!"

Haru put a firm hand upon the shoulder of Braxus. "Let us hope that it does not come to that, my friend. Now enough talk of business and death. Girls… dancing girls are what we need now." Haru clapped his hands again and bellowed out commands in Khoshite and several young beautiful women appeared. Thinly veiled in gossamer, they sprang to dance, the bells upon their ankles ringing and their finger cymbals clanging.

By the time Argus, Braxus and Tarrak exited the hall of Haru Pesch, the sun had sunk below the peaks of the valley, leaving Rho Thule shrouded in darkness. As the mist and fog thickened the night air, Tarrak led Argus and Braxus through the village to the inn where they were all to bed down for the night.

Upon entering the tavern portion of the inn Braxus exclaimed, "It has been a long and dry journey, my friends. Let us partake in more wine before we dream of dancing wenches."

Tarrak looked at Argus questioningly. Argus shrugged his shoulders. "I see no wrong in it. Let us sit. Tarrak, take this and bring us some libation." Argus handed Tarrak some coin as he and Braxus found a table. Soon Tarrak returned with a jug of wine and three tankards. They all began to drink and speak of the impending caravan journey of the day to come.

The tavern was filled with Khoshites; mostly men, except for a few whores that obviously worked the tavern. There was one exception that Argus took note of: a lone man sitting in a dark corner of the pub who was most obviously not from the land of Khosh. He was a large muscular white man whose long golden locks flowed onto a fur hide draped over his shoulders. The hide appeared to be that of a grey wolf. Under the hide was a black leather cuirass with a raised image of a lion's head in the center of the chest piece. Leather bracers on both forearms accentuated the rippling muscles of his arms. He wore a large leather belt about his waist with wolf's hide loin covering and leggings. His boots were of fine leather tailored in the west, most assuredly not the work of any craftsman of Khosh. The grips and hilts of two crossing swords on his back stood out from under the hide draped around his shoulders. He appeared to be a fairly young man judging by his physique, but the blond mustached and bearded face seemed to exhibit that of a hard and sullen man who had seen many adventures. He paid no attention to the two brawling Khoshite miners wrestling on the floor beside him as he stared into a tankard with fixed gaze. One of the whores tried to entice him but was swiftly sent away with a push of his hand.

"A toast!" blurted out Braxus. "To the great Almec Khan for paying us so handsomely for guarding his caravan."

As Braxus and Tarrak lifted their tankards Argus looked to them, puzzled. "What? Oh yes, to the Khan," replied Argus, clanking his mug against the others.

Braxus looked at Argus questioningly. "What has your mind frozen, brother?"

Argus, with eyes still fixed upon the blond warrior, responded in a half whisper. "You see the blond man at the corner table sitting alone?"

Braxus and Tarrak both cast their gaze towards the man. "The Aiserian?" asked Tarrak.

Argus gave Tarrak a nod of affirmation. "He came to Rho Thule some moons back. He was employed by the great Khan as a caravan guard. But he only did this for a couple of trips and since then he has stayed here at the inn. I suspect him to be a fugitive of the western kingdoms. I can think of no other reason an Aiser from the north lands would venture to a place such as this." Argus lowered his voice. "A fugitive to some but a legend to others. I swear by the goddess Mira that this man is familiar to me. Do you have knowledge of his name, Tarrak?"

"I know not the man but I have heard him referred to as the White Lion. It is told that he killed many bandits in a raid of the last caravan he guided back to Khotar. After that he returned here and has been in Rho Thule ever since. How is it that you think you know this Aiser?"

Braxus poured himself another tankard of wine. "Yes! Do tell how you come to know this White Lion."

Argus responded with his stare still fixed upon the Aiser. "I know nothing of a White Lion. I know this man by his Arcanian name of Tarsus."

Braxus almost choked on his drink in recognition of the name. "You mean Captain Tarsus? The undefeated gladiator of Xanthar?"

Argus kept his eyes firmly placed upon the man. "Yes, Captain Tarsus of General Triverius' Imperial Legion."

Tarrak cast a puzzled look towards Argus. "You know this man personally?"

Argus leaned forward towards the center of their table and looked Tarrak in the eyes. "General Triverius was one of the greatest leaders Arcania has ever known. If not for him Arcania would not be the great and rich empire it is today. He led the Arcanian army from victory to victory expanding the kingdom for Domicus, the king of Arcania. It was General Triverius that reversed the outcome of the war against Skythia and caused Nimneth, the ruler of Skythia, to come to terms with Camoria and eventually agree to the peace treaty that is now in place. Tarsus was his adopted son. I know not the man personally but served in the Imperial Legion of General Triverius under the command of Captain Tarsus, so I have laid eyes upon him many a time. I am sure I have placed him well for the lion's emblem on his leather is also familiar to me."

"You said he was the adopted son as if he is no longer claimed by this general?" asked Tarrak, who had become extremely interested in this topic.

Braxus leaned back and sighed. "By the gods, you have opened the barrel now, Tarrak. Prepare for story time. You see, our friend Argus here loves to spin a good tale whenever given the opportunity. Go ahead, let words fly, brother."

"Yes, Argus," said Tarrak. "Please, tell me of this gladiator captain."

Argus took a sip of wine and leaned back a bit. "It is said that Tarsus was but a small lad found on the battlefield during the Arcanian conquest to expand into the north lands of Aiseria. It was rumored that he had been raised by wolves until that time. General Triverius took him under his wing. One tale I have heard was that Triverius felt compelled to take him in because of the death of his wife and son during childbirth. Another tale is that he felt remorse for the many Aiser that lay dead in the north lands because of the frontier expansion, and out of pity he adopted the boy. No matter which, the boy was raised from that point on as an Arcanian, even though he was obviously an Aiser. Something that did not set well with some in the king's court I am sure.

"Triverius saw the boy educated in all ways. Art, languages, philosophy and most of all, the art of war. He grew big and strong and became very suited to the blade at an early age under the guidance of a truly great general. But the boy was headstrong and did not take well to domestic life in the capital of Xanthar. He trained with all manner of weapons and became fixated on entering the gladiatorial games in the arena at Xanthar."

"I thought only slaves fought in the arena?" interrupted Tarrak.

"Calm your horses, boy!" Braxus interjected. "Let the man spin his tale. Believe me, he will not leave out a thing." Braxus chuckled and lifted mug to mouth again.

Argus took another sip of wine. "It is not only slaves that fight as gladiators. There are many that fight for fame and fortune. And much of both will be had if you win the hearts of the crowd in the arena."

Tarrak could not hold his tongue. "So you have been to the arena and witnessed these games?"

Argus snickered slightly. "No! I have never even been to Xanthar, let alone witnessed the gladiator games. But I have heard the tales of Tarsus and his exploits in the arena. He was maybe the youngest to ever compete of free will. And he is one of few that earned all the accolades possible for a conquering gladiator. He was undefeated and well known for execution-like climaxes to most of his matches. After advancing himself as far as possible and earning every laurel attainable within the arena he then joined the Arcanian Legion under the command of his father General Triverius. It was about that time that Camoria and Arcania became allies. Domicus, king of Arcania, realized that if Camoria lost the war with Skythia that Arcania would then be next in the path of Nimneth's army. So Domicus and Thalon, the king of Camoria, signed their pacts with each other and Domicus dispatched General Triverius and his Imperial Legion to the Camorian borders to help repel Nimneth's Skythian horde. Tarsus was now a captain under his father and won many a great battle in the war at the Camorian-Skythian border. I had the honor of fighting under the same banners as that man and have watched him lay waste to soul after soul on the battlefield.

"The tide of war was turned against Nimneth and he sent emissaries to King Thalon to speak of peace negotiations. General Triverius spoke outwardly against such a peace treaty, claiming it to be a ruse to gain time for another Skythian build-up of arms and men to once again surge into the lands of Camoria. He also advocated advancing on Nimneth's army, driving them not only back into their lands but to expand the border of Camoria as punishment for invading in the first place. It appeared that General Triverius had the ear of King Thalon, for the negotiations were at a stalling point as we continued to push those painted Skythian bastards back into their dark lands.

"Then came a dreadful and fateful night. Triverius was assassinated in his own tent while he slept. His throat cut from ear to ear, so I was told. No alarm was heard until the next morning when one of the general's servants found him in a pool of his own blood. The news ran through the encampment very quickly and Tarsus was soon in his father's tent surveying the situation. He had every guard that was on watch that night brought before him one by one. And one by one he slew each and every guard. But it was the captain of the guard that he took special time with. We heard his screams for hours as Tarsus slowly vivisected the man until his screams were silenced forever."

Braxus raised his mug and slapped Tarrak on the back. "I told you, did I not? He has the tongue for the telling of tales. Go on! Tell him the rest of it, man."

Argus looked at Braxus with a slight bit of disgust. "You should not forget that we are to rise early and guard a caravan tomorrow. It might be wise if you slow your intake of wine."

Tarrak was still eager to hear the rest of the story. "Tell me what happened after that. I must know why the fates have led this man to hide in a place such as this."

Argus cast another gaze back at the blond warrior and continued his oratory. "Well, I think all of us in the Legion understood full and well why Tarsus did such a deed. It should have been impossible for anyone to murder Triverius without one of the guards knowing. The only answer possible in my mind is that the captain of the guard was bribed, maybe the rest of the guards as well. Tarsus was only exacting vengeance upon those responsible. King Thalon, though, was appalled by the brutality of his actions against the guards. When Domicus got word of the tragedy and how Tarsus retaliated against his own troops, the king demanded that Tarsus be arrested and brought back to Xanthar to face judgment himself. I think he assumed that because he was not truly of Arcanian blood that he would not be fairly treated, so when Domicus' men came to arrest him, Tarsus slew them all and disappeared into the night. All of his father's estates and lands were absorbed by Domicus. All of the accolades of the arena that Tarsus had earned were erased from memory by removing the statues of his image from the arena halls. He was proclaimed fugitive by King Domicus with a handsome reward placed upon his head if delivered to the king's court either dead or alive. And it was soon after this that King Thalon, weary of the war and bloodshed of his people, agreed to the treaty with Skythia."

Braxus filled up his tankard, once again slurring his speech. "And now it appears that we have unraveled the mystery of where Captain Tarsus ran off to."

Argus stood up and grabbed the tankard from Braxus' grasp. Braxus started for a moment. Argus looked sternly at Braxus and said, "You have had enough, my friend. Both of you, await my return."

Argus grabbed his tankard also and walked across the tavern to the blond warrior's table. He put one mug upon the table in front of the man in leather and furs. Before he could even mutter a word the Aiser sprang like a panther. Argus dropped the mug as he was wrested to one knee. Holding him from behind with a vice-like grip, the Aiser drew from his boot a half-foot long dagger that swiftly came to rest at the throat of Argus. Braxus sprang from his seat to come to his comrade's aid, but Argus quickly raised a hand gesturing to Braxus to stay back.

"You would have your purse bulging with bloody coin, eh? How about I fill your purse with your own blood? What say you?" said the Aiser.

Argus did not move a muscle. "I but wished to share a drink with a fellow Legionnaire and brother in arms," he stated calmly. "I served under thy father in the Skythian war and only sought to toast a great general whom I hold in highest esteem. I do not seek vengeance or coin, and your deeds of past are most honorable in my eyes. I implore you to let me live, my lord. I meant no ill of thee."

Tarsus slowly released Argus from his grip and sheathed the dagger back in his boot. "I can't be too careful in these times," he said as he sat back down at his table.

Argus took to his feet again. "Apologies. I did not mean to alarm thee, my lord Tarsus. I only meant to pay respects to thy father whom I hold to heart as a great man."

Tarsus slowly raised his head to gaze into the eyes of Argus. "He was a butcher like myself. Now begone before I change my mind and slit your throat."

Argus' only response was to give Arcanian salute with fist upon his own chest. He then returned to the table where Braxus and Tarrak were showing relief that Argus was still among the living. "Let us call this a night and look to the task of the next day's light." Argus' words were a bit shaky.

As the other two rose from the table Braxus exclaimed, "Was that my mug or yours that spilled? And is that mine or yours still left in front of that barbarian?" Argus glared at Braxus, who smirked back. They made their way out of the tavern area and up the stairs to the sleeping quarters. "The next time you decide to commit suicide by pissing off an Aiser, let me know in advance, would you? Oh, and by the by, you have a small cut on your throat." Braxus chuckled as Argus slapped him on the back of the head.

"Mind yourself, my friend. That is a true legend who is torn between worlds. Can you not feel the pain that is smoldering in his soul?"

Braxus chuckled again. "All I could see was the end of Argus until your sweet tongue saved your ass." Tarrak could not hold back the laughter at that statement. Even Argus began to laugh slightly as they sought out their quarters.

* * *

The next morning came with Argus, Braxus, Tarrak, and the three Khotarian soldiers leaving Rho Thule with the camel and mule caravan. Several merchant traders were to be found among the travelers along with servants of both sexes and carts of ore, hides, and many jugs of wine. One cart held a special cargo chest of fine gems that would be polished and sold at extremely high cost once it made its way to Khotar. Such a treasure trove would be of great interest to the Khoshite bandits. They would have much to trade with other tribes and also the Tarranian pirates who roam the Sea of Baal if they could seize it.

At the entrance of the Khijar Pass they rendezvoused with the Khotarian Guard that was left encamped there, which consisted of twenty-five foot soldiers and fifteen mounted cavalry. Another day passed and they broke camp and began the long journey on the caravan trail to the Oasis of Tijem, the halfway point to Khotar. For three more days the caravan traveled with the guard keeping watchful eye for raiding bandits, but none were to be found. The days had been brutally hot and windy and the nights very cool with the chill of the desert night air.

This day the sun was unimpeded by clouds, causing the temperature to soar and the sweat to pour. The sun was beginning to decline in the west and the heat was taking its toll on one and all traveling with the caravan. Water was always under ration while traveling the caravan trail, for the only constantly flowing watershed to be found between Rho Thule and Khotar was the Oasis of Tijem. Braxus continually rode up and down the ranks of the caravan upon his white and black Paint, commanding the troops not to drag their feet and keep alert. This journey was proving more difficult than the trek to Rho Thule. The winds of the desert were becoming unforgiving and the dry heat was draining the energy from man and animal.

Braxus rode to the front of the column, joining Argus, who rode a brilliant white Arcanian stallion. With his armor gleaming in the sun Argus was a majestic sight compared to the other soldiers within his command. Braxus reined in his steed and joined pace with Argus, mumbling complaints. "By Helos and his bed of bones! These men of the Khan's are mere images of soldiers. They know nothing of forced march. Unfortunately I think we shall have to make camp soon before all drop from heat and exhaustion."

Argus turned in his saddle and looked back at the caravan column. "I suppose you are right, Braxus. I was hoping to make more distance this day, though. We are still maybe three days out from Tijem."

Suddenly Braxus nudged Argus with his forearm. "Argus, look! It is Tarrak. He seems to be in a mighty hurry." Argus swung back around in his saddle to see Tarrak riding his brown steed at a dead run from further up the trail where he had scouted ahead. Argus raised his hand in gesture for the caravan to stop. Tarrak came speeding up to Braxus and Argus, reining in his frothing horse in a cloud of dust. Sweating and panting, Tarrak excitedly reported, "My lords, bandits are coming from the south up the trail as we speak."

Braxus grabbed the arm of the young Khoshite with his enormous hand, shaking him slightly. "Settle your nerves, boy, and tell us what you have seen."

Argus handed the lad his leather water pouch and Tarrak began to talk after taking a large drink. "I saw twenty, maybe thirty, well-armed bandits on horse heading this way. They wear the red sashes of Saris Borga's tribe, the most ruthless bandit tribe in all of Khosh. I fear we are doomed."

Just as Tarrak said those words Braxus pointed up the trail to the southern horizon. From out of a rising cloud of dust the bandits could be seen riding toward them.

Argus began barking orders. "Braxus, you know what to do. Form the carts into a circle of defense. Tarrak, see to it that the people are gathered within the circle. Tell the Khan's soldiers to form ranks and prepare for engagement. Assemble the cavalry here to me."

Braxus had just turned his mount to the rear and spurred it on when out of the earth itself, on both sides of the caravan, sprang dark-skinned Khoshite bandits wielding knives and scimitars. The bandits rose from out of holes that had been dug in the ground. They had covered themselves and lay in wait for the appropriate moment to strike. Panic immediately struck most of the people of the caravan. Women screamed and ran to and fro as a dozen of Saris Borga's men poured out of their holes, attacking any human that moved. They were all scantily-clad, with red sashes, loin cloths and sandals only. They pounced upon the Khotarian soldiers with the fury of wild animals, blades slashing through padded armor into flesh and bone.

Argus watched with amazement as the bandits sprung from their hiding places. He drew steel while Braxus trampled one bandit under his horse's hooves. The Bull caved in the head of another with his sword, blood and brains spewing from the wound.

Argus wheeled his horse around and sped down the opposite side of the caravan from Braxus, chopping and cleaving the enemy as he rode. His intent was to assemble the cavalry to turn and intercept the oncoming horsemen from the trail to the south, but his troops were scattered the length of the caravan already and engaged in combat with the rogues that had caught them off guard. He continued to ride towards the rear of the column, hacking down bandits as he came upon them, but something caught his attention to the west. After sending an opponent to the ground with the kick of his boot he took a brief moment to look into the sinking sun. Looking directly into the sun made it difficult to focus but he soon realized another group of horsemen was approaching the caravan. They appeared to be a large contingent. Argus turned back just in time to see the man he had put to the ground rise again. Without hesitation Argus plunged the point of his *gladius* into the man's face, ending his life instantly.

Argus surveyed the situation quickly. It appeared that, even though faced with heavy losses, the Khan's soldiers were faring well against the attackers and few bandits were left on their feet. Braxus rounded the end of the caravan and sped his horse towards Argus, still hacking at the enemy as he yelled out, "There are more, Argus! We are flanked from the rear."

Argus yelled back at him, "And still more to the west… look."

Braxus looked to the west and saw the oncoming horsemen. "No time to circle the carts," he said. "We must brace for the attack now."

"Tarrak!" screamed Argus. The young lad raised his head out from hiding in one of the carts. In a commanding voice Argus said, "Tell our horsemen to dismount and take positions on both flanks of the caravan to the north and south. And tell these foot soldiers to gather to me. Do it now, Tarrak!"

Argus rode to half length of the caravan column, swinging his sword in the air and yelling out, "To me, men! To me! There is no way out of this but to kill or die!" Most likely none of the Khoshite guards even understood him. "Brace yourselves, lads, and make them pay for their arrogance with their blood." Tarrak repeated commands in the native tongue from within the cart and many of the infantry soldiers came to Argus' side, preparing to accept the onslaught of the horsemen headed directly for them.

The sound of the horses' hooves became audible to Argus as they approached even closer. Then the cries of agony and death resounded from the front of the caravan. Argus turned quickly to see that the horsemen from the south had just reached the front of the caravan. Braxus was there, fighting alongside some of the Khan's cavalry against more than thirty bandits on horseback who were equipped with long spears and scimitars. But there was nothing Argus could do to help them, for the horsemen to the west were almost upon them as well. He only had enough time to yell out one last command. "Send them all to the underworld!" Then the oncoming horsemen collided with the line of the Khotarian soldiers. The sound of metal clashing on metal was deafening. Excruciating cries of pain and agony rang out from the wounded and the ground was rapidly becoming stained with a river of crimson up and down the span of the caravan.

The Khan's men were dropping at an exponential rate. Both defensive lines at the head of the caravan and on the west side were breached. Now the bandits were riding and rampaging through the ranks of the whole of the caravan. It was now nothing more than an open brawl with the numbers of the caravan defenders dwindling rapidly. Braxus had been thrown from his horse during the assault on the front of the column but he managed to dispatch his assailant. He made his way back towards the center of the caravan where Argus was doing his best to stand his ground against fearful odds. And the odds were now becoming even worse due to another group of mounted bandits from the north entering the fray.

Argus, still mounted upon his steed, was locked in combat with two bandit riders, one on each side of him. He swung his sword furiously, slashing across the chest of one bandit and dismounting him. He came back across with his swing too slow, leaving himself open. His other opponent's scimitar found its mark across his chest. Luckily the blade did not cut its way through his Arcanian cuirass, merely denting the armor. But the blow was sufficient enough to launch him from his saddle and onto the ground. Stunned, Argus rose as quickly as he could, but as he looked up he saw the mounted bandit with scimitar raised above him preparing to deliver a fatal blow. Argus began to raise his sword to block the blow but he knew that his effort was going to be too late. And then a streak of black horse flesh swept between Argus and the mounted bandit. Argus was sent reeling backwards, but he managed to stay on his feet. As quickly as the blur of black came it was gone. Remaining in front of him was the bandit slumped on his horse, his head dangling from his shoulders by a thread of bloody flesh.

Argus regained his composure and was astonished to see the fugitive Tarsus running his black stallion headlong into another bandit's horse, both of his *gladii* swords singing their death song as one red sash after another fell lifeless to the ground. Tarsus wheeled his horse back around, dispatching another bandit with a mighty swing. He spurred his horse on and returned to Argus, yelling at him, "Get mounted, man! This battle is lost and your only hope is to survive this slaughter is escape to the east."

Argus looked upon him with confusion. He tried to stammer out words of concern for the caravan, but was interrupted quickly by Tarsus again. "No time to think, man! You are outmatched. Do as I say or die here." Tarsus spurred his horse on again and met another bandit rider, chopping the rogue's spear in twain with a backhand stroke of the sword in his left hand and following it with a mighty forward stroke of the sword in his right. The blade cut clean through the bandit's spear arm and a spray of red ichor splashed upon Tarsus and his horse. The arm flew to the ground, still twitching and clutching what was left of the spear. The bandit let loose a scream of agony and fell from his mount, bleeding out rapidly.

Argus ran and mounted his steed just as another bandit came riding towards him at full gallop. By now Argus had regained his senses and his composure. He reared his stallion up with its hooves striking at the oncoming horse and rider. The bandit's horse winced at the sight of the attacking war horse, giving Argus the advantage of position. As the magnificent white horse came slamming its hooves down to the earth Argus struck, his sword finding the lower jaw of his assailant. A shrill gurgling sound emitted from the man as blood and teeth flew from his face.

Argus looked for Braxus. He was standing on one of the carts slashing away at riders as they sped by. "Braxus! With me!" screamed Argus as he grabbed the horse's tethers from the bandit he had just cleaved. He jerked on the reins and spurred his own horse on. As they took off towards Braxus the bandit fell from the saddle and lay limp on the sand, his smashed jaw hanging from his face. Argus rode by the cart and Braxus jumped onto the bandit's horse. They both turned and rode towards Tarsus, who was still dealing crimson death to more of Saris Borga's men.

Tarsus turned to see Braxus and Argus riding up to him. He yelled at them, "If you wish to live, follow me." He kicked the black stallion hard. It sprang into action and launched into a full run eastward towards the steppes and the Himla Mountains.

"I wish to live!" cried Tarrak, who jumped out of the cart and ran up to Braxus and Argus as they rode by. Braxus reached down and grabbed up the Khoshite scout and flung him up and onto the back of his horse.

Argus looked back over his shoulder toward the caravan as they raced away on their mounts. There were only a few of Almee Khan's men left alive that he could see and it appeared as though they were being struck down at that very moment. Bandits tore through the carts and rounded up the scattered camels and mules. Slaves were taken captive and he could see some of the female servants being ravaged by several of the red sash ruffians. His heart sank as he realized he had failed his mission. He had lost his command, and as far as he was concerned, his honor also. Just before he turned forward he noticed an especially tall and muscular Khoshite bandit, with red turban upon head, standing on one of the carts staring directly at him and his retreating companions.

* * *

Night was beginning to fall as the stars crept into view in the darkening desert sky. Not a word had been spoken between any of the four while they rode as fast as their mounts could be spurred to. Tarsus finally stopped his black steed and wheeled about, looking for any signs of pursuit. Argus and Braxus slowed their horses to a halt with Tarrak still clutching onto Braxus from behind. The horses were frothing from the run but the heat of the day was starting to subside. Tarsus climbed down from his saddle and knelt in the sand. Braxus helped Tarrak down from the back of their mount. "We must let this poor excuse for a horse rest. By the gods, those bastards skewered mine back there."

Argus dismounted as well and approached Tarsus "My lord Tarsus, we… I… owe…"

Before another word could spring from the lips of the Arcanian, Tarsus raised his hand in a gesture of silence. "Listen." he whispered. They all remained silent for several moments. "I had a suspicion but now I am sure. We are being followed."

Argus strained to look into the desert night. "How can you tell? I can't see anything out there."

"I can hear their horses. It would serve you well to take inventory of what food and water you have. We will need to ration what there is, I am certain." Tarsus stood up and grabbed one of three water pouches hanging from the horn of his saddle. He threw the pouch to Tarrak. "Here, boy, see to it that the horses get equal shares of half of that."

Tarrak looked at Argus as if to ask if he should obey. Argus nodded, saying, "Do what he says, Tarrak."

The towering Camorian known as Braxus the Bull came to the side of Argus and Tarsus. "What would they have of us? They already have the caravan. What else is there?"

Tarsus looked at the brute of a man and spoke with a dark husky voice. "They want you. You would both make fine trophies for the likes of Saris Borga. Every westerner that he kills or captures grows his fame and charisma amongst the tribes. Plus, our horses and western steel are much more desirable than what is normally found in Khosh. Or maybe they just want that horse of yours back."

Braxus chuckled a bit. "The wonders of the gods never stop. A northman with a sense of humor."

Braxus began to introduce himself to Tarsus but the Aiser interrupted him mid-sentence. "I know who you are. Little is left to secret within a place like Rho Thule."

"How is it that you came to our aid, my lord?" asked Argus. "And maybe even of more interest to me—why?"

Tarsus turned to the east and began to lead his horse while calmly answering. "You called me a brother in arms. I had forgotten that I had any. Now we must push on, for the bandits of the Red Brotherhood will not rest till they overtake us. They are not far behind."

"How many do you figure are tracking us?" asked Braxus.

Tarsus quickened his pace a bit. "If I know Saris he will send no less than a dozen of his best men. And if he feels you a notable prize he may even come after you himself. If that is the case, then we can expect many more on our heels. We will proceed on foot for a time until the animals have rested enough to ride again."

Across the desert sands Tarsus and his newly acquired comrades pressed on through the night, only stopping briefly to rest and share what little water they had with their mounts. Tarsus was better provisioned than the rest with water and food. Tarrak had mere bread scraps hidden away in his shirt but no water. Braxus had some form of hardtack and jerky in a sack found on the bandit's horse along with one water pouch. Argus had no provisions aside from a lone water pouch that by now was half empty. His bedroll and saddlebag had been lost during the battle at the caravan. Tarsus repeated his warnings to preserve their water as much as possible. Just before dawn Tarsus stopped and shared about half of the oats that he had with all three horses. Every so often he would stop to listen and peer silently into the chilled night behind them.

As the sun rose above the mountain peaks far to the east, the light of a new day lit up the desert sand with sparkles and gleams. Tarsus stood straight legged in his stirrups, raising himself up as high as he could. He peered out across the barren terrain, eying a faint cloud of dust behind them to the west. Tarsus beckoned to the others, who were all looking very worn and tattered from the flight. "They will be upon us by midday if we do not make haste." He spurred his horse and as he passed the others he gave each of their steeds a slap on the hindquarters.

"Why not stand and fight?" Braxus bellowed.

"I am sure it will come to that, but it shall be in the place of our choice." Tarsus yelled back. "If we can stay ahead of them long enough to make it to the rocky steppes, then we may find higher ground that we can defend."

Onward they rode, the horses weakening with the rising temperature as the morning passed on. White foam formed on the steeds as they struggled for good footing in the sand and baked broken ground. A gust from the northeast began to blow. Tarsus halted his black stallion, looking back to the west and then to the north. The bandits were closing fast. Now the riders themselves were visible. Tarsus gave another look back and forth between the approaching riders and the northeast.

"I make them twenty or more. Too many to face on open ground. We will never make the steppes before they overtake us. We have only one chance, lads. There seems to be a storm brewing there." He pointed towards the northeast. Swirling clouds of sand could be seen in the distance.

Argus questioned the Aiser. "You plan to lose them in the wake of the storm?"

Tarsus spurred his horse, saying, "If not, then blind them to our blades." He directed his stallion toward the ever-growing storm as Argus and Braxus looked at each other.

"Will we not also be blinded to theirs?" Braxus asked sarcastically.

They both kicked their mounts after Tarsus. Tarrak hung onto Braxus, screaming, "The gods have forsaken us. If the Red Brotherhood does not kill us, the wrath of the sands shall."

The velocity of the wind increased and blew sand everywhere, making visibility somewhat poor. But as Tarsus glanced back to their rear he could see the bandits were nearly upon them. The gusts became even stronger and a whirlwind of sand blew against them, obscuring anything at a distance. It was difficult to even see each other. The sand began to sear into their faces and exposed flesh. They pushed on as the sandstorm gained intensity, doing the best they could to guard their faces from the blowing sands that felt like needles.

They could no longer run the horses in the gale and vision was limited now to only the length of a pull cart. The black stallion of Tarsus began to pull to the right again and again. The bandit horse that Braxus and Tarrak rode stumbled upon a seemingly rocky ledge protruding out of the ground. Tarrak fell off the horse, landing on his back with a yelp. Braxus stayed the mount and regained control.

Tarrak struggled to his feet. He looked about him and then announced to the others, "It is a wall… I think… or what remains of one."

They all gathered together for a moment while Tarrak hopped back upon the horse behind Braxus. The wind was nearly deafening at this point. Tarsus yelled to the others, "My horse believes there is water in this direction. Stay close to me."

Tarsus let his steed guide him as they slowly entered what seemed to be ruins of walls and buildings. Perhaps they were ancient remnants of a settlement or village of some sort. As they continued further along they happened upon more and more broken walls made from large limestone blocks. Soon it became obvious that this had not been a mere village but a somewhat large city. There seemed to be no structures with roofs left, however. Tarsus halted the group when he found a wall that was large enough and well positioned to protect them from the storm. It stood about twice a man's height. They hunkered down and clung close to the wall, trying their best to keep the horses protected from the raging sands blowing all about them.

Tarsus handed the reins of his horse to Tarrak. "Guard him well, boy." Tarsus drew in close to them all, speaking in a hushed and husky voice. "Speak not. I believe the bastards are still at our heels. Draw blade and prepare to deliver." Tarsus then disappeared into the blowing sands as silently as a cat.

All three heeded his words and drew their swords. Argus and Braxus, both giving control of their horses to Tarrak, took up positions at each end of the wall that protected them from the storm. Tarrak stayed snug behind the wall holding the tethers to the horses, shaking with fear. Still it was impossible to see more than a few feet in any direction as the wind and sand blew with even greater might. The wind howled furiously, but Braxus thought he caught ear of horses on the opposite side of the wall. His shield had been lost in the caravan raid, but he still had his weapons to defend himself with. He gripped his medium length sword in his right hand and a large hunting knife in his left. He poised himself ready to strike anyone coming around the corner of the wall.

The sudden sounds of a horse braying and the crashing of stone alarmed Braxus. He felt the blocks of the wall beside him heave as two large sections of stone tumbled down beside him. To his surprise he saw a brown horse sprawling on the ground. Then a dark skinned Khoshite fell beside it with a gaping wound from shoulder to chest. The horse scrambled to its feet and ran out into the blowing sands. Braxus took a brief look at the bandit to make sure he was dead and noticed the red sash wrapped around his waist. "That has to be the gladiator," Braxus thought to himself. He sprang around the corner of the wall, still being pummeled by the wind and sand, with one thought in mind. Tarsus was on foot, so if it rides a horse, kill it. He saw a faint outline in the blowing sand and raced headlong toward it. As he closed in he could tell it was a horse with rider. With a mighty leap he crashed into the rider and embedded his sword into the man's chest. The horse bucked and ran as the two combatants fell to the ground, the Khoshite already dead. Braxus ripped his sword out of the man's chest and tried to gather his sense of direction. He headed back towards where he thought the wall was. He could hear horses but with the howl of the storm he was not exactly sure from which direction.

Two mounted bandits seemed to manifest out of the sand to Braxus' left. They headed straight for him, both riders brandishing throwing spears. As they prepared to throw, a figure on foot slid in front of the second rider's horse with the speed of a striking panther, slashing at its legs with two Arcanian *gladii* swords. The horse's legs buckled when struck, and the rider toppled from the saddle as the mare slammed face first into the ground. Tarsus was upon the dismounted bandit instantly, delivering a blow with each sword that left the head crushed and faceless.

The other bandit managed to loose his spear at Braxus, who tried to dodge it without success. It penetrated into his left side, breaking ribs, but still the man-giant unleashed hell upon the bandit, slashing at his leg as he rode past. Braxus' sword found flesh on both horse and man. Entrails gushed out of the horse's side and blood sprang from the deep cut in his assailant's leg. Both rider and horse toppled to the ground in a pool of blood. Braxus pulled the spear out of his side with a groan of agony. He hurled it into the chest of the wounded thief, killing him instantly.

Braxus spat at the dead bandit and then fell to one knee, holding tightly onto his punctured leather armor. Unfortunately the spear tip had not hit any of the metal banding on his leather armor, but had pierced deep into his side. He was losing blood rapidly. Tarsus came to his aid, helping him to his feet. He half-dragged Braxus back to the wall where Tarrak and Argus still were. When they arrived they found Argus standing over another bandit with red sash lying dead on the sand, blood streaming out of the wound from his partially severed neck. The great white stallion of Argus was on the ground, mortally wounded with spear in neck. None of the other horses were in sight. Tarrak clutched at the wall in absolute fear with his scimitar on the ground before him.

Argus started as he saw Braxus and Tarsus approaching. "Braxus, you're hurt?" inquired Argus.

"I can still fight," Braxus barked back.

Tarsus leaned the wounded Camorian against the wall and immediately went over to Tarrak and lifted him to his feet by his shirt. "You lost my horse? I should kill you right now! But I may need to eat you later, since you lost all our food and water also."

Tarrak answered in terrified voice, "It is this place. It is haunted by the souls of the dead. I can feel them. I have heard of this place. I know it to be evil. We must leave here at once, my lord."

Tarsus threw the boy to the ground. "You spineless sack of wine. There is no such thing as ghosts or even gods. You are just a coward, believing in tales old women tell to scare children." Tarsus looked to Argus. "We must find refuge from this storm. I am fairly certain there are more of Saris Borga's men still here sniffing for our blood. Let us be-gone and try to find more suitable cover."

Tarrak and Argus helped Braxus with each of his arms over their shoulders. Tarsus led the way through the wind-choked ruins of what must have been streets and marketplaces in some distant past. It seemed everywhere they turned they ran into ruins of a great city that had once thrived forgotten ages ago. The storm still raged on and Braxus was nearing unconsciousness.

Tarsus cried out to the others. "Come. I think we might have something here." They followed and to their astonishment they found themselves standing on a stairway of stone. The stairway lead up to a building, a temple, possibly, of architectural design that was not familiar to them. It appeared that the roof was intact, promising protection from the elements. They ascended the stairs and entered the large archway into the structure.

A sigh of relief could be heard from all as they entered into the dark of the building, leaving the storm behind. Braxus was still clinging to life and consciousness though he was now covered in his own blood. Argus did the best he could to tend his wound and stop the bleeding.

Tarsus peered into the darkness of the structure they had entered. He found what seemed to be a rotten piece of furniture that was an ottoman or divan, at one time, and scavenged the wood from it. He produced flint and cloth from a small pouch fastened to his belt, and proceeded to ignite a fire some distance from the entrance.

While Tarsus made torches out of the furniture, Argus removed Braxus' banded leather armor and bloodied shirt. He used the shirt to make a bandage for his friend.

Tarsus handed Argus a crudely made lit torch, keeping another for himself. "We need to venture further into this place," he said. "So as not to be discovered by the remainder of the bandits."

As Tarsus extinguished the fire he had started, Tarrak began to panic. "No, my lords, we must not go further into this place! It would be the doom of us all and our souls will be trapped in the netherworld for the ancient ones to feast on." Tarrak was overwrought and shaking with fear. "I would rather face the storm than the perils of this forsaken place."

Argus walked over to Tarrak and smacked him hard across the face with the back of his gauntleted hand. "Boy! I am of strong respect for your overseer Haru Pesch, but you try my patience with such cowardly actions and talk. Now what in Mira's name do you speak of? Answer! Lest I hush your rantings with my steel."

"Aye, my lord, I am a coward when it comes to the ways of sorcery and magik. I am guilty of that."

Braxus gurgled a laugh. "You are not worth the piss of a dog, Tarrak. You have not raised blade once against our attackers. You cower in carts or in corners, hiding like a rabbit."

Argus looked at Braxus. "You... save your breath." Argus turned back to Tarrak. "You! Tell of what you speak now."

Tarrak looked to Argus in stark fear. "I cannot, my lord. To even speak of it inside these walls could awaken an evil that would devour us all."

Tarsus shook his head in utter amazement. "Just off the mutt before we are found out. Bring the body with us. We will need food eventually."

Argus drew his sword and placed the point against Tarrak's chest. "That is a very tempting idea that I will surely entertain if words do not spill from his mouth."

"Very well, very well," hurried Tarrak. "But let it be known that I..." Before he could make another sound Argus pushed the tip of his sword harder against the scout's chest. "All right, all right... I will tell."

Argus backed the steel away from Tarrak's chest and the lad began to talk. “In the times of the Old Ones when Cthul and Yog ruled the dark lands that are now known as Skythia, there was an ancient race of people that lived here when this place was full of fertility and not the barren desert that it is today. They built a great city called Tehm where they ruled with fair hand and guarded a great red gem of power. It is said to glow and beat like a heart and whoever possesses it can rule the world with its powerful magik. It was housed in a temple such as this, as the story goes, and guarded by dragons that would devour anyone who would dare try and take the jewel. My friends, I am most worried that we may have stumbled onto the forgotten city of Tehm. We are in grave peril of our souls being trapped in the underworld while dragons gnaw upon our bones. So you see, my lords, we must not stay here.”

Braxus snickered again, despite the pain. “The boy tells a story almost as well as you do, Argus.”

“We must venture forth into the heart of this place now or run the risk of discovery,” Tarsus said. “Either kill the mutt or bring him, but we must do it now.”

Argus pushed his blade against the chest of Tarrak again. “Either come with us and help Braxus or I kill you here where you stand. Your choice, for I cannot let you leave for fear of giving up our position to those marauders.” Tarrak shook his head in understanding as he helped Braxus to his feet. “Tarrak, did I mention you are not worth the piss of a dog?” said the Bull of Camoria.

With makeshift torches burning in hand, Tarsus and Argus led the way through the dark deeper into the bowels of the structure. After moving through several different chambers they happened upon a large room with a ceiling so high that even the flickering torchlight would not illuminate it completely. Large chiseled stone pillars stood at intervals in support of the ceiling.

Tarsus reconnoitered the area and instructed Tarrak to ease Braxus onto the floor next to what appeared to be some sort of ornately carved altar. It appeared to be marble, but it was difficult to tell in the dim torchlight. It was obviously ages old, but still the stone under the dust remained smooth and polished to the touch. As Tarsus brushed away decades of dust from the side of the altar, carved images were revealed. They marveled at artistic engravings of tall naked warriors with tridents riding in chariots and scenes depicting a king and queen sitting upon thrones with tall ornate headpieces and flowing robes.

Argus once again tended to Braxus. The wound had finally stopped bleeding. Tarsus found a dusty ragged tapestry and more rotted wood chairs and converted them into a campfire, illuminating the large room much more. It was a great hall with mammoth pillars. Just beyond the altar, up a small set of stairs, were two large wooden chairs that resembled the ones from the engraved fresco on the altar. Braxus fell to slumber as Argus and Tarrak sat and leaned back against the altar, exhausted and spent.

Tarsus still seemed alert and kept a watchful ear and eye out as he positioned himself against one of the pillars. It appeared there was only one main entrance into the hall. He looked to the others. "We will at least be able to see or hear anyone approaching from here," he said softly. "Rest and I will take the first watch." Argus and Tarrak both fell into deep dreamless sleep almost immediately, feeling secure that Tarsus would arouse them were danger to approach.

A quarter of the day passed before Argus was awakened by Tarsus' hand covering his mouth. The hand was slowly removed as Tarsus whispered to him, "There is another passage behind the thrones. I have heard noises from within." Argus slowly rose from the floor. "I have also felt the dampness of water and keened to its scent from within this passage as well. We must have water or we shall surely perish. I think we should investigate."

Argus looked to Tarrak and Braxus who were still slumbering on the floor. "I will go with you my lord," whispered Argus.

"We all must go," said Tarsus with a stern look on his face. "Tarrak would bolt in a moment left here with Braxus."

Just then the voice of Braxus could be heard in hushed tone. "I will have no part of laying here while there is fun to be had. And Tarsus is right, that spineless snake would run at first chance." Braxus extended his hand to Argus as the Arcanian helped him grunting to his feet.

"Are you fit enough to fight, man?" asked Tarsus.

"If the noises you heard are those maggots with the red scarfs then you will have need of all our blades," replied Braxus, wincing.

Tarsus gave the man a look of respect. "You would do well in the arena, Argus! Wake your mutt up. Keep him quiet, even if you must silence him forever."

Argus nodded in affirmation as he clasped his gauntleted hand over Tarrak's mouth, waking him with a nudge. "Make a sound and I will send you to the afterlife. Now go before me, quietly."

Tarsus led the way with torch in one hand and sword in the other, his second sword sheathed upon his back. The four approached a large moldy and dusty tapestry hanging upon the wall. Tarsus drew back the tapestry from one corner to reveal a passage leading into darkness. The corridor of polished stone was only wide enough for two men side by side. The torchlight flickered down the empty passage as Tarsus stopped suddenly, listening intently. A scratching noise could be faintly heard from further down the hallway. Tarsus slowly and silently crept on with the others close behind. Stealthily the four made their way to a doorway at the end of the corridor. Torchlight danced across the floor and walls of a small antechamber. The room was completely empty except for another doorway on the opposite side. Tarsus crossed the room cautiously, the others a few steps behind.

As the group crossed the threshold of the archway, the torches illuminated a balcony-like landing with stairs leading down to another level of a large room. As they approached the stairs Argus spotted two braziers supported by iron stands on each side. They still contained oil, so he extended his torch into the one closest and it began to blaze brightly. Tarsus lit the other and the chamber became fairly well lit.

They stood atop the stairs looking down onto the bottom level. "By the stars, what treasure is this?" proclaimed Braxus.

They all stood frozen in amazement as they gazed upon a stone pedestal in a pool of water in the center of the lower level. Upon the pedestal was a small stand made of iron rods which bent and entwined to form a holder for a red palm-sized jewel that was covered in dust and cobwebs. The four descended the steps, with Argus providing the encouragement Tarrak needed in the form of a forceful push. They found more braziers around the lower level of the chamber. They lit them, causing eerie shadows to dance upon the walls.

Tarsus bent down to the pool of water and tasted a bit from his hand. "It is fresh water. There must be a spring or well below." After taking several gulps from his palm, he splashed water on his head and face and then shook his golden mane. All three of the others quickly joined Tarsus at the pool, partaking of the refreshing water.

Then the scratching noise was heard again and all four men started and held their positions, watching and listening intently. The noise appeared to be coming from back up the stairs by the wall next to the archway. Argus approached the stairs slowly with Tarrak behind him.

Tarrak looked up at the wall. It was covered in artistic inscriptions, though they were not very discernible due to the amount of dust. He brushed the dust away, exposing a giant fresco of men being eaten by large lizard-like creatures. "Aieee!" Tarrak cried out. "By all that is holy, this is the city of Tehm, and that is the gem I told you of! We must escape now before the dragons come, just like it is pictured. For the sake of our souls, do not touch that gem!"

Argus started towards Tarrak. "You fool! Shut your mouth!" He reached for Tarrak, but the Khoshite scout was spooked beyond rationality at this point. He bolted up the stairs and out the archway before Argus could even react.

Argus pursued, but stopped abruptly upon hearing a blood curdling scream. The body of the young scout fell back through the archway and landed on the floor with a thud, blood spurting up from a gaping wound in his chest. Right behind the body of Tarrak came a tall Khoshite, bloody scimitar in hand, lumbering through the doorway. His head was wrapped in a red turban and a red sash adorned his waist. Argus recognized the man as the tall Koshite who had stood in the cart during the ambush and watched him flee as the bandits ransacked the caravan. Several more bandits came flooding through the archway.

Obviously the leader of this band of rogues, the tall bandit with the turban leaped off the landing while slashing with his scimitar at Argus. The Khoshite landed as gracefully as a cat upon the floor of the lower level. He had missed Argus by a hair's breadth due to the Arcanian ducking under his swing. Braxus ran towards the Khoshite leader, swinging his sword furiously. The rogue parried the move and kicked out at Braxus' chest, sending him to the floor.

Suddenly the room shook and dust billowed off of the wall by the stairs as whirling and grating sounds echoed through the chamber. The wall began to rise as noises of metal upon metal could be heard from behind it. Tarsus, moving with the speed and agility of a mountain panther, unleashed both of his *gladii* blades upon the bandit leader. Both warriors began trading blows, each one met by the other's steel. Argus was defending himself from the other bandits as the wall rose even higher. From out of the opening hurried a huge scaly-skinned beast, bright red and yellow stripes running down its back. The monstrous creature measured the length of two or more men and its girth was enormous. A red forked tongue slithered out and back into its mouth. Without delay the thing lunged towards the bandits on the landing at the top of the stairs. Two of the bandits jumped down to the lower level while the others, staying on the top landing, tried to fight the beast with scimitars and spears. The giant lizard snapped its powerful jaws around one of the Khoshite warriors, ripping flesh and breaking bone with ease. Blood spewed from the man's wounds and drenched the floor of the balcony. The monster chomped its massive jaws twice and then flung the lifeless and mauled body of the Khoshite across the floor while its tail swept the feet out from under another.

Argus, seeing Tarsus embroiled in battle with the red sash leader, leaped off the stairs towards the two bandits who jumped from the balcony. With both hands gripping his sword hilt, Argus came crashing down on the first Khoshite, knocking him to the ground. With great agility Argus rolled towards the other rogue. A lightning quick swing opened the man's abdomen, his bowels spewing to the ground. Argus then wheeled about as the other bandit scurried to his feet. Both men's swords clashed, sending sparks into the air. The rogue reared back to make another pass with his sword when his head flew from his shoulders, crimson gore pulsing out of his headless neck. The body fell limp to the floor, revealing Braxus with dripping sword in hand behind him.

The wall was still rising and from within the depths of the darkness beyond, a second enormous lizard beast came thundering out and down the stairs. With his wound reopened and his bandages drenched in ichor, Braxus gave out a hellish yell and ran headlong at the beast, chopping at its head with blow after blow. The skin of the monster was like armor, and the hacking of steel upon it had very little effect. Argus ran to join the foray against the beast. The monster turned quickly and its sweeping tail caught him full in the chest, hurling him to the floor by one of the braziers. Braxus dodged the mouth of the giant creature and with great force he stabbed upward with his blade, trying to impale the lower jaw of the monstrosity. The creature was quick, though, lowering its head and opening its jowls to strike. Braxus' sword missed the lower jaw and entered the mouth of the beast, penetrating through its palate. But this did not stop the monster's jaws from snapping and the razor-sharp teeth of the giant lizard clamped down upon the head and back of Braxus as he hung onto the sword's hilt. The jaws snapped open and shut several times in rapid succession as crimson sprayed from the broken body of Braxus. With another chomp the body of Braxus was bitten in half and his lower extremities fell to the floor in a pool of red liquid and entrails. The enormous lizard reared its head back, chomping and swallowing the other half of the body, head and all.

Argus jumped to his feet, screaming with horror and anger. He launched himself into the air and brought his sword down with savage force, planting the point of the blade deeply into the back of the monster's neck just behind its head. The beast thrashed about furiously. One of its claws slashed across Argus' chest, ripping through his metal cuirass and tearing through skin, causing serious injury. Argus hit the floor hard. Even though he tried to regain his feet immediately he fell back to the floor, his life blood seeping out of his wound. The giant lizard finally stopped thrashing in its death throes, succumbing to eternal slumber at the base of the stairs.

Tarsus found his assailant to be a formidable foe. Even though Tarsus was wielding two swords the Khoshite was making good showing with just one. With one expert move after another the bandit pressed Tarsus towards a corner of the room. Finally the rogue's sword found its mark, slicing into Tarsus' forearm. Luckily his leather bracer protected him from serious harm, but it was forceful enough to rend the sword from his grip, sending it clanging upon the stone floor. A glaring look of fury smoldered within the blue eyes of the Aiser. He swiftly leaped upon the wall from the corner and pushed off with his feet, spinning and coming downward with a strike of a *gladius*, implanting the blade deep into the body of the Khoshite through the top of his shoulder, into his torso and out through his chest. Crimson flowed out of both wounds as Tarsus wrenched the sword back and forth, making sure that there was no life left in the man. He unsheathed the blade from the body and spat upon the corpse.

Tarsus grabbed his other sword from the floor and turned to survey the rest of the situation. He ran to Argus and pulled him to his feet. "Can you move?" asked Tarsus. The wounded Arcanian nodded in affirmation. Tarsus helped Argus maneuver around the dead lizard and up the stairs, where two bandits stood their ground against the other monster. Several Khoshites with red sashes lay brutally mauled and bloodied about the balcony. Tarsus did not delay and quickly dragged Argus along with him as they went back through the antechamber and out into the dark corridor leading to the great hall. They quickly passed through the pillared hall and through the other rooms until they reached the main entrance to the temple.

The two ex-legionaries emerged from the temple to discover the storm had ceased and night had fallen. Blood covered both of them as they made their way through the ruins of Tehm. Finding a good place to rest, Tarsus eased Argus to the sandy ground. Tarsus then stood up, placing two fingers in his mouth and whistled loudly. He knelt back down and pulled the torn metal cuirass off Argus and inspected his wound. Then to Argus' surprise, the black stallion of Tarsus galloped up to them. The Aiser grabbed a water pouch from the saddle horn and men and horse quenched their thirst for the moment. Argus laughed for a second but stopped abruptly due to the pain it caused.

Coughing, Argus spoke in strained voice. "You knew your horse was not lost!" Tarsus smirked at Argus but did not respond verbally as he bandaged the wounds of the Arcanian. "How do you suppose those dragons survived all this time? Maybe magik? Or maybe some dreadful curse of the ancients kept them alive to guard that jewel."

Tarsus finished tending to Argus' wound. "If you wish we can go back and find out," he replied sarcastically.

Argus chortled a bit, wincing in pain once again. "No, I think I like it out here. That other dragon probably ate the last of the marauders and is still roaming that forsaken temple."

After a short span of time Tarsus lifted Argus into the saddle. They started off into the desert, Tarsus leading the black warhorse on foot. Neither of the warriors uttered a word for some time until Argus finally spoke with a weak voice. "Am I to die, my lord?"

Tarsus stopped and walked back to the Arcanian. "No, my friend, you shall live. We will skirt the steppes to the south until I am sure that we are out of the reach of Saris Borga's men. Then we will turn back to the west and make our way to the oasis of Tijem. There you can rest and recoup your strength before we head on to Khotar. We have enough water and food in my pack to get us through."

"That tall bandit with the red turban. Was that Saris?" asked Argus.

Tarsus chuckled a bit. "No, he was but a lieutenant. But I must admit the man put up a good fight. He was, let's say… challenging."

Argus sighed. "I have lost my friend Braxus. I have lost the caravan and all my men. My lord, I am of mind to think death would be better than having to face Almec Khan with explanation of failure."

"Death will come to us all one day," Tarsus said. "'Tis better to look it in the face than to show it your back. Braxus will be missed but he died a warrior's death and an honorable one."

"Tarrak is dead too."

"Bah! Tarrak was not worth the piss of a dog, as Braxus said. But

Tarrak was correct about one thing."

"You mean the dragons?" asked Argus.

"No! Those were not dragons, but overgrown lizards. What I speak of is that he was correct that touching the gem would bring about doom." Tarsus produced the finely cut red jewel from a pouch at his belt. "You see, when I saw Tarrak fall dead I snatched this pretty rock. It was then that the gears could be heard moving the wall. I am fairly confident that by removing this gem I set into motion the release of those reptiles. But you need not worry about Almec. I know him and you shall return with something much more valuable to him than his caravan."

The two exhausted and aching mercenaries continued traveling into the chill of the night. The sky was alive with sparkling light from the wash of stars above. "I owe you my life more than once, my lord," spoke Argus. "From this day forward, if I live, I am your man, my lord."

Tarsus stepped back a few paces and put his hand on the leg of Argus. "You fought well and it simply is not your time yet, my friend. You will survive this. And from now on no more of this 'my lord' foolishness. If you do not wish to call me by name, then call me brother."

Argus looked up to the starlit sky and smiled.

Beneath Dead Lake

By Geoff Blackwell

Wings beat the air and feathers danced around Ituanhi, dirt and sand stinging her face. She pushed against the assault, slipped beneath the talons that raked at her face and pressed her sword against a neck covered in gray, downy feathers. A shriek split the air, then all went silent as the struggle abated. Ituanhi's heart convulsed at the avian face that stared back at her. It was as if humankind had spread his seed into hawks or eagles. It was one of the winged people from the desert highlands, beings that were the subject of horrific tales around the children's story circles. As Ituanhi steeled herself for the kill, she met the creature's eyes. They held a spark of intelligence... and fear.

"Are you a demon?" Ituanhi asked.

The bird-creature lay trembling for several heartbeats before replying in a voice punctuated by chirps and trills, "I am Seraffi." Ituanhi knew then that she couldn't kill him, this frightened creature who spoke in her tongue and stared up at her with liquid amber eyes.

"Are you alone?"

"Myself, myself! Seraffi gone, catching the sky, dancing with the wind."

"I want to let you go. But if you try anything, I'll cut you. I swear it by my gods and yours." Ituanhi hoped that she meant it.

"This *my* resting spot," the creature protested.

"I don't care."

After a pause, the Serrafi gave her the slightest of nods.

Ituanhi withdrew her blade, keeping an eye on the skies above and the nearby rocks where she had intended on camping for the night. The Seraffi's pulse raced beneath her. She rolled away, weapon still poised. He sat up, stretching his arms. It was then that Ituanhi noticed the limpness in his left wing, wretchedly twisted, dragging in the dirt. "You're hurt," she said.

He stroked the feathers gingerly. "No wind-dancing for me." He lifted his face to the dying sun and cried *Kiii-hiii!* in a voice loaded with grief. Ituanhi shuddered. Nestled within that avian cry was a sadness and longing which rang frighteningly human to her ears, the way a soldier might weep for a loss of limb. Pity surged through her, pity for this creature who had ambushed her. Inwardly, she cursed her emotions.

"I have bandages and medicine," she said. "I'm called Ituanhi, daughter of Ferengal of clan Makkar."

The bird-man scrunched his face, perplexed. Finally, "I'm born Anemiki, son of Illias-ka. Your words are strange. 'Medicine'?"

"Yes, for healing. Mending. Maybe I can help." She withdrew a strip of white cloth from a pouch on her belt.

After some coaxing, Anemiki allowed Ituanhi to look at his damaged wing. About ten inches from the tip, the bone veered away in a painful direction. "I'm going to reset the bone, then bind the wing to your body," she said, passing him a stray hunk of wood. "This goes in your mouth."

He gave her a blank look. *"Kiii?"*

"It's going to hurt."

It took her three tries. By the time Ituanhi tied off the bandages, the sun had sunk behind the hills, leaving the sky bruised black, pricked by the light of star and moon. The Seraffi lay against the rocks, panting. Ituanhi scrounged for more scraps of wood and managed to build a small, comfy fire. Anemiki's head perked up as she roasted a stick of dried iguana meat, shielding it from the wind with her hands. His tongue slid across a row of pointed teeth.

Ituanhi handed him a piece. "Hungry?"

He chomped it down and she allowed him a swallow from her canteen. She shook it when he had finished, grimacing at the dim slap of water within. "How long have you been stranded here?" she asked.

"Two suns, two moons," Anemiki said, cooing up at the crescent scar above them. "Seraffi are gone now."

"Why? Where are they going?"

"To the great green. Beyond brown sand, over the long blue," he pointed to the hills, outlined against the final throes of dusk. "Nesting-grounds once there. Not safe anymore. Stolen. No place for Seraffi here now."

Ituanhi pointed to his wing. "And that?"

"Hunting. Had a mistake," he hugged his legs against his chest. "Seraffi without wing is dead Seraffi. How my mother cried!" He tipped back his head and crooned a sad melody. Ituanhi's skin tingled as the song fluttered amongst the breeze. The final wavering notes seemed to hang in the air a few seconds longer than they should have before disappearing into the last glimmer of twilight. An eon of chill silence descended upon them, and Ituanhi pulled her robe close to keep from shivering.

"My father died," Ituanhi said. "He was a soldier."

It was not what she had meant to say. She'd simply wanted to break the silence with a word of condolence for her new companion. Instead, words spilled from her mouth in a flat, untouched monotone. "He went away to fight against an enemy clan and was slain during a raid. My uncle took me and my sisters in and promised to care for us. Once he realized how much of an expense three girls would be upon his household, he sold us as wives into the harem of a mountain lord. When the ashes and personal effects of my father were returned, I took his sword and ran away with whatever else I could carry. I escaped, but I left my sisters behind." Her fingers dug into the hilt of her sword as she spoke. "They wouldn't come with me. They were too scared. I *tried.*"

Anemiki whistled and shook his feathered head. "Sad words, Ituanhi. But I know this." He pointed to the sword. "You have a long talon!"

Ituanhi cracked a smile. When their tiny fire smoldered into embers, Ituanhi laid on her back and gazed into the star-pricked sky, tracing old constellations with her eyes until her Seraffi companion kicked up a chirping snore. How funny, she thought, that the two of them should meet like this. He, left behind by his own people. She, running away from hers. If she believed in things like fate, she might have called it a sign. As she drifted into sleep, she dreamed of dust and darkness and scaly things.

Ituanhi awoke to Anemiki shaking her by the shoulder. "Thunder in the ground," he hissed as she rubbed the grit from her eyes. Dawn was only just peeking over the horizon, throwing wan light upon the craggy ground.

Anemiki seemed anxious, as far as she could tell. "Listen, listen!" he said, scratching at the ground with his foot-claws.

Ituanhi gave him a curious look and pressed her ear to the dirt. Her heart jolted and she stood up, wide awake. "Riders," she said, and set about gathering her belongings.

Anemiki cocked his head and gave her a questioning chirp. "My cousin Darsaan is after me," she said.

"You are hunted?"

"I thought he'd given up a few days ago."

The Seraffi stood. "We go away."

"If they are riding stalkers, we can't outrun them. Is there anywhere we can hide?"

Anemiki paused and regarded the landscape with darting glances. "Yes, hide. Cracks in the ground. Not far, not far." He pointed toward the hills that had once belonged to his people. "Dead Lake. Not a good place."

Ituanhi peered in the direction she had traveled from. Already a cloud of dust could be seen to the south. Beyond this, the solitary peak of her homeland speared up from the ground, leagues away, in stark contrast to the surrounding flatlands. "Anything is better than back *there,*" she said.

It was two hours of hiking beneath the rising sun before they reached the place that Anemiki had spoken of. Unlike the sharp badland crags, the route leading to the Seraffi hills was smooth, dusted with a blanket of silt and painted in dull layers of red, orange, white and brown. Ituanhi thought back to the way her father had once described the land surrounding the faraway coasts.

They crossed the hills until the landscape dipped before them in a wide, dusty bowl. Formations of stone climbed the sky in crooked columns, bearing the same layered hues as the walls of earth which surrounded them, dotted by small caves.

"Once filled with water, say the elder ones," Anemiki hissed.

Their path took them down, down, down the water-smoothed slope until the ground near the center split into wide cracks. A large fissure gaped before them, a hideous wound in the bed of the dead lake. Anemiki went forth with halting steps and peered into the darkness. It was a grim-looking hole, filled with dust, shadows, and a foul damp stench.

"I don't like this," she said, wrinkling her nose.

"Kah! Nor me. But if we quiet, if we careful, we safe."

Anemiki lowered himself into the darkness, foot-claws first until he was out of sight. Ituanhi paused before the entrance, hands clammy, mouth dry. Humankind was not meant to go into a place like that. Even as a child or adolescent, she never dared to explore the abandoned caverns and shadow realms of her mountain home. A sharp crack and a *Hiyah!* from behind made her turn. At the rim of the earthen bowl were seven, no, eight shapes: white-cloaked riders upon pale green stalkers. They rode with haste, the men goading their reptilian mounts with whips, shouting and hollering. The rider in the lead wore a red tunic of nobility. It was Darsaan, come across nearly two weeks' worth of sand to fetch the runaway bride. Already she could see his grin of triumph as he urged his steed.

It was all the convincing Ituanhi needed. She scrambled into the opening, her boots scraping against stone. Below her, Anemiki hissed for quiet. Within ten nervous steps, the outside world became nothing more than a cloudless blue scar overhead. Ituanhi found herself surprised, for the earthen chamber was wider than she'd originally judged. A small staircase had even been worked into the path under her feet. Who built these steps, in what dim era? She didn't dwell on such thoughts.

Anemiki waited for her in the spot where the final flecks of daylight yet reached. Beyond him, the passage diverged three ways, each one as dark and forbidding as the other. She shuddered.

"Ituanhi-ki, we could sneak this way, lose them." Anemiki's voice was so quiet that she could hardly make out the words. "Some paths lead back outside."

"Where do the others go?"

"Down."

"Cousin Ituanhi!" a voice shouted from above. Her blood froze. It was Darsaan. "You have ran far enough. Come out and return home with us. It's a crime, keeping your new husband waiting for so long."

Ituanhi clenched her teeth until her jaw throbbed. As she began to shout back an obscenity, a hand covered her mouth. "*Khii*, say nothing," Anemiki whispered into her ear.

Heavy feet shuffled above. "The stalkers won't go any closer, sir," said another voice.

"You stay here then," Darsaan said. "The rest of us will go down and drag her out."

Anemiki took Ituanhi's hand and led her beyond the light into total, wretched darkness, as stealthy as a ghost. A symphony of crunching dirt and rustled tunics chorused behind them. Anemiki had chosen the left-forking path and he strode ahead with sure steps, pausing only momentarily to sniff or possibly to drag his claws across the cavern wall. Confused voices rose in the dark behind them. "Light a torch you fools, and split up," said the voice of Darsaan. The two vagabonds hurried their pace, slowing only for the Seraffi to scuffle vaguely at the stone walls around them.

The complete and utter blackness flooded Ituanhi's senses, solid smoke, everlasting night. It damped her soul, closing in on her from all sides. It was as though she breathed darkness instead of air. The rotting smell of the tunnel threatened to choke the life from her throat and lungs. As Anemiki's path lurched from right to left to right and back again, her entire sense of direction shattered, replaced by a dull, weary numbness which twisted her guts like damp rags. She began to gasp in small, frantic breaths, her heart racing in her chest. Her foot slipped on a loose pebble and she fell, a feeling that Ituanhi would forever remember as pure, infinite oblivion, before crashing against the hard, dusty nothingness of the cavern floor, wheezing, coughing, burning with pain. A pair of gentle hands helped her back upon her trembling legs. The voice of Anemiki cooed to her. "Everything is so dark and close," she said, finding his hands again.

A fierce crack shattered the nightmare stillness, reverberating and ringing against the stones.

Anemiki squawked. *"Kiiii!* Thunder below earth?"

Ituanhi shook her head. "It's a gun. A weapon."

More shots, faint voices shouting. No one had caught up to them yet, what were they firing at?

"*Kahiii!* What kind of weapon speaks the tongue of lighting?" Anemiki's grip on her hand slackened for a moment and he sniffed the air. "Oh no," he moaned.

A pained scream in the darkness.

"What's happening?" Ituanhi asked. Anemiki tugged her hand.

"Fly! Hurry!"

Before Ituanhi could protest, the Seraffi picked up his run and the two of them renewed their race between shadow and stone. Anemiki seemed more frantic than before, barely pausing, his show of stealth from earlier forgotten as the tunnel rattled with the sounds of talon and boot and breath. Through the depths of the world they fled, woman and winged demon, through what Ituanhi would have sworn was the underworld itself. She barely noticed the deepening miasma of filth until she found herself barely able to breathe again. Another family of sound began to chorus through the tunnel: the padding of small feet and an evil hiss that rose and fell like some unholy tide.

Without any warning, Anemiki quit his run. Ituanhi stumbled right into him, and the two went down against the rocks together. Ituanhi groaned, clutching at her shoulder. It would be bruised fiercely, should she ever see again.

"What happened? Why have we—"

"Ksssss! Quiet!"

Their voices expanded *outward*, echoing into a vast expanse. Within that expanse, the dull chorus of hissings rose, punctuated by reptilian chatter. The place reeked of slime. The blood in Ituanhi's limbs went dead cold. Claws scraped against stone all around them, drawn by their commotion.

"Anemiki..." Ituanhi said, trembling.

"Ituanhi-ki, I had another mistake. Time for your long talon."

"Can we run?"

"Too late."

The pair rose to their feet, unsteady in the darkness. Ituanhi found her sword hilt and drew it forth. The blade hissed against the leather like a living thing and the threatening noises before them drew back for a brief instant. The sword shook in her dirt-scorched hands even as she fell into a fighting stance. Anemiki stepped in, back-to-back against her, his feathers brushing the back of her neck.

Within that perfect tableau beneath the earth, a galaxy of images and memories surged through her: the warm yet hardened faces of her parents. Her two baby sisters, naked and burbling as she helped wash them in a basin after a rainfall. Her mother, unable to rise from the disease that swept through her body like a desert twister and left her dead in a matter of days. The only time she saw father shed tears. Exploring the dunes just outside the village with a young man she fancied, an apprentice potter. A rare desert rose, discovered and picked by her youngest sister. The strange, faraway expression her father wore as he waved goodbye, riding with the rest of his company to his final raid.

Each burst of recollection struck home like a bullet. Despite this, Ituanhi managed to steady her breath and her hand. In the midst of the terror and the horror writhing in her guts, a new realization filled her with a sense of courage: a violent end beneath the dead lake would be better than a life spent in servitude.

Together, the unlikely duo stood poised, waiting for death.

Then, more new sounds emerged from the tunnel behind them. The crash of boots against stone. The wheeze of strained breath. A distant scream, human.

Ituanhi turned and saw an orange star, blazing and bobbing, filling the chamber with dull, frantic light. The harsh face of Darsaan went beneath it, along with three others. Her cousin's face twisted and churned in a mixture of deep breathing, curses, and stark, livid fear. It all dripped away when he locked eyes with Ituanhi. Grim determination overrode everything, then.

One of Darsaan's three men disappeared from the light in a flashing instant. Ituanhi blinked, wondering if he'd ever been there at all. And then the man's wretched shriek of terror pierced all senses, and Ituanhi noticed the hunched, shadowy figures tailing behind them. In the orange light she saw the flash of scales and baleful slitted eyes. And teeth, so many teeth.

Darsaan's torch revealed a second tunnel, veering away from the massive cavern of creeping death. A slim hand gripped Ituanhi's and pulled her as Anemiki tore into the newly-lit pathway.

The hisses and titterings became a sonic wave of reptilian fury. Ituanhi turned and looked for just an instant into the great cavern they'd just left, and wished she hadn't.

Once, as a child, she had seen a hive of quartz snakes; a great pile of slender lizards huddled together, surrounded by slime and piles of veined white eggs that gazed up at her like sightless eyes. She'd had nightmares about it long afterward. The torch-lit glimpse into that putrid chamber had been far, far worse than any of that.

They ran. Ituanhi found her feet and Anemiki led her in a full-tilt scramble, once again keeping one claw on the left-side of the wall. Up ahead, the cavern split in twain. The rotting, evil stench was thick and pervasive here. Dark, slim nightmare shapes spilled from the right side of the tunnel. They screeched and charged as the pair approached.

Anemiki veered left, releasing Ituanhi's hand and swiping with his talons at the creatures as he passed. There was no room for Ituanhi to swing her sword, so she held the long edge before her as a shield, slim and sharp. Small, wriggling creatures threw themselves upon her, tiny claws pricking her thighs and forearm. With her free hand she withdrew a knife and plunged it into rank flesh. The hissing monsters recoiled for an instant, and the pair broke through. Against her better judgment, Ituanhi glanced back as the beasts surged upon the three men pursuing them. The match flames extinguished as the men jerked into action. Tittering noises swelled and men screamed, weapons blasting in panic. The noises of hurt and dying humans filled the caverns and a dread chill crawled up Ituanhi's spine. She pushed herself faster, running without any regard for balance or stealth, keeping her left hand against the wall as she'd seen Anemiki do. Panicked footsteps and reptilian hissing pursued them. Again Ituanhi stumbled and again she rose sobbing, her fear and panic blocking the sting of her scratches and bites.

The path tilted upwards. White-gold light from the outside world teased her eyesight. A tiny cavern mouth opened up ahead, blue skies shining. The profile of Anemiki ran before her with slight limp, dark patches of blood smearing one leg. He reached the opening and crawled out of sight. She threw herself into it, scrambling between the dust and dirt and stones as light and color flooded her world. Again the taloned hand gripped hers and pulled. Ituanhi coughed and sputtered into the open air. The tunnel had spat them out on a slope, around the other side of the dead lake. Below them stood the eight stalkers and their guard. The riding lizards were restless and jumpy and their guardian held a rifle in his hands, looking anxious.

"The stalkers," Ituanhi said, starting down the slope.

The warrior on guard gaped as she ran at him. Ituanhi forced herself not to look behind her at the scores of slithering beasts that were surely pouring from the bowels of dead lake. The lone rider flung himself into the saddle of one stalker and spurred the panicking creature into motion.

Darsaan, bloodied and battered, burst free from the cave and screamed "Wait! Wait, damn you!" Behind him, the serpentine, tittering creatures followed. Sunlight glinted from black scales. Triangular heads and slim, coiling tails followed behind them as they leaped down the slope, raptorial and ferocious. Ituanhi's guts heaved at the memory of their hatchery, deep beneath the lake bed.

As they approached, the stalkers bolted in panic. Ituanhi tugged on the nearest set of reins.

"We ride these things?" Anemiki screeched.

"Yes," Ituanhi said as she scrambled into the saddle. The stalker snapped its teeth, hissing and fidgeting. Anemiki stood frozen, staring at the lumbering beast. Realizing that he had probably never ridden another creature before in his life, Ituanhi reached out, shouting "Take my hand!" Anemiki did so, swinging his legs awkwardly into the saddle. "Hold on tight," she said, whipping the reins. The stalker needed little encouragement to run as the black tide of claws and scales swept toward them.

From the corner of her eye, Ituanhi saw Darsaan fling himself upon the saddle of the final straggling mount, kicking out at a black creature who snapped at his boot. Their stalker's lumbering steps became powerful strides and they cut a line between the stone pillars as the hordes of dead lake gave chase. A line of the awful reptiles teemed from a cavern to their right. Ituanhi struggled with the reins, veering away from the marauding devils. The land sloped higher and higher and Ituanhi grit her teeth as though the stalker's efforts were her own. With a final stride, they were away. Waves of sand and dirt rolled before them as they left the dead lake behind. The screeches of the black lizards faded, unable to keep their pace. Darsaan tailed close behind as they raced across the open desert. Ituanhi cursed the creatures for failing to kill her cousin.

The Seraffi's arms were wrapped tight around her belly, his face burrowed between her shoulder blades. "Anemiki, you know this area," Ituanhi said. "Where can we go?" Before he could reply, gunfire rattled the air. Their stalker screamed and tumbled, flinging Ituanhi from the saddle. Bright lights scattered across her vision and pain burst through her shoulders and spine. She looked up just in time to watch Darsaan's stalker plow toward her, Anemiki tumbling to the dirt and disappearing beneath its charging feet.

Darsaan brought his stalker to a halt before Ituanhi. He held a pistol in one hand. His thin mustache curled above his lips in a cold sneer. "Found you, bitch-cousin."

Ituanhi staggered to her feet, drawing her father's sword. "I'm not going back. Not with you. Not to uncle, nor the pig in his mountain keep."

Darsaan snorted. "True enough. You've become a consort to demons. It will be a mercy to kill you now." He tossed his spent gun to the dirt and dismounted, drawing his own sword. "It was terrible," he said, words drenched in mock drama, "we found her dead; raped by winged demons and her corpse mauled by lizards. We were forced to fight our way out. I was the only survivor."

He advanced, sword aloft. Ituanhi felt a chill which settled into the marrow of her bones. She had been trained in the martial arts by her father but she had never fought in wars or bloody campaigns. Darsaan had every advantage upon her. "Uncle will be furious if you come back without me," she tried.

"Oh, certain people will stomp up and down their halls for a time, true. But what's one lonely wench in this wide world really worth? Now come here and die, cousin."

His blade arced downward, meeting hers. The clash of steel rang loud and clear in the open sands. Darsaan came at her again and each parried blow jarred Ituanhi's arms to the bone. Any attacks of her own were turned aside almost playfully by her cousin.

Darsaan's next attack opened a short gash in Ituanhi's forearm. "First blood," he said, grinning. Ituanhi would have cursed him had she any breath to spare, but the weight of everything—running away, finding Anemiki, crawling through the dark, escaping the black lizards and swinging swords beneath the desert sun, it all caught up to her. Sweat trickled from her forehead and her limbs trembled like jelly.

A failed thrust left her wide open. Darsaan's hilt slammed against her sternum, knocking her windless to the ground. He stood above her, silhouetted by the sun. He touched the tip of his sword between the rise of her breasts and stooped down. As he opened his mouth to speak, a stone struck the back of his skull. Darsaan fell sideways as a rush of gray-white feathers and flashing talons sprung upon him. The Seraffi's wings dangled twisted and useless behind him as he loosed an avian battle scream.

Despite the Seraffi's surprise attack, Darsaan was a natural fighter. He grabbed hold of Anemiki's wrist, twisted until the bird-man squawked, then wrestled him to the ground. He climbed on top of the squirming Seraffi and drew a knife. The blade sparked against the sunlight.

Ituanhi didn't think. As Darsaan raised the knife for a killing blow, she was on her feet, sliding her father's sword into his guts. Her cousin looked at the hilt protruding from his belly. His mouth dropped open. The dagger fell from his fingers and he slumped to the ground, twitching, bleeding, dying.

Silence descended, broken only by Anemiki's pained chirping.

"Your long talon is sharp, Ituanhi-ki."

Ituanhi said nothing. She stared at her hands. Rather, the blood upon them, exemplified by the scarlet tones of the falling sun. She trembled. "I've never killed before."

"No? Not hunted before?"

"That's different. Hunting is surviving."

"If you didn't kill him, would we survive?"

Ituanhi wrinkled her brow and grunted. She wasn't in the mood for tough questions. "What about you? Are you hurt... oh!" She gasped. Anemiki's white plumage lay limp in the dirt, caked in a pallet of browns, blacks and reds. The bandage that had secured his broken wing was long gone, and now both of his wings contorted in wrong directions. "Oh,

Anemiki…"

He looked at his ruined wings. His liquid eyes betrayed little. "Won't move," he said. "Now a land-dancer, like Ituanhi-ki."

Her heart deflated. "Anemiki... I'm so sorry."

He sighed. "Sad, yes. But, you dance without wings, stalker-lizards without wings. Lake snakes, even. Perhaps Seraffi too."

Anemiki acted strong, but Ituanhi knew the weight of being flightless and never rejoining his clan must fall upon his shoulders like the weight of the sun. Tears bit at the corners of her eyes and, embarrassed, she turned to blink them away. If she could give him anything, it wouldn't be her pity.

"What of the lake snakes?" she asked, the thought suddenly occurring to her. Anemiki looked back across the wind-swept dunes. The sunken bowl of the dead lake was barely a shadow in the ground perhaps a mile away. He hissed.

"They like the darkness. Bind my wings, Ituanhi Longtalon, then we go."

Ituanhi retrieved her sword from Darsaan's corpse and searched him and the packs of the dead stalker. She found bandages and a short length of rope and provisions.

" 'Ituanhi Longtalon'?" she asked as she secured Anemiki's wings to his body.

"*Kiii!* Name for a warrior!"

Ituanhi laughed.

They found Darsaan's stalker nearby. The two companions, vagabonds from different races, for different reasons, saddled up and rode away as the last rays of the sun fell behind the hills, casting the spires of Dead Lake into darkness.

Thannhausefeer's Guest

By Howie K. Bentley

The wine-dark sea swallowed the remains of the scattered wreck and retched up a lone figure too strong to die just yet. Breakers rolled in under the gray sunless sky and cast the man face down on the snowy shore. All about him lay bleached human skulls and assorted bones scattered alongside desolate rocks and boulders.

The man's long black hair stuck to his bearded face. He wore a waterlogged cape of giant silver wolf skin and drenched accoutrements fashioned from various other animal hides. His sword still rested in the scabbard slung over his back, and a dirk hung in its sheath at his hip. Echoes of the splintering ship and the screams of dying men staining the deck red with blood rang in his thrumming eardrums.

The man gasped for air—his chest rattling—breathing in the stinging salt air and spitting up acrid brine. He slowly raised himself on all fours and struggled to get to his feet. Drops of bright crimson pattered down onto the back of his left hand and the floor of the barren shore. He touched his moist warm forehead and looked at his hand. From the looks of the blood and the throbbing in his skull he had suffered a pow erful blow to the head.

His vision was blurry, and he staggered and fell—tried to raise himself up again. He caught a flash out of the corner of his eye of a billowing white gown blowing in the wind. The woman leaned down, and he wrapped his arm around her. She braced him and helped him to his feet.

Rolling his head to one side, he glanced at her, his vision wavering in and out. Flaxen hair framed her pale-skinned classic beauty with high cheek bones and full red lips that seemed to have never smiled. Her icy blue eyes looked through him upon dim netherworld vistas far beyond the realm of man. She appeared familiar, but he didn't know who she was. They had walked for only a moment when she languorously raised her right arm and pointed to the colossal citadel at the top of the hill in the distance.

"You must go there," she said in the monotone of a black lotus dreamer. He nodded his head and did not argue. He knew he was bleeding from a head wound and winter had set in. It was best that he find shelter and a warm place to dry.

A massive splash just to the rear of the ship and walls of sea rose up and washed over the deck, drowning some crewmen and throwing others overboard. A crash like lightning followed by a thunderous roll. The galley's bow shot up and twisted, and the ship exploded from bow to stern. Planks flew high into the air. The main mast collapsed, and the lines dangled high above the galley like striking serpents.

I was hanging onto the gunwale–shouting, he recalled. *Where was I going?*

Helped along by this single strange woman with her white gown blowing in the wind, the lone survivor of the shipwreck faded in and out of consciousness. Somehow, he traversed the distance from the shore and was nearing the titanic edifice at the top of the hill.

Trebuchet! One shot hits us and we're sinking! he remembered shouting and clenching the gunwale.

The ship exploded. Men screamed as the mast crashed to the deck and crushed them. The tattered sail whipped in the wind. The deck ran red with the blood of the men who weren't immediately cast into the sea.

Yet I live. Here I am, but where am I?

Lying at the top of the steps and leaning on his arm, the shipwreck survivor pounded his fist on the door that climbed high into the sky. His head fell to one side, and he rolled onto his back and mustered all of his strength to knock yet again on the towering door to the castle. The woman in white was nowhere to be seen. A loud slamming—and the door creaked open as the injured man's head fell back. He slid into black oblivion as if it were a hot bath on a cold winter night.

* * *

"You took quite a blow to the head and lost some blood, but the cut wasn't as deep as we thought," a woman's voice said.

The man's hand shot out and gripped her by the wrist.

"It's all right," she whispered. "I just need to replace the poultice on your forehead. The salve has done wonders for you in these last two days."

"Two… Two days?" The man mumbled, becoming aware of his surroundings, his blurred vision gradually clearing.

"My sword?! My cloak?!" he exclaimed.

"Your sword is in its scabbard in the corner, and your cloak and clothes are hanging over by the fire. They are surely dry by now."

The fire crackled and gave off a pleasant aroma of well-seasoned cedar.

"Are you cold? I will get you another blanket."

"No," he mumbled, reaching for her. "Shipwreck. Trebuchet fired… Trebuchet fired on us."

She smiled down at him as though he was a child. "There was a shipwreck, but I don't know anything about a trebuchet. I think you are still getting over the fever dreams. You were restless most of last night. So, you came from the wrecked ship? Were there any other survivors?"

The man looked off into the distance, trying to peer back through the misty veils of time and recollect the events of recent days. "No. Only I survived the attack."

The woman's bell-like laughter rang throughout his sleeping chambers. "Maybe the gods of the sea attacked you. There was a terrible storm on the evening you showed up at my lord's castle. My name is Lydiana." She gently brushed his chest with her hand.

He could now see her clearly. Flaming red hair that rippled like waves in the sea fell to her waist. She had piercing blue eyes set back in a handsome face, and her bright blue velvet gown hugged her voluptuous feminine form.

The man's brows furrowed as if he was trying to find a solution to an immediate problem.

"What is your name, man from the sea?" she asked in a childlike voice.

"I… I don't know."

"Well, how about I call you Manannan? You look to be a Tuath, and it is said that Manannan mac Lir is the sea god of the Tuath je Danaan."

The man remained silently pensive.

Her tinkling peal rang throughout the room again, and she said, "Manannan it is!" and turned and left the room.

A boulder splashed behind the galley far to the rear—then another. He was gripping the gunwale shouting, "Boulders! They are shooting boulders at us!" The third one connected! The ship exploded into splinters from bow to stern.

The smell of food nearby reminded him he hadn't eaten in a long time. His attention returned to the room, in which he lay, with a crackling fire and a beautiful woman tending to him. Lydiana had returned carrying a tray loaded with roasted boar, boiled potatoes, and a freshly baked loaf of soft warm bread. She sat the tray on a nightstand by the bed and went over to a shelf and removed a bottle.

"A vintage red wine. Forty years old," she said as she crossed the room, uncorking the bottle.

"A big strong warrior like you doesn't need a cup. Just take the bottle and drink it. I bet you are used to taking whatever you want." She licked her lips and cast a wanton glance at him.

"Once you have eaten and rested a little more, I will give you a bath; and we can see if I am right.

"Tomorrow you will meet the lord of the realm, Thannhausefeer. He is hosting a competition. Warriors from all over come to pit steel against steel. The last man standing will be generously rewarded by my lord with all of the gold and jewels the champion can carry away in his ship."

"I saw no ships on the shore, woman."

"They only arrived yesterday. Thannhausefeer wants to meet you on the morrow. He is a great admirer of warriors such as yourself, and I am sure he will want to see you compete in his games."

"And if I refuse to fight?"

Silence filled up the room like the belly of python that had just swallowed its prey. The crackle of the fire even seemed to get quieter as if it were sentient and wished to hide. Lydiana fixed her burning blue gaze on him. "Manannan, my lord is a generous man; but his anger is terrible."

Her eyes softened, and she went over to him and gently ran her hands across his chest and torso and down to his groin. "But let's not worry about that right now. Let's get you cleaned up and nice and relaxed for tomorrow." She smiled at him—a smile he did not return.

* * *

Manannan marveled at the colossal archways, doors, and vaulted ceiling as Lydiana led him down the corridor to the great hall where the Lord of the Realm held court. The roof was supported by columns that raised the ceiling high into the sky—at least twice the height of any castle he had visited until now. The hall was abnormally wide, and he guessed that the walls were nearly twenty feet thick. Torches the length of spears blazed in sconces high up the walls beyond his reach. He could hear the clash of weapons down the hall.

"What strange architecture," he commented.

Lydiana's eyes narrowed, and she smiled as if enjoying a private jest. They hadn't gone far when she veered off to the left into the monumental archway opening into the great hall.

Two men were engaged in conflict—broadsword against battle-axe—and droplets of blood and sweat were flying; but that did not interest Manannan so much as what sat in the center of the table stripping meat from a human femur. The man was at least twice Manannan's height of six feet, and his massive girth filled out the Giant's scintillating golden throne that was wider than Manannan was tall. Men—some of them armed and armored—sat in long-legged chairs to either side of the Giant observing the games. They looked like dolls on a shelf sitting alongside the behemoth. The Giant, engrossed in watching the two men hack each other to death, paid no heed to Manannan and Lydiana.

"Thannhausefeer?" Manannan asked her.

"Indeed!" Lydiana replied. Her azure eyes beamed, and she grinned—her cheeks like apples.

The Giant's red, square-cut mane was a shock of tangled hair held back by a massive leather band encircling his head. The head band held a large polished oval of azurite centered in front. Cold blue eyes bore into the two warriors endeavoring to deal death to each other. Thannhausefeer's crimson beard fell down his chest and was braided at the ends by ornaments fashioned from the stringed bones of human fingers. Enormous steel sinews rippled under the deceptive roll of fat that partially concealed them. He was dressed in a silver-studded black tunic that fell below his waist and white wool britches. His boots were made of stitched animal hides and were as big as panniers. Red spiked leather gauntlets covered his forearms. He wore no crown; he needed none to proclaim himself the master of his demesne.

Thannhausefeer's golden throne was embedded with rough-cut jewels. Sapphires, rubies, amethysts, and numerous others glinted in the dim sunless light that filtered through the window high above in the dingy hall. The Giant carried no weapons on his person, but a broadsword the length of two horses hung on the wall behind his gleaming throne. Logs crackled and popped in the tall fireplace on the south wall of the chamber, vanquishing the winter chill.

A young bearded blond warrior wielding a broadsword bled from myriad wounds and gasped for breath. His axe-wielding opponent's visage was obscured by a silver-studded executioner's hood made of black leather. The hooded figure was splattered with blood, but most of it wasn't his own. The armor the swordsman had entered the contest in was of inferior quality to that worn by the axe-wielder and had been mostly hacked away by now.

"At him, Kurlick! The fight isn't over until one of you falls!" Thannhausefeer's voice rolled like thunder and reverberated through his chamber as he continued to gnaw the remaining meat from the femur.

At the Giant's command, the yellow-haired warrior hastily looked for an opening and took it. With all of his remaining strength, he moved in with a disemboweling thrust. His opponent had anticipated his next move and side-stepped the man's broadsword just in time. Twisting and coming back through with his battle-axe, the Executioner severed the man's head from his body with one blow. The head spun through the air and landed on the table in front of Thannhausefeer.

"Yes! That's it!" The Giant's laughter rumbled throughout the hall, shaking the feasting table as he pounded his fists on it. Thannhausefeer fervourously smeared droplets of blood on his face from the decapitated head. He reached into a large copper cauldron sitting on the table next to him and threw gold coins at the feet of the axe-wielding Executioner.

"Congratulations, Donthar! Three victories yesterday and two so far today. You may yet live to sail away in your ship with enough wealth to buy your own kingdom!"

The Giant pounded his fist on the dining table again and shouted, "Arrival!"

Four raven-haired beauties in brightly colored gowns appeared from the corridor to the right of Thannhausefeer's throne and started to carry away Kurlick's head and body.

"I marked the page for that one in my book. I knew he would fall next. See that the meat is prepared strictly by the guidelines that I have set forth, or you know what will happen."

The women hurried away.

Thannhausefeer turned and acknowledged Manannan and Lydiana for the first time since they had entered his chamber. "Ah! A new warrior enters the game! You are just in time for the chance of a lifetime. What is your name, Champion?"

The man stood studying Thannhausefeer in silence for a moment. He noticed the Giant begin to fidget and become irritable, but it did not faze him.

"I am Manannan," the warrior said after a long pause.

"Where are you from, Manannan, and how did you hear of my games?"

"I came from the sea."

"The sea?"

"The ship I was sailing in was wrecked. Everyone drowned but me. I know nothing of your games but what I just saw."

"Well, no matter, Manannan from the sea. Sit with us awhile and observe. I am sure you will find what we do to your liking if you have yourself ever shed blood for a living, and by the look of that sword you carry and the scars on your face, I am certain that you have.

"Bring mead and a plate for our new guest!" Thannhausefeer called over his shoulder.

Manannan relaxed his hand on his dagger hilt. "I don't eat the flesh of my own kind, Giant."

"Neither do these men who sit with me, Man from the Sea." Thannhausefeer's face reddened, but otherwise he showed no emotion. The Giant spoke with obvious restraint; his voice dropped lower, and he added, "Be careful not to fall in battle in this hall."

* * *

The two champions squared off, warily circling each other in the middle of Thannhausefeer's chamber. One was bald, save for the horse tail of hair done in the manner of a circus mare sprouting from the top of his head. His name was Tarkatha the Bull. Clad in only a loincloth and low boots of animal hide, he brandished a wicked curved scimitar in his fist. His yellow skin glistened with oil. Tarkatha snarled, and his nostrils flared around the large golden ring set in his nose.

The other man was Prince Pellipedes of the Sathzarian Isles. He had gone in secret to Thannhausefeer's castle. Though the Prince was learned in the arts of war, Pellipedes's father, King Diodedes, forbade him to ride into battle. Pellipedes didn't care about a shipload of treasure: he only wished to impress his father. The Prince, well trained in the double-sword art of A'Tom, wielded a blade with each hand. He was dressed in mailed hauberk, colorful silken finery, and a green silk band, which encircled his head. Every lock of light-brown curly hair was in place, and he had a thin mustache; but by the whirling sword dervish he presented to his opponent, all present could tell the Prince was no mere dandy.

Tarkatha feinted, and Pellipedes jumped back slightly, though his expression remained calm and his blades kept whirling. Pellipedes's blade licked out like a striking serpent, and rivulets of blood fell from Tarkatha's upper arm. The Bull seemed not to notice and answered with a slash aimed at Pellipedes's midsection. The Prince jumped back again. Tarkatha closed in and slashed. This time the point of his scimitar connected with Pellipedes's abdomen and tore through mail, raking the Prince's skin.

Pellipedes came in, twin swords spinning; and Tarkatha artfully dodged having his arms shorn from each side of his body. The Bull looked as though he was performing a dance to avoid the Prince's flurry of steel. Tarkatha aimed another disemboweling thrust, and the Prince backed up to avoid having his innards spilled on the floor.

Manannan was so engulfed in the combat taking place before him that he didn't notice himself and Thannhausefeer as they sat side by side, swilling mead and slamming their drinking jacks down in unison as though it were choreographed.

Tarkatha blocked Prince Pellipedes's left-hand blade with his scimitar and slammed a booted foot into Pellipedes's face when the Prince went for too wide of a stroke with his right-hand sword. The Prince stumbled, trying to regain his balance, and fell. As Pellipedes leapt to his feet, Tarkatha moved in and slit the man's throat with the point of his scimitar. The Prince fell back to the floor gurgling as the blood jetted from his jugular.

"Outstanding!" Thannhausefeer boomed. "Here we see age and experience has just vanquished extreme martial skill until now untried in the face of death!

"Arrival!" the Giant bellowed, and the four dark-haired beauties appeared again. "This one is to be prepared for his funeral, but I don't think that is what Tarkatha has in mind."

Thannhausefeer addressed Tarkatha the Bull, "You have done well, warrior; and I keep my promise to you. You shall have Pellipedes's body to do with as you like while you bed the one of your choice tonight."

Tarkatha looked at the four women who had come to carry away the corpse, and with a quick snapping motion of his arm thrust his index finger at one of the young women. She couldn't have been more than sixteen years old. The girl began to tremble.

"You will go with Tarkatha and Pellipedes's corpse tonight, Rose-Athelind!" the Giant croaked like an enormous bullfrog.

The girl fled back through the corridor weeping.

"Remember: there is nowhere you can run to escape my will, woman!" Thannhausefeer's laughter reverberated through the chamber. He turned his head, looking back through the archway where the girl had just run. "I make good my promise to Tarkatha this night!"

Manannan quaffed deeply of his cup and sat back relaxed in his chair to the right of Thannhausefeer. A gong sounded at the back of the chamber, and a man appeared in a black studded tunic much like the one Thannhausefeer wore. The man's closely-cropped black hair set above a low forehead that had sustained a number of sword gashes. His face was smeared with dark-blue and green paint of woad that did little to conceal the scars deeply etched into his countenance like a roadmap to Hel. The warrior wore leggings of animal hide and a scabbarded sword and dirk. He stood at attention in front of Thannhausefeer and his table of warriors—all, Manannan had surmised, there to compete for the shipload of wealth the Giant had promised the winner.

"Care to cross swords with General Krothess, Manannan from the sea? I think I need to see some proof of your martial skills before we go much further. The way you are swilling my mead supply, I soon shall have none left if I do not find a diversion for you."

The warriors sitting at the table laughed in unison at the Giant's jest.

Manannan drained his cup and squinted his eyes at the General, smiling lopsidedly. He slowly got up from his chair beside Thannhausefeer and walked around the table to meet General Krothess.

The wind whistled off Manannan's blade as he whipped his sword from its scabbard. General Krothess drew his sword and stepped into a fighting stance. Krothess made the first move with a blow aimed at Manannan's head. Manannan ducked the general's blade and drove Krothess back and back, raining blow after blow upon the General's sword. Krothess threw up his blade just in time to keep Manannan's blade from splitting his skull. Momentarily the two warriors stood pressing steel on steel. The stench of the General was overpowering. He smelled like an amalgamation of sour clothes, dung, and rotten wood.

The boy stunk of sour clothes and was a whole head taller than him, but he still gave a good account of himself. He had suffered the big boy's taunts and torment for far too long.

He heard his mother calling his name to come to supper as he hit the bully with a stick he had hidden in the woods in anticipation of the fight with him that afternoon. The big boy lay on the ground, unconscious and bleeding. From then on, he never saw him in the woods surrounding his house again.

I just heard my mother calling my real name, but I was so busy fighting that I didn't hear what it was, realized Manannan.

Manannan braced himself and shoved the General backwards. Before Krothess could regain his bearings, Manannan slashed through Krothess's hands where they gripped the handle of the man's sword. The General's left hand was ruined, and he shifted his sword so that he only wielded it right-handed. With a stout blow, Manannan knocked Krothess's sword back so that the man was unprotected and cleft the General from collarbone to sternum on the return. General Krothess fell to his knees, blood frothing from his mouth, then headed over.

Manannan cleaned his blade on Krothess's clothes, and returned it to his scabbard. "You might want to wash that one well before you eat him, Giant. He stunk pretty bad."

Thannhausefeer sat in silence, his eyes shifting back and forth from Manannan to Krothess's corpse on the floor of his great hall.

"Arrival!" the Giant boomed.

* * *

Lydiana lay asleep next to Manannan. After the two of them had sated their lusts she quickly dozed off. Manannan was spent, but his mind raced back through time trying to force open doors to the past for the answers he needed.

Lydiana had offered herself, nay, forced herself upon him. As he had taken her from behind, he looked down at her. When she turned her head to look back at him, it wasn't Lydiana but the Woman in White who had brought him from the shipwreck to Thannhausefeer's castle. The woman gritted her teeth; covering her entire back was a tattoo of a large wolf. His eyes moved from the wolf to her perfect pale visage; her ruby lips smiling up at him.

"To show you I will always remember you…" she moaned.

Mannanan jerked awake and sat up in bed. Lydiana mumbled something and rolled over only to fall back asleep.

I am not Manannan! She just said my name. But who am I?

The harder he tried to come away with what he needed to know about himself, the more the woman's voice receded into fast-fading dream. The tattoo of the wolf spread out across the woman's back was the last thing he remembered as he slipped yet again through the gates of slumber and behind the wall of sleep.

Steel on steel clashed! Horses' whinnies and neighs blended with the screams of men. Battle-axes shattered helmets, and fine-pointed blades pierced corselets and spilled vital organs upon the ground. Maces crashed into skulls, and brains seeped out onto the frozen earth. Every minute, men died in scores. The tide of battle had turned against them. Realizing this, he threw his head back and shouted to the sky. The pain was at first excruciating, however brief, then he fell to his knees and his perception changed. His senses were heightened to ecstasy, and everything around him moved in slow motion.

"Wake up, Manannan!" Lydiana shook him.

"What did I just say?" He was trying to remember the words he had called out in the throes of nightmare.

"I don't know. You were speaking some sort of gibberish. It sounded like a chant. You aren't a sorcerer are you, Man from the Sea?" Lydiana pounced on him playfully, revealing her ample alabaster cleavage. She licked his lips, sticking her tongue in his mouth.

"Today is the final day of the games. Thannhausefeer will want to get an early start. And if you are lucky, you will sail away with a shipload of treasure at dawn on the morrow."

"And if I am unlucky, woman?"

Lydiana looked down and cast her glance away from Manannan.

"Will you come away from this island with me, Lydiana?"

"It cannot be," she sighed.

"Why?"

"My place is here, tending to Thannhausefeer's affairs and warming his bed. He does you honor by allowing you to sleep with me."

"This man is a monster! A cannibal! Why do you stay with him?"

She looked away from Manannan as she spoke. "My mother was cast up from the sea in a shipwreck, just like yourself. She died giving birth to me. She was all too human…"

"And your father?"

Lydiana—nostrils flaring—turned her piercing blue eyes on Manannan.

"Thannhausefeer!"

* * *

Knives formed a whirling silver ring before Thannhausefeer and the three warriors sitting at the Giant's table. Dwarfs with twisted limbs clad in colorful dyed sleeveless wool tunics sat behind Thannhausefeer's throne playing a gay tune on flutes made of human bones and drums fashioned from skulls stretched with human hide. Lydiana entered through the door at the back of the chamber and came over to sit in the empty chair to Manannan's right.

"He is good, isn't he, lover?" she spoke into Manannan's ear and nodded at the fool dressed in bright red and green silk tights covered in diamond-shaped patterns. The man's face was calm and stoic under the tall conical-shaped hat he wore. Standing across from the Giant, the dagger-whirling juggler looked like an obnoxious toy that a hateful child derives great pleasure from slowly destroying.

"That's enough, Jobenox! It is time to fight again!" Thannhausefeer rumbled.

The fool kept the daggers whirling as he turned to go and exited through the main archway of the great hall, his face set as stone.

"You were late to Thannhausefeer's table. What you did not hear is those daggers are all dipped in poison. The merest scratch—and the fool dies. He puts himself into a trance when he performs." Lydiana raised her eyebrows but elicited no response from Manannan other than a grunt.

"Well, well. There are three of you left: Donthar the Executioner, Tarkatha the Bull, and Manannan, the Man from the Sea. I think it is high time we see who gets to carry away a shipload of treasure at dawn tomorrow," the Giant bellowed.

The gong sounded and Thannhausefeer's voice boomed again, "Tarkatha and Manannan!"

The two warriors walked around the table, and broadsword and scimitar hissed from their scabbards like metallic serpents. Both men stepped into fighting stances: Manannan, holding his heavy broadsword two-handed, and Tarkatha the Bull, holding his wicked curved blade in his right hand. Tarkatha was the first to strike, feinting, then aiming a blow at Manannan's inner thigh. Manannan brought his broadsword around and blocked Tarkatha's blade, nearly sending it spinning from the Bull's grip. Tarkatha leapt back and grasped his scimitar with both hands. Thannhausefeer roared with laughter at the man's overconfidence. Sweat beaded Tarkatha's forehead, rolling down into his slanted black eyes.

Broadsword and scimitar engaged in a quick succession of lightning-fast strokes. Manannan's sword missed splitting Tarkatha's head by a fraction of an inch, and Tarkatha answered with a blow that would have severed Manannan's arm had he not stepped back. Even so, Tarkatha's blade sliced through Manannan's shirt and broke the skin.

Tarkatha brought his blade down and over. Manannan stepped aside, and Tarkatha's sword hissed another blow on the return. Manannan blocked the blow and made an arc with his broadsword. Manannan's steel bit into Tarkatha's hamstring, but as the Bull went down on one leg, he brought his sword back through at Manannan's lower torso. Manannan knocked the scimitar from Tarkatha's grip and struck the man's head from his shoulders with a single wide sword stroke.

Manannan held the yellow man's head up, and showed it to Thannhausefeer, then dropped it on the floor.

"Say 'hello' to Pellipedes in Hel, Tarkatha!" Manannan mumbled.

Thannhausefeer's fat belly rolled with laughter, and he clapped his hands. Only three of the serving girls appeared this time to take away Tarkatha's corpse and mop the combat area. Manannan noticed that Lydiana had left the room. He went over to sit by the Giant and quaff deeply of his mead cup.

Thannhausefeer was nothing more than a tyrannical oversized cannibal, but—by Fenris!—his mead was good; and killing was thirsty work!

Manannan's hand instinctively brushed the giant silver wolf's pelt thrown over his back like a cape while half-emptying his cup with one pull.

"Best go easy on your cups, Man from the Sea. You fight Donthar the Executioner next, and he is not so happy with you. Ever since he showed up, he has been wanting to bed Lydiana; but I gave her to you. Now, she is going to show him something to send the fire coursing through his veins." Thannhausefeer nodded his head as the flame-haired beauty appeared before the Giant's table.

Lydiana grinned and her lust-filled eyes met with those of the Giant as they shared more than just a private jest. The dwarfs introduced the tune with a drum beat that reached into the primal area of the brain governing the procreative drive, and the flutes joined in with an eerie minor-key melody. The music bespoke the dangerous seduction of beauty, and Lydiana began slowly and sinuously undulating her hips. She cupped her hands to the slender silver brassiere barely covering her firm breasts and spun in a circle billowing her green gossamer skirt.

All three men, including Thannhausefeer, watched, enspelled. Lydiana thrust her hips, and the drums became more aggressive; and the music louder. She ripped the fabric from her lower body and sensuously stepped out of it like a serpent shedding its skin. Manannan's cup stopped before it could reach his lips as he sat motionless staring at what was beneath the skirt: another skirt of coarse material with the drawing of a wolf inked upon it. He had seen it before. It was the tattoo on the woman's back; the woman from his dreams.

He suddenly recalled the woman from his dream say, "To show you I will always remember you… Argantyr!"

Argantyr? That is my name! Argantyr—Argantyr Faoladh as I am known in my homeland of the Tuath je Danaan! And King Argantyr Fenris in the northlands of Skaldavia where I rule!

Lydiana thrust her hips faster and faster, and the wolf's head jerked and thrust at Manannan-Argantyr, faster and faster! Memories rushed forth and retreated like lightning bolts flashing across the sky and vanishing. Lydiana removed her scant silver scaled top, and her firm bare breasts jiggled.

Even over the music Argantyr could hear the sound of Thannhausefeer swallowing as the giant leaned over and told him, "How do you like her skirt? A gift to my daughter! I have to commend the tattoo artist who put that wolf on the girl's back. He was exceptional! I traded for the woman taken in a raid, but there was an obedience problem that took great measures to correct. Oh! She screamed and screamed but was defiant to the end! Donthar there is normally excellent at getting someone to do what he wants. He removed her skin while she yet lived, when he was here about a month ago."

"The trebuchet! One shot and he's sinking us!" he had shouted as he clenched the gunwale.

I can see through the mists on that fog-bound hill! I can see what was on that hill as clear as day now! There was no trebuchet! It was him! The Giant was standing on the hill throwing boulders at us! He knew King Friodere had sent us to rescue his daughter, Friona! My love! Friona! I was too late to save you, but I am not too late to avenge your death!

Argantyr saw the looks exchanged between Thannhausefeer and Lydiana.

The Giant knows I have come here to kill him. With the luck of the Tuath, he still thinks that I don't know who I am. Best to let him keep thinking that until I am ready.

Argantyr's eyes met Lydiana's, and he arched his eyebrows and smiled, drinking deeply of his cup. With a gesture from his hand, Thannhausefeer signaled for the dance to stop. The music was cut short, and Lydiana suddenly ceased her wicked gyrations. With a gesture from Thannhausefeer's hand, Lydiana turned and left the room. The gong sounded. No further words were needed. Argantyr and Donthar met in front of Thannhausefeer's table.

Whoosh! Donthar's axe went at Argantyr, and he ducked the deadly blade. Again and again Donthar the Executioner came on, and his axe blade bit empty air, coming ever closer with each swing. Of a sudden, Argantyr lunged forward; and splinters flew from the Executioner's axe as Argantyr's blade hacked into the handle. Blood ran in rivulets from Donthar's fingers down the handle of his battle-axe. He switched his grip on the weapon, and when he did, Argantyr's broadsword ripped through Donthar's hauberk and made a shallow gash in his chest as the Executioner leaned back.

The two men slashed at one another like rabid dogs. Argantyr bled from gashes in his chest and upper arms, and Donthar's hauberk was shredded. The Executioner's blue tunic was soaked with his own blood as he bled from what would have been several fatal sword strokes aimed at a slower, lesser warrior.

Donthar brought his axe over and down in a stroke to split Argantyr's head open had it not been for the man's panther-like reflexes. Donthar slammed the haft of his axe into Argantyr's ribs with a blow that would have knocked most men to the ground. Argantyr kicked Donthar in the midsection and knocked him back a few paces. Wind whipped off Argantyr's blade, but Donthar caught the blow on his axe handle, more splinters flying. Argantyr closed in, and the two of them stood straining, broadsword and battle-axe locked together momentarily, legs braced and pushing the two warriors into one another, steel on steel. Argantyr grunted and pushed Donthar's axe back a few inches towards the warrior. Then, a few more inches.

"Now, Executioner, you don't face a helpless girl in steel manacles for you to torture at your leisure! You face King Argantyr Fenris! Know that her name was Friona, and I loved her! That is why I am going to kill you; then the Giant!"

Argantyr could see Donthar's eyes go wide inside of his hood, then Argantyr ripped the hood from Donthar's head revealing a face disfigured by chemicals and war. Argantyr head-butted Donthar, and the man fell sitting on the floor, blood streaming down his face. But even with his vision obscured by a broken nose, the Executioner was a dangerous man. No sooner had Donthar hit the floor than he was swinging his mighty axe-blade at Argantyr's legs. Argantyr leapt high and came down with a blow from his broadsword that split Donthar's head like a melon. Bits of skull flew up and pelted back down, and brain matter seeped out onto the floor of Thannhausefeer's great hall.

Argantyr's ears rung, and his head throbbed from the head-butt he had delivered to Donthar. The memories burst through his brain like water from a broken dam.

Thannhausefeer overturned the massive table to his feasting hall and bellowed. The chamber rumbled as if it were in an earthquake.

"Aye! The jig is up, Giant! You know why I am here, and I know that you didn't plan on anyone leaving the Isle of Bones with any of your treasure!" Argantyr shouted, plucking the dagger from the belt at his hip and throwing it into Thannhausefeer's left eye. The Giant roared with pain.

Argantyr clutched his wolf-hooded head in agony. "I remember! Damn you, Giant! I remember! *Freae Nome gonastre! Kreedolph hgnome Fenrir! Krynestrees Ryedorf! Hoathehe Fenrir!*" Argantyr shouted and fell to one knee as the transformation began. His face contorted and stretched. His clothes ripped, and he instantly expanded in size, silver hair sprouting from his skin. An elongated snout burst from his face, opening wide a mouthful of deadly razor-like fangs.

Thannhausefeer had managed to pluck the dagger from his eye. He picked up his throne and threw it at the Werewolf, but the creature had already moved from its spot and passed by the Giant, ripping a chunk out of his inner thigh with its deadly fangs. Thannhausefeer's knee buckled. He stumbled backwards and reached for the enormous broadsword on the wall. The Werewolf lunged at the Giant. It stood as nearly as tall as Thannhausefeer on its hind legs. The beast locked powerful jaws on the Giant's face and Thannhausefeer clumsily dropped his sword as Giant and Werewolf tumbled across the floor.

Blood filled Thannhausefeer's eyes from his savaged face, and he could no longer see. He felt along the beast's fur for its throat and clutched at empty air.

"You've blinded me! Damn you!" The Giant felt for his table to brace himself. Trying to stand, his face gored, and his right eye hanging from its socket, the Giant fell, slumping to the floor.

Thannhausefeer heard the padding of feet coming down the hall towards his chamber. He heard the heavy breathing of the beast within the great hall and an almost human sound of laughter coming from the Werewolf. It sounded like the sawing of wood.

"No! Lydiana! Stay away!" Thannhausefeer shouted.

The Giant's daughter screamed. It was too late. The monstrous supernatural wolf gripped Lydiana in its powerful jaws and slung her like a rag doll. She crashed into the wall, and there was a thump and the snapping of bones. She screamed again. The Werewolf locked his jaws on the woman and slung her a second time; another thump—and more bones crunched.

The creature dragged her over beside of her father. Lydiana was unable to move and lay gasping for air but still conscious. Raising himself up on one arm and mustering his strength, Thannhausefeer grasped his enormous broadsword and swung it single-handedly where he heard the Werewolf laughing, but the blade cut empty air; then the beast had its front paws on Thannhausefeer's chest, tearing the Giant's throat out. Lydiana could hear Thannhausefeer's screams segueing into gurgling as blood frothed from his mouth and ran onto the chamber floor. The Werewolf quickly slung Lydiana out of the way so she would not drown in the blood gushing from the dying Giant's mouth.

* * *

Argantyr rocked on all fours, clad only in the giant silver wolf skin. Crimson flowing from the dead Giant's blood matted Argantyr's dark hair and beard, streaming down his naked chest and torso.

Armies had fallen before Argantyr and his hosts, and the ending was always the same. The pain of the man becoming the beast and becoming the man again. *Why should it be any different this time?*

The wounds sustained in the fight with Donthar were quickly healing; the transformation from man to wolf and back to man always insured a quick recovery in the aftermath of battle.

He clutched at his stomach and retched up blood and bits of the giant's flesh. While the beast enjoyed consuming the blood of his enemies, the man had little taste for it. It had been the price of empire.

Once the effects of transformation back to a man had subsided, Argantyr rummaged the antechambers of Thannhausefeer's castle and managed to find enough dead warriors' garments and furs that hadn't yet been disposed of. Some of them were an ill fit, but Argantyr managed to make the best of a bad situation. He had done it before. Generally, he prepared before a battle with a fresh change of clothes; but this time circumstances hadn't allowed for it.

Argantyr could hear the woman's heavy breathing. He went over and knelt down beside her.

"Manannan, I didn't want you to die. I wanted to sail away with you, but I knew he wouldn't let me go. He kept me here as… as a memento of my mother." She gasped, sucking in air.

Argantyr knew that Lydiana had probably thought about running away with him, but he also knew that she had enough of the cruel Giant's blood in her that she enjoyed the suffering of others.

Argantyr cradled Lydiana's head in his left hand so she could see him as he spoke to her. "Listen, woman, my name is Argantyr. That dead woman whose skin you danced in belonged to King Friodere's daughter, Friona. I loved her." With his last words, Argantyr slammed his dagger down into Lydiana's chest. The blow made a thumping sound like a melon struck by a hammer, and blood jettisoned up from the quietus. The woman strangled on the blood frothing from her mouth. Her rheumy eyes widened as she looked upon the *House of Shades*; and then Lydiana expired.

With his sword slung over his back and his dagger at his hip, he listened for movement amidst the silence of Thannhausefeer's castle. His wolfen senses were still strong and warned him of no impending danger, but he left his scabbard tip untied. It always paid to be cautious.

They must have hidden themselves away after hearing what went on in the great hall. It is just as well. I long to be free of the madness of Thannhausefeer's castle and leave this Isle of Bones.

* * *

Argantyr paced the smoky snow covered shore as he looked upon the burning ships crumbling to ashes. Thannhausefeer had set fire to them all.

A ghostly figure appeared on down the shore, barely in his line of vision under the dim sunless sky. The stinging winter wind whipped the woman's billowing white gown and blonde hair. He couldn't make out the features of her face from such a distance with the biting wind blurring his vision. He followed her on down the shore for a while but never seemed to gain any distance on her. She raised her arm languorously and pointed to a ship sailing just on the horizon. By the red and white striped sail with the banner of the great bird of prey in the center, Argantyr knew that it was one of King Friodere's Sea Hawks, and therefore friendly.

"Ho! Sea Hawk! It is Argantyr Fenris! Ho!" he called to the crew of the ship.

Argantyr could see them lowering a lifeboat and men filing in it to row ashore. Though he surmised that reason had told King Friodere that his daughter was probably dead by now, Argantyr knew there was still hope in his friend's heart. He dreaded breaking the news to the old king. If Friodere had only summoned Argantyr to look for her sooner…

While he waited for the rescue boat Argantyr scanned the shore for the Woman in White, but there was no sign of her.

The Chamber Of Juleptsu

By Jaron Evil

Gorrim spun the five-foot shaft of the rune-covered battle-axe, sending a whorl of blood and ichor spiralling from Krella's enchanted double blades. Grimly, he surveyed what could be seen of the cavern's shadowed depths in the flickering red-orange of the torches lining the stone walls at irregular intervals. This wasn't the main chamber, he knew; large as it was, he was well aware that the ancient priests and acolytes of the god Juleptsu would never have trusted ultimate guardianship to a few score misshapen subhumans and their pets.

Absently, he rested the head of the battle-axe on the chest of the corpse he was using as a platform to improve his vantage point, and shook the blood from his hands. Some of it was his—he was bleeding slowly from numerous small wounds he'd taken to his arms and shoulders in the short but furious battle he'd had with cavern's defenders. His dwarven chainmail was rent in spots, as even the *kythrandir* links could not withstand the primordial fury and iron jaws of creatures Time should have erased long since. He'd also acquired a small slash to the left side of his jaw, and it stung abominably—likely a bit of venom in the wound, he realized. Most of the blood was that of his foes, he noted with savage satisfaction.

The body on which he stood was that of one of the *Fenriksyr* dogs he'd decapitated in the defenders' initial onslaught. Like most of his kind, he was actually shorter than the measure of Krella's haft. The dead (and nicely foreshortened) *Fenriksyr* was, in fact, merely the topmost of an impressive pile of corpses and body parts, subhuman and canine, but the dwarf did not hesitate to use the remains to improve his perspective and plan the next phase of his search. The dog's body was huge, even with the fearsome head removed: the creature was a sort of Hel-hound, taller at the shoulder than Gorrim himself when standing on all fours, and nearly as broad across the chest as the dwarf, whose musculature and strength were legendary already among his own kind.

Not that he cared for such things particularly, but the name Gorrim Guar-Mortik was already known, was whispered in places where one did not speak the names of others aloud.

Though there had been no other living soul to witness what had taken place in the cavern, it was grim and bloody testimony to Gorrim's great strength and martial skills, as augmented by the ancient fey magic imbuing the blades of Krella, the Headsplitter, that fully twenty of *Fenriksyr* lay dead in their own blood, with twice that number of their powerful but stunted subhuman masters, their curving hook-tipped blades beside them.

He considered his options. The small bit of canine venom in the wound on his jaw was irksome, but not enough to slow his reactions or cause permanent damage, and his dwarven mail, which hung nearly to his knees and covered him from throat to wrist, nullified the effects of any venom that might have otherwise accompanied his other wounds. *Kithrandyr* chain was highly prized for ample reason. He felt fatigue only slightly, and it was leaving him quickly. The cavern was far beneath the surface of the world in which he normally moved, and he was a dwarf. His people were of the earth's depths, and the mystical millennia-long ties of dwarven-kind to the mineral-rich depths, passive though they were said to be, were reasserting themselves in him.

Despite the dangers of the task he'd accepted and the arcane forces aligned against him, he felt strangely at home in the depths. He could sense the cavern's roof far above him, and knew just how far the walls extended around him. He could even sense the location of the final doorway, far across the cavern, the portal through which he would gain access to the Chamber of Juleptsu… if he survived whatever additional surprises the accursed priests had built into the cavern in which he presently stood.

He became aware of the earth as a Presence, a source of power on which he might be able to draw, though he would have to rely on instinct alone. He felt as though the Presence might be female in nature, motherly, and just for a moment, it was as if a soft hand had touched his brow. It must, he was sure, have been his imagination. The wound on his jaw did seem less painful…

By the gods, he thought, time to get moving. He'd been attacked by the dogs and their masters almost immediately on entry to the cavern. He was still close to the entrance, their bodies piled under and around him. The flickering torchlight revealed that the entire scope of the fight had fallen within a semi-circle of lighter stone around the entry, a clear line of demarcation from the dark, shadowed floor beyond it. The cavern's defenders had been stupid, clustering near his entry point and giving him plenty of victims within Krella's lethal arc, instead of using the shadows and the cavern's size to their advantage.

Clambering down from the pile of corpses, he picked his way to the inner edge of the semi-circular boundary. The light of the torches was poorer here, but it appeared that neither body parts nor even a single drop of blood had touched the floor of the cavern outside the lighter stones.

Perhaps, he mused, the defenders had not been quite as stupid as he thought. Showing his teeth, he lifted Krella high and began to chant softly in the dwarven Old Tongue. After a few moments, the axe-head began to glow with a soft blue-white radiance. As Gorrim continued to chant, the sweat beginning to stand on his brow, Krella's light—for in truth, Gorrim had summoned the Light of the Fey—intensified, illuminating a much larger area before him.

This, he well knew, should have been impossible, just as it should have been impossible for any dwarf to wield Elven weapons forged aeons before, and by the highest of Elven magics at that. Nor should Krella have responded to language other than High Elven. Dwarfs and elves, though they'd occasionally been forced to cooperate over the millennia, still regarded each other with deep suspicion and intense dislike, if not outright hatred.

But Krella had fallen to his hand with the death of an enemy, an Elven assassin. The weapon had spoken to his spirit; his spirit had answered, and there was a strange bond between the dwarf and the near-sentient axe. He had long since ceased to question it. Rather, he had accepted it and was grateful for it.

The idea that the link between dwarf and mystical weapon might bespeak a strange and arcane destiny awaiting him in a shadowed future did not even occur to him. Gorrim was, after all, a dwarf.

His destination, the portal to the Chamber of Juleptsu, was before him, diagonally to his right at a distance of perhaps two hundred paces. Krella surrounded him in a luminescent blue-white sphere of perhaps thirty paces in diameter.

So, he thought. Minimal time to apprehend and repel attacks from the darkness around him. No way, save by his other senses, to detect a possible attack from above or below, or to forestall magical attacks.

He had known it would not be easy.

He would not have had it otherwise.

It was time. He leaned Krella blades-up against the corpse of another fallen dog, and began by gathering seemingly random items from the cavern's floor, within the half-circle of lighter stones: loose pebbles, bits of metal, primitive charms from the necks and bodies of the subhumans—all small, hard items that he deposited in a small pouch. He also selected four of his enemies' vicious, hooked knives, thrusting them into the wide, studded belt about his waist.

One of the dead subhumans had carried a small oaken shield, round, and bound in iron. That, too, he took for himself, loosening the crude binding straps and thrusting through his left arm, chain and all. Then, by Krella's light, he began casting items from his collection of pebbles, bits and pieces, one by one, in the direction of the portal he sought, cautiously stepping forward as the pebbles and bits he cast before him provoked no response.

One never knew when a misstep might trigger a trap for the unwary.

His tension grew with every step, but there were no hidden traps, no sudden attacks or waves of hostile magic. By the time he'd crossed the cavern, anticipating attack with every step, his muscles were tight with tension and he could feel the sweat trickling down his back beneath his mail and protective leather under-jerkin. The air had grown thick, and his surroundings had grown all too quiet, the sound of the cast pebbles seeming ridiculously loud as they bounced on the cavern's floor.

Krella's light revealed he had reached the far wall, and he could sense the Chamber of Juleptsu before him, though his eyes told him he was facing a blank wall. He hesitated, and then cast a pebble at the wall itself. When nothing happened, he snorted and threw a second, larger rock with more force. To his astonishment, his second throw actually appeared to leave a small crack in the wall, a crack that began to grow and spread of its own accord, crumbling the surrounding stone. Fragments of the wall hit the floor of the chamber. In Krella's otherworldly glow, the fallen shards of stone began to move slowly in his direction.

"Gurni's beard!" he cursed aloud. No sooner had the oath left Gorrim's blood-stained lips, than the fallen stone fragments had become spiders, hungering for his blood—and they no longer moved slowly, scuttling at him with terrifying speed, poison visibly dripping from their mandibles.

He was not afraid of spiders, and the sole of his boot made quick and messy work of the eight-legged crawlers. There were those, he knew, even among warriors, who might have been paralyzed with fear. He was not one of them. The ugly arachnid was no real threat to him, though they did serve as a warning for what might await in Juleptsu's hidden nest.

He considered his situation before risking entry into the dark portal revealed by the shattered wall. The *Fenriksyr* venom was causing his jaw to pulsate with pain yet again. Pulling off the steel gauntlet on his right hand, he dug a thick forefinger into the wound and scooped out something wet. Flicking it onto the ground, he saw it was a combination of coagulated blood and green ichor. Ignoring the pain, he dug at the wound again, causing it to bleed more heavily, and he persisted until he saw only fresh blood on his fingers. Satisfied that he'd rid himself of as much venom as possible, he pressed on the wound firmly for a few moments to slow the bleeding. Better, he thought. Much better.

The moment of his confrontation with Juleptsu was almost upon him. First, he checked his weapons, seeing to Krella's edge and the security of his borrowed shield, and then he shrugged once or twice to settling his chainmail about his massive shoulders and chest. He slipped the gauntlet back onto his hand, and flexed his fingers into a mighty, steel fist.

He was ready. He spat, seized Krella firmly, and deliberately stepped forward to the portal, the axe lighting his way as he passed through it. He was prepared, Gorrim told himself, to challenge the old god in his very lair. Truly, he knew not the meaning of fear, though he did not move without caution. The world held much more fell things than *Fenriksyr* and spiders in the deep places of the Black Earth, as he well knew. Juleptsu, black ancient of the depths, was among the darkest of beings.

The portal led him down a long, narrow corridor that opened into another torchlit chamber, vast and circular. The torches' wan purple flames cast a sick and unearthly light—clearly, the work of conjuration with dark magics that inspired dizziness and nausea. Not surprising, Gorrim considered, given what little was known of Juleptsu's true nature. Even the air seemed tainted. The room was silent, save for the faint dripping of water. Thick, scabrous webbing depended crazily from the ceiling, casting malevolent shadows.

This is too easy, he thought, knowing the chamber to be a trap. He began moving toward the chamber's center, Krella at the ready. The sound of sliding stone turned his attention to the portal through which he had entered. It was now closed, as if it had never been open at all. Trapped inside the Chamber of Juleptsu, he became very aware of three things: the echoed dripping of water, the sound of his own breathing, and the gentle metallic hum of Krella, his truest companion, ever-willing to tear his foes asunder. The axe knew what was transpiring, he was certain; the hum indicated that it was responding to hostile magic, countering what it could.

As Gorrim approached the centre of the room, Krella's glow revealed a circular obsidian pillar he'd never have seen in the torchlight—it seemed to absorb the dull, flickering glow, remaining virtually undetectable in the dim chamber unless one bumped into it. He held Krella closer, and saw that the pillar was deeply carved with prophetic tellings in what he knew to be a runic language, and an ancient one. Gorrim spoke several tongues and could make out some of the symbols, but he could not cipher the meaning of the carved scripts themselves.

Whatever this dark speech is, he thought, time must've forgotten long ago.

As he studied the carvings upon the pillar, the skin on the back of his neck began to prickle, and Krella's glow intensified. From far above, there came a sudden, eerie chittering, and it was clear that he was not alone. He held Krella high, using the Light of the Fey to see what new horror stalked him from above.

Something struck his arm with great force, knocking Krella from Gorrim's grasp and sending it flying across the chamber with such force that the axe embedded itself into the wall. There was a rush of air as a heavy body dropped near him, landing lightly on eight spined and curved legs, each longer than Gorrim was tall. He had to tilt his head back to get a glimpse of the terrible face of his foe in the dim light. With Krella's light extinguished, it took a moment for his eyes to adjust.

Gorrim found himself face-to-face with a great and terrible spider, ready to devour its prey, its eyes bulging and mandibles dripping foul-smelling, poisonous ichor. Gorrim grunted angrily, and leaping forward, drove his gauntleted fist directly into the spider's maw, sending a large fang flying free. The empty cavity spurted black blood and ichor, and the colossal spider hissed in rage, and leaped back out of range, gathering itself. Krella was far from Gorrim's hand, and his newfound oaken shield became the only defence against its certain retaliation.

To his shock, the spider spoke.

"I have not tasted dwarf for a millennium. Take solace in the knowledge that you will be enjoyed!"

So—here was his foe, in the flesh. "Juleptsu," said Gorrim, almost smiling. "You've been an infection in the body of the earth for far too long. I will end your immortal life, or die in the attempt—and in that case, you're likely to choke to death on me, you disgusting insect."

He pulled a hooked knife from his belt and threw it at Juleptsu, who merely suffered a scratch on his blackened face from the shoddy weapon. The spider laughed.

"Shall I begin?" he hissed.

Gorrim cursed the crude blades of his would-be dispatchers under his breath.

Perfect, he thought. Poorly weighted curved blades are useless for throwing, lunkhead. He needed Krella, and between him and the axe was Juleptsu, the Spider God, the Dark Ancient himself.

Juleptsu pounced at the dwarf, cracking the shield and knocking Gorrim over. His leap took him over the dwarf's head, and one of his black legs bypassed the shield and struck Gorrim a glancing blow to the jaw, dislocating it, and worsening his wound. But instead of taking advantage, Juleptsu backed off as Gorrim roared in pain, clearly taking sadistic pleasure from the damage he'd inflicted. He even raised one foreleg and beckoned to the fallen dwarf, inviting him to try again.

The dwarf got to his feet, grabbed his jaw, and shoved it back into place. The crunch of bone was audible throughout the chamber. Gorrim grimaced, spitting a blood-stained molar upon the floor. He spat blood and shook his head, and then focused on the Spider God. He'd been lucky, he knew: if the foul poison oozing from Juleptsu's mandibles had touched his bare flesh, he'd already be writhing in death agony, and he couldn't be certain that even the magical protection against poison that was fused into each link of the *kithrandyr* mail would be enough to withstand the Dark Ancient's taint. His piercing green eyes grew cold and flat, and he stretched his great muscles, his joints cracking as he did so. He bared his teeth at Juleptsu in a humourless smile. "Thanks," he grated, his voice like gravel. "I needed that."

He suddenly charged forward, running at the great and repellent arachnid with shocking speed. The Spider God crouched low, its two forelegs raised in anticipation, as if to embrace the charging dwarf. Then, at the last possible instant, Gorrim crouched low as he ran, gathered himself and leapt, his short legs straightening with a snap and propelling him up and over the hissing monster.

Instead of leaping to meet him, Juleptsu reacted in shock as the dwarf used his own tactic against him. The arachnid reached up with a single foreleg in an attempt to knock the airborne dwarf to the chamber's floor. As he sailed over Juleptsu's head, Gorrim reached with his mailed right hand, seizing the tip of Juleptsu's upraised foreleg in his iron grip and twisting with all his strength and the weight of his own mailed body as he flew past the startled god. Whatever Juleptsu had believed about dwarfs, he clearly had not understood Gorrim's capabilities.

Like all the males of his kind, Gorrim was short but massively muscled and boned. His weight was considerable, and he was fully mailed. He had propelled himself into the air with great force, like a dwarven missile, a living weapon. His hand had wielded Krella's weight for years; it had swung a dwarven hammer effortlessly and endlessly. He had never been defeated in the annual dwarven wrestling competitions, and the force of his grasp had caused more than one opponent to break down in agony or sprawl senseless before him.

Nothing in Juleptsu's experience could have prepared him for what occurred next: with a rending snap, the Spider God's foreleg shattered at multiple points, its tip completely crushed in Gorrim's steel fist. Juleptsu screamed in agony, skittering sideways, his foreleg flopping before him with ichor spurting through broken chitin. That natural armor might have turned aside an ordinary sword-blade, but even the Spider God's supernatural form could not withstand the torqueing power of the mighty dwarf's grasp.

Gorrim flew well past his foe, righting himself in mid-air and landing with a roll and the harsh clanging of *kithrandyr* mail. He skidded to a halt at the far wall, exactly at the spot where Krella's massive haft stood out from the stone. Casually, he turned and regarded Juleptsu, who was crouched low some distance from him, nursing his shattered foreleg and trembling in pain and rage as he returned the dwarf's gaze.

Without taking his eyes from the loathsome creature, he reached up and put a hand on the axe haft. The weapon did not come free. Turning, he raised his other hand to the haft and appeared to struggle, still not looking away from Juleptsu. Then, when he detected a change in the tone of the creature's hissing—perhaps a note of relief—he dropped both hands and spoke.

"You think still to kill me, Old One? Or perhaps you think to escape me because I cannot make use of my weapon? That is it, isn't it? I've done what no mortal creature has ever done to you. You think perhaps you may still destroy me, but you would rather retreat and heal yourself while I seek to free myself from this cavern." He paused, then hawked and spat, his spittle blood-tinged. "You said it had been a thousand years since you tasted dwarf. You've forgotten quite a lot about my kind. We are famed for many things—our strength, our tolerance for pain, our ferocity, perhaps even our own tastiness," he continued in an amused tone. "But we're best known for the dwarven sense of humour. I myself, for example, am an extremely funny fellow. Let me demonstrate." He bared his teeth in a humourless snarl.

With that, Gorrim reached up again with his right hand, grasped Krella's haft and effortlessly withdrew the weapon from the solid rock wall. The axe-head came free with an appalling screech of metal on stone, its luminescence restored as soon as the undamaged blades left the rock. He leaned forward, waved Krella in Juleptsu's direction, and winked. "You see?" he laughed. "I was just pretending. I really am a very amusing dwarf." He stopped laughing and his visage grew cold, vicious. "Now," he whispered as the Spider God shook and hissed, "it is *I* who shall begin."

Juleptsu moved, not waiting for the dwarf's attack. With his shattered limb flopping uselessly before him, he used the seven good limbs remaining to him to launch himself to the nearest vertical surface. He hit the gently curving wall lightly at more than double Gorrim's height from the ground, and scurried up, his speed only slightly diminished. He charged around the circular chamber, his movements erratic, in an attempt to fool Gorrim's keen eyes in the darkness. But the dwarf was used to the world beneath the surface of the Black Earth, and his eyes, keen though they were, became secondary to his other senses, grown sharp from years inside the mountains. His hearing was extremely acute, as was his sense of smell.

Juleptsu could not keep from the air of the chamber the taint of his own poison or the foulness of the ichor which flowed within him. Nor was he used to coping silently with the flaming agony of the damage Gorrim had inflicted in shattering his foreleg.

From his vantage point high on the wall above the dwarf, he saw the dwarf inhale deeply, could hear the beating of the dwarf's heart as it pumped fresh, red blood through Gorrim's veins. He sensed the dwarf's breathing change, sensed the dwarf's energy coalescing, focusing inward in some strange manner he did not fully grasp. Gorrim tilted his head slightly to one side, his eyes blank, as if listening to a voice only he could hear. The vast muscles in his arms appeared to relax, and he held Krella loosely in his grasp, standing in a pool of tranquillity defined by the light of that cursed axe. Juleptsu did not relish the prospect of Krella's kiss, god though he might be.

With a good deal of pain-inspired caution, Juleptsu now descended slowly and silently from fresh webbing above the dwarf, cursing to himself with each spastic movement of his shattered limb. He no longer wished to play with his prey; he no longer wished to risk further injury by ending the dwarf between his powerful mandibles, especially as the socket that had housed his missing fang ached insanely, interfering with his control. Instead, the chitin on his back split open, and he extended his stinger—a curving ten-foot reticulated column of chitinous armour tipped with a hollow, hooked appendage through which he was capable of pumping large quantities of lethal poison into his prey. It was to be hoped, he thought to himself, that Gorrim would not know he possessed this weapon, would have no plan to resist it, focused as he had been on Juleptsu's mandibles as the spider god's primary weapons.

Gorrim, for his part, was simply waiting. He found himself in a strange state of calm readiness, despite the fact he could no longer see Juleptsu. It didn't matter; the smell of the Dark Ancient pervaded the chamber, but it was slowly growing stronger above him, and slightly to one side. He could hear, faintly, the friction between the broken pieces of chitin on the shattered foreleg. He leapt to his right, spinning left to face the spot he was sure Juleptsu would hit the ground and raising his shield arm.

He was almost in position when Juleptsu's stinger lashed forward out of nowhere, piercing through the dwarf's shield at the leading edge and deep into the back of Gorrim's clenched hand where his gauntlet had slipped forward to expose flesh. He howled with agony, his features contorted and his face grey with the shock of the wound. Juleptsu laughed and ran back up the wall to enjoy the dwarf's agonizing death from a safe vantage point.

Throwing the pierced shield, Gorrim fell to his knees, senses reeling. Clinging desperately to consciousness, he grasped Krella far up on the haft, near the blades, and forced his envenomed hand against the ground. He knew what he must do, or Juleptsu's venom would surely carry him to the afterlife. Without time for thought or breath, he roared his anger as he brought Krella down with tremendous speed and force upon his wrist, severing his hand before Juleptsu's venom could spread within him. So great was his stroke with the rune-graven axe that the heat and pressure from the blade sealed the wound as Krella passed through flesh and bone to sink a blade into the solid stone of the floor.

Immediately, his head began to clear, though the pain of the amputation was staggering. But he was a dwarven master warrior, and no conventional wound save a lethal blow could keep him down for long. He had acted before the venom had spread; he would have known were that not the case because he'd have been dead or dying by now. He took several deep breaths, and slowly got to his feet, picking up his severed hand as he did so.

Juleptsu, meanwhile, had scuttled back down the wall, sure the battle was his. He regarded Gorrim, disbelieving—the wretched creature was standing, and strongly at that.

"That was a good trick. You deserve a reward," said Gorrim, tossing his severed hand into the spider's face. The creature's hiss of outrage was deafening in the chamber, and it scuttled back momentarily. Gorrim immediately took advantage, bending and wrenching Krella free of the floor in a single, fluid motion.

They charged at each other with mortal intent, the sound of their impact explosive. To Juleptsu's outrage and growing alarm, Gorrim did not get knocked back when they clashed together, nor did he stagger. Hissing wildly, he bit madly at the dwarf's handless arm, only to find that *kithrandyr* was, as it had ever been, much stronger than it looked, and the fiery acid of his own venom burned between his jaws. Gorrim, not even flinching, began hacking away with Krella where Juleptsu's loathsome head met his body. His chain was indeed protecting him from death by poison, thank the gods, so Juleptsu's bite brought only pain—an intense and ugly pain that galvanized him, prompting him to swing Krella with even greater fury, the fey blades unequalled in all the world.

It only took three more vicious, single-handed strokes before Krella penetrated the spider god's natural armour, and Juleptsu began spurting black blood and vile green ichor. Immediately he released the dwarf's bloody left arm and scrabbled back in a vain attempt to put distance between them.

Gorrim would not be denied. His axe swung one final time, severing half of Juleptsu's head in a veritable explosion of ichor, dark foulness and exploding arachnid brain.

The Dark Ancient was dead, yet his body driven by arcane impulse, convulsed and writhed. The corpse began to twist onto his back. Gorrim kept hacking wildly at the spider, each strike imbedding itself in Juleptsu's lesser armoured underbelly. After twelve axe strikes, Juleptsu ceased to move, and Gorrim paused for breath, exhaustion finally beginning to take him. He looked coldly into the spider god's faceted eyes, now dim and lifeless. The stench of the foul liquids pouring from the corpse was unspeakably vile.

Gorrim glanced around the dark chamber, swaying from pain and blood loss as he did so. The female presence he felt before grew. It was beneficent, he knew, and powerful—very powerful. It seemed stronger than ever, and grateful. The purple torchlight flickered and then strengthened, changing to a normal and vibrant orange. The walls began to crumble around him. The ground shook from the force of falling stone, though not a single fragment touched him, and Gorrim's gaze drew wide as the falling obsidian debris hit the ground and immediately became dust. The carcass of Juleptsu hardened, turning white, and then to stone. A thin smile emerged behind the dwarf's long red beard. One final time, he brought down Krella upon the stone carcass, shattering it into thousands of pieces.

The black stone pillar in the center of the room shed its obsidian skin, as if by fire, revealing a large glowing crystal. Gorrim fell to his knees before it, humbled, knowing he had rid the Black Earth of a dark, ancient magic. Could it be…?

"Earthmother," he began cautiously. "Is it You, truly? After so long? Your foolish son before did not dare to believe…" He could sense assent, forgiveness, and unaccountably, a trace of amusement. "For too long have You been under this poisonous curse. Thank You for helping me to set You free." He paused, and then suddenly smiled. "As one of your children, I am not usually this modest." The sense of amusement intensified, but it was tempered with deep and abiding love, and a profound gratitude.

Gorrim's arm began to tingle. He looked down, eyes growing wide. Before his eyes, in but a moment's time, his left hand reappeared, uninjured and unblemished. It tingled more intensely, as if it had merely fallen asleep for a time. A tear rolled down his cheek as he clenched his new hand for the first time.

"My gratitude, Earthmother, for this, and all Your blessings, now and ever." He had no more words, and of course, the Presence did not speak. But he knew Its love, gratitude and protection would be with him. Always.

There was no barrier to his departure. Slowly, painfully, he made his way back to the corridor, through the outer chamber, and thence through the long and convoluted caverns to return to the mortal world above. The Black Earth was a vast terrain, littered with demons and other fell things that dwelled below and above the surface, but as the sun rose to crest distant mountains with its majesty, Gorrim knew the Earth-mother had been given back a small piece of her great dominion. The thought made him smile.

Cosmic Horror

The Riddle Master

By Ernest Cunningham Hellwell

It is with great trepidation that I create this memoir. But it occurs to me it might be a way to rid myself of the demons of my mind. When the uncertain aspects of life become overwhelming I resort to the pen. And a master of the pen I am indeed! I am an author by profession... but to my continual discomfort, not a wealthy one. And it appears that in times like these I not only resort to the pen but also the elixirs that help blur the pain of my suffering soul. It is my opinion that such evils have brought me to where I am today and I must breathe these words onto this parchment to exorcise the wicked dreams that have been wrought upon me. For I find myself looking over my shoulder, reeling from the shadows of my own thoughts.

The weaving of this web of a tale begins at a pub that I frequent from time to time in Baltimore called Ryan's. I had stopped in that night with my dear friend, Mr. Frederick Thomas, to confer upon some business matters. I was not in the best of moods for I was deeply discomforted by my financial situation. And this was to be the topic of which I would return to several times during our conversation that eve.

Not long ago I had published my second public effort, a book of poems of my own creation. It was originally published while I was in the Army where I managed my way up to the rank of Sargent Major of the Artillery, which is the highest rank an enlisted man can achieve. To my displeasure my name did not even appear on the book as its author. I procured an early discharge from my army unit so that I could enroll in West Point Military Academy. This I did in July 1830 but was discharged from the academy in February of 1831. It was through the help of some of my classmates at West Point and other friends and family that I raised enough money to publish the book of poems again. This time I added a few more poetic tapestries, but most importantly, the book was published with my name upon it.

Unfortunately neither one of these publications made me any money to speak of. So I have resorted to working as an editorial assistant here and a journalist there with different publications. I had entered four short stories into a contest at the *Philadelphia Saturday Courier* to no avail. Not only did my stories not win the contest but the devil of a publisher saw fit to go ahead and publish my stories without paying me anything.

It is a foul world, this business of writing and publishing, for since I submitted the stories to the contest the publisher announced to me that they were now the property of the *Philadelphia Saturday Courier* and that they could do with the stories as they pleased. There should be laws to protect the writer from such criminal thievery.

Ryan's is not a place one would acquaint with the higher classes. For that matter it was more of a putrid place but it was one of the few establishments that I was not indebted to. I had most recently acquired the taste for absinth, and Ryan's was a pub that had no qualms serving such libation. Mr. Thomas and I were seated at a table in the back corner of the pub. I must admit to having many drinks, putting myself in a fairly blurry state of inebriation. I was getting a might boisterous as the night lingered on, with my howling about unfair business practices by the publishers and the fact that I seemed to have chosen the most difficult of careers to make a suitable living at. I remember blurting out something in the manner of "I would give anything to prove to the world what a literary master I am."

It was at that moment from a table across from us that a gallant-looking gent with jet black shoulder-length hair and a dark complexion rose from his seat. He had a finely trimmed mustache and the eyes, oh, the eyes were like green emeralds peering at me with an intensity that chilled my bones! Finely dressed was he with a black suit and red shirt under a vest with gold embroidered paisley patterns. He was tall and looked formidable in physic. He approached our table and with an eerie, deep voice he spoke, "So it would be anything that you would give to have this wish?" He spoke with a foreign accent of some sort. It was not something I could place but it sounded European. Now having lived in the coastal regions of the eastern part of these United States, I was very familiar with the accents of immigrating Europeans, but this man's accent was not completely discernible to me.

I responded to my inquisitor with a rather unfriendly tone due to my disposition at the time. "Would there be some reason, albeit unknown to me, why I should share my wishes with an uninvited stranger?"

He stood tall at our table looming over me and with that strange low voice he spoke again. "It is possible that I can help you attain that which you seek, my good sir." And then he bowed to me almost like an Oriental would. Even though I was disturbed by his presence I found him extremely intriguing. As he rose erect from his bowing gesture he asked, "May I join you gentlemen? I would be honored to purchase the drinks for the length of our conversation."

Considering my financial stress at the time and the fact that Frederick had purchased most of the drinks so far that evening I decided to entertain this odd man. So I stood and introduced myself and Frederick and then politely offered him a seat at our table. He bowed again and then introduced himself to us as Mr. Leviat as he took a chair at our table.

"That sounds like a French name, my good man!" I exclaimed. "Where do you hail from, sir?"

He replied back with an indirect answer to my inquiry, "I am from many places. A shore does not exist that I have not set foot upon. My travels are vast and I have been exposed to all cultures around this world. It is because of where I have been and what I have learned that I can support the claim of being able to help you with your… let us say, predicament."

Our newly found acquaintance raised his hand and motioned to the barkeep to supply the table with another round of drinks. "So you are a writer, yes?" His question almost sounded more like a statement and he really did not supply me with sufficient time to respond. "It is an admirable profession but not usually a lucrative one. I could not help but overhear your conversation about the difficulties you have encountered so far in your field of endeavor. May I be so bold to ask… are you good?"

Before I could speak Frederick came to my rescue as any good friend would, I suppose. "He is not just good. He is a rare poetic talent that the world has never seen the likes of before. I have faith that he will be recognized for his literary genius one day and I myself will do anything I can to help him become discovered."

The tall dark man spoke abruptly. "So you are his agent?"

"Uh… no," Frederick replied. "I am just a good friend that believes in the stroke of this man's pen."

The man leaned back in his chair. "So there is no agent but avid desire I feel. Ah… our drinks."

The barkeep appeared with a tray carrying a bottle of absinth and two glasses, one of which he placed in front of me and the other before our newfound acquaintance. I did not even see the dark man reach for his money but he produced a more than ample amount for the barkeep. Our server's eyes opened wide and as he retreated he exclaimed, "If there is anything else you need, good sir, you have just to call. My name is Ryan."

Before the innkeeper could utter another word Mr. Leviat said with a bit of an aristocratic air, "Yes, yes, if we have need of thee you will know. Now begone, for my friends and I have business to discuss."

At that moment I actually began to like this mysterious man. He was obviously a man of means and was willing to treat those beneath his level as such, a trait that I considered impressive. As the barkeep humbly exited back toward his counter our new drinking comrade reached inside of his jacket and produced a small bottle of dark liquid and looked at me. "I see you too appreciate the effects of a stronger drink than most." I would not really call this an astute observation from our newfound companion but a truism none the less. "May I have the honor of sharing something with you that will enhance the absinth to an even higher level?" He pulled the small cork from the mouth of the bottle and started to act as if he was going to pour it into my drink when Frederick pulled my glass back and we both looked deeply into those green eyes with concern. "Oh... how rude of me!" exclaimed the dark man. "I will show you it is safe." He began pouring a bit of the dark substance within the bottle into his own drink. "You only need add a touch and the effects are quite wonderful. It is called laudanum and is derived from the poppy... poppy tears as it is sometimes called, lachryma papaveris, Papaver somniferum. I will drink first so that you may understand that it will be of no harm to thee." He downed his glass and then gave me a questioning gaze waiting for my approval to let him add the elixir to my own. I gave him a nod and extended my glass, as did Frederick, but with much more hesitation than I.

We had several drinks at our new companion's expense as he continued to tell us of exotic lands in the far east and abroad where customs were much different and strange compared to the ways of the new world. His demeanor was very theatrical, you might say. His gestures were amplified by the fact that his lingual capability was extraordinary. Obviously an educated man, but when I inquired of him where he gained such knowledge, he simply replied that he was a world traveler and that he acquired such understanding through his dealings with man around the globe.

It did not take long before the effects of the laudanum made my head swirl in a hazy way that I had never experienced before. It was then I noticed that Frederick had succumbed to the night's carousing and had slipped into slumber with his head resting upon the table top. Mr. L. looked him over for a moment and then exclaimed, "He will be fine. I assure you, my good man, there is no need to worry over him. Now shall we proceed to the matter at hand and discuss your wishes?"

I am not one to confide in strangers but in this instance I believe the night's drinking was getting the better of me and caused me to drop my guard in the presence of this stranger that completely intrigued and enticed me to wonderment. I'm sure my words were slurring as I spoke, telling him that what I really wished was to be recognized as a great writer. How I was sick of seeing authors of trash being hailed as genius and wise. And just as my ranting was beginning to get loud, my dark mysterious comrade put a finger to his lips. My voice was immediately silenced but it was very strange indeed for I am not sure that I willed myself to stop talking.

"I have connections!" exclaimed Mr. Leviat. "It is I who can make thine wishes reality. But you must make your wish explicit so that I can be precise in rendering your desires."

"What?" I began to laugh almost hysterically. "Are you some kind of djin escaped from his lamp and searching for a master?"

His response was fast and direct. "I am no djin, and this offer I do not bring to you in any manner of jest. I am extremely serious when I say that I can deliver what you wish for."

I stopped laughing, for this man's sincerity was genuine. "And what is in it for you, Mr. Leviat? Everything and every man has a price. What is yours?"

Mr. L. rose from the table, placing his hands upon its top, leaning in and looming over me, his black mane dangling between my face and his. "There is always a price, is there not? And I am no different than any other, for I too have a price." He sat back down as he poured us another couple of drinks. "My price is rather simple, actually. I only ask two things of you. First, you must prove to me that you are indeed the literary master that you claim to be. So I propose to render a riddle to you. You do know what a riddle is?" The look of consternation upon my face was apparent at having been asked such a condescending question. He then continued, "As I said, I will compose a riddle for you to solve, and if you are successful I will grant you the one thing that you seem to desire most. But you must be precise in your wish as I aforementioned. So what would your wish be, my good sir?"

Now at this moment I was doing my best to stifle the laugh that was about to roar out of my throat. But I controlled the urge and instead I decided to humor this green-eyed stranger. I told him that my wish would be to become one of the most well-known and respected writers worldwide for centuries to come.

The dark man immediately motioned to Ryan. When the barkeep came to our table Mr. L. requested a pen and ink. Ryan quickly scampered off to the back room and came quickly with a bottle of ink and a dip pen along with some paper. "The parchment will not be necessary... I prefer my own." Mr. L. then deposited another healthy sum of money into the barkeep's hands and exclaimed, "Now leave us be, man. Can't you see we have important business at hand?" The keep scurried away counting the money. In all honesty I have never seen Ryan so subdued by anyone. Usually his demeanor was that of an arrogant ass.

The stranger pulled a piece of parchment from inside his jacket and began to write. I noticed that the parchment had a very strange and porous look to it. Thicker than normal and a much darker color to it than that of which I was accustomed to. His left hand was so quick at writing that I could only see a blur. I was sure it was my level of intoxication that was affecting my vision. The room was starting to tilt slightly but I felt wonderful. The combination of the absinth and the laudanum was exquisite. Then I came slightly to my senses and realized that he had not told all yet. "My dear sir, you said there were two things you would ask of me. I only remember you mentioning one."

He stopped writing and looked sternly into my eyes. "If you prove to be unworthy of the wish and do not solve the riddle by... let us say, the stroke of midnight tomorrow, then you will forfeit your eternal soul to me to do with as I wish."

This time I could not stifle the laugh. It blurted out of me like a volcano erupting. I reeled back in my chair laughing exorbitantly. I stood up and started to announce to all in the pub what an absurd thing the man had just said, but to my surprise, there was no trace of anyone in the pub except for myself, the dark man, and Frederick still slumbering upon the table top. Not even Ryan was present. That was highly unusual, for he ruled his keep, like all other tavern owners, and rarely left his post. I looked at my timepiece and it was still early in the night, not quite yet midnight. I was befuddled and unsure what to think. I could not remember seeing anyone escape the confines of the pub. It had not been overcrowded, but I was sure that there had been a good number of patrons in the establishment just minutes before.

I fell back into my chair in bewilderment as the dark stranger spoke to me again. "I see that you doubt my earnestness. But what do you have to lose, my good sir? A little time pondering a poetic riddle. There is no one here to see you enter the deal and your friend is quite asleep and unknowing himself. So there is no chance of anyone belittling you for humoring me and my little game. You see, I too consider myself a poet of sorts. And I wish to challenge you to this battle of wits. You say you are a master of the pen. Well then... prove it. You don't seem to be a religious man so maybe you don't even believe that you possess a soul. And if that is true then I would have nothing to gain even if you don't solve the riddle. You portray yourself to others as a literary genius. I say you are not the master. It is I that am the master, and if you don't enter into this agreement with me then I will reward myself highly with feelings of conquering you without ever having to write the riddle at all."

Now this was a statement that needed rebuttal. And there was only one way to prove to this knave that I was the writer and literary giant that Frederick had claimed me to be... and that was to accept his offer, no matter how absurd it was, and dissect the riddle which he would create. There was a slight sense of caution within me, but very slight. He did appear to be a highly educated person but I still had the utmost confidence in my own capability in such a challenge. And even though I did not really believe he could make my wish come true, I did take careful notice of the amount of money he was throwing around that night, and the thought occurred to me that if I proved myself a worthy adversary to this man that there was a chance of securing some form of financing from him.

So I leaned forward onto the table and said to him, "Very well then, I will accept your challenge, but if I solve your riddle then you will have to help me attain my wish."

"If you solve my riddle then your wish will become reality," he retorted back to me. "I have drawn up the agreement here and all that is left to seal the pact is for you to make your mark upon this parchment."

I reached for the pen and in a blurred moment the table shook and my dear Frederick's arm convulsed and sent the ink jar and pen plummeting to the floor. "Oh, what a shame... there is no ink to sign your pact with now," I said with a facetious sound to my voice.

Within an instant the dark man grasped my right arm and plunged it to the table top with a thud. I started and attempted to rise, but could not. "The ink we need is within you!" he said in an even lower tone than that of before. My eyes were fatigued but I could have sworn that I saw his index fingernail instantaneously grow at least an inch. Then he used it to cut into the palm of my hand he held captive. I flinched instinctively but I could not break his clutching grip. Blood instantly poured from the wound as he turned my hand over and slammed it down upon the parchment on the table top. "It is done then!" I heard him exclaim.

I rose quickly and my first impulse was to lay waste to my assailant but the night's activity finally caught up to my body and my head began to reel. I could not keep my balance, and as I fell back into my chair blackness closed in upon me.

I must have only been out for a very short while, because when I woke, I immediately looked at my timepiece to see that it was only a few minutes past midnight. Frederick was rising out of his slumber as well, but looking very pale and definitely not able to make it to his home of his own volition. I gathered him up and as we left the drinking establishment I noticed that still there was no one to be seen within Ryan's. And no sign of our strange riddle master either. I hailed us a carriage and made sure that Frederick arrived at his home safely. I then returned to my living quarters as well. I was not affluent enough to afford my own residence, but due to family ties, I was staying with relatives and was allowed a small study in their home to pursue my life's dream of being a writer.

When I arrived back at my dwelling I was still very inebriated and almost to the point of passing out again. I stumbled my way into the study, shut the door, fell upon the sofa, and began to drift off into slumber. My thoughts were scrambled. Mysterious visions, reenactments of the night's pandemonium, were coursing through my head. I kept asking myself if it had even happened the way I was remembering it. It all seemed to be such a hazy or foggy event in my mind that I was not even sure if it was real. Perhaps I was just now becoming enabled again from a drunken night and I had hallucinated the whole thing. But then I looked to my hand and indeed it was cut and there was still dried blood within my palm. I began brooding over the events and chose to believe that I must have cut myself on a broken glass at the pub or some similar event. And then I thought to myself that our strange Mr. Leviat, if he really existed, did not even inquire as to my address. So it seemed that there would be no riddle to solve after all.

Then at that very moment I heard what seemed to be a shuffling sound immediately outside my study door. I was sure I felt a wisp of wind, but as I rose and lit a lamp I saw that all the windows were shut and secured. Approaching the door, I noticed that a piece of parchment had been slid under it. It was old and thick and looked very similar to the type of parchment that Mr. L. produced out of his jacket at the pub. I unlatched the door and flung it open, looking wildly both ways down the hall outside my study. The lamplight flickered and shadows danced across the hallway walls but other than that there was nothing. Nothing but the parchment left on the floor. I picked up the paper and unfolded it. And to my astonishment it was a riddle in the same style of handwriting that was upon the contract that Leviat had rendered my blood upon. How in the world had this man found me? I sat at my desk and pondered the situation. It took me a few moments but then I decided that he must have somehow followed me from the pub. I told myself that I must have been too drunk to notice. And so therefore I must not have locked the front door when I arrived home. I sat at my desk for a while convincing myself that this must be what had happened. But how could I be sure?

I sprang from the chair at my desk and ran out of the study and to the front door. It was at this point that the sheer horror of the whole thing started to ebb into my mind. The door was locked from the inside and there was no way to lock the deadbolt from without. I immediately ran through the house to the back door and it also was latched with the deadbolt. I stumbled back to my study and shut the door. What the Hell was happening here? How was all this possible? I sat back at the desk and began to read the riddle on the parchment. It read thus:

What lies in the dungeons of holy men's fears?
For what would kings cower and men drown in tears?
What brings death and pleasure, growth and decay?
What makes life worth living, who's the master today?

My nerves were rattled and I reached for the bottle in my desk drawer. I drank and studied the parchment. It seemed to have an almost leathery feel to it but more pliable. It appeared somewhat stained with age but yet still supple as if newly prepared. And what of the riddle inked upon this odd paper? A riddle that asks "what" all through the piece just to change direction at the end and ask "who."

I poured myself another drink and then one more as I stared incessantly at the poem reading it over and over. I do not know how long I peered at the parchment before a cloud of blackness consumed my head and sleep overtook me.

I awoke in an extremely groggy state of mind the next day. I managed to clear my head somewhat after attending to some personal rituals, and as I was returning to my study, I remember thinking to myself that I must have just been really drunk to the point of hallucination, or that maybe I just dreamed the whole thing. But upon returning to my sanctum, there it was. The parchment with the riddle etched upon it lay on my desk top. I had not hallucinated or dreamed the events of the night previous.

I felt a rush of blood to my head and a very light sensation fell upon me. I weaved my way to the sofa and threw myself onto it. I was completely bewildered and somewhat in denial, but at the same time I felt an urgency of fear at the possibility that this dark man would come for the answer to this riddle at midnight. And even more so that if I could not decipher the correct answer that I would lose something that I had not clearly decided that I had in the first place: my supposed eternal soul.

After some time my head cleared even more and I became somewhat alive again with the help of a little hair of the dog. At one point I had grabbed my jacket and started out the door to visit Frederick about the whole thing. I stopped myself though, realizing that Mr. Thomas had been unconscious throughout the whole of the deal with our eerie traveler of the world. I went back into the study, sat at my desk and produced the bottle out of the drawer again. I looked at the grandfather clock that stood in the corner as it chimed the sixth hour of the evening. I had slept much of the day away in recovery from the night's drinking and it would appear that the laudanum had a bit of a hangover effect as well.

I think it was then with each chime of the clock that I realized that I had been challenged and that if this man thought he could get the best of me, then he chose the wrong person to battle wits with. I grabbed the parchment, chose my course, and set myself to solving the riddle. Still frustrated with the two directions of questions in the poem, I decided to concentrate on the first three lines because of the question "what" being the most recurring between the two. I pondered the verses as the clock's chime reminded me of each passing hour. And with the passing of each hour I felt an ever-growing fear of something closing in on me... like the shadows of my own mind were suffocating me. Another chime... nine o'clock... and another... ten o'clock... and still I had no solution to the puzzle of words.

Then the eleventh chime came. Only one hour left. I became intolerantly restless and could not seem to focus on the task at hand. I was perspiring profusely and as I looked to my hands they were shaking uncontrollably. I threw down another drink and poured myself back into the words of the riddle searching for the answers. I could not help but continually look to the clock in the corner, seeing the minutes elapsing as the pendulum of the clock swung back and forth, back and forth. It was almost as though each motion of the pendulum was bringing my demise closer and closer.

There would be moments that I thought I would have the answer to the first part of the riddle but then I could not combine the answer with the question of "who" that appeared in the last phrase. I looked to the clock again and it was forty minutes past the hour of eleven. I then figured that if I could not solve the riddle I would be damned if I was going out without a fight. So I prepared my pistol with powder, cap, and ball and placed it upon the desk. I also took my cutlass, from my army days, out of its scabbard and leaned it against the side of the desk.

As I was about to sit back down at the desk I felt a chill crawling its way from the nape of my neck down my spine. I felt a bit of a breeze from behind me and I whirled about. To my astonishment, my eyes fell upon the black haired Mr. Leviat, standing before me just inside the study door.

I trembled in fear at the sight of the man. I know I had locked the door to my study and yet it remained shut even at that moment. How could he have entered the chamber without me knowing? I could not move or even utter a word. I was frozen in utter disbelief of my own eyes. He took a step closer to me and said with that low hypnotic voice, "So I think you have not solved my riddle, yes?"

I looked upon the clock and the hands exposed the time to be thirteen minutes till midnight. I finally found my voice and blurted out, "It is not midnight yet, you fiend, and my soul is not for you! How dare you invade my premises!" I grabbed the pistol from atop the desk and cocked it, pointing it directly at the chest of Mr. L. "I am not afraid to use this, sir!" I said, almost screaming.

He took another step towards me. "Then use it, for I have come to collect on our contract," he said in that strange accent.

I pulled the trigger and the cap fired, billowing smoke into the room, but the powder in the barrel chamber never ignited. As I threw the pistol aside and reached for my cutlass I heard such a sinister laugh from the man that it rung in my ears like an echoing cave. I picked up the cutlass and wheeled about, thrusting the blade most of its length into the chest of my challenger. He stepped back one step and looked down at the sword I had impaled him with.

I saw no blood, and to my utter disbelief, he seemed to turn into some sort of apparition of mist and smoke. The cutlass fell to the floor and before my eyes the devil reformed from mist back into flesh and clothes. I stumbled back into the corner with my back against the clock. I looked up and back to see the time was now nine minutes to midnight. My heart was racing, pumping blood through my veins at an incredible rate. I tried to speak but the words would not form.

The fiend took a few steps closer towards me and as those weird green eyes gazed into mine he spoke. "You are asking yourself who I am right now, are you not? And in just a matter of minutes you will have your answer, my supposed master of the words. For I knew you would fail our little contest and not be able to provide me with what we agreed upon, leaving me the master of your soul, you pitiful creature."

It was that precise moment that has amazed me well beyond all the other fantastic and bizarre events that had taken place. For he gave me the clues, I'm sure without intending, with his very own arrogant words. It all seemed to make perfect sense to me very suddenly, like the realization of an incredible story idea. I looked back at the clock again as the minute hand clicked another notch towards the midnight hour.

I turned to the… well, I was positive that this was no man before me now. So henceforth I will refer to him as the demon. I turned to the demon and straightened my clothes a bit, gaining back my usual tepid composure. I stepped forward and placed myself face to face with my challenger and with my own style of arrogance exclaimed, "You think yourself the riddle master, eh? It is not midnight just yet and so therefore I still have the chance to solve your feeble attempt at a riddle."

I could see a bit of a startled look in the face of the demon as I continued on with my little speech, while also keeping a close eye on the clock in the corner of the room. "The first part of your riddle was easy and written like that of a simpleton. The last line was, to be honest, a bit of a challenge, but not that difficult either." I heard the clock's minute hand shift again and I took a brief look towards it to see I had four minutes left before midnight struck. "You said you wanted two things of me. It was child's play to figure that your riddle was also in need of two responses. What lies in the dungeons of holy men's fears? For what would kings cower and men drown in tears? What brings death and pleasure, growth and decay? What makes life worth living? All of this can be answered with one word my good… whatever you are. And that word is *reality*."

The demon stepped back and suddenly the fiend's eyes were no longer green but more like obsidian orbs. "That is but one answer, mortal," he said shrilly. "As you admit yourself, there must be two."

"Oh, yes I understand full and well," I continued, trying not to show the enormous amount of cowardly fear that was ebbing up within me. His face, within inches of mine, was changing. The human look that it once possessed seemed to be melting away, along with the clothing as well. I heard the clock's minute hand shift again. "The next part is what gave me a little trouble, but as I said before, not that much. You see, you are not the riddle master today or any other as far as I can tell. I am the riddle master and I am the master of my own destiny. So who is the master today? It is I and I believe you owe me my wish."

I will never in my days forget the shrieking cry that came from the demon at the moment I spoke those words. It was the most hellish sound I have ever heard. The demon's body and head lunged towards me growling and screaming and then suddenly there was a huge circling gust of wind that blew like a whirlpool within the study. I grabbed onto the bookshelf and clung to it as this maelström of wind funneled through my chamber. I looked into the center of this whirlwind to see the demon had changed completely and no longer resembled any human form of life, nor the devil I had expected. No horns or red spiked tail, but a grotesque figure like that of a burnt body with the skin still melting away from the bone. In an instant there was a burst of wind that seemed to explode within the study and suddenly I found myself alone with the room seemingly untouched.

I loosened my grip on the bookshelf and looked about the study. I picked up the pistol from the floor along with my cutlass, rounded the desk, and somewhat fell back into my chair. I started to shake a bit and quickly retrieved the bottle from my desk, putting it to my lips without even bothering with a glass. I looked up to the ceiling, still trying to comprehend the gravity of what had just transpired. I sat back up and pulled my chair in toward the desk when I realized there was something missing from the desk top and also something new upon it. The parchment with the riddle was gone and where it had been was a small bottle of laudanum just like the one the demon had in the pub. Was this my reward? Was this my wish? How could that be? I asked to be a famous writer that would be renowned throughout the world for centuries to come.

I dare not share this episode of my life with anyone, not even my dear friend Frederick, for I would surely be taken by all as a madman. And I suppose that I should have had a bit more care in the wording of my wish, for I realize now that what I wished for could come at any time and not necessarily during my lifetime. But then again, maybe my time of true recognition is upon me, for a story of mine won a contest award in the *Baltimore Saturday Visiter*, and I have just secured a job as assistant editor of the *Southern Literary Messenger* in Richmond.

There is one thing, though. That period of my life still haunts me. I cannot seem to drown the dreams away. I have such horrific dreams now. Visions of the grotesque and macabre. They plague me and I have found only one thing that will keep the dreams from recurring and that is to pen them to paper. So the nightmares come and the only saving I have from them is to write them down. That is why I am penning this now. It is in the hope that the haunting horror of it all will somehow vanish and I may still have a chance to live and love like a normal person. But if this was to be found it would mean the end of my writing career, I am sure, so I will hide it in a secret compartment of my desk in the study here in Baltimore. I will be leaving for Richmond soon and hopefully this will mark the end of the horrific and nightmarish dreams that persist in haunting me night after night.

I still have to wonder if I shall ever encounter the demon again. Or for that matter how many others there are like it within our realm. It is unbearable knowing what I do and not being able to talk openly about it to even my closest of friends or family. But I cannot and will not speak of this to anyone and so therefore it shall be a secret that I take to my grave. Blessed be those who have seen what I have.

E.A.P.

Eve's Grave

By Scott Waldrop

What knew I of the grave before? Its knowledge became mine and befouled me to the core in all aspect. It's with no little grievance and pronounced trepidation for fear of The Dead's retribution that I endeavor to recount the summer of my youth during which I set forth upon the great southerly vanishing point. This was a highway of highways that lured the gamut of guileless romantic adventurers to humanity's most sordid detritus, from extreme north to southernmost tip, upon the New World's vast eastern coastal stretch. It was then whence the blackish devil and I chanced upon one another for the first time, and were ultimately entwined in an enduring dance of morbidity. It was there that the said devil's four spectres of doom taught me their lessons. Never before was there a more oppressive space, a vacuum of light, and a vacuum of positive nature, than was its dwelling hideaway consigned to obscurity in the marshy wastes. I have not spoken of the account and have gone as far as to feign indifference towards airy and otherworldly matters for a lifetime until now upon my impending expiration, that I'm obliged of abject cosmic terror to purge the dark energy which has nested within me and clutched at me indefinitely since those early summer days and persisting into decrepitude. The restrictive nature of language constrains my availability to convey to you what unwanted knowledge has been imposed on me. The forthcoming explanation of my strife will prove an infinitesimal measure, and therefore a tentative aim, to convey upon you what abominable revelations lie crouched in wait behind our illusory supernal vault. Notwithstanding full acknowledgement that I offer myself to the derision of the rational preponderance, I own my last words and so pen them disposed they may be my prime legacy and perchance they should ever be displayed alongside my effigy. That I bequeath to pseudo-intellectuals an innumerable eons' recreation of mockery to my memory is of superficial concern. For me, it is certainty that a dark spectre of unlimited power and distance catalyzed my creeping destruction. It was this inhuman spirit hailing from an unrecorded dystopian antiquity that prodded me through an existence of misery and unto me, cast it the cruel destiny of a violent plunge into final singularity. Forgive me as my delivery ebbs and flows betwixt elegance and drunken blather, as the resurrection of memories here within have driven me to imbibe the poison fire spirit, notwithstanding a myriad dubious antidote. If nothing else, derive from this that a serpent is ever-crawling through Eden and that every man dies pathetically.

In a recent past obscured by machinery and contractual obligation, I was a wayward youth with unquenchable wanderlust. The southern coach roads and their associated lore long-solicited my every thought. I conceived beyond doubt the private conviction that in some remote bog, lecherous and cadaverous nymph-sirens splayed upon a lichen-crusted rock ushered me and telepathically inoculated me with festering obsession. Their beckoning surmounted incessantly and manifested itself as a fever—soon to which I would succumb. I made haste to embark whilst unknowingly accepting this spectral invitation into oblivion, though my sojourn began without incident nor omen indicating the malady I had been slowly coming to intersection with since birth. It was a season when the fetters of adolescence had been removed and an open road provided a canvas with which to paint a personality out of visceral experience and dormant desires. Months were spent in a marinated swoon indulging in orgiastic liberties and seeking out all manner of vice. I made the crevices of ill repute my own and compartmentalized several lifetimes of perverse self-absorption into fleeting moments. I, pandemonium incarnate, liked to laugh about peering into the abyss as it stoically reciprocated admiration. My uncanny observer knew we were respectively closing in on one another for eternity and once within its clutch, the beast-thing saw it fit to plant within me a longing for purpose. I dried sober and surrendered my path to whatever whim this magnetic and seemingly guardian force required.

The genesis of my so-thought enlightenment afforded me a rapturous perspective and consistently positive philosophy on all I observed. Miracles within miracles abounded within plain sight and were absorbed deliciously into a joyful, grateful heart. With sunlit dust rising from the shadows of its ancient travel ruts, the great southern road before me offered a quintessential hinterland beauty, flanked on each side by olden agrarian charm and graveyards full of old beloved slaves. Oleander and magnolia sweetened the air as nearby mangroves would occasionally accompany the bouquet which inspired one's lungs to full capacity with assurance that the air here was surely nothing less than a medicinal wonderwork of Mother Nature. I basked in this rustic opulence while passing Baptist churches and cross-crested shanties beaming with celebration and hope of a glorious hereafter.

I was given these fleeting last moments of solace merely so that the insufferable daemon may confiscate them and hold me evermore with their memory intact. I was given them so I may be marked by bitter loss. This would be the first demonstration by it which's tutelage I was forcefully given to and obliviously marched towards. The gloaming came dour upon that dirt road on the eve of my perpetual fall. The firmament's gradation from the late afternoon's amber-honey to amethyst transitioned with unnatural suddenness as if an act perpetrated at the caprice of some mad black magician. The air lingered stagnant and was suspended in that twilight shade. I was hypnotized by the proliferation of softly floating glowworms which were cast against cool lavender for an inordinate stretch of the hour hand. The pattern of time frayed, stiffened, and died though I was unaware. As I traveled on, my mood turned as I awakened to my peril. Black shapes revealed themselves leering behind hoary tree trunks, materializing and vanishing sporadically and with great secrecy. They occupied my thoughts profoundly and influenced my observations making me aware of a polar shift in my personality. The scenery took on a dark overtone when the ugly intuition came to me that those with mere hope are servants to the torturous thoughts that nihilism or undreamed horror aren't also potential fates henceforth this world. Subsequent to my neurotic and anxious foreboding, all things leaned negative and with feverish pitch. Deep I rode into waning light and cypress wood where willows faithfully thronged my path on either side. I had vague concern that they may be phantom sentinels with the capacity to snatch me of their own autonomy—predatory and without warn. Upon the eldritch and gnarled bark were crudely fastened planks containing biblical verses imploring travelers to repent. As I went on, the weather-stained boards were appearing on most trees, making it apparent that I was in the space of ill-minded religious zealots:

"Prepare to Meet Thy God"
—Amos 4:12
"Strive to Enter at the Straight Gate"
—Luke 13:24
"Repent"
—Mark 6:12

In a sunlit church these words could bring comfort, but in the dark woods the messages on signs appeared more as death threats rather than spiritual suggestion. My unbridled fear rendered any altruistic motives of their creator mute. The arcane scrawling heightened the oppressive pitch in atmosphere to a tangible and choking crescendo. I needed nothing more than to hide away from the maddening wood. I fled down the next available side path and raced furiously over its root-gnarled clay until it opened upon a moonlit grove. There calmly stood something against the midnight sky.

Usurped by eons and the ever tenacious southern flora stood the faltering carcass of a once venerable manor house. Dangling precariously upon its now single hinge, the Lamp Light Inn's moniker poignantly fluttered in the still air. I was bemused, beholding the structure an odd marriage of antebellum grandeur coupled with the pitiful finite inevitability of materialism. Its forlorn majesty was surely an icon to phantoms yet fable to flesh. The spell of this transfixing juxtaposition burst as I was mesmerized anew to a beckoning distant glow deep within house's innards. With unintelligent stare I could scarce perceive a whisper of sickly yellow light stuttering with autonomous frenetic energy in that country darkness. Something was inside. Inasmuch as the notion of encountering its inhabitants was acutely appalling, lethargy compelled me onward to the loathsome mansion. As I approached closer, an ominous nausea enveloped me while the slithering reek of grave slime went from what I first believed to be a figment of imagination to a dawning grim certainty.

Once at the threshold I had scantly a moment to take in the edifice before I slipped into some phantasmagoria. I was immediately intoxicated to a pathetic state at what can only be defined arbitrarily as the will of a strange and extremely evil dominance. Near the door I beheld the visage of a ghoul-man glowering pallid behind milky glass, and framing a first floor windowsill to create a most hideously repelling portrait. I fancied that the image would evaporate faintly and materialize with a sickly breath-like quality in its rhythm. Somewhere inside and far beyond the white imp, the yellowish incandescence continued to flicker with sporadic unpredictability. This house, this light, and the white face were all I knew as I went forward. One foot falling bewilderedly before the next, I was puppeteered by some thing undefined. I regretfully must reprove my own articulation as to presume said "thing" could even be given this cryptic and arbitrary label albeit for lack of human comprehension, my decided language suits the purpose of a distant attempt at conveyance.

My host opened the door and revealed himself floating. He wore a retarded countenance with a plastic grayish complexion. I had no option but to acquiesce in his strange offer to visit with what horrors await within, and fell forth into their funereal carnival. Inside I was first besieged and rendered prostrate by the unmistakable and sweetly fetid miasma of a rampant vermin infestation. Once regaining composure, I discerned that the walls around me were swollen pregnant and amorphously animated. I was possessed of dire suspension that all manner of night creature teemed and writhed in copious volume inside the lime plaster. I peripherally perceived in my mind's eye that the presence of a myriad squirming and intelligent invertebrate glowered at me unseen and comprised the bulk of the house's bones, as some strange ecosystem unified by psychic bond and shared malevolence towards those who they capriciously deem unfavorable. The bleak-skinned imbecile took my hand and pulled me languidly towards one of the many blackened corridors afforded by the main foyer which was itself in a state of mortuary draped-shadow and a void of unnatural blackness. I drunkenly slumped forward, submitting to the tug of these mortal remains which slinked towards a north facing hall; an entry point I felt was taken without pretence, intelligent conjecture nor device. With dull wit, my guide imbued within me the knowledge through its graven cold clasp, that it matter not which path we begin for each and all are but a macabre tangle permeated by undesirable wisdom of which I'm obliged to obtain upon this grand tour. A black so deep in its saturation suffocated my perceptions so that nothing save tactile cues engaged any inferences as to my present course or surroundings. Spongy floorboards made malleable by funk moisture, sagged underfoot as my boot sank into what must have once been wood, now long-since transmogrified into more of a mildewed niter which blossomed a noxious cloud with each dreaded step. One hand in the clutch of my skeletal host and the other fumbling in nothingness, I twitchingly and tentatively reached out nervous fingers, dismaying at their touch upon foul walls coated viscous with gastropod trails and gossamers moistened by the sultry crypt air. The blind neverness in which I found myself being escorted through agitated my thoughts to a degree that the mind eventually belched forth a secession of crazed notions which would spree across my mental plane and take chase after a next series of demented inner monologues. I was a schizophrenic infant crouched, cornered, and impotent for fear of the primeval elementals taunting me and touching at my flesh. Finally in that primeval darkness a lesser dark suggested itself and my eyes fixed upon a faint contour that I desperately needed to be more than a wishful apparition projected by an ill mind. Oh gramercy! Oh gramercy! My strife hath boundary indeed! That sick, yellow, flickering, vertical and oblong illumination did sleepily manifest itself from darkness over the expanse of twenty minutes to twenty years; know not I which nor care for I gazed upon it warmly and comforted for it proved a reprieve from my ever-surmounting madness. There indeed was natural science upon which to rely and I was clearly healing from some intoxicant I unwittingly ingested. No. Crestfallen, I crashed back into phantasmagoria as its bony hand held fast to my right wrist whilst a sharp phalange from its other hand scratched new life lines into the palm of my left, altering and dictating my hitherto fortune to misfortune. Vapid and dumb whilst I gasped at my mutilation, my diviner gestured toward the light. Telepathically I understood I should now pass through the first of four doors to dark perception imposed by the void-thing.

Once through the door I vaguely noticed that I walked upon a downward gradient as mildewed cellar air entered my lungs. It was odd that I may be descending into a basement without negotiating a stairwell but the house had its own personality and it disoriented its inhabitants as it saw fit. There stood I in a sanatorium's laboratory kept company by my grey-faced clod companion. The bilious yellow luminescence continued its stormy and stroboscopic game revealing and then quickly confiscating its shocking reveals back to pitch black. Chamber-pot-funk oppressed the atmosphere. One couldn't guess when nor what the next scene would unfold. Depending upon where I found myself in my anxious circular craze, the sudden light exploded upon a most eclectic freakshow of macabre oddities. In the flickering confusion there flashed menacing taxidermies of cryptids such as gigantopithecus and what may have been a serpentine whale. After undeterminable hours, there did appear the next revelation as mason jars containing pickled beasts with abominable deformities became to be and evaporated back into the void. A blackness saturated far beyond the totality of color gave way to some conceptually abstract spectrum until there was dim light in which the asylum collectively breathed life again, although it may have been a simple recording of the past. As vivid as it was, I could not discern what truth there was in the phenomenon. An innumerable mob of pinheads with milky blue cataract eyes were continuously seizing and foaming at the mouth, trapped in unwanted life. I extrapolated that these dispossessed mongrels were forcibly kept for experimental purpose. They were of a singularly poor stock. A dunce-capped fool played the theremin as the half-witted revelers cavorted en masse and were presided over by The Plague Doctor of Nijmegen whom they referred to as "The Great Overshadower of All." The bird beast before the troglodyte throng attended a table containing an assortment of grimy implements arranged with psychotic organization. Contrary to their presentation, these were but corroded medical tools patented in an age of ignorance. To employ them at present would be vicious barbarism. The Plague Doctor confirmed the worst, calculatingly selecting the oxidized ecraseur then turning to his prey. He brought the crude scissor-thing over her and then hovered long enough for the feebleminded cauldronhead to dumbly observe that menacing device. She shuddered, drooled and droned as she locked mask-eyes with The Doctor, who by giddy bodily language displayed that he was gaining droll amusement from terrorizing the fool. Her naked body was fettered tight against a cold steel medical table with parched leather restraints which held her sufficiently still despite her shaking horror. The beak-nosed masochist brought his tool to her open loins and when her screams came, blood trickled from the table's bloodletting hole. Trickles gradually flowed into a faithful babbling. The Doctor worked vigorously until her blood fell meaty. As her agonized drivel waned, there slowly plopped upon the floor the pathetic crowning precipice of a crimson gore pile. I gasped and crushingly gripped my guide's skeleton hand, imploring it to know if there were rime or reason as to why I bared witness to such senseless abomination! I hadn't a split second's reprieve before my emaciated, grey, plastic-complexioned, and retard guide gestured towards a freshly unfolding horror which instantaneously commanded my attention in a darkened corner of the infirmary. I trained upon a scene in dark so deep I need adjust my eyes until sensory adaptation took hold and the hazy outline of a nun-hag-with-patient-form filled out of the blackness. The outlined figures were accented by ember glow from a nearby crematory chamber. The presence of vermin pestilence came creeping into my feelings via weird perception which I was only beginning to understand. The nun-hag held an old man amputee, diagonally suspended by his one foot while she wiped the waste from his unmentionable regions. He was covered in small black insects which moved quickly about his brown body and were beginning to transfer onto her forearm. He sadly looked at me fully conscious of his poignancy. The odor of insect feces and geriatrics lingered heavier and the shriveled little man remained fixed upon me communicating a sense of warning. I felt the bugs upon my skin. The roach-reek unyieldingly gained strength and the perpetual molestation of biting insects upon me indoctrinated me into a new meaning of madness. Maggots under his skin made it quiver and once punctured by the hag-nun they gushed forth, releasing a traumatizing death stench. The nun-hag began to feed the gaping furnace jaws with the little man. I fell faint as my mind and body surrendered to terror.

My spirit was utterly broken of despair to wake in the basement of that unholy house. Sleep was so sweet, and I fully expected to wake safely in the house of my nativity far north from here. My only consolation was that all traces of the ghastly asylum scene were absent and the great room was empty save the wet filth caked upon its foundation stones. If I was unsure that I may be standing before the portal to hell, my subsequent experience was to provide me with total conviction. My dumb guide was mindlessly floating in circles waiting for my eyes to open. Preempting my thoughts of escape, the gray retard seized my wrist and swept me to a remote shadowed basement corner. It dumped me at the threshold of what appeared to be an anomalous grotto or what may be the burrow of a fair sized animal. It was indeed a well if not all three guesses were true. Another certainty regarding this odd little hole is that it stretched to extreme depths and as I gazed downward, I had the intuition that it was nothing less than a shaft to a vast subterranean realm. A sick luminescence pulsated far away down that hole. That living glow was from the same supernatural family as the one which lurked above in the loathsome mansion—albeit this one manifested itself in the hue of a nauseous green. The stench of serpent musk issued forth from the hole's mouth as if those dank green netherworlds were looking back up at me and released an offensive sign of acknowledgement. A soft-whistling wind began deep below and increased in momentum until I gradually perceived that it was not a wind but a vacuum. The revelation struck panic in me as there was scant an object to cling to before the great shaft inhaled me. I was now numb to surreal terror and submissively accepted my descent with suicidal abandon, the grey retard faithfully tumbling behind me. Eventually the shaft opened and we plunged through open air for an undeterminable passage of silent dark moments until breaking some surface and submerging into a bacterial soup. One would expect to be forced to abysmal fathoms by our great momentum, yet having only sunken into the viscous ectoplasm but a few yards, it was apparent that the only consistency in this realm was its inconsistency in the laws of physics and the learned-in-general. My head emerged and the green bioluminescent glow revealed none but a low-hanging fog upon the gelatinous and primordial substance through which I laboriously treaded as some dull suction came from beneath. For a fleeting moment I felt the vindication of fortune when I aimlessly propelled myself in a random, fear-guided, blind direction, and with little effort my hand chanced upon a muddy bank. My fingers clenched into the warm rotting leaves and clay as I pulled myself from the gelatin. Looking back, I saw that the gray-thing (now my only shadow in this dark world) hovered above the surface as though he never submerged into the slime with me at all.

I laid in filth and observed my surroundings, resting with anxiety over the next phenomenon that was sure to come to antagonize me at any moment. I puzzled over how I had lost my measure of time and was oblivious as to how I had transcended from the indoor world of that loathsome mansion to this new lost realm of the outdoors—let alone how I may ever return to the open road from whence this grim misadventure originated. The subterranean world opened around me as the fog vaporized at cue. Above me loomed a gnarled tree canopy of Spanish Moss-draped willow with invasive serpentine vinery woven throughout. Arboreal beasties, alien in their lankiness, precariously dangling by long arms, crept back into the lofty bramble once noticed. At eye level there stretched before me a dismal swampscape. Poisonous groundcover blanketed the archipelago of diminutive terra firma humps protruding from the misty bacterial broth simmering on the horizon. Upon the rotted knob upon which I sat, tenebrous berms teemed with ostensibly intelligent cottonmouths which writhed, and hissed, and expelled putrid glandular stench in outward aggression towards me. The world around me droned low with the cacophony of a myriad distant and frightfully arcane varmint. Ape woops of the wampus and grassman were particularly perturbing. Some sounds were weird copies of familiar macabre ones, comparable to the ghostly whip-poor-will, and the katydids of late August who sadly usher summer's end. In every direction, bulbous frogs on mucky toadstools grew to grotesque prepositions—whose saucer eyeshine flickered in the blackness beyond my visibility. The bald cypresses appeared to all be stricken with malignant outgrowths which resembled the tube nests of mud dauber wasps with diameters suggesting them a product of a prehistoric Permian Period. On tiny islands in the nebulous distance I squinted to discern they may be littered with diagonally standing totems resembling bony newt people. About the cryptic figures danced orbs of foxfire which I intuitively knew to be jealously protective spirits. Shoals of glassy-scaled and eyeless fish swirled and transfixed me as I peered into their stagnant slop. These creatures inexplicably filled me with hatred, save that I fancied them all the devils' imps and familiars. The Grayman remained patiently hovering over me, familiar with and disinterested in his environs. Surmising I had absorbed enough, he sluggishly lifted me by the underarms and took me on a languid flight above the infirm bubbling wastes. Below the archipelago became a sinuous and stippled outline resembling its various crawling denizens. What purpose did the Grayman have for me now? I feebly lifted my neck to behold in the distance the craggy spires of a distant promontory issuing forth from the sleepily wiggling gel, and presiding almighty over the Great Dismal Wastes. The atmosphere became insufferably sticky as we neared the menacing ascension, and faintly increasing in volume, came the chants of some Neolithic religion resounding from its island shores.

The heights above the promontory's craggy shores was a place The Gularian Priestesses wouldn't dare. Their ritual was protective. Both of these notions were discerned solely of my newfound and pronounced conviction in my own clairvoyance, though I knew not from where these women came nor where they went when they were finished. Surely they could not dwell here for prolonged periods as the rock was permeated in extreme evil. The Grayman suspended me directly over them and they continued their rite, consummately, and ignored our presence. Were they spectres or were they amongst us spectres? White-eyed and with obsessive repetition they swayed amongst the flames and spoke with wyrd tongue:

"Oh Miss Green Teeth of The Well…
…She'll surface when it swells…
…You've given your goods to the witch in the woods…
…You could turn back to being good which you probably should…
…Lest she pull you down to Hell!"

Their ritual had dramatic effect as a densely defined circle of the tree canopy withered and far beyond, in simultaneous succession, the cloud cover dissipated to reveal a waxing-horned-red-moon. Lunar rays shot their ugly glow with spotlight efficiency on the devil's rock and seized the ritually induced opportunity to menace their beholders. The gray retard floated us to the rock's precipice and dropped me into a phosphorescent pool which collected in its highest spire. It was there I would encounter the murderous bog woman.

She had been there forever—this and the following I inferred from new perception. I was in Miss Green Teeth's den. Through said perception (and now I knew it to be dark perception), I first met the limp-wristed troglodyte with fidgety zygodactylous digits and gore-slathered lips: humanoid, yet predating hominids. Her home made me vomit in terror as my surroundings gave new meaning to swamp horror. I retraced her history through psychic energy embedded on all I touched. Black jelly egg sacks bobbed in brackish water where she knew the children couldn't be found. She relished in absconding with them into the night whence she emptied their bodies of life so they may sour with her evermore. She laid them in the willows where the marsh tides could carry their bodies out to skeletonize in the silt and rotting hyacinth. Her bog was littered with petraglyphs from some antediluvian epoch of beforetime. That ancient rock graffiti depicted the most peculiar beings whose form contradicted earthly evolution. After puzzling at them, unsure of what the eye initially saw, I saw that they were clearly engaged in lowly acts of depravity—taboo even at a primate level. In dire desperation, I implored higher forces that I not encounter this lowly thing!

She surfaced, and I saw her in all her grim tangibility for the first time. She was quintessentially unhealthy and so thoroughly disgusting in appearance I implored that we not be fashioned by the same universe, let alone exist in the same. She further encroached half-bodied before me and reached out malevolently so as to snatch me and steal away with me to her cold, cold riverbed den. She wickedly and yearningly stretched and clutched at the air between us. Her rank breath wheezed with the overexertion of an animate corpse. That malignant breath whistled through craggy olive teeth, reeking of a wet and feral mongrel coupled with a midsummer's hot garbage pile. Inasmuch she was intolerably fetid, she moreover was matted—generally stringy, and the personification of all things swamp-crawly. Outrageous repulsion gasped forth from my involuntarily agape mouth as the noxious breakwaters retracted to reveal her lack-there-of entirety; a half body with gangly arms and wagging tailbone that squirmed with the annelids mining the rancid meat remaining on her rib cage. Her mossy, withered, and rotten-pear-like breasts drooped dismally as pubic algae swayed from her underarms. Her sodden skin was speckled with lentigines and fishy spots. Pollywogs thronged and nibbled about her in the brownish substrate. A raspy hiss strained from her gullet in demonstration of her gruesome lust for me to writhe and cavort eternally in the sludge with her. Black energy evenly flowed from her. I mawkishly longed to return to a time when I was ignorant to her being. At present, I was vaguely distracted by the realization that I had not felt the Grayman's presence for some time at which point I had the morbid revelation that he had crept inside of me. I was but his possessed vessel and my limbs moved of another's volition. This great teacher of fear and depravity took embrace of the putrid Miss Green Teeth and down the vortex we slid—to be abducted, defiled, and held in abeyance in the yawning gloom for eras upon eras.

I awoke in an arid chamber with the detailed and unwelcome memory of my age in the bog whilst betrothed to the rotted, sodden halfbody. I remembered-in-dream how the humidity had dissipated and the halfbody mummified to stillness and finally her grisly croaks and whistles were forever mercifully silenced. The Grayman hovered calmly in the darkness near me. His dull luminescence provided the nearest margin of light required to espy that I may be in some crypt, as I softly felt, whiffed, and perhaps saw whirls of grave dust blowing through the total darkness of some boundless mausoleum of the long foregone. I strongly perceived that I was hidden deep near the center of eternity where the world's core perpetually burned. I felt certain that from my coma I had wholly metamorphosed into an empath, telepath, and clairvoyant. I perceived that I was now entombed with The Fool King. I was obliged to press forth and convene with this third spectral tutor and absorb his select mastery of forbidden insight. Down the Neolithic catacomb corridors we went, guided by the Grayman's spectral emissions on a gradual slope towards chambers untouched by light nor wind. Crumbling relief statues flanked the corridors depicting the self-serving existence and maudlin demise of a lord ignored by history. It was here that I learned the particulars of his regrettable life's journey. Trailing behind him was an innumerable herd of sycophants whom he collected as treasure and surrounded himself with. Their procession stretched the length of a vast desert land. I felt I walked amongst and with them, as I observed the raised carvings by the light of my old supernatural travel companion. Onwards we trudged slantingly downwards towards the black star's heat source. I and the lowly followers shadowed The Fool King, better to indulge him on his march of wanton destruction than to obstruct its path with one's futile polemics. Winding through stygian promenades, the weak-hearted kept in step with one another as the serpent's head pointed his finger and consigned his kingdom's denizens to poignant fates. On a moment's whim he commissioned, by quick and arrogant gesture, titanic effigies in his likeness to stipple the map in profusion and where under a myriad spurning candidates fornicated under command of the king for his absurd merriment. The aforementioned facts were made clear from the stories told in stone coupled with my uncanny sight, yet it was the latter of my perceptions which completed the forthcoming assertions about The Fool King's character—for as I drew nearer to his place of final rest, I felt his ugliness look upon my own soul. He was a man who only knew himself through his alter ego. A disgrace to his venerable bloodline whose name he solely bastardized, he was an unbridled exhibitionist with the predisposition for petulance and entitlement. If there was humility within him it dwelled as a schizophrenic split personality, long abandoned and bricked up in a solitary dungeon. He only did good to make himself feel good. His comprehension of altruism was by superficial definition. Precious life fleeted before him punctuated by petty gloating and the conviction that others were designed for servitude. In the end people watched uncaringly as he slowly died. The Fool King refused to admit that he could feel himself rotting. He stupidly smiled while death was near. In the end of all endings, there came to completion an era seers came to view as The Drastic Tragedy. There was a between period when civilization lay dormant, approaching a new age of control as another's kingdom would rise to a time which would be classic. Beneath the ruins glowed the tenacious embers of possibility—a future on to which beloved leaders and valiant heroes came to rule and inter the memory of The Fool. As I finally stood at the threshold of his tomb I realized he lived still in some fashion. His lunatic reign spawned and dispersed everlasting phantoms upon the land as well as the collective unconscious of tomorrow. Through my mind's eye I saw the desert highway he haunted. It was a path that meandered as far as the eye could see—and was littered with the eclectic pieces of a million broken hearts that all belonged to him.

Behind a crusted portcullis left half ajar lay the throne of The Fool King entombed with what remained of his various treasures. What once must have been an opulently appointed chamber was now reduced to ransacked disarray. His glittering objects were plundered, yet he and his cohorts' skeletal remains were intact and organized in a diorama scene which was presumably customary of some long-forgotten Neolithic funeral rites for nobility. Desecration was all around except for the ghoulish sumptuous feast in which they remained suspended. My clairvoyance offered glimpses of harried robbers nervously hoarding jewels and unable to do their work for anxiety of his empty eye sockets bearing down on them. He had been interred with a legion of warriors and whores on skeleton horses which also cast reproving and cursing eyes upon the intruders of the ages. Some of them held brittle blades while others clutched parchments of absurdly anachronistic obligations and deeds. The resplendent austerity of his tomb did nothing to resonate with his general disposition in life nor legacy. He was a lowly worm. He was a true louse amongst men. He was inflated to capacity with a sense of self-importance. His presumptions peeled the skull beneath his grin to simple men, which made him an impotent leader. His stately countenance rendered him soft in their eyes. I returned gaze with those eye sockets whilst standing there transfixed in their story. In my peripheral perception I saw his eyes bright as they were in life and exchanged intent gaze with the liar. In our shared trance the veil became transparent. The cancerous Fool King was ultimately destitute, yet still he jealously clutched his gold while he died. He passed into history the forgotten and tearful jester. He moved towards the great black hole and into final singularity making his strife on earth insignificant. He was only a bit of grave dust in the wind. Sand in the nitrogen cycle. The spell of the liar's eyes was lifted. I spiraled into a fourth and final descent. I fell into the inner void of the burning black star's core where dwelt Ebezura.

Her name was Ebezura the Soothsayer of Tales. She was a waif with a skein. The palmystress appeared famine-stricken as she wove word and yarn. She was a conduit to the channel of the gods. All about her were ritualistically-placed purple-black candles and votive figures depicting a hoary snake goddess. She possessed an encyclopedic mind with the ability to eloquently tell winded epics, as if casually relaying the facts in common discourse. She had been waiting for me eternally. She greeted me with fungal tea and she shared tales relayed to by her oracle companions. She sang Cassilda's song of Lost Carcosa. She spun her tangled mess and told me tales meant to leave men insane, sadder, and wiser. She then told her own saga in detail, albeit in a broken lyrical dementia. It told tales of the saintly days of yore as well as of things yet to come. It was the tale of all of us. It was Ebezura's Tale and it went as such:

"Phantom Black from far beyond is lost and never free
Look below to find the truth once tossed into the sea

We are the ones who wage the wars, we are to be, and were before
Into the night at morning light, we are the suns who lost the light

We wayfarers want your steel, join us!
We are the future, please believe
Our prophets tell us that when we die death's a journey
No pearly gates or burning in the fire

Bones are breaking under hoof
Dormant monsters longing for a chance to live again
We pulled you from the mire and we gave you life again
Now give yourself for battle as the search for truth begins

Meet the masters guiding your fate
Eyes are burning as they crack their whips
See the forgotten with frozen stares
Longing for the light that was never there

A world on its knees still can't believe
The moans of the rising dead ride on the breeze
When all things come to an end it's a chance to live again
The sound of the raging winds calls to me
The winds call to me for a chance to die and be free

And the light at the end of the tunnel is just a gate to reality
And your life that flashes before you is the start of eternity

We soldier into blackness beyond the ivory lights
We brave the bleak hereafter and exit on through time
We're riding on The Never's storm and march amongst the now
The crushed remains of cursed things lie scattered in dust clouds

We are the only ones when time begins
We only cut the ties to get a chance to live again
We're always wandering and will withstand ever passing time
It always circles back to where we began

A trial fire raging and it's nigh the time for why
Witch or whore, no matter no more, who's been brought here to die
She shape shifts in the night world, a place so steeped in myth
Seize her rose, remove her clothes, she's marked six sixty six

Now you're going to know what it's like to go below to total dementia
You'll make the final mistake and end upon the stake
Me and you, my only friend, were here, and here again
The sun and the moon were the same for a moment in time

No angel hides away for long
Bad angels don't fly away but do fly away from home
Me and you with the best of life
A princess in the nexus of time

We want it to be all the things we foresee
We hate when it goes differently
You know if they knew all the things that we do...
They would pray for us both fearfully

Imprisoned in a world of make believe, my mystery believer
Mystery believer, at the edge of the river, you can run forever
Mystery surrounded you from conception into death
Would you call it a lie or would a miracle astound you?

Where are you heroes now that this world's come full circle?
Winners and losers still kill and sell their souls
West of the sunset cities one waits for the end of time
While on the horizon, soulless rulers sign the hammers down

She'll wake from a slumber so sweet to kiss the dawn when dark angels sing
She's a forgotten myth spreading her wings
You've thrown out your gods so return to the dark

Willing souls speak soft into the darkened light

But the love they've always had remains unproved tonight
The Master of Evil sends a message to us
Eyes in the darkness are staring at you and you fear all the evil they'll do

On the ringlet clouds of dawn the stranger came
The mists were rising and the moon was dying
Dark angels bowed to pray

It made a dark and lonely place to hide itself
Demise was spiraling and the raven crying
Yet no evil could be traced

A sleeping village wakes to a strange presence
Familiar at side beyond the quagmire
The spell poisoned the air

The bishops held their ground with cross and spike
The windows boarded, their sorts were sordid
All life seemed doomed to die

We're prepared to stand and face the evil in this place
With the cross and gall of flame, its power compels you
We're prepared to set ablaze this place where you like to play
Psychotic mobs set to lay waste with intent to kill you

Beneath the mystic graves it waits to wake
Macabre collection of spirits resting
Will spree once found again
Beware their charming ways and the things they say
The devil's armoire holds toys of torture when evil wants to play

You came to see the underworld and you know the bargain indeed my girl
You'll find light so white, so now down you go
You'll have the best of the Earth and it will be yours alone

You silly child, I'm wild, it seems you've fooled yourself

I've finally placed you in an urn upon my shelf
You were the whore who wore the clothing of a nun

There's no excuse for all the evil games we play
Kidnap the unicorn and take its horn away
You want some wisdom and I've got some to lend
I'll give you some of mine. I'll bestow the kiss of death

When the lost cities are finally found and the unicorns are all slain for their horns
We wait for the winds of the end in a wasteland of woe

Bastards with the power to destroy won't fill the world with fear evermore
As red skies ignite we'll take into flight to strike down the kind and the cruel
We ride Armageddon with our wings ablaze as approaches the age of our rule

We're the angels of the fire and we'll burn you to our hearts' desire
You're all on the run for the night is ours
We're a mystery and a reason to believe
We're a promise kept from the torn page of history
We bring fire and death. We leave with nothingness left

Some thousand epic trips ago we passed the word to see who'd show
The curse dispersed to far off lands and we journeyed there to make our stand
We drank from ale horns

Dark star's fury lights up the sky and shines on through the night
Travelers and dead men fought by our side
I am possessed by thoughts that are not my own
They've lead me far to things unknown"

I awoke many years later in a peaceful mangrove. Pussy willows dreamily swayed in the high tide. Catfish cavorted in spectacular leaps beyond the breakwaters. The sweet grass and cotton were high in the distance behind me. Not unlike Rip Van Winkle, I was surely missing asleep for generations though I felt virile and ageless. As the blood flowed more steadily I came to realize my condition was less than the serene exterior I comforted in. My exposed skin was savagely bloodied from some erstwhile insect molestation. A foot was sodden in a puddle nibbled at by pollywogs. My life force had dripped and coagulated at my feet where it was imbibed by the pulpy ground. I stood to face a world sadder and with a troubled brow. Throughout life I was a followed and haunted person. A destroyer demon cast its looming dark upon me and delighted in holding me down. Extreme evil plagued me with night terrors and in the waking hours attracted to me poltergeist companions. It was called upon and would not stop until it ran its course which constituted my lifespan. Early in life it introduced me to the four ghouls of Revelations. As I passed into the final light, there at the tunnel's end materialized the vision of an ancient orchard where-through a serpent slithered. Four cadaverous siren nymphs splayed themselves upon an ancient tomb on which were carven the three letters EVE.

That Than Which There Can Be No More Terrible

By Michael Scalzi

Dr. Dendrite's lectures on the philosophy of religion were his specialty, and in the eyes of his graduate students, would likely be his downfall. His recitations of medieval arguments for God's existence, the problem of evil, and his own highly original theodicies had become the frequent subjects of academic debate, gossip and playful imitation among the university's graduate and elite intellectual populations. Yet as impassioned as Dr. Dendrite's apologetics were—extending far beyond a seasoned professor's dutiful defense of the text—they also retained the capacity to muddle his otherwise unbreakable concentration and crystalline logic, rendering him as obstinate and single-mindedly obsessed as a ranting politician. During these philosophical fugues he was given to frequent fits of fallacy, eruptions of erroneous argumentation as well as rhapsodic rants, both pedestrian and pedantic—all of which he'd have easily dismissed as sophomoric or sophistic under less intellectually imperiled conditions.

Medieval theological arguments, steeped as they are in the principles of Aristotelian and Platonic metaphysics, manage to employ their share of quasi-logical "rabbit in the hat tricks," i.e. arguments that either bamboozle the reader with "pretzel logic" (the twisting of relationships between ideas and definitions until they appear to produce a valid conclusion), or ask them to accept a few simple premises and then hit them with a conclusion that appears to follow, but at the same time goes far beyond what they promise. Both of these techniques tend to leave the reader vaguely dissatisfied with the conclusion drawn, yet strangely unable to articulate why.

Ian Fichte was a proud member of the "fallacy finders" club: an informal distinction denoting the young brilliant minds found in the front row of every philosophy lecture, scrutinizing every point of discussion to death with overly-literal interpretations of text, nit-picking minute points of logic, and generally attempting to ruffle the mismatched tweeds of stalwart professors. Such biting criticisms as "anachronism," "confirmation bias," or the ultimate coffin pin in any ethical position: "the naturalistic fallacy" (the claim that no ethical term can be explained by mere approval or disapproval) were among their daily arsenal. The standard *modus operandi* for young philosophers had become negative: an attack on all preceding positions. Rather than creating new ideas—a practice which the academe had deemed trite and nigh-impossible at this late stage in the shelf-life of secondary research, it was sufficient to simply react—to present a contrasting pale. After all, it's the positive claim that ultimately bears the burden of rational argument. Defense of a negative is not nearly as difficult a task; it's simply a lack of belief—a healthy skepticism requiring no further defense.

Ian sat in the front row of every one of Dr. Dendrite's lectures, remaining particularly attentive during the recitations of theological arguments. While the rest of the class sank into its customary dogmatic slumber, Ian's shrewd sensibilities were titillated by the hylomorphic doctrines of the Scholastics and Neo-Platonists—both subjects he had mastered previously by methods both formal and autodidactic. The subject of today's rant was the formal syllogistic proof of God's existence, otherwise known as the "classic ontological argument" as formulated by St. Anselm of Canterbury in his famous *Prosologium.* And a rant it was. As Dendrite set up the premises of the 11th century argument he paced the half empty hall with a military pomp and swagger that resembled the goose-step; footnotes and corollaries jettisoned from his tongue, fanning off in all directions like philological shrapnel. Contrary to the cold, dispassionate flavor of the original argument's form, Dendrite's interpretation, or perhaps more aptly put, *performance* of the argument far exceeded St. Anselm's original in both depth and character of presentation, and all but confirmed Ian's long-standing suspicion of Dendrite's crypto-thespianism. He questioned how the rest of the students could manage to wistfully doze off or stare at their smart phones with such a spectacle before their eyes and ears. He found the ontological argument fascinating, and Dendrite's rendition of it only buttressed this opinion.

The argument itself, to Ian's mind, was a good example of a logical "rabbit in the hat" trick. There was something seemingly trivial about the way the conclusion landed in the lap of the interlocutor, giving her no choice but to assent to its positive claim, yet unable to resist a gnawing sense of gut-skepticism. It seemed a preposterous and arrogant piece of reasoning on several levels, yet it was extremely difficult to articulate even to one's self exactly what was wrong with it. Atheist Richard Dawkins, in his pseudo-philosophical bestseller *The God Delusion* compared it to a childhood playground anecdote, in which one child plays a little trick of the "na-na-na-na" variety on his classmates. English philosopher Bernard Williams simply called the argument "invalid" (i.e. the conclusion does not follow from the premises). Ian found the argument to be valid, but perhaps unsound, in that the conclusion does appear to follow from the premises, but the truth of the premises is highly debatable. Dendrite's moderately augmented version of the argument was presented as follows:

"Premise one simply states that it is a conceptual truth that God is a being than which none greater can be imagined—that is, the greatest possible being that can be imagined. Whether or not you are willing to accept that there is such being, the argument asks only that you admit that the idea of the being than which there can be no greater exists as an idea in the understanding. It is a concept that you can clearly grasp and understand." And indeed it was an understandable concept, thought Ian, whether or not it is a believable proposition in "reality" (i.e. outside of the understanding).

Dendrite's second premise was a little more challenging:

"A being that exists as an idea in the understanding and in reality, is necessarily greater than a being that exists as an idea in the understanding only. For instance, imagine the idea of an ice cream cone, just the idea of an ice cream cone, in your mind. Now imagine the idea of the ice cream cone in your mind, and in your hand as well, at the same time. Which is greater? The idea of the ice cream cone in the mind alone—or the idea of it in your mind combined with the actual item in your hand, and then in your stomach as well?"

The majority of the class conceded that, indeed, it was greater to have the ice cream cone both in the mind as an idea, and in their hand as a reality. Dendrite went on:

"Thus, if what we have agreed to in these two premises is true: that the being that exists as an idea in the understanding and in reality is greater than a being that exists only as an idea in the understanding, then the being than which there can be no greater cannot exist only as an idea in the understanding, for then we could obviously imagine a being that is greater than the being which there can be no greater. But, by definition we cannot conceive of a being greater than the being than which there can be no greater—for it is a contradiction to suppose that we can imagine a being greater than the greatest possible being. Therefore, this greatest possible being must necessarily exist."

At the end of this brilliant recitation of a somewhat perplexing piece of reasoning, half of the class remained silent and understandably vexed. The other half appeared to at least get the logical "feel" of what was being presented—if not convinced of the truth of the conclusion. To Ian it was somewhat convincing, in that the argument seemed to have the uncanny ability to slip through the logical fingertips of the interlocutor when presented in this conversational form. It really only asks you to assent to the two initial premises:

1. That she is capable of understanding the idea of "the being than which there can be no greater," i.e. the greatest possible being. It is not asked that the reader/listener imagine what this being would be like, or what it would be like to be this being, or even to believe that this being must or even could exist (in this initial premise)—only that she is able to clearly grasp the idea of the being than which there can be no greater. The majority of readers will readily assent to this premise. In the words of Anselm:

Hence, even the fool is convinced that something exists in the understanding, at least, than which nothing greater can be conceived. For, when he hears of this, he understands it. And whatever is understood exists in the understanding.[1]

2. That a being that exists both in the understanding, conceptually, *and* outside of the understanding in "reality" (both as a mind-dependent and mind-independent substance) is necessarily greater than a being that exists only conceptually in the understanding. This premise is usually accepted by the majority of readers as well, although it may often require further explanation than is presented in the original argument:

And assuredly that than which nothing greater can be conceived, cannot exist in the understanding alone. For, suppose it exists in the understanding alone: then it can be conceived to exist in reality; which is greater.[2]

Once these two premises have been accepted by the reader, she has only to attend to the contradiction produced by attempting to deny the existence of the being than which there can be no greater (known as a *reductio ad absurdum*, i.e. an argument which concludes in a contradiction). If the reader is able to clearly conceptualize the idea of a being than which there can be no greater, and admit that this being would be even greater if it existed outside of the mind as a real being, as well as in the mind as an idea, then they have only to attend to the logical contradiction produced by the denial of this being's existence outside of the mind. If the being does not in fact exist outside of the mind as well as within it (if the being is not realized, but remains only conceptual), then the two premises become incompatible; the greatest possible being cannot be the greatest possible being if there is an even greater possible being.

Ian had first encountered the argument about three years earlier, in his private studies. He was mystified, as many others had been before him, by the arrogance of the conclusion that one can prove the existence of an infinite substance by merely forming the concept of it in their mind. There was something fallacious about it in either a formal or informal sense, but he couldn't quite put his finger on what it was. The most obvious problem, to Ian's mind, was that between the first and second premise the argument appears to switch from a proposition about the idea or concept of a being to a proposition about an actual being, i.e. from proving that an idea exists, to proving than an actual being exists. And on this basis it may be concluded that, rather than proving that God exists as an actual being, the argument proves only that the idea of God exists. But it must then be admitted that the argument proves that the idea of God exists inside and outside of the mind as well—and what would it be like for an idea to exist outside of the mind? Is there such a thing even possible? A mind-independent idea? Ideas are by definition mind-dependent, and therefore any claims that the ontological argument only proves the existence of an idea, yet one that exists outside of the mind, is a manifest contradiction.

Also, there is the famous objection presented by the 11th century monk Gaunilo. Gaunilo claimed that the logic used in the ontological argument could be applied to an idea of anything at all—that is, the *perfect idea* of anything. Being a contemporary of Anselm, Gaunilo was able to respond directly to his argument, proposing that Anselm swap the idea of the greatest possible *being* for the idea of the greatest possible *island*, and on that basis prove by the same argument that the island than which there could be no greater must necessarily exist. Gaunilo's island than which there can be no greater is described as "the island which is more abundant with riches and delights than any other possible island." This argument fascinated Ian just as much as the original, and Anslem had a chance to respond to it: his reply was that *sheer quantity* of "riches and delights" (or of any other thing) can always be exceeded. This is premised on Aristotle's denial of the possibility of a true infinite, i.e. it is impossible to count upward to an actual infinite number. When dealing with quantities there can always be one greater—therefore infinity is purely conceptual, never actual. So the greatest possible island, when characterized as greatest on the basis of its unsurpassable abundance of riches, could always be greater in actuality, and therefore remains purely conceptual, and never actual. This resonated with Ian, being a devotee of Aristotle, but it also seemed that all Gaunilo would have had to do was to swap the island's criterion for greatness from sheer *abundance* to beauty or tranquility, or a less quantifiable, more qualitative property.

As these thoughts flooded Ian's mind (for minutes at a time, broken up by attending to the lecture) Dr. Dendrite fielded objections to Anselm's argument for the better part of an hour. Several students had broken their slumbers and reacted, as they invariably will to the ontological arguments, with great passion and fervor. One student argued that a concept simply can't prove the existence of something, i.e. that Gaunilo's objection stands up against the argument, even in its quantitative form. Another argued that a "greatest possible thing" is necessarily finite and bounded, in that its "that which there can be no greater" status is able to distinguish it from other sorts of things—and is therefore disqualified as a theistic deity (for the theistic deity, by definition, possesses *infinite being*). But Dendrite disarmed them at all turns—he seemed, like many tenured professors, to have "canned" responses to all possible attacks (and these were not the most ferocious of attacks by any means).

Ian was not planning to weigh in on the subject—not today. Dendrite was on fire, and he could think of nothing that would stand against his counterarguments. Even Kant's famous objection that existence is never a predicate or quality of an idea (and therefore adds nothing to its concept) seemed less than rival to the power of Dendrite's rejoinders. *But then it hit him. It hit him hard.* What if the positive character of the argument was reversed? What if the same logic demonstrated in the ontological argument was used not to prove the existence of the *greatest* possible being, but the *worst* possible being? Would the argument not possess the same strength in the negative? In fact, would it not be even *more* convincing in the negative? The more Ian thought about it (running it through his mind at lightning speed for what was probably no more than twenty seconds) the more he was convinced of it. It was practically apodictic ("apodictic" being one of those fancy philosophical words associated with Immanuel Kant, meaning: "necessarily conceived as true upon clear conception in the mind"), and more so than in the positive!

Ian was exalted, and simultaneously terrified. He stared down at his desk. Then at his note pad, his pen, the cover of Anselm's *Prosologium.* Then he made his move. Without raising his hand he inquired sharply: "What if we can imagine the idea of the being than which there can be no more terrible?"

Dendrite looked up from the brooding plod of his wide-stepped pace, squinting through bifocals in Ian's direction. "I mean," continued Ian, "if we are able to clearly understand the idea of the being than which there can be no more horrible, and grasp it conceptually in our mind—and assent to the fact that that being would be more horrible if it existed both in the mind conceptually as well as outside the mind in reality—then does it not follow that that being must exist in reality?"

The class continued to stare at Ian. Dendrite's expression further intensified—his stare moved to the floor, to the table on which his text laid. It struck Ian for the first time that Dendrite was truly convinced by the logic of the ontological argument—the intensity with which he pondered this new negative version only testified to the fact that he took the logical force of the *reductio ad absurdum* very seriously.

"In fact," Ian explained further, "one of the common objections to the original argument denies that the idea of a being existing in the understanding alone is necessarily a lesser being than one existing in reality. But a being than which there can be no more horrible, or terrible, would *definitely* be more terrible if it existed in reality. I can clearly comprehend the idea of the worst possible being: the most terrifying, evil, disgusting, contemptible being possible. It is clear to me what these words mean, and although I do not wish to come up with an image to accompany them, the concept of this being is clearly apprehended by the mind. Now surely if the idea I have of this being were realized there is no question that it would be *much, much more terrible* than it is as a mere idea inside my mind—in fact it seems even more certain that it would be all the more terrible if it were realized than the greatness of the greatest possible being would be if it were realized—and therefore all the more convincing that this being must exist in reality."

It was true that the argument seemed much more convincing in the negative. It was hard to put one's finger on exactly why, but it was clear to Ian that Dendrite was now convinced of this disturbing addendum to the ontological argument. The fact that this being could, and in fact must (by the logic of the ontological argument) exist in reality, was a much more powerful realization for some strange reason than the realization of the existence of the greatest possible being. And it was the fact *that the certainty of the sharp increase in the manifest terribleness of this being if it were to exist in reality, rather than in the mind alone* that was responsible for the certainty that it must exist. The realization that one must assent to this being's necessary existence—not the worst being in existence, but the worst *possible* being—the most terrible being that could exist in *any possible world*, or accept the logical contradiction which arises from its denial, appeared to be more than Dendrite's superior yet delicate sensibilities could suffer.

Professors often shudder and stir at the well placed jabs of their brighter students, but subsequently regain their composure, rejoining with a zinger of their own, or more often "bloviating" their way around the objection with grand postures and big words. Dendrite did neither. He was clearly vexed by Ian's argument, and just as clearly convinced of its logical efficacy. His pacing resumed silently. Clearly he was disturbed, put off—completely broadsided by this bizarre yet highly convincing argument. He shook his head. He stirred and took his glasses off, wiping them with his breast-pocket handkerchief which he then applied to his moistened brow. In a highly transparent attempt to laugh it all off, he exclaimed: "Well, that's really quite an interesting point, of course, I do see your point… It is rather… ummm… interesting. You have created quite a conundrum. In fact… my God…" he exclaimed, now drenched in sweat and making little effort to compose himself. "You seem to have stumbled upon something quite, well… quite… I'm at a bit of a loss to…" Dendrite chuckled nervously, this time under his breath. "I'll have to think… I… aaugh… I'll have to get back to you… that will be all for today—"

Dendrite abruptly left the room. The students looked at each other, and then at Ian, who began to laugh nervously. He had a desperate urge to discuss the argument further with Dendrite. It was not going to leave his mind. He was not entirely convinced of it, of course—he was never entirely convinced by the original ontological argument—but there was one thing he was sure of: *Dendrite was convinced*—clearly convinced of the necessary existence of *the being than which there can be no more terrible.* He had obviously been much more convinced by Anselm's ontological argument than Ian had previously realized, and, on that basis, was even more convinced by this new version. He could only imagine that Dendrite was now staring at the walls of his office, trying desperately to un-convince himself of the sheer logical necessity of the existence of this horrible being, and perhaps just as desperately to rid his mind of accompanying images.

Ian left the classroom no less abruptly than Dr. Dendrite had moments before. Dendrite's office was in the same building, two floors up. Ian took the stairs—thoughts of violence and terror racing through his mind as he climbed. When he got to Dendrite's door it was hanging open. The first thing he noticed was a swift draft blowing into the hallway. Upon entering he saw no sign of Dendrite, but then noticed broken glass all over the desk, spilling onto the floor. The large window facing the street was shattered. Something large had obviously been hurled through it. Ian retreated to the door and shut it, falling back against it in a doomed attempt to deny what he was surely about to confirm. Slowly he stepped towards the window and stuck his head through the shattered pane, only to confirm his greatest fear. Dendrite's tweeds were ruffled for the last time, around his twisted, motionless body on the sidewalk four stories below. The fear was too much—the reality of this most horrible being was incontestable. Only a fool would attempt to deny it.

* * *

Sources:

[1] St. Anselm, *Proslogium; Monologium; an Appendix in Behalf of the Fool by Gaunilon; and Cur Deus Homo*, Translated From the Latin by Sidney Norton Deane, B. A. With an Introduction, Bibliography, and Reprints of the Opinions of Leading Philosophers and Writers on the Ontological Argument (Chicago, The Open Court Publishing Company, 1903, reprinted 1926)

[2] ibid.

Author's notes:

My first attempt at philosophical fiction was made at the age of 19, when I composed the tedious story of a graduate philosophy student who drives himself insane, entitled *A Rhetorical Apocalypse*. It surely did justice to its namesake though a more pithy title such as *A Literary Dis aster* might have been more appropriate. I printed up a few copies with a little paper cover and submitted it for review to the *Fact Sheet Five*, in which it received a moderately pleasant review. Several people (among them at least one incarcerated individual) actually ordered copies and wrote me letters in response commenting on the story and its philosophical/horrific content. Hopefully this current effort is, if not better, at least slightly more mature, readable, entertaining, etc. I composed it (after having driven myself insane as a graduate student, and becoming a philosophy teacher myself) mostly as a teaching tool for my Philosophy of Religion students, as supplementary reading to St. Anselm of Canterbury's Twelfth Century *Ontological Argument*. The obvious Lovecraftian flavor of the story is simply there to make it more fun to read (and write). I don't think I could ever publish standard academic philosophy papers—for lack of interest and perhaps talent, so this is as close as it gets.

Mystery Believer

By Scott Waldrop

"Ghosts are real. They're here. I've seen them." The utterly random and bizarre assertion issued forth from an unfamiliar voice punctuating the still night air and permeating the group's collective energy with adrenal trepidation. The bellowing halted a marathon of tall-tale-telling, one non-believer regaling the next with preposterous fancies toned with sardonic mockery. The night-cutting utterance was followed by an even more commanding and darker inflected truth: "Your mysteries are my mundane." The voice was rustic, generally obtuse and blunt in timbre yet possessed of a puzzlingly singularly articulate nature. The flames' frenetic illumination contorted the shadows upon his already hideous visage, shape-shifting it to and fro to create a cinematic gallery of grotesque masks, much to the pointedly nauseating terror of his hostages. They collectively gasped aloud as the stranger materialized from the edge of the wild. From the spaces where black and orange shadows contort and contrast his form filled out—out of the real country darkness. Down from true north he came. He was thin-skinned and albeit he gazed at them through milky cataract eyes, he seemed to stare straight and true to his target as he tallied each onlooker from garb to soul. From his entire body hung unusually long hair tangled with gory bones. The matted rot which precariously dangled from him was pasted with upchuck and reeked of wet dog. No doubt he was a transient who had traipsed downward from The Mildew Mountains and was all too happy to chance upon a group whom he could impose his incoherence upon. Inasmuch as they were appalled by the gray grizzled mongoloid, they were taken by his silver tongue. In his clutch, transfixed by the crazed man's command over them, the fireside captives were all but the arrested prostrate recipients of his eldritch knowledge. The forest revelers now a sable throng, dripping sweat and tear, were statues in ice and a variable cromlech weathering against an ever-intensifying hellpyre fueled by the incantations belching forth from the blathering stranger's fetid tongue. To intervene with his spell would be precipitous and result in blunder though his prisoners knew not why. It was a truth told to them in their mind's eye. His power compelled them to listen to his tale.

And he spoke unto them: "Some are The Grim. They harkened from remote antiquity. They are the ones who walk in league with The Death

Gods and slip into our channels during our weak moments. They will the wild upon The Earth. Others are but benign analogs of residual trauma stained upon crude matter. A whisper of what was once a parent's purpose abruptly extinguished at the caprice of chance and damned to traipse sad corridors on an eternal quest for mother. No matter dark destroyer nor guardian nymph, they all are characterized by their strangeness. You close your eyes in dark meditation and try to realize a colour that no one knows the name of. Such is the true nature of ghost. Endeavoring to know them is vain pursuit as their ways are purposefully made inaccessible to us by whatever governing force dictates all that whatever thing experience is. Know this! The following is a true story. A wiser man once told me that a song is nothing more than three chords and the truth. This is my song. This is my song to my ghost. These are my three chords devoid of pomp, caprice, and all things superlative." His voice decayed in epic sustain, and somewhere in that starshine ether, his words and their images were conveyed via the mind's eye unto that lowly campfire throng. Through a tunnel cosmic and saturated beyond perception, the stranger's life unfolded casually and vividly in their respective dreamscapes from its genesis on. Through a waning conduit to reality he spoke, "You will find improvisational truths here. Since my emergence from the womb I have walked a canopied subterranean path of none but singularly bizarre phenomenon." Their minds were bridled and placed within placid remembrances of the venerable mongoloid.

Now to The South. Before he transmogrified into his current state he began as any child—fresh, abounding with potential, and doted on by a myriad relation who believed in him. He was born on a Wednesday to a psychic mother who kept cursed black sand in decorative bottles. In his nursery hung a poem proclaiming Wednesday's child to be full of woe. He was predisposed to gloom. His colic would tear his parents apart. Despite this bleak inevitability, he entered the springtime of life with abundance and sun. His youth was marked by high tides under ephemeral glances of heaven painted rich Carolina blue and smeared soft peach by carousing spirits in the sky. Girls in cultish white dress lead him down the shell-laden beaches. He remembered their kind faces and not their names nor identities. Their mousy locks sheen with youth, they danced wildly with abandon in the origin surf winds. They were stranger kin. They were telepaths. They imbued him peripherally and abstractly via astral energies with the encouraging truth that it's never too late to be brand new. They disappeared hovering beyond the beach into the shadow of pine where through their lullaby of high cotton and jumping fish faded into the deep wood. With their dissipation came the crossing crescendo of a soft organ's cadence floating ever gently across amber fields, and once again he was hand in hand with the elder woman en route to a strawberry patch where spat forth Clovis points from its hoary depths when black soil drank the August rain and purged its secrets. It was the edifice that presided over this tranquil montage that bonded the energy of the past and present. It was perhaps more human in spirit than the humans themselves. Any thing or place maintained by humans becomes personified—this is pointedly true of houses as they become living and breathing things pulsing with the energy and will of their inhabitants who smear their life force into their fiber through loving maintenance. The tending humans pamper crude matter until it teems with life force. It teems with the limitless shoals of wriggling little souls. Without the human they're incarnate. The human brings them into being and indubitably provide the materials with love and fastidiousness until they ultimately expire, leaving the domicile alone to languish woefully and vainly longing for their keepers' return. And unto this journey of perpetual longing the house returns to nature, tearfully, moss-eaten, sodden and bowing, until its final death rattle while gently it lists under the pressure of one final funeral shroud of snow. A pile of brittle timber imbued with the swollen emotions from births, deaths, and holidays celebrated by the long since deceased. It begins to cough. It begins to shake. It is languishing, starving, and naked not unlike a cadaveric prisoner of war. Now just a pile of bones and residual psychic discoloration on the soil as the area and remnants themselves are ghosts as its ghosts who once loved in it and loved it.

Such was the venerable colonial haunt and its country labyrinth hedges which belonged to him the child and him alone during the long rays of summer. There he pioneered old barns where remained the restless spirits of war horses, crumbling fire pits where his forbearers leisured, bean bins with hiding serpents, and sandboxes with ancient toys encrusted in the red clay beneath the beach sand. Ominous and ever-present in the distance was land ceded by evil spirits where Indian burial mounds callously lay level in the wake of diesel belching behemoths. This land was also his yet never dared upon. The house's foundation served as the bowels to an innumerable and forgotten number of structures before it. It was more a yawning and indifferent hole in the ground, a sepulcher pit and a general portal rather than a proper foundation. The property's land records long ago inexplicably went missing. This colonial revival house of his parents' parents was where he first perceived "them." A dim and distant warning, lurking and knocking upon its slimy limestone underbelly was ever-encroaching—ill fungi-like, tenacious and patient as it dwelt. In its third floor southeastern bedroom he'd remain wide awake, staring at walls painted pale blue which took on bizarre luminescent properties as the moonlight played its spectral trick upon them. This paint was ancient and harkened back to days gone when children now dead fancied its then vibrant hues. Now they stood bleached and neglected, yet untouched for nostalgic and unbearable memories of those long since dead kin. As a child (in some abstract perception) this wasn't lost upon his developing conscious. His bedroom window afforded a wide view of a moonlit garden and its well where gray spectres would dully float, dart and sometimes dance upon the bowling green when the night's atmosphere felt tentative and fitful to the little one.

He saw these dark wonders as beauty and it in no way broke nor oppressed his effervescent spirit. He took the uncanny as mundane drudgery and weird phenomenon as commonplace occurrence. At five years of age he told his mother to look under a dank niter-coated rock in the forest under which she discovered gold. It was not that he knew what was under the rock—rather than merely a compulsion to suggest she check, as perhaps by random obsession or driven by exterior forces. He had not the words to articulate the inner monologue then no more than he ever would into decrepitude. All things weird seemed to cavort around the child. Where he went there was the weird. He was integral, center, and perhaps the very vortex from whence it came and where it flourished. He always had strange neighbors. There was a house in his midst where two women lived. They kept the company of psychics, all of whom (it was relayed in rumor) informed them that there was a shockingly beautiful yet melancholy spirit in their house. A wide-eyed gypsy prophet said a barn once stood where the house now was. It was perched upon a precipice cresting a dramatically steep hill. It would have been an obvious lookout point to scroll the rolling Carolina landscape of the agrarian days. She—waiting eternally for her beau to return from the great war of aggression, unbeknownst to her that what few shreds of his mortal remains could be scraped from the gory true northern soil were hastily and carelessly cast into a nameless mire amongst a motley disarray of skull and limb, none belonging to the next. She would go to that barn to weep where its soil routinely drank her brackish cascades which fell with profusion. Moreover, there was a soldier's headstone in a grove all but fifty yards from where the little boy laid his head on his pillow each night and went to sleep only to become a conduit to all the spiritual vortex on spree in his tiny world. There was causal connection between this weathered stone and the ghost girl of the barn. His metaconscious assured him of this, though it was never outwardly contemplated.

His neighbors were a carnival of oddities indeed, but oh, how there was one clan but the worst! They dwelt across the fields and their boundary could be seen through the hoary bubbly pane of his bedroom window—the woods wherein the ebony witch dwelt. Oh that witch, how she gave him a fright! She lived beyond the great dismal bog in the distant woods wherefrom the wild dogs barked. She was the skeletal officer of two retarded waifs, aggressively reclusive and without spouse. She would oft creep to the wood's edge and besiege those she chanced upon with unsolicited words which were always vague and foreshadowing. A singular vivid memory of seminal origin within his metaconscious, the boy recalled, was her cryptic words issued with a raised crooked boney finger, pointing as they croaked droll from her rancid mouth gaping below sunken dead eyes. "Don't let my children poison your mind." He knew she was attempting to manipulate him as those are the silver-tongued words of deception giving itself away to the savvy. He knew it to be the opposite and the mongoloid children were innocents.

The Indians constantly kept candles burning on the left side of their cabins which faced in her hut's direction so as to illuminate and sanctify their domiciles against her negative energy. Superstition ran rampant in these hinterlands. Some lit their dwellings against her out of pure intuition without any exposure to folklore regarding such matters. It was a simple primal necessity. It was at an early age he became metaconscious. He pondered what was at the forefront of one's mind and what was abstract and peripheral. The forest Indians and common people all had their mantras and maxims. He wondered if the common folk understood the seminal genius of their metaphors or if they simply repeated them in blind servitude to the colloquialisms of their birthright. They, the troglodyte hinterland rovers who indulgently blathered their maxims—was it feigned wisdom? Was it total complacency of speech such as their literal interpretation of scripture? He felt that it was most likely they traipsed through their lives with utter complacency in perspective. Surely he thought, profound truth and revelation was lost and/or at best transmogrified, through their injudicious heaping of superfluous fluff upon their language. He couldn't help but dwell on the words carefully chosen through discourse and how they resonate throughout life. One should use analogy sparingly and with precision he believed, as they are the exposing calculation of one's intellect. His inquiry into such matters drove him quite often to the brink of sanity. His path into strangeness had begun early on indeed, and his cup flowed over with beauty in cosmic weirdness of which he imbibed to excess.

His honorary induction into the metaphysical community came in the form of their family ghost and its nocturnal sprees. It brought all into question and commensurately answered all question. Phenomenon of all sort followed. He received sporadic psychic shivers at utter random. He was certain of callous pedestrians crossing his grave in some remote future. The notion that he indeed was dead and unaware, such as his dead companion, became an intrusive notion that walked with him in his shadow as his shadow walked with him at night darker than any other umbra. As an empath he absorbed the negative, tense energy in any environment or situation. The clashing of beasts such as a steed rearing before the wolves of the woods gave him a spell and would leave him emotionally drained, having absorbed all the fear and aggression of each respective animal spirit's soul. He endeavored greatly not to faint after such incidents. With revelation shifted the paradigm slowly gradating in the metaconscious—his reverence for dark beauty became entwined with humble fear. A foot dangling from the side of the bed was a liability as skeletal hands seizing his ankle in the small hours, imploring him to comprehend their undead plight, wasn't removed from the spectrum of possibility. He was told folk tales by the elders which he knew the truths of instinctively. He knew of the old decrepit murderer man who was said to be ghoulishly emaciated, shoeless, with ragged pants and stringy hair, carrying a long knife and would lurk the wood along the ancient creek bed where rusted oddities lay submerged and multitudes of unusually plump frogs became trapped in the frozen water during winter without explanation save witchcraft. He saw the twin girls in the Carolina woodland found hanging from their eye sockets in a well in their Sunday dresses. He knew Obadiah Payne, the ghost of a sea captain who angrily rattled anchor chains in the attic. Vague remembrances from strange childhood tales would define him in the broader scheme. These tales were passed down from an earlier age. He was the accidental child born of old parents. This made his childhood a strange recollection from another era—alien to his own—and him an old soul. He himself was antiquarian and anachronistic by nature and birthright.

Matters became darker as the true elemental and oppressive destroyers crept through him. Him, the portal. His parents' relationship deteriorated due to the psychic maelstrom raging out of control, and his mother went forever missing and estranged, casting herself into the wild with drooling dead-eyed dementia. In her place a grizzled hinterland matron of the common folk was called upon to tend to the boy as his father toiled. Loathsome, wretched and simple was she. She was no consolation gift in place of a missing mother. His mother figure had been ruthlessly downgraded from an elegant, soft-spoken belle to the lowliest human detritus devoid of compassion and possessing little more intellect than the gastropods trudging the hinterland's stone walls. The grizzled matron came with her dim adult son as an obligatory companion and he seemed destined to be in her care into their respective expiration. The boy learned that The Dim and Simple tend to teeter on the extremes of the spirit plane. This particular Dim one was a void of light and goodness. He was a vile and dull clod, with a generally incestuous aura, whose soul—if that is indeed was what inhabited his shell—was the most basic of evil. He had a predilection for prowling and voyeurism—in particular during the night, on the outside looking in, behind window panes, and through the eyes of grotesque masks. He was never without weaponry of some sort which was the most unsettling detail about him. He would creep up to the attic at twilight and rifle through the family's belongings, eventually chancing upon a chest of Hallow's Eve decor. From its dusty depths he exhumed and procured the faces of skeletons and devils which he ran his dirty fingers over, drooled upon and cooed at upon their exposure to his lamp's evil orange glow. He absconded with them to his hideaway and would employ them in the evenings to leer at and menace the boy while he ate supper and slept. The boy paid no mind as he was charged with psychic strength and guardian spirits. In defeat, The Dim Evil One in his mask traipsed into a village where he fancied a girl. He became the monster outside her window at night. One night the glass eventually shattered. It was penetrated by his crude weaponry—and without the vile details, it suffices to say that the girl was reduced to bloody gore. The Dim Evil One would hang and the boy slipped away to fight the psychic storm another day albeit prematurely older and wiser.

In his bedroom at night the boy heard distant trains rumble and whistle which served as a reminder of people moving as he lay stagnant—strange thoughts indeed for a youngling. He was restless and the darkness saw this as weakness. From the intense quiet of the starshine ether moments between wakefulness and sleep, there was some inexplicable great violence in that serenity as to suggest that this state of consciousness was an entry into the psychic maelstrom. The great quiet violence was that which can only be defined as an immense evil in its size and infinite power. This was clear to him though indefinable and not the sort of thing worth discussing with others. The dark energy compelled him oft to malicious behavior that he would reprove himself from as he knew the black energies were gaining strength and he was slipping. Nonetheless in haze he would catch himself tossing wriggling serpents from on high upon the common folk below or creeping upon unsuspecting victims and sending needles into their backsides. Mercifully, the universe opened opportunity to balance the light against dark as it was announced by his father that they were to travel true north to where a new sea was said to exist by voyagers, and the land thereabouts was rife with abundance and pure potential. So upward traveled they, leaving behind the high tides and agrarian glory for the steel-vaulted firmament and tumultuous rhythms of the great northern monstrosities of humanity, unto which the boy was cast upon a psychic theater he was well-prepared to wage battle upon. Up north the venerable brick colonial was exchanged for a cottage perched dramatically upon a terrace where the view was scenic and expansive. There were northern farmlands to explore, conquer and cede. And here, in that old cottage basement was found a planchette and spirit board. His new friends implored him that it was to be left unmolested, but the boy employed it with addiction. It gashed his conduit's opening, flooding where he walked with storm and strife. The boy reinterred the ghostly device into the cottage's slimy sub-basement nitre amidst the psychic turmoil and it was great fortune that a new kindred companion was to soon enter the stage.

The grizzled matron of the hinterlands was mercifully replaced by a noble old world Germanic woman who was pointedly eccentric, and fed the boy's intellect. She was built of the objective, analytic, and stern emotional disconnect he craved in companionship, yet she was airy and ethereal such as he. "There is something here," she at random one day announced to the boy as she strung his garments on a rope in the washroom. She looked upwards at the second story floorboards and professed, "I hear footsteps up there when I am alone during the day, and I don't like whatever it is." The boy just stared at her. It was the first time another had acknowledged at-point-blank this particular mundane piece of existence. She told the boy that the house stood on a battleground and that the ghosts of war break things in the night. The boy knew this and the two were briefly silent in mutual understanding. She then went to the mantel and took down his own portrait and brought it to him, placing it before his face so as to make him look into his own eyes. She covered his mouth in the portrait with her finger and said, "I see your eyes are full of sadness and you too can see it when your smile is covered." She knew as he, that he was Wednesday's child.

As it happens with all folk common and exceptional alike, childhood waned in a bleak pale dawn revealing a stormy horizon. The noble Germanic woman abandoned the boy as had all parental figures when the phantom maelstrom intensified and he was left feral with back against the blackness, where he was left to fend off the wolves of humanity with the torch-scepter of his own spiritual creation. Thrust into this frenzied and wild world at half strength, the suffocating blackness couldn't be held at bay. He was enveloped by groaning shadow elementals. They held him down and terrorized him in the night. They blurred his meta-conscious in the day, presenting the elixir bottle with the devil lurking in its bottom. "Won't you partake in this last offered cup?" screeched one of the void figures. "Or disappear into the potter's ground?" offered another. They all looked on craftily rubbing their hands together, such flies plotting to inoculate carrion with their eggs. Without understanding or memory of doing so, The Youth having been left to his own devices, partook and the psychedelic befouled his spirit evermore. He descended the proverbial rabbit hole, was there arrested, and was to be suspended within its yawning toxic chasm until lessons enough were learned to devise a means of escape and redemption. At the bottom he found himself in dark spaces. Early upon his entry, a veteran denizen of the night who was hobbled and deformed by his own depravity offered the prophetic words, "If you start down this path you will meet the worst of This Earth." With abandon he went forward into the thicket and into a world of slime-coated blackened crags choked by menacing night-purple flora possessed of autonomous minds and nervous systems. A horizon-wide black entity mountainously filled the distant landscape—its true nature only recognizable in the mind's eye such as in dream—and also such as in dream, the descent down this path was punctuated by the ever-present sensation of being chased by ghosts albeit the stark lonesomeness was hefting an unbearably heavy load on the soul. He was a conduit within a conduit. This mystery was confounding even to an individual who relates to all things nether and arcane. Warm hues were all but forgotten to comprehension. What is orange? Nothing should be orange. It's the most loathsomely cheerful of hues. In that cracked brain flourished the rampant kudzu of psychic illness. Obsessive thoughts harnessed him then unbridled him and left him dilapidated. Some think that a thought forgotten must not have been important enough to remember. But what if this ebbed on the side of err? What if a profound and precious truth was tragically realized fleetingly and just as soon lost in that phantasmagoric swoon? One can never say, albeit golden-aged truths were exhumed from cosmic grave dust in this wasteland of terror, and devastatingly slipped through a porous mind fluttering into the ether once again—laughing—knowing their chance for rediscovery was an abstract concept akin to the meaning of what can only be measured in words as "beyond impossible." Here, you visit places only accessible via dream. A dream is all you need to go there albeit a special and exceedingly rare one. You may only be given this dream but once. Such were the games the elixir played on his soul. His mind was left fractured beyond recognition. Peering into himself, he found a broken mirror that he couldn't make sense of. The reflected pieces were generally chaotic and each deconstructed. He had to endeavor to leave this place and find another to quietly repair this damage. Somehow he had known content as a youth. Was this a luxury not to be afforded to one devoid of innocence or could it be reclaimed? Determinedly he arose and with weak constitution and retarded mental fortitude, quested epically to find where through the light may be penetrating the canopy of this dismal bog he was hopelessly lost within.

At length he discovered that this place was adamant that he not leave. It worked its charm. Small glistening ectoplasm droplets manifested from neverness and transfixed him as they magically floated through the air. Droplets undulated into diminutive spectres and marched in undead procession, aphid-like yet humanoid, amongst the thorn-crested highways flanking that dank tunnel. Beings with only a whispered resemblance to anything familiar darted in shadow. He resisted its trance grasp and willed the apparitions back to neverness from whence they came. The scepter glowed with might. It all started with a proactive move and the gumption to make a choice with conviction. He must go one way or the other. Both ways are black and only the heart could choose. Nonetheless, he was resolute. He would return to a time of dark beauty. He would hold power over mystery. And above all, he would return to a time when he believed in himself and everyone believed in him. He moved forward! Into undreamed wastes he braved The Nausea Terra Firma.

The stench came slowly and then steadily. The Sewage Thing would faithfully molest his olfactory senses throughout his journey, shadowing him with tenacity. Along the trail he paralleled the ancient aqueducts where from emanated the dull miasma which filled his lungs and mind. Breathing heavy with cardiovascular strain he shuttered to contemplate the poison wastes entering his lungs, moving into his bloodstream and seeping into his every fiber. The miasma oppressed his very spirit which was entrapped within its now mortally polluted temple. Eventually the thorn canopy opened into what appeared at first to be a rolling moonlit meadow save that proving upon a moment's acclimation, it was but a fossil-vaulted chasm lit alone by some spectral force. It was, however, a meadow inasmuch as alien flora akin to grass grew there albeit the substrate (whatever chemical agents it was composed of) more closely resembled the sheen black coat of a horse as its gloss defined the contours of the topography. Unlike the terra firma of reality, this took the form of deep water in suspended animation. Upon its glassy ebony banks thronged an innumerable herd of ground fauna which moved in concert as would a vast shoal of fish. It was a field full of rabbits. There was contradiction in them. Something ordinarily docile and sweet took on menacing attributes in their multitudes. They stood ears perked, venerable, stoic and watchful. They were imbued with godly hyper intelligence, had supernatural powers and were merely choosing to be seen. They were dangerous fauna and were the apex predators here. "They kill most who pass them," The Mind's Eye whispered. He passed through their realm and into dense forest which with sporadic inexplicability opened upon strange ritual groves where cromlechs from a living remote past protruded from sweet electric green mosses. This was the last lost grove oasis the forest would reveal, and unbeknownst to the traveler, he entered the dark indefinitely. As the electric moss and spectacularly abstract fungi creepily grew before him—slowly yet with animation—he entered into the land of sodden despair.

In this new and even stranger world the rain was a persistent delicate mist that coated everything in its midst incessantly. It was ever-present, ever-moistening, and ever-maddening. The world gave no visual cues as to direction for the monotony of dark brown to black was all-enveloping in this prison of ever-decomposing wet wood. Dead snakes were all around. They were grotesque vipers of storybook variety from distant lands. It was alarming to know that they resided here in such profusion. One would think such a fabled and fearsome night-creature would be an oddity, but indeed the forest was teeming with them. It came as some condolence that he was only observing the unlucky deceased specimens but it was commensurately bothersome to extrapolate that these numbers were a reflection of their still-living kindred. The environment itself had psychoactive properties and made travel difficult as its flora perfumed anything animate with noxious dope which incubated surmounting terror of the most abject and personal sort within him. Moreover, there was a creature under his feet that followed him under the soggy rot at length. It wriggled and jostled the spongy bark below. Surfacing only feet before him was an unnaturally large and blackish amphibious monstrosity. It was king in this dreaded swamp kingdom where things tend to grow bigger. It stared at him. Preposterous saucer eyes gleaned intellect with indifference. It consumed him and into obscurity he lay dormant in black suspension. Eons upon eons elapsed as he floated in magic sleep.

In death he awoke to find a glowing golden hue illuminating an exquisite face. "Are you an angel?" he asked. She smiled and silently wiped away the ugliness from him. Her love warded off evil. She stayed with him at length and days would become years. The night terrors returned to him but hunkered in the dark corners of his chamber and loathsomely glowered, unable to penetrate the positive energy provided by The Angel. But lie in wait they did until there was a moment of weakness as angels too must sleep from time to time. The Angel slumbered and her protective powers lay dormant with her allowing a wrinkled portal to begin creeping open. Once the portal was opened they rushed to his side and forced the elixir down his throat and it surged back into those long detoxified veins. He walked with the ghosts. All the best of The Earth that surrounded him withered and all approached The Wretch with ambivalence. The only haunted house one is forced to dwell within is one's own shell. And thus, his domicile and sanctuary was the embodiment of both, and both were commensurately toxic. All was being lost. The house was alive with evil. In its dark spaces where the gossamers collect, crawling things held clandestine congregations. Deep in its sodden beams cavorted an abominable orgy of slimy wriggling bugs, destroying it with their procreating, and devouring it from the core. In the grey garden outside, flowers grew in profusion amongst the tombs of deceased pets. There was still something positive here in the roots. The light and dark pulled against one another each in desperation. Others would try to occupy the house but it would only be bridled by its masters. Its window panes were etched and permanently emblazoned with the visages of its beloved former occupants who once looked out of them to see the children of summer, the frosts of October, the freshly fallen snow, and first birds of spring. Its blessed chambers resonated with their whispers, the energy of Christmases past, and the energy of funerals past unique to the lineage of its long dead caretakers (a lineage other than their own). They were intruders. The Living were the uninvited guests. They were creating an alien energy, making static and turbulence upon the veil between two worlds. They feared its attic. They feared its basement. They feared the creeping white roots which tenaciously and firmly grasped the crackling underbelly of its sodden beams. They would attempt repairs but were appalled when they exhumed the legions of annelid and aphid which swarmed taking outrage at their exposure. In these unseen nether regions of the house a silent menace was ever-present, ever-expanding, gripping and claiming with each passing moon. The intruders gathered themselves. They were determined to restore the old thing as it beckoned to them with its seductive might. They began to peel ajar a single floorboard from its parlor. With a crack, the innards revealed themselves for the first time since lost antiquity. There, exposed infinite blackness wherefrom lethargically and dumbly arose the deep, dull, obtuse, and brutish odor of many-a-thing eternally rotting. They gasped! Their terror was ever so pointed and ever so abject. The intruders aborted and fled in weeping submission, now the recipients of unwanted cosmic wisdom which was ever-metastasizing and ever-expanding in their minds. Those feeble minds! Those finite minds where the vortex will reach critical mass and fracture their souls to no return. The man was left alone in his haunted house. He dwelt there for time immemorial and from antediluvian antiquity remained dull and silent until the house returned to nature and the spirit found himself a satellite island in alien waters which had long-since drowned the lush terra firma where the venerable edifice stood in times undreamed. He was stranded and fatigued in the center of that black lake. He could see both sides. He saw where he started from. Looking back to his journey's genesis there was still a discernable scene of sunny shores and firefly-catching innocence. The other side which he was languidly treading towards was a gnarled embankment, offering little hope of liberation from the murky waters and only offering little but certain encounters with night creatures. Cold patches where the current brought fluctuating temperatures—as if some leviathan were agitating deep primordial areas or the water's undead—were closing in underfoot to touch upon his flesh. He circumnavigated the toxicity. He became strong for the last time and swam across the great black lake in reverse and to a king's return to summer shores.

The captive revelers revived from their collective swoon to discover this message etched in ash amongst the slow pulsating embers: "In each mystery there's something true and never too late to be brand new." Distant in the real country darkness, where faintly discernable firefly lights spangled the oily blackish night canvas, there deep within decayed the whisper of childish woops resonating through the forest. And believers collected themselves and took their first step out of that EVIL EVIL night.

Red Ochre

By James Ashbey

I used to wish that I were less inquisitive, and that I could travel through life without the perpetual urge to follow every mysterious and sinister thing to its hiding place. But here at the end of it all, now that I know what rich rewards await the curious, I regret nothing.

The shelves of the Institute of Archaeology Library in Bloomsbury are replete with wonder of many kinds, and it is all too easy to wander there and become lost in the marbled corridors of the past. On one such visit I found myself lifting from the shelf W. F. Hermann's *Chthonic Cults of Prehistory;* an obscure volume which bore no relevance to my studies, but whose irresistible name and charming red leather binding spoke to that childlike thirst for fantasy which in some of us never truly dies.

I sat with the book for some time, and before long became convinced that much of what passes for erudition in contemporary academic circles is mere pretence. Professor Hermann's far-reaching study of the earthen powers once known to mankind is a scholarly masterwork, and it left me in no doubt of the shocking unity of the cultic practices that prevailed across much of the world at civilisation's dawn.

In particular I was drawn to a sequence of coloured plates illustrating the homogenous nature of early burial custom, and above all the use of red ochre as a funerary dressing. I learnt that, from the Outer Hebrides to the Levant, early humans covered their dead with that ruddy pigment before sealing them in caves or grave pits. The book's photographs showed all manner of skeletons, some surrounded by primitive earthenware, others lovingly adorned with shell jewellery and semiprecious stones, but all of them stained a dusky red-brown; the unmistakable hue of red ochre.

I left the library with reluctance, conscious of the onset of evening and my expected attendance at a dinner engagement, but I could not take my mind off what I had read and seen. I offered little conversation to my fellow diners that night, being too lost in reverie concerning ancient funerals and the primal prayers that must have accompanied the throwing down of the ochre. Above the hubbub of the restaurant and the pervasive drone of road traffic, I fancied that I heard the pulsing of crude percussion and the sullen mourning chants of peoples at one with Nature.

The following day I raised the subject of ochre burials with my lecturer, and was surprised to be curtly silenced for pursuing "outmoded" avenues of scholarship. I was told that Hermann was a "fringe academic" whose work had been stripped of all credence by subsequent generations.

Undeterred, I resolved to seek out some of Hermann's case studies for myself. I visited the British Museum and spent hours gazing at red-brown bone fragments and pottery sherds, feeling like a pilgrim who has reached his long-sought shrine. The evidence seemed irrefutable: our distant, scattered sires all possessed a deep and uniform belief in the power of red ochre... but what kind of power? Was it the sort of transient symbolism that prevails in modern ceremonial—hollow pomp to feed the vanity of the living—or was it something deeper, more hard-wired, toppled from its former preeminence and enduring only as the faintest of yearnings that the clamour of modernity compels us to ignore? I had to find out.

Obtaining red ochre is a simple task. Artists and craftsmen have always used it in abundance, and it remains the primary colourant in many paints and textile dyes. Doubtless the scale of my order prompted a raised eyebrow when the ledger clerk of A. Macey's Fine Arts on Jermyn Street came to balance his books, but by then I was well advanced in my researches.

The ochre was delivered as powdery bricks, each wrapped in linen and labelled with its country of origin. Most of the stuff was French by birth, from the famed quarries of Roussillon, though some of the parcels hailed from South Africa, Mexico and even New Zealand.

The Roussillon ochre I unwrapped with almost episcopal solemnity. Alone in my small London garret I exposed the rich pigment to the lamplight and sat staring at it for some time, reluctant to disturb that which the grinding continents made for us so long ago. At length however my mission prevailed and I proceeded to smear my body with the red mineral, mixing in a little water as I went. Once my skin was entirely coated, I lay down upon my thin scholar's mattress and slept.

Mammoths!

I must tell the tribe. The furs are heavy on my shoulders, but I can still run. Not far to Hrulskala, *the lookout rock—from there they will hear my hunting horn. I will sound the mammoth-sound.*

Here is Hrulskala, *and now the horn…*

Yes, the sound flies well. The hunters will hear me, wherever they roam in the Snow Trees. Even Umyi will hear me, deep in the caves, where she suckles our second son. She will know that Roga is the meat bringer.

Ah, my breath-clouds come quick, the hunt-thrill is in me. The flint is sharp on my spear.

Again the mammoth-sound! The women will cook the red flesh on skewers. Death will flee from our caves.

Like the stain of sin, red ochre is devilishly hard to wash out. In the lectures I attended over the following weeks I cut a ragged figure, swaddled in unseasonal layers to hide my nightly experiments. I'm sure my lecturer saw enough though—he that had poured such scorn on W. F. Hermann's great work—saw the earthy pigmentation around my eyes, saw how my fair hair was turned russet at the roots, saw the redness beneath my nails which no amount of scrubbing would shift. Saw these things and logged them.

Once all the Rousillon ochre was gone, I progressed to the South African. By now my bedsheets and mattress were utterly dyed, but the effect only served to please me; every night I climbed into my own red-stained grave pit, alike to those photographed in Hermann. I was one with the red skeletons and walked on higher planes.

The fighting is done, the savage ones are beaten off, laid low. My heavy club did well, broke many heads. The quick ones ran like scared gazelles, back across the savannah, to tell why so few return.

Gom is dead though. I saw them open his ribs with their hunt sticks. I will dig him the best of beds, high in the hills the giants made. He will sleep with his favourite stone axe and our best foraging pots. We will throw the red ochre on him, and he will wake up in the Sky Land. I will meet Gom again.

By day I was a thoughtless drone, trudging along furrows ploughed by countless miserable beasts before me. At night I was free to stoke the fires in my soul, to see through the eyes of the dead and walk in their footprints. I came to understand the allure of the opium dens, and found a fresh respect for those who would dream their lives away at the expense of earthly achievement. For what are a few years of wealth and status against even one glimpse of the divine?

My lecturer had no right to doubt the findings of Hermann! The way he glared at me each day, saw the giveaway stains… such scepticism always gets engulfed by greater events and forgotten. No one remembers the last leaf of autumn; we say only that winter has come.

Next I wore Mexico. I opened the Mexican parcel to find a vivid ochre looking and smelling every bit like the holy ointment it was. It was darker than the French and South African batches, and needed more water to be spread evenly across the skin, but soon I wore it all over. I stood in front of my mirror for many minutes, admiring the high priest I had become, face blood-red and fearsome, eyes like sharpest obsidian slicing through the gloom. A deathless power was unearthed, reborn. Only sleep would wake it.

The Moon lights my way, knows my purpose, kisses the keen blades of my mace. I know my foe sleeps in the vast jungle, somewhere beyond the grey rivers, up in the canopy he has built himself a nest. The Moon is with me, the gods are with me… I can already taste his blood. I will rub the red soil on his body and offer it to the mountains. The rains will follow.

The papers have called me a mad servant of nightmares. They have dubbed me the Nightwalker, the Dreaming Killer. If such is true, then I would rather dwell in the land of dream than remain in this colourless kingdom of toil. Professor Hermann has shown us that there is a means of lifting the veil, known to all peoples in the happier times of the ancients, and cruelly hidden from us by the fog of centuries. Yes, red ochre strips the waking world away, and lifts the curtain on a land of infinite possibility.

It is small wonder that our forefathers coated their deceased with the pigment, knowing that they bought them safe passage to a blessed otherworld, starlit and peaceful, where Death never treads. For the same reason I rubbed my lecturer's still warm flesh with the fine Mexican ochre, shortly after finishing my priestly task, so that he might enjoy eternal life in the realm he disavowed.

Tomorrow I will hang, and I can only hope that enough of the ochre has settled in my pores and follicles to evade the mandatory bathing that will come first. The noose shall set me free, and I will return finally to that oldest and purest of heavens, once known and loved by all.

Darke Manor

By Jaron Evil

"One man enters, naught but his shadow emerges…" It was these cryptic words of warning that drew my morbid curiosity to that run-down dwelling. Wretched it was, dilapidated and crude, high atop a blighted hill, within the town limits of Autarch. A mansion of sorts, though it is doubtful that many desired to take up residence within its walls. It was the thrill of impossible possibility that lured me, one rainy and fateful autumn noonday, to brave its darkened corridors. Who I am, where I have been, and what things I have seen before coming to this particular moment in my life are inconsequential and have no bearing on my tale. For what seems forever, my name has been of little interest to anyone. For this reason above all, I am simply known as Traveler.

So where should my story begin? Perhaps first I should mention the conditions under which I labored when I stumbled into what had long since become known to the locals as Darke Manor.

Of the ecstasies and tribulations of hallucinogenic narcotics, much has been written. One may learn extensively about the immediate and protracted effects of such substances, though eloquent descriptions whether structured by the essayist or painted by the poet—hardly come close to conveying the horrors and majesties of the murky realms into which the inspired and oft melancholic dreamer is transported. To this day, I could tell neither what possessed me to indulge in such dubious activity, nor what thoughts drove me to indulge my dark habit before entering… the house. That *bleakest* house.

I am a hapless individual, and I suffer deeply from ennui. Apart from some unwanted internal residue of an instinctual need for survival, which need is only human in nature, I feared neither phantasm nor death. Truth be told, I think the greater part of my being would have welcomed the latter, rather than fearing it. Perhaps only a traveler such as I, a bleak man, might find what I seek in Darke Manor… or so was my thinking at the time.

The tale I am now about to impart is true. This I swear by whatever God resides in the heavens. Could the sum of my terrifying experiences be the result of my hallucinatory habit?

Perhaps.

Only perhaps.

The door slammed behind me with an echoing crack that shook the cobwebbed walls. For a moment, my surroundings seemed mystifying, as if my vision were utterly out of focus; but slowly I realized my lone presence in a long-abandoned room lit by numerous windows, many with cracked or absent panes. Of the exact nature of the room I could not say, for my mind raced with both unsettled thoughts and the dark influence of foreign substances. There was a mangy bearskin rug, a rotting wooden rocking chair, and a fireplace with a stag's antlered head mounted above it. The drab wallpaper had been torn in places, and water coupled with mold stained it near the tears and in the corners of the room. Of these things I was aware, though they were not uppermost in my thoughts. Rising above every other impression in my mind came an increasing fear of the unknown—a fear that was alien to me, but that nonetheless gnawed at my brain, sending chills down my spine to a greater and greater degree because I could not analyze its source. I breathed in deeply to calm myself. The air was thin and musty, smelling faintly of mildew.

All was still, silent, save for the relentless beating of rain through the gaping windows. Gathering my wits, I let my eyes scan the room a second time, noticing more detail than in my initial glance. The eyes in the head of the bearskin rug, disturbingly lifelike, were staring directly into mine, with what seemed dire intent. My mind told me, logically, that the bear was not alive. All my instincts, however, told me in spite of this, it was aware of my presence. The stag's head above the fireplace had its mouth slightly agape, revealing yellowed teeth. To my disgust, a spider crawled out of its mouth and into its nose. There was a closed door on the far wall, and although this was not immediately relevant to me, it soon would become so.

The room was cold from the wind gusting in through the broken windows, carrying leaves and other debris, and spreading the bits about the rotten hardwood floor. I approached the fireplace and found it already stocked with fresh wood. I paused, distracted—yet as odd as this was, it failed to stop me from fishing the matches out of my pocket and lighting the fire. Orange flames flickered and began to warm the room. Turning my attention to the rocking chair, I chose to make myself comfortable. As I moved, I noticed, suddenly, the eyes of the skinned bear on the floor following me!

Anyone else might have fled in terror; however, I was in such a state that I was unable to trust my eyes, as I knew all too well the tricks they could play upon an intoxicated mind. I chose to ignore the rug, and instead turned my gaze back to the closed door on the far wall. I stared intently at the crack between the door and the floor. All I saw was the blackest darkness, though I swore I could hear whispering emanating from behind the door. At first, I thought it was merely the fire crackling over the constant thrumming of the rain and the wind's whistling, playing more tricks on my excited imagination, but the longer I sat in the rocking chair, the more I became convinced it was two voices whispering back and forth, and definitely coming from behind the door.

I stood up and tiptoed across creaking floorboards towards the door. Kneeling down, I placed my ear next to it in silent eagerness. As I did, the whispering ceased immediately. I glanced back to the opposing wall and realized I was now in a room with only the one door! The door through which I had entered the house was gone, as if it had never been there. The gnawing fear I had felt before returned, this time to raise the hairs on the back of my neck. I ran to where the front door had been, and felt the wall in its place. My mind swam, the metallic taste of fear sour in my mouth, until I convinced myself aloud that it was the drugs playing with my perception. To this day, I'm not sure if I truly believed my own words, but I managed to calm myself and allowed my breathing to return to normal. I approached the closed door once again, this time reaching out to grasp the doorknob. It was now the only exit from the room, so it would be only a matter of time before I would be forced to go through it in any event. Perhaps it was an inner need to be in control of my own fate, or possibly a readiness to welcome my own death, that caused me to open the door at that moment. It mattered not. I eased it open with a loud creak and found myself at the foot of a long and precarious stairwell leading upwards into darkness.

For a long moment, I simply stood there and stared upward, as strange and terrible shadows, whose very presence was inexplicable in the already black stairwell, crept menacingly downward toward me. To my dazed and drug-induced vision, the shadows seemed to coalesce into nightmare shapes with long arms and ragged claws, eager to grasp my person. They swarmed about me, drenching me in darkness, and then flowed around and past me into the room, casting out the waning light from the windows and snuffing out the fire. I waited another short moment for my eyes to adjust to the darkness, which they eventually did. It was then that I chose to brave the stairs.

Step after step led me upward in a seemingly endless ascent. I climbed forever, turning back only once to see how far I had come. The door was naught but a faint and tiny dot at the base of a myriad of never-ending stairs. I could not correctly sense the passage of time, for it seemed to me hours since I had begun the journey up the mountain of steps. More time passed, slower than ever it had, or so it seemed. Several times within the passing hours, I had to pause to catch my breath. Eventually, at long last, I could see the top step in the far distance. My legs ached madly, and my heart was pounding—not from fear, but exhaustion. Time seemed to stand still, and after an indeterminate period (it might have been moments or hours), I finally reached the summit of the stairwell, only to collapse, my legs refusing to work for a second longer. My feet felt blistered inside my shoes, and the sweat soaked all my clothes. Glancing down the stairs brought me to tears, for I saw then, and only then, that I had climbed thirteen steps to the second floor of the house. The door below was shut once again.

I rolled onto my back, sweating madly, refusing stubbornly to accept my experience as reality. For a moment, I thought myself crazy. What spectral jest was this that would void the mind of reason in such a manner? Whatever the main cause, I was now certain that the mind-altering substances I had so unwisely consumed were not the only elements present to work their deviltry on me.

The gnawing fear returned.

I was no longer buried in blackness. With a quick glance around the shadowed and ruined room that lay at the top of the stairs, I immediately noticed the large mirror hanging on the closest wall. Weird symbols had been scribed crudely upon it, but it was not until I struggled to my feet and approached more closely that I was struck by two undeniable facts that shocked me to immobility. The symbols had been written in blood, and what had been written was, in fact, in English—save that the message was backwards, down to the letter, as if it had been written by someone on the other side of the mirror. Nothing, however, worked more negatively on my fevered imagination than the import of the message itself. Spelt backwards: "MOTHER, HELP ME. I CAN'T GET OUT. PLEASE HURRY, HE IS COMING BACK."

How was it possible that my brain could conjure such a fantastical thing? Despite the lies I told myself to remain calm, deep down I knew it could not, not of itself. Was I dreaming? Was this whole experience a nightmare? If I had not but barely survived to recount my tale, I might well have ascribed it at the time to the fevered actions of a troubled but sleeping mind.

I stared at my reflection, obscured by the chilling backwards message. My eyes revealed the fear I had tried so hard to suppress. I reached towards the reflective glass, touching it lightly. It was cold as ice, and to my astonishment, not solid! My arm disappeared into the mirror as if I had dipped it into a pool of reflective liquid. A numbing sensation crept up my arm and into my shoulder, causing me to convulse with a sudden burst of panic. I attempted to withdraw my arm from the looking glass, but could not. On the other side, something gripped me by the wrist and would not release me. Its visage did not appear in the mirror, but whatever thing it was, I could feel the grasp of a hand too large to be human.

The sense of dread I had felt earlier, which for so long had been foreign to me, became a harsh reality, deepening on the instant to a mortal terror. I began to scream as I struggled violently to free my arm from the mirror of peril. I could not free myself, despite the fear-inspired strength with which I tried—but suddenly, that which held me released its numbing and unseen grip on my arm, sending me stumbling backwards. I would have fallen abruptly, but for a small writing desk that shuddered awkwardly as I backed into it. Out of sheer panic, I reached for the first solid object I could find, a large leather-bound book on the desk's surface, and violently threw it at the mirror, which in turn shattered into a thousand pieces.

My heart pounding, I leaned on the desk, struggling to slow my racing pulse. Gradually regaining my composure, I inspected my arm carefully. It seemed unscathed on cursory inspection, and the numbing pain of the monstrous grip was fading quickly. I wasted no more time in returning my attention to the shattered mirror and to the book itself, which lay among the shards of leaded glass.

The book had fallen open to a random page where it lay in the midst of the mirror's fragments. Picking up the book, I read the page, and discovered that what I held in my hands had long ago been someone's diary.

August 21st, 1832

My son Nathaniel is missing, though I can still hear his faint screams from somewhere within the house! Oh dear lord, please let me find him. I have searched every inch of this damned household to no avail. Where is my son?

August 22nd, 1832

Screams awoke me in the very earliest hours last night. I leapt from my bed and followed them all the way to the stairs, where they stopped. I broke down into tears and went back to bed. I turn all my devotions to my beloved Nathaniel, praying that he is safe from harm and that he will return…

August 23rd, 1832

I think I am going mad. I saw Nathaniel today, staring at me from within the hallway mirror. He did not say a word; he simply stared back at me as I wept…

My reading was interrupted by the sudden sound of footfalls. I gasped involuntarily; then, glaring wildly around my dim surroundings, I held my breath, not wishing to make a sound. The sweat on my brow stung as it ran into my widened eyes. I could now make out that the room connected on its far side to a hallway adorned with various portraits that lined its walls. At the far end a figure stood, though I could not tell if it were man or woman. The figure seemed to glide, though the sound of footsteps still echoed down the hallway towards me, growing louder with each pace. I became too petrified to move, and grasped the diary in my arms tightly, not knowing what else I might do. The figure stopped five feet before me. It was only now I could make out in the dimness the visage of a middle-aged woman, whose face seemed locked in a perpetual, unblinking stare. Wide-eyed and silent, her eyes burned into mine.

"Who are you?" I asked the woman. A short silence passed between us before I received an answer. When I did, the voice was low and coarse, as if she were ill.

"I am the lady of the house, Mistress Isabelle Gaffney," she said. In such a terrifying predicament, for which I may affix blame only upon myself, or rather upon the wicked curiosity that compelled me to enter the house in the event, one might find comfort in regaining some human contact. I found none in this grim meeting. I was not certain that the contact was indeed human.

"Have you seen my son?" The woman asked me. Too dumbfounded to verbalize a response, I merely shook my head. Keeping my place in the diary, I thumbed back to the beginning, and my suspicions were confirmed.

"The Diary of Mrs. Isabelle Gaffney" was inscribed on the inside cover in a beautifully written cursive. Quickly, I turned back to my previous spot in the book, and read the next entry. It was dated several days after those I had already read. It was also the final entry in the tome.

August 27th, 1832

Nathaniel's visage has appeared in the mirror for the past several days. I cannot bear it any longer. These strange and torturous visions, products of my failing mind, will not end—my torment is unending. I fear my son is dead, and I can neither bear the agony of his absence nor endure the fantastical visions that wrack me without respite. I am damned; God forgive me for what I must do.

Looking up from the pages, I stared coldly into the widened bloodshot eyes of Mrs. Gaffney. A spectre she may have been, but knowing this with certainty actually calmed me—as I have said, I feared no phantasm, no mere departed mortal spirit. She turned her back to me and slowly glided back down the hallway, footsteps again resounding. I followed her.

As I trailed after the ghost of Mrs. Gaffney, the long and narrow hall seemed to stretch out longer before my eyes. This I attributed willingly to my hallucination, though truly, I had seen so many incredible and frightening things, I could not be sure. There were more portraits on the walls. The further down the hall I went, the darker my surroundings seemed to become, yet I was fully aware that the eyes of those depicted in the portraits were following me. I stopped only once, briefly, to admire a large painting of a lone figure standing in a forest clearing. Red eyes of wild beasts gleamed their hunger at the figure from between dense trees. A crude yet detailed and eye-catching painting it truly was.

Darker still the hallway became, until I was blindly following only the sound of the footsteps. I heard the sound of a door creaking open and, in darkness, I followed the footsteps through it into what I deemed to be another room. All became silent save for an old clock which ticked away the seconds, the sound lulling me into a fleeting and uneasy calm. That momentary respite was quickly shattered by the resounding report of the door suddenly and without warning slamming shut behind me. Startled, I leapt forward several paces and bumped into something low and solid, though I could not tell what it was.

The clock kept ticking, dully, rhythmically, and my pulse responded in a strange counterpoint, the pressure in my veins increasing dangerously.

I was transported from mere discomfort to crippling pain in a matter of some few moments. My temples throbbed with agony, as if my skull were about to split. It was a rising crescendo of torment, the likes of which I have experienced neither before nor since. I was convinced, almost, that I might die of it then and there.

I gasped, and breathing in filled my nostrils with the reek of death. Remembering, finally, the matches in my pocket, and shaking from the spiking agony that all but immobilized me, I retrieved them and lit one in front of my face, terrified of what I might find in the room around me. The absolute shock and revulsion I felt as I stood staring at the putrefied corpse of Mrs. Isabelle Gaffney, suspended from a ceiling beam by a noose around her neck, will forever be with me and will haunt my dreams.

The match died, and I found myself in blackness again.

The clock kept ticking. My head pounded, the pain hardly abating.

In the dark, I struggled to slow my racing heartbeat. I fumbled with the matches, eager to light another. At long last, I stilled the shaking of my hands sufficiently that I could do so. I looked about me. This had been Mrs. Gaffney's bedchamber, and chill of fear again gripped my spine—but why, now that the instant of terrible shock at seeing her rotted corpse was past? Gazing around by the flickering match-light, I found the room otherwise to be as expected. It was dusty and old, long untenanted by a living soul—a place of old death. But there was something… I suddenly realized the fear I felt was brought on by instinct, the source being my sense of proximity… I was not alone in the chamber of Mrs. Gaffney's death!

The match died.

The clock stopped ticking, as if time were frozen, and I was abandoned to an eerie silence.

I expediently attempted to light another match. Feeling only one left in the box, I removed it and struck it. I held it out in front of me, the orange flame flickering from my panicked panting.

I spun around to the sound of light scratching at the door, as if a cat were on the other side, though the scratching was too high up on the door to be caused by a household pet. I took a deep breath, and attempted to calm myself in some measure. I would have reached out to open the door, but the sense of an alien Presence suddenly grew much stronger—terrifyingly so. I turned back to the room and to Gaffney's hanged corpse, in time to witness grinning, ghastly lips lean in from the blackness into the light of my match and blow out the flame. In that very second, the face I saw was that of a ghoul. In its eyes I saw the entrance to Hell, and I stand amazed that the very fabric of my mind was not completely torn to fragments by the sight.

All was instantly black around me as I fell to the floor, curling in on myself, screaming for the end of the nightmare. When I had then given over to fear, and was certain of my impending doom, there was… something. A shift? A ripple in the fabric of being? I do not know. I know only that in that moment, I was somehow transported. My fear turned into shock when I lifted my head, squinting in the brightness of full daylight, to find myself outside, out of the cursed house, in the center of a forest clearing. Tall, densely grown trees surrounded the clearing, reaching high toward white fluffy clouds that decorated a bright blue sky. The sun was shining, and for a moment, I felt a combination of confusion and relief.

Much to my dismay, this was to be short-lived. As if fueled by the wrath of God himself, the clouds grew denser and darker, erasing both the sun and blue sky from sight. Thunder crashed sullenly, and rain soon followed. As if a great eclipse were in progress, the day grew dark… *very* dark, until the dense trees surrounding the clearing were themselves part of the blackness. The darkness, the cold and biting rain, the thunder, all seemed to bode further ill, and I paced about the clearing for a time, uncertain of anything.

I failed to grasp the true nature of my situation until a myriad of glowing red eyes hungrily stared at me from within the darkness between the dense trees. I recalled the curious painting I had stopped to observe in that long ominous hallway, whilst shadowing the ghost of Mrs. Isabelle Gaffney. Only then did I comprehend my predicament as it truly was, both unbelievable and undeniable. I was *in* the painting!

One may well speculate as to how powerfully I was affected by this realization, but foremost in my thoughts was the question of how I would return to the real world, or even if I would be able to do so. When dealing with matters of the supernatural or of an impossible nature, logical thinking becomes a tool without function or purpose. All I could do was simply pray that what I was experiencing was brought on by my perception-altering addiction.

In my dire situation, I ran to a nearby tree and began to climb. The beasts began to emerge from the surrounding woods. They were unlike anything described in any dark, esoteric, or fantastical book I have ever read. Roaring and terrible, clearly both carnivorous and extremely hungry, these slavering, nameless creatures surrounded the tree I climbed with haste. I glanced down but a single time, and saw below me a sea of fangs, tusks, claws, and raven-black fur. Some of the beasts walked on all fours, while others were bipedal, but all hungered for my blood and eagerly waited below for me to fall.

I climbed higher and higher. It was not long before the bipeds among them started climbing after me. The higher I climbed, the easier it became, to the point where branches became interlaced in front of me. Before I realized what was happening, the tree I was climbing had become a ladder. I looked above me to see that I was approaching a wooden ceiling with a square entrance portal to which the ladder led. I hurried my climb, as the snarling nameless ones below drew closer. I struggled to move as fast as I could. As I approached the square entrance portal, I could feel the body heat of the nightmare creatures panting on my heels.

With all dispatch, I climbed through the square portal. Shutting the door and locking the latch, I found myself back in the damned shadowed manse, but this time in what I could only surmise was the attic space. It was a barren room with no windows and a single small entry door. I allowed myself a moment to catch my breath and gather my thoughts.

For a long while, I sat there in the empty musty room, contemplating my escape. Eventually I gained the courage to undo the latch to the small entrance and slowly open the door, justifiably fearful as to what I might find on the other side. It was really too much for me in my now-weakened condition: all that was before my disbelieving eyes was Void—blackness, an infinite abyss of nothing.

"Hello?" I called out. The response was a never-ending echo that faded slowly but never quite vanished, becoming instead part of a faint murmur, as if all the words ever spoken were somehow echoing dimly in the endless blackness. My head swam with dizziness and vague memories of old quotations I had once read about staring too long into the abyss.

I shut the door, and lay down on the floor of the attic. Exhaustion overtook me, and before I could stop myself, I was firmly in the arms of Morpheus.

When I awoke, I was no longer in the attic, though my immediate environment was not obvious to me. I was no longer prone upon the floor; I found myself in a narrow bed. My head buzzed with the annoying headache of newborn sobriety, though I must say that it was a very welcome change from the horrendous intoxication I had induced in myself the day before.

The room was dark, though inexplicably lit dimly by an unidentifiable source. On first glance, it seemed to be a child's room. Colorful, playful wallpaper lined the walls and there was a feeling of calm in the room. Yawning, I swung my feet off the side of the bed.

My ears became filled with the sound of crackling paper. Before I could even grasp what was happening, the wallpaper began rotting off the wall before my very eyes, revealing the drab, decaying walls beneath. Strange words, in a child's writing, adorned them. The first one my eyes caught had been written in what appeared to be red crayon:

"There is a monster under my bed," it read. My eyes grew wide as a green scaly hand grabbed me by the ankle from under the bed and began ripping at my flesh. Whatever strange creature it was, it roared like bear, which shook the bed. With great effort, I freed my leg from the monstrous grasp and bolted for the door, abyss on the other side or not. I began laughing hysterically. It was rather an odd moment to find myself laughing. I believe it was the result of an irresistible fear slowly eating away at my sanity. A cold sweat ran down my brow as I giggled madly.

Running through the door plunged me into blackness. My memory over events at this juncture now grows hazy. I remember falling forever into nothingness, as the ebon blackness of a great void closed about me. My screams were the only sound to be heard, echoing endlessly in all directions. Those echoes were the last thing I remember before waking to find myself here.

Four padded walls and a ceiling; that is all I now know. I am being watched and I must conclude this narrative, before they realize I have scribed my account in my own blood upon the walls. They say I have become insane, but I know the truth. I myself was warned of the truth at the outset: "One man enters, naught but his shadow emerges…" It had been these very cryptic words of warning that drew my morbid curiosity to that dilapidated dwelling, and now as I have discovered, the selfsame words that foretold my present misery. I am the mere shadow of a man, and the path of the shadow is one of no return.

Darke Manor, as I have recounted, is not a place for the faint of heart or spirit, for its horrors are strange and terrible. Experiences such as mine may seem impossible, and I must say that I scarcely believe them myself, as my sanity is now in question. I know not the line betwixt fantasy and reality anymore, and perhaps the events I have described truly were chemical visions or the fabrications of a diseased mind. In the end, it is only my word, and there is no proof to be found.

If any lesson might be learned from my sorry tale, it is only this: tempt not the impossible, for if you do, the impossible materializes and hunts its prey—it will find you, doubt it not. Do not seek to discover all that lives in the world of shadow, for there is a price: you will walk, as I now must, forever in shadow.

The Key

By Mike Browning and D.M. Ritzlin

Before I attempted to operate the time machine, I sat back and reflected on how I got to this point and all the strange things that happened in sequence to bring me to where I now am. It all seemed so prearranged; but how could it be, since I was about to change everything? If this piece of alien machinery really did work the way I thought it would, I would become the first person in known history to successfully travel through time. I, Dr. Allen William Magus, would go back to the beginning of Christianity. I planned to arrive at the time when its influence took hold and changed the calendar to what was commonly known as AD or *Anno Domini* (but is now *After Death).* That is when true corruption took over and began to control the masses, and it is how we ended up in World War III with religions competing for domination of the world. No one saw it coming until it was too late. The Christians against the Muslims against the Buddhists. Yes, even a sect of Buddhists involved themselves in the holy holocaust. Each religion battling for supremacy over the others, all in the name of a God of Peace!

The governments let it all happen. It was an amazing form of population control that put the mighty exactly where they wanted to be. The people, obeying the edicts of their own religious leaders, destroyed each other with the help of a government-created war plague. They released clouds of radiated gasses into the atmosphere. It spread relentlessly and caused global chaos. Nearly two-thirds of the population of Earth was destroyed in a matter of weeks. I will never forget the sight of swollen bodies infested with radioactive roaches, their bright green glow illuminating the night. People tried to crush the things, but it was no use, for they were burned to the bone by the bodily fluids of the horrible vermin. There were millions of them everywhere, feasting on whatever was left.

I was very fortunate. In my older years I'd bought a nice secluded piece of land that included a small hill with a cave underneath. I used the cave as my private laboratory to conduct various experiments of unusual nature. Solitude was a necessity as I could no longer tolerate my meddlesome colleagues. I made the cave into a nearly impenetrable fortress, so when the chaos hit, I was ready. There was just enough time to seal myself inside before the nuclear gas attack occurred. I spent weeks holed up in my lair, waiting for the deadly gasses to subside. My fortress offered me sanctuary not only from the poisonous vapors, but from any religious maniacs, government officials, or atomic mutants who would want to harass me. In order to take my mind off of the world's terrible doom, I put myself to work. I spent that time building myself a protective whole-body garment that functioned as a much more advanced type of hazmat suit. It would shield me from just about anything that was left out there—or so I thought!

The United Nations seized control of what remained of the world's governments. Their reign didn't last long.

Not more than a month after the initial release of the nuclear gas strain, a huge alien spacecraft appeared in our atmosphere over the Atlantic Ocean. Within hours several smaller droid ships were spewed forth from the huge mothership and began a mass decimation of what was left of this poor planet. This was now a true war of the worlds. We were too devastated to fight back and although we did try, it looked hopeless. We had no idea what we were up against. We didn't even know what planet the invaders came from. I presumed they were from another galaxy.

Battles raged above the planet between the droid ships and the meager air forces of Earth. Missiles and laser beams streaked across the sky, causing such annihilation that it seemed as though the very heavens would crumble. Earth scored a minor victory in a skirmish not far from my fortress. One of the smaller droid ships had been shot down and crashed right on the other side of my hill, so after the battle I donned my protective suit and went to investigate the wreckage. I thought if there was hope for Earth's survival, it would be on that ship. Perhaps I would find a weapon we could use against them.

Crossing the short distance to the ship safely was no easy task. I took great pains not to step on any of the hundreds of radiated roaches skittering across the rocky terrain. One wrong move and I would crush one of them underfoot. My protective suit might have been strong enough to prevent their acidic juices from burning me alive, but I didn't know for sure. I didn't want to find out the hard way. I moved slowly in trepidation. Some of the horrible things crawled over my body and I had to pick them off with great caution.

As I approached the smoldering crater where the ship lay, I saw various mechanisms clearly of unearthly origin strewn about the wreckage. The largest one was of humanoid shape, which I deduced to be the ship's robot pilot. It was made of a surprisingly lightweight metal, the likes of which I had never seen before. Implanted it its chest was a strange glowing symbol which upon further examination I determined to be its power source. The symbol immediately struck me as having some kind of mystic significance, although its specific nature was beyond the limits of my knowledge. I have dabbled in occultism, but it is not one of my main areas of expertise. I proceeded to dismantle the ship and searched for any salvageable parts. Due to the lightness of the material, I was able to carry a good amount of it. I headed back to my cave fortress as quickly as I could. More droid ships might appear in the sickly yellow sky at any time, and I wouldn't want to be caught out in the open should such an unfortunate event occur.

Shortly after my return I felt a sharp pain in my left bicep. With great dismay I discovered that a radiated roach had gnawed its way through my suit and into my arm! My suit had failed me. Nauseated, I extracted the grotesque thing and threw it into an incinerator. I checked myself for more of the foul insects. No others had penetrated the suit, but one was enough. I immediately felt my body start to weaken and wither.

I desperately wracked my panicked brain for a way to survive. I could only think of one thing that might save me, and that was a long shot: my orgone accumulator. Orgone, the universal life force energy, was dismissed as pseudoscience by my snobby former colleagues. It frustrated me that I was unable to prove them wrong, as my device never functioned properly. If it failed now, it would cause me not just frustration but death. But what did I have to lose?

I entered the chamber of the accumulator and shut the door behind me. I could feel little positive effect. My cells were decaying faster than the orgone could regenerate them. I had bought myself a little time, but ultimately it would be no use. What else could I try?

My fevered mind was struck by a flash of insight. The technology from the ship! There had to be something of use amongst the items I brought back. Hastily I pawed through the stuff, but the alien nature of the items was too far beyond my comprehension. Lastly I came to the robot, its head hanging loose. It gave me a strange idea…

Within a few hours I was no longer completely a man. I was something greater.

By infusing my human brain with the robot's memory banks, I had given myself super-intelligence. The functions of all the alien technology I had acquired became clear to me. With my new enhanced brain, all the scientific problems that had confounded me seemed ridiculously simple. I began grafting parts of the robot onto my slowly rotting body.

My left arm was the first to receive the upgrade. Although the roach bite only affected a portion of my arm, I thought it best to replace the whole thing, as the infection was spreading quickly. Amazingly, I was able to successfully operate on myself even under the influence of a strong anesthesia. I merely put myself on auto-pilot and let the robotic portion of my brain do the thinking.

The left arm was in place, but why stop there? I repeated the process on my right arm, and then both my legs. I might be more machine than man, but what did that matter? I was alive, with greater intellect and physical strength than I ever had before. I felt invincible. I felt… godlike! If only my former colleagues could see me now! Ha, the fools would be so jealous! But in all likelihood they were probably dead, so it was no use to gloat.

The next task at hand was to build a weapon to defeat the aliens. By combining parts from the ship with my prototype for a portable orgone accumulator, I devised a powerful blaster. By focusing the orgone in a beam, the target would become overloaded with energy and explode. I found it mildly humorous that an invention originally intended for healing purposes had been modified into the deadliest of weapons.

A realization hit me. Even if I could destroy the aliens with the orgone blaster, what good would it do? Earth was in ruins. Billions were dead. Civilization was in utter disarray. So I began to think. What would be the most significant thing that I could do to change all this?

The answer was simple: build a time machine. Now that I had a supply of alien technology and the ability to understand it, it could be done. I was able to manufacture everything that I needed to create to make my projects work from the parts of that alien space ship. It was almost like it was meant to happen to bring everything to this point in time.

With my new hyperintelligence I calculated the turning point in history when the event occurred to forever mark the change of a whole system that had been in place before recorded history. It was the birth of Jesus Christ, a messiah who was used in a corruptive way to change time as it was being recorded back then in order to serve a certain religion's need for control. Once the world went from a lunar calendar to a solar calendar, the entire history of the lunar period of the Earth was slowly erased by this religion, so that they could create their own history and conquer the people with fear. It was the perfect plan and their sheep fell for it, thereby creating a new religion that has been steeped in bloodshed from its beginning to the present day in AD 2026. So the ultimate time period to go back to in order to change history would be the night of Christ's birth. I would eliminate the Messiah in his birthplace in Bethlehem under the North Star shining bright!

I had a mission with a goal that was going to change the fate of the world, a mission that must be carried out no matter what. There could be no emotions involved to hinder this mission in any way. With my new technology-infused brain it was now second nature for me to control my emotions. It was as simple as turning off a switch.

With my goal in mind I set the chronometer to September 28th, 1 BC (the true date of Jesus' birth) and the coordinates to exactly where the North Star was over the Earth on that night. If I did not miscalculate I would end up somewhere close to the manger scene described in the Bible. But still I had some doubt. It was clear that I might end up in a place or time that was no better than what was left of the planet that I was leaving in AD 2026, if this machine even worked at all. I brought with me several things that would help me survive for quite a while wherever I might end up, such as food and, of course, my trusty orgone blaster.

I hesitated briefly before turning on the machine. I heard a peculiar whirling sound, as if thousands of insects were fluttering all around me. It made me feel extremely light headed and almost dizzy. I took my chest power piece out and stuck it in the main panel board of the time machine. It lit up bright green, much brighter than I had ever seen it glow before. Yellow sparks began flying out of the symbol in the circle, followed by an energy field. It was glowing so brilliantly by this point that I thought it would explode. Just as I was about to turn it off, it started emitting a strange high-pitched whine, but like no pitch I have ever heard before. I thought the deafening sound would drive me mad. The energy field The Key created began expanding. Soon the whole time machine was enveloped inside of an electrically charged ball of lightning bolts. I felt myself literally coming apart into millions of small particles, but I still retained my basic shape. Suddenly the whole energy-encompassed time machine started sinking into the floor, almost as if melting, and a huge white flash with a bang was the last thing the human part of my brain remembers. The computerized part of my brain, however, was filled with fantastic imagery. It was like I was witnessing history backwards. I saw major events of the world unfold before me, but in a reverse order. The moon landing, the fall and rise of the Third Reich, the colonization of America followed by its discovery by Columbus… Each image passed by as fast as the speed of light, but still left an imprint on my mind.

The thoughts slowed down for a couple seconds, then the sounds of whining and whirling came back with full force. The heat inside the machine was tremendous. I could tell I was traveling at an excessively high rate of speed. Everything flashed again with a thundering sound as I felt all the separate particles of my body pull themselves back together into a solid form. Wherever I might be, I was whole again and had survived.

The machine was still glowing from the heat of its… otherworldly reentry, I suppose you could call it. As the smoke started to clear I could tell that I was on solid ground, in a desert with a million stars above shining brightly. I had never seen such starlight before. Had the machine taken me back to a time before pollution?

I noticed three figures standing in the not too far distance staring at me and my time machine. Certainly it must have made quite a spectacle. I pulled The Key to the time machine out and put it back in my chest piece. It began to glow again as a new wave of energy surged through my entire body. The feeling of invincibility returned. I stepped out of the time machine with my orgone blaster in hand and I started walking towards the three figures. As I approached, they knelt down and put the baskets they were carrying out in front of them in offering to me. They spoke to me in tones of awe and reverence. My enhanced brain let me understand every language there ever was so I was able to converse with them.

"It is a miracle!" said the eldest. "The prophet had written that the Messiah would appear in Bethlehem. A great distance we have traveled, following your fiery chariot. Your appearance is strange to me, O Lord, but I have seen you come from Heaven with mine own eyes. We bestow upon you gifts of frankincense, myrrh, and gold."

I looked down at the three men who abased themselves before me. I said, "You got the wrong guy!" and blasted them into nothingness. I felt not the slightest regret about slaying the three Magi in cold blood. It was necessary. If they had known that I was coming to destroy the Messiah they were so desperately seeking, they would have tried to stop me.

It wasn't a very long walk until I could see a small farm in the distance and I knew it was exactly what I was looking for. As I got closer the sheep started bleating pathetically. They could sense that I was a paranormal intruder. The bleating sounded to me like cries of desperation, but it fell on deaf ears, for I was on a mission to destroy the Messiah in his birthplace. Wasting no time I drew my orgone blaster and kicked open the door to the stable. Inside I found a man, woman, and child. The second I came through the door I pointed my blaster at the man and woman and pulled the trigger, completely obliterating them. At that point I realized that there was nothing to stop my mission. All my plans and work were about to come to fruition. This realization brought the human emotion back into my brain and I was temporarily overwhelmed by the immensity of its implications. Overcome with hysteria, I began to laugh maniacally as I blasted the Messiah right in the manger.

Now the fate of the world and history as I had known it was forever changed. I have the power to rule the entire planet! All who dare oppose me shall die by the sign of The Key!

Nautical Adventures

Blue Mistress

By Geoff Blackwell

Cyrill Derx gave the knot of his lifeline a tug for reassurance and dived over the *Orphan*'s railing. He heard the voice of the captain screaming at him before all went cold and dark and wet as he plunged into the sea. The water stung his eyes as he peeked into the depths. Further ahead, something *glimmered*, a fleetingly human shape that he had seen from the deck of the ship.

Derx kicked out, propelling himself towards his target. He reached out, wrapped his fingers around an arm. The skin was heavy and tough, like water-smoothed stone. As he gathered the strange figure into his arms, his lifeline tugged against his hips, dragging him backward and jarring the breath from his lungs. Water filled his mouth and he struggled, vying for breath even as his shipmates sought to pull him from the sea.

He broke the surface, gasping with animal panic. The figure he had rescued hung limp in his arms. It was a young woman, but one unlike anything Derx had seen before. She was fully nude, with blue-black skin studded by crystalline shapes which glinted like stars in the night sky. A cascade of dark green hair hung from her head. She was unconscious, sapphire lips slightly agape, a smooth, slitted bump of a nose barely rising from her face. Her body twinkled, even under the cloud-blanketed skies. Was she made of gems and precious stones?

The young sailor heaved her limp form over one shoulder and the sailors pulled him onto the *Orphan*. The deck shook with angry footfalls and the scarred face of Captain Beiran Stormchaser hovered over Derx.

"What in the blue hells were you thinking?" he snapped. "Where do you get off, boy? What…" his words melted away when he saw the unconscious sea-woman.

"Ocean pearls," he managed.

The crew babbled in a free-for-all of curses and prayers in whatever language came naturally to them. Beiran Stormchaser enjoyed variety in his crew, so long as the sailors could get around the more common Southroot tongue. First-mate Vlannir shouldered his way alongside Beiran, pausing when he saw the glittering girl.

"A deep-dweller," Vlannir said, mystified. His leathery face held a mixture of childish wonder and adult fear. "Blow me down, lads. A real deep-dweller!"

Derx thrust a protective arm over her body as the sailors leaned closer with hungry looks in their eyes. One man was on the verge of drooling. A lithe, naked girl made from jewels? Some dreams *did* come true.

"Deep-dweller?" Derx asked.

"Ancient people of the water," said Beiran. "Legends say they were here long before mankind crawled onto dry land, even before the mountains rose from the ocean depths to create the first continents. Islanders from Broxas worship them as gods." His broad fingers twitched at the hilt of his sabre.

Derx, raised in a strict Houjana household and unused to the ways of others, shook his head. "That's impossible, people can't live underwater. And the papyrus of Hojo tells us that the Iron Men sculpted the mountains at—"

Beiran slapped his shoulder, cutting him off.

"Boy, take a good look at her. That's right, take a good, long look. Now look me in the eye and tell me that creature laying there was born and bred on dry land like you and me. The sea is older than any holy book, and she has twice as many secrets."

Vlannir tweaked his blond beard with two fingers. "Moving beyond religious debate, what do you propose we do with her, Cap'n?"

"Young Derx is going to put her back where she belongs."

Dismay clouded Derx's face. He opened his mouth to speak, only to be cut again by Beiran's sharp eyes.

"Some things belong to the sea. The Blue Mistress has a way of getting her own back," the captain growled.

Beiran Stormchaser turned back to the quarterdeck, hollering the crew back into action. The crowd around Derx reluctantly dispersed, muttering amongst themselves, watching Derx from the corners of their eyes.

Vlannir knelt beside Derx. "Come, mate. Let's get this done."

Derx didn't budge. "She's unconscious, Vlannir. Maybe she's hurt, dying. We could help her. What harm could she be to anyone?"

The first mate sighed and gripped the boy's shoulder. "Just let it go. I've been sailing with old Stormchaser for nearly two decades, and I've seen enough places and things and wonders to make me renounce me own gods. Nothin' ever surprises the captain, and he always seems to know what's right when it comes to the sea and her charms. Got a knack for it, he does. If he thinks it's for the best, he's probably right."

Vlannir stood and nudged Derx with his boot. Derx gazed a long time at the twinkling sea-woman and ran his fingers across the richness of her skin. Soft and bumpy; she felt more like fine shoe leather than stone.

His ruminations shattered as the *Orphan* rattled and shook. The ship lurched starboard, the waves boiling around her. White-crested spray flew from each side, dashing Derx and Vlannir's faces. Twoscore voices rose in shock and confusion.

"A reef?" Derx said, spitting out water.

"I'll swear by the Blue Mistress, that was no reef," Vlannir replied. He gave the sea-woman a dark look. A great bellow rumbled from below the ship. Vibrations crept from the floorboards into Derx's feet, through his spine, buzzing in the top of his head. It was a deep, nightmare sound. No living thing should have been able to make such a noise.

Then the sea exploded.

It was as though a series of volcanoes came to life beneath the ocean. A forest of limbs erupted from the waters, clammy-gray, mottled in brown. Some skinny, like twigs of trees, others wider than a man's thigh. People cried out as the creepers slithered, climbing the sky or feeling their way around the *Orphan*'s railing like blind worms.

"Guns!" screamed Vlannir, already priming his pistol. A limb like some titanic slug groped toward them. He cranked the key, heard the click and aimed. Smoke and fire burst from the gun, tearing a ragged hole in the slimy skin. Foul green ichor oozed from the tentacle, which wriggled and retreated away from the ship.

The scent of burning powder filled Derx's nose as more weapons blasted the attackers. He didn't have a gun, for he hadn't saved up enough money to buy one worth having. The extras were in the cargo hold, at the other end of the ship. He pulled a knife and stabbed at a creeper near the railing. Vlannir was in the midst of reloading when a gurgling scream came from port. Gennain was caught in a tug o' war between the lifeline at his hips and the tentacle wrapped around his throat. More of the gray-brown creepers rose to collect him or pull him apart, whichever came first.

Vlannir swore and rushed to help, drawing his blade. All around Derx, sailors engaged the tentacles with gun or sword. Beiran and several other men had formed a tight knot on the quarterdeck, hacking and slashing and howling like lunatics. With only an unconscious deep-dweller by his side, Derx felt horribly alone. He put the blade of the knife into another creeper before hefting the woman over his shoulder and making for the door of the cargo hold.

Put her down somewhere safe, then grab a gun and return to fight, he told himself. A sailor named Kyvar went down, four creepers wrapped around his chest and legs, dragging him overboard. He locked eyes with Derx for an instant, but he was too far away for any help. Kyvar gave one yelp of terror before disappearing into the waters. He hadn't been wearing his lifeline.

How do you win against a beast like this? By amputating each and every tentacle? Derx shuddered when he thought of what might be waiting at the other end of those creepers.

The mess of mottled limbs thickened. They seemed never-ending, climbing above the surface of the water in great towering spires of flesh. They wrapped themselves around the ship, coiled amongst the rigging. The timber groaned beneath the strain. Derx heard the voice of Beiran Stormchaser shout "Fire!" and the cannons below deck, a half-dozen on each side, bellowed at the base of the tentacles. A roar of fury loosed from beneath the water and the jungle of tentacles recoiled, disengaging from the the ship. A hearty cheer went up from the crew.

"Shut yer traps and reload," Beiran said over the hubbub. "It'll come back for more and it'll be pissed!"

Derx stiffened when Beiran caught his gaze before glancing at the deep-dweller in his arms. The captain's face became a mask of rage. He stomped down to the primary deck and shoved Derx against the mizzenmast, snarling. "I told you to put her back in the water, boy. I told you that the sea would reclaim her own."

"She's not even awake, captain. How will she survive?"

Beiran took a handful of Derx's shirt. Up close, his face became a geography of scars on his lips and cheeks. "Damn you, boy, it's not our problem! Who knows what kind of politics happen under the ocean depths without our knowledge, what wars are fought beneath the seas? We're in barely-charted waters as it is. By bringing her up here, you've disrupted their balance, and we're involved now. I will not have my men killed and my ship crushed into flotsam just because *you* decided to fancy some pretty woman from the water."

A noise spread out around the *Orphan*, like mountains groaning into place, like foghorns droning in the distance. The captain hissed. "Here it comes."

The sound echoed away, leaving deathly silence in its wake. The men looked around the water with faces pale, weapons poised, shaking in their boots.

The weight on Derx's shoulder shifted. A blue-black arm flexed, sparkling fingers stretching out. A pair of liquid amethyst eyes blinked up at Derx, strange, without pupils or iris. He could feel those pale, violet eyes boring into his own, the intelligence behind them. His gaze remained locked upon her as she slid from his shoulder to stand upright, nearly six feet tall.

Beiran took a step back, sabre poised. The girl paid him no heed. Instead, she opened her mouth. A smooth, amorphous note slid between her lips. It held, sustained and unwavering, a siren's croon filling the air. For a moment, all other sound bowed before it.

The sailors paused, rapt by her voice. Even as the thick creepers rose from the waters, the note remained. Then it disappeared beneath a symphony of curses, gunshots, and sword-blows. The deep-dweller started across the deck, irregular steps, like a babe in the midst of learning to walk. Despite her alien gait, she carried herself with grace and poise. Instinctively, Derx reached out and took her hand. She walked on without acknowledging him, seemingly oblivious to the violence and chaos surrounding her. She side-stepped the foremast, singing again her lonely motif. Her voice filled Derx's ears, pushing the noise of the battle and the roaring seas far away into a dreamlike distance.

The creepers became more deliberate and focused in their movements. The slim ones picked their way closer, following the sound of her voice. The massive, suction-lined pillars sprouted higher and higher into the cloudy skies. A sailor whose name Derx didn't remember fell across their path, a trio of creepers coiled around his limbs. As they drew close, the creepers untangled themselves and stretched out, seeking to touch her. The man lay where the creepers had left him, vomiting and gasping. Derx stepped over him without pausing. They passed Vlannir, Gennain, and a knot of other sailors, who stared at the two of them as they went by.

The pair reached the bow of the *Orphan*, hand in hand. Creepers lapped at their naked feet. The deep-dweller climbed onto the bowsprit, the wind whipping at her hair and clawing at the masts. The creepers coiled about her legs.

The girl pulled her hand from Derx's grip and she crouched on the bowsprit. Her song rose to a series of higher pitches, steady and smooth despite the wind and the bucking of the ship. The gray tentacles spiraled around her body, forming a slimy nest of living flesh around her until Derx could barely see her anymore. The singing came to an abrupt halt, and the sea exploded again.

A silvery shape reared from the water in front of the *Orphan*. A nightmare of a creature, a mountainous bulk of gray skin, lined with creepers, writhing and twisting like living fur. At the front of the creature, a row of black orbs stared unblinking. They were limitless black pits, filled with ancient memories and cold, unyielding hunger. They were eyes that stared at Derx and said *you are nothing. You will rot away into the dust and dirt from whence you came. We endure.*

The terrible eyes rolled backward, and a gaping cavern opened in front of the ship. A cavern filled with teeth.

The creature exhaled, flicking pungent mucus upon the ship's bow. It reeked, worse than rotting fish in a waste-choked city gutter. The creeper cocoon bearing the sea-woman lifted from the bowsprit.

"No!" Derx screamed. He lunged at the wall of creepers, cutting with his knife and tearing with his fingers. Sickly green blood spattered his tunic and hair.

The beast let loose a rumbling moan, and the eyes turned upon him again. Even though they looked no different than before, Derx could *feel* their ire. He wasn't a threat. He was a minor nuisance. Insignificant, but annoying. A tree-trunk creeper disengaged from the rest, and jabbed Derx in the chest, pinning him to the deck. It pushed down, hard.

Derx groaned beneath the weight. He stabbed it again and again and again, but it made no difference. His ribs screamed out in pain, as though they were filled with needles.

He was going to die here, crushed like a beetle. Because some underwater woman made his heart flutter.

The great beast roared again, rattling Derx's eardrums, but this time, it was different. The roar contained real pain, real anger. The whole ship rattled from the sound. The weight retracted from Derx's chest. He lay there, choking. Every breath he took burned. A chorus of shouts rose from the crew and he rolled upright to look. The gray monster from the depths thrashed about the water's surface, tentacles flapping in the air. The throes of the beast sent waves crashing against the *Orphan*. What was happening?

Then he saw.

Spears protruded like pale stalks from the head of the monster. Green blood fizzed out like a leaky keg and the water off the starboard bow churned and boiled. A pair of silver-blue fish broke the water, side by side. Long tusks spiraled from their mouths. A crude chariot with no wheels rose to the surface in tandem, attached by a harness, a pair of men standing upon it. Their bodies were encrusted with a sort of white, bone-like carapace, arranged like plate armor. Beneath that, blue-black limbs glistened. One of them whipped the harnessed fish with sea-weed reins and a sharp cry; the other held a long lance of bleached bone. As the chariot neared the thrashing beast, the man drew back, aimed, and threw. The lance sailed into the air, puncturing a black eye.

A terrific howl surged through the air and the water. The living cocoon holding the deep-dweller opened and she fell upon the bowsprit, clinging to the ropes.

Derx hauled himself upright and climbed over, offering the girl his arm. She hesitated and cocked her head, her violet eyes not comprehending. He grabbed her and pulled her to the deck as more chariots rose from the sea. The bone-armored warriors and their mounts circled the great beast, hurling their spears from afar and hacking with swords of sharpened stone. The monster swept about with its creepers, knocking a handful of them from their chariots. Within minutes, the sea monster had been overpowered and driven back into the depths. Whether it was dying or retreating to nurse its wounds, Derx had no clue.

The chariots, at least a score of them, made a phalanx and approached the *Orphan*. The crew stood, guns and sabres in hand, fidgeting with trepidation.

"Hold steady," Beiran growled to the sailors. "Move a goddamned muscle, and you're fish food."

Derx took a step back, leading the girl by the hand. She gave him a funny look, but didn't resist. In fact, Derx would have sworn that the shadow of a smile played upon her lips.

The first of the sea-warriors climbed aboard. He, naked as the woman under his armour, was tall, perhaps seven feet in height. His dark skin glittered with a scintillating, gem-like quality. Multicolored algae encrusted the nooks and crannies of his armor. In one hand he carried a wicked bone sword, single-edged, broad and serrated. In his other hand he carried a bronze tiara, studded by a rich hexagonal sapphire. On his own head the warrior wore a similar crown, decorated with a ruby. His eyes shone pale turquoise, hard and opaque. Behind him, half a dozen warriors climbed over the railings, spears in hand.

With purposeful steps, the bone-clad warrior approached the rabble of sailors, gaze locked on the woman. The crew stepped back to let him pass. Even Derx, who had defied a mouth of toothy death not ten minutes earlier, stepped aside.

The warrior bent down on one knee before the girl, presenting the tiara. She laughed, a joyful, bubbling sound. She took the tiara and placed it on her head.

"The Blue Mistress," someone whispered.

"Queen of the deep!"

"Ocean pearls," someone moaned. The sailors buzzed nervously until Beiran shushed them.

The ruby-crowned warrior stood up, offering the Blue Mistress his arm. Before Derx could stop himself, he hissed. The Blue Mistress stopped and turned to him, those amethyst eyes of hers scanning his face.

She leaned in. Her lips brushed against his cheek.

A shiver crept into the top of Derx's skull. It crawled into his throat, shimmied down his spine, shot through his legs, and landed in his toes. His knees quivered beneath him. The world fell away, bone quiet.

The Blue Mistress pulled away and went to her retinue. They hoisted her into one of the chariots and she disappeared beneath the water without a backwards glance. The ruby warrior gave Derx what might have been a bemused look, then nodded to the assembled crew before following his queen beneath the waves.

When the deep-dwellers had all disappeared, the crew turned to stare open-mouthed at Derx. Beiran elbowed them all aside and jabbed Derx in the chest, which still smarted from the creeper attack. "I'm not entirely sure what just happened, but you'd best thank your lucky stars, boy." To the crew at large: "Anyone hurt?"

"Tunjan's got a dislocated shoulder and Januu's got a few cracked ribs. No sign of Nujakki or Camosun," Vlannir said. "I saw that thing take you down, Derx. You all right?"

"Kyvar was pulled under," Derx said in a pinhole voice. "I saw it drag him away. I couldn't help him."

The crew stood silent for a moment. Hats were removed from heads.

"They were decent men and fine sailors," Beiran said after a time, "but they knew the risks. Derx, you will pick up Kyvar's duties, Vlannir will show you the ropes. That should keep your foolish head away from women and shiny things for a while. There will be plenty of that in the future. If you don't get us all killed, that is."

Beiran turned on his heel. "All right, you sheep-shagging bilge rats, back to work! The crystal caves of Xalxattar won't find themselves!"

Derx stood there, feeling rather stupid and sorry, his eyes lost in the ever-shifting ocean. Vlannir slapped him on the back.

"I think old Stormchaster has taken a liking to ye, mate."

Derx glowered. "I'm not in a joking mood."

"No jokes," Vlannir said, laughing. "The old bastard can't resist someone who shows him something he's never seen before!" The first mate leaned close to Derx, his voice lowered to a conspiratorial whisper. "What was it like? A kiss from the Blue Mistress?"

The clouds parted. The sun was falling beyond the edge of the world. Soon, the night sky would glitter with secrets. Secrets like the deep-dwellers, in their ancient kingdoms below the waves.

"Cold," Derx said, grinning, "and wet!"

The Pirate Prince of Tarran

By Ernest Cunningham Hellwell

It was a time when many deities ruled the minds of men across the lands. A time when kings and queens were the final justice for all. When the art of war was changing due to a few ingenious metallurgists who had discovered how to make weapons of steel. A time when legends were born from the doing of heroic deeds and the spilling of blood.

The salty water of the Sea of Baal erupted in a heaving spray as the two wooden sailing vessels collided, both shuddering from the impact. The sound of oars breaking and hull splintering filled the air as the pirate galley, *Seventh Son*, careened into the starboard side of the Camorian merchant ship. Flying from the mast of the galley was a black flag with white skull and crossing red scimitars painted upon it. It was a stout ship built for speed and battle which the Camorian merchant vessel had no chance of outrunning.

Behind the port side rails of the main deck stood a row of pirates forming a wall with round wooden shields. Thirty plus Tarranian corsairs in light leather armor crouched behind them. With gritted teeth and blades drawn the corsairs all looked to the forward part of the deck where stood, partially shielded by the railing, a tall dark skinned Tarranian man of early age. His straight cut shoulder length hair was black as a moonless night. Upon his head was a red bandana that contrasted brightly with the white bloused shirt that was tucked into tan colored pantaloons. A black sash was tied around his waist. A dagger was sheathed on the outside of each of his high top leather boots. He carried one other curved dagger with an ornate gold scabbard on the left side of his waist wedged between body and sash. The open lapel of his shirt showed a hairless, muscular chest. His handsomely rugged face was smoothly shaven. A lengthy scar above his left eyebrow was prominent, but even more noticeable were his bright green eyes, seeming to almost gleam in the sunlight.

He peered through the peg posts of the railing as arrows coming from the merchant ship began to hit shield and rail, yet none found their mark. With a hint of a smile he looked down to the bald, full bearded Tarranian corsair kneeling beside him.

"Hajish. Send them our regards." Then he turned back towards the men upon the deck and yelled, "Archers at the ready!" Immediately upon hearing the command a dozen men with bows stood up behind the others and took aim. Seeing the bowmen ready Hajish gave the next command: "Loose." The flight of the arrows could be heard above the heads of the other corsairs followed by a few frantic screams of pain from the merchant ship as several arrows reached their intended destinations.

Hajish partially stood up and looked over the railing. "My lord Amahl, look! They scurry about like lambs before the slaughter."

Amahl glared at Hajish. "They are lucky to be afloat after that hit. Words shall be had with the steersman when this is done."

"Your will, my hand, O Prince," replied Hajish.

Amahl looked forward and saw the bow of his ship almost even with the other. "Keep those archers busy and loose the grapples."

Instantly Hajish turned back to the men. "Archers, fire at will. Pick your target." And then yelling across to the buccaneers kneeling upon the deck: "Grappling hooks away."

A dozen men rose up among the ranks of the pirates, swinging and hurling ropes with iron hooks attached over the shield wall to the other ship. Several men on each rope pulled them taut and began reeling in the merchant ship toward the *Seventh Son*.

Some arrows from the merchant's crew were now proving accurate, leaving one dead with an arrow to the head and two wounded. One of the pirates was struck in the shoulder but still manned his post on the end of a grapple's rope, helping draw the ships together.

As the hulls finally met, Amahl laid a firm hand upon the shoulder of Hajish. "Planks now."

Hajish stood up straight. "Boarding planks away. Let's go, let's go!" The shield wall parted in spots along the rail as more men rose up from the ranks of the corsairs with long, thick planks of wood, slamming them down across the railings of both ships. As soon as a plank was in place, others with large wooden mallets drove long iron nails into the planks to hold them to their own rail. More arrows from the merchant deck found their targets, leaving two more buccaneers dead and another wounded. The merchant crew was sustaining greater casualties due to the extreme accuracy of the Tarranian bowmen.

Amahl reached down and picked up the tulwar that was leaning against the rail next to him. "Hajish, let's go have some fun."

Hajish raised his own scimitar overhead and screamed out, "Boarding parties attack! Shields first! Attack! Attack!" Every corsair on the deck rose up hollering and howling. The shield-bearing men were the first to run across the planks, their spears jutting out in front of them, clearing a path for the ones behind.

Hajish looked back to the bowmen. "Archers, up top!" The dozen archers shouldered their bows and quickly climbed the mast's rigging, taking up positions to continue their aerial barrage of the opponents' deck. Some shield carriers were well met by the merchant crew with men from both sides falling, wounded or dead, to the waves below. But most of the shielded corsairs burst through the defenders and onto the deck of the merchant ship. A few of the corsairs had thrown smaller hooks on ropes into the rigging of the enemy vessel and were swinging across, holding on with one hand while brandishing a sword with the other. The Tarranian pirates were now running across all planks onto the merchant ship's deck. Steel connected with flesh and blood began to flow.

"Behind me, my Prince," said Hajish as he leaped onto the nearest plank. Just then a small hook on a rope flew over Hajish's head and into the rigging of the other ship.

"I shall see you over there," laughed Amahl as he swung past Hajish toward the other ship's deck.

Hajish, with a look of consternation on his hard face, pushed his way across the plank, toppling the men in front of him onto the enemy's deck. "Out of my way, you dogs! Protect the captain."

Swinging onto the deck of the merchant ship, Amahl crashed his tulwar down on a Camorian sailor's head, spilling brains and blood. Releasing his grip on the rope, he tumbled in a rolling fashion onto the wooden deck, ending up on his feet in a battle ready stance. Faced with two Ca morian sailors, Amahl sprang with lightning speed and sank his Tarranian steel into the gut of the opponent to his right. Leaving his blade in the man, Amahl rapidly stepped inside of the other sailor's swing, grabbed him by the throat with his left hand, and at the same moment drew the dagger from his right boot. Showing his strength, Amahl lifted the man off his feet with one arm while driving the dagger deep into his ribs, turning and twisting the blade until death was obvious. Extracting the dagger, he let the corpse fall to the deck and looked down at his crimson stained shirt with a grin.

Amahl gazed up to see two more Camorians running headlong toward him, one with sword and the other with iron tipped pike. Amahl pulled out the dagger from his left boot. Before he could hurl it at the assailants a few of his own corsairs intercepted them with deadly blows. Hajish made his way to Amahl's side while half a dozen of the Prince's men created a defensive perimeter around them. Hajish, also covered in Camorian blood, panted heavily. "I wish you would not do that, my lord."

Amahl snickered a bit while he sheathed his daggers and then retrieved his sword from the dead man's body. "You know what to do and what we are looking for, Hajish. Make haste, for I feel this scow listing to starboard. I fear she is taking on water. Go below. Free any Tarranian and Aiser slaves and we shall meet at the stern."

"Aiser?" questioned Hajish, confused.

"Yes, Aiser. Now go, you lummox."

Hajish turned from Amahl, slightly shaking his head. "Your will, my hand."

As Hajish and several other corsairs battled their way to the stairs leading to the lower deck, Amahl raised his tulwar above his head, yelling "All right lads, this hunk of driftwood is almost ours. Make way aft. I want to see the rest of this boat."

By this time the merchant ship's deck was strewn with wounded and dead from both sides. The Camorians had suffered more casualties and the corsairs now controlled the bow of the vessel. Tarranian arrows once again rained down death from the *Seventh Son*'s rigging. The sounds of battle rang out with the clang of metal on metal. Battle cries and screams of agony reverberated along the deck as Amahl and his men hacked their way to the stern, leaving a trail of crimson gore in their path.

The remaining Camorian sailors had rallied in front of the helmsman's platform, mounting a strong defense. Amahl set eyes upon the man who was obviously the leader of the defenders, a semi-aged but well-built Arcanian wearing a leather cuirass of a Legionnaire. Amahl moved toward the white-skinned Arcanian commander. "Away! He is mine. This one is for my blade only."

The Arcanian had short graying hair that was beginning to thin. With a thigh length tunic under the cuirass, bracers of leather and padded leggings, he appeared well clad for combat indeed. He was drenched in blood, not of his own, which told Amahl that this man could be a formidable foe. The two men squared off with each other, Amahl with his Tarranian tulwar and the Arcanian with a *gladius*.

Amahl extended his left arm toward his opponent, holding his hand palm forward with thumb, index and second fingers raised together, forming the alpha sign. He then spoke sternly to the ex-Legionnaire in the shared tongue of the Arcanians and Camorians. "I see you were a Legionnaire. I can tell by your broken beak and the scars upon your face that you have earned your life many times. I presume you have been employed to protect this ship by the merchant called Morro. Look around you, man. It appears that I have won the day. If you lay down your weapons I will be merciful and spare your lives. What say thee? Wilst thou surrender this deck?"

The Arcanian grimaced. "I will never surrender to a pirate dog like you," he responded angrily. The Arcanian then spat at Amahl and lunged to attack. Amahl, with the quickness of a jaguar, parried the blow. With a rapid swirling motion he used his tulwar's blade to wrap his assailant's sword arm into an arm bar. Forcing the Arcanian's arm up with one fast and fluent motion, Amahl drew the curved dagger from his waist with his left hand and plunged it deep into the now exposed armpit of his adversary. With a look of surprise upon his face the Arcanian gasped, dropping his *gladius* to the deck. Amahl released his tulwar and grabbed the Arcanian by the throat with his right hand, gripping it tightly. Amahl drew the man in close to him, speaking nonchalantly in normal voice. "I don't like the word pirate. I prefer corsair." Then with a violent twist of the dagger he rendered the ex-Legionnaire lifeless.

The Arcanian's corpse slumped to the deck in a pool of blood. Amahl picked up the *gladius* and his tulwar. He looked around to see the last of the Camorian sailors throwing down their weapons and surrendering. The corsairs began rounding them together, making sure they were all disarmed.

Amahl's second mate, Kaleeb, approached the Prince. His light leather armor was covered in blood and he had a fairly deep gash on his left forearm. Kaleeb was a small man and not as muscular as many of the corsairs, but he made up for it with speed and agility. His long black, curly, matted hair was soaked as red droplets sprinkled about from his mane. "The upper deck is yours, Captain."

"Good," replied Amahl. "Take some men below to help Hajish."

Kaleeb's response was to point his bloody scimitar towards the stairway to the lower deck. Amahl turned to see Hajish and his men emerge from the bowels of the ship along with seven Tarranians clad in loincloth only, some still in chains and shackles. Also with them was a very large and muscular Aiser with long straight black hair, also wearing nothing but a loincloth. There was one more with Hajish and his men, a short, chubby Camorian clad in expensive robes. "It appears Hajish has found your man, my Prince," remarked Kaleeb.

Just then the sound of wood crackling and splintering startled the corsairs. The merchant ship lunged and began listing hard to the starboard side. Amahl looked at Kaleeb with wide eyes.

"Not good," Hajish yelled across the deck to Amahl. "The hull is breached. She's taking on water fast."

Amahl turned to Kaleeb, pointing the *gladius* at the dead Arcanian. "I want that armor." Kaleeb responded with an affirmative nod of the head. "Then get all of our men back to the *Seventh Son* before we find ourselves in Neptula's treasure chest."

"Aye, Captain," came back Kaleeb. "And what of the prisoners?"

"End them," Amahl replied with no reservation.

Kaleeb turned to his men and gestured with his hand across his throat. They did not need to be told that meant "no mercy." In moments the captured Camorian sailors lay dead amongst the other bodies on the deck.

Amahl quickly sprinted across the now slanting deck, yelling, "Gather the wounded and help them back to the ship. Make haste before this wreck takes us and the *Son* down with her." With alacrity the corsairs began evacuating the conquered Camorian merchant ship. It was now a race against time, for the grappling lines were beginning to cause the Tarranian galley to list towards the sinking ship. "Leave the dead mates," Amahl yelled to his crew. "Neptula will entertain them now."

Hajish ran up to Amahl. "My Prince, you must go now."

"Not till they are all away," said Amahl sternly. "Did you find it?"

Hajish grinned and reached into his leather armor, showing him the end of a scroll. Amahl nodded affirmatively as the last of his buccaneers made their way back to the *Seventh Son*. Amahl and Hajish leaped across from the merchant ship onto their own, yelling "Cut the lines."

Kaleeb repeated the orders. "Cut those grapple lines now. Steer to starboard. Port side oarsmen, push off." Kaleeb ran to the iron grating in the middle of the deck and yelled again to the crew in the hull. "Port side oars, push off from that ship, unless you bastards want to swim."

The grappling ropes were severed and the galley lurched to the starboard side, then back to the port side, eventually evening out. "Port side oars, row now. Row, you dogs," yelled Kaleeb.

Hajish ran as fast as his thick and heavy body would allow towards the helmsman's perch, bellowing "Hard to starboard, hard to starboard" the whole way. The *Seventh Son* slowly began to distance itself from the sinking vessel. Amahl yelled "All oars full ahead." The galley veered away from the doomed merchant ship and the whole crew, even the wounded, watched as the craft dove into the depths of the sea.

Amahl slowly walked to mid-ship, surveying the state of his crew. Many were wounded, some critically. His eyes narrowed as he bellowed out orders, pointing the *gladius* at the Tarranian slaves from the merchant ship. "Get the manacles off those men. Take the injured below and get them to the barber." He then examined Kaleeb's wounded forearm. Ripping off one of his own bloody shirt sleeves, Amahl made a quick bandage for the gash. "Get that looked at," he ordered.

The burly Hajish came lumbering across the deck towards Amahl and Kaleeb. Two other corsairs followed, firmly escorting the tall, lanky Tarranian that had been piloting the ship. They all stopped before Amahl as Hajish tossed the pirate's saber and knife to the deck beside the Prince. Amahl approached the steersman who was still being restrained by the two corsairs and spoke. "Was there something unclear about my intentions to capture that ship which is now in the belly of the sea?"

All eyes of the crew were upon their captain as he began slapping the palm of his hand with the blade of the sword he had taken as a prize.

"O Prince, it was not of my doing," the helmsman nervously replied. "The starboard oarsmen did not stop rowing soon enough and there was a gust of wind from the west that sent us into the other ship."

Amahl began nodding his head up and down, slightly, with a reassuring grin. "Ah… so in truth you were not at fault?" asked Amahl.

"Aye, O great Prince, it was beyond my control."

Amahl stabbed the *gladius* into the deck, leaving it standing erect and wobbling as he addressed the steersman again. "Very well, then. It is decided." A look of relief came over the face of the tall Tarranian, but in a mere moment changed to dismay as the blade of Amahl's curved dagger sliced through his throat, an arc of blood streaming from the jugular. "Seafood," Amahl angrily growled to the two men holding onto the gurgling man. With crimson pumping out of his neck, the man collapsed as the two corsairs dragged the dying helmsman to the ship's rail.

Hajish leaned in close to Kaleeb, whispering, "It appears that was the wrong answer." Kaleeb shook his head back and forth, chuckling. Hoisting the now limp and lifeless corpse, the two corsairs hurled the body over the side into the waters below.

Amahl looked to the faces of his crew members. "That man cost us the prize that we all fought and bled for. Let it be known that those who do not accept the responsibility of their own actions shall have no mercy from me."

Amahl wiped clean his dagger blade upon his remaining shirt sleeve and looked toward Hajish. "Who is now piloting my ship?"

"Hasahn is, my Prince," answered the first mate.

"And why was he not at the helm during the attack?" Amahl questioned again.

Kaleeb interjected quickly. "My Prince, it was you that insisted that Hasahn lead the aft boarding party."

Amahl returned his dagger to its scabbard and grunted with a bit of a laugh. "So it was."

Hajish gave Amahl an I-told-you-so sort of look, saying, "Your will, my—"

"Yes, yes, I know. My will, your hand. Let me see the map."

Hajish pulled out the rolled-up scroll from his leather armor and handed it to Amahl with a grin. Amahl unfurled the map that appeared to be made of a thin, soft, leathery material. He squeezed and rolled the material between his fingers.

"Is it?" asked Hajish.

"Yes," Amahl answered. "It seems to be a map tattooed upon human skin."

Kaleeb and Hajish smiled as Amahl handed them the map and walked across the deck to where the plump prisoner was held at blade's point. Amahl towered above the short Camorian of fair skin. His pug smoothly shaven face shown of desperation and fear. "You will need me alive to read Skulpa's map for you," he stammered nervously in the Arcanian language.

Hajish barreled across the deck and backhanded the Camorian across the jaw, sending the man sprawling to the deck with bloody lip. "Do you not know whom you are before?" roared Hajish in the Arcanian tongue, with a strong Tarranian accent. "You are in the presence of Prince Amahl Hammid Ahkba, seventh son of Drakos Saleem Ahkba, Grand Malik of Tarran. You shall not speak unless spoken to. On your feet, swine." Two corsairs lifted the split-lipped Camorian up off the deck.

With steady eyes of green, Amahl met the man's gaze and spoke in near perfect Arcanian. "So this is the merchant called Morro." Amahl grabbed the jaw of Morro in his left hand with an iron grip. "Tell me again why it is that your life should be spared."

Sweat poured down the brow of the merchant. "You will need me to read the pirate Skulpa's map," he replied shakily. "It is written in the ancient language of the Dahkmahl. A long forgotten type of hieroglyphic writing that disappeared when their island sank into the Sea of Baal ages ago. I can read these glyphs. You need me."

Amahl released Morro's jaw and turned to Kaleeb, taking the map from him. "We all know the tale of the dreaded pirate Skulpa of Tarran," he said, turning back to face the merchant again. "How he amassed a great treasure trove from his escapades upon the high seas. How he hid this great fortune in a cave on a remote island guarded by a demon he summoned with his dark ancient magik. And as the tale goes, he had a map tattooed on the back of his first mate. This map, as you have said, also contains directions written in the age-old and nearly lost glyphs of the Dahkmahl culture. It is said that when Skulpa was captured by the Arcanians they found the map on the back of the first mate, so they had his back skinned and the map tanned to preserve it. But no one could read the ancient writings on the chart. And yes, I still have need of you for the moment, but maybe not for what you have said. Hajish, where did you find this map?"

Hajish pondered a brief moment. "It was on a table in his quarters where we captured him."

Amahl turned back to Morro and with a half mouth grin blurted out, "Remove his garments. All of them." The corsairs holding Morro stripped him naked, leaving his clothes lying in a pile on the deck.

"Hajish, Kaleeb," commanded the Prince. "Search those garments well and pay special attention to those boots."

Both men started tearing through the clothes. "What are we searching for, my Prince?" Kaleeb asked in Tarranian.

Amahl answered in similar tongue. "You will know when you find it. I tell you, look carefully at those boots."

Amahl addressed Morro as Hajish and Kaleeb each began ripping the stitching out of the boots. Switching back to the Arcanian language, Amahl spoke in a very calm manner. "You see, Morro… any normal treasure hunter would have been fooled by all of this. I mean, the map is for sure a tattoo on human skin and the glyphs upon it are definitely that of the Dahkmahl. Unfortunately for you, though, I am a man of learning, educated in the palace of my father. I know how to read the writings of the Dahkmahl and the glyphs on this map are nothing but senseless combinations that have no meaning. Whoever made this map most likely copied the glyphs from the original out of order in an effort to make a decoy map that did not give up the true words of the original. It does bring to mind one question: Whose back was used for this one? Now what I wish to know is whether you were duped by this obviously fake map, or if you were the one that had it made."

"My Prince," interrupted Kaleeb, brandishing another human skin map. "As you said, Captain. It was in the lining of a boot."

Amahl took the map and looked at it intently for a moment, then looked back at Morro. "So now I have my answers."

Morro became slightly indignant. "So now I suppose you will slit my throat as you did your own man?"

"No," returned Amahl. "I will not kill you." The Prince stuffed the map into his sash and then, reaching down with his right hand, locked his grip on Morro's penis and testicles. Morro let out a scream of pain as he was led by his manhood across the deck to where the Tarranian slaves and the Aiser had just been freed of their shackles.

Amahl released his grip on Morro's genitals and kicked him to the deck amongst the men who had been his slaves. "As I said, I will not kill you," explained Amahl. "Your fate is now out of my hands, for I am giving you to these men." Amahl then spoke to the seven Tarranians and the Aiser in the tongue of Tarran. "He is yours, lads. Do with him as you please, but take your time. Remind this pig of all the time you spent under his whip." All seven of the freed Tarranians encircled the merchant, with some picking up the remnants of the chains they had worn. In moments Morro's screams of agony rang out.

Amahl approached the large, thickly-muscled and fair-skinned Aiser. His long, straight, black mane was wet. From the scars on his chest and back it was evident he had been under the lash. He was not participating in the slow demise of the merchant Morro. Hajish quickly stepped to the Prince's side, hand at the ready on the hilt of his sheathed scimitar.

Amahl questioned the north man in fluent Aiser. "Do you not speak Tarranian?"

The Aiser looked at Amahl directly in the eyes with amazement, answering in very good Tarranian. "I understood you."

"Then why not have your revenge upon that pig?" Amahl returned.

The Aiser not once took his gaze away from the green eyes of the Prince. "I find no honor or challenge in execution," answered the north man.

Amahl gave a low grunt with a bit of a laugh attached as he walked back over to the *gladius* sword still stuck in the deck. He pulling the sword free and swaggered toward the stairs to the lower deck, barking orders. "Square those men away when they are finished with that swine Morro. Get them food and wine. Clean up the Aiser and bring him to my quarters."

"Aye, Captain," responded Hajish and Kaleeb in unison.

Amahl started down the stairs, still growling commands. "Bring us about on a course of east by southeast for now. I need time to study this chart. And bring me a basin of fresh water. All mates in my cabin at sunset. I need a drink." Then the voice silenced as the door to the captain's quarters slammed shut.

* * *

A short time passed and Amahl had just finished cleansing himself of the gore from the foray when a loud knock resounded from his cabin door. "Enter," said the Prince. Hajish, still covered in dried blood, entered and shut the door behind him.

Oil lamps suspended from the ceiling on swaying chains lit the chamber. Though the room was somewhat cramped, the woodwork was ornate and expertly carved. A rope hammock swung slightly on one side of the room and on the opposite wall was a shelf of scrolls and charts. In the center of the chamber was a small but exquisitely crafted desk where Skulpa's map of human skin lay unrolled with the captured *gladius* on top. Three short wooden stools were in front of the desk, while behind was a throne-like chair with red cloth cushions on seat and back. Upon the wall behind the desk hung a beautiful tapestry depicting the image of the Tarranian goddess Kaleesh, with her six arms and six legs, holding tulwars in each hand. Just below the tapestry was a table with a water basin, silver goblets and two small casks of wine. Next to the table were chests reinforced with straps of iron and securely sealed with a key lock.

Amahl put on a vest of fine red material with golden dragons embroidered on the lapels and back. With no shirt on underneath, his very fit frame was showing some scars from battles and encounters past. He wore tan pantaloons with a fine leather belt about the waist and a pair of calf-high black boots.

Amahl sat in his chair behind the desk and studied the map. "Well, Hajish, it appears there is true substance to this legend of Skulpa's treasure after all."

"Aye, Captain," replied Hajish. "So you can actually read those symbols?"

"Indeed I can, my friend," answered Amahl. "And what I have read is very interesting. The map itself is a chart showing where the island is located, and then the glyphs give specific directions from a bay on the west coast of the isle to the cave where the treasure lies. It says here the treasure cannot be seen unless you bring the sun. I am fairly sure that means we will need the light of fire. It also goes on to say that upon the rocky finger of death is where what one seeks can be found. The last glyphs read as a challenge to survive the wrath of the magik demon that was raised from the abyss to protect the treasure."

As Hajish eyed the chart section of the map, Amahl noticed the bloody state of his first mate's armor. "You fought well today, my friend. As did the others. Let us hope it was worth it. What of our casualties?"

Hajish straightened up. "Fourteen dead and as many wounded. A few of the injured will most likely perish before the morrow."

"And Kaleeb's arm?" inquired the Prince.

"It is being attended to as we speak. The Aiser is outside your door under guard. You requested him brought to you for some reason," Hajish said, somewhat confused. "I understand your urge to free our brother Tarranians from enslavement, Amahl, but what care do you have for the Aiser? They are but barbarians and are no concern of ours."

Amahl stood up, adjusting his vest. "Let's just say for now that I have a curiosity. Bring the north man in and dismiss the guard."

"Dismiss the guard, my Prince? But…"

"You think that I and an ox of a man like you cannot handle one Aiser?"

Hajish stepped towards the door, exclaiming, "Your will, my hand, but I must tell you that when we arrived to free the slaves from the oars, he had already broken loose and killed most of the Camorians that were in that section of the lower deck single handed."

Amahl thought for a moment. "Did he resist you and your men?"

"No, my Prince. Maybe it was our numbers, or the fact that we were killing Camorians also and freeing some men from the oars."

Amahl motioned with his hand. "Well, bring him in and let us have measure of this barbarian. And Hajish... the guards will not be needed."

Hajish opened the door, muttering, "Your will, my hand."

Hajish brought in the large Aiser who was now clean but still wore only a tattered loincloth. The well-sculpted muscles of the north man's thick arms and legs rippled with every movement. He seemed to be close to the same age as the young Prince but stood a head taller.

The first mate dismissed the three corsairs that had accompanied him, but not before whispering to them to remain close at hand. After closing the door Hajish stated firmly, "Know your place here, barbarian. You are in the presence of Prince Amahl Hammid Ahkba, seventh son of Drakos Saleem Ahkba, Grand Malik of Tarran."

Amahl chuckled. "You must excuse the manner of my friend Hajish. He just loves saying that. We were both raised in a much different atmosphere than this. You may call me Amahl." Hajish, with hand on sword hilt, rolled his eyes, shaking his head back and forth slightly. "And what shall we call you?" asked Amahl.

"I was given the name of Mottar Gundarson," said the north man. He had once again fixated upon the green eyes of the Prince while answering. His body seemed to tremble as he spoke to the Prince. Amahl quickly sensed that the man was deeply afraid of him, yet the Aiser still stared intently into his eyes.

Amahl reached out to put his hand upon the man's shoulder, saying, "What is it, man?"

The barbarian backed away from Amahl's touch, stumbling backwards into the shelf of scrolls and maps. In a fearful tone, Mottar replied, "Are you not a demon? Are you not about to eat my soul?"

Hajish broke out in laughter. Amahl backed away from Mottar, explaining, "I assure you I am no demon. Just a man who has no use for your soul, lad. Come, sit down and we shall drink." Amahl motioned for Mottar to sit on one of the stools as he circled the desk and poured three goblets full of wine. "I have questions for you, and I am sure you have questions for me."

Mottar composed himself and slowly sat on the center stool before the desk. Amahl raised his goblet. "Let us drink to our victory today and to your freedom."

"Freedom?" asked Mottar, puzzled.

"Why, yes," replied Amahl. "What thought you, man?"

"I presumed I would be enslaved at your oars. That is until I saw your eyes. I have never seen the likes but I have heard tales of soul eaters. Demons with green eyes that feed on the souls of men."

Hajish laughed again, wiping wine out of his beard.

"That sounds like my father," exclaimed Amahl as he took a big gulp of wine.

Hajish raised his goblet. "I will drink to that, my lord."

"You, my friend, would drink to anything," Amahl jested. Hajish laughed a bit again, nodding in agreement as he took another pull off of his goblet.

Mottar took a drink and relaxed a little as he began to realize that Amahl was no demonic threat. After a taste of the wine he downed the remainder from his goblet in two big gulps. Amahl refilled the goblets as Mottar spoke. "May I ask of you a question?"

"Of course. I expect you have many, as do I."

"Well, my lord Amahl," said Mottar, "I understand why you would free the men of your own lands, but why me? There were many others from other lands chained to the oars of that ship that went to a watery grave. Why is it that I did not share the same fate?"

Hajish looked at Amahl with curiosity, saying, "I, too, would like to know this."

Sitting back in his chair, cradling his goblet, Amahl pondered for a moment before answering. "What I am about to tell you I have not shared with anyone. Not even my best man here, Hajish." A very interested look came upon the burly first mate's face. "Some time ago we captured a Camorian merchant ship much like the one we just lost today," Amahl continued. He drank his goblet empty and slammed it down onto the desk top. "By the many arms of Kaleesh, I would like to kill that bastard steersman all over again. What was his name?"

"He was called Sirhan, my Prince," answered Hajish. Amahl filled his goblet again.

"Well, let it be known that henceforth no man of that name shall ever be allowed on my deck again. I didn't like him anyway. He had the look of an assassin." Amahl took another drink from his wine and resumed his tale. "As it was, that merchant ship was one of Morro's, and the captain's tongue loosened quickly in trade for his life. It was then that we learned of Morro possessing Skulpa's fabled map. He was also kind enough to tell us what port city in Camoria Morro frequented the most."

"So did you spare the captain's life?" asked Mottar.

Hajish and Amahl both laughed. "So to speak. We did not kill him but we put him ashore on the Isle of Red Death off the coast of Tarran. The island is where victims of the plague are shipped to from our homeland. After selling the merchant ship and the cargo for a good sum of silver at the Port of Bahglesh in Tarran, we refitted the *Seventh Son* and made sail for the coast of Camoria. We anchored in a cove a distance south of the Camorian port city of Barros. Even though Hajish objected strongly, I put to shore alone and set out to sneak into the city in hopes of acquiring information of Morro's whereabouts. My plan was to pass myself off as a Khoshite merchant, but I was careless and I'm sure my accent gave me away. It was the first time I had ever set foot on a western kingdom's soil, and the dialect of Arcanian that is spoken in Camoria is slightly different than what I was familiar with. When found out I made a good showing of myself to my aggressors, but a lucky blow to the head rendered me unconscious. When I awoke I found myself in chains.

"I will not bore you with all the details, but it was an Aiser who enabled my escape and in more than one instance saved my life. I offered this Aiser reward for his service, but all he requested of me was to extend the same kindness to any other north man that I may meet in my travels. This is why you have your freedom now. I promised this man, my savior, to treat all other Aiser as brothers in arms. But according to our own Tarranian traditions, that man still owns my life, and I told him so. If it ever were necessary I would spend my life for his."

Hajish walked around the desk and poured himself another drink. "And why by Neptula's tentacles did you not tell me of these events?" he grumbled. "You told me you just had a run in with the locals at a tavern."

Amahl gave a quirky smile answering, "Well, that was truth. I just did not tell the whole of the tale, my friend. You would have never let me hear the end of it."

"Oh, I promise you, my lord, the end of it is far from heard now for certain," Hajish spat out.

Amahl filled Mottar's cup again. "So now, how it is you came to be a slavc on a Camorian merchant ship?"

Mottar looked up, still amazed by the emerald eyes of the Prince. "There is little to tell, my lord. When I was young my father taught me how to fight. He was a hunter, and then a leader of men when the clans stood up against the invading Arcanians. It was for naught, though. The Arcanian Legions were too vast in numbers to be repelled. My village was sacked and burnt to ashes. When they came they had my father's head upon a pike. We tried to fight them, but it was mostly the aged along with women and children left in our village. The men had all gone to defend us to no avail. I did my best, but I was young and was subdued. I did kill two of those Legionnaires before they took me, though." Mottar was becoming agitated and tense, but he quickly changed his demeanor after taking a deep breath. He continued speaking in a shallow voice. "I saw my mother raped and then gutted like a deer. The old and the infants were all slaughtered. The young girls and boys, I among them, were all tied together and led for many days' journey to the coast. It was there that I was put on the auction block and sold to the highest bidder. That happened to be Morro. I have been on that ship ever since."

The three men were silent for a few moments before Hajish blurted out, "They must have fed you well!"

Mottar looked at Hajish with a hint of a grin. "My father was a big man and the rowing has kept me fit."

Amahl grunted with a bit of a laugh. "How is it that you speak Tarranian so well?"

Mottar extended his empty goblet. "I learned from the men you freed. What will become of those men?"

"They will be given the choice of joining the crew or returning to Tarran the next time we make port in Bahglesh," said Amahl, filling Mottar's goblet. "We have another destination first, though. In the meantime they will be well provided for and given duties among the crew to earn their keep. You see, I don't believe in slavery. Even our oarsmen upon this ship are a part of the crew and get fair shares of the booty."

Mottar took another drink. "So what becomes of me, then?"

Amahl spoke with the air of sincerity. "My brother, in your case your will is my hand. You are a free man now to choose your own fate. We can put you ashore in the north of Aiseria where the Arcanians have not ventured if it is your desire. Maybe Bahglesh would be more to your taste. I can offer you fine quarters and lifestyle there. Or if you see fit, you may join us. Roam the seas in search of booty and adventure and spill the blood of Camorians and Arcanians whenever possible. You don't have to decide right now. You will have ample time to ponder your future."

Mottar stood up and placed a closed fist upon his chest. "I need no time to ponder such a choice. I am yours, my lord. You freed me from bondage and I somewhat understand your ways and I shall honor them. Therefore I owe you my life and freedom. Most of my days have been spent on the sea. Maybe it is the Fates that have provided me to you."

Hajish rolled his eyes, saying, "Just what we need, another philosopher."

Amahl stood up and extended his right arm in friendship to Mottar. "So be it then. Welcome aboard the *Seventh Son*." They clasped each other's forearms in a brotherly embrace across the desk.

"There is something that puzzles me, my lord," asked Mottar. "Why does the son of the great king of Tarran lead a band of pirates on the seas?"

"I prefer to call ourselves corsairs," answered Amahl. "Pirate just sounds so base, don't you think?"

Amahl sat back down at his desk. "Hajish, I think all is good here now. Get yourself cleaned up and remember, all mates here at sunset."

"Are you certain?" asked Hajish.

"Yes, I am certain. And check on Kaleeb while you're at it, and send food and more wine. We shall all dine in here tonight."

Hajish slowly exited the captain's quarters saying, "Your will, my hand."

Amahl let out another partial grunt and laugh. "He says that when he questions the wisdom of my decisions. You see, Hajish grew up with me in my father's palace in Serba. He is a bit older than I and his father was one of my father's greatest commanders. We both learned the art of war together at the hands of the finest swordsmen in all of Tarran. I consider him more friend and brother than any of my own family. My father, Drakos, was also the seventh son of his father. As you can imagine, being the seventh in a line to the throne you would think there is little chance of ever assuming the title of Malik. As it was, two of his elder brothers met their doom in battle against the Khoshites in the days when we were trying to invade Khosh. As his own father drew closer to death from old age, his brothers, one by one, died of questionable circumstance. There were nine brothers in all. Not all of the same mother, though. You see, we are allowed many wives where we are from. Even the two younger brothers met an untimely and suspicious demise. And so Drakos became Grand Malik upon the death of his father. Oh sure, people secretly think that Drakos usurped the throne from his siblings and made sure none did that to him by removing the threat of his younger brothers as well. But no one dares speak of it openly. My father rules with an iron fist and all who oppose him usually regret it.

"I had a normal life of a Prince until a sorcerer by the name of Morbis gained my father's confidence. Morbis used my acutely different eyes as an excuse to cast suspicion upon me. You see, my father's eyes are also green. So with Drakos being convinced of a possible future in which I would repeat his evil deeds to gain the throne, he exiled me to the city of Bahglesh. Hajish was commanded to accompany me as my protector and my brothers were forbidden to enter the city. Of course I had all I needed there, but my life was becoming a bore. I had studied and trained all my life and for what? To sit in a palace mansion in Bahglesh for all my days? No. The call of the sea and adventure was too strong. So I had the *Seventh Son* built. Hajish and I mustered a good crew and off we went sailing into the Sea of Baal. Since then we have profited greatly from our adventures and amused ourselves with living a life on the open sea where we choose our own path in life. I speak of freedom, Mottar, son of Gundar, and it is sweet to the senses even if you have to fight for it."

Mottar sat back down, cocking his head sideways. "I feel a bit strange, my Lord."

"It is the wine, my friend. You will get used to it."

A loud rap upon the door and the bellowed announcement "Hasahn" resounded simultaneously. The cabin door flew open and a mid-sized Tarranian man of good build burst through the doorway. He sported no shirt, only a gold medallion on a chain about his neck. High top black boots he wore with white pantaloons tucked into them, accompanied by a wide leather belt with scabbard and scimitar about his waist. "Did you see how my men handled those Camorian bilge rats?" Hasahn threw himself up into the hammock, continuing on without waiting for response. "They didn't have a chance against our Tarranian steel." He unsheathed his scimitar and stuck it into the ceiling, still babbling on. "Kaleeb and I ended many lives today, but I think he is slowing down.

You know he took a wound today in the arm. The barber says he'll be all right, though."

Amahl broke Hasahn's ranting. "This is Mottar, son of Gundar. Mottar, this is Hasahn, my third mate and reader of the stars."

Hasahn jumped out of the hammock, leaving his sword waggling in the ceiling. Abruptly sitting down on a stool beside Mottar, he put a hand to his chin as if to ponder something. "Ahhhhh. So this is the Aiser. I hear we are to be friends." Slowly Hasahn's ponderous look turned to a smile. With a sudden slap on Mottar's back he exclaimed, "Well then, welcome to the Brotherhood of the Red Corsairs."

Amahl handed Hasahn a goblet of wine. "Do I not get to announce anything on this ship?"

"Nope. Hajish tells all," said Hasahn, taking the goblet. Ah, good, I'm starving."

At that moment two beautiful dark haired Tarranian women entered through the open door, carrying large silver trays of fruit and fish. Amahl cleared the *gladius* and map from the desk top. He handed both to Hasahn as the women placed the trays upon the desk.

Mottar looked at Amahl questioningly. "You allow women on your ship?"

Amahl let out yet another of his grunted chuckles. "Of course we allow women on board. We bow to no man or superstition. Plus they are very nice, are they not? Life is to be lived and enjoyed my friend, because it does not last that long. And if you have the means… why not?"

Another woman came in carrying a cask of wine. She was dressed as the others in a thin colorful gown and jeweled chains of gold about her neck. Amahl smiled at the raven haired beauty, saying, "Isbetha, my friend Mottar here shall be sleeping with you tonight. I do not believe he has ever shared the company of a woman before, so see to him well, my sweet."

"As you wish, O Prince," said Isbetha as she bowed her head.

Hasahn nudged Mottar with his elbow. "Lucky man." Then he looked to Isbetha, saying, "I will bring him to you when we are finished here. Now get your asses out of here." Hasahn jumped up, chasing the women out of the room and slapping them on their posteriors with the flat of the *gladius*. The girls giggled as they exited. He turned back into the chamber, remarking, "This has very good weight and balance, Captain. But I think I still prefer a curved blade."

Amahl walked over to Hasahn, taking the sword from his hand. "I saw a man wield two of these expertly once," he said, admiring the blade. "I have now but to find another so I can try to master his technique. But look at the chart, Hasahn."

"By the stars!" yelped Hasahn. "We know where this cluster of islands is. We have been just off its shores before."

Kaleeb then entered the chamber, door still standing open. In his arms was the armor of the Arcanian that Amahl had slain, which he placed below the hammock. "What are you barking about now, Hasahn?"

"Your mother's terrible cooking," Hasahn quipped back.

Kaleeb ignored the remark and headed directly to Mottar. Kaleeb was dressed in clean banded leather armor with a thigh length blue tunic underneath. A new bandage was about his wounded arm. "So you are Mottar," he said, eying the man up and down. Kaleeb was the smallest of all the buccaneers, and standing together made Mottar almost appear as a giant. "I am Kaleeb, second mate to the Prince. As long as you stay alert and do what we say, we will have no problem. Understood?" Mottar shook his head in affirmation as Kaleeb continued. "Good. Now tell me, are all north men as big as you?"

Before Mottar could answer, Hasahn bit again. "Everyone looks big to you, Kaleeb."

"Shut up, dog," snapped Kaleeb. "I'll have you swabbing the deck tonight."

"I would eat your mother's cooking before swabbing a deck for a mangy cur like you," said Hasahn, smiling as he tossed Kaleeb a piece of fruit.

Hajish then entered the room, closing the door behind him. "Thanks for waiting for me, mates."

Hasahn jumped back in the hammock, looking at the chart of human skin in one hand while holding a piece of fish in the other. "We have learned to get an early start before you have a chance to devour it all."

Amahl whistled sharply with two fingers in his mouth. "Listen, lads. Hasahn, the Arcanian's cuirass looks as though it would fit you. It is yours. Kaleeb, the bracers are for you since you like to use your arms as shields."

Amahl stood up and handed Hajish a full goblet of wine. "We have the treasure map of the pirate Skulpa. By my calculations, with fair weather, we can be at Skulpa's island in four days' time. Hasahn will chart us a corrected course by the stars tonight. So here is to Skulpa and his treasure. May it be as vast as legend tells." He raised his goblet and drank. The other men did likewise, except for Hasahn, who was still studying Skulpa's map in the hammock.

"Can any of you make out these squiggly marks on here?" he asked.

Hajish looked at Amahl. "And this is whom you wish to pilot your ship?" he asked. All began to laugh at the puzzled Hasahn.

"What? What did I say?"

* * *

The weather did not cooperate as hoped. It was not until the sixth day when the *Seventh Son* finally reached the isle that was noted on the map as the hiding place of Skulpa's treasure. The lookouts scoured the western shoreline for the bay described on Skulpa's chart. The shores of the isle were comprised of cliffs and clusters of grey and black jagged rocks jutting out of the waters. Eventually an opening in the cliffs was discovered: an inlet, between cliff faces, that fed into a large bay with a beach of silt-like sand.

Hasahn expertly maneuvered the Red Corsair's galley through the narrows and into the bay where he easily grounded the bow of the ship into the soft sand of the beach and dropped anchor. Two gangplanks were extended down to the beach from both sides of the bow. Kaleeb and some of the corsairs speedily disembarked and established a defensive line along the beachhead. A lookout from atop the galley's mast watched intently across the jungle tree line just beyond the beach.

After Kaleeb and the lookout gave the "all clear" signal, two hunting parties were dispatched to seek fruit, game and fresh water. Meanwhile, Amahl assembled another search party on the beach with Skulpa's map in hand. The group consisted of six archers, six shield bearers with spears, and ten men at arms all equipped with swords, torches, lanterns and several small casks of oil to replenish the light sources. Each corsair also carried a water pouch and food enough for three days. Hasahn, Hajish and Mottar were also assembled for the expedition. Amahl charged Hasahn with leading the archers while Hajish would command the others. Amahl and Mottar took the forward point position of the party.

It was mid-afternoon when Amahl's expeditionary party set out to the south along the beach heading toward the cliffs. Along the way Mottar kept grabbing handfuls of sand and examining them. The Aiser was still scantily clad, but with newly made leather loin covering and sandals with leather strapping around the calves.

Amahl observed the large woodsman's ax Mottar carried with him. "I offered you the pick of any weapons in my armory, and this is what you choose?" asked Amahl.

"I have no experience with curved blades, my lord, so the choice seemed to make sense," answered Mottar.

Amahl let out a half grunt and laugh. "We will have to teach you the ways of the blade, my friend. Or at least get you a better looking ax." The two men laughed together as they continued along the beach.

It was dusk by the time the party reached the cliffs where the beach ended. Amahl motioned the men to halt, saying, "We shall camp here tonight, lads. According to Skulpa's directions, we are to follow this cliff face inland to the east till we reach a cave. Then a lengthy trek in the dark from there. No wine tonight, men. I need all alert and able in the morrow."

The night passed without incident, as did the early morning trek into the jungle along the cliffs. By mid-morning the group had come to discover the cave entrance within the cliff face. After oiling the lamps and torches, they were lit with flint and steel and the party entered the cave mouth.

The cave was dank and damp and much cooler than the temperature outside. The light from the torches and lamps caused eerie shadows to dance about upon the walls and ceiling. It was like a natural tunnel, winding and weaving through the rock with the width varying as the corsairs slowly and cautiously proceeded on. "Always to the right hand path," exclaimed Amahl as they passed other openings and passages along the route.

With the passage narrowing to the width of two men shoulder to shoulder, Amahl stopped and remarked to Mottar, "Do you smell that? It's the smell of sea water. By my best reckoning we turned back to the west long ago and are now within the belly of the cliffs well out beyond the beach."

Mottar put finger to mouth as if to request silence. After a moment he said, "I thought I heard something like water splashing ahead of us. How would one come to find such a place as this?"

"Obviously Skulpa had a taste for exploring and adventure," answered Amahl. "This is something I can understand. Does not this whole journey make you feel alive?" Amahl slowly pressed onward with the Aiser at his side.

After a short distance the passage opened up and the group's flickering lights shone upon what appeared to be a vast chamber with a very tall ceiling. The smell of sea water flooded the nostrils of all as the sound of water slapping the rocks emanated from all around. With the rest of the party filing in behind Mottar and their captain, the torch and lantern light illuminated the cavern even more.

Before them was a very large circular pool of water with a diameter the length of four galleys. They could faintly make out the rocky shoreline on the opposite side of the pool as their firelight gleamed its reflection off the water.

"My lord Amahl," said Mottar, pointing his torch at what appeared to be a natural path along a ledge to his right. "You said the right hand path, did you not?"

"That I did," answered Amahl. "Lead on, man."

Mottar took the point, carefully navigating the ledge with Amahl and the others all close behind in single file, circling the outer edge of the pool. The ledge opened up to a large flat area of rock that had a smooth surface.

Mottar stopped abruptly. "We are not the first here, my lord."

Amahl stepped up beside Mottar and saw a large stack of aged timber of the type that could be used to build a campfire. Underneath the pile of tree limbs were the remnants of another fire that had burned long ago. Amahl pondered for a moment. "Interesting," he said.

After dispersing his men to either side of Amahl and Mottar, Hajish joined them, inquiring, "What do you make of it, my Prince?"

"It appears that someone intended on returning and did not," answered Amahl. "Throw some oil on it and set it aflame. Let us have a better look at this place." The fire was lit and as the flames grew, so did their field of vision throughout the cavern. It had a dome-like ceiling forty men tall. The pool was almost perfectly circular except for a small peninsula of rock that jutted out from the cavern wall into the water almost directly across from where they entered.

"Captain," said Hasahn. "Upon that finger of rocks I think I see something."

Amahl strained his eyes, trying to see clearly in the flickering light from the fire. "What is it?" Amahl asked. "What do you see?"

"It looks like material from a sail, or maybe a flag."

Amahl looked at Hajish and then Hasahn. "Give me two spear bearers and two swordsmen. Have them bring torches and lanterns. Mottar and I will investigate. You two, stay here with the rest of the men."

Orders were followed and Amahl, Mottar and the four corsairs walked towards the base of the rocky cape. "I have never dreamed of a place like this," Mottar exclaimed.

They reached the water's edge at the base of the rocks extending into the pool. Amahl reached down into the water and brought his fingers to his lips. "Definitely sea water. There must be a tunnel beneath the cliffs connecting this pool to the sea."

Amahl led the way as Mottar and the four other men followed him onto the rocks of the promontory. In the center of the cape was part of a ship's sail that was covering something beneath it. Amahl unsheathed his tulwar from its scabbard and used it to carefully lift a part of the sail. He peeked under it, then let the canvas drop, saying, "Remove it, lads." Mottar and the corsairs obliged by drawing back the material, exposing a large stack of chests brimming with gold and silver coins as well as jewels and gems sparkling in the fire light. Weapons of all kinds from different lands lay in a pile amongst the cache of riches. A long moment of silence passed as the six men stood in awe of what had been unveiled. Amahl sheathed his tulwar and bent over, picking up a silver goblet from one of the chests. He spoke solemnly. "My faith in legendary tales has been renewed, mates. This Skulpa was obviously a hero amongst pirates."

Mottar lowered his torch over the pile of weaponry. He placed his woodsman's ax down and picked up a one handed battle ax from the assortment. The ax he held was expertly crafted with a glaive-like hand guard. The grip was wrapped in leather and small sapphires were crafted into the edges of the pommel. The other buccaneers seemed more interested in the chests as they raised their torches and lanterns to have a closer look.

Amahl turned and yelled out victoriously to the remainder of the party at the large campfire. "Hajish! Skulpa's treasure is ours." The words reverberated throughout the cavern. Just as the returning cheers from the men at the fire resounded, the water erupted at the tip of the rocky cape. Before Amahl could react, something large hit him with massive force, knocking him down onto his back. The silver goblet flew out of his hand but he still retained the torch. Amahl raised the burning torch in front of him as he scurried to his feet, seeing the legs of one of the corsairs kicking to and fro, at eye level, but where the man's torso should be were the jaws and face of a large serpent-like creature with a neck three or four men long protruding out of the water. A spray of blood shot out of the monster's mouth as it gulped down the rest of the pirate's body.

The face looked like an eel with tentacle-whiskers on each side of its nostrils. The creature's jaws were large enough to hold three men inside. Its greyish-blue skin was scaly, but more reminiscent of a snake than a fish.

Amahl quickly drew his tulwar and screamed, "Fight or die, mates!" He lunged forward, stabbing the torch towards the monster's face. He was joined by a corsair with shield and spear on his left and Mottar on his right. Mottar swung his newly found ax in an overhead arc, embedding the blade in the creature's neck right below the head. He ripped the ax out of the wound and a stream of dark red ichor spewed onto him. Amahl, upon seeing this, yelled, "If it bleeds, we can kill it." But the injury did not seem to faze the monstrosity. It lurched its head towards the men, snapping its saber sharp teeth at them. All three of the men narrowly dodged the oncoming jaws. Without hesitation Amahl once again jabbed the torch into the face of the creature, followed by several quick blows to its head with his tulwar. His blade cut through the snakelike skin but met bone as well. Even though the strikes drew blood, they seemed to have little effect on slowing down the monster.

The serpent-like thing recoiled slightly from the flame of the torch and Amahl's attack but then, with fast fluid movement, dove back towards the men. Once again Amahl barely escaped the snapping jaws and laid two more blows to the head. The creature thrashed its head back and forth viciously, knocking Amahl and Mottar off their feet.

The other three pirates stepped forward, attacking with spear and sword. Two of the corsairs jabbed their spears into the face and neck of the horror. The other struck with his scimitar and then brought his lantern crashing down upon its head. The lantern broke into pieces, spreading oil and flames over the head of the beast. With fire dancing about its face and eyes, the abomination raised its head high above the combatants, letting out a shrill hissing sound. At that same moment the water erupted on both sides of the beast. Amahl and Mottar regained their feet as two more serpent-like heads, identical to the first, rose out of the pool on each side of the original. One could now see part of the creature's large blue and grey body as it rose up further from the water and onto the tip of the cape. All three necks were conjoined to the same body.

"By Ymir, it is a sea hydra!" yelled Mottar.

Another of the corsairs screamed out, "It's Skulpa's magik demon."

"Nonsense!" roared Amahl. "Magik does not bleed."

The hydra's center head, still aflame, flailed about as the two other heads attacked the men on the rocks. To Amahl's right Mottar picked up a straight short sword from the pile of weapons and ran like a berserker at the head nearest to him. The monster's jaws opened wide and in an instant clamped around the man with the scimitar. As the hydra's jowls snapped shut blood sprayed into the air, leaving only the man's severed legs upon the rocks. Just as the hydra head swallowed, Mottar leaped onto the back of the beast's neck, driving the short sword to the hilt into the flesh of the terror. Straddling its nape, Mottar hung onto the sword and began ferociously hacking away at the back of the hydra's neck and head. The monster reacted, raising its head up, violently trying to dismount the Aiser. Mottar clinched his muscular legs around the thing's neck while hanging onto the sword, continuing to deliver blow after bloody blow with the ax.

To Amahl's left the other newly risen head swooped in to strike. The two remaining corsairs, both with shield and spear, stabbed furiously at the hydra. The force of the thing's attack was too much to be reckoned with. One of the men was sent sprawling backwards onto the rocks while the other stood firm, trying to block the creature's jaws with his shield. Alas, the defensive move proved ineffective as with a snap of the hydra's teeth, the man's arm was bitten off at the shoulder. The hydra swallowed the arm and the shield together. With each heartbeat of the wounded corsair, blood pumped in a stream from his shoulder. "I hope you choke on it!" he screamed in both agony and anger. With his last bit of strength the brave Tarranian threw his spear with all his might at the hydra's face. The last thing the corsair saw before he fell dead into the water was his spear protruding from the eye of the hydra.

Amahl, taking advantage of the moment, dropped his torch and leaped to the water's edge, attacking from the blind side of the beast. Wielding his tulwar in both hands, the Prince delivered a powerful blow deep into the neck of the hydra. The monster's neck and head crooked around so it could see its assailant with the one good eye. Seeing Amahl it rose up, jaws open, preparing to attack, just as a half dozen arrows sailed through the air into the neck and head of the monstrosity. The hydra reacted instantly, turning its head in the direction the projectiles had come from.

Like a raging bull Hajish came running onto the cape, yelling, "The eyes, Hasahn, the eyes!" Hasahn had moved his archers up to the edge of the pool and they were now rapidly firing arrows into the sea horror. Hajish ran out beside Amahl with lit torch in one hand and a small wooden cask of oil in the other. "Behind me, my Prince!" he yelled. As Amahl retreated Hajish hurled the cask of oil, shattering it upon the rocks. Tossing the torch onto the oil soaked rocks, Hajish drew his scimitar as he pushed Amahl back from the flames that were now blazing up between them and the hydra.

The remainder of Hajish's men ran out onto the promontory and encircled the Prince and his first mate. The hydra head, with spear still embedded in its eye, recoiled from the flames. Stretching its neck the full length, it snapped its jaws at the archers on the shore, but they were just out of reach. More arrows were launched from the archers' bows at the hydra as Hasahn directed their targeting. "Hit the eye, you scurvy dogs," Hasahn yelled at the bowmen.

The center hydra head immersed itself under water, extinguishing the fire that had engulfed its face. It then reared back up out of the pool, its wounded eyes looking like melted jelly. Blinded, the head thrashed about, wildly snapping its massive jaws. As the head slammed down onto the point of the cape, Hajish seized the opportunity and ordered his men to attack. The corsairs swarmed around the head of the creature, stabbing and slashing away at it with spears and swords. Just by chance the blind head still managed to grab onto one of the attacking buccaneers and gobbled him up. The intense onslaught of steel finally took its toll on the horrific face and head of the beast. Its serpentine neck slowly retreated, crimson ichor gushing from its wounds. The body of the hydra slid back into the pool with its three hideous appendages slowly following. More volleys of arrows were launched at the head with the spear protruding from its eye. Hasahn could be heard swearing at his archers. "You bastards are pathetic! The eye, damn you, the eye!"

The fire was still blazing upon the rocks on that side of the peninsula as Amahl, Hajish and several of the bruised and battered corsairs advanced to its point. Amahl pointed his dripping tulwar to the third hydra head which was still swaying in all directions. Hajish and the men looked on, seeing Mottar riding the monster, still hanging onto the short sword embedded in the back of its neck. The Aiser was swinging his battle ax, chunks of hydra flesh flying off his blade with each intense blow he delivered. Blood was spewing from the nape of the grotesque being's head where Mottar had concentrated his attack. The corsairs, one and all, watched in awe. The hydra retracted its heads back into the dark waters of the pool, taking Mottar with them. The north man continued hacking with all his might as he vanished into the depths.

A few moments of silence passed and then Hajish spoke in a low tone. "Damn. I was just getting used to the lad."

Amahl continued to stare into the pool as the waters settled. "He probably saved our lives, along with the man who set the thing on fire. Where is he?"

"Uh… he didn't make it, Captain," answered the last remaining corsair that accompanied Amahl. The spearman was bloodied and banged up from being dashed into the rocks.

Hajish put a hand upon Amahl's shoulder. "Come, my Prince. Let us return to the safety of the shore in the case of that thing's return."

One of the other corsairs added, "What if there's more than one?"

Just then Amahl stepped further out on the rocks, exclaiming with exuberance, "There! Look there." Coming out of the water not far from the point of the rocky cape was Mottar. He was struggling to swim, as if he was pulling something along with him or perhaps wounded badly. Amahl stepped out into the water on the rocks that sloped down into the pool, extending his arm out to Mottar as he approached the point. Hajish followed also, reaching out for the Aiser. As Mottar came up out of the water he let out a mighty yell, his muscles rippling and straining, as he heaved a severed head of the hydra upon the rocks in the shallow where Amahl and Hajish stood. Still clinging onto the ax, breathing heavily, he looked up to Amahl asking, "May I keep it?"

Amahl had an ear to ear grin upon his face as he obtusely answered, "What? The head? I suppose, if you really want it."

Mottar gave Hajish a puzzled look as they helped him back up onto the rocks of the cape. Amahl let out a half grunt, half laugh, adding, "Of course you can keep the ax, and anything else you wish that is upon these rocks. You have more than earned it, my brother."

Amahl turned to the remaining corsairs. "It's been a good day's work, lads, and I don't think our friend shall be returning. But in case there are more of those things, I think we should make haste in moving this booty over to the campfire." Hajish instantly started giving orders to the men.

Amahl, leaving the peninsula, walked over to Hasahn who was yelling at his archers. "You bilge rats couldn't hit the side of a galley in dry dock." Hasahn, seeing Amahl approaching, ran to him, embracing his arms in his hands. "My brave captain, methinks you should learn to run. I am pleased you are in one piece. And our barbarian? Is he all right?"

"Amazingly, he is still in one piece also," Amahl answered.

"Amazing is an understatement," said Hasahn. "I have never seen anything like that."

Amahl also clasped Hasahn's arms in his hands, and with one of his typical partial laugh and grunts returned, "By the gods, I have never even heard of anything like that before. Have your men help retrieve the treasure."

"Aye, Captain," said Hasahn. Turning to the archers, he said, "You see lads, since you are useless as bowmen, you now have to work for a living. Get over there and help your mates, and put your backs into it." The archers filed off to help carry the treasure.

Amahl said to Hasahn, "I owe you, brother. If not for your first flight of arrows, I think I would have been seafood."

"I think it is we who should thank you for learning how to read those squiggly drawing things on the map," Hasahn answered back. They both laughed as Hajish and Mottar joined them.

Hajish bowed and waved his arm as if to introduce someone in the Princes' Court. "May I present Mottar, son of Gundar." Hasahn bowed to the Aiser, who was confused by their humor. "Go ahead, lad," stated Hajish.

Mottar bowed to Amahl, saying, "My lord, I found something amongst the treasure that I think belongs to you." Mottar handed Amahl two perfectly matched *gladii*, both with identically cut emeralds in the ends of the pommels. Amahl took the swords and immediately swung them, checking the balance of the blades. Mottar added, "Now maybe you can master that technique you spoke of. And if so, maybe you would see fit to teach me. You see the gems? They match your eyes, my lord. A sign from the Fates that you were supposed to be here, and these swords your prize from the gods."

Amahl gave Mottar a friendly gaze. "Thank you, my brother. They are perfect."

Hajish then said to the others, "I've been thinking…"

"We are doomed for sure now," Hasahn interrupted.

Hajish smacked Hasahn in the chest. "Shut up, swine." Hasahn moved backwards a bit, chuckling as Hajish continued. "How do you suppose Skulpa and his men got the treasure out there without being eaten? He assuredly knew about the sea hydra because of what he wrote on the map."

"I had wondered that also, my friend," Amahl answered. "I would expect that Skulpa did run into that beast. It is high tide now. He most likely waited for low tide to move the booty onto the rocks, when the water level was low enough that the hydra could not reach them."

Hasahn snickered, somewhat amused. "Too bad you didn't think of that till now. We could have done the same thing."

Amahl gave a very sincere and serious look at Hasahn, blurting out, "Now where would the fun of that have been?" There was a brief moment of silence until Amahl smiled and began to laugh. Then they all erupted in laughter with Hajish raising his scimitar into the air exclaiming, "Here, here."

Amahl clanged the blades of the *gladii* together, announcing to the others, "All right, you barnacles, we've work to do. After that booty is moved I want two runners sent back to the ship. Have them bring more men, litters to carry the loot, and more oil. Send out a party to chop more timber. I want fires all over this place. No more surprises." At that moment Mottar dropped to his knees with exhaustion setting in. Amahl knelt beside the Aiser. "Get to it, lads. I'll see to him."

Another full day passed before all of Skulpa's riches could be extracted from the cave and carried to the ship. Fires all about illuminated the cavern extremely well now. As the last of the corsairs were preparing to exit the cavern, Amahl, Hajish and Mottar all stood where the treasure had been on the rocky peninsula. Looking out across the now lower pool, Amahl thought out loud, "I wonder what other strange terrors live in the depths of Neptula's chambers?" He knelt down on one knee and placed a single gold coin upon the rocks, then covered it up with the piece of sail that covered the treasure originally.

"My lord, why do you make this gesture?" Mottar asked.

Amahl stood back up. "Oh, this is no offering, mate. You, see I plan to keep the map in my quarters on the *Seventh Son*. I'm sure news will travel that Morro and his ship have disappeared and I'm also sure that we are not the only ones that knew he had Skulpa's map. So if we don't tell of its finding, the legend will live on. The search for the map will continue by many. And when the day of my defeat and end comes, my vanquisher will hopefully find this map and go to all the trouble of translating the directions and making the journey here to Skulpa's Isle. But instead of vast riches they will only find this one piece of gold. And maybe a sea monster, too."

"So you would have your joke on them even after your death," Mottar said in a thoughtful manner. "I see the truth of it, though sinister it may be."

Hajish put an arm around Mottar and gave him a brotherly hug, chuckling, "Know ye now more or not, my brother? Know ye now more or not?"

Stormchaser

By Geoff Blackwell

Derx lowered his ale and scowled at the lad who approached his table. A Molorzian, young and nervous, his eyes darting away from Derx's gaze. Around them the tavern thrived in a cacophony of toasts and jeers and fighting words.

"You want something?"

"Er, beggin' your pardon Captain Derx, but, thing is, you see, er—"

"Spit it out or move along, lad. Men are trying to drink."

"Beg your pardon," the youngster muttered again. "I don't mean to disturb. My mates and I, we only wanted to ask you about the *Orphan*, sir."

Derx looked past the youth to the far end of the tavern. Three other young soldiers sat staring and whispering to one another. He sighed and drummed his swarthy fingers against his mug. "My crew is full, son."

"With respect sir, we wanted to ask about her previous owner. The Stormchaser."

The captain's fingers halted mid-drum. "Where did you hear that name?"

The lad's mouth opened, closed, then opened again. "Well, the sailors talk. One of my mates heard about it. We were just wondering, is all."

Derx gulped down a mouthful of ale before replying. "Beiran Stormchaser," he murmured. It was a name he hadn't uttered in… how long? A decade? He wiped his mouth on his sleeve. "He was my captain."

The Molorzian's eyes lit with curiosity. "When? How long ago?"

"I had barely seen fourteen summers when I stepped aboard the *Orphan* for the first time. We sailed together for six… no, seven years. The Molorzians were barely an empire in those days."

"So what of the *Orphan*? Did you have to fight Stormchaser for it? Did you win it in a card game? Steal it?"

The captain raised an eyebrow, his gaze flickering back to the three youths at the other table. They were watching him and their friend intently. A handful of coins lay stacked upon the table.

Derx chuckled. How indeed? Memories in obscure nooks of his mind dusted themselves off. A few lines from an old seafarer's song rose to the front of his mind, a song he hadn't heard since his days as a freebooter.

There had been the roar of guns. Seething winds. Ocean spray; the tang of blood. There had been—

—*"Fog!"*

Derx could just barely hear Beiran's voice over the roar. He felt air rush against him as cannon-shot flew past his shoulder, crashing into the ocean beyond. Beside him, Janirro went down wheezing, clawing at a hole in his chest. Derx dropped his rifle and knelt, tearing a scrap from his shirt and pressing it into Janirro's wound. It soaked red in seconds and the injured sailor gurgled and choked and died upon the deck. The world thickened with greyness.

The fog engulfed the *Orphan* in a silver shroud. So thick, Derx couldn't see the deck of the ship, couldn't see Janirro's twitching body. The shouts and cries of men and the report of guns carried on but they seemed lost and far away, like a dream, a memory. Then silence became the world. The ship, the wind, the violence of the ocean, it no longer existed.

Derx stood up, alone in a world of clouds. Cupping his hands around his mouth he shouted for Vlannir, Gallad, Trizna, Beiran, anyone. He felt his tongue form their names but he couldn't hear the words. He shouted louder, harder. He screamed so fiercely that he could taste blood in his throat.

All around him the mist contracted, became heavier, constricting his movements like some nightmare snake until Derx thought it would crush him and splinter his bones. It crawled into his mouth, up his nostrils. He couldn't breathe—he choked and retched without any sound.

The world melted into shadow and oblivion.

The first thing Derx did when he regained consciousness was stagger to the railing and vomit. His vision carrouseled around him and his legs trembled like jelly. He fell to the deck and passed out again. As the darkness closed down upon him, his thoughts lingered on the smooth rocking of the ship, the gentle splashing against the hull, the dimness of the sun, the distant cry of sea fowl.

His face suddenly stung. Derx groaned, and it stung again. He opened his eyes and saw three blurry faces peering down at him against a grey haze. He blinked. The three faces converged into a single familiar one. It was first mate Vlannir, his bearded face etched with worry.

"Ocean pearls, lad. I thought you were a goner."

"What happened?" Derx said, voice creaking and raw. The fog had lifted, though the clouds still turned restlessly above them. "Did we escape?" For an instant his guts turned to stone. "Are we dead?"

"Couldn't tell you, mate. As soon as we hit that fog…" Vlannir trailed off, shaking his head.

The *Orphan*'s deck was a mess of fallen weapons, chunks of splintered wood and toppled bodies. Some sailors staggered upright, some crawled. Some lay silent. Janirro's body lay where he'd fallen, Derx's scrap of fabric still stuffed into his chest. Blood stained his clothes and his eyes hung halfway open, misty in death.

"I tried to save him," Derx said.

Vlannir took a long look at the corpse and shook his head. "You did what you could." He held out a brawny arm and helped Derx to his feet.

Silver light filtered through the clouds. Up ahead, a mass of land approached, a bleak shoreline where rocks jutted skyward like rotting teeth. The land stretched before them in a shallow beach, then reared into high hills and barren cliffs, their peaks painted white by more of the low-hanging mist.

"Where are we?" asked Derx.

"I haven't the faintest idea, mate."

"Where are the enemy ships? What the hell happened to us?"

Vlannir shook his head.

Derx looked around, trying and failing to fix his bearings. He saw Beiran Stormchaser up at the quarterdeck, hands at the wheel. The captain's eyes were wide and wary, his jaw set tight. Vlannir and Derx set about reviving the rest of the *Orphan*'s crew. Most of them woke up much in the way young Derx had, others cursing and thrashing as though the ship was still under attack. Some of them wouldn't wake up, even a few who had no visible wounds. The confounded sailors pointed to the island and whispered. None had seen or heard of this place before, even those who had been born and bred on the deep southeastern waters. They could only sit and wait as the pebbled shoreline drew nearer and nearer.

"Captain, we've lost nine of our own," Vlannir said, breaking the silence of the crew.

"Drop anchor at bow and ready the landers," Beiran said, his eyes fixed on the land before them.

Vlannir stared in shock. "Are you mad?"

Beiran blinked and finally tore his gaze from the horizon and gazed down at his crew. He stared at them and started down from the quarter-deck.

"Do you know this island, Captain?" someone called out.

The captain's eyes flickered back to the sloping landmass ahead of them. "Maybe. But maybe not. I need to see. Prepare to land!"

With defeated movements, the sailors went about the task before them. Derx and Vlannir hauled the corpses into a row and Trizna, the ship's doctor, shrouded them in weighted blankets one by one. There had been Janirro, a bit younger than Derx, hailing from some unnamed hamlet in Umbrioch. Cerridwen, who came from Ireheart, a fishing town in Varachne. They'd called her "Cerri" for short. Also Hurald, Nahwhey, and Gloan and more. All the dead faces were covered by a scrap of blue silk as the *Orphan* laid anchor and the landing boats were prepped.

"We go ashore. Bring weapons and a day's rations," Beiran ordered.

Vlannir ripped a foul curse and stood before the captain. "Beiran, we've got nine dead here. Their spirits deserve their rites."

The Stormchaser looked upon the shrouded bodies, probably for the first time. He gave the waiting beach another glance of quiet longing, then he spoke:

"Brothers and sisters of the sea, we release you, we thank you, and our strength ebbs without you. Rest beneath the waves."

It was weak, but it was the best that they would get.

The bodies were dropped into the water with less reverence than was usual for such an event. The crew stood and watched with hands over hearts until the last ripples swept away. Then they collected their guns, sabres and knives and assembled onto landing boats to be lowered into the sea. A pair of coughing, weakened sailors volunteered to stay aboard the ship. Derx took the same lander as Beiran and Vlannir, the first to hit the water, oars dipping and pushing.

The island, with its pebbled shore and ragged cliffs, was the most bleak and lonely piece of creation that Derx had laid eyes upon. It was as though the entire scene had been painted in meticulous shades of grey. From the rocks on the beach to the surrounding waters to the clouds above, dismal and dull. The fog that had nearly suffocated the *Orphan* lingered above them like an intangible monster, wrapping the sun and the skies beyond in its silver claws. Derx shivered. Despite the sad monochrome of the place, Beiran Stormchaser was a man rapt. The old captain sat, tweaking his beard with one hand, green eyes unblinking, scanning the horizon until the hull of the boat crunched against stone. They disembarked and strode upon the beach in the same silence they had rowed with, their captain not even waiting for the rest of his crew to land. The beach inclined into a steady hill and the pebbles underfoot were replaced with hard-packed dirt.

As the crew ascended the hill, the mist drew closer, thin wisps kissing the tops of their heads. Derx caught himself holding his breath, remembering the fog that had descended upon the ship. The mists were thinner now than they were then; he could see the faintly sketched silhouette of Beiran trudging ahead of them.

"Captain," Vlannir said. It was the first anyone had spoken since they'd left the ship. If Beiran heard the first mate, he made no indication. "Captain Stormchaser," Vlannir said again. "What are we doing here? Talk to us, mate."

Still no response. The captain soldiered on through the fog.

"We've lost nine sailors today and we don't know this place. Look at us. We're in no shape to go hiking in some strange land. We need to rest up, and—"

"Vlannir," the captain said. He'd stopped walking. "What lies on the other side of this hill?"

"What? I don't know, but I'm pretty damn sure it can wait until later."

The rest of the crew stared in shock. Vlannir was the Stormchaser's right hand man. They'd stood together on every word until now. He would have defended the captain and his orders to death and beyond in spite of Beiran's sandpaper personality and eccentric ways. As far as Derx knew, the two men had been sailing for decades and had seen most of the world together, charted and uncharted. Vlannir must have been truly shaken by things for him to talk back to the Stormchaser now. Beiran gave him a long look, curiously devoid of emotion. "Then you can wait. But I want to know. I *need* to know."

The Stormchaser resumed his walk. Vlannir gaped after him. The first mate looked upon the rest of the crew. Tired, puzzled faces peered back at him. With a hopeless shrug Vlannir followed his captain and the crew gradually fell into step behind. Derx could hear the captain singing an old song to himself up ahead.

"... One more sea to sail..."

The mists grew thicker as they hiked, caressing Derx's cheeks. His heart began beating faster as he remembered the way the mist fell upon him on the ship, the way it had swelled and made the rest of the world disappear.

"... One more hill to scale..."

White tendrils coiled around his shoulders, thighs, chest like the touch of ghosts. Behind him, he heard another sailor slip and fall, boots scuffing the dirt. The sound was faint, so far away. Everything felt small and insignificant and Derx cursed himself for blindly following the crazed Stormchaser.

"... One more star I've never seen..."

He couldn't turn back. The mist thickened in Derx's nose, enveloping his world in white and grey. His heart thundered against his ribs, his skin writhed. The men around him choked and gasped and sputtered and the world seemed to compress around Derx until his body felt ready to buckle and then in a final, fleeting instant—

—the fog lifted, and the world returned.

The crew and their captain stood at the hill's crest, panting, eyes bloodshot. The barren landscape fell away in all directions before them. From their vantage they could see across the entire island, tiny and bleak as it was. Derx had trouble believing that a single living creature made its home here, for there was nothing but dirt and stony greyness and wind. The only thing of note on the other side of the hill was a lagoon, a bowl of water seemingly cut into the land, leading back into the sea on the other side. In the lagoon sat a ship, wreathed in mists.

She was a mighty galleon, raven-black, with five milky sails and her masts spearing through the fog. Below the bowsprit was a grand figure-head in ebony. Derx squinted. It was the fine figure of a woman, her lower torso that of a squid. She held a sword, poised as though she were charging into battle and leading the rest of the ship behind her. At the edge of the lagoon sat a landing boat. Three figures stood alongside it. They were waiting.

Beiran stared at them. Derx might have imagined it, but he would have sworn he saw a tear roll down the captain's cheek. His eyes echoed radiance and joy. It was the look that Derx imagined ancient prophets might have, believing they'd looked upon the gods themselves. The captain descended the hill with nervous steps towards the lagoon. The trio of men below were a striking bunch: tall, thick of hair, weighed down by gold and weapons and fine clothes. Waters lapped at their boots. As Beiran approached them, one stepped forward, beaming. "Beiran my friend," he said. "It's good to see you after all these years." He looked at the rest of the crew. "Ah, Vlannir is here too. How you've grown, my boy."

Vlannir blinked. "Is that…?"

"Triloche," Beiran said. "I thought you were dead."

The man called Triloche winked. He motioned to his companions. "This is Oullain Windermere, my own captain, from an age ago." Oullain bowed his shaggy, silver-streaked head.

The third, a black mountain of a man with thick clumps of hair dangling past his shoulders spoke next, in a voice that could have commanded demigods. "I am D'ianno Cawtooth, captain of *Ocean's Sword.*"

Stark silence followed. A strange mixture of both reverence and fear crept over Derx. Every sailor knew of D'ianno Cawtooth and his ship. This man had ventured out into the seas and discovered most of the charted world. He and *Ocean's Sword* had become stuff of legends, told across all the civilized countries where there were ships and waters to sail upon. He had also lived three hundred years ago.

"Beiran Stormchaser," D'ianno said. "Are you a true man of the sea?"

"Yes."

"What do you sail for?"

Beiran frowned. "What do you mean?"

"What do you seek on the water? Riches and wealth, fame and fortune? Wine and women?"

The Stormchaser was silent for many heartbeats. A breeze moaned and gave life to the sails of the ebony ship. Finally, he answered:

"To find out what's on the other end of the ocean, the other side of the seas. To seek the things that other men have never seen, or even dreamed of."

Hairs prickled on the back of Derx's neck. D'ianno and Oullain shared a look, then nodded to Triloche. "Stormchaser, will you join us upon *Ocean's Sword?*"

There was a collective intake of breath from the crew. Vlannir's mouth dropped open.

"Where are you bound?" Beiran asked. His voice cracked.

"To the edge," Oullain Windermere said. "Where the sea meets the sky, the place between dreams and reality, where only the best brothers of the sea will reach."

"We need one more to complete the voyage," Triloche said.

All eyes were on Beiran. Even the wind held its breath. His face was unreadable, his gaze dancing from the three old captains before him to the black ship resting in the lagoon. He turned to gaze upon his crew. He looked each sailor in the eye. When his eyes met Vlannir, Derx thought that the first mate might collapse.

Beiran stepped towards Triloche and the others.

"No!" Vlannir cried. "Don't leave us stranded here, Beiran."

"Don't be a twit," Beiran said with a snort. "You can work a ship just as well as I can. The crew loves you, Vlannir. There's no one better."

"You can't go. We were going to see the world together, remember?"

Beiran faced him. "I'm weary of our world. The more of it I see, the smaller and more sickening it becomes. The *Orphan* is yours. Take care of her. She's the closest I've had to a bride." He turned back to the lagoon and the shadow ship in the distance. "Besides, I know a good time when I see one."

Vlannir fell to his knees, broken. Beiran stepped into the lagoon and into the landing boat. "You'll never be able to return," D'ianno said, his voice colored with warning.

The Stormchaser grinned. "Thank the gods for that."

With huge and hearty laughter, the four captains stepped into the boat. As the oars rose and fell, Beiran Stormchaser, navigator, adventurer, freebooter, master of the *Orphan*, went to *Ocean's Sword* and never looked back.

It was a time before Vlannir pulled himself together and started back over the hill, the crew falling into place behind him. The fog bothered them no more. Derx looked back once they reached the top of the hill. The lagoon sat empty, waters shining amongst the lonely grey rocks. No one spoke a word about what had happened until they reached the *Orphan*, where Vlannir promptly appointed Derx as first mate. They hoisted anchor and slipped away from the nameless island and through the mists. Seasons rolled into years. People changed. Sailors who had seen too much drifted away and broken men left the sea life behind. But some stayed. Money changed hands and—

"—Captain Derx?"

Derx blinked. The tavern sounds returned in a swell of tinkling glass and rough laughter. The Molorzian lad stood before him, puzzled, eyes wary. Derx shook his head, dislodging a memory. "What's that?"

"The *Orphan*, sir?"

Ah, yes. Derx looked the lad over again. He couldn't have been more than eighteen summers. Barely a man, in the land where oil and powders and science were replacing the magic and mystery of the open waters. Barely a man, but still too old for fairy tales and sailor's myths.

"The old captain retired and I bought the ship from him. Cost me a damn fortune, but I've paid my debts."

The youth looked maybe a little disappointed as he shuffled back to his friends and Derx felt a tiny pang of guilt for robbing him of a story. To be fair, Derx hadn't lied to the boy. It was just that the *whole* truth… well, he wasn't sure of the truth himself. Sometimes, it felt like his time with Beiran Stormchaser had only been a dream, woven by strands of silver cloud and patched with mist. Captain Derx hummed the old song again as he dropped a few coins on the table and quit the tavern.

…One more sea to sail…
…One more hill to scale…
…One more star I've never seen…

The Voyages of Caleb Blackthorne

By Byron A. Roberts

Part I
Into the Dawn of Storms

"Like thunder roared the cannon's ire, booming o'er the waves,
Sundering the corsair's boards, to bloat unfathomed graves.
A golden prize the seas disgorged, beneath the sunset's gleam;
Steel and shot to glut the sharks and bless old England's queen!"

(Old privateer's shanty, as sung by Captain Caleb Blackthorne's crew)

ENGLAND: DURING THE REIGN OF ELIZABETH THE FIRST...

The man entered the darkness of the narrow alleyway, his keen eyes rapidly adjusting to the gloom. Pale moonlight gleamed dimly upon the basket-hilted broadsword which hung in its black leather scabbard at his side, and the man curled his fingers around the weapon's leather grip as he strode further into the shadows. A slender snaphaunce pistol was thrust into his wide belt, alongside a double-edged dagger. The man was clad in a thick wool shirt edged with golden braid and a toughened leather tunic, while a threadbare grey cloak was draped about his broad shoulders. Studded vambraces bound his sinewy forearms, and he wore black breeches and high boots of buckskin. His greying hair was drawn back into a tight ponytail, and a light beard adorned his scarred and weathered features. His pale blue eyes glimmered, reflecting the guttering torchlight which shone from a nearby doorway.

A bloated rat scurried across the alley, disgorged from its hiding place as twin shadows stirred suddenly in the black. The grey man smiled as two figures emerged from the darkness to bar his way.

"A nice evening, is it not?" the grey man said, his voice deep and unwavering.

Offering no reply, one of the figures pushed his hand into the folds of his tattered shirt and produced a notched basilard. The other, a swarthy man with a hook nose, drew a cruelly curved falchion and adopted a fighting stance.

"You lads might want to think twice about this," the grey man growled.

"How much coin you carrying, old man?" the hook-nosed figure snarled, brandishing his blade.

Instantly, the grey man's sword hissed from its scabbard and swept forth in a ruinous arc. A shrill cry pierced the night and the falchion fell to the earthen floor of the alley, along with the hand that held it.

The swarthy brigand stumbled back aghast, blood coursing from the cloven stump of his wrist.

The grey man smiled a cold, mirthless smile. "Tell your mates you faced Captain Caleb Blackthorne this night," he hissed. "And that you were damned lucky to escape with your worthless life."

Screaming an oath, the brigand pitched headlong into the shadows of the alleyway, leaving a trail of night-dark blood in the dirt to flank his boot prints.

Blackthorne levelled his bloodied steel at the remaining assailant. "Join him and live. Stay, and die. Your choice, sirrah."

The man cursed, hefting his blade and lunging clumsily forward. Blackthorne's steel sang once more in the night, and the brigand dropped his basilard and crumpled to the earth, scrabbling in vain to stop his entrails spilling forth from his rent and riven belly.

"A poor decision," rumbled Blackthorne, wiping his sword on the filthy shirt of the dying man before returning the blade to its scabbard. He stepped over the quivering body and continued down the alleyway in silence.

At length, Blackthorne arrived at an arched oaken doorway, into which had been carved an elaborate arcane sigil. In the gloom of the shadowed aperture, the pictogram seemed to glow with a faint blue luminescence. Caleb touched the sigil and the grating sound of an ancient lock echoed in the alleyway. The great door yawned ponderously open and Caleb shuddered as he stepped into the cold, stygian blackness beyond.

"Welcome, Captain Blackthorne," a sibilant voice said, as if from a great distance. "I'm pleased you were able to keep your appointment."

"I wouldn't have missed it," Blackthorne said. "I just hope you have the answers I seek."

A shimmering replica of the blue sigil suddenly appeared before

Blackthorne, illuminating the nighted gulf and revealing a narrow stone tunnel. The coruscating symbol hovered briefly before the captain's eyes, then sped away into the darkness, searing a path through the void.

"Pray, follow," the voice intoned.

Blackthorne tracked the lambent glyph for what seemed an interminably lengthy span of time, the dark stone walls of the tunnel never varying in their appearance, and no other alcove or doorway being discerned. The temperature in the benighted passage decreased steadily until he began to feel an almost preternatural chill permeate his muscular frame. Finally, the tunnel terminated at a huge wooden door with brass hinges and an elaborate handle fashioned after the form of a serpent poised to strike. The cerulean sigil settled into the centre of the door, pulsed once with a fell radiance, and was gone. Blackthorne considered trying the serpent to gain entrance to the room beyond, but a great creaking and grinding noise stayed his hand. The door groaned slowly and inexorably open, clouds of dust and debris billowing from its frame, until at last Blackthorne found himself gazing at the chamber concealed beyond its hoary threshold. The room was large, and ornately furnished. A myriad candles provided illumination, but still the chamber's corners and many alcoves were shrouded in shadow. Countless books and scrolls adorned the many shelves lining the walls, and an array of strange trinkets and artefacts, the origin of which Blackthorne could scarcely guess at, gleamed and glowered in the half-light. A collection of paintings, maps and charts hung from the sanctum's panelled walls. In the centre of the room was a wooden desk, upon which were scattered gems and crystals of varying shapes and sizes. The desk seemed to groan beneath the weight of a vast assortment of tomes, grimoires and scrolls. One book in particular drew Blackthorne's gaze. It was bound in oily green leather with tarnished metal hinges, and its mold-mottled cover sported a curious motif resembling a single, closed eye. The sight of the eldritch tome caused a chill to run through Blackthorne's body, though he knew not why.

Seated behind the desk, partially wreathed in shadow, was a man. He was clad all in black, his robes rich and voluminous, and a black skullcap covered his head. He sported a white, pointed beard and his face was creased with lines of age and wisdom.

Blackthorne stepped warily into the room and offered a perfunctory bow. The man's eyes gleamed in the candlelight as he regarded his visitor.

"Welcome, Captain Blackthorne," the man said, "Pray sit, for you have travelled farther than you know."

"Thank you, Doctor Dee," Blackthorne said, easing into a wooden chair before the desk. "I appreciate this audience."

Doctor John Dee smiled and interlaced his slender fingers. "Not at all, captain. I found your missive most interesting, and have much to divulge to you on the subject."

Blackthorne leaned forward in his chair attentively.

"But first, I trust your journey here was uneventful?"

Blackthorne's eyes narrowed. "I was waylaid by some cutpurses, but they were swiftly dealt with. In truth, I found your sorcery far more unnerving."

"Please forgive my penchant for the theatrical," said Dee. "I find the Cerulean Key is a most effective security measure, and one can never be too careful these days. This great city is darkly astir with perfidious plots and villainy."

"Not to worry, doctor. Such fell abilities are precisely why I seek your counsel."

"Of course," said Dee, leaning back in his ornate chair. "Oh, before I forget, Her Majesty has asked me to convey her gratitude concerning your recent maritime exploits. The Spanish gold you seized has bolstered the security of the realm immeasurably."

"You can tell the queen that I'm at her disposal," Blackthorne replied. "If I can serve her in any way, she has but to ask."

Doctor Dee nodded. "I'm sure she will be delighted to hear it. The privateers have grown more bold of late, prowling the waves and posing a great threat to our merchant vessels. Mayhap that's something you can offer assistance with?"

"Buccaneers and pirate sloops are no match for my sea-wolves," Blackthorne said. "The bellies of sharks from Gibraltar to Tortuga are swollen with the ravaged flesh of all who've sailed against me."

"So I've heard, captain. Yours is a formidable ship, if the tales are true."

"Indeed she is," Blackthorne rumbled. "The *Starfire* has consigned many a vessel to the fathomless depths, and she has the battle scars to prove it."

"And long may she sail in England's service," Dee said. "Which reminds me, our mutual acquaintance, the venerable Captain Drake, sends his regards."

A humourless smile curled Blackthorne's thin lips. "I'm sure he does. I'll be raising another flagon with that wily old pirate soon enough, I'll wager."

"Of that I'm sure," smiled Dee. "Now, on to the matter that brought you here to my sanctum."

Blackthorne's brow furrowed as Dee lifted a small obsidian mirror from the desk top and proceeded to gaze into its darkling surface. Then he suddenly fixed the captain with an almost fever-bright glare.

"Long have I peered into the scrying mirror, Caleb Blackthorne. Much have I seen. We are dealing with powerful magic, and baleful gods who were ancient long before the Antediluvian Scrolls were ever committed to crumbling parchment. A terrible curse has befallen the immortal soul of a man, a tortured soul to which the whims of fate have bound you inextricably. Black vengeance spawned this curse, and the path to breaking it will be a perilous one indeed."

"What more?" Blackthorne breathed. "What must I do? The dreams are becoming more vivid with each passing night."

Dee sighed. "All in good time, Captain. But first, I require your thoughts. I must experience these dreams through your own mind's eye."

"And how precisely will you achieve this?" Blackthorne asked guardedly.

The doctor extended his hand to position the obsidian mirror directly before Blackthorne's eyes. In the eldritch depths of the polished glass, a panoply of hues seethed and roiled, swirling like mist upon a midnight sea. Blackthorne drew back in apprehension.

"Pray relax, captain," Dee said. "This will not be painful. Not for you, at any rate. Gaze into the deeps of the crystal. Concentrate on the vista before you. We will walk the dreamscape together, and its secrets will be divulged."

Blackthorne stared at the lucent glass, the dancing colours seemingly reaching out from the glimmering portal to encompass his field of vision. Pulsing tendrils of light writhed before his eyes, and he felt a great weariness descend, enveloping him in a mantle of opiate bliss. Then, the trappings of reality melted away like hoarfrost before the rising sun, and the radiant maelstrom of colours engulfed him.

Two moons glowered like the eyes of a great silver serpent, gazing balefully down upon the battlefield. Scores of slain auric-armoured paladins were strewn across the frosty plain, their riven corpses surrounded by the shattered remains of countless marginally human creatures. Spatters of blood stained the coruscant snow like crimson blossoms; a mosaic of vivid red agleam in the lambent moonlight. At the centre of the battle's ruinous aftermath, near a circle of brooding trilithons, towered a fearsome figure clad in black chitinous armour, a huge horned helm concealing his visage, a twisted and bloodied black great-sword in his fist. Twin red orbs burned behind the eye-slit of his helm like ireful embers.

"Ah, the raw scent of carnage and still warm blood," the dark warrior rasped, his voice at once sepulchral and sibilant. "Soon the worms shall gorge themselves upon the flesh of the slain. A grand tapestry of slaughter has been woven this night. 'Tis a pity that none survive to tell their tale in my wake."

"You have not yet won this battle, arch-fiend!" came a resounding voice. From the deep shadows strode a lone paladin, his silvern armour spattered with viscid black ichor, his once bright sword now dark with impure blood. "Your time has come. Prepare to die, spawn of the Z'xulth!"

Pitiless laughter welled in the dark giant's throat. "Do you truly aspire to thwart me, godling?" he seethed. "You are but a mote of dust in the Great Eye of the Universe! You are nothing!"

The knight stopped some ten yards from his foe, levelling the tip of his star-forged blade towards the fuliginous figure. "We shall see."

"I have shattered the gleaming citadels of Lemuria, and have given ancient Atland to the sea," the dark warrior hissed, hefting his cruelly serrated sword. "Ere long, I shall raze the lofty spires of the Serpent Kings to the tundra and grind the bastions of the First Ones to dust! The world shall tremble at my tread. The Star-gods themselves shall fear my name!"

The knight snapped shut the visor of his crested helm and started forward. "You talk too much, devil. Tonight, the crows pick your bones clean!"

Their blades met with a juddering impact, blue sparks blossoming from the clash of steel. The weapons sang with a martial howl of battle, each razor-edged blow ravening for blood. The dark giant parried the paladin's blows with disdainful ease, pushing his foe back with each brutal riposte. With a guttural snarl, the towering fiend swept his black sword at the knight's head, but the warrior's blade blocked the deadly arc and their searing steel became locked in a grinding cacophony of pattern-welded death.

The stygian fiend suddenly drove his gauntleted fist into the knight's helm, staggering his valiant foe. The ebon blade arced down again, but was thwarted once more by the paladin's sword. A pitiless storm of thunderous strokes rained down upon the knight, each blow driving him inexorably back, each bone-jarring strike taking its terrible toll. Then, with one final dire and deadly flurry, the black demon hammered the knight to his knees, and at last the warrior's sword shattered into countless silvern shards. The great black blade hissed down unchecked, biting into the knight's pauldron, rending the armour and sundering the flesh and bone beneath. Blood erupted from the terrible wound in a crimson fountain, and the knight's ruined sword arm fell limply to his side. The malefic warrior laughed, the sound vile and cold.

"And so it ends, wormcast," he growled, his reddened sword poised for the deathblow. "Your crusade ends here. Your realm falls tonight."

"Mayhap," the knight rasped. "But I'll not travel the dark road alone!"

From the ornate hilt of his broken sword, the paladin swiftly pulled a slender dagger of lambent blue steel. With the last vestiges of his fading strength, he drove the blade into the armoured abdomen of his nemesis. With a resonant crack and a gout of green ichor, the steel bit deep into the darksome giant, striking true to embed itself to the shining hilt. The fiendish warrior bellowed a bestial cry and fell back, thick black smoke billowing from the wound.

"Sorcery!" he seethed. "Treacherous cur!" The demon sank to his knees, dropping his serrated sword. Green flames now leapt from his riven armour, and black blood pulsed from the wound in viscid gouts.

The knight pushed himself to his feet with great effort, taking up his foe's twisted blade. The terrible weapon was heavy in his grasp, and a fell radiance seemed to emanate from the sword, as if the dark steel crackled in protest at being wielded by the knight. Summoning all his remaining might, the paladin drove the vile blade into his adversary and swept the black giant's head from his shoulders. A searing flash of green light and a deafening sound like a thunderclap accompanied the blow, and the armoured head toppled to the earth and rolled to a stop at the knight's feet. The fiend's body slumped prone to the ground and lay still, save for the tendrils of black smoke issuing from the corpse's cloven neck. The paladin threw the unclean blade to the earth and kicked the severed head away, staggering several steps before he himself sank to the frosty earth of the battlefield. Slowly, he removed his helm and wiped the sweat and blood from his azure eyes. Darkness clouded his vision and a great weariness enshrouded him. A vista born of nightmare roiled before his mind's eye; an endless realm of slime-flecked cyclopean temples, and the malefic fiends which dwelt within those hoary stone vaults. He saw the freezing black reaches between the stars, and the vile grotesqueries which bred and blasphemed within their ultra-stellar tombs, their aberrant minds ever astir with thoughts of vengeance and diabolic hatred. And burning above that charnel-world of chaos and lunacy, a sinister black sun pulsed and thrummed its siren-call of terror to the desolate void.

"Death comes for you, my love," came a cold, seductive voice from the massing dark. "You have bested my war-hound, but you have not saved your son."

The knight peered into the gathering gloom to see the sinuous form of a slender woman approaching him, traversing the frozen earth like a gossamer ghost. Her flesh was snow-pale, her lips full and blood-red, and her raven-black hair fell unadorned to her waist. He gazed into her midnight eyes, and saw the glimmer of ophidian malice that dwelt there.

"Why won't you lift the curse, witch?" the knight whispered. "I've done all you've asked."

"This is only the beginning," she purred, kneeling before him and gazing into his grim eyes. "The endless cycle of death and rebirth. Can you summon the strength to return from the void? Will you conquer death to save your son?"

She pressed her lips to his, a loveless kiss, cold as the grave.

"Damn you!" the knight rasped. "May your maleficent soul walk only in dark places!"

"Alongside yours, for all eternity," the woman laughed, the sound melodious but more chilling than the song of the north wind. And then she was gone, disappearing into the night like a serpentine spirit.

Then, the knight closed his eyes, his head sagging forward. And darkness engulfed him.

Blackthorne awoke with a jolt, the vortex of colours swiftly dissipating before his eyes. Dee lowered the obsidian mirror, his face ashen pale, a sheen of sweat upon his furrowed brow.

"Yes, that was most enlightening, captain," he said quietly, rubbing at his temples. "I see now the full severity of your plight."

"Then tell me how I may rid myself of these visions," Blackthorne said. "I'll pit my blade against man or devil to break this curse, and find out why I'm embroiled in such a web of black sorcery!"

Dee's expression darkened. "It's sorcery, to be sure. Hoary spellcraft of such power that this world hasn't seen its like since twin moons spun coruscant around our tellurian sphere."

"I've been slain by gladius, scramasax, longbow shaft, claymore, and countless other weapons which in truth are beyond my ken," Blackthorne growled. "I remember every blow, every mortal wound, every death. Why, doctor? What fell forces are at work here?"

Dee interlaced his slender fingers and nodded. "A dangerous voyage lies before you, captain. The answers you seek are not far from England's shores, but many are the foes ranged against you, and they will not give up their secrets easily."

"Cold steel and cannon fire have a way of persuading even the most reticent of people to divulge information, doctor," said Blackthorne, the traces of a smile touching his lips.

"True enough, mariner. But steel and shot alone may not avail you against the fiends you will face. This evil is born of the chaosphere, and you will need all the preternatural assistance you can muster to overcome it."

With that, Dee produced a small ebony box from a compartment in his desk. Almost reverently, he removed a wedge-shaped crimson crystal from its velvet-lined interior. The precious stone had been affixed to a slender golden chain and the gem glimmered seductively in the candlelight, its multifaceted depths ablaze with a rutilant glow.

"This is a key. Guard it well. You will know the door which it opens when you find it."

Blackthorne took the crystal, his cold eyes reflecting its blood red radiance. Swiftly, he looped the chain around his neck and tucked the amulet out of sight behind his shirt. "Where do I begin?"

Dee took up a leather cylinder from the desktop and handed it to Blackthorne. "Within is a chart which will guide your vessel, and a map once you make landfall. Follow it carefully, and you will find that which you seek."

Blackthorne opened the cylinder and removed a stained, tattered scroll from within. He carefully unfurled the scroll and studied the chart etched upon its yellowed surface. Then he smiled and returned the scroll to the cylinder, tucking into his broad belt. "Anything else, doctor?"

"Just a warning, captain," Dee whispered. "Go with care. Trust no one. I fear I can tell you no more."

Blackthorne rose from the chair. "Then you have my thanks, doctor. I hope we meet again."

"We may, Caleb Blackthorne. The scrying mirror does not yield its cryptic secrets lightly. But before you depart, tell me… are you a religious man?"

"I hail to the gods of the sea," Blackthorne replied grimly. "Whichever ones bring my ship and my crew safely home."

"Of course you do," Dee said. "A most prudent theological stance, given your line of work. I hope those gods protect you. Farewell."

Blackthorne nodded and turned to leave. Then he stopped and pointed to a large map which hung on the chamber wall, partially concealed in shadow.

"One last thing, doctor, if you will. I'm curious. That chart depicts a shore I've never seen, and I've sailed farther than most."

Dee smiled. "No man has seen that shore in ten times a thousand years, captain. 'Tis fabled Atlantis, a realm long since devoured by the pitiless seas."

Blackthorne laughed, the sound devoid of humour. "Ah yes. Atlantis. A legend known by every mariner."

"More than a mere legend, captain. Mayhap I shall show you the splendour of the Atlantean realm, if you return."

Blackthorne moved to the chamber door. Before stepping across the threshold, he turned once more to face John Dee. "I look forward to that, doctor. Farewell."

Then, he disappeared into the darkness of the tunnel beyond.

* * *

The inn was almost empty when Caleb Blackthorne stepped through its wide doorway. Several sailors were seated at the bar and a serving maid was tending the guttering fire in the large stone hearth. Three unconscious bodies were sprawled upon the filthy, straw covered floor.

A huge, heavily muscled man suddenly appeared before the captain, thrusting a jug of ale unceremoniously into his hand. The man's ruddy face was harshly weathered and he sported a braided red beard and close-cropped hair. Hoops of gold adorned his ears, and his green eyes gleamed with the joviality of intoxication.

"Is the word given, cap'n?" the man thundered.

"Aye, Drustan, it is given," Blackthorne said, taking a long swig of the ale. "We have our destination. We'll return to the *Starfire* with the dawn, and sail before the week is out. There's much I have to tell you, when my deck is beneath my feet once more."

The red-bearded man lifted his own flagon and drained its contents in a single swallow. "Then may the gods smile on us. Time yet for another round!"

Blackthorne's attention suddenly turned to the inn's entrance as a swarthy, hook-nosed man staggered through the door. The man's right hand was missing, and a filthy blood-stained bandage covered the stump of his wrist. Five men followed him into the building, all of them armed with daggers, rapiers and falchions.

"There's the whoreson!" the hook-nosed man bellowed as he spied Blackthorne. "The one who took my hand and butchered poor Albert! Gut him boys!"

The men advanced, weapons ready.

Drustan threw aside his flagon and hefted his notched cutlass. "A friend of yours?"

Captain Caleb Blackthorne smiled as his fingers curled around the hilt of his sword. "An acquaintance from earlier this evening. Time to take the rest of him. Piecemeal, if needs must!"

Blackthorne's steel hissed from its scabbard, and the battle was joined.

The raven-haired woman watched the brawl in the tavern from afar, the images shifting and shimmering in the great obsidian mirror before her. She studied the graceful, martial movements of the grey-haired swordsman as he engaged his foes, admiring his skill with the slender blade, marvelling at the deadly economy of his fighting style. In an instant, two of the assailants were down, their blood staining the filthy floor of the inn. The swordsman's towering companion clove the third brigand with his cutlass, the force of the blow almost shearing the man's head from his shoulders. The grey man disarmed the fourth warrior and sent a pitiless thrust into the buccaneer's belly, the tip of his steel emerging from the spine in a red arterial spray. The giant red-bearded fighter parried a blow from the fifth warrior with contemptuous ease and hammered his notched blade down through the man's shoulder. The steel swept down into the man's ribs before it was dragged free amidst a shower of dark blood and shards of bone. Finally, the grey-haired swordsman faced the one-handed man alone. Naked fear illumined the swarthy brigand's eyes, and the grey man's steel flashed cruelly in the torchlight, instantly opening a gaping furrow in his neck. The grey man moved in close to the dying thief and spoke to him as he sank to the bloodied floor, but the woman could not discern the words he uttered. Abruptly, she waved her hand and the image in the glass swiftly faded, swallowed by a deep, swirling shadow. She turned to the imposing figure that loomed behind her, gazing up into the man's crimson eyes. The woman smiled as she reached out to stroke the man's azure flesh, her slender fingers tracing the contours of his sculpted musculature, lingering over the hard lines of his broad chest. A web of veins pulsed beneath the man's blue flesh, agleam with a faint cerulean luminescence.

"An enigma, this mortal," she whispered. "Caleb Blackthorne is merely a vessel which houses the soul-shard, one of many such hosts over the centuries. And yet he is something more. Why does this one remember? I cannot fathom his role in this. His true nature is unknown to me, but he may yet prove to be of some use in our grand undertaking."

"He will bleed and die like all the rest," the giant man rumbled, his voice deep and cold.

"Dreams have compelled him to seek the truth," the woman breathed, pressing her lips close to the man's ear. "Dreams sent by my former paramour. The spells are strong, but my curse is stronger."

"I will wait for this mortal," the dark giant hissed. "He will be no match for me. I will send his ship to the depths, and carve my name in his flesh."

The woman moved her hand to gently stroke the jagged scar which encircled the giant's bull neck. "I have remade you for this task, my love. I have recovered your soul from the pit so that you may fulfil your destiny. Do not fail me."

The azure man's rutilant eyes narrowed. "The scion cannot hide forever. I will have my vengeance."

The woman fixed the giant with a cold, baleful gaze. "You will, my love, you will."

And a serpent's smile curled her blood-red lips.

Part II
A Voyage on Benighted Seas

From the log of Captain Caleb Blackthorne:

Entry I:

Damn these treacherous seas! To what cursed, devil-haunted expanse of ocean has Doctor John Dee's hoary chart guided us? Four days out from Southampton and the tempest struck; the brooding black clouds massing in an obsidian sky, the heavens roaring their thunderous ire as rain like arbalest bolts lashed the deck, all while a searing demoniac wind threatened to rend our sails and splinter our lofty masts. But we are no strangers to the storm, and our oaken prow drove onwards through the tumult, cleaving the murderous waves to carry us through the ravening vortex. As suddenly as it had descended upon us, the witch-storm was gone; the wrath of the heavens mercifully spent, our battered vessel a living testament to the cruel whims of the pitiless oceans. Now, the sea is like ebon glass. The corposant haunts the rigging. Only a noisome wind conjured from the east deigns to fill the Starfire's sails, pushing us ever onwards to our baleful destination.

Entry II:

The nights here are preternaturally black, as if the moon herself seems reluctant to shed her silvern light upon the fathomless depths. And by the gods, such dire fiends dwell in those lightless ocean vaults! Strange and squamous beasts whose passing is marked only by the faintest glimmer of green in the stygian water; bloated, tentacled things writhing and slithering through the pitch, their luminous eyes peering up from the gloom and promising some unspeakable, insidious malignity yet to be wrought. The brood of the mythic Leviathan? The vile children of the fabled Kraken itself? Or mayhap something far worse… the dread spawn of the arch-fiend who sleeps and dreams in death within the basaltic tombs of the ancient sunken city? Bah! My musings get the better of me, I fear. And yet, the red jewel given to me by the old wizard sits ill about my person. Does it truly whisper to me in the fevered depths of the darkness, or is that naught but the endless creak of the boards and the sighing of that fell wind in our sails? Each night I have dreamt of the vortex, that desolate black maelstrom in which all briny devils dwell; but in place of the sea is an endless void of shimmering stars, and the infernal reaches of an eternal abyssal night. Surely some shuddering nameless blasphemy lurks and seethes in that blighted bitumen gulf!

Entry III:

We are not alone. Thrice now have we spied the Black Ship prowling the waves behind us, trailing us like some vengeful ghost; a predator locked in its spectral pursuit as it hunts us across these wine-dark seas. 'Tis an argosy of the deep night, appearing and disappearing like mist, ever poised on the distant horizon like a darkling sentinel, never closing, never altering its course save to match our own. Who sails aboard that shadow-ship? Who commands its unseen mariners to dog our wake and track us upon this eldritch voyage? I harbour an uneasy feeling that we shall find out ere long, as Doctor Dee's counsel warned that we would encounter a myriad deadly foes on this grim expedition. The crew are fearful, murmuring. But they are stout and hardy men of the sea and they will not shirk their duty. At any rate, our cannons are primed, and our blades are sharp. We stand ready.

Entry IV:

As Dee's crumbling chart promised, we discovered the island on the sixth day, surrounded by its wreath of lambent mist, nestling in a ring of crystal clear, azure water. The heat is damnably oppressive! The sun beats pitilessly down upon us now. Such an infernal clime as this should not exist so far north. Strange black birds soar above the isle's twisted trees on great leathern wings, bellowing their vile cacophony to the unheeding sky. We make ready. I have given the order to drop anchor and launch the pinnance. What perfidious villainy awaits us on this emerald atoll? What answers shall I find here? Aye, destiny beckons. My sword is honed.

* * *

The verdant maelstrom of the jungle seemed to press ever more heavily upon the men as they hacked their way through its teeming, sweltering depths.

Growling an oath, Captain Caleb Blackthorne hefted an ivory-hilted cutlass and hewed a path through a mass of twisted, quivering vines. His buckskin boots were soaked through, and his wool shirt and leather tunic clung to his muscular frame, sodden with sweat and the perpetual kiss of the crawling green. At his side was his deadly basket-hilted broadsword in its black leather scabbard. An ornate snaphaunce pistol was thrust into his wide belt, while a long-bladed dagger rested in its sheath at his hip.

Sunlight filtered down through the vast canopy of titanic trees which loomed above the men, casting a dappled golden glow upon the jungle floor. The constant, maddening drone of the seething forest was an insistent cacophony in Blackthorne's ears, as the coarse cry of unknown birds mingled with the hum and chatter of countless colossal insects which swarmed blackly in the writhing shadows.

Caleb stopped, running his fingers through his sweat-matted grey hair and taking a swig of tepid water from a goatskin gourd which hung from his belt. Then he wiped his beard and pulled an ornate leather cylinder from the folds of his shirt. Removing a crumbling parchment from the cylinder, he studied its yellowed surface and turned his gaze skyward, shielding his blue eyes against the fragmented sunlight. Nodding silently, he secreted the ancient map and once more took up his stained cutlass, pressing on into the crushing embrace of the jungle.

Five men followed Blackthorne through that vast sea of flaying fronds and gnarled, mossy boles. They had been handpicked to follow their captain ashore into the impenetrable vault of towering trees and treacherous undergrowth, and they were amongst the finest fighters ever to sail aboard the far-famed ship called the *Starfire.* Warriors, buccaneers and steel-hard men of the sea; each a master of the cutlass, basilard, arbalest and wheel-lock, each the veteran of a score of sea-fights in every wild weird clime from the cliffs of Dover to the dire shark-glutted waters of Cape Horn.

Gunnar, the heavily muscled blond reiver from the snow-shrouded Jarldoms of the North, strode through the jungle carrying his huge rune-carved battle-axe, its iron head curved like the beak of a deadly bird of prey. His voluminous flaxen beard was braided into a trident configuration, each plait secured by a bronze ringlet. The burly Northman's scale-mail cuirass gleamed in the half-light, and a black leather patch covered his left eye.

Kattikouda, the ebon slayer from the beast-haunted plains of distant Nubia stalked the undergrowth like a hunting cat, clad in his panther-skin tunic and wielding his cruelly serrated twin short-swords with their polished rhino horn hilts. A leather thong adorned with lion's teeth hung about his great scarred neck.

Ryo, the steel-thewed shadow-assassin from the mythic isles of the far Orient, marched silently through the green labyrinth, garbed like midnight and gripping his ornate razor-edged katana, its slender hilt bound with blackened shark-skin.

At the rear of the column, Drustan the red-bearded Celtic giant trudged sullenly. He swatted an insect the size of a sparrow which had settled on his corded forearm and a luminous yellow ichor instantly exploded from the creature's shattered carapace. Scowling, he wiped his befouled hand on his black breeches, clutching his great notched cutlass ever more tightly.

"I hate this damned place," the Celt growled. Rivulets of perspiration ran down his face, stinging his eyes and collecting in his crimson beard. He had stripped off his leather jerkin to march bare-chested through the jungle, and his powerful frame was now studded with leeches and black beetles.

A lean, sandy-haired young man with a hefty matchlock slung over his shoulder and a bronze-panelled arbalest in his grasp turned to Drustan, taking a moment to survey the myriad duelling scars and old wounds which had carved their mute testimony upon the clansman's flesh.

"Well, at least we finally made landfall," the man said, checking the slender snaplock pistol holstered at his belt. "After that storm hit us, I'd have sworn the captain had lost his way."

Instantly, Drustan gripped the young man's shoulder in a vice-like grip, his green eyes blazing like emeralds in the jungle.

"The captain has never been lost, boy!" he hissed. "He can tell where the *Starfire* is by the colour of the sea beneath her keel and the tang of the wind in her sails! Remember that."

The man nodded, cradling his arbalest to his chest and grinning broadly. "I'll not forget, old man," he said, turning to resume his march through the clawing undergrowth.

Drustan called after him. "Get yourself a blade, young Malachi. You may be the best marksman I've ever known, but that matchlock's damn near useless in this cursed damp!"

"Mayhap," Malachi replied. "And yet it'll serve well enough as a bludgeon if need be!"

Drustan cursed loudly and moved slowly up the column, finally reaching Captain Blackthorne and matching the muscular Yorkshireman's long purposeful stride. "Much farther, cap'n?"

Caleb cast a wary glance at the undergrowth, one hand on the hilt of his broadsword, the other still curled about the ivory grip of his cutlass. "No. If Dee's map is to be trusted, our destination is near."

"Thank the gods!" Drustan spat. "This bastard place is eating me alive."

Caleb nodded. "There are eyes upon us, old friend. Something's been watching us since we came ashore."

"I've felt it. But beast or man? I can't fathom."

"We'll find out, ere long," Blackthorne said, hacking at a tangle of broad green fronds with his blade.

"Do you really think you'll find the answers you seek on this cursed isle?"

Blackthorne sighed, shaking his head. "I don't know. But it's my last hope, Drus. The visions are becoming more powerful. Oft have I gazed upon thronged battlefields, seemingly through the eyes of another. I have seen vast cities, raising their jewelled spires to the stars. I have witnessed giants locked in pitiless combat with gods, and demons slaying paladins beneath the baleful light of two moons. I have seen gold-girded legionaries clashing with massed hordes of painted tribesmen on the heather, and armies of shining knights waging war beneath a rainbow sea of billowing banners."

Caleb's hand suddenly lashed out to grasp a mottled red snake which was encoiled around a mossy bough overhanging their route through the jungle. Dragging it free of the branch, he studied its scaly head intently.

"Venomous?" asked Drustan.

"I imagine so," Caleb replied. He hurled the writhing serpent far into the undergrowth and resumed his trek.

"The dreams… visions or whatever they are," Drustan said. "You're slain in every one of them?"

"Aye," Blackthorne replied. "Always, like a wolf hunting its prey, death has stalked these vistas. Each waking dream, each crystal memory ends with a mortal wound or a ruinous death blow. I remember each time I've fallen in battle, and always the last thing I see before death claims me is that dour sentinel astride his great winged steed who silently observes each descent into oblivion. Who is he? What does it mean? I fear my wits are being lashed like a vessel on a storm-wracked sea."

"Fear not. We'll discover the secrets of this blighted place," Drustan said. "That old astrologer had best be right!"

"I pray he is. Sometimes I feel I've lost myself. Where do the other lives end and mine begin? By the gods! I swear I've been known by many names, old friend. Though the only one I recall is Blackthorne!"

Drustan was silent for a moment, then he grimaced and prised a bloated leech from his massive shoulder. "Well, whatever we find here, this voyage should vex your rivals if naught else."

Caleb turned to the clansman, a wicked gleam in his icy blue eyes. "Damn right! That nefarious old pirate Drake's never set foot here, and that's a fact!"

* * *

At length, the jade labyrinth of enormous leaves and cyclopean boles began to thin somewhat, until the corsairs found themselves in a clearing ringed by jagged black branches which seemed to encircle the glade like dolent sentinels. Littering the grassy floor of the green expanse were bleached and broken bones of all shapes and sizes; fragmentary remains of large animals, birds, and certain other skeletal ruins which appeared vaguely human in origin. Blackthorne kicked idly at the cloven skull of a horned creature which to his eyes seemed to resemble the fleshless head of both a bull and a huge man, apparently fused together in some abhorrent corruption of nature. He shuddered and turned to the exhausted men who had assembled behind him at the perimeter of the clearing.

"We're here, lads."

At the far side of the charnel-dell a dark stone structure squatted ominously, its slimy carven edifice starkly at odds with the verdant morass which surrounded it. Some forty feet tall, the black shrine was encarved with strange glyphs and sigils the likes of which Blackthorne had never before beheld on all his voyages to the distant shores of the known world. Fashioned in a vaguely pyramidal shape, the structure's top most reaches had been hewn down by the assault of both time and the elements, and fragments of mossy black rock now lay strewn at its base. At the centre of the hoary ziggurat a single monolithic doorway brooded, sealed tight by a vast slab of stygian stone. And in the middle of that carven panel was a small, wedge shaped aperture.

Blackthorne reached into the folds of his shirt and produced the glimmering red jewel which had been given to him by Doctor John Dee, still fastened to its gold chain about his neck. The bright sunlight danced in the gem's rutilant depths, and its multifaceted surface seemed to glow with a crimson luminescence.

"The good doctor said this was a key," whispered Caleb. "Well, I think we've found the door."

The red jewel seemed to thrum in Blackthorne's grasp, a discernible heat building in its crystalline deeps and warming his calloused palm.

"Come on. This is what we're here for," Caleb said, striding towards the desolate black temple.

The mariners warily followed their captain across the bone-strewn expanse, their weapons held ready.

"What men built this?" asked Malachi, still clutching his arbalest to his chest. "It looks ancient."

"Mayhap no men ever laid these stones," growled Drustan, gazing at the darkling edifice with apprehension.

"Do you think there's treasure inside?" Malachi said. "Gold? Jewels? There could be anything in there!"

"Aye lad, that's what worries me," Drustan replied.

Captain Blackthorne halted before the basaltic black door, gripping the red jewel tightly.

Malachi brushed his hand along the contours of the mossy stone, his brow furrowing. "It's cold. Nigh on like ice."

"Stand back," said Caleb. He unfastened the jewel from its chain, carefully bending the golden claws which secured the gem. Slowly, he pressed the crystal into the aperture in the centre of the black door. With a barely audible click, the jewel was pushed home to fit perfectly into the tiny, recessed alcove.

At once, the relative silence of the glade was shattered by a great grating and grinding din, and the black door slowly began to rise. A cloud of dust billowed forth from the shadowed rim, and fragments of moss and stone crumbled to the earth. The stone slab continued its noisy ascent until it had disappeared wholly into the black edifice above. Beyond the threshold, utter darkness roiled and writhed.

"What a waste. Do you think we'll get that gem back?" Malachi asked, crestfallen.

Drustan grinned at the young man. "Forget the bloody jewel, laddie. It was a fell thing anyway. At any rate, your treasure trove might lie within."

Blackthorne turned to the assembled mariners. "Drustan, Malachi, come with me. The rest of you, wait here. Give us an hour, and if we do not return, come after us with steel and shot. Be ready for anything."

Gunnar, Kattikouda and Ryo silently took up their positions, vigilantly flanking the doorway of the time-worn shrine.

"We should fashion brands," said Malachi. "I've flint and tinder in my pouch."

Blackthorne stared into the brooding black maw before them. In the ebon depths, he could barely perceive a faint azure glow illumining the void.

"We might not need torches, boy. Follow me."

And he stepped boldly into the glooming embrace of the darkness.

* * *

The dank, shadowy captain's cabin of the great black galleon was illuminated only by the light of a single, guttering candle. The oaken walls were mould-mottled and dripping with sea-water, and the slimy black deck was encrusted with barnacles and other assorted detritus of the fathomless oceans. Dark, multi-legged crustaceans skittered and scurried through the muck, and the eerie creak of the ancient boards filled the darkness with its ceaseless dirge.

In the centre of the cabin stood a huge man, clad in a suit of blackened chitinous armour. His pauldrons were fashioned in the shape of twin skulls, their toothsome maws frozen in a perpetual rictus grin. His gauntlets were spiked at the knuckle joints, and each finger ended in a talon of black iron. Slowly, he removed his great horned helm and placed it on a low, rotting table before him. The man's flesh was azure, and the veins at his temples seemed to glow faintly with a cerulean luminescence. His head was shaven and his eyes were bloodshot, seemingly aglow with a gentle crimson radiance. A jagged scar encircled his great corded neck.

"I summon thee, black empress," the man hissed, his voice deep and sepulchral. Taking up a phial of green glass from the table, he moved to a black metal brazier that had been wrought after the form of a coiled bipedal serpent, its clawed feet splayed upon the salt-stained planks in the corner of the cabin. The man emptied the contents of the phial into the gaping mouth of the iron serpent, and at once a great cloud of acrid smoke billowed forth, filling the cabin with a sickly-sweet odour. Slowly, the tendrils of smoke rising from the brazier coalesced into something resembling human form. Then, amidst the writhing plumes, the ghostly image of a beautiful, black haired woman appeared. The woman's subtly slanted violet eyes gazed at the azure giant from beneath her raven tresses, and her full lips slowly curved into an alluring smile.

"Speak, Maalech Xul." The woman's sibilant voice came to him as if from far away. Her tone was soft, almost melodious, yet tinged with an unnerving edge colder than hoarfrost.

"The mortal has reached the shrine," the giant growled. "He seeks that which lies within."

The smile faded from the woman's face and her ophidian eyes narrowed malevolently. "Let him take it, then seize it from him. The soul-shard endures within this one, and his dreams persist. He may yet prove to be of use to us. Bring him before me. I would speak with this man... this Caleb Blackthorne."

"You wish him intact?" Xul said, a note of vexation in his voice.

"Yes. There is yet power in the transference gem I bestowed upon thee, is there not?"

Maalech Xul produced a small multi-faceted jewel from a hidden compartment within his gauntlet and studied its crystalline surface. The gem was dark green in hue with black veins running through its murky depths like a spider's web, and it glowed faintly in the flickering candle-light. He nodded and secreted the stone once more. "And when he has fulfilled his purpose?"

The smile returned to the woman's face, then her mouth curled into a sly and fulsome pout.

"Then you may do with him as you will. Take his head and send his ship to the abyss, if it pleases you."

"It shall be so," Xul said tersely.

"And how fares your crew, paramour? Does my spellcraft yet hold them in thrall?"

"They serve and obey, as you said they would. The dead ask no questions and seek no recompense."

"Then command them well. Our time approaches. All for which we have striven shall soon be within our grasp. To fail me would be… unwise."

With that, the smoke dissipated and the image of the woman rapidly faded.

Maalech Xul moved to the table and took up his helm once more. Finally, it was time for trenchant steel and slaughter. At last, the predator would descend upon the prey and redden its ravening jaws. Smiling mirthlessly, he secured his curved, serrated sword in its scabbard and strode out onto the deck of the great black ship.

* * *

Caleb, Drustan and Malachi stood transfixed in the small circular chamber, each of them gazing in awe at the centre of the ancient stone room.

"By the gods, will you look at that!" exclaimed Drustan.

The black walls of the chamber were inscribed with glowing blue sigils which cast an eerie lambent light upon the three mariners. But what enthralled them so completely was the object which glimmered at the heart of the shrine's inner-most sanctum.

A magnificent silver sword hung suspended in a coruscant cocoon of shimmering azure light, its mirror-like blade sparkling with pulses of electrical energy. The sword's cross-guard had been fashioned to resemble two great wings, and its hilt was bound with gleaming platinum wire. The pommel was a colossal sapphire which shone with a glorious, crystalline radiance, and arcane symbols and strange runes had been etched into the adamantine steel of the luminescent blade.

"It's beautiful!" whispered Malachi. "What a jewel!"

Caleb strode silently to the radiant sword, ascending a low circular stone dais above which the fulgid weapon thrummed and sparkled. Slowly, almost reverentially, he extended his hand. As his fingers passed through the ethereal shell of dancing light, he beheld a sheen of frost suddenly encase his wrist and knuckles, but he felt no sensation of cold. Then, steeling himself, he boldly grasped the hilt of the sword. Instantly the sapphirean pommel burned brighter, glowing with a near blinding blue energy. A lance of white light crackled forth from the gem and touched Caleb's forehead with its searing brilliance. A myriad vivid colours abruptly exploded before Blackthorne's eyes, and a tremendous sound like the roar of the ocean filled his ears. Then, the confines of the stone chamber melted inexorably away around him, and Caleb surged headlong into a raging maelstrom of seething, ephemeral light.

From the writhing vortex of colours, an incredible vista rapidly coalesced before Blackthorne's eyes, and he found himself gazing down upon a vivid dreamscape which quickly crystallized into razor sharp focus. Below him, two great armies were separated by five hundred yards of arid, sun-scorched plain. Harsh sunlight danced on the countless swords, spear-points and helmets within the massed ranks, and heat rose from the dusty earth in shimmering waves. Two hundred yards to the east of the opposing legions, a huge black pyramid brooded, its darkling stone surface appearing to wholly absorb the pitiless solar rays.

The smaller force was assembled beneath an array of huge banners emblazoned with the device of a winged horse rearing against a field of azure, and the mighty sigils billowed in the gentle breeze which caressed the desert expanse.

Astride a dun-white charger at the centre of the army's front line was a man with the regal bearing of a king. He was resplendent in silvern chain-mail, gleaming vambraces and greaves, and a bejewelled open-faced helm crowned by a plume of white horsehair. A ruby red cloak trimmed with white tiger fur hung about his shoulders. In his grasp was a mighty lance which crackled with cerulean energy, its honed tip aglow with arcane power.

Mounted at the noble paladin's side was a younger man, armoured in gleaming steel plate and wielding a familiar sword with quillons fashioned after the form of silver wings. His hair was the colour of the sun and a golden circlet ringed his snow-pale brow.

Despite the clamour of the great armies, Caleb found he could hear perfectly the words spoken by those he beheld.

"And so, it has come to this, my son," the older man said, a note of sadness in his deep and powerful voice.

The younger man turned in his saddle. "We have no choice, father. This battle must be fought. The witch must be vanquished, lest the realm be lost."

Then, Blackthorne's dream-gaze slowly swept the enemy ranks. Men they most certainly were not. Each black clad warrior's frame was hunched and twisted, their long limbs unnaturally jointed, their vile pallid faces toothsome and vulpine. And at the vanguard of that dark army, a giant of a man sat deathly still atop a huge, heavily muscled black steed. He was armoured head to toe in black, and at his waist was scabbarded a huge cruelly curved sword with a single crimson jewel set into the pommel. Beside him, astride an unearthly midnight horse, was a woman swathed in stygian diaphanous robes. Her cloak billowed like a shadow, and her raven hair was darker than the frozen heart of a long dead sun. Her violet eyes were fixed on the young man who rode with the opposing force, and they shone with the cold malice of a serpent.

Caleb saw the kingly warrior shake his head sorrowfully as his gaze fell upon the woman. "This is what you have wrought, queen of lies, vile empress of deceit! Well, your treachery ends here. You have sown the wind… now shall you reap the tempest!"

"Beware, father," the younger man said. "You know full well the extent of her powers. She plots something this day. Her true intent is yet unknown."

"Behold her vassal army, my son. Look upon her cursed war-hound, the energumen beast Maalech Xul. The perfidious magicks she has conjured to bring forth that vile abomination are an affront to the gods! She has defiled the sanctity of the Nine Temples with her blasphemous diableries!"

"The Cerulean Phalanx stands ready, father. Shall we send the herald?"

"No, Araklion," the man replied wearily. "The time for diplomacy is long past. All that remains is red war and the bitter song of cold steel!"

Caleb at once realized that he had seen more than one of those mighty protagonists before. Prior visions had revealed to him the armoured paladin and the dark knight, most recently when he had allowed Doctor John Dee to share his dreams via the astrologer's ancient scrying mirror. During that communion, Blackthorne had witnessed the demise of both warriors following a brutal battle upon a desolate plateau of frozen tundra, and with grim certainty he knew that the vista below him represented a point in time before that slaughterous confrontation. And the shadow-wreathed succubus… Blackthorne would never forget that beauteous but sinistrous countenance! But who were they? What momentous events did their ethereal appearances portend?

The dreamscape suddenly shifted, the armies melting away into darkness. Abruptly, a new image manifested before Caleb's eyes. The sun had set, and night had enshrouded the ghostly battlefield. Two moons now cast a lurid light upon the desert expanse. Now, Blackthorne gazed upon a sea of ruined corpses, and at the centre of the charnel-vista, the prone body of the young warrior Araklion lay surrounded by the riven bodies of a score of slain foes. His silver sword, its bright blade now befouled by blood, was at his side. The raven-haired woman knelt beside him like a shadow, a cruel smile upon her lips. Slowly she produced a green jewel from the shimmering folds of her black robes and held it to the fallen youth's brow. The woman hissed a sibilant incantation in a tongue Blackthorne could not fathom, and the green gem instantly pulsed brighter, bathing Araklion's body in an emerald light. Swiftly the woman withdrew the crystal and rose to her feet, her cloak rippling about her lissome body like black mercury. Suddenly she looked up, meeting Blackthorne's dream-gaze. Her eyes shone with a baleful fury, and her ruby lips drew back in a malefic snarl. Searing agony tore through Caleb's incorporeal body as he stared into the ireful depths of that ophidian glare, and the eldritch vista abruptly faded, becoming swallowed once more by a tumultuous storm of vivid, fulgid hues…

Blackthorne was torn painfully from his reverie, reeling with the intensity of the vision. Immediately, Drustan's powerful arms had hold of his captain's shoulders.

"Steady, old horse," the clansman said. "We lost you for a moment there." Caleb shook his head as the last vestiges of ethereal light dissipated before his eyes. He was still holding the great silver sword.

"The son!" he exclaimed. "The soul of the boy, doomed to roam the void, haunting the battlefields of eternity. And the winged steed is his father's sigil!"

"Which means what, precisely?" snapped Drustan. "What did you see?"

"This blade," Blackthorne hissed, hefting the gleaming sword. "His blade! It has revealed to me the truth of this malediction. I know now what I must do. Break the curse, and free the boy!"

"How exactly are we expected to do that?" Drustan asked guardedly.

"Before now that was beyond my ken, clansman. And yet, the events of the dreamscape have divulged at least some of their secrets. These are not mere mortals who haunt my visions, but titans! Warriors possessed of such power that they doubtless seemed as gods to the men of their era. Gods of steel and storm! John Dee named them as such, and I believe it!"

"Gods?" spat Drustan. "Feh! This all smacks of mummery to me! Are we to meddle in the affairs of immortals now?"

Caleb nodded solemnly. "Mayhap, old friend. At any rate, I am certain it is no less than a king who appears to me in my dreams… a god-king whose numinous realm has long since fallen beyond time and the meagre reckoning of human history!"

"This all sounds rather perilous," Drustan muttered.

"I hold a facet of the boy's soul within me," Caleb said. "To liberate myself from this purgatory I must undo a dark deed wrought many thousands of years past. The woman! By thunder, what a vile villainess! I know not who she is, but her hatred burns bright, reaching across the aeons like a shadow beyond time. An undying malice!"

"So, it's witchery, then?" scowled Drustan.

"Aye. It is she who has woven this dire spell of sleepless malignity, though as yet I know not why."

"So be it. Where are we bound?"

"For a sea no ship may sail, I fear," whispered Caleb.

Drustan's brow furrowed. "What mean you by that?"

"When we tread our oaken boards again, I'll disclose my intent. But for now, back to the ship!" Caleb turned and made for the chamber's darkling entranceway, pausing before the threshold. "Where's the lad?"

"Here!" came Malachi's voice from the shadows. The young mariner was busy filling his pockets with an array of small blue gems which were strewn beneath the glowing glyphs engraved in the sanctum's walls. "These are sapphires, I'm sure of it!"

"Get a move on," Drustan growled. "Best not to overstay our welcome here."

"Scared, old man?" Malachi chided. "Not like you to be afraid of the dark."

"It's what may dwell in the dark that worries me, whelp. Besides, I seem to recall it was you who nearly got us killed last summer when you were prising gems from the wall of that pharaoh's tomb!"

"How was I supposed to know that damned jackal statue would

spring to life?" said Malachi indignantly. "At any rate, those baubles bought us a fortnight in the flesh-pots of Araby and scored us six new culverins for the old girl's deck, plus a new jib-sail to boot!"

"He's right, I'll warrant," Caleb said. "And the lads deserve some spoils from this voyage. A ship doesn't sail on goodwill alone, after all."

"I think I've got them all," Malachi said, pocketing the last of the blue shards and rising to his feet. "Not as splendid as the pommel on that pick-sticker, captain, but they'll do!"

"Come then," Drustan said. "It's getting colder in here, and darker."

The lambent runes in the black stone were fading as the three men made their way from the chamber and into the pyramid's main entrance tunnel. As they emerged into the bright sunlight, Gunnar turned to them, clearly relieved.

"A fine sword," the Northman said, eyeing the ornate blade in Caleb's grasp. "Nothing happening out here."

"Good," Caleb replied. "Now we return to the beach!"

Drustan nodded. "And if we get back to the ship without incident I'll down a flagon of rum tonight in praise of the gods and every blessed ancestor ever to bear my name!"

The corsairs began to move swiftly across the clearing and back to the verdant embrace of the jungle.

Then, from behind them, there suddenly came the sound of splintering boles and snapping vines. The men spun to face the black pyramid once more and beheld the trees on the far edge of the clearing swaying and bending, as if forced down by some colossal, unseen force. A tremendous bestial roar abruptly thundered from the shadows of the jungle; a guttural sound unlike any animal the mariners had ever heard on their far-flung voyages to the distant forests and unmapped atolls of the world.

"Oh, that doesn't sound good," whispered Malachi, all colour draining from his face.

With a final resonant crack of rending wood, a nightmare shape erupted from the breached wall of trees which ringed the bone-glutted glade. Standing twelve feet in height, the creature resembled one of the great hulking apes of the southern continent, save for its matted fur which was dun-white in hue. Its massive shoulders and arms rippled with iron-hard muscles, and where the ivory hair did not cover its colossal frame, a hide of scaled grey skin encased its abhorrent body. The creature's head was small and vaguely simian in appearance, but its cavernous maw was studded with yellow fangs each the size of a basilard. Both of its gigantic paws terminated in a set of reddened talons, and its burning feral eyes were fixed on the men as it lumbered forth from the jungle. Another guttural roar thundered from the monster's slavering jaws; a bone-chilling bellow sounding at once bestial and yet unnervingly human.

"I knew it!" snarled Drustan, hefting his cutlass. "It couldn't have been that bloody easy!"

"Behold the god of the Bulgani!" shouted Kattikouda, lifting his twin short-swords with barely concealed glee. "Many are the tales told of him amongst the tribes of my southern brethren. The mighty spirit of the great apes made flesh! It is a rare honour to battle him!"

"That's no ape!" Ryo hissed, sliding his katana from its lacquered scabbard. "Run or fight?"

"Pray, run!" said Malachi, clutching his arbalest. "That would be my vote."

"Too late!" Caleb growled, as the towering beast loped inexorably towards them. "Stand your ground, men of the *Starfire*. Bring the fiend down!"

Instantly, Malachi loosed a bolt from his arbalest which flew true to embed itself in the scaly chest of the onrushing creature. Its charge not halted in the slightest, the white ape tore the metal projectile from its body, leaving not a trace of blood to mark the bolt's brief presence.

"Scatter, and slay!" Caleb shouted, pulling his snaphaunce from his belt. With a thunder-crack report, the ornate pistol bucked in the captain's hand, a gout of flame and a cloud of smoke billowing from its barrel. The lead ball took the creature square in its sloping forehead, but left no discernible wound. "Black powder won't avail us, it seems!"

"The edge it is then!" snarled Gunnar, raising his axe and barrelling towards the beast. "Slake your steel, in Odin's name!"

The Northman's eyes were aglow with the bear-sark rage as he engaged the great white ape. He drove his curved axe into the beast's midriff with the force of a thunderbolt, the steel biting deeply into the scaled flesh. Howling in pain, the ape-thing lashed out at Gunnar with a great taloned paw, the glancing blow sending the blond reiver reeling to the ground. Spitting blood, Gunnar rolled instinctively to narrowly avoid a crushing fist which hammered the earth beside his head. He hefted his axe once more and surged to his feet, leaping beneath another vicious swipe of the monster's bludgeoning paw.

Instantly, Kattikouda vaulted to the creature's massive back like a great jungle cat, bringing both of his short swords down in a deadly arc to pierce the beast's hairy shoulders. The ape lurched forward and seized hold of the Nubian's leg in an iron grip, dragging him free and hurling him effortlessly across the glade to crash heavily to the ground some twenty feet away.

"This thing won't die easily!" bellowed Malachi, running to Kattikouda's aid and hauling the dazed tribesman to his feet. Three ragged gouges in the Nubian's muscular thigh were pulsing with bright blood. Frowning, Malachi swiftly unslung his long matchlock rifle from his shoulder and opened the leather pouch at his belt.

"Then it'll die hard, laddie… but die it will!" Drustan growled, spinning his notched cutlass and loping towards the fearsome creature. "Together, Northman!"

Gunnar ducked beneath another deadly swipe of the ape's talons and thundered his axe into its massive forearm just as Drustan pitched headlong at the beast's legs and drove his cutlass into one of its scaled knees. The creature bellowed another ear-splitting roar and lashed out again, its great fist striking Gunnar with a juddering impact and sending him scudding across the bone-strewn earth. Snarling an oath, Drustan spun and thrust his blade at the ape's matted groin, the cold steel biting deep. Instantly a massive paw surged down and took hold of the clansman's throat, lifting the red-bearded giant from his feet. Drustan found himself flailing mere inches from the creature's nightmarish maw, feeling the ape's foetid breath hot on his face. The vice grip tightened inexorably and shadows began to writhe before the clansman's eyes.

Suddenly a single resonant thunderclap echoed through the dell and the ape-thing's head snapped backwards. The beast immediately released its hold on Drustan, howling with a cacophonous mixture of pain and fury.

Gasping for breath, Drustan cast a glance across the clearing to see Malachi grinning broadly, his matchlock's muzzle billowing with plumes of white smoke.

"That's one you owe me, old man!" the young mariner shouted gleefully.

"Mayhap," Drustan rasped, his tongue slick with blood. "But it took you long enough to fire that bloody noisemaker!"

The shot had taken the beast square in the eye and staggered it, albeit only fleetingly. Lurching backwards several steps, the ape shook its shaggy head and grunted as the shock of the impact dissipated. Its eye was yet intact, and for all the dire and ruinous wounds the creature had suffered, still not a single drop of blood had escaped its hulking frame. The ivory behemoth bared its yellow fangs and beat a savage tattoo upon its granite chest, and another ear-splitting roar resonated throughout the glade.

Suddenly, a black clad figure appeared before the beast like a shadow. Ryo sprung lithely at the giant ape, his katana shimmering in the sunlight. With preternatural speed, the assassin leaped and spun about the monster like a whirlwind, each razor stroke of his searing steel opening a gaping bloodless wound in its grey hide. Evading every swipe of the simian juggernaut's paws with disdainful ease, Ryo wove a graceful and scintillant web of death around the creature, his sword striking pitilessly like an adamantine viper. Finally, the assassin delivered what should by rights have been a death blow to the creature's bull neck, his blade singing with a single sustained note of crystalline beauty. But the great ape merely howled in rage and defiance at its diminutive assailant, its eyes aflame with feral hatred.

"Yaiba, tanegashima… yakunitachimasen!" the assassin hissed, leaping gracefully back to the edge of the clearing. "This is not a natural thing. It does not bleed. It will not fall!"

"Press the attack!" Caleb bellowed, discharging his snaphaunce once more to no avail. "Give no quarter!"

With blood running freely from the ragged furrows in his neck, Drustan limped to where Gunnar was climbing unsteadily to his feet. "Can you still fight, lad?"

The Northman lifted his axe, wincing as a sharp pain tore through his midriff where his scale-mail cuirass had been riven. "Aye," he said, grinning wolfishly. "A few cracked ribs I'll wager, but I'll yet go down hacking!"

"We shall die here," said Kattikouda, readying his short-swords as he prepared to attack the beast once more. "So, may we die well, and honour our ancestors!"

Grim faced, Caleb suddenly holstered his pistol. "Stand down, mariners!" he boomed. "No mortal weapon can slay this beast." With that, he hefted the argentate sword and strode to face the monster, the rays of the baleful sun glimmering in the weapon's sapphirean pommel.

"What makes you think that meat cleaver will do any good?" Drustan called to him.

"Nothing else has worked," Caleb replied.

The simian colossus grunted, shook its huge head and immediately charged at Blackthorne, its mammoth fists striking the ground like iron mallets with each loping stride.

Caleb adopted a fighting stance, his brow furrowing as he felt the hilt of the sword growing strangely warm in his grasp. The crystal pommel seemed to glow with a cerulean radiance, and he began to discern a low humming sound emanating from the blade. Then, he felt the bombinating sword tremble in his fist, and to his astonishment narrow tendrils of blue energy suddenly manifested to dance along the length of the glyph-scored steel. Smiling, Blackthorne looked up at the charging behemoth and raised the radiant blade high. And with a final deafening roar and a resonant snap of its jagged jaws, the ape-thing was upon him.

A sound like a whip-crack abruptly rent the air, and with a blinding blue flash the ancient sword met the granite flesh of the colossal creature. Caleb channelled all his might into the ruinous blow, the force of the tremendous strike rendering his muscular arms momentarily numb. With a blossom of blue sparks, the glowing steel sheared through the beast's shoulder and down to its sternum, cleaving the grey hide with preternatural precision. Blackthorne was pummelled from his feet by the impact of the clash, rolling beneath the ape's legs and rising instantly to one knee, the sword still tight in his grasp.

The ivory beast crashed thunderously to the earth beside him, sending up a cloud of dust and a shower of soil and shattered bone shards. The ireful mass of fur and sinew scudded along the ground for several feet, leaving a great furrow in the grassy terrain. A heartbeat later and the mammoth creature was finally still, save for a plume of acrid smoke which billowed from the terrible wound in its twisted, ankylosed frame.

Blackthorne rose to his feet and warily approached the fallen monster. No blood issued forth from the riven carcass, and amazingly the beast's flesh seemed to be petrifying before his eyes; transmogrifying into a dry grey husk devoid of any semblance of life or hue. Swiftly, the great ape crumbled to dust, leaving naught but a mound of fine dun-white powder upon the churned earth of the jungle clearing.

For long moments, no one spoke. Then, Drustan bellowed joyously to the cloudless sky. "Thank the gods!"

Kattikouda made the sign of the protective horn across his chest, and Ryo offered up a silent oath to the heavens.

"There is more to that sword than meets the eye," Gunnar said, gazing at the glimmering blade in awe.

So it would seem," Caleb replied. "Be proud, my sea-wolves. You've faced black sorcery this day and shown your mettle. But I fear we have little time to celebrate. Now, let us return to the ship and leave this thrice-cursed atoll behind us."

"I like the sound of that!" Drustan said, grinning broadly.

Malachi shouldered his matchlock and stared uneasily at the great mound of pale dust before them. "What if there are more of them out here?"

"Shut up, boy," growled Drustan, and shoved the youth roughly towards the waiting perimeter of the shadowed jungle.

* * *

Blackthorne emerged from the tree line and stepped onto the narrow beach, shielding his eyes against the sudden glare of the sand. The return trek through the jungle had taken longer due to the wounds suffered by Gunnar and Kattikouda, and the sun now hung lower over the distant horizon. The ship's pinnance waited, drawn up on the shore of a broad lagoon which had afforded the most secure sounding to make landfall.

Drustan pushed his way clear of the undergrowth and halted beside Caleb, breathing heavily and tugging at his sweat-matted beard.

"At last. I swear we've trudged thirty leagues this day, if a yard," he muttered as the remaining mariners appeared from the dank perimeter of the jungle behind him.

"And there she is," Caleb said, pointing out to sea. "Not a more beautiful sight in all the world!"

The *Starfire* was anchored beyond a jagged outcrop of volcanic rock, floating serene and splendid in the sparkling blue water. A heavily modified carrack, the ship was seventy feet long and armed to the teeth. Her deck bristled with a bewildering array of guns, all cast of bronze or iron. The arsenal of cannons, demi-cannons, culverins, sakers and falconets studded the vessel's oaken body, the larger weapons thrusting menacingly from the gun-deck's ports and the smaller armaments swivel-mounted on the rails. The ship was square-rigged on the foremast and mainmast, and lateen-rigged on the mizzenmast. Her stern was high and rounded and sported a lofty aftcastle behind the transom. She boasted a low forecastle with a slender bowsprit jutting from her blade-like prow. A figurehead of an ornately carved dragon adorned the stemhead, fashioned after the fearsome serpents of the ancient northern drakkars which once prowled the rivers of Blackthorne's ancestral city of York.

And high on the masts and stern of the sleek warship, the far-feared blazon of the *Starfire* fluttered in the gentle breeze; a grinning, helmeted skull with two crossed battle-axes behind it. That ireful red and sable flag was known far and wide across the trackless waves; the dreaded pirate's bane… the legendary scourge of the seven storm-wracked seas!

"Aye, she's a blessed thing, to be sure," Drustan said, gazing at the distant ship with an expression akin to love.

"She's firing!" exclaimed Malachi, pointing to where a cloud of white smoke had suddenly billowed from the ship's gun-deck. Scant seconds later, the sound of the cannon's salvo reached the mariners, and their eyes followed the arcs of the cannonballs as they sped out across the waves.

"There!" Gunnar growled. "From the witch-fog!"

Caleb stared out far beyond the jagged outcrop to where the low bank of eerie, nebulous mist perpetually encircled the island. Slicing the blue water like a ghostly leviathan, the Black Ship suddenly emerged from the fog, its ragged sails billowing, its iron bow guns blazing.

"That spectral hulk's found us!" Drustan bellowed. "I feared as much!"

"Get that bloody pinnance in the water!" Caleb thundered, racing to the shoreline. "I'll be damned if my girl's going to trade broadsides without me on her deck!"

* * *

Standing at the bow of the great black galleon, Maalech Xul fixed his rutilant gaze on the *Starfire* and the verdant isle beyond. A cannonball howled past the black mainmast and pitched into the azure water at the dark vessel's stern. He raised a gauntleted fist and pointed to the anchored carrack. "Cripple that damned ship!" he seethed.

A black clad mariner with pallid alabastrine skin and glazed, lifeless eyes moved to stand beside the armoured giant. "And the crew?" the sailor rasped.

"There is one whom I seek. I want him alive. The rest can feed the sharks."

Xul gripped the hilt of his curved black sword tightly. "Haul him before me in shackles, if needs must! But bring me Caleb Blackthorne!"

Part III
The Scion at the Gate of Eternity

Caleb Blackthorne surged through the acrid cannon smoke beclouding the quarterdeck of the *Starfire* and felt a rush of adrenalin course through his lean, muscular frame. His basket-hilted broadsword was scabbarded at his side and his ornate snaphaunce pistol was thrust into in his wide leather belt, along with his slender double-edged dagger. In his hand he brandished the scintillant silvern sword which he had seized from the hoary shrine deep within the verdant vaults of the jungle atoll, its platinum bound hilt thrumming gently in his calloused grip.

The visceral thrill of battle shone bright in Blackthorne's blue eyes as he felt his ship's keel lurch beneath his feet and heard the rattling and luffing of her great sails high above him.

"Fire!" he bellowed, brushing several errant wind-whipped strands of greying hair clear of his furrowed brow. "Give the foe a full broadside!"

The fearsome array of bronze and cast-iron cannons studding the ship's starboard gundeck spoke as one, hurling a keening storm of death out across the cerulean waves where the black galleon was cleaving the water towards the *Starfire* like a tenebrous leviathan. Three balls hammered home into the fore-peak and jib boom of the vessel, sending up razor blossoms of wooden shards and iron fragments. The rest of the ordnance plunged into the roiling surf.

Blackthorne leaped past the capstan to the gunwale where a burly mariner clad in a tallow-stained jerkin and goat leather breeches hung precariously over the rail, his powerful hands gripping the ship's knotted oakum ropes.

"Quartermaster O'Rourke!" Caleb shouted. "Grand job! You beat to quarters like true dogs o' the sea. Never yet has any scurvy sloop caught my girl at slumber!"

O'Rourke flashed a black-toothed grin which creased his swarthy, wind-weathered face. The quartermaster's salt coarsened hair was bleached white from years of sailing the sun-seared seas of the world. "The lookout on the mainmast spotted her, cap'n. Hands to braces and anchor hauled before she got off a shot! Our thirty-two pounders had the first word, and have been hot since you clambered o'er the tumble-home!"

Blackthorne clasped the man's broad shoulder. "You've earned your grog tonight, old horse!"

Then he gazed out to sea at the black ship which was swiftly closing on them, watching its ragged sails billowing in the sultry dusk wind. At just over a hundred and forty feet, she was twice as long as the *Starfire*, and boasted a jutting rostrum and an oddly gnarled bowsprit. All four masts were rigged to the gallants; square rigged on the fore and main-mast, lateen rigged on the mizzen and bonaventure, and everything from the freeboard to the gunwale was darker than pitch and midnight. The fore and aftcastle were similarly hued, and the ship's cannons were bared like the blackened teeth of some abyssal devil of the briny deep. And yet to Blackthorne's battle-seasoned scrutiny, something about her was very wrong indeed. The ship looked ancient and mould-mottled, as if it had been dragged dead and rotting from the very bottom of the ocean. The sails were nigh on ruinously tattered, and how the wind caught them sufficient to drive the hulk onwards to rend the waves was beyond his ken. Strangely, the myriad cracks and fissures in the sea-sodden timbers also seemed to glimmer faintly with an eldritch viridescent luminescence, the source of which Caleb could scarcely guess at.

With a start, Blackthorne suddenly caught sight of the mariners who were positioned along the ship's deck and hunched in her jibs and rigging. They were pallid and emaciated shades; gangly wraiths cast crudely in the forms of men with skeletal frames and scabrous flesh acoil with a plethora of slithering and skittering denizens of the fathomless deeps. Clad in rags and the long-corrupted garb of the sunken dead, the cadaverous crew of the ghostly vessel were seemingly devoid of all semblance of light and life. And then, Blackthorne spied the stygian giant who stood like a carven marble titan behind the black bowsprit. Encased in jagged chitinous armour and wielding a fearsome serrated sword he recognized from his waking dreams, Caleb knew in an instant who it was that commanded the benighted argosy.

"Maalech Xul! The demon from my darkest visions!" Blackthorne hissed.

"Volley inbound!" bellowed O'Rourke, as the twin bow guns of the galleon suddenly blazed with a relucent green radiance. Two black spheres howled from the corroded cannons of the foe and arced inexorably towards the *Starfire*. The first shot sailed cleanly between the masts to crash into the water beyond the gunwale, but the second thundered into the aftcastle with explosive and ear-splitting magnitude. Wood and bone shattered at the point of impact, cloven timbers and riven flesh scattering across the oaken deck in a viscid red rain.

"Topsails and gallants!" barked Blackthorne. "Boatswain! Get the wounded below-decks to Butcher Tavistock! They'll bleed his sawdust red, but his surgeon's knives might yet save their blessed hides!"

The crimson bearded clansman Drustan lumbered to Caleb's side, his bull neck still red raw from the talons of the great white ape which the mariners had faced on the jungle isle.

"She's a fell ship," the Celt growled. "Will our cannons avail us against this witchery?"

Caleb's blue eyes narrowed. "We'll sink that bitch with iron and faith, my friend!"

"How many guns do you think?"

"At least fifty, by her size and how she sits. I'll wager twenty demi-cannon, twelve culverins, some eight demi-culverins, with the rest being sakers and fowlers."

"We're outgunned."

Blackthorne scowled. "But not outmatched!"

"She turns!" O'Rourke boomed. "Seeking to bring all her guns to bear!"

"Hard to larboard!" Blackthorne thundered. "Hands to braces and we'll show them our mettle!"

"We can yet outsail her and batter her hull to shards," Drustan said. "We've a reload time of a minute flat with six men per gun."

"She's fast, for such an ungainly hulk," mused Caleb. "She's got a good rate of knots on that keel, wind be damned. Something unnatural propels her. But my gut tells me she doesn't aim to sink us. They mean to board."

"To what end?"

Caleb hefted the gleaming arcane sword, marvelling once again at its polished, rune etched blade and its ornate quillons which were fashioned in the form of two mighty silver wings.

"Mayhap this?"

"Mayhap *you,"* Drustan replied, his craggy brow arching.

"Let them come alongside and grapple, damn it all!" Caleb said, tightening his grip upon the gleaming sword. "'Tis the fiend from my fever-dreams who strides that deck. I would have hard words with him. But first, we'll tear a few more holes in her black hull!"

"In the jungle you said you knew our next port of call," Drustan said. "Where do the visions drive us next?"

"Where no chart or navigator may guide us, and perhaps where I alone may tread," growled Blackthorne, gazing grimly at the black ship. "Into the belly of the beast!"

* * *

On the forecastle of the darkling galleon, Maalech Xul hefted his great black sword and scanned the heavily armed carrack maneuvering before him.

"There you are!" he growled as he discerned Caleb Blackthorne standing defiantly upon the quarterdeck, silver blade in hand. "The hunt draws to an end, at last!"

The dark giant's chitinous armour glistened with a sheen of salt spray, his great black cloak billowing like the leathern wings of a colossal bat. Sea water dripped from the twisted maws of his skull shaped pauldrons, giving the disquieting impression that the leering effigies were salivating at the prospect of the impending clash.

Another barrage of cannonballs thundered from the *Starfire's* gunports, shrieking towards the ghost-ship like a swarm of ireful ironclad hornets. This salvo struck home with a deafening cacophony of rending wood and screaming metal, shattering the foremast, the mainyard and a vast swathe of the quarterdeck in a shower of blackened shards. A score of silent, pallid mariners were rent horrifically asunder by the volley, their limbs torn from their decaying bodies and their vulpine skulls splitting to spill their noisome contents to the ravaged deck planks. Dark green ichor exploded forth from the riven corpses, spattering the vessel's barnacle encrusted planks like a malignant and foetid tide.

And the black ship sailed inexorably on.

"Blast this cursed vessel apart board by board if you must, human," Xul hissed. "I shall yet bear thee to the Black Spire!"

The armoured titan secured his huge horned helm and watched as the stygian galleon's jagged prow clove the sea like a ravening shark, bringing the vessel ever closer into position to flank its tenacious quarry. "Stand ready to sling hooks," Xul thundered above the rattle of the ragged sails and the roar of the churning sea. "Kill all you can, but Blackthorne is mine alone!"

* * *

"Prepare to repel boarders!" boomed Caleb as the black ship hove near. "Courage, lads… these fiends are the devil's progeny, but they'll still fall to steel and shot! Now, stand fast and send them back to the briny vaults!"

"Man those breech-loaders on the rail!" Quartermaster O'Rourke barked. A score of men leaped instantly to the swivel-mounted bronze fowlers on the gunwale and made ready to fire.

Drustan slowly bared his great notched cutlass and smiled, the expression wholly devoid of mirth. Glancing towards the aft of the ship, he saw the young marksman Malachi take position by the mizzen mast, his long matchlock rifle poised.

The Nubian bladesman Kattikouda crouched by the capstan like a hunting panther, his twin shortswords with their rhino horn hilts twirling in his hands, his claw-raked thigh bound with a filthy linen bandage.

The blond bearded reaver Gunnar stood at the forecastle, his deadly curved axe glimmering in the rays of the setting sun. The Northman still wore his scale-mail cuirass, steadfastly ignoring the dire wounds he had suffered during the battle with the great white ape.

The black garbed assassin Ryo was perched upon the foreyard like a shadowy bird of prey, his razor-edged katana with its shark-skin hilt agleam like a single silver talon.

Many mariners waited at the bulwarks, blades and guns ready. Others had climbed to the rigging and the spars with their weapons honed and primed for combat.

Caleb Blackthorne dragged his basket-hilted broadsword from its scabbard and rested the blade upon his shoulder. In his other hand he still held the coruscant rune-etched blade from the island shrine. Grinning wolfishly, he vowed both blades would soon drink deep of the impure blood of this deathless assembly of gangrenous fiends who now dared waylay his ship. The men of the *Starfire* were the veterans of countless sea-duels from the White Cliffs of Dover to the black volcanic crags of the southern isles, and there was nothing that sailed upon or swam beneath the seven seas that these doughty sea-wolves feared!

The black ship loomed ever closer, close enough that the vacant, staring eyes of its corrupted charnel-crew could clearly be seen, and several of those vile mariners crouching in its rigging were now hurling twisted iron hooks attached to slimy ropes.

"Give them one more for good measure!" bellowed Caleb gleefully.

The demi-cannons on the *Starfire*'s larboard gun-deck thundered their martial report once more, and two hundred pounds of iron, limestone and flint tore into the rotting boards of the black galleon with a sublimely deafening cacophony. A billowing storm of smoke enveloped both decks and a shower of wood, metal and worm-eaten flesh rained down like a sepulchral tempest.

With a titanic grating din, the freeboards of the two ships met, the wood grinding together like the clash of two great primal predators from the dawn of time. The crack of the timbers was ear-splitting, as the spars and rigging of the twin behemoths were wrenched and riven, splintering and snapping free from the shackles of the masts and decks. Iron missiles whistled down from the spars as the black ship's mariners struck like baleful shadows, leaping from their vile vessel to befoul the deck of the English carrack. The fearless corsairs at the *Starfire*'s bulwarks met the onslaught with a purifying storm of bright steel, raking and rending the aberrant fiends as they pounced hissing from the rigging. Cutlasses and pikes clove grey flesh and clattered on the gunwales, while matchlocks and breech-loaders hurled hot iron death into the gangrenous, nightmare tide of onrushing hell.

Caleb drove his basket hilted blade into the pallid face of a snarling fiend as he felt his ship rock beneath his buckskin boots. The cankerous mariner crumpled beneath the blow and Blackthorne spun to parry a cutlass strike from another boarder before sweeping his silver longsword upwards to cleave the creature from its hip to its sternum. The ravaged body was rent in twain by the mighty strike and fell to the deck in two rotting halves, its darksome entrails erupting to writhe upon the viscera-strewn planks like a mass of steaming eels. A vile face twisted in a rictus grin suddenly reared up before him, and Caleb swept the feculent head from its bony shoulders amidst a torrent of dark green blood. Embedding the point of his basket hilted blade momentarily in the carrack's deck, Caleb tore his snaphaunce from his belt and with a thunderous crack and a plume of smoke discharged the weapon into the decomposing face of another shambling fiend. The creature's head instantly exploded in a noxious shower of black ichor and yellowed bone, the decapitated body collapsing to the boards in a tangle of spindly limbs and filthy rags. Throwing the pistol aside, Blackthorne swiftly unsheathed his slender dagger and hurled the honed blade unerringly into the milky, clouded eye of a bloated purulent form which was clambering awkwardly over the gunwale. The creature's malformed head snapped backwards and it plummeted into the churning sea between the two embattled vessels. Caleb then took up his sword once more and leaped again into the thick of the fray.

All around him, the foetid mariners were falling to the bright steel and withering shot of the carrack's crew. Gunnar's pitiless axe-blade was black with gore, and Kattikouda's short-swords struck again and again like twin cobras. Malachi's matchlock and snap-lock found their marks unerringly, and Ryo's searing katana wove a scintillant and graceful tapestry of death. Drustan clove the legs from one undead mariner and split the head of another from its crown to its chin, a slurry of maggot-wreathed grey brain matter blossoming from the splintered skull.

"Give no quarter, wolves of the sea!" Blackthorne bellowed. "Drive these cursed demons back to their shark-haunted graves!"

And then, like a colossal ireful shadow, Maalech Xul leaped from the rail of the ghost-ship to the deck of the *Starfire*, his midnight cloak billowing, his vast curved sword whirling.

"Caleb Blackthorne!" he roared, his guttural voice tomb-cold. "I have come for thee!"

Two mariners fell instantly to that black sword, their bodies seared to red ruin by its cruelly serrated ebon steel. A matchlock ball suddenly impacted Xul's great horned helm with a resonant crack, only to ricochet harmlessly from the blackened crown.

Caleb turned solemnly to face the armoured giant, his dripping blades poised.

"You," he growled. "The spectre from the dreamscape, finally made flesh. Long have I awaited this meeting."

Dark laughter welled in Xul's throat and a crimson light shone balefully from the eye-slits of his helm. "Indeed, human? Come, then. Let us commune at last!"

The silver sword met the black blade with a resounding metallic clarion and a blinding shower of rutilant sparks. Blackthorne's steel suddenly blazed with cerulean energy, the hilt thrumming ever more intensely in his grasp. In response, Xul's blade shone with a fiery green glow, viridescent tendrils of witch-power crackling along its length. The two weapons became locked in a grinding, relucent contest of arcane might, each razor edge shrieking and keening its eldritch defiance. The ageless swords of light and shadow, meeting again in their time-lost battle of good and evil!

"I've faced that cursed sword before," Xul rumbled. "Long before your ancestors crawled from the primordial mire. The soul of its former wielder now lies sundered and scattered to the abyss."

"I've seen you die in my dreams, devil," Blackthorne spat. "I mean to take your head again this day!"

Snarling, Xul drew back for another ruinous blow and Blackthorne arced the silver blade up for the parry, the resultant clash sending a shockwave of pain along the length of his sword-arm. Desperately, Caleb swept his basket hilted broadsword into Xul's chitinous cuirass, the strike rebounding harmlessly from the surface of the blackened metal.

The dark giant hissed and forced his opponent's auroral blade down, pressing his inhuman weight against Caleb's guard.

"You are no match for me," Xul growled, the crimson embers behind his helmet's eye-slits blazing brighter.

Gritting his teeth, a sheen of cold sweat upon his brow, Blackthorne felt himself being pushed inexorably down by the preternatural strength of the armoured fiend. The two blades hissed and crackled with arcane fire, bright sparks blossoming from the steel. Lances of agony tore at Caleb's arm and shoulder. He fell slowly to one knee, an invisible and oppressive wall of cold spectral force hammering pitilessly at his body.

"I am not so easily bested," Blackthorne rasped.

Summoning the final vestiges of his fading might, Caleb roared an oath and drove the point of his basket-hilted broadsword viciously into the area between Xul's cuirass and pauldron, ramming a full eight inches of steel into his foe's inhuman flesh. With a bestial howl, the dark giant fell back, gouts of dark blue blood erupting from his riven armour. Blackthorne instantly leaped to his feet and hammered the silvern sword's edge into Xul's midriff, the incandescent steel scoring a great furrow in the jagged cuirass. Blue flames exploded from the scarred breastplate and Xul stumbled backwards several paces. Pressing his advantage, Caleb lunged forward and swept the silver sword in a lateral arc towards the giant's helm, seeking to cleave the beast's head from his body. But with malefic speed, the black blade flashed up to meet the blow. A sound akin to a thunderclap rose above the tumult of the surrounding battle, and a cocoon of searing light instantly enveloped the two combatants like a lucent shroud. Trapping his foe's shining blade and pushing it down, Xul's taloned gauntlet suddenly lashed out to grasp Caleb's forehead, and a bright green glow abruptly flared where the riveted black iron met the captain's flesh. Instantly, Blackthorne's knees buckled and his broadsword clattered to the deck, his body slumping insensate into the grip of his darksome opponent. Swiftly, Xul scabbarded his black sword and wrested the silver blade from Blackthorne's lifeless grip, securing it at his belt. Then, he swept Caleb's frozen, immobile body effortlessly up onto his great shoulder.

"Steel is not the only tool at my disposal, human." he rumbled. "We have an appointment with my mistress… one which we must keep."

From a compartment in his gauntlet, Xul produced a small black stone which sported a lattice-work of green veins running across its polished surface like a sinistrous spider's web. Raising the jewel before him, he hissed a sibilant incantation in a long-dead arcane tongue. Instantly, a shimmering portal manifested before him, rending the air like a gaping, glowing wound in the fabric of reality. Beyond the eldritch gateway, a myriad radiant hues swirled and roiled like a vast spectral maelstrom. A tremendous howling sound accompanied the sorcerous threshold, like the rushing of some fell, unholy gale. The dark giant stepped towards the pulsing portal, still bearing the motionless body of Caleb Blackthorne.

Suddenly, in a blinding flash of folded steel, the adamantine blade of Ryo's katana swept cruelly down upon Xul's outstretched arm. With a clamorous crack and a plume of acrid smoke, the blade severed the armoured limb cleanly and the arm fell to the blood-stained deck, still bearing the green jewel in its gauntleted grasp. Xul roared in pain and rage, the inhuman sound terrifying in its bestial ferocity. With torrents of dark blue blood erupting from the terrible wound, Xul surged headlong into the arcane portal, disappearing wholly across its shimmering threshold. In an instant, the glowing doorway disappeared, contracting like a fuliginous iris until nothing but a writhing tendril of green mist remained to mark its passing.

All about the *Starfire*'s deck, the vile undead mariners abruptly collapsed, their ancient weapons clattering to the boards, their ankylosed frames crumpling motionless to become nothing more than piles of tattered rags and muculent bones. The clamour of battle swiftly subsided and the carrack's corsairs watched in astonishment as their insidious foes fell before them. Scant seconds later, every single one of the ruined corpses was swathed in a shroud of greenish light, all of the grisly remains swiftly disappearing to leave naught but a fine alabastrine powder which was quickly dispersed by the whispering sea wind.

"The captain!" Drustan boomed as he loped to where the severed arm lay oozing upon the deck. "I could not reach him in time to give aid!"

"This blow was all I could render," Ryo said, kicking at the rent limb. "The throngs of the *kyonshi* kept my steel busy."

Suddenly, the air was filled with the din of rending wood and twisting metal, and the mariners turned to see the great black ship begin to shake and judder violently. In an instant, the vessel became wreathed in a viridescent glow, its masts and boards splintering and crackling as if being crushed in the vice grip of a colossal unseen hand. Moments later the galleon was gone, the azure sea churning and bubbling where once its fell keel had floated.

Scowling, quartermaster O'Rourke picked up the severed arm and gingerly prised the green and black jewel from its dead grasp.

"Sorcery!" he spat. "I saw the devil use this stone to open the witch-portal!"

Gunnar moved forward to peer at the gently glowing rock, his scale-mail cuirass slick with black blood and viscera. "Where did that fiend of Nifelheim take him?"

"And can we follow?" growled Kattikouda, wiping his befouled blades.

"Loyalty is the watch-cry of this crew," Drustan said. "Each of us owes his life ten times over to Caleb Blackthorne. If there is even the remotest chance we can travel the same path to retrieve the captain, we are honour bound to try, no matter where that infernal path may lead."

Malachi carefully took the stone from the quartermaster and held it aloft, gazing at the crystalline green veins which sparkled faintly in the light of the setting sun. "This is the key to opening that cursed door," he said. "All we need to do is fathom how to use it."

* * *

Caleb Blackthorne awoke to find himself lying prone on a small islet of black volcanic rock surrounded by a silent, wine-dark sea. Shedding the last vestiges of his sorcery induced slumber, he rose slowly to his feet and discovered that his wrists were shackled by a pair of lucent green manacles which seemed as incorporeal as mist, but which no amount of straining could serve to loosen in the slightest. Gazing upwards he beheld a vast blue sky devoid of clouds, boasting a baleful burning sun which glared down upon him like a single searing eye.

"Good. You have awoken," came a sepulchral, ice cold voice.

Caleb spun to see Maalech Xul standing several yards behind him, the winged silver sword secured at his belt. Dark blue blood pulsed steadily from the cloven stump of the giant's elbow where his chitinous black couter had evidently been sheared clean through.

A wry grin curled Caleb's lips. "Lose something?"

Xul levelled the point of his serrated black sword at Blackthorne's head and strode menacingly towards him. "Silence!" he barked, an edge of vexation in his voice. "You find yourself in the domain of my mistress. Come now and meet your destiny. Behold the Black Spire!"

Caleb turned to gaze out across the basaltic islet, swiftly discerning a narrow black bridge which stretched over the motionless water and on to the distant horizon. Beyond the dark causeway's farthest extent, rippling and shimmering in the heat-haze, he beheld a vast cyclopean structure which towered skyward like a sinister talon of smooth black stone. The stygian spire was colossal, easily two hundred feet tall, and at its pyramidal pinnacle was a gigantic green orb which pulsed and burned with a fell viridescent fire.

Xul roughly took hold of Caleb's arm and proceeded to shove him in the direction of the ebon tower. "Move."

Blackthorne began to trudge silently along the narrow bridge, the sun beating pitilessly down upon him. The dark giant strode wordlessly at his back, leaving a serpentine trail of blue blood upon the bitumen stone.

"I have seen your vile mistress in my visions," Caleb said, glancing back over his shoulder. "She is the perfidious architect of this curse which plagues me. You should know I mean to bring her to task over her dire misdeed."

Xul laughed darkly. "She has seen mighty empires rise and fall, and witnessed the birth of gods in the ultra-stellar wombs of eternity. Why she seeks an audience with the likes of you is beyond my ken, but rest assured you pose no threat to her, lowly human. She is as far removed from you as your mewling race is from the worms which writhe beneath your feet."

"And you, Maalech Xul," Caleb growled. "You are no vaunted champion of a noble queen. You are naught but a fawning lapdog to a petty slattern… an impotent slave to a sorcerous harlot whose insidious plots are doomed to ignominy and failure!"

A myriad flecks of light abruptly exploded before Blackthorne's eyes as Xul drove his iron-sheathed fist into the base of the mariner's skull. Caleb fell heavily to the blackened stone only to be hauled violently back to his feet by the incensed titan.

"Speak again, wormcast…" Xul whispered, "and I shall kill you where you stand, the wishes of my mistress be damned!"

Caleb smiled silently and continued his trek through the oppressive and desolate vista.

At length, the dark sea of silent glass subsided and gave way to an arid coastline. The bridge too abruptly terminated upon a shore of bone white sand, the unbroken dunes stretching as far as the eye could see. Huge fragments of ancient statuary lay strewn upon the scorched terrain; colossal representations of gods and demons whose ageless dominion had long since fallen beyond the immemorial bounds of time and memory, leaving only the broken sun-bleached stone to stand as mute testament to their hoary divinity. And ever, the brooding monolithic spire loomed inexorably closer.

Eventually, Blackthorne found himself within the blessed shadow of the black monolith, thankful for the respite it offered from the merciless scoring of the solar glare. The spire was smooth as obsidian, and yet it did not reflect a single lucent ray of the sun, rather seeming to wholly absorb and negate the illumination afforded by the searing sphere.

Xul slowly raised his curved sword and instantly a rectangular doorway manifested at the tower's base, shimmering into existence upon the surface of the aphotic stone. The armoured fiend pushed Caleb towards the benighted threshold. "Enter."

Blackthorne strode silently into the shadowed interior of the spire. Instantly, the withering heat of the desert dissipated to be replaced by a preternaturally icy chill. The stone walls of the construct's inner reaches were black as coal, shot through with fulgid emerald veins which cast a limpid glow upon the tesserae tiled mosaic floor. In response to a sibilant whisper from Maalech Xul, a column of green light sprang suddenly from the semi-darkness, cocooning the two travellers in a shell of pulsing energy. The shroud of witch-fire burned momentarily brighter, illumining the gloom with a fell radiance. Scant seconds later, the pillar of light was gone and Blackthorne found himself in the centre of a vast circular chamber with walls of glittering obsidian. To his left gaped a vast and shimmering ovoid portal, beyond which could be seen the distant motionless sea and the jagged bridge which had borne him to the desolate tower. Immediately below the great window was a shallow pool of ink-black water encircled by a low perimeter of rough-hewn cimmerian stone, and from the centre of the pool rose a large mirror encased in an ornate frame of ebony.

As his keen eyes adjusted to the half-light, Caleb peered further into the tenebrous depths of the shadows before him and gasped. In the easternmost sector of the circular crystalline chamber, upon a carven dais, brooded a great black throne hewn from fulgent onyx. And upon that darkling throne reclined the sinuous, night-clad figure of a beautiful, lissom woman. Her diaphanous robes sparkled with the forlorn rays of long dead stars, and her lustrous tresses were blacker than the void between worlds. The woman's flesh was whiter than virgin snow, and her eyes shone with a seductive fathomless malice colder than the abyss. Her fulsome lips were red as blood, and as Blackthorne gazed enthralled upon the woman's mesmerizing beauty, those glistening lips curled in a cruel serpent's smile.

"Well, the view's improved, at any rate," Caleb muttered.

Maalech Xul removed his horned helm and cast it angrily to the blackened floor, revealing the great jagged scar which encircled his bull neck. "Great queen," he grumbled, "as bidden, I have brought this mortal before thee."

The dark giant strode towards the caliginous dais and the smile abruptly faded from the woman's face as she beheld the oozing stump of the demon's riven forearm.

"By all the black gods of the Chaosphere! I grow weary of remaking you, sirrah," she hissed malevolently, her voice husky and colder than hoarfrost. "'Tis no small task to weave the spells needed to heal that hulking form!"

"Battle exacts a heavy toll, even upon one such as I," Xul growled, his rutilant eyes narrowing as he took position at the left-hand side of the throne.

The woman sighed exasperatedly. "Why you cannot simply inhabit a human host is beyond me."

"My previous experiences with mortal shells have proven less than satisfactory, as well you know," rumbled Xul. "A human mind may exert a modicum of control over me whilst I dwell within its corporeal frame. That is something I will not tolerate. Thus will this ersatz form suffice for now. And this scheme of yours had best be worth the price I've paid."

The woman glanced briefly at the giant's chiselled azure features before returning her attention to Caleb. With a casual wave of her slender hand, the lucent shackles binding the mariner's wrists instantly disappeared.

"Please accept my apologies, Captain Blackthorne," she purred, her voice akin to the slither of serpentine scales on eastern silk. "I do hope I have not overly inconvenienced you. I trust your journey to my sanctum was not too arduous."

"Not at all," Caleb smiled, rubbing at his chafed wrists. "It was absolutely delightful."

The woman nodded. "And pray forgive me for the rather unsavoury means by which I ensured your apprehension. Reanimating the dead in such considerable numbers is invariably a vulgar and distasteful exercise, but regrettably in this instance it was the most efficient method at my disposal."

A grim scowl crossed Caleb's weathered features. "Many good men perished at the hands of those rotting aberrations. 'Tis but one more crime for which I mean to hold thee accountable."

The black-clad woman's eyes sparkled with the faintest hint of amusement. "Indeed, captain. Perilous has your voyage been, and long have I watched thee. Know now that you stand before Queen Tanit Vyperia, the divine Adelinda Coaxoch Ophidia, Seventh wife of Amaalphagus, Beguiler of Zurra, Bane of the Grand Arbiter of Temporal Jurisprudence, Sorceress Supreme of Lyonesse, Majestrix of the Praesidium of Ys, former paramour of the Lemurian Emperor, Scourge of Atland and Immortal Consort of the Demon Lord Maalech Xul."

"Well that's certainly a mouthful," Caleb grinned. "How should I address you... *your majesty*?"

"Have a care, worm!" boomed Xul. "Maintain a civil tongue in the presence of Queen Vyperia or I'll wrench it from between your bloodied teeth!"

"You really should muzzle your attack dog," said Caleb. "He's an ill-tempered beast, prone to biting."

Xul immediately lurched toward Blackthorne but was stayed by the merest gesture of Vyperia's delicate hand. Then she smiled and crossed her lissom ivory legs, her robe falling partially open to reveal the flawless eburnean flesh of her thighs. Her long sable boots hugged her perfect calves and Blackthorne felt a powerful surge of arousal as he gazed at those toned and shapely limbs.

"You are an enigma, Caleb," Vyperia said. "Initially you were naught to me, simply another nameless host in an endless succession of unremarkable mortality. But then I looked closer, and the conundrum became apparent. You alone of all the soul shard's vessels retain full memory of each existence in the aeons old cycle of death and rebirth. I wonder why this is the case?"

"We men of York are made of stern stuff," quipped Caleb. "In truth, I've also been watching you, though not by choice. My dreams and visions have been most vivid, and I've learned much of late as to their origin. This cruel curse you've woven. End it now, witch. I won't ask twice."

Melodious laughter sang from Vyperia's lips and she leaned forward in the onyx throne, her gown falling open still further to afford a fleeting glimpse of her ample alabastrine bosom. Blackthorne's blue eyes blazed with desire and he clenched his calloused fists.

"You are a bold one," Vyperia breathed. "Eventually I came to the conclusion that your dreams were the result of my former paramour manipulating the filaments of the temporal web from far beyond the veil of shadow, though to what end I cannot presently guess. He is a troublesome one, bearing his great grudge against me as he does."

"Heavens forfend anyone could possibly harbour thee any ill will," Caleb muttered.

Vyperia flashed a pearlescent smile and regarded Blackthorne intently. "Still, it brought you to my attention, if naught else. Ever since I learned your name, I've been peering deep into your soul. You are a man of action and of honour, a warrior, a leader and even a lover in your own unrefined way. I've looked back upon your ancestors and gazed into the

Glass of Far-Seeing to witness your descendants; those hardy souls who will bear your name across the generations to come. One in particular distinguishes himself as a scholar and an adventurer, although we have insufficient time to sing his praises today, I fear. Yes, you are a rare gem. A wolf among sheep. But wolves can be tamed, or slain."

"This wolf won't suffer either of those fates," Caleb growled. "Mark me on this."

Vyperia reclined upon her carven seat once more. "By now you've fathomed that your soul is intertwined with the essence of another. A prince. The son of a man who styled himself a god and who once shared my dominion as well as my bed. He spurned me once, long ago… before Atlantis sank beneath the waves. He forsook our star-born trysts in favour of a mortal woman. Imagine that. A queen's affections scorned for the crude embrace of a common doxy. Ah, well. Hell hath no fury, as one of your more erudite countrymen shall very soon write. Or something very similar, at least."

Blackthorne scowled. "Are you saying that this malediction is the result of a lovers' tiff? Gods, women truly are all the same, be they serving wench or empress!"

Vyperia's smile faded. "A singularly unenlightened observation, Captain Blackthorne. At any rate, I of course wrought my vengeance. Not upon the man, but upon his son. The son he sired with the mortal drab. It was a rather imaginative curse, I must admit. The soul of his progeny scattered to the cosmic winds to be reincarnated in the bodies of warriors across the millennia. Ever destined to live, to die, to be reborn. My former paramour's suzerainty was a glorious if minuscule antediluvian islet, his people the forebears of the Atlantean race. Much as your little island has a strong strain of Atlantean blood running through the veins of its denizens. In keeping with this vaunted heritage, the vessels I chose for the soul shards all shared the same ancestry. The devil is in the detail, after all."

"Ah, 'tis passing strange, but this explains much," Blackthorne said.

Vyperia's delicate brow arched. "Many were the battles I fought with my former consort. Our armies clashed in pitiless combat times beyond reckoning. You see, I knew he would ultimately have his son with him upon the battlefield, to share what scant glory he perceived would be his to seize. He was an arrogant man and I am a patient woman. And yet my night-spawned forces were always destined to prevail, particularly after I conjured the energumen fiend Maalech Xul to lead my legions."

Xul's carven jaw set silently and a dark scowl crept across his azure countenance.

"At length, I finally wove my curse upon an arid battlefield in the brooding shadow of the Black Pyramid. And mere months later, Maalech Xul slew my former paramour and his last remaining paladins upon the frozen tundra beyond the ancient Temple of the Serpent Kings."

"But not before losing his head over the matter," Caleb said. "It seems he has a penchant for shedding body parts."

Xul remained silent at the remark, although his crimson eyes narrowed to malefic slits.

"But forgive me, my dear captain," Vyperia said. "You have brought me a gift, have you not?"

Maalech Xul grudgingly proffered the silvern sword with its winged crossguard and Vyperia reverently took the mighty blade, holding it aloft to gaze admiringly at its canescent steel.

"The sword of Araklion," she whispered. "It has been a long time since I laid eyes upon this star-forged blade. I claimed it as a trophy following my victory, only for it to be stolen from me by the nefarious Lord Angsaar centuries ago and sealed away in a hoary shrine, safeguarded by potent spells even I could not negate. Thank you for returning it to me, Caleb. And well done on besting the Ghulgani. Many before thee had tried and failed."

"It was nothing," Blackthorne shrugged. "I confess I have yet to fathom that fancy pig-sticker's significance in all this, but I had expert assistance divining its location."

"Ah yes, the old wizard of Logres," Vyperia said. "I believe he now calls himself John Dee, does he not? He knows much, that one. More than he cares to divulge. I shall visit him one day, for he too may ultimately prove to be of use to me. But for now… shall we reunite this splendid bauble with its true and rightful owner?"

Vyperia gestured to the darkened southern sector of the chamber and instantly two black braziers flared to life in a blaze of green flame. The shadows swiftly melted away to reveal a great sarcophagus which had evidently been carved from a single colossal diamond. The coruscant casket was bound upright to the obsidian wall by blackened chains, and its polished surface shone with crystalline clarity. Within the glittering tomb Blackthorne could clearly see the body of the young prince Araklion, his pale face serene and frozen in a deep, death-like slumber. A golden circlet ringed the youth's noble brow, holding his auricomous locks in place, and he was still clad in the gleaming ornate armour which Caleb recognized from his waking dreams.

"Such a handsome young man," Vyperia whispered. "So much like his father." Releasing her grip on the argent sword, she hissed a fell word of power and the blade instantly moved to the sarcophagus as if borne by an unseen spectral hand, ultimately coming to a stop to hover before the entombed prince's somnolent form. "Now, my dear captain," Vyperia said, fixing Caleb with her hypnotic gaze once more. "I have rather an intriguing proposition which I would dearly like to put to you."

At this, Xul glanced sidelong at Vyperia, his iron-clad hand bunching slowly into a fist.

Blackthorne raised a quizzical eyebrow. "Indeed, lass? This should prove interesting. Pray, continue."

"This desolate place," Vyperia purred, raising her hand to indicate the black spire's gloomy interior. "In truth, it is little more than a prison. A domain in which I am undeniably supreme, but a glorified gaol nonetheless. Over the centuries, my power has waned inexorably, and where once I strode the glorious kingdoms of the antediluvian world unfettered, now I dwell here unable to traverse the boundaries between realms unaided. The dissolution of my dominion and the inevitable toll wrought upon me by the countless battles with my myriad foes has essentially stranded me here, much like a mariner shipwrecked upon some blighted atoll on an uncharted sea. That and certain spells cast by my enemies intended to shackle me here indefinitely. Damn the thrice-cursed Chaos Liege! A pox on the machinations of Angsaar and his treacherous magicks!"

Blackthorne watched with interest as the woman's momentary rage dissipated, her composure swiftly returning.

Vyperia sighed heavily. "Once, this was a sublime haven, a glorious and verdant paradise to which I oft times sojourned in order to replenish my arcane power. Now, it is an arid and lifeless wasteland… a time-lost void between worlds where I may watch and wait, but scant little else. For centuries I have observed the realms of men, watching their fleeting empires rise and fall, beholding their ascent from primitive barbarism to sovereign mastery of this fragile globe. And ever have I schemed and plotted, devising and setting into motion certain plans for my liberation and the reclamation of my rightful divinity."

"Truly, my heart bleeds for your plight," Caleb growled.

"Why, the energy I expended in weaving the spellcraft to send Maalech Xul forth into your world alone nigh on exhausted me and sorely drained my reserves of mana," Vyperia hissed, an ireful edge colouring her husky voice. "Which at length brings me to my point, and the true reason why I summoned you here to this darkly gilded cage."

Both Caleb and Xul now stared at the woman in rapt and silent anticipation. "Your realm... your England. Long have I watched its war-like inhabitants and studied its disparate tribes. Through the ages I have witnessed your island's ascent from the mire of the barbaricum to its present state as a far-reaching nation with ever growing ambition, replete with a plethora of hardy souls bred to perpetuate that martial aspiration. I have seen the future of your people and I have witnessed their unification and the colourful banners of their empire driven proudly into the far-flung territories of the world, the glory of conquest forging a dominion upon which the sun will not set for centuries to come. The destiny of your people is to embody the greatest imperium the world has ever seen, greater than that of Atlantis and Koord, more far reaching even than the Achaemenid, Macedonian and Roman Empires at their glorious heights. Your island is prophesied to shape the realm of men, Caleb. In a few short generations, your Britain will rule the world."

A wide grin flashed across Blackthorne's bearded face. "Well, if I had a flagon of ale, I'd certainly drink to that."

"To be blunt, I wish to be a part of that glory," Vyperia said, her ophidian eyes narrowing. "I wish to rule once more. I have watched your queen, the flame haired wench with the heart of a shield-maiden and the tenacity of a she-wolf. Her tenure on the throne will sow the seeds of empire. Her rule will hone the engines of both statecraft and warcraft alike so that subsequent kings may further that ambition and fully seize the grand destiny of conquest and colonization. I mean to have a hand in this."

"How?" frowned Caleb. "By your own admission you are trapped here in this sweltering purgatory. How can you hope to achieve what you seek?"

Vyperia smiled once again, her dark eyes gleaming with a fathomless cunning. "With your assistance, I can transfer my immortal essence into the body of your queen. I can assume control of her mortal shell and rule from her throne, compelling and empowering the realm to ever greater and more lofty heights of glory. This is my destiny, Caleb. Where oncc I ruled, there shall I rule again. As once I conquered, so shall I conquer once more."

"I see," Caleb rumbled. "In truth, I expected as much."

"I shall manipulate the temporal eddies to accelerate the currents of history, subtly influencing their ebb and flow to bring about the desired goals that much quicker. 'Tis no small task, to be sure. But know that I have wrought such plans before with great success."

"I don't doubt it," Caleb said. "I have of late come to appreciate the extent of your ambitions and your capabilities."

"And you, mariner," whispered Vyperia, leaning forward in her carven throne. "Once you have willingly borne my spirit from this spire in a shard of my Soul Crystal, you will act as my vessel and convey me to the court of your red queen. I shall do the rest. All I require from you is the means to travel beyond the veil and make contact with your sovereign's regal flesh. It will be a relatively simple task, and none too gruelling for you."

"Not an overly fortuitous swap for you, aesthetically," grunted Caleb.

"Oh, my true body will be quite safe here, my dear captain," beamed Vyperia. "Frozen in a sorcerous sleep and very well protected, awaiting the day when I return to claim it, once my arcane powers have been replenished sufficiently."

Blackthorne folded his arms across his broad chest. "Indeed. And what could you possibly offer me, to make such an act of high treason worth my while?"

Vyperia chuckled and reclined seductively in her crystalline seat once again. "Why my sweet, simple Caleb… you shall be my king, of course! You shall rule by my side! You will be nothing less than my right hand as I seize my glory and dominate the peoples of the world!"

A malefic growl welled in Maalech Xul's throat and he turned fully to face the lissom woman. Blackthorne watched this movement silently and his muscular body tensed.

"You see, I shall require a man such as yourself to assist me," said Vyperia. "A man familiar with the minds and hearts of the people. A guardian to protect me as I recover from the rite of possession and assume the arduous mantle of queen. In return, I shall grant thee a modicum of immortality and bestow upon thee power hitherto undreamed of. Think of it! A lowly sea-dog reigning as a king beside his deathless queen for all eternity!"

Caleb glanced again at Maalech Xul. "And where does your loyal hound fit into this perfidious scheme?"

Vyperia laughed cruelly. "Oh, he doesn't. I fear his usefulness is at an end, his purpose all but served. Where I am bound, I shall need far more than a demon's shade dwelling in the crudely cast patchwork body of a man as my vassal. Maalech Xul shall return to the infernal abyss from whence I summoned him, his role duly fulfilled."

A moment of ominous silence enshrouded the shadowy chamber. Caleb warily took a single step closer to the onyx throne. Vyperia still gazed at him expectantly, her eyes sparkling with anticipation. And Maalech Xul slowly leaned in to his mistress until their faces were less than an inch apart.

"I have heard enough," the azure skinned giant growled. "Now you will learn that my favour is not so lightly discarded!"

With terrifying ferocity, Xul's gauntleted hand lashed forth to encircle Vyperia's eburnean throat. His iron clad fingers tightened and the woman's dark eyes widened in pain and shock.

"You would have this mortal wormcast by your side?" the demon hissed. "So be it. You can be together forever… in death!"

Vyperia's delicate fingers scrabbled at the colossal hand in vain. "You… dare?" she rasped, flecks of blood speckling her fulsome lips.

"I dare anything!" Xul boomed. "I am Maalech Xul, Deathbringer of the Z'xulth! And you will pay the price for your betrayal!"

Desperately, Vyperia raised her left hand and a violet luminescence suddenly flared about her slender fingers. With a blinding flash and a resonant crackle, a writhing lance of energy suddenly erupted from her palm and smote the armoured giant fully in the chest. Maalech Xul was hurled twenty feet by the arcane blast, his great frame spiralling across the chamber to strike the obsidian wall with a sickening impact. Lucent tendrils of power encased his body like the strands of a spider's web, and acrid smoke began to rise from the joints in his chitinous black armour. Slowly, his powerful body began to sag in the vice grip of the sorcerous filaments, his cuirass glowing red where the searing magical fingers were scoring the black breastplate. Finally, he crumpled heavily to the floor to lie motionless upon the cold stone.

Vyperia slumped in her throne, dazed and disoriented, her ivory fingers brushing her bruised and bloodied throat.

In an instant, Caleb bounded across the chamber to where the crystalline sarcophagus sparkled in the gloom, swiftly taking up the great silver sword once more. The blade thrummed and bombinated in his grasp, its platinum bound hilt warm to his touch.

"The chains, Blackthorne!" came a faint voice, suddenly echoing within Caleb's mind as if from some immeasurable distance. "Sunder the chains!"

At once, Blackthorne recognized the sibilant spectral tone which whispered through his consciousness. It was unmistakably the voice of Doctor John Dee! "Grand to hear from thee again, good doctor!" growled Caleb, tightening his grip upon the gleaming sword. "And most timely indeed is your ghostly missive!"

With one sidelong glance at the onyx throne, Caleb swung the great sword in a mighty arc, shearing through the black chains which suspended the fulgid diamond casket. With a deafening din akin to the shattering of glass, the sarcophagus struck the black floor and exploded into a thousand gleaming shards. And yet the body of the young prince Araklion remained upright and untouched, the fragments of crystal passing through his form as if they were nothing more than lucent rays of moonlight. Then, a cerulean glow suddenly enveloped the somnolent body of the prince, bathing his serene frame in a gentle spectral light. Caleb stepped back, gazing incredulously at the ghostly image of the sleeping youth.

"Has that done it, lad?" he whispered. "Is this bloody curse lifted? Or must I slay that damned witch to boot?"

Suddenly, a great noise like the rushing of a storm-wracked ocean filled the darkling chamber. Turning to the onyx throne where Vyperia still slumped insensate, Caleb beheld a great vortex of shimmering light abruptly manifest before the carven dais. Lances of writhing electrical energy flashed within the eldritch maelstrom, casting a sapphirean glow about the cavernous room.

Vyperia stirred and gazed up at the caesious vortex before her, her eyes widening in stark fear. And then, coalescing in the lambent depths of the swirling light-storm, a fantastic image appeared.

"By Aegir, Llyr, Mazu, Ahti, Sirsir and Poseidon!" whispered Caleb incredulously.

The form of a great winged steed had manifested within the maelstrom, white as snow with eyes of searing blue fire. Upon its broad back was an armoured man wielding a silver spear which crackled with cerulean energy. An ornate crested helm concealed his features, but Caleb was in no doubt as to the identity of the eldritch rider. As he watched spellbound, the mighty paladin extended his gauntleted hand silently toward Vyperia.

"Forgive me, Tyberion," the witch rasped, trembling. "My love!"

Her terrified gaze suddenly focused on Blackthorne. "Help me, Caleb! I beg of thee!"

Still brandishing the silver sword, Caleb strode to the side of the onyx throne, shielding his eyes against the glare of the lucent vortex. "I dare say there's nothing I can do for you now, girl."

"You sublime fool!" hissed Vyperia. "I could have made you a god amongst men!"

"A god?" said Caleb, his brow furrowing. "No, lass. 'Tis enough that men might dream of being kings, without aspiring to the power of gods. And in truth, I've no desire to be a king, either. Too much hassle, not enough freedom."

Bitter tears welled in Vyperia's dark eyes. "We could have ruled the world together!"

Caleb frowned, leaning in close to the woman's beauteous face. "I sought no part in your tyrannical plot. Although just between you and me, I confess I did consider your proposal for a fleeting moment." With that, he planted a lusty, lingering kiss on Vyperia's ruby lips. "Farewell, dark queen!"

Then, Blackthorne took hold of the woman's slender arm and hurled her into the swirling maw of the effulgent portal.

Instantly, the shining paladin gathered Vyperia in his lucent embrace and deposited her roughly across the saddle of his winged mount. Then, in a blaze of azure light, the form of the young prince Araklion suddenly appeared astride the steed behind his father, a gentle smile illumining his noble face. The armoured king nodded once to Caleb in silent gratitude and lifted his hand. With a flare of white light, the silver sword in Blackthorne's grasp abruptly vanished and immediately reappeared within the hand of Araklion.

Caleb slowly stepped back from the onyx throne as the portal began to shimmer and fade. Then, as abruptly as it had appeared, the coruscant vortex was gone, leaving only a faint humming and a gentle whisper of icy wind to mark its passing.

"And that's the end of that, I'll wager," sighed Caleb wearily.

The mariner wiped his brow and glanced about the chamber, searching the shadows for an exit from the black spire.

"Well played, mortal," boomed a sepulchral voice from the gloom. Caleb spun to see Maalech Xul striding toward him, his charred and blackened armour emitting plumes of acrid smoke, his great twisted sword in hand. "The seductress is gone. Now all that remains is for you and I to have our reckoning."

Caleb smiled mirthlessly. "It wasn't my fault you trusted the witch, you great lumbering moldwarp! I don't suppose you'd simply be content to call the tally even?"

Xul laughed, the sound dark and devoid of humour. "I think not. You've been a thorn in my side for quite some time now. There is no means by which you may leave this place. I considered simply leaving you here to rot, but I would derive scant satisfaction from such a minor gesture of mercy. No, I shall enjoy taking your head before I return to the abyssal realm."

Blackthorne raised his empty hands. "You appear to have me at a disadvantage, demon. I find myself without a blade, which is a rare thing indeed for me. Care to settle this by wrestling, or mayhap fisticuffs?"

"Enough talk!" thundered Xul, lunging forward with his black blade raised. "Die, human!"

Suddenly, a titanic thunderclap shattered the silence of the stygian chamber, and a vast section of the obsidian wall exploded to rain jagged black fragments upon the stone floor. Caleb whirled to the shimmering ovoid window which overlooked the arid approach to the spire to witness a sight which caused his heart to soar like a raven upon the winds of dusk. In the distance, beyond the twisted bridge which stretched across the wine dark sea, the sails of the *Starfire* billowed gloriously, a huge shimmering portal pulsing brightly at her stern. The ship's bow guns flared again, their booming report echoing across the desolate expanse.

"Gods blast me for a madman," Caleb shouted joyously. "The whole bloody ship, no less!"

Scant seconds later, the cannon balls reached the spire and tore another section of the black stone asunder with an ear-splitting crash. The shockwave hurled Caleb from his feet as massive chunks of rock and crystal erupted from the tower's walls and scattered all around him. Maalech Xul stumbled as huge fragments of obsidian tumbled from the structure to assail his armoured form, the explosive impact rending a great fissure in the floor beneath his feet.

"That cursed scow won't save you!" Xul snarled, lurching towards Blackthorne with his benighted blade awhirl.

Caleb scrambled to his feet in time to see a colossal section of the tower's lofty interior crumble lazily from its perch, spiralling downward in an inexorably slow and graceful arc. With a sickening crack, the vast slab of broken stone struck Maalech Xul and hammered the dark giant pitilessly to the rubble strewn floor. Xul's blade tumbled from his grasp as the massive fragment pinned him against the onyx throne, his ravaged armour splitting to disgorge great gouts of dark blue blood.

"This... is not... the endgame," Xul rasped, azure liquid bubbling from his lips. "I am eternal... I cannot die!"

As Caleb watched, the rutilant glow in Xul's eyes slowly guttered and died, and his great armoured frame finally fell silent and still. Then, from the giant's gaping mouth, a writhing tendril of pitch black smoke billowed forth and swiftly disappeared into the tenebrous shadows of the sundered black tower.

"I believe I've overstayed my welcome here," Caleb muttered. Glancing toward the northern section of the chamber, he saw that a great ragged aperture had been torn in the aphotic stone floor through which he could barely discern a faint glimmer of sunlight. Evading further fragments of razor edged crystal which were still plummeting from the upper reaches of the spire, he leaped to the fissure and peered into its murky depths. An expanse of bright sand could be seen amidst the shattered stone, and he knew instantly that he had found his exit.

"Praise the gods!" Caleb whispered. "But damn it all, I won't leave empty handed!"

Blackthorne turned to where the shattered remnants of Araklion's crystalline sarcophagus lay strewn upon the riven floor and bounded to the nearest glittering fragment. Taking up a vast chunk of lucent diamond, he scrambled back to the yawning fissure and leaped headlong into the darkness. For long seconds he tumbled down the rough-hewn tunnel, its jagged edges tearing many shallow wounds in his flesh. Then, his feet struck hot sand and he finally rolled clear of the black monolith's ruinous embrace.

Caleb sprinted across the arid sand for several hundred yards, not daring to look back. Finally, he halted his desperate flight and glanced breathlessly at the great obelisk. Huge cracks were gaping in the spire's smooth black stone, writhing like shadowy serpents from the base to its lofty pinnacle. As Caleb watched enthralled, the viridescent crystal at the structure's summit collapsed, falling and shattering upon the stygian pyramidion. With a thunderous crack, the entire eastern face of the spire suddenly buckled and crumbled, tumbling downward in a billowing cloud of dark smoke and debris. A heartbeat later, the entirety of the sinister structure began to utterly disintegrate, groaning its ireful defiance as it crashed to clamorous, earth-sundering ruin upon the desolate sand.

For many lengthy moments, Caleb Blackthorne gazed at the wreckage of the tower, every painful breath drawn in a ragged, dust-choked gasp. Then he turned silently and began the long walk to where the *Starfire* waited in the sun-scorched distance.

From the log of Captain Caleb Blackthorne: Final Entry...

The dreams have ceased, the curse has been lifted. Many weeks have passed since that fateful day in the desolate spire and I still find myself at a loss to explain much of it. My crew fathomed how to use the demon's magic stone in a timely fashion, bless their salt-scored hides! They sailed the Starfire through the witch-portal they'd conjured and opened fire on the only thing they saw on that blighted horizon; the obsidian obelisk of the dark queen. Although they had no knowledge of my whereabouts and therefore relied on gut feeling and instinct, I am thankful that they dealt with the quandary in the manner best fitting their status as wolves of the sea; with cold steel and cannon fire! Fortuitously, the arcane orb contained just enough potency to transport us back from that sweltering limbo to navigate familiar seas once more. Those brave souls who perished in the battle with the witch-woman's unhallowed dead were buried at sea; their bodies duly committed to the fathomless depths, their noble spirits unshackled to rove, feast and slay with the glorious fallen legions of the Sea Gods and sail the vast oceans of eternity until the end of time. As for we who survived this benighted expedition, our voyage home was far less perilous than had been the outward trek, as if the ire of the fell forces which opposed us had been duly spent with the sundering of the maleficent curse. The colossal diamond which I looted from the tower, along with the sapphires which young Malachi seized from the jungle shrine, have enabled me to fully repair and refit the ship, as well as bestow upon each and every member of my crew a generous share of the booty. Those who suffered wounds during the battle are now all but healed, and I've enlisted a few more hardy privateers to man my oaken deck. On the morrow I shall visit Doctor John Dee once more, and fully relay to him the fantastic and harrowing events of this eldritch argosy. His most recent letter to me which I received via messenger at Southampton revealed that he had been able to witness at least some of my confrontation with the seductress via his scrying mirror, and I thank the gods that when it mattered most, his words of counsel were far from cryptic! He also relayed to me the disquieting news that the Queen has been acting somewhat odd of late; strangely out of character and prone to becoming lost in a cryptic reverie complete with vivid recollections of an ancient time before the great flood devoured the realms of pre-history. I am most concerned by this disclosure and during my audience with the Doctor I intend to quiz him extensively on the ill-omened matter. What's more, word has reached me that the old sea-dog Drake is marshalling a fleet to sail against the Spaniards at San Juan, and I fully expect to helm my girl as part of that righteous expedition! After that... who can say? Many are the mariners' tales of uncharted atolls and exotic climes waiting to be discovered by a sturdy ship and a doughty crew such as mine. The seas are vast, and our sails are broad. I know beyond any shadow of a doubt that there are yet more wonders awaiting us beyond the distant horizon. Aye, the siren call of the open ocean is strong in our hearts and our minds, and I am certain that the voyages of the Starfire are far from over...

ABOUT THE AUTHORS

Born in 1986, **JP Abboud** can recall several confrontations and ruined relationships in the name of Metal. An introvert's love of paranoid sci-fi and solipsistic fantasy dream hazes punctuated his stint fronting maniac cult **Borrowed Time**. He is working now in the Epic Metal band **Gatekeeper**. He will die eventually.

James Ashbey has been a member of various heavy metal bands, including **Solstice** (England), **Lethean** and **Craven Idol**. He sees many parallels between weird fiction and heavy metal, and enjoys working creatively in both fields.

Howie K. Bentley is the guitarist, lyricist, sole composer, and founder of two heavy metal bands: **Cauldron Born** and **Briton Rites**. He became an avid reader as a teenager in the early 1980s upon discovering the fantastic tales of Robert E. Howard and Edgar Rice Burroughs. Howie has had a number of sword-and-sorcery and occult fantasy tales published in recent years. He resides in his home state of Kentucky, where he spends his days and nights writing epic prose about barbarians and wizards and dreaming of the days of blood and thunder. For updates on his fiction, visit https://www.amazon.com/author/howiebentley.

Max Birbaum, born in 1989, is a German author and musician. During his studies of philosophy and history he has released three books in the German language and two albums as the guitarist of **Lunar Shadow**. Among his literary idols are names such as Tolkien, Robert E. Howard, Clark Ashton Smith and Lord Dunsany.

Geoff Blackwell is a guitarist and keyboardist currently living in Vancouver, Canada. He has played in several bands including **Gatekeeper** and **Scythia**, has appeared on no less than ten physical recordings and makes his living teaching music and performing in bands, musical productions, and as a studio musician. His primary inspirations are Robert E. Howard, Frank Frazetta, Quorthon, Thin Lizzy, and Ayinger Celebrator Dopplebock. He'd like to thank DMR for letting him appear in this book, plus family, friends and bandmates of past, present & future for all their support.

Mike Browning is a metal drummer/vocalist that has played in several well-known bands. He was a founding member of the legendary Florida death metal band **Morbid Angel**. His run in that band lasted from 1982 to 1986. In 1987 he briefly played in **Incubus**. Later that year he formed **Nocturnus** which lasted until 1992. In 1990 **Nocturnus** put out *The Key*, a science fiction/horror concept album. The story "The Key" is based on that album. Mike has reactivated the band under the name **Nocturnus AD** and have released an album entitled *Paradox*.

Jaron Evil was born in Vancouver, Canada and has appeared on more releases than most would credit him. He has been the bassist for tech death titans **Archspire**, guitarist and vocalist for space metal band **Eismond**, and under the moniker Vultyrous he has been the lead vocalist and rhythm guitarist for symphonic black metal band **Artep**. A diverse multi-instrumentalist, Jaron also has several solo projects under his belt including **Funeral Fornication** (black metal), **Ringbearer** (Tolkien-inspired dark ambient), **Almuric** (power/doom metal), **Bio-Mech** (80s sci-fi synthwave), and others. He is always working on new music.

Ernest Cunningham Hellwell was born in Wichita, Kansas. An avid reader at an early age, his interests in writing and music both manifested in high school. It was at Wichita High School North that he met **Mark Shelton** in a creative writing class. During this time Ernest conceived and wrote the story "The Riddle Master." Shelton was so taken with the story that he later put the tale to music in a song of the same title. It was released on the album *Crystal Logic* by his epic metal band **Manilla Road** in 1983. Ernest made his musical debut to the public in 2011 as the bassist on the **Manilla Road** album *Playground of the Damned*. Shortly thereafter E.C. and Mark established the band **Hellwell**. His stories were never published until his tale "Acheronomicon" was included with the release of the first **Hellwell** album *Beyond the Boundaries of Sin* (2012). The second **Hellwell** album, *Behind the Demon's Eyes*, was released in 2017.

D.R. Lackner is a multi-instrumentalist and oil painter. His creative output can be seen and heard as the guitarist, vocalist, lyricist, and cover artist for the epic heavy metal band **Legendry**. His work in all mediums revolves around fantastical realms of sword and sorcery, and takes inspiration from Robert E. Howard, Manilla Road, and Frank Frazetta, among countless others.

Joe "Deathmaster" Minichino is a vocalist/guitarist, and the founder of Italian epic Heavy Metal band **DoomSword**. Born in Lombardy, Italy, he has a life-long passion for medieval history, fantasy and Heavy Metal. Joe is greatly influenced by Moorcock, Howard, Poul Anderson, Cirith Ungol, Manilla Road, Bathory, Frazetta, and Whelan. He adopted his pseudonym from a Warlord EP. Joe has also released albums with **Agarthi**, **Fiurach**, **Gjallarhorn** and **Fury'n'Grace**. He has lived in Cork, Ireland since 2004. He'd like to thank Rowena O'Sullivan, Rory O'Kelly and Sean Musick for proofreading/feedback on his story.

Byron Roberts is the vocalist, lyricist and founder of the UK extreme metal band **Bal-Sagoth**. An English Literature graduate, Roberts conceived **Bal-Sagoth** as a symphonic black metal project built upon an elaborate fantasy and sci-fi oriented lyrical concept, inspired by the novels, short stories, comics and movies he grew up with, particularly the classic pulp stories of Robert E. Howard and H.P. Lovecraft. The lyrical mythos of the **Bal-Sagoth** universe goes far beyond the band's six album discography, encompassing novellas, short stories, and even graphic novels. For more information on Byron's work, visit www.bal-sagoth.net and www.byron-a-roberts.co.uk.

Mike Scalzi is the singer, lead guitar player and founding member of **The Lord Weird Slough Feg**, as well as a philosophy instructor at Diablo Valley College, San Ramon, California. Scalzi was born and raised in Central Pennsylvania.

Birthed and raised in the San Francisco Bay Area, **Chris Shoriak** was exposed to many different forms of music and art, which quickly became his biggest interests. Moving to the Pacific Northwest, his love for fantasy was tempered within the iconic scenery, pristine shorelines, and ancient redwoods. After several years and several music projects he moved out to the lush, snowy mountain-town of Flagstaff, where he met several like-minded musicians who shared in his vision of **Ice Sword**; thusly began his long-awaited dream of a power/fantasy metal concept-band/project.

Jason Tarpey is a musician and blacksmith from Boerne, Texas. He is the vocalist for **Eternal Champion**, **Iron Age**, and **Graven Rite**, the latter featuring the song "The Summoner's Pit" which inspired his short story "Vengeance of the Insane God." He also operates Hammerhall Forge, where he creates his hand-forged iron works.

Scott Waldrop was born in Winston-Salem, NC, grew up in Washington D.C., and lives in Raleigh, NC, with his wife Mary and son Scottie. He plays guitar in **Twisted Tower Dire** and **Walpyrgus**.

COMING SOON

Karnov, Phantom-Clad Rider of the Cosmic Ice by Matthew Knight, Howie K. Bentley and Byron A. Roberts - Returning from battle, the warrior Karnov discovers his family murdered and his homeland ravaged by vampyres. Aided by witchcraft and sorcerous allies, will Karnov's powers and burning lust for retribution be enough to avenge his loved ones, or will undead wraiths corrupt the earth forever? Classic horror film atmosphere meets pulp-style swashbuckling adventure in this action-packed epic.

Wulfhere by A.B. Higginson - In the Dark Ages of England, kingdoms were ready to be carved out by any with the ambition and might to do so. The mightiest ruler of all was Penda, Lord of Mercia, a man as strong as he was ruthless. He had no equal in martial prowess, excepting his son Wulfhere... Originally serialized in the pages of the legendary pulp magazine *Adventure,* DMR Books is proud to present the first-ever publication of this historical novel in book form.

ALSO AVAILABLE

The Road to Infinity by Gael DeRoane – Aran Dyfar's wanderlust leads him on a quest to discover the mythical Road to Infinity. Along the way he encounters friends, monsters, and wonders beyond imagination. A picaresque adventure sure to please fans of Jack Vance's *Dying Earth* and *Lyonesse* series.

Heroes of Atlantis & Lemuria – Classic tales of adventure from the sunken lands! Includes five Kardios stories by Manly Wade Wellman, all three Lemurian tales by Frederick Arnold Kummer, Jr., and a hard-to-find Leigh Brackett story set in Mu.

Printed in Great Britain
by Amazon

82889721R00263